Richard Holt Hutt

The National Review

Vol. 17. July and October 1863

SALZWASSER VERLAG

Richard Holt Hutton, Walter Bagehot, Robert Theobald

The National Review

Vol. 17. July and October 1863

Reprint of the original, first published in 1863.

1st Edition 2022 | ISBN: 978-3-37500-410-1

Verlag (Publisher): Salzwasser Verlag GmbH, Zeilweg 44, 60439 Frankfurt, Deutschland
Vertretungsberechtigt (Authorized to represent): E. Roepke, Zeilweg 44, 60439 Frankfurt, Deutschland
Druck (Print): Books on Demand GmbH, In de Tarpen 42, 22848 Norderstedt, Deutschland

THE

NATIONAL REVIEW.

VOL. XVII.

JULY AND OCTOBER 1863.

LONDON:

MDCCCLXIII.

THE NATIONAL REVIEW.

CONTENTS OF No. XXXIII.—JULY 1863.

THE NATIONAL REVIEW.

CONTENTS OF No. XXXIV.—OCTOBER 1863.

THE NATIONAL REVIEW.

JULY 1863.

Art. I.—THE EARLIER LATITUDINARIANS: FALKLAND, CHILLINGWORTH, HALES.

Proceedings, principally in the County of Kent, in connection with the Parliaments called in 1640, and especially with the Committee of Religion appointed in that year. Edited by the Rev. L. B. Larking, M.A., from the Collections of Sir Edward Dering, Bart., 1627-1644, with a Preface by John Bruce, Esq., F.S.A. Printed for the Camden Society, 1862.

Clement Walker, in his History of Independency, records a rather curious circumstance which happened at Walton-on-Thames at the beginning of Lent 1649. The minister had preached in his parish-church after dinner, and had prolonged his sermon till twilight. When he came down out of the pulpit, into the church came six soldiers, one of them with a lantern in his hand and a candle burning in it, and in the other hand four unlighted candles. The parishioners would not allow him to mount the pulpit, or to address them in the church; he therefore adjourned to the churchyard, and the people followed him. He then and there told them that he had had a vision, and had a message from God to them, which they were to receive on pain of damnation. First, the Sabbath was abolished as unnecessary, Jewish, and merely ceremonial. Secondly, tithes were abolished as not only Jewish and ceremonial, but a great burden to the saints of God, and a discouragement of industry and tillage. Thirdly, ministers were abolished as anti-Christian, and of no longer use when Christ descended into the hearts of his saints, and his Spirit enlightened them with revelations and inspirations. Fourthly, magistrates were abolished as useless, since Christ had come among men in purity of spirit, and had erected the kingdom of his saints upon earth. Each of these constructive anathemas the soldier had intended to accompany by a symbolical act, that is to say, by putting out one of his candles; but, as he explained to his wondering audience after each phase of abolition, the wind was so high that he could not light his candle. One candle, however, he had safely burning away in the lantern; and of this also he had a use to make. Fifthly and lastly, he put his hand into his pocket and pulled out a Bible. "Here," he exclaimed, "is a book you have in great veneration, consisting of two parts, the Old and New Testament. I must tell you, it is abolished; it contains beggarly rudiments, milk for babes; but now Christ is in glory among us, and imparts a fuller measure of his Spirit to his saints than this can afford; and therefore I am commanded to burn it." So, taking the candle out of the lantern, he set the leaves on fire; and then, putting out the candle, he cried, "and here my fifth light is extinguished."

Extravagances such as this were congenial to a few excited spirits in the army, but had no attraction for Englishmen in general, even when the nation had tasted blood and developed its most extreme propensities. Much less was this sweeping removal of all ordinances contemplated by the men of Kent and the Kentish men who in 1640 and 1641 petitioned the knights of the shire or the House of Commons on account of their ecclesiastical grievances. They inclined evidently to the Presbyterian type, which allows the minister considerable power over his flock, but also intrusts the flock with a very tight hold on its minister. In several cases the only grievance of which they complained was the very scanty income with which the services of a good curate or vicar were rewarded. In one instance the petitioners, having preferred certain articles against their curate, are soon after anxious to recall their petition, confessing that it was precipitately sent "at the instigation of a malignant humour," and that their curate was "very able, sufficient, and painful in dispensing the word of God," though he had seemed to carry himself somewhat too loftily towards them. In one case an elaborate series of charges against an incumbent palpably breaks down; in another, the parson pleads guilty to human infirmities, including a little occasional intemperance. No subject of complaint is so frequent as the ministers railing-in the holy table, placing it altarwise, and obliging communicants to receive at the rails. Occasionally disputes about tithes crop up, such as were frequent in all times till the memorable era of the commutation. In several cases the congregations profess themselves to have been scandalised by doctrines contradicting that of Calvin; and it is objected to the minister of Crayford that he, "drinking with certain gentlemen at the Bull in Dartford, did confidently affirm and say he was persuaded that the first motion and inclination of the heart to any sin without consent, was not sin." But if the men of Dartford were curious in theological distinctions, the men of Chatham could not appreciate a joke; for they informed the House of Commons that their curate, being urged by the apostle's words that his duty did consist in preaching, and being instant in season and out of season, replied that "in season" was preaching on Sundays in the forenoons, and "out of season" was preaching in the afternoons. But we need not linger among the grievances which came in different ways under the cognisance of Sir Edward Dering, himself a most unskilful and unhappy meddler in the controversies of those times. The interesting volume printed by the Camden Society, in which these particulars are contained, will help those who are curious in such matters towards furnishing that mental picture of the civil war which every educated Englishman should try to draw distinctly for himself, with appropriate details for the background. At present we would call the attention of our readers to the memory of three men, each important during that eventful period in politics, in religion, or in both; each venturing to think for himself; and each having the greater claim on the regard and respect of posterity, as having risen superior to interest and party, and preferred independence to success.

Our trio consists of a nobleman and two clergymen; and the nobleman shall have due precedence. Lord Falkland has been as fortunate in history as he was unhappy in life, going down to posterity in that magnificent eulogium of Clarendon. But Clarendon must not be trusted implicitly with regard to Lord Falkland or any one else. The shrewd politician was too keen a partisan to write history without colouring it. His enthusiasm for Falkland was genuine and well founded; but it did not so disturb the usual balance of his mind as to keep him from tampering a little with Falkland's portrait. It was not enough that his friend should have shared his loyal principles, should have toiled for the king as secretary of state, and died for the king at Newbury: it was necessary also that his opinions on other subjects should be assimilated as far as possible to those of the conservative Hyde. As Clarendon was not fond of alluding freely to the liberal sentiments of his own youthful days, he veils as far as possible the avowed liberalism of his friend. He did not wish the firm supporter of the king to appear as the opponent of the temporal power of bishops. He attributes to him a change of opinion of which there is much reason to doubt if it ever took place. It is, of course, both natural and probable that a man like Falkland, independent, conscientious, and scrupulous, might think different measures expedient at different times, and might change his opinion in many particulars as well of things as of persons. Nothing is more likely than that, as Clarendon narrates, he asserted this right of judging and acting according to the occasion, when Hampden pressed him with a charge of inconsistency. But it is often found that the greatest firmness in principle is exhibited by those who repudiate consistency in details; and there is every reason to think that Falkland did not at all vary in his general view of episcopacy. Two of his speeches in the House of Commons in reference to that subject are extant. The first was published in 1642, and has been more than once republished since in the interest of those who either disliked bishops altogether, or feared the jurisdiction of the order. The second was published in 1660, as a valuable document on the side of those who favoured a moderate episcopacy. The first speech was in support of the bill for excluding the bishops from the House of Lords; the second was against the utter abolition of bishops. The earlier speech is a deliberate and pointed attack on that portion of the bench which was most fully represented by Laud. In consequence of his father's connection with Ireland as lord-deputy, and his own residence in the island and education at Dublin, Falkland had strong views of his own respecting Irish affairs, and detested the policy of Strafford. But to detest the policy of Strafford was also to condemn that of Laud. He raised his voice against both in the House of Commons. No one can doubt to whom he alludes when, in attacking "some bishops and their adherents," he remarks: "We shall find them to have been almost the sole abettors of my Lord of Strafford, while he was practising upon another kingdom that manner of government which he intended to settle in this; and after they called him over from being deputy in Ireland to be in a manner deputy of England, to have assisted him in the giving of such counsels, and the pursuing of such courses, as it is a hard and measuring cast, whether they were more unwise, more unjust, or more unfortunate; and which had infallibly been our destruction if, by the grace of God, their share had not been as small of the subtlety of serpents as of the innocency of doves." In a well-known passage he inveighs against them as having been the destruction of unity under pretence of uniformity; as having brought in superstition and scandal under the titles of reverence and decency, and having defiled our Church by adorning our churches. He declared that their apparent work had been "to try how much of a papist might be brought in without popery; and to destroy as much as they could of the Gospel without bringing themselves into danger of being destroyed by the law." But he never for a moment included episcopacy in his censure of certain bishops. Of the order he said in the same speech, "I do not believe them to be *jure divino,* but neither do I believe them to be *injuriâ humanâ.* I neither consider them as necessary nor as unlawful, but as convenient or inconvenient." He was confident that the House would "not think fit to abolish upon a few days' debate an order which hath lasted (as appears by story) in most churches from Christ to Calvin, or in an instant change the whole face of the Church, like the scene of a masque." His second speech is in thorough keeping with the first. He repudiates the necessity of episcopacy, while insisting on its expediency. Its grounds, he said, were ancient, general, and uncontradicted in the first and best times; episcopacy had agreed very well with the constitution of the laws and the disposition of the people; and Englishmen had lived very happily and gloriously under that form of government. But he expresses, at the same time, his dread of the encroachments of ecclesiastical jurisdictions, and mentions the *jus divinum* only to protest against it. It was a saying of his, that "those who hated bishops, hated them worse than the devil; and they who loved them, did not love them so well as their dinner." He himself had no hatred either of his dinner or of bishops; but he loved neither so well as liberty and truth. He resisted their extravagant pretensions as firmly as Hampden or Pym; and he thought ecclesiastical courts quite unlike the seventh heaven.

No satisfactory biography of Falkland has as yet been written; and this for obvious reasons. The material is not very abundant; and most persons who are tempted to begin the search are disappointed with the nature of the material which they find. The advocates of the Long Parliament as opposed to the king, the admirers of Hampden, Pym, or Cromwell, are not attracted by a decided royalist who died fighting in the king's army, and has even been suspected (though, we believe, without a shadow of reason) of being privy to the king's attempt to seize the five members. Those, on the other hand, who approach Falkland from Clarendon's point of view, expecting to find in him a stanch advocate for all that is generally meant by "Church and King," if they weigh the facts of his life fairly, will probably feel themselves disappointed. We all know the sad unbuttoned man, negligent of his person and careless of his life, abrupt in manner and conversation, and grown into a perfect habit of uncheerfulness, who, when sitting among his friends, would, after deep silence and frequent sighs, with a shrill and sad accent, ingeminate the words *Peace, peace.* But we must not judge of his life by its closing days, by the opinions of his later companions, or by the sentiments of his friend and panegyrist. The quick little man, full of spirit and learning, at once a soldier and a scholar, nice in dress, sharp in retort, epigrammatic in diction; imprisoned in the Fleet in boyhood for some outbreak of youthful passion, and not without some suspicion of gallantry even at the time of his death; fond of freedom, and watchful against the encroachment of authority; loving learning much, but reason more; taking the king's side actively, but not with the spirit of one who thinks that his cause is wholly good and must conquer; a Christian, rather than a churchman; very outspoken against bishops and episcopal abuses; and accused, with however little reason, of Socinianism, can scarcely, at the distance of two hundred years, gain the hearty attachment of conservative students who admire the Caroline divines. Were he alive now, and a member for the University of Oxford, his seat would be as insecure as that of Mr. Gladstone. Cautious men would scarcely account him "safe;" and suspicious men would breathe some hint of heresy. His house at Great Tew was indeed "a college in a purer air;" but it had no touch of a cloister. Intellectually, as well as physically, its atmosphere was very different from that of St. John's at Oxford.

But the burden of the civil war lay far more heavily on Falkland than the part which he played in theological controversy. To this he was partly attracted by his intellectual activity, and partly forced by the circumstances of his family. His mother was a Romanist; his two younger brothers, while yet children, were stolen from his house and carried beyond seas, that they might be brought up in the same belief; and his two sisters, as Clarendon says, anticipating a modern term, were "perverted." It is not surprising that under these circumstances he took up his pen and attacked the papal infallibility. But his attack is that of a chivalrous combatant who wishes to defeat his adversary, but not to disgrace him unfairly, or to ply him with reproachful words as auxiliaries or substitutes for better weapons. "I have ever thought," he says, "that there should be as little bitterness in a treatise of controversy as in a love-letter; and that the contrary way was both void of Christian charity and human wisdom, as serving only to fright away the game, and make the adversaries unwilling to receive instruction from him, from whom they have received injuries." "I desire," he elsewhere says, "that recrimination may not be used; for though it be true that Calvin hath done it, and the Church of England a little (which is a little too much),—for *negare manifesta non audeo, et excusare immodica non possum,*—yet she, confessing she may err, is not so chargeable with any fault as those which pretend they cannot, and so will be sure never to mend it."

And he reckons among the chief causes which make so many leave the Church of Rome, "this opinion of damning so many, and this custom of burning so many, this breeding up of those, who knew nothing else in any point of religion, yet to be in a readiness to say, To the fire with him, to hell with him; as Polybius says of a certain furious faction of an army of several nations, and consequently of several languages, *μόνον τὸ ῥῆμα τοῦτο συνίεσαν, βάλλε*—they all joined only in understanding this word, throw at him."

It is not easy to estimate with exactness the literary obligations of Chillingworth to Falkland. He used his library, and had the advantage of his conversation; perhaps, as has been asserted, he availed himself directly of his learning. For Chillingworth had not the reputation of being a very learned man. It is said of him that he did not study much, but that when he did, he did much in little time. Yet he was not exactly the man to take his learning at secondhand, while he was just the person whose learning was liable to be underrated. Falkland wrote easily, like the gentlemen of his day; did not trouble himself much about the structure of his sentences, and admitted at once a classical allusion, or a Greek quotation, if it came ready to his hand. But Chillingworth was a disputant by profession, and looked warily to his tools. He used, we are told, to walk much in Trinity College gardens, keeping, as he walked, a sharp look-out for some unhappy victim whom he might entangle and baffle with his logic. Like most effective arguers, he trusted little to abstruse research, and much to retort and homely illustration. He threw off the old scholastic armour entirely, and relied on a rapier and his own bare arm. Indeed, that skill in intellectual fence which was the strength of the controversialist was the weakness of the man. On one occasion, we know, being worsted by a Jesuit controversialist, and convinced by experience that he was not infallible, he inferred too hastily that the Church of Rome was. But he gained little satisfaction from his half-year's communion with that Church, and his very brief sojourn among the Jesuits at Douay. It is said, indeed, that he did not find himself sufficiently well treated among the Jesuits; that they made him porter, to try his temper and exercise his obedience, and that he could not stand the test. And this is probable enough; for Chillingworth was hasty, impetuous, excitable; and the Church of Rome is quite wise in driving from itself the quickest wits, if they cannot be thoroughly broken to harness. A little contemplative leisure, in a position in which he could not conveniently find an opponent with whom he could argue, may have combined with letters from his friends in England to convince him that there were two sides to Roman infallibility, as to most questions, and that on the side which he had not hitherto explored there was a precipice of huge and fatal assumptions. So he came back to England and to Protestantism, to argue still, but to use argument more wisely than before. Once, perhaps, he argued for the sake of argument; now, he argued for the sake of truth. As to truth, he found, like most persons who endeavour to discover it mainly by force of reasoning, that it was much more easy to discover where it was not than where it was. He never persuaded himself that, in returning to Oxford and to the Church of England, he came back to another but a smaller Rome, which claimed the right to suppress inquiry and to silence conscience. His restless, sceptical mind had doubts about many things, and about the Church of England among the number. There were points of her formularies which he found great difficulty in assenting to; and as a controversialist he defended, not his own Church, but Protestantism in general. Seeing, as he did, plainly, and with his own eyes, popes against popes, councils against councils, some fathers against others, and the same fathers against themselves; having searched for interpretations of holy Scripture, delivered by tradition from the Apostles, and having found few or none, he discovered no certainty but of holy Scripture only for any considerate man to build on. In believing holy Scripture to contain all necessary truth, and in this belief only, he found, as he avowed, rest for the sole of his foot. And, therefore, ignoring alike for the time the doctrine of Luther and Calvin and Melancthon, the Confessions of Augsburg and Geneva, the Catechism of Heidelberg and the Articles of the Church of England, he declared the Bible, and the Bible only, to be the religion of Protestants.

The Religion of Protestants a safe Way to Salvation was published at the close of 1637. Laud was then in the full swing of his power. In the June of that year Prynne, Burton, and Bastwick had been sentenced in the Star-Chamber, and had lost their ears. In July Laud's old rival, Williams bishop of Lincoln, had been censured in the Star-Chamber, fined 8000*l.*, imprisoned at the king's pleasure, and suspended by the king's commission. In August a royal proclamation had declared that processes might issue out of the ecclesiastical court in the names of the bishops; and that a patent under the great seal was not necessary for the keeping of the said ecclesiastical courts, or for the enabling of citations, suspensions, excommunications, and other censures of the Church. Resistance to the liturgy was beginning in Scotland, and an anonymous libeller had fixed his libel on the south gate of St. Paul's, declaring that the Church of England was a candle in the snuff, going out in a stench; but the Archbishop of Canterbury kept his candlestick conspicuously on high, and trimmed the snuff with sharp scissors. His feelings with regard to the foreign Protestant churches were a matter of common notoriety. A few years before, he had endeavoured to force the English factories in Holland, Hamburg, and elsewhere into exact conformity with the English liturgy. He had effectually discouraged the attendance of the English ambassador at Paris at the Huguenot church at Charenton. He had robbed the French, Dutch, and Walloon churches in London, Norwich, and Canterbury of that free use of their own discipline which had been wisely granted to them by former kings and tolerated by former archbishops. Not even his close and intimate relations with the king and the royal family could induce him to allow a draft of the royal letters patent on behalf of the banished ministers of the Palatinate to pass unchallenged, in which it was asserted that the religion of the Palatine ministers was true, and the same with our own. It might well have seemed a bold thing in Chillingworth to publish his pronounced opinions in the face of one whose strong hierarchical ideas were backed by the unflinching exercise of arbitrary power. A divine without preferment, and with the stigma of recent Romanism clinging to his name, he made common cause with Huguenot and Calvinist in England and abroad, when the archbishop had recently oppressed and discouraged them. Poor Bishop Hall, only two years later, was severely criticised by Laud for not being strong enough on behalf of bishops in a book whose very title proclaimed "the Divine Right of Episcopacy;" yet Chillingworth was connecting the Church of England with bodies which held episcopacy to be contrary to the law of God. Laud was strong for the value of tradition as an interpreter of holy Scripture: Chillingworth's watchword is "the Bible only." Laud was adding forms to the liturgy in England, and endeavouring to enforce its use in Scotland: Chillingworth had not only scruples as to some of its contents, but would gladly have seen some new form of worshiping God proposed, which was taken wholly out of Scripture. But in this, as in so many other cases, things as they were differed widely from what we might have expected. Laud was throughout the patron of Chillingworth: it was to Laud that Chillingworth ascribed his reconversion to the Church of England; it was Laud whom, two years before the publication of his book, he had feared to offend by declining Church preferment; it was to examiners appointed by Laud that Chillingworth submitted his book for approbation before it was published. Such are the facts, strange as they may seem at first; facts which can be adequately explained by no mere personal ties between Laud and Chillingworth, and which find their parallel in the relations between Laud and Hales, of which no similar explanation can be given.

A happy man this Chillingworth—one might have thought who read history by snatches, and knew only that he had powerfully asserted the supremacy of the Bible, and had retained the friendship of Laud,—a happy man, with friends on the right hand and the left: unlovely, of course, to Papists, but dear to Puritans; not perhaps agreeing exactly with rigorous Calvinists and strict Presbyterians, but fighting powerfully on their side against Rome, and defending the charter of their spiritual freedom; an ally without the camp, if not a friend within it; a herald who could go from Geneva to Canterbury with a flag of truce, receiving honour in both places, and free from the fear of personal danger. His friendship with Laud might need accounting for; but who could wonder if the Presbyterians, disclaiming all tradition, and finding their own dear polity in the Bible, welcomed with all their heart this champion of universal Protestantism, and embraced him as a scriptural Christian? Poor Chillingworth! he had probably few hopes of this kind himself, knowing the Puritan temperament far too well. Certainly the history of his later days tells quite a different tale—a tragedy, in which there is real suffering, and much to offend the sensitive mind, and to which the perverse and fanatical intolerance of the principal actor gives, by its sheer intensity, a kind of unconscious humour.

Chillingworth, it seems, was of opinion that war was unlawful; and accordingly, with an inconsistency which may surprise us in so keen a logician, thought that he would do his best to put an end to it by a little ingenious fighting. He had been at the siege of Gloucester, though it is not quite certain in what capacity—whether as spectator, chaplain, or amateur engineer. Be that as it may, in December 1643 he accompanied Lord Hopton into Sussex, to make experiments with a military engine which he had invented, and which was to move so lightly as to be a breastwork in all encounters and assaults in the field. We are not informed how this modern application of *testudines cum pluteis* succeeded against the enemy; but we know that the experimental trip was most disastrous in its consequences to Chillingworth. He fell ill on the expedition, and was left at Arundel Castle, which was retaken in January 1644 by the parliamentary forces under Sir William Waller. Clarendon tells us that he was most barbarously treated by the rebels, and died shortly after in prison. But this is only Clarendon's way of putting it. Chillingworth was, we suppose, liable to imprisonment by the laws of war; but, on account of his illness, he was treated with more consideration than the other prisoners. They were sent to London, but Chillingworth was removed to the bishop's palace at Chichester, where he received much attention and kindness, as he acknowledged in a codicil to his will.

But the poor sufferer met with a fate which was not the less cruel because inflicted by one who really meant to be kind. He was spared by the Presbyterian soldiers, but he was killed by a Presbyterian divine. What Horace prophesied jestingly of himself was gravely fulfilled in Chillingworth; he was literally talked to death. The garrulous person who slew him was Cheynell; a man of learning, probity, ability; a despiser of wealth, and given to hospitality; one who had himself suffered loss in these unhappy times; but also, as Chillingworth found to his cost, the most zealous of doctors, and the most orthodox of Presbyterians.

Cheynell was a member of the Assembly of Divines; he had lately published a work accusing Laud, Chillingworth, and their adherents of Socinianism; he was come on a preaching excursion into Sussex, when the current of war drifted him to Arundel Castle. When the castle fell, and Cheynell found Chillingworth within it, he interceded with Sir William Waller on his behalf. We may omit details, transport Chillingworth without further delay to Chichester, and bring Cheynell there to visit him in his illness. Happy indeed would it have been if the Christian had come to the sick man's bedside, leaving the controversialist behind.

The defect of Chillingworth's constitution, we learn from Clarendon, was "his sleeping too little and thinking too much, which sometimes threw him into violent fevers." It was abundance of sleep, and complete freedom from disturbance, that he needed on his sick-bed at Chichester; but these simple remedies were not granted him. Cheynell, on his first visit, thought that the patient might need repose, and therefore spared him for the time. But he soon returned; and after telling Chillingworth that he did not desire to take him at the lowest, when his spirits were flatted and his reason disturbed, asked him whether he was fit for discourse. He answered with a "yes" which even Cheynell perceived to be faint; and accordingly they went straight to an argument, of which we have only Cheynell's account, and which, as we rather sympathise with Chillingworth, we have no wish to inflict upon our readers. Indeed, times have changed; and the matter which then kept the invalid awake might now send the strong man to sleep.

To be brief, a long discussion followed, from which the sick man never fully rallied. Cheynell gave him many more visits;

but he seldom found him fit to discourse, because his disease grew stronger and stronger, and he weaker and weaker. Occasionally, however, Cheynell contrived to throw in a hard question; and Chillingworth, whenever it was possible, referred him for answer to his book. At last Chillingworth died, after suffering, to an uncertain extent, a torture like that which is inflicted in China on some criminals, who are never allowed to sleep. Then followed the grave question of his burial.

Was he to be buried as a Christian at all? As he had not answered Cheynell's questions satisfactorily, he was not supposed to have made a full and free confession of Christian religion. Besides, he had taken up arms against the Parliament, and was thought by some to have been guilty of his own death by his foolhardiness, and therefore to be *felo de se.* But Cheynell could not go all lengths with those who would have denied Chillingworth the semblance of a funeral; for, as we shall see presently, he wished a funeral to take place, and himself to perform some solemnities on the occasion. And yet he would not himself bury Chillingworth, as he avows in his account of the transaction, giving reasons to justify his conduct. He had never given Chillingworth the right hand of fellowship, but had freely and constantly protested against these damnable heresies, which he had cunningly subintroduced and vented in this kingdom. He knew that Chillingworth had once been a Papist, and he believed that his subsequent conversion was a pretence. He differed from him in fundamentals, and therefore did not feel himself a member of the same Church. He had a shrewd suspicion that prayer over the dead was likely to lead to praying for them. Besides, Chillingworth had expressed a wish to have some part of the Common Prayer-Book read over his grave; and Cheynell objected to the Prayer-Book in general, and to the Burial Service in particular. He believed that it was absurd and sinful to use the same form of words at the burial of all manner of persons, as insinuating that they were all elected, all rest in Christ, and that we have sure and certain hope of their salvation. In short, Cheynell wished to subject the dead, as well as the living, to the pure Presbyterian discipline; he could not understand that when the soul of a fellow-sinner had left the body, it was not for man to judge the departed, much less to pass sentence on him. He dared not express a hope on a subject on which no Christian has any right to despair. Not content with proclaiming God's eternal enmity to sin, he felt it his duty to act in a way which would convey the impression of his eternal enmity to the sinner. Thus armed with a harsh and unholy theory, he forbad his lips to utter those good and solemn words, which express so wonderfully the dim and mysterious hope which rises naturally in the Christian heart at the sight of a corpse and a coffin. He refused to bury Chillingworth as he wished; but still he was to be buried, and the question remained, where.

Chillingworth, at the time of his death, was chancellor of the cathedral-church of Sarum, and held also the prebend of Bricklesworth, which is attached to that chancellorship. There is reason to think that this preferment was much more honourable than lucrative, but it had its pleasant associations. Hooker, for instance, had not many years before held a stall in the beautiful cathedral of Salisbury; and Bricklesworth is Brixworth in Northamptonshire, a place remarkable for the exceeding antiquity of its church, which appears to be really a fragment of a Roman basilica. But Cheynell had probably no eye for architecture (if he had been so blessed, could he ever have been a fellow of Merton College, and then have become the strictest of Puritans?); as a rigorous Presbyterian, he could not have cared much for Hooker; and he would probably have regarded the Roman bricks at Brixworth only as an additional mark of the beast. As to burying Chillingworth within the chancel of Chichester Cathedral, either because he was chancellor of another cathedral, or simply because he was a priest, he jeered at the very idea. "Being *cancellarius,*" he says, "it was conceived that he should be buried *intra cancellos,* and rot under the altar, near the pot of incense, that the constant perfume of the incense might excuse the thrift of his executrix,—*ossa inodora dedit.* . . . . But some more serious conceived that this desire of burying him *intra cancellos* was but the issue of a superstitious conceit that the chancel, or *sanctum sanctorum,* was more holy than other places, and the carcass of a priest as sacred as that holy ground; and it was their opinion that a modest and well-grounded denial of this request would be the most effectual confutation of that superstitious conceit." As these more serious persons had their way, it was arranged that Chillingworth should be buried in the cloisters; and there Cheynell met the corpse, which he refused to bury. The conclusion of his invective will suffice our readers. "I refuse"—this is his own report of his own words—"to bury him myself; yet let his friends and followers, who have attended his hearse to this Golgotha, know, that they are permitted, out of mere humanity, to bury their dead out of our sight. If they undertake the burial of his corpse, I shall undertake the burial of his errors, which are published in his so much admired yet unworthy book." Then follow some words of bitterness against Chillingworth, which we need not quote. Cheynell soon returns to the book in these words, suiting, of course, the action to the word: "Get thee gone thence, thou cursed book, which has seduced so many precious souls; get thee gone, thou corrupt rotten book, earth to earth, and dust to dust; get thee gone into the place of rottenness, that thou mayst rot with thy author and see corruption. Touching the burial of his corpse," he continues, "I need say no more than this. It will be most proper for the men of his persuasion to commit the body of their deceased friend, brother, master, to the dust; and it will be most proper for me to hearken to that counsel of my Saviour, 'Let the dead bury their dead, but go thou and preach the kingdom of God.'" And so he went from the grave to the pulpit, and preached on that text to the congregation.

It is hard to think that the kingdom of God which Cheynell preached was exactly righteousness, and peace, and joy in the Holy Ghost. The malignants at least, whom he left standing by the grave when he went off to the pulpit, must have been of a very peculiar constitution, if the straitness of his zeal did not kindle in them the bitterness of aversion. They may have been royalists of a very common type, caring little for any form of religion; some of them may have been like that Sir Edmund Varney, whose sad, thoughtful face, thanks to Vandyke, we could see at the British Institution last summer,—the gallant standard-bearer who fought for his king because he had long eaten his bread, but owned privately to having no reverence for bishops. Yet for the nonce they must have become Episcopalians of the strictest sect, if they could gain that distinction by disgust at the Presbyterian brotherhood. To agree with Chillingworth was to distrust tradition, to insist on the supremacy of Scripture, to uphold reason and private judgment, to claim community with foreign Protestants, and to deny the divine right of any hierarchical system. These were far from the sentiments of Laud; yet they were, practically, further still from the school of Calvin. Compared with this tyranny of Geneva, even the rule of Rome would seem tolerable at a distance, and that of Canterbury would be embraced as absolute freedom.

But it may be thought that Cheynell was not a fair specimen of his class. He was a hot and violent man, and at one time of his life at least was not without a suspicion of madness. Be it so; he was an extreme man in one direction, as Laud was an extreme man in another. His conduct at the grave was about as characteristic as the conduct of Laud in the ecclesiastical courts and the Star-Chamber. But he had real Christian virtues, little as they showed themselves at the burial of Chillingworth; and far from being rejected by the Presbyterians as an unfair representative of their opinions, he was put forward by them as one of their leading men. In the previous year he had published his treatise on the "Rise, Growth, and Danger of Socinianism," in which he had vehemently declared that the religion upheld by Laud was "not the true pure Protestant religion, but a hotchpotch of Arminianism, Socinianism, and Popery." Before he had time to correct the proof-sheets, he was summoned to preach before the House of Commons on the monthly fast, and sounded "Sion's memento and God's alarum" to the full satisfaction of his hearers. In 1646 he was sent to Oxford by parliament, with six other divines, with authority to preach in any pulpits of the University for six months, in order, as Neal quaintly words it, to "soften the spirits of the people." In 1647 he was made one of the visitors of the University, that he might reform by force the body which he failed to persuade. In 1648 he was appointed president of St. John's,—a most strange successor of Laud,—and Margaret professor of divinity. If he could not retain these preferments, it was the fault, not of the Presbyterians, but of the Independents. He is a fine, and therefore an exaggerated, specimen of his class,—orthodox among the orthodox, violent among the violent, earnest among the earnest. We cannot say that all Presbyterians were like him; but we may safely say that the Presbyterianism of that day was very much like him indeed.

Perhaps, as a mere representative of opinions, more objection can be taken to Chillingworth than to Cheynell. Chillingworth was no doubt hateful to the Presbyterians as a royalist as well as a divine. And his adherence to the king was no matter of pure theory. Whatever were his speculative objections to war, they were overruled by a practical disposition for fighting. His head, as Cheynell said, was full of engines as well as of scruples; he was not only a malignant clerk of Oxford, but also the queen's arch-engineer and grand intelligencer. Thus in his case political questions became inextricably mixed up with religious differences. When Cheynell wished to press him home in argument, he chose for discussion the thesis, *Is tyranny God's ordinance?* It was just possible for a quiet thinker, even in those troublous times, if favoured by fortune, insignificance, or a patron, and uniting the wisdom of the serpent to the harmlessness of the dove, to escape the notice of the diligent searchers after delinquency, malignity, and heresy. John Hales, who gained the title of "ever memorable" while toiling after something better than fame, is not quite a case in point; for he lost his fellowship at Eton in refusing to take the Engagement. But he had been allowed to retain it for a time without taking the covenant, and so far serves to show that the Presbyterians could make some approach to tolerance. But his history also proves that Laud, with all his faults, could sometimes rise above mere tolerance, and could be actively and decidedly liberal.

Associated as John Hales was with Falkland and Chillingworth, he differed from them in one respect, which constitutes for the most part a bar to intimate friendship. He was a much older man. He was probably a student at Oxford when Chillingworth was born, and was appointed by the University to deliver the funeral oration of Sir Thomas Bodley when Falkland was only three years old. The two younger friends died within four months of each other, being respectively a little more than thirty and forty years old; but Hales lived on another twelve years, and passed the allotted age of three score years and ten. Falkland fell in battle; Chillingworth died from the consequences of a siege; Hales, stripped of his preferments, and not allowed to act as private tutor in a family, because to give him board and lodging would have amounted legally to harbouring a malignant, spent his last days in the house of an old servant, and was in an undesirable sense a *helluo librorum*, living on the proceeds of a partial sale of his library. His long life had not been without variety. He had been a fellow at Merton, like Cheynell, but many years before Cheynell's time. He had been Greek lecturer in his college, and Greek professor in the University. He had been the principal reliance of Sir Henry Savile in preparing for the press that fine edition of St. Chrysostom, which is unhappily too full of contractions for degenerate moderns to read. He had attended Sir Dudley Carleton, ambassador to the Hague, as his chaplain; had been present at the Synod of Dort, to which he went as a Calvinist, and at which, upon the well pressing of St. John iii. 16 by Episcopius, he "bade John Calvin good night." But he was not of that false and untrustworthy temper of mind which flies immediately from one extreme to the other. A model convert, he was still among Calvinists as a Calvinist, and could use freely their technical phraseolgy, while he gave it a moderation which was his own. He knew when to speak and when to hold his tongue; indeed, if he erred at all in this respect, it was on the safer side of saying and writing too little. He published nothing except his oration at the funeral of Sir Thomas Bodley. When once he preached at St. Paul's Cross, he began by saying that he would not have been seen (he quite despaired of being heard) in that conspicuous pulpit, if he had had in his power the choice of his ways and the free management of his own actions; with no thirst after popular applause, he felt that a small, private, retired auditory better accorded with his will, and he believed that it better accorded with his abilities. He even declined to undertake the cure of souls, so entirely did he devote himself to study. But his thoughts and his reading had no narrow or unworthy object. Once he was obliged, to some extent, to discuss his own conduct and principles; and then he wrote as follows: "The pursuit of truth hath been my only care ever since I first understood the meaning of the word. For this I have forsaken all hopes, all friends, all desires, which might bias me, and hinder me from driving right at what I aimed. For this, I have spent my money, my means, my youth, my age, and all I have, that I might remove from myself that censure of Tertullian,—*suo vitio quis quid ignorat?* If with all this cost and pains my purchase is but error; I may safely say, to err hath cost me more than it has many to find the truth; and truth itself shall give me this testimony at last, that if I have missed of her, it is not my fault, but my misfortune."

The pursuit of truth, even in matters of religion, is sometimes conducted in a hard unsympathetic spirit, with little apparent love of God or man. But this was not the case with John Hales: in seeking truth, he found peace, the sister of truth. His soul, he said, in the opening words of his last will and testament, which was written in his closing days of poverty and trial, had long been bequeathed to the mercies of God in Christ, his only Saviour. Towards man he was alike tolerant in opinion and kind in practice. He would often say that he would renounce the religion of the Church of England to-morrow if it obliged him to believe that any other Christian should be damned, and that nobody would conclude another man to be damned who did not wish him so. His behaviour was full of the same overflowing charity; he was remarkable for his liberality to the poor, and for his general kindness and courtesy. Aubrey, who called on him at Eton after his sequestration, and found him living at an inn when ejected from the college, was received by him with much humanity. He describes him, at the time of the interview, which was within a year of his death, as a pretty little man, sanguine, of a cheerful countenance, very gentle and courteous, dressed in a kind of violet-coloured cloth gown with buttons and loops, and reading *Thomas à Kempis.* He was apparently a proficient in the philosophy of "tips," to an extent which would have delighted Mr. Thackeray; for we hear incidentally of his giving, in his poorer days, ten shillings to three Oxford students who called upon him when on a "frolic on foot" from that University to London. A year after his death, Pearson, who was in time to be Bishop of Chester, and a great authority in dogmatic theology, wrote an introductory notice to his *Golden Remains,* in which he could scarcely abstain from the language of unmixed panegyric. Hales, he informs his readers, was not only most truly and most strictly just in his secular transactions, most exemplarily meek and humble notwithstanding his perfections, but beyond all example charitable, giving to all, preserving nothing but his books to continue his learning and himself; of a nature so kind, so sweet, so courting all mankind; of an affability so prompt, so ready to receive all conditions of man, that it was nearly as easy a task for any one to be so knowing, as so obliging. One spot, indeed, in an almost faultless character, the shrewd and discerning Pearson—who contrived, with better worldly success than Hales, to be successively chaplain to the drunken Goring during the civil war, incumbent of a City church in the time of the Commonwealth, and rector, prebendary, archdeacon, master of Trinity, and bishop after the Restoration—thinks that he discerns, though he scarcely ventures to indicate it. "He took, indeed," observes Pearson, "a liberty of judging, not of others, but for himself; and if ever any man might be allowed in all matters to judge, it was he who had so long, so much, so advantageously considered, and, what is more, never could be said to have the least worldly design in his determinations."

A man like this, so learned, so wise, and so peaceable, was not likely to set up for a great discoverer of truth, and to trouble the world with his crotchets. His friends, indeed, complained of that genial and indulgent silence which had no touch of reserve; and we knew from Clarendon that he often said, with regard to certain points on which his sentiments differed from those which were generally received, that his opinions, he was sure, did him no harm; but he was far from being confident that they might not do others harm who entertained them. He himself, in one of his sermons, alludes pleasantly to a tale told by Julius Agricola, who, writing *de animantibus subterraneis*, reports of a certain kind of spirits that converse in minerals, and much infect those that work in them. Their manner when they come is, to seem to busy themselves according to all the custom of workmen: they will dig, and cleanse, and melt, and sever metals; yet, when they are gone, the workmen do not find that there is any thing done. So, observes Hales, fares it with a great part of the multitude who thrust themselves into the controversies of the times: they write books, move questions, frame distinctions, give solutions, and seem sedulously to do whatsoever the nature of the business requires; yet, if any skilful workman in the Lord's mines shall come and examine their work, he shall find them to be but spirits in minerals; and that with all this labour and stir there is nothing done. Devoted as he was to avoiding the fault which he censured, and to working out quietly his own fine vein of pure gold, he was once, and once only, at all entangled in controversy. There is matter suggestive of reflection, both in the occasion and in its issue.

Hales had, apparently for the use of Chillingworth, written a small tract on schism, contained in less than two sheets of paper. It was passed from hand to hand, till, to the surprise and annoyance of its writer, it reached the Archbishop of Canterbury. Its opening words could scarcely have been pleasing to Laud. "Heresy and schism, as they are commonly used, are two theological scare-crows, with which they who use to uphold a party in religion, use to fright away such as, making inquiry into it, are ready to relinquish and oppose it, if it appear either erroneous or suspicious." As Laud read on, he must have found matter as little to his mind. Hales had been accustomed, in common discourse, to say that it was only pride and passion which kept the Christian world from agreeing upon such a liturgy as might bring the world into one communion; all doctrinal points upon which men differed in their opinions being to have no place in any liturgy. He wrote to the same effect in this little tract. "Why may I not go," he asked, "if occasion require, to an Arian church, so there be no Arianism expressed in their liturgy? And were liturgies and public forms of service so framed, as that they admitted not of particular and private fancies, but contained only such things as in which all Christians do agree, schisms on opinion were utterly vanished. For consider of all the liturgies that are, and ever have been, and remove from them whatever is scandalous to any party, and leave nothing but what all agree on, and the evil shall be, that the public service and honour of God shall in no wise suffer. Whereas, to load our public forms with the private fancies upon which we differ, is the most sovereign way to perpetuate schism unto the world's end. Prayer, confession, thanksgiving, reading of Scriptures, administration of sacraments in the plainest and the simplest manner, were matter enough to furnish out a sufficient liturgy, though nothing either of private opinion or of church pomp, of garments or prescribed gestures, of imagery, of music, of matter concerning the dead, of many superfluities which creep into the Church, under the name of Order and Decency, did interpose itself."

The clear and distinct assertion that, in cases of separation among Christians, those who would impose burdens on others and enforce an unnecessary conformity are really responsible for the schism; the evident longing for a simple, scriptural, and comprehensive liturgy, encumbered with a *minimum* of ceremonies; the strong censures on episcopal ambition, as the great cause of frequent, continuous, and bloody schisms; and all this in a curt, abrupt, and telling style, compressing much matter on two sheets of paper, could not easily be overlooked at Lambeth. Laud sent for Hales, whom he had known of old. Heylin, who happened to be at the palace that day, gives an account of their meeting, which can be trusted up to a certain point: how the archbishop and Hales, about nine o'clock in the morning, adjourned to the garden till the bell rang for prayers; how, when prayers were ended, they returned to the garden and stayed there talking till dinner-time; how, when dinner was over, they resumed the old work in the old place, and did not desist till the archbishop's presence was required by some great people, when they both came in, high-coloured and almost panting for breath—enough to show that there had been some heats between them, not yet fully cooled. But Heylin, whose great object was to varnish Laud's portrait, did not care much for accidentally bespattering that of Hales. He insinuates that Laud on this occasion secured the loyalty of Hales to the Church of England by his arguments, strengthened by a chaplaincy at the time, and riveted into conclusiveness by higher preferment afterwards. Clarendon, though singularly unlike Hales in temper, tastes, and opinions, represents him as acting in a way far more consonant with his character; as answering the inquiry, if he wanted any thing, by saying that he had enough and desired no additions; and as afterwards with great difficulty persuaded to accept a canonry of Windsor, because he knew that his means were already equal to his wants.

The canonry, we know, did not long stay with Hales; and when Laud's time of trouble came, Lord Say and Seal quoted against the archbishop the opening words of Hales' tract on schism. But the student probably parted readily with the preferment which he had been slow to accept; and the primate on his trial could hear without a blush the words of an honest man with whom he was far from agreeing in opinion, but whom, from motives which perhaps he could not analyse, he had in former days protected instead of injuring.

Two hundred years and more have passed since the men with whom we have been holding converse have passed from this earthly scene. No fanatical soldiers disturb the church or churchyard of Walton-on-Thames, preaching intolerable doctrines and extinguishing symbolical candles. The name of Dering has lately been before the world in consequence of a contested election between a Conservative-Liberal and a Liberal-Conservative. Our interest in the great men of the civil war has extended from their opinions to their bones. Falkland, happier than Hampden, sleeps in a tomb at Great Tew, of which no one can even conjecture the place, and is safe from literary or surgical examination of his skeleton. Chillingworth still rests in the cloisters of Chichester Cathedral, unvexed by Cheynell and not startled even by the fall of the spire. A black marble monument in Eton churchyard covers the remains of Hales. Laud was interred with the rites which he loved in the church of Allhallows Barking, when his head had been severed from his body. Cheynell—well, graves and funerals are not exactly sacred to his memory, and we have not cared to inquire of the place or manner of his interment. Yet the dead still speak and live. Hales is "the ever memorable," even with those who knew nothing of his *Golden Remains;* Chillingworth argues as clearly as of old, if not quite so disputatiously; Falkland steps forward with a sad grace from the eloquent pages of Clarendon. As for Laud, his handiwork is visible in almost every church in England. The holy table stands altarwise in the chancel, protected by a decent rail from the hats of irreverent men, the satchels of careless boys, and the misdoings of profane dogs. A ceremonial more strongly resembling that of Rome than any thing which Laud ventured on is practised in the Church of England when the clergyman and the congregation like it, and sometimes, unhappily, when the clergyman likes it and the congregation does not. The Star-Chamber and the High Commission Court are indeed no more; but Laud has been more powerful to liberate than ever he was to enslave. His blood washed away from High Churchmen for ever the "horrible decree" of Calvinistic reprobation. Cheynell, too, exists, but far more altered; mild, gentlemanly, aristocratic, very probably even, to his own surprise, a bishop. By degrees, after the day of Black Bartholomew, the old Presbyterian element reconciled itself to the Establishment; first endured episcopacy and the liturgy, and then embraced them. And Low Churchmen, too, thanks to brave John Wesley, have rejected Calvinism. At the sacrifice, it may be, of logical consistency, but with an accession of moral and spiritual strength which more than compensates for such a sacrifice, the doctrines of free grace are now taught without any attempt to thrust a single soul by necessary consequence into the pit of unutterable darkness. And yet old tendencies still exist, old sympathies, old affinities; and the modern representatives of Laud and Chillingworth are essentially much nearer to each other than either to the most softened likeness of Cheynell.

Let us suppose three tolerably defined specimens of the three modern schools—High, Low, and Broad—to meet together with a view to forward some work into which the directly religious element enters,—to approve of a curate, it may be, or select an incumbent, or regulate the religious instruction of a school or college. If the three men are by nature equally frank and unsuspicious, there is little doubt which of the trio would feel the earliest theological misgivings. In the heart of one of them would rise up on the first disputed point a question addressed to his companions, Are you converted? His own conversion is, of course, a postulate under the circumstances. But how would a modern Falkland, or Laud, or Chillingworth answer such a question, if it dropped, as it were unconsciously, from the lips of a modified Cheynell? Falkland might say that he was honestly bent on doing the work in hand, and might be told that honesty was not the spiritual mind. Even an appeal to a text of Scripture—"We know that we have passed from death unto life, because we love the brethren"—might not be accepted as satisfactory from a common mortal. Who, Cheynell would ask, are the brethren? and what were the time and place of the supposed passage? Laud might suggest that he was a baptised Christian, and might hear in reply that the grace of baptism was only a charitable hypothesis. Chillingworth might say something about the light which lighteth every man, and would be consigned at once to the outer darkness of the heathen.

The school which thus erects religion on experiences, and ignores so many forms of high and unconscious goodness; which declines to accept results if it cannot see processes, and disbelieves the divine life of man if it cannot trace its history, often shows a partial sense of the danger of its own position. There is something terrible in staking so much on a few facts of religious consciousness. A man whose own faith is the warrant of his hope, whose present trust in God turns upon some past phase of his inner history, who is sure that he is now in the right way mainly on the ground that some time ago he certainly turned out of the wrong one, had need have a good memory, and a good deal of obstinacy too. His religion is not only personal, but individual; and his past convictions are a part of his present faith. Out of a few texts of the Bible he constructs his tests of a standing or falling church, a standing or falling soul; collates these texts with certain passages of his life, and then—woe to him who would shake his confidence in either. If he is thoroughly in earnest, he is essentially a moody and morbid man. We know his thin rigid face, every line of which is hardened and drawn out in the endeavour to fix the soul on a few supposed truths, even at the danger of rejecting all other truth as falsehood. He is suspicious and solitary; for he knows that his shibboleth is easily caught, and is often repeated by hypocrites. He may have a few chosen companions whom he can trust; but he cannot throw himself unsuspiciously abroad among the glorious company of the saints and the noble army of martyrs.

They were sincere, no doubt, in their way; but he has great doubts about their vital Christianity.

The most narrow and exclusive Laudian, who having signed the Articles on the ground that they must be right, because such men as Andrews and Cosin and Bramhall have signed them before him, betakes himself to a medieval book with massive clasps, and fancies, as he chants Gregorians out of it, that every Christian of orthodox repute before the unhappy Council of Trent was exactly of the same opinion as himself, may be further from the truth than the modern copy of the Puritan, and yet can reach it by an easier and more open road. His world of thought is small and artificial, distorted in its facts and maimed in its proportions, a feeble copy of God's world; still it is a world, a cosmos; a thing of order and degree, of variety, of multiplicity, of law; full of spirits, angels, powers, authorities, hierarchies, not a thin line of connexion between the soul and God. If, as his knowledge enlarges and his feelings deepen, he escapes in an early stage of transition the superficial fascinations of Rome, he may grow naturally and almost insensibly into broader and deeper views of truth. He will still love the Church, though he has ceased to see an essential connexion between the Church and any one form of Church-government; he will respect, and wish others to respect, the sacraments, while not regarding them as charms; while admiring the types of holiness which were received in former days, he will not despise the peculiar shape which goodness may assume in his own day; he will feel that living and breathing men are as sacred as those whose bones are encased in shrines and reliquaries, and that righteousness and peace have not changed their nature in escaping into the world from the cloister. He will love the chant, the psalm, the solemn rite, the old seat of religion, the home of medieval learning, as truly as of old, and more wisely; without any taint of superstition, he can keep in its niche the image which the Puritan would break, and view without horror an apocryphal saint in a painted window; but still, as he pays the due tribute of respect to Jerusalem and even to Gerizim, he will not fear to trust himself to that spirit of Truth which is also the Spirit of God.

But the keen observer of events of the day will need no precedents from the seventeenth century to prove that those who in the nineteenth century seek for enlightened tolerance in the Church of England must look for it rather High than Low; and an analysis of the process which has of late led many, and will yet lead more, from dull, dry, unsympathetic orthodoxy to the loving freedom of truth, has no necessary connexion with Falkland, or Chillingworth, or Hales. Let us return briefly to our old subject before finally quitting it, and see the spirit of intolerance sitting by the side of the death-bed, not only torturing the victim, but also hardening the tormentor, by leading him to forget alike the extent of human ignorance and the scale of divine operations, and to strive with feeble yet obstinate hands to bring together those great events which God has put far asunder—the hour of death, and the day of judgment.

Chillingworth had, at least for a time, several scruples respecting the formularies of the Church of England; and one of these shall be stated in his own words. "The damning sentences in St. Athanasius' Creed, as we are made to subscribe it,"—thus he writes to his friend Sheldon,—"are most false, and also in a high degree presumptuous and schismatical. And therefore I neither can subscribe that these things are 'agreeable to the Word of God,' seeing I believe they are certainly repugnant to it; nor that the whole 'Common Prayer is lawful to be used,' seeing I believe these parts of it certainly unlawful; nor promise that 'I myself will use it,' seeing I never intend either to read these things, which I have now excepted against, nor to say 'Amen' to them." Unhappily the answer of the future archbishop to the remarkable letter from which this passage is an extract is not extant. It is probable, however, that he succeeded in palliating, if he could not wholly remove, Chillingworth's scruples; for the discussion between the two friends extended to other subjects connected with the Articles, on which it would not have been worth while to enter while this great issue remained unsettled; and Chillingworth, within three years of the date of his letter, did, on his admission to the chancellorship of Salisbury Cathedral, "willingly and heartily subscribe to the Thirty-nine Articles, and give his consent thereto."

His case was, to all appearance, a very common one. On inquiry, he found that he could assent to the formularies of the Church of England with an explanation; and he assented accordingly, wishing all the time that their sound meaning was more obvious, and that they did not need to be explained. Their letter, he saw, was fatal; but he knew that an apostle had said as much of the letter of holy Scripture itself. He could himself employ upon occasion (and an apostle could do so too) the damnatory language of ecclesiastical dogma; but it was foreign to the ordinary tone of his mind, and conflicted unpleasantly with his matured convictions. He was much more inclined to abstain from judging, that he might not be judged, than to condemn others in the hope that he might be saved himself.

On this man, always of a tolerant and charitable disposition, and especially now, when he felt that he was dying, longing to be at peace with all men, Cheynell, on finding him one day a little more hearty than usual, made an onslaught with a terrible question—Did he conceive that a man living and dying a Turk, Papist, or Socinian could be saved? Chillingworth wished to decline the controversy, but in vain; Cheynell persisted in tormenting him, though he gained for his pains only this answer from Chillingworth respecting Turk, Papist, and Socinian, that he did not absolve them, and would not condemn them.

Half of the answer Cheynell dismissed with a sneer. It was frivolous for Chillingworth to talk of absolution; priest though he was, he could not absolve them if he tried. With the other half he professed himself gravely dissatisfied. If he could only have extracted an anathema from the lips of the dying man, he would have had some hope of his salvation. And one passage in Chillingworth's works had encouraged him to think that he might be successful in the attempt. In replying to one of his most formidable assailants, Chillingworth had written as follows: "You charge me with a great number of false and impious doctrines, which I will not name in particular, because I will not assist you so far in the spreading of my own undeserved defamation; but whosoever teaches or holds them, *let him be anathema!*" On these latter words the eye and the memory of Cheynell fixed themselves, as on something sound, wholesome, and satisfactory, occurring in the midst of a hotchpotch of Arminianism, Socinianism, and Popery. And when the dying man declined to repeat the formula, Cheynell expresses his fear lest "Mr. Chillingworth grew worse and worse, and would not anathematise a gross Socinian." Poor Cheynell! incapable of perceiving that if there be a time for cursing, there is also a time for abstaining from curses; that a dying man has something better to do than to condemn the gravest errors of his neighbour, and that the heartiest anathema directed against a heretic is a miserable substitute for the faintest faith in a Saviour.

Within two months after the death of Chillingworth, the trial of Laud began. But had the archbishop been able to leave the Tower, and to visit his dying friend and godson, we can imagine some of the incidents of the visit. He would have come, Prayer-Book in hand, and would have turned to the Visitation of the Sick. As he used it, he would very probably have indulged in sundry gestures and bowings, and have longed in his heart for the oil of unction. Still he would have been faithful to its words; and when he came in its course to inquire whether the sick man believed as a Christian man would or no, he would simply have rehearsed the Apostles' Creed, and have asked Chillingworth if he believed it. The sick person having answered, "All this I steadfastly believe," the archbishop, or any other minister, must go on to other matter. The clergy of the Church of England have no reason or excuse for forcing on the sick and dying the language of scholastic distinctions and ecclesiastical censures. The Apostles' Creed must suffice them when they admit the babe into the Church at baptism, or strive to strengthen those who are ready to die. The Athanasian Creed is an occasional incident in morning prayer; it never touches font or altar, or blends itself with even the skirts of a sacrament. Falkland and Hales and Chillingworth, we cannot doubt, would gladly have dispensed with it. Laud might have comforted himself on its removal, with the reflection that the Councils both of Ephesus and Chalcedon had forbidden any addition to the Nicene Creed; an archbishop of Canterbury, not long after Laud, wished the Church well rid of it. It has become offensive in the course of two hundred years, even to the more judicious successors of Cheynell. Its days in the Church of England are surely numbered; and though it is too much to expect that churchmen of strong conservative instincts will be pleased at its final disappearance, yet their children of the next generation will take up a prayer-book which contains neither the State Services nor the Athanasian Creed, and rejoice that their good fathers had not their own way in all things.

Art. II.—PROFESSOR CONINGTON'S HORACE.

The Odes and Carmen Sæculare of Horace translated into English Verse. By John Conington, M.A., Corpus Professor of Latin in the University of Oxford. London: Bell and Daldy.

The Odes of Horace translated into English Verse. With a Life and Notes by Theodore Martin. London: Parker, Son, and Bourn.

Horace occupies a peculiar position not only in Roman poetry, but in the history of Europe. As a poet he stood on the boundary-line between the objective poetry of the earlier Romans, and the more subjective poetry of the Empire. More than any other man he may be called the art-poet of Rome. More than any other man, without sacrificing the objective form of the antique, he embodied that reflex play of conflicting feelings which accompanies every culminating civilisation, and which is essentially subjective. Horace first, as a poet, began to muse over his own feelings, and to play with his own experience. When Montaigne sat in his arm-chair spinning his own soul for future generations, he merely did in uncouth gothic style what Horace had taught him to do in the perfection, but also in the trammels, of ancient beauty. It is true that, when compared with later Europeans,—with Shakespeare or Schiller, with Shelley or with Goethe,—Horace's writings seem strangely shallow and meagre, as no doubt to him theirs must, could he have read them, have seemed the ravings of madmen or sick girls. But all proportion kept, if we compare Horace with other ancient authors, Latin and Greek, it is impossible, we think, not to feel that he is, by comparison with them, essentially subjective, and already, though with a youthful hand, unconsciously busy interpreting the self-inspection and self-dissection of his time. The key-note of his character in this respect (oddly enough, for it cannot have been by design) appears in his dedication to Mæcenas. The "sunt quos juvat"—words which, somehow or other, have served to stamp the feeling of the difference of human tastes ever since, and which ticket the ode in the schoolboy's mind—describe the very essence of his character. Let Lucretius describe the mysteries of creation uncreated, and Virgil her outward beauties; let Plautus set the manners of his countrymen in action; Horace is absorbed in his own feelings and those of the men around him, whom he personally knows. His classical conventional imagery is mere conventional drapery, a pure make-believe that he is sailing in the clouds. No man really hugs the ground closer, or is more intent upon the actual living throng about him. The real secret of Horace's hold upon later European thought arises precisely out of the living reality of his experience, coupled with the translucency of ancient forms, which made them readily intelligible. And it would be difficult to point to any set of feelings in modern society, the germs of which are not to be found in Horace, invested with that peculiar freshness which belongs to every first crop. His position as a freedman, belonging to the mercantile class, gave him an insight into the whole tract of sentiment arising out of the jealousy between the political aristocracy and the plutocracy of his day. All that he writes is written with a living personal feeling which is unmistakable. Every phase of this multiplex social conflict was minutely and vividly familiar to him. He was born tolerably well off. Like many a young man, he took the noble and loyal, but losing side. He tasted comparative poverty. He was by whatever train of circumstances reconciled to his victors. He became partly dependent upon their good offices. He adopted their politics. He preached poems to their adversaries, his former friends. He rose to the enjoyment of universal popularity. He kept his personal pride. In a word, he passed through every vicissitude which could make the life of his time a living reality, vividly and personally familiar to him in its most fleeting and evanescent details. Another man passing through the same train of events might not have written as Horace, but assuredly without his experience Horace would never have written as he did, or become the household author in the hands of what may be called the European "man of the world."

It is this singular combination of ancient art and complex personal feeling which makes Horace so peculiarly untranslatable. Had he written poems for the sake of writing poetry and not to express his feelings, they would have been much more imperfect (judged by the highest standard), but probably much more translatable. The source of their perfection—their personality—is also one cause of the impossibility of adequately rendering them,—their intensely conversational tone, differing only from spoken language by the more exquisite crystallisation of forms, and a certain additional care and apparatus. Whether he begins, "Lydia, dic per omnes te deos oro," or "Nullam, Vare, sacra vite prius severis arborem,"—whether he wards off, with averted head, the "brutal crowd," or asks Asteria, why she weeps for Gyges,—there is almost always and throughout a strictly spoken tone. And this of all others, though apparently the smallest difficulty in the way of the translator, is absolutely insuperable. To translate Horace into English which shall preserve his feeling, yet sound like the English addressed by one Englishman to another, is an impossibility. If any one will satisfy himself of this, let him compare the fiery and talented distortions of Mr. Theodore Martin with the cool, wary, and wonderfully elaborate translation of Professor Conington. It is not too much to say, that in nine cases in ten, Professor Conington comes infinitely closer to the tone of Horace than Mr. Martin, and in nine cases in ten he is still at an infinite distance from the original. Who would ever, in any English form of address, say:

> "O, wont the flying Nymphs to woo,
> Good Faunus, through my farm," &c.?

The Latin is in the quietest form of colloquial appeal:

> "Faune, Nympharum fugientum amator,
> Per meos fines et aprica rura
> Lenis incedas," &c.

In this instance Mr. Martin has the advantage:

> "Faunus, lover of the shy
> Nymphs, who at thy coming fly,
> Lightly o'er my borders tread," &c.

This is better just because it is more simple and natural. But after the unlucky first line, Professor Conington falls on his feet again, and proceeds more soberly, if not as happily as usual. Mr. Martin's second stanza is all in the plunging style:

> "When December's Nones come round,
> Then the cattle all do bound
> O'er the grassy plains in play."

This "when," "then," "bound," "round," hop-skip-and-jump translation is manifestly alien to the easy, serpentine, conversational tone of the Latin:

> "Ludit herboso pecus omne campo
> Cum tibi Nonæ redeunt Decembres
> Festus in pratis vacat otioso
> Cum bove pagus."

But in order to place the conversational character of Horace's style more strikingly in view, we ask our reader's leave to print one of the odes without the rythmical division into lines, as if, in fact, it were prose:

"Ad Leuconoën.

Tu ne quæsieris, scire nefas, quem mihi, quem tibi finem dî dederint, Leuconoë, nec Babylonios tentaris numeros. Ut melius, quicquid erit, pati, seu plures hyemes, seu tribuit Jupiter ultimam, quæ nunc oppositis debilitat pumicibus mare Tyrrhenum. Sapias, vina liques, et spatio brevi spem longam reseces. Dum loquimur, fugerit invida ætas. Carpe diem, quam minimum credula postero."

There is in these lines an undulating grace and variety, an ease, a refinement, and a coincidence of sense and metre so exact, that the rhythm seems to differ at every step. In other words, the metre has followed the sense, a humble handmaid following her mistress with a basket of flowers; the sense is not manacled in the metre, like a rogue in the pillory. Compare with the Latin Mr. Martin's version of the same ode, which we also print as prose:

"Ask not of fate to show ye—such lore is not for man—what limits, Leuconoë, shall round life's little span. Both thou and I must quickly die! Content thee, then, nor madly hope to wrest a false assurance from Chaldean horoscope. Far nobler, better were it, whate'er may be in store, with soul serene to bear it. If winters many more Jove spare for thee, or this shall be the last, that now with sullen roar scatters the Tuscan surge in foam upon the rockbound shore. Be wise, your spirit firing with cups of temper'd wine, and hopes afar aspiring in compass brief confine. Use all life's powers, the envious hours fly as we talk. Then live to-day, nor fondly to to-morrow trust more than you must or may."

It is impossible to read these lines without smiling. They are the best burlesque of the Latin that could probably have been written, if the intention had been to *mock* every single thing Horace had said, step by step. And in saying this we are not at all exaggerating our real meaning. Surely the trundle and mockery of the balladic rhythm is unmistakable. It almost seems to carry with it a jeering, flouting tone, admirably suited to the rollicking banter of Don Gaultier's ballads, where the very essence of the poetry is its mocking and phantomlike unreality, but wholly alien to the sobriety and intrinsic reality of Horace, who hardly ever, if ever, strays very far from the tone of spoken language.

Another remarkable feature is the Tennysonian workmanship of Horace, the "callida junctura," the exquisite art of imparting freshness and novelty to common words by a slight change of usage without ceasing to be classical. The "oppositis *debilitat* pumicibus mare," the "spem longam *reseces*," the "*carpe* diem" (*plucking* the day), the "*credula* postero," are all exquisitely graceful, new, yet transparently clear. The other expressions are unforced, simple, and polished. There is absolutely nothing hackneyed or trivial. But in the English, such expressions as 'asking of fate' 'to show *ye*,' 'such lore,' 'nor madly hope,' are all on the boundaries of bad taste.

Professor Conington's version steers much nearer the original, both in ease, grace, sincerity, and variety:

"Ask not ('tis forbidden knowledge) what our destined term of years, mine or yours; nor scan the tables of your Babylonish seers. Better far to bear the future, my Leuconoë, like the past, whether Jove has many winters yet to give, or this our last; *this*, that makes the Tyrrhene billows spend their strength against the shore. Strain your wine, and prove your wisdom; life is short; should hope be more? In the moment of our talking, envious time has ebb'd away. Seize the present; trust to-morrow e'en as little as you may."

This is, in tone and feeling, much more like Horace. We add another example in the same form:

"Ad Venerem.

Vixi puellis nuper idoneus et militavi non sine gloria. Nunc arma defunctumque bello barbiton hæc paries habebit, lævum marinæ qui Veneris latus custodit. Hic, hic, ponite lucida funalia, et vectes, et arcus oppositis foribus minaces. O quæ beatam, Diva, tenes Cyprum, et Memphin carentem Sithonia nive, Regina, sublimi flagello tange Chloën semel, arrogantem."

The tone here is evidently more jocose, and the trip of the rhythm exactly fits the fun of the poet. But for all that, the general tone lies near the temper of animated but polished conversation. How different are the following lines,—

"Of late I've been leading a life of flirtation, and trophies have won that I care not to show. But wooing and winning are only vexation; I'm heartily sick of the business. Heigho! My spurs having earn'd, I'll lay down my armour and hang up my lyre, ne'er to touch it again, on this wall by the left hand of Venus the charmer,—the sea-goddess Venus that sprang from the main. Quick, quick! pile them here, while the fit is upon me; the torches, the tabors, the arrows, the pike, and the crowbar, which oft-times an entrance hath won me to beauty that only to valour would strike. O goddess, o'er Cyprus the sunny who reignest, fair queen of soft Memphis, oblige me and touch with your scourge that minx Chloë,—the scornfullest, vainest,—just so as to frighten, but not hurt her—much."

Is not this just in the tone in which a clerk would hum a comic song to himself, with his hands in his pockets, on his way to his office? Here again the Oxford professor has the advantage in dignity, sobriety, and taste:

"For ladies' love I late was fit, and good success my warfare blest. But now my arms, my lyre, I quit, and hang them up to rust or rest. Here, where arising from the sea stands Venus, lay the load at last, —links, crowbars, and artillery, threatening all doors that dared be fast. O goddess! Cyprus owns thy sway, and Memphis, far from Thracian snow. Raise high thy lash and deal, I pray, that haughty Chloë just one blow."

The word "lady," however (as in the next ode, "sire" for "pater"), gives a disagreeable touch of gentility to the ode. "Defunctumque bello barbiton," a beautiful expression, is lost. So is "carentem Sithonia nive." So is the exquisite emphasis of the final word, "arrogantem;" which seems so to have touched Mr. Martin's poetical sensibilities that he unburdened his swollen feeling in the following paraphrase, "that minx Chloë,—the scornfullest, vainest,—just so as to frighten, but not hurt her—much."

Professor Conington has dwelt at great length upon the question of the choice of metre in translation; a question which has engrossed the attention of recent scholars in a great degree. He says, "The question what metres should be selected is of course one of great difficulty. I can only explain what my own practice has been, with some of the reasons which have influenced me in particular cases. Perhaps we may take Milton's celebrated translation of the Ode to Pyrrha as a starting point:*

* We give the Latin, with Milton's translation, and also Professor Conington's; a comparison between which will doubtless prove interesting to our readers.

"AD PYRRHAM.

Quis multa gracilis te puer in rosa
Perfusus liquidis urget odoribus
    Grato, Pyrrha, sub antro?
        Cui flavam religas comam,

Simplex munditiis! Heu! quoties fidem
Mutatosque Deos flebit, et aspera
    Nigris æquora ventis
        Emirabitur insolens,

Qui nunc te fruitur credulus aurea,
Qui semper vacuam, semper amabilem
    Sperat, nescius auræ
        Fallacis! Miseri quibus

Intentata nites! Me tabula sacer
Votiva paries indicat uvida
    Suspendisse potenti
        Vestimenta maris Deo."

Milton's Translation.

"What slender youth, bedew'd with liquid odours,
Courts thee on roses in some pleasant cave,
    Pyrrha? For whom bind'st thou
    In wreaths thy golden hair,

Plain in thy neatness? O, how oft shall he
On faith and changed gods complain, and seas
    Rough with black winds, and storms
    Unwonted shall admire!

Who now enjoys thee credulous, all gold,
Who always vacant, always amiable
    Hopes thee, of flattering gales
    Unmindful. Hapless they

To whom thou untried seem'st fair! Me, in my vow'd
Picture, the sacred wall declares to have hung
    My dank and dropping weeds
    To the stern god of sea."

Professor Conington.

"What slender youth, besprinkled with perfume,
    Courts you on roses in some grotto's shade?
        Fair Pyrrha, say, for whom
            Your yellow hair you braid,

So trim, so simple? Ah! how oft shall he
    Lament that faith can fail, that gods can change,
        Viewing the rough black sea
            With eyes to tempests strange,

Who now is basking in your golden smile,
    And dreams of you still fancy-free, still kind,
        Poor fool, nor knows the guile
            Of the deceitful mind!

Woe to the eyes you dazzle without cloud
    Untried! For me, they show in yonder fane
        My dripping garments, vow'd
            To him who curbs the main."

"There can be no doubt," Mr. Conington says, "that to an English reader the metre chosen [by Milton, the iambic] does give much of the effect of the original; yet the resemblance depends rather on the length of the lines than on any similarity in the cadences. But it is evident that he chose the iambic movement as *the ordinary movement of the English poetry ;* and it is evident, I think, that in translating Horace we shall be right in doing the same, as a general rule." We agree, more or less, with these remarks; and if we were to generalise the difference between Mr. Martin's and Professor Conington's versions and their comparative success, it would be that Professor Conington has in general chosen a metre that lay closer to our spoken language; whereas Mr. Martin, betrayed by his enthusiasm and misled by his previous habits as a successful balladist, has habitually, in his translations of Horace, fallen into metres which, however they may differ from one another, are essentially balladic and rotatory, and essentially, therefore, antagonistic to the prevailing temper of Horace's odes. Professor Conington goes on to say, "Anapæstic and other rhythms may be beautiful and *appropriate* (?) in themselves, but they cannot be *manipulated* so easily; the stanzas with which they are associated bear no resemblance, as stanzas, to the stanzas of Horace's odes." With this, also, we agree in the main, except in so far as the word "appropriate" seems to imply, theoretically, that the same metre in one language would be "appropriately" rendered by the same metre in another. To this we should demur. It may, and it may not. Thus, for instance, we hold that the hexameter in English lies at the opposite pole of the hexameter in Greek. In the present imperfect state of our knowledge of the mirage of analogies, which constitute the association of sound with sense, it is impossible to determine accurately what is the exact metre which, if the proper words could be found, would be the nearest approximation to the sense and sound of any combination in another language. But so much seems evident, that it may happen quite well, and perhaps constantly, that, if found, the metre of the particular combination in each case would be different to what it is in the original language. The truth is, that in translating an ode of Horace, what takes place is something like this. The translator casts about for a metre; he is influenced in his choice by that particular expression which has impressed him most strongly. There are always expressions which strike the translator, and shake his mind as a tree is shaken. One or two ripe fruits fall at the first touch; the rest are sour, and he cannot ripen them for the nonce, because their maturity depends on broader causes than those coincident with the extent of his own mind,—namely, on the difference of climate, as it were, of the two languages. Or, to use another metaphor, whatever may be the particular note which furnishes a key to the translator in his choice of a metre, that note will jar with most of the others. But it may be said that this doctrine would operate equally against the possibility of writing truly natural poetry of any kind. And unquestionably an immense quantity of the poetry palmed off upon mankind is forced and unnatural, and it dies accordingly. There is a process of natural and national churning, if we may so say, of poetical metres and idioms in every language subject to development and not already dead,—a process which goes on insensibly, and independently of any particular poet. A casual spark in a particular mind sets fire to a long train of antecedent feeling; and instantly a number of expressions, which have been long and silently preparing, crystallise by a process of natural selection into ripe and natural shape round some particular subject. These are growths, and they live. But their number is comparatively small. The painful efforts of any one man to force into bloom his own obscurer thoughts, only result in distortion and end in premature death; for in any one metre, at any given time, in any given language, there is only a certain accumulation and reservoir to tap, greater in one metre and less in another, as the case may be. To return to Mr. Conington.

"I have, then, followed," he continues, "Milton in appropriating the measure in question to the Latin metre, technically called the fourth Asclepiad; at the same time that I have *substituted rhyme* for blank verse, believing rhyme to be an *inferior artist's* only chance of giving pleasure." In other words, Professor Conington's modesty frightened him into putting a chime of bells round the neck of his Muse in order to reassure himself, and her, under the eventful unexplored prospect of appearing side by side with the august shade of Milton. He will forgive us for thinking this was a mistake. Milton himself must smile at the bells, however he may love the Muse. Professor Conington's modesty rather stands in his way. With all due deference to his knowledge of himself, we must emphatically deny that he is, in any sense, "an inferior artist." He may not take rank with Milton as an epic, or with Horace as a lyrical, poet; but as a translator he is a very distinguished artist indeed, and very far placed above the necessity of adorning his verse with the baby jingle of rhyme. Having said this, we will add no apology for not following him into the speculation about the respective merits of "alternate and successive rhymes," and "the effect of interlinking, so natural in a stanza." He proceeds: "Taking an English iambic line of ten syllables to represent the longer lines of the Latin, an English iambic line of six syllables to represent the shorter, we see that the metre of Horace's 'Scriberis Vario' finds its representative in the metre of Mr. Tennyson's 'Dream of Fair Women.'" We shall quote a few stanzas of this ode to enable our readers to judge more conveniently:

"*Dream of Fair Women.*

* * * * * *

That man, of all the men I ever knew,
  Most touch'd my fancy. O, what days and nights
We had in Egypt, ever reaping new
  Harvest of ripe delights,

Realm-draining revels! Life was one long feast.
  What wit! what words! what sweet words, only made
Less sweet by the kiss that broke 'em, liking best
  To be so richly stay'd!

What dainty strifes, when fresh from war's alarms
  My Hercules, my gallant Antony,
My mailed captain leapt into my arms,
  Contented there to die!

And in those arms he died: I heard my name
  Sigh'd forth with life: then I shook off all fear,
Oh, what a little snake stole Cæsar's fame!"

* * * * * *

"*Scriberis Vario.*

Scriberis Vario fortis, et hostium
Victor, Mæonii carminis aliti,
Quam rem cunque ferox navibus aut equis
    Miles te duce gesserit.

Nos, Agrippa, neque hæc dicere, nec gravem
Pelidæ stomachum cedere nescii,
Nec cursus duplicis per mare Ulyssei,
    Nec salvam Pelopis domum,

Conamur, tenues grandia; dum pudor,
Imbellisque lyræ Musa potens vetat
Laudes egregii Cæsaris et tuas
    Culpa deterere ingenî.

Quis Martem tunica tectum adamantinâ
Digne scripserit? aut pulvere Troico
Nigrum Merionen? aut ope Palladis
    Tydiden Superis parem?

Nos convivia, nos prœlia virginum
Sectis in juvenes unguibus acrium,
Cantamus, vacui, sive quid urimur,
    Non præter solitum leves."

Professor Conington's Translation.

"Not I, but Varius: he, of Homer's brood
  A tuneful swan, shall bear you on his wing,
Your tale of trophies, won by field or flood,
    Mighty alike to sing.

Not mine such themes, Agrippa; no, nor mine
To chant the wrath that fill'd Pelides' breast,
Nor dark Ulysses' wanderings o'er the brine,
Nor Pelops' house unblest.

Vast were the task, I feeble; inborn shame,
And she, who makes the peaceful lyre submit,
Forbid me to impair great Cæsar's fame
And yours by my weak wit.

But who may fitly sing of Mars array'd
In adamant mail, or Merion black with dust
Of Troy, or Tydeus' son by Pallas' aid
Strong against gods to thrust?

Feasts are my theme, my warriors—maidens fair,
Who, with pared nails, encounter youths in fight;
Be Fancy free or caught in Cupid's snare,
Her temper still is light."

Mr. Martin's Translation.

"By Varius shall thy prowess be
In strains Mæonic chanted,
The victories by land and sea,
Our gallant troops, led on by thee,
Have won with swords undaunted.

Such themes, Agrippa, never hath
My lyre essay'd, nor bold
Pelides' unrelenting wrath,
Nor artfullest Ulysses' path
O'er oceans manifold;

Nor woes of Pelops' fated line,
Such flights too soaring are!
Nor doth my bashful muse incline
Great Cæsar's eulogies and thine
With its thin notes to mar.

Who, who shall sing; with accents just,
Mars' adamantine mail,
Or Merion grimed with Trojan dust,
Or him who, strong in Pallas' trust,
Made even immortals quail?

Heart-whole, or pierced by Cupid's sting,
In careless mirthfulness
Of banquets we, and maidens sing
With nails cut closely skirmishing
When lovers hotly press."

We have made these quotations at length, because the comparison of the two translations with Horace and with Tennyson is full of interest the closer we look into them. It cannot fail, we think, to strike any scholar on the most cursory glance how much nearer the tone of Mr. Conington's rhythm lies to the Latin than Mr. Martin's. Nor does it seem any exaggeration to say, that when we compare with

> "Scriberis Vario fortis, et hostium
> Victor, Mæonii carminis aliti,"

the lines

> "By Varius shall thy prowess *be*
> In strains Mæonic chanted,"

we are again instantly reminded of the dandling motion of a person chanting to an infant. The effect is necessarily at the opposite pole of the grave courtesy and studied simplicity of Horace, a courtesy always heightened by the ineffable varnish of *bonhomie,* nowhere more conspicuous than in Horace, and the invariable accompaniment of the highest breeding. It is a curious thing, too, to observe how perpetually the plunge of the rhythm betrays the translator into exaggeration in translation. Perhaps the temper of mind which led to one naturally resulted in the other. Be this as it may, to take an example out of five thousand,

> ". . . . . pulvere Troico
> *Nigrum* ; . . . ."

a beautiful and powerful application of the simple word "black," Mr. Martin distorts into "grimed," which, besides a tinge of vulgarity, misses the true grace and vehemence of the original. Mr. Conington said well,

> ". . . . . *black* with dust
> Of Troy . . . ."

We look in vain in the translation of Mr. Martin for the true poetic touches of the ode. "Carminis *aliti*," "gravem Pelidæ stomachum cedere nescii," "*sævam* Pelopis *domum*," "*imbellis* lyræ Musa potens," "laudes *culpâ deterere ingeni*," are all smothered in commonplace: "*strains* Mæonic," "swords *undaunted*," "*gallant* troops," "*never hath my lyre essay'd*," "*woes* of Pelops' *fated* line," "*soaring flights*," "*bashful Muse*," "*careless mirthfulness*,"—all which are certainly not English poetry, and equally not Horace, than whom no poet, perhaps, departing so little from the analogies of spoken language, ever illustrated more abundantly and with a more inconceivable wealth his own precept:

> "Dixeris egregie, notum si callida verbum
> Reddiderit junctura novum."

It would be a very interesting inquiry to ascertain, by a comparison with other Latin authors, whether there is a single line of Horace which does not contain one or more of these "*callidæ juncturæ*," entirely his own.

It is in this that the science of Mr. Conington, and his discipline, his fine perception and his reverence for his author stand him in such good stead. There is, indeed, a little too much of the stately academic courtesy in such renderings as "Not I, but Varius," which is as much a distortion of "Scriberis Vario," as "grimed" is of "nigrum." "Not mine—no, nor mine," reads affectedly, and has a faint tinge of clap-trap. "*Dark* Ulysses" gives a Christian view of Ulysses alien from that of the ancients. They rather liked and admired Ulysses. He was a sort of legendary spoilt child and *enfant terrible* among heroes; a quaint cross between a Homeric Columbus and a Homeric Munchausen. They never mention him without a grin of satisfaction, not at all rendered in "*dark* Ulysses." "Pelops' house *unblest*" is feeble for "*sæva* Pelopis domus," and again introduces a Christian element, in which the, here, truly "*dark*" and bloody savagery implied in *sæva* is drowned in attar of roses or holy water. There is something really very simple, unaffected, yet fine, in the "tenues grandia," for which "my weak wit" is conceited and falsely modest. "Tenues" refers less to Horace himself, or his wit, than to the character of his subjects. If there is the faintest sidelong glance at himself, it is magnified a thousand times in "my weak wit."

Professor Conington may fairly say that it is a choice of difficulties; and so it no doubt is. We congratulate him heartily upon having overcome so many. It is no small achievement to have given a translation of Horace which Latin scholars can read with attention and with genuine pleasure; and the careful comparison of which at every step, while it cannot fail to increase their insight into the poet's meaning, must impress them not only with the impossibility of the task, but the wonderful science and maturity with which Professor Conington has dared to cope with it.

ART. III.—WITS OF THE FRENCH REVOLUTION.

Œuvres de Chamfort, précédées d'une étude sur sa vie et son esprit. Par Arsène Houssaye.

Galerie du XVIIIe Siècle. Par Arsène Houssaye.

Histoire de la Presse en France. Par Eugène Hatin. Vol. VII.

Esprit de Rivarol. Paris, 1808.

Causeries du Lundi. Par M. C. A. Sainte-Beuve. Vols. III., IV.

THE reader, whose historical zeal carries him to the earlier numbers of the *Moniteur Universel*, as they appeared during the weeks of the Terror, finds himself confronted by one of those half-comical, half-revolting contrasts, for which human nature—and especially French human nature—shows from time to time so strange a capacity. In one column he will peruse the long morning list of victims of the Conciergerie,—old men and maidens, rich and poor, strong and weak, alike swept promiscuously away under the ruthless ban of hostility to the commonweal, and, ere their doom printed, already on the road to death. In the other, as he turns shuddering away, he will be detained by an almost equally long list of "to-night's entertainments,"—grand scenic tableaux, emblematic ballets, hippodromes *à la Grecque*, masked balls, the comic opera, the successful vaudeville, all proceeding with complete regularity, and all apparently in the greatest possible request. What, he will exclaim, must be the innate frivolity, the cruel indifference, the latent barbarism of a race which saw nothing strange in such an appalling mixture of tragedy and farce! Were they men or fiends who could be thus easily amused, while death hung over each, and the pavement outside streamed with kindred blood? Who but the traditional "tigre-singe" could skip away, yet bloody-handed from civil slaughter, to applaud the nimble feet of some venal Terpsichore, or the quips and cranks of some fashionable buffoon?

We shall run the suspicion, we fear, of the same sort of inhuman versatility if we invite our readers to a less grave, but scarcely less characteristic, aspect of the French Revolution than that with which history has rendered them the most familiar. Friends and foes for the most part, though differing wide as heaven and earth in all beside, have depicted it in the light of the sublimest of human tragedies. Whatever else a sympathising or a hostile critic judged it, both regarded it as colossal; and colossal in a sense that forbade, as if half profane, the notice of those collateral topics which, in meaner matters, might appropriately claim attention. The scale of action was heroic, the performers demi-gods or demi-fiends, and praise and censure alike assumed a tone of fitting gravity and respect. The half-frantic vehemence of Burke, the curses of an army of Tory denunciators, the shrieks of political or religious cowardice, the vindictive Conservatism—which in our own days has dwindled down to the Cassandra-like maledictions of a single maudlin peer—for a long while accustomed Englishmen to regard that strange series of events as a catastrophe whose Titanic proportions overwhelmed the sense,—an outrage at which heaven and earth might stand aghast, and which struck mankind with awful silence,—a conflagration, lit with no earthly flame, blazing at our very doors, and too full of grand results, one way or the other, to our species, for any language but the impassioned cry of hope, the solemn denunciation, the groan of horror and despair. At length the flames died down, the smoke cleared away, and it gradually became perceptible that the universe remained intact. The calm, half-humorous genius of Carlyle, piercing through the golden haze of rhodomontade, and fathoming the shallows of many a tempest-ridden tea-cup, marshalled the facts of the story into artistic shape, reduced heroes and demons alike to strictly terrestrial proportions, and proved that the grand convulsion of French society, when cleared of fictitious embellishment, was the handiwork of no superhuman agents, but of irritable, passionate, and, in many cases, extremely feeble men; that vanity, jealousy, and a host of petty instincts had at least as much to do with it as the grander passions of our nature; and that though, in the evolution of the drama, some natures beyond the ordinary standard of daring and ability disclosed themselves,—and one intellect at least of the very highest order rose upon the surrounding chaos,—yet that most of its results could be accounted for by the activity of commonplace emotions working in a host of inferior minds, and had a side which was far more ludicrous than either terrific or sublime. A few striking personages stand of course foremost on the stage, and vindicate in more than one instance the doubtful honour of monstrosity. Louis XV., an effete Sardanapalus, grovelling daily deeper in his sensuality; Orleans, rubicund already as if with a Tartarean glow; Danton, a portent of ferocious power; Mirabeau, shaking his lion-like locks, and preparing, as a giant refreshed with wine, for the subjection of a pigmy race; the stately Austrian lady, imperial in her very weaknesses, falling queen-like and undismayed amid curses and gibes; Corday, hurrying in joyful enthusiasm to her perilous emprise; Roland, in her white robe and flowing locks, confronting her accusers, or returning from the tribunal in more than stoical dignity to announce her doom,—these are indeed the conspicuous personages of the tale, but they are not the whole; nor did their earnestness for good or evil, their strength of will, the intensity with which they felt, the scale upon which they acted, represent the true character of the great mass of Frenchmen. Behind them stand inferior performers, and it was these, after all, that made the Revolution what we know it to have been. An attitude of mind the very reverse of majestic, a childish passion for display, an insatiable thirst for flattery, an exquisite sensitiveness to the sting of satire, a passionate and unthinking rebellion against the inequalities incidental to human society,—such was the thin soil out of which the Revolution sprang, such were the motive principles which shaped its onward course. It was natural enough that a generation bred in an atmosphere like this, should, when it came to be engaged in any considerable undertaking, become from time to time bombastic, theatrical, and extravagant. It was equally natural that men of such a cast, trained by the tradition of centuries in the habits of brilliant conversation, and wielding a language of incomparable neatness and pliability, should carry the art of effective rejoinder to the utmost possible perfection, and should assign to witty and epigrammatic language a controversial importance which less impressible natures find it difficult to understand.

This was conspicuously the case in Revolutionary France. A large section of society, elevating drawing-room repartee into a standard of thought, accepted a witticism as a refutation, and considered that a thing ceased to be true when it began to look ridiculous. The salon life of Paris—the paradise of an army of ambitious idlers—engendered a tone of mind in which far less attention was paid to the accuracy with which an idea was thought out than to the elegance with which it was expressed. To achieve a social success was for the aspirant to fame the most imperative of all necessities, and for this neatness, brilliancy, promptitude, were alone essential. A race of men grew up astonishingly skilful in the fence of words, masters of forcible, pithy expressions, but superficial in knowledge, shallow in thought, and utterly innocent of all earnest intention. They breathed the poisoned air of a vicious society, whose refinement but gave a piquancy to systematic heartlessness and crime. They carried their convictions just so far as the fine ladies, whose smiles they sought, considered it in good taste to follow; their scepticism began in restlessness, and ended in a sneer; their philosophy was the cynicism of faded voluptuaries; their ambition, to live in the mouths of a fashionable coterie; their keenest pleasure, to transfix a rival with the envenomed weapon of a sarcastic epigram. The criticism passed by one of them upon another might with justice be applied to the whole class of which both were members, and serve as the epitaph for a school of wits: "Superficiellement instruit," writes Chamfort of Rulhières, "détaché de tous principes, l'erreur lui était aussi bonne que la vérité quand elle pouvait faire briller la frivolité de son esprit. Il n'envisageait les grandes choses que sous de petits rapports, n'aimait que les tracasseries de la politique, n'était éclairé que de bluettes, et ne voyait dans l'histoire que ce qu'il avait vu dans les petites intrigues de la société." The French empire was, according to the famous definition, a despotism tempered by epigrams. The fashionable creed of a large section alike of its assailants and supporters might be described as cynicism set ablaze with wit.

Two men, conspicuous champions on either side, may be accepted as the types of the class above described; and their performances, although already the object of more literary zeal than their importance might seem to merit, are yet so amusing, and at the same time throw so real a light upon the true history of the times, that we make no apology for introducing them in detail to our readers' attention: Rivarol, the champion of the departing régime; Chamfort, the fanatic of equality, and the assiduous composer and collector of revolutionary facetiæ. The delicate pencil of M. Sainte Beuve has already sketched the characters of both, and enabled us to understand the real affinity of thought and disposition which, under a superficial appearance of antagonism, bound the two men together, and stamped them, though fighting in different camps, as in reality kindred natures. Both have left a long list of excellent stories to attest the justice of a contemporary reputation, and the humour of each will be best appreciated by being introduced in connection with the principal circumstances of his career.

The society which, half way through the eighteenth century, excited the aspirations of an ambitious Frenchman, was no longer that of Versailles. To the court of Louis XV. survived nothing but the tedious ceremonial and the complete depravity of his great-grandfather's period. The intellectual prestige, which lent a refining splendour to the great monarch's reputation, had vanished along with everything else decent and respectable. The palace was as gloomy as it was corrupt; "quant à la gaieté," says the historian, "il n'en était plus question, le foyer de l'esprit et des lumières était à Paris." Madame Campan, indeed, with the applausive servility of a royal servant, informs us that the king knew how to jest, and occasionally honoured his dependants with witticisms which proved "la finesse de son esprit, et l'élévation de ses sentiments." As specimens, however, of the one and the other, she gives the stupid slang terms by which the Sovereign was pleased to designate the four princesses who had the misfortune to acknowledge his paternity; and she suggests that his répertoire of indelicate phraseology was sedulously enlarged by reference to the dictionary when in his mistresses' society. It is pleasant to turn from such a scene to the dignified reply made by M. de Brissac, one of the few courtiers to whom decency had not come to be a joke. The king was rallying him upon the sensitiveness he displayed as to some matrimonial catastrophe. "Allons, Monsieur de Brissac, ne vous fachez pas; c'est un petit malheur; ayez bon courage." "Sire," said the injured husband, "j'ai toutes les espèces de courage, excepté celui de la honte." The arrival of Marie Antoinette no doubt infused a new spirit into the dull routine of wickedness which had hitherto prevailed at court. Monsieur de Brissac again figures as the author of an appropriate rejoinder. "Mon Dieu," cried the young dauphiness, as the crowd surged under the balconies of the Tuileries, "Mon Dieu, que de monde!" "Madame," said the courtier, "sans que Monsieur le Dauphin puisse s'en offenser, ce sont autant d'amoureux." Full of playfulness and vivacity, the young princess herself was ready and elegant in conversation. Shortly after her arrival at Versailles, she made private arrangements to supplement her extremely defective education: "Il faut," she said, "que la dauphine prenne soin de la réputation de l'archiduchesse." It was in no such innocent recreations that the king's remaining powers were meanwhile expended. His notorious excesses excited scandal, alarm, indignation. The base of an equestrian statue, in the Place Louis Quinze, was guarded by four figures representing Peace, Prudence, Strength, and Justice: an unknown hand wrote under it,

> "O la belle statue! O le beau piédestal!
> Les vertus sont à pied; le vice est à cheval."

Vice at length dismounted for the last time, and the terrified courtiers prepared for a new allegiance. The details of that terrible deathbed are universally familiar: one story, however, may be worth recording. It is a scene enacted between the Duc de Villequier, first gentleman of the chamber, and Monsieur Androuillé, the head surgeon to the court. The king's disease, it will be remembered, rendered it almost certain death to go near him. The duke thereupon politely suggested to the doctor that it was his duty to open and embalm the body. The doctor professed his alacrity for the task, but he added: "Pendant que j'opérerai, vous tiendrez la tête; votre charge vous y oblige." The duke said not a word; and Louis the Fifteenth, it is perhaps superfluous to state, was buried unopened and unembalmed. The new court had hardly opened when the young queen's daring spirits, her impatience of ceremonial, her girlish caprices,—above all, the political intrigues amid which she lived,—began to endanger her popularity. Her contempt for etiquette scandalised the fine ladies, and obtained for her the perilous nickname of "Moqueuse." At her first mourning reception after the king's death we find one of the ladies of the court squatting down behind her, pulling her companion's petticoats, and endangering the gravity of the whole proceeding. The epigram which appeared next day might have warned her of the danger of petty indiscretions:

> "Petite reine de vingt ans,
> Vous qui traitez si mal les gens,
> Vous repasserez la barrière,
> Laire, larila, larila, laire," &c.

Four years later her enemies had gathered courage, and the feeling against her was deeper and less concealed. The birth of her daughter gave rise to a host of cruel pleasantries, in which the royal family were unhappily the readiest to take a part. The Comte de Provence held the child at the font. "Monseigneur," he said, when the grand Almoner inquired its name, "cette question n'est pas la première que vous avez à m'adresser; il faut s'enquerir d'abord les père et mère." The Almoner, astonished, said that that question was asked only when doubt existed as to the parentage of the child; "personne ignore," he added, "que madame est née du roi et de la reine." "Est-ce votre avis, M. le Curé?" the count sardonically asked, turning to the Curé of Notre Dame. The audience stood aghast; and the Curé, in fear and trembling, strove to close so embarrassing a scene. The disrespect did not stop here; the City Authorities aped the impertinence of the Court: and the queen, at last vexed beyond endurance, uttered an impatient sneer at the contemptuous delay with which the birthday fêtes were organised. "The magistrates," she said, "are resolved, I suppose, to defer them till the little one is big enough to dance at them herself." The fraternal affection thus curiously exemplified on the part of the queen's brother-in-law was the subject of a drama dedicated in this very year to the queen, which placed Chamfort, already the darling of Parisian drawing-rooms, in the full sunshine of imperial favour. For fifteen years he had been labouring at his tragedy of *Mustapha and Zéangir;* and in 1776 it was for the first time acted at Versailles. Its success was complete. The tender intimacy of the two brothers, who defy all attempts at separation, and perish at last in each other's arms, affected the king to tears. The queen summoned the fortunate author to her box, and announced, in terms so gracious that, as he said, he could never either forget or repeat them, that a pension was to be conferred upon him. "Madam," so ran the courtier-like dedication of the piece, "the indulgent approbation with which your majesty has deigned to honour the tragedy encourages me to present it to you. Your goodness has rendered the design still dearer to my gratitude. Happy, Madam, could I consecrate it by new efforts, justify your benefits by new undertakings, and find grace before your majesty more by the merit of the work than the choice of a subject." Let us see what manner of man it was whose courtier tongue could run so glibly in the conventional phrases of servility.

Born, a natural child, in 1741, he bore the name of Nicholas, and as such was entered, in the position that became his low estate, at the Collège des Grassins, in the Paris university. His appearance bespoke sensitiveness, energy, and enthusiasm; his delicate nostril, his blue eyes lighting up in instantaneous vivacity, his flexible and touching voice, gave the impression of a finely strung, highly nervous organisation. His abilities were not slow in making themselves felt, and the young scholar soon carried every prize before him. All thoughts of the church, the natural career for one so circumstanced, were speedily resigned; and some youthful indiscretion brought his career as a collegian to a close. The world was all before him; the escape from the thraldom of orders delightful; and Chamfort, secure of pleasing, and with all the qualities to command success, threw himself with courageous recklessness upon society. Literary employment, however, was not to be had; famine knocked loudly at the door; his mother was looking to him for bread; and the young adventurer, in despair, applied for the place of clerk to a procureur. The procureur discerned the superiority of his petitioner, and made him tutor to his son; but he soon found his household in disorder. "Enfant d'Amour, beau comme lui, plein de feu, de gaieté, impétueux et malin," the new-comer proved a very troublesome inmate; and we next find him travelling into Germany in the capacity of private secretary to some provincial millionnaire. This plan, however, answered as badly as the last; and Chamfort returned nothing richer, except for the discovery "qu'il n'y avait rien à quoi il fut moins propre qu'à être un Allemand." He now began to work seriously at literature, and in 1764 brought out a little comedy, in which the fashionable doctrines of an ideal primitive perfection were carelessly worked into an amusing shape. Belton, an erratic Englishman, is wrecked upon a savage shore, and lights on Betty, an interesting and unsophisticated young lady, who provides him with sustenance, introduces him to her father's cave, and finally accompanies him to his home. Belton's wavering virtue is relieved at the fortunate moment by a charitable Quaker, who provides a dowry and insists on a formal marriage, much to the astonishment of Betty, to whom priests and lawyers are still novelties. "Quoi," she exclaims, "sans cet homme noir, je n'aurais pu t'aimer!"

The pretty trifle succeeded, and Voltaire, in expressing his approval, indoctrinated the young author with that supreme contempt for his countrymen which became in after life the leading principle of Chamfort's creed. "Our nation," he wrote, "has emerged from barbarism only because of two or three persons endowed by nature with the taste and genius which she refuses to all the rest. We must expect the race, who failed to discover the merit of *Athalie* and *Misanthrope* to continue ignorant and feeble, and in need of the guidance of a few enlightened men." Chamfort's next efforts were directed to the Academy; and a few years afterwards, in the *Eloge de Molière*, one of his successful compositions, he, for almost the first time, gave evidence of that "âpreté dévorante," that dreary view of life, and that cynical dislike of society, which pointed all his later witticisms. What, he asked, would be the task of the Molière of that day? "Verrait-il, sans porter la main sur les crayons, l'abus que nous avons fait de la philosophie et de la société ; le mélange ridicule des conditions : cette jeunesse, qui a perdu tout morale à quinze ans, toute sensibilité à vingt ; cette habitude malheureuse de vivre ensemble sans avoir besoin de s'estimer: la difficulté de se déshonorer, et, quand on est enfin parvenu, la facilité de recouvrer son honneur et de rentrer dans cette île autrefois escarpée et sans bords ?" Unfortunately, in decrying the times, Chamfort was but sketching his own career. He had thrown himself with disastrous vehemence into all the worst pleasures of a corrupt capital: the women among whom he lived were the fitting priestesses of a cynical creed: none of his sayings accordingly are tinged with a fiercer scepticism than those which relate to feminine infirmity. "Il faut," he says, "choisir: aimer les femmes, ou les connaître: il n'y a pas de milieu." "Pour moi," he writes elsewhere, "je recherche surtout celles qui vivent hors du mariage et du célibat: ce sont quelquefois les plus honnêtes." Many of his stories are in illustration of the same ungallant theme :

"Mademoiselle du Thé ayant perdu un de ses amants, et cette aventure ayant fait du bruit, un homme qui alla la voir la trouva jouant de la harpe, et lui dit avec surprise, 'Eh ! mon Dieu ! je m'attendais à vous trouver dans la désolation.' 'Ah !' dit-elle d'un ton pathétique, 'c'était hier qu'il fallait me voir.'

L'abbé de Fleury avait été amoureux de Madame la Maréchale de Noailles, qui le traita avec mépris. Il devint premier ministre; elle eut besoin de lui, et il lui rappela ses rigueurs. 'Ah ! monseigneur,' lui dit naïvement la maréchale, 'qui l'aurait pu prévoir ?'

Un homme était en deuil de la tête aux pieds : grandes pleureuses, perruque noir, figure allongée. Un de ses amis l'aborde tristement : 'Eh ! bon Dieu ! qui est-ce donc que vous avez perdu ?' 'Moi,' dit-il, 'je n'ai rien perdu; c'est que je suis veuf.' "

Thoroughly prosperous in the best society, Chamfort was gradually becoming a revolutionist at heart : it was the fashion in aristocratic quarters to deride aristocracy ; and a little play, *The Merchant of Smyrna*, published by him in 1770, carried the taste so far, that its author, in after years, pleaded it as a proof of his democratic tendency. The fun of the piece turns on the perplexities of a slave-merchant, who has encumbered himself with several unsaleable purchases; amongst the rest, a German baron and three abbés. They are so useless that he dares not even expose them in the market. Here is a conversation in the same spirit. Hassan is interrogating one of the captives, a Spaniard, as to what he is:

"*L'Espagnol.* Je vous l'ai déjà dit, gentilhomme.
Hassan. Gentilhomme ! je ne sais pas ce que c'est. Que fais-tu ?
L'Espagnol. Rien.

Hassan. Tant pis pour toi, mon ami; tu vas bien t'ennuyer.—(*à Kaled*) Vous n'avez pas fait une trop bonne emplette.

Kaled. Ne voilà-t-il pas que je suis encore attrapé! . . . . Gentilhomme, c'est sans doute comme qui dirait baron allemand. C'est ta faute aussi: pourquoi vas-tu dire que tu es gentilhomme? je ne pourrai jamais me défaire de toi."

Whatever his real convictions, Chamfort, for the present, was a thorough courtier in behaviour. M. Sainte Beuve quotes a pretty epigram which he composed about this time for the King of Denmark's arrival in Paris:

"Un roi qu'on aime et qu'on révère
A des sujets en tous climats:
Il a beau parcourir la terre,
Il est toujours dans ses états."

Before long his failing health drove him from Paris, and the young wit found amusement and hospitality awaiting him at several fashionable watering-places. At Barèges he not only recovered his health, but had the luck to charm four fine ladies, who loved him "chacune d'elles comme quatre," and whose kindness melted for a while even his determined acerbity. One of them especially he enumerates among his other blessings, as entertaining for him "all the sentiments of a sister;" and he adds cheerfully, "il me semble que mon mauvais Génie ait lâché prise, et je vis, depuis trois mois, sous la baguette de la Fée bienfaisante." I can tell you, writes one of his admirers, that M. Chamfort "est un jeune homme bien content; et il fait bien de son mieux pour être modeste." His humility must have been still more severely tried when the Duchess de Grammont, one of his four admirers, introduced him at court, and his successful tragedy secured him, as we have seen, the favour of the queen. He now seemed at the zenith of success. Besides his pension, the Prince de Condé had given him a secretaryship; a seat in the Academy secured his position as a writer; the best drawing-rooms in Paris were at his command; and Madame Helvétius, who held a sort of "literary hospital," was delighted to have him for an inmate. An uneasiness of soul, however, was beginning to mix gall with his cup of enjoyment, and Chamfort became restless, moody, and miserable. The very honours that were showered upon him seemed fraught with indignity; his rank as a successful man of letters was agonizingly equivocal. "Je ne voudrais," he said, "faire comme des gens de lettres qui ressemblent à des ânes ruant et se battant devant un râtelier vide." The idea that he paid for his dinners by his bons-mots robbed them of their charm; the disproportion of his own fortune to those with whom he lived drove him mad with jealousy. He detested, yet could not bring himself to resign the society in which his talent shone so brightly; he found himself the plaything of a wealthy class, and he could neither tolerate nor abandon his position. "Il est ridicule," he exclaimed, "de vieillir en qualité d'acteur dans une troupe où l'on ne peut même prétendre à la demi-part."

At last he determined to fly; but not before he had intensified his passion for equality, and his hatred of the class which had loaded him with favours, to a degree of malignity which nothing but actual suffering could explain. "Je ne suis pas un monstre d'orgueil," was his apology to a friend for his retreat; "mais j'ai été une fois empoisonné avec de l'arsenic sucré. Je ne le serai plus: 'manet altâ mente repostum.'" An interval of comparative felicity awaited him. He had met at Boulogne an aged beauty, of the Duchess of Maine's household, talkative, witty, and cynical as himself; and the two lovers retreated, in misanthropical attachment, from a world which they agreed in detesting. After six months the lady died, and her husband returned to Paris with a real sorrow added to his list of imaginary grievances. "When I wish to soften my heart," he writes, "I recall the loss of friends who are mine no longer,—the women whom death has snatched from me. J'habite leur cercueil; j'envoie mon âme errer autour des leurs. Hélas! je possède trois tombeaux!"

Less than ever inclined for the subserviency of social life, and fretting daily more and more at the heavy chain of patronage, Chamfort found opportunity, before the outbreak of the Revolution, to escape from the hospitality of an aristocratic friend, and to ensconce himself in more congenial quarters in the Palais Royal. Mirabeau was devoted to him, fired his spirit with something of his own enthusiasm, and carried him into the full tide of the new movement. Chamfort, delighted at his emancipation, embraced his new creed with all the ardour of a neophyte; his former friendships were discarded, his favours forgotten. "Ceux qui passent le fleuve des révolutions," he said, "ont passé le fleuve de l'oubli." Henceforth he became the oracle of republican clubs, and lent his wit to the cause, which always had his sympathies, and now claimed his open allegiance. His services, as an ally, were speedily appreciated. One morning he visited the Count de Lauraquais: "Je viens de faire un ouvrage," he cried. "Comment? un livre." "Non, pas un livre; je ne suis pas si bête; mais un titre de livre, et ce titre est tout. J'en ai déjà fait présent au puritain Sièyes, qui pourra commenter à son aise. Il aura beau dire; on ne se ressouviendra que du titre." "Quel est-il donc?" "Le voici: 'Qu'est-ce que le Tiers-Etat? Tout. Qu'a-t-il? Rien.'" Another of his contributions was the famous cry: "Guerre aux châteaux! Paix aux chaumières!"; and the horrors of September elicited from him no other apology than the inquiry, "Voulez-vous qu'on vous fasse des révolutions à l'eau de rose?" It is easy to conceive the satisfaction with which, for the first time, he allows his taste to follow its natural bent. He abounds in good stories, pointed at an incapable ruler, the follies of an aristocracy, the pride of birth, the slavery of a court.

"M. D— disait, à propos des sottises ministérielles et ridicules, 'Sans le gouvernement on ne rirait plus en France.'

On demandait à une duchesse de Rohan à quelle époque elle comptait accoucher. 'Je me flatte,' dit-elle, 'd'avoir cet honneur dans deux mois.' L'honneur était d'accoucher d'un Rohan.

Un courtisan disait, à la mort de Louis XIV, 'Après la mort du roi, on peut tout croire.'

Dans les malheurs de la fin du règne de Louis XIV, après la perte des batailles de Turin, d'Oudenarde, de Malplaquet, de Ramillies, d'Hochstet, les plus honnêtes gens de la cour disaient, 'Au moins le roi se porte bien, c'est le principal.'

Un prédicateur de la Ligne avait pris pour texte de son sermon, *Eripe nos, Domine, à luto fœcis*, qu'il tradusait ainsi, 'Seigneur, débourbonez-nous.'"

Chamfort's posts and pensions were of course soon swamped by the revolutionary tide, but his zeal was only quickened by the loss. He was one of the first to enter the Bastille after its capture, and he talked with Brutus-like severity of the sacrifices which a patriot should be prepared to make. For some time he acted as secretary to the Jacobin Club; but the growing ascendency of Robespierre and Marat drove him once again in the direction of the Conservatives. To this period we may refer his translation of *Fraternité ou la Mort*, which he said should be rendered "Sois mon frère, ou je te tue." He found his most natural leaders in the Girondists; and Roland, in rearranging the Bibliothèque Nationale, appointed Chamfort to a post in connection with it. He now turned the full blaze of his satire against the Convention; and there were of course plenty of ready listeners to inform the state conspirators of the sarcasms of their new assailant. His friends warned him of his peril, but he relied upon his reputation as a Liberal. "N'ai-je pas," he cried, "hautement professé ma haine contre les rois, les nobles, les prêtres, en un mot tous les ennemis de la raison et de la liberté?" At last he was denounced and imprisoned. Scarcely had he recovered his liberty, when a second arrest showed the complicated dangers of his position and threatened him with a more protracted confinement. He resolved to escape it by self-destruction, and mutilated himself, horribly but without effect, both with pistol and razor. Before he was dragged to prison, he dictated and signed, all bleeding as he was, the following theatrical declaration: "Moi, Sébastien Roche Nicholas Chamfort, déclare avoir voulu mourir en homme libre plutôt que d'être conduit en esclave en prison." He lived to appear before the Tribunal, and was at length partially enlarged. His nervous system, however, had received too great a shock, and the carelessness of his physician hastened his end. He died with a characteristic sentence on his lips: "Ah, mon ami," he cried to the Abbé Sièyes, "je m'en vais enfin de ce monde, où il faut que le cœur se brise ou se bronze!"

Melancholy alternative; but happily the verdict of philosophers of the Chamfort school ought to count for less than nothing in our estimation of existence. He had shut himself off from the really interesting side of life. Government, religion, marriage, death, the unseen world, all the great springs of human action, all the tenderest sentiments of human hearts, were to him but so many whetstones on which to sharpen the glittering razor of his wit. Mephistopheles himself might envy the icy heartlessness of the glittering epigrams in which his contempt for each was crystallised. His wit fed upon himself, and merrily proclaimed his own degradation: "L'homme est un sot animal," he said, "si j'en juge par moi-même." His estimation of mankind at large was equally unflattering: "Le public, le public, combien faut-il de sots pour faire un public?" The best thing to do with society was to leave it. He preferred solitude to the company of his fellow-men, "parce que je suis plus accoutumé à mes défauts qu'à ceux d'autrui."

"Je demandais à M——, pourquoi, en se condamnant à l'obscurité, il se dérobait au bien qu'on pouvait lui faire. 'Les hommes,' me dit-il, 'ne peuvent rien faire pour moi qui vaille leur oubli.'

M. D——, pour peindre d'un seul mot la rareté des honnêtes gens, me disait que dans la société l'honnête homme est une variété de l'espèce humaine.

M. de Lassay, homme très-doux, mais qui avait une grande connaissance de la société, disait qu'il faudrait avaler un crapaud tous les matins pour ne trouver rien de dégoûtant le reste de la journée, quand on devait la passer dans le monde."

The verdict of after-times is disposed of with a single sneer: "La postérité n'est pas autre chose qu'un public qui succède à un autre; or vous voyez ce que c'est que le public d'à présent."

His feelings about religion were tinged with all the bitterness of the period; and the sarcasms which he poured out so freely upon this world, lost none of their sting when directed against the next.

"On s'habitue à tout, même à la vie. La Fontaine, entendant plaindre le sort des damnés au milieu du feu de l'enfer, dit: 'Je me flatte qu'ils s'y accoutument, et qu'à la fin ils sont là comme le poisson dans l'eau.'

A propos des choses de ce bas monde qui vont de mal en pis, M. L— disait, 'J'ai lu quelque part qu'en politique il n'y a rien de si malheureux pour les peuples que les règnes trop longs. J'entends que Dieu est éternel; tout est dit.'"

We conclude with two stories of less gloomy import, and good specimens of Chamfort's lighter order of fun. The first sounds as if it owned the parentage of Molière.

"On disait à Délon, médecin mesmérist: 'Eh bien, M. de B— est mort, malgré la promesse que vous aviez faite de le guérir.' 'Vous avez,' dit-il, 'été absent; vous n'avez pas suivi les progrès de la cure: il est mort guéri.'

Le maréchale de Biron eut une maladie très-dangereuse: il voulut se confesser, et dit devant plusieurs de ses amis: 'Ce que je dois à Dieu, ce que je dois au roi, ce que je dois à l'état.' . . . Un de ses amis l'interrompit, 'Tais-toi,' dit-il, 'tu mourras insolvable.'"

The examples already quoted will suffice to give an idea of the cold, hard, metallic glare of a genius which, like Chamfort's, was unenlightened by earnest thought, softened by no humanising emotion, and devoid of all inspiring sincerity. His witticisms glitter about him like a cascade of sparks, emitting neither distinct light nor creative heat; his very polish is suggestive of sterility; and the smile which his humour suggests is quickly succeeded by a wearisome sense of deliberate heartlessness, hopelessness, and indifference.

We turn with relief to a mind more instinct with purpose, and certainly not less entertaining in performance. Rivarol was pronounced by no less a judge than Voltaire to be "the Frenchman *par excellence* of his day;" and even without so authoritative a verdict, it would be impossible to overlook the numerous particulars in which he typified the tastes, if not always the convictions, of his countrymen. His short career—for he died at forty-four—explains the incomplete and fragmentary nature of his works; but, besides his extraordinary conversational reputation, which raised him to the dignity of a professed improvisatore, he has left enough behind him to assure neutral critics of his readiness, versatility, and resource, and to justify his biographers in claiming for him admission to that shadowy temple of fame in which those who, but for adverse chance, might, could, should, or would have been among the leaders of mankind, receive the languid honours of conjectural admiration. He was born in 1757, in a village in Languedoc, and, as the eldest of a family of sixteen, was very speedily impressed with the imperative necessity of securing a livelihood. The father, though coming of good Italian stock, and by no means without education, had descended to the inglorious but profitable business of an innkeeper. The circumstance was not forgotten when Rivarol, in after times, surrounded by an eager and revengeful army of literary enemies, stood forth as the champion of aristocratic rights. Even those who profited by his talent could not help sneering at the hand which defended them. Once in a well-born crowd, at the first outbreak of the Revolution, Rivarol was descanting with an air of importance on the dangers of the times. "Nos droits," he cried, "nos priviléges sont menacés." "*Nos* droits?" cried the duc de Crequi, who was standing by. "Eh bien, qu'est-ce que vous trouvez donc singulier en ce mot?" "C'est votre pluriel," replied the Duke, "que je trouve singulier." The young aspirant to fame, however, was too sure of his powers to be easily abashed, and he contrived that his first literary task should call attention to his hereditary respectability. Coming to Paris, and apparently absorbed in frivolous amusements, he was in reality working hard at a translation of Dante. "C'est un bon moyen," he told his friends laughingly, "de faire ma cour aux Rivarol d'Italie;" and elsewhere he explains, "J'ai traduit l'Enfer de Dante parceque j'y retrouvais mes ancêtres." The undertaking of so ambitious a task bespoke already the lofty designs which were concealed under affected manners and an ostentatious indolence. Success soon smiled upon his hopes. His graceful manners and imposing delivery procured him an easy triumph in several literary cafés, especially "Le Caveau," where a set of brilliant talkers were accustomed to meet. In 1784 he acquired an almost European celebrity by carrying off the prize offered by the Academy of Berlin, under the auspices of Frederick the Great, for the best treatise on the universality of the French language, and the probable causes of its continuance. The essay, though as rhetorical and high-flown as was natural under the circumstances, implied a real critical faculty, and was the means probably of directing its author to a line of grammatical inquiry on which he subsequently grounded other and far deeper speculations. The laboured enjoyments of Parisian salons and a life of polished dissipation were, however, beginning to tell upon his powers, and before his thirtieth year he began to complain of diminishing versatility. "Ma vie est un drame si ennuyeux," he writes, "que je prétends que c'est Mercier qui l'a fait. Autrefois je réparais dans une heure huit jours de folie; et aujourd'hui il me faut huit grands jours de sagesse pour réparer une folie d'une heure." His judgment as a critic, and his never-failing loquacity, placed him, however, daily in a more conspicuous social position. His taste in authorship was delicate, sensitive, and correct, and the judgments he pronounced were tinged with a real literary enthusiasm. "Les gens de goût sont les hauts-justiciers de la littérature. L'esprit de critique est un esprit d'ordre; il connaît les délits contre le goût et les porte au tribunal du ridicule; car le rire est souvent l'expression de sa colère, et ceux qui le blâment ne songent pas assez que l'homme de goût a reçu vingt blessures avant d'en faire une." The critical activity thus explained and defended led him before long to undertake a systematic onslaught on a host of insignificant poetasters, who at this time crowded the booksellers' windows with worthless productions. This was the *Petit Almanach de Grands Hommes*, a sort of prose *Dunciad* in which the chief literary culprits of the year were, under a transparent veil of bombastic eulogy, held up to well-merited derision. As with the victims of Pope's immortal satire, time has already effectually completed the assailant's purpose, and the heroes of the *Petit Almanach* are for the most part only known to fame by the very instrumentality which was intended for their more speedy consignment to oblivion.

Rivarol had now, however, graver employments before him. Immediately upon the outbreak of the Revolution, he made the choice which interest, taste, and prejudice, alike recommended, and stood boldly forward against the advancing current of democracy. A journal named *Politique National* was the organ of the most enlightened Conservatives, and to this Rivarol contributed the most forcible, and certainly the most sagacious, expositions of the existing crisis which had as yet appeared upon his side of the controversy. With a vehemence which lost none of its effect by being polished and antithetical, he denounced the jealous vanity of the bourgeoisie, as being, rather than the sufferings of the mass, the true cause of disturbance. Though the slave of his own brilliancy, and too epigrammatic to be invariably correct, he gives from time to time satisfactory evidence of his real thoughtfulness and political insight. For one thing, he thoroughly appreciated the gravity of the statesman's task: "La politique," he said, "est comme le sphinx de la fable—elle dévore tous ceux qui n'expliquent pas ses énigmes." The follies of his own party did not escape him any more than the crimes of his antagonists. Upon the blind tardiness of the court he was especially severe: he pointed out the futility of concessions withheld till their worth and efficacy is lost: "La populace de Paris," he writes, "et celle même de toutes les villes du royaume, ont encore bien des crimes à faire, avant d'égaler les sottises de la cour. Tout le règne actuel peut se réduire à quinze ans de faiblesse, et à un jour de force mal employée." He observed of the aristocrats, the men who forgot nothing and learnt nothing, "qu'ils prenaient leurs souvenirs pour des droits:" of the anti-revolutionary alliance, "ils ont toujours été en arrière d'une année, d'une armée, et d'une idée." On the other hand, the contempt for the mass, which with Chamfort exploded in a sneer, became in his mind a guiding principle in speculation, and satisfactorily explained the social phenomena of the time: "Le peuple," he said, "ne goûte de la liberté, comme de liqueurs violentes, que pour s'enivrer et devenir furieux." "Le peuple," so runs another of his maxims, "est un souverain qui ne demande qu'à manger: sa Majesté est tranquille quand elle digère." Here is another still more trenchant in its tone:

> "Il n'est point de siècles de lumière pour la populace; elle n'est ni française, ni anglaise, ni espagnole. La populace est toujours et en tout pays la même—toujours cannibale, toujours anthropophage; et quand elle se venge de ses magistrats, elle punit des crimes qui ne sont pas toujours avérés par des crimes qui sont toujours certains."

The genius of Burke himself might have rejoiced over the concise and nicely-poised weightiness of such apothegms as these:

> "La populace croit aller mieux à la liberté, quand elle attente à celle des autres.
>
> Les nations que les rois assemblent et consultent, commencent par de vœux et finissent par des volontés.
>
> La philosophie moderne n'est rien autre chose que les passions armées de principes.
>
> Tout philosophe constituant est gros d'un jacobin: c'est une vérité que l'Europe ne doit pas perdre de vue."

Another and less successful project was the publication of the "Acts of the Apostles," a gigantic squib, intended to show the proceedings of the revolutionary leaders in a ridiculous aspect: but the joke was on too large a scale, and too long supported to suit the fastidious taste of Parisian readers, and in its present shape defies the most enterprising student by its insupportable dullness. Rivarol, however, was not allowed to continue his literary championship undisturbed. In 1790, he found it expedient to attempt escape, but failed to elude the vigilance of the patriots, and only two years later succeeded in making his way to Brussels, Amsterdam, and ultimately London. He now set about the most serious enterprise of his life,—his *Théorie du Corps Politique*, on which he was still engaged when, some years later, his mortal illness overtook him. The object of the work was to combat the doctrine—which Rousseau had rendered fashionable—of the sovereignty of the people. Defining power to be organised force, sovereignty to be conservative power, and the people to be essentially unconservative, he demonstrated with a lucidity, for which every good Tory should revere his memory, the truth that the true governance of society must be vested in the hands of the aristocratic few. Society, however, still stole him from his tasks; and we have an amusing account of the troubles of an unfortunate publisher who, during Rivarol's subsequent residence in Hamburg, had actually to keep him under lock, to expedite the composition of a long-promised preliminary discourse to a new dictionary of the French language. It was doubtless far more agreeable to dictate to fine ladies than to be the slave of a printer's devil; and Rivarol would not do the one so long as he had the least chance of enjoying the other.

At Hamburg he appears to have lived in an agreeable and somewhat dissolute society. The animal spirits of Emigration, he said, fled thither for refuge; and we may infer that merriment was not the only characteristic of the expiring régime which the high-bred exiles carried with them to their new abode. Rivarol, no doubt, knew extremely well how to enliven supper-parties, where manners were good and morals indulgent, which were graced by the gentle radiance of "des yeux de velours," and the sophistries of controversialists more lovely than immaculate. Once, for instance, we find him parodising the mixed greediness and patriotism of Lally-Tolendal. "Oui, messieurs, j'ai vu couler ce sang,—voulez-vous me verser un verre de vin de Bourgogne?—oui, messieurs, j'ai vu tomber cette tête,—voulez-vous me faire passer une aile de poulet?" &c. &c. One can fancy the glee with which such a scene would be enacted to a royalist audience, and the witticisms which it would suggest at the expense of revolutionary gourmandism.

Here, too, among other excitements, Rivarol fell in with the most fervent of all his admirers. Chênedollé, at this time young, romantic, burning with literary enthusiasm, and a hero-worshiper of the devoutest order, was as enraptured as a priest of Apis with a new-found calf, at the discovery of so worthy an object of adoration. Four years before, the young poet had joined the party of the Emigrants, had served for two campaigns under royalist banners, and had arrived in Hamburg, early in 1795, a fugitive from the arms of his victorious countrymen. His zeal for greatness was hot, his temperament of the order that is familiarly described as "gushing;" and the neighbourhood of so great an intellectual celebrity threw him into a fever of excitement. Already the *Héloïse* of J. J. Rousseau, the *Georgics* of the Abbé Delille, the *Arcadia* of Bernardin de Saint-Pierre, above all, the graphic descriptions of Buffon, had excited ecstasies of wonder and delight. All these, however, were as nothing to his latest passion. Several chance meetings with Rivarol at the fashionable restaurant of the city, and a few brilliant expressions stealthily overheard, intoxicated the young votary almost to the verge of insanity. "I saw, I thought, I dreamt nothing but Rivarol: c'était une vraie frénésie, qui m'ôtait jusqu'au sommeil." After six weeks of frantic expectation, an opportune friend volunteered to introduce him to "the king of conversation." The young poet arrived in a ludicrous state of mixed nervousness and satisfaction, which he has delineated with unblushing fidelity, and which M. Sainte-Beuve, in his sketch of "Chateaubriand and his literary friends," has preserved entire. Nothing can be more graphic than the account given by Chênedollé of the much-desired interview, or more characteristic of the inordinate pretentiousness, vanity, and bombast into which the triumphs of society and a long course of flattery can stimulate a nature for which really grave pursuits possess no charm, and which honest criticism has never curbed into decent self-restraint. Chênedollé might well tremble, for Rivarol was not only a great talker, but a fine gentleman, and affected the graceful condescension of one who belonged to the innermost and most refined circle of the Parisian world. He launched forthwith into a friendly criticism of his visitor's latest production, and promised him a speedy growth of power in the invigorating sunshine of his own society. "J'espère," he said, "que nous ferons quelque chose de vous. Venez me voir, nous mettrons votre esprit *en serre chaude*, et tout ira bien. Pour commencer, nous allons faire aujourd'hui une débauche de poésie.'" Hereupon began a marvellous display of versatile loquacity. Starting from the first principles of his theme, the orator maintained that the savage and the poet are one: both speak by hieroglyphics, though the latter moves in a larger orbit, and enjoys a more extended range of vision. Armed with this idea, and enlarging it gradually to the proposition, that art should aim at nothing short of the infinite, Rivarol performed prodigies of dexterity, dazzled his auditors with a sparkling cascade of metaphor, analogy, and retort, quenched their occasional dissent with an authoritative "point d'objections d'enfant," and charmed them no less by the melody of his voice than the cogency of his reason into fancying themselves for a while the favoured visitors to an intellectual fairyland. After dinner, however, still greater wonders awaited them: the party adjourned to the garden; and Chênedollé has invested the scene with the classical dignity due to a Platonic discussion. The sun was sinking to the west, the sky was clear as that of Greece, the foliage rivalled the plane-trees of the Academy, and the modern Socrates began to talk, and this time upon no abstract theme. Rapidly surveying the writers of the century, he passed a trenchant, searching, and, it must be confessed, somewhat uncharitable judgment upon each. Against Voltaire especially he evinced a sort of personal animosity, and, as his panegyrist observed, "pushed jealousy very far." The *Henriade*, he said, was nothing "qu'un maigre croquis, une squelette épique, où manquent les muscles, les chairs, et les couleurs:" the tragedies are cold and glittering philosophical treatises; in the style there is always "une partie morte:" the Essay on Manners an elegant but barren and untruthful sketch,—a miserable parody of Bossuet's immortal discourse. "One must needs," continued the critic, "be very *médiocre* oneself to imagine that there is nothing beyond the thought of Voltaire: "rien de plus incomplet que cette pensée: elle est vaine, superficielle, moqueuse, dissolvante, essentiellement propre à détruire, et voilà tout. Du reste, il n'y a ni profondeur, ni élévation, ni unité, ni avenir, rien de ce qui fonde et systématise." In support of so rigorous a sentence the literary culprit's works were next reviewed in detail, and some stinging sarcasm, like a drop of aquafortis, bestowed on each. Buffon was the next to suffer: "Son style a de la pompe et de l'ampleur, mais il est diffus et pâteux: on y voit toujours flotter les plis de la robe d'Apollon, mais souvent le dieu n'y est pas." Chênedollé's enthusiasm must have died away, as one by one his favourite descriptions were analysed and disapproved. That of the Dog was too long; "not characterised by the splendid economy of style of the old masters:" the Eagle was not sufficiently vigorous or masculine: the Peacock especially provoked the critic's indignation at its insufficiency; it was diffuse, yet incomplete; "cela chatoie plus encore que cela ne rayonne;" to paint this 'opulent oiseau,' one ought, he said, "to dip one's brushes in the sun, and shed the colours on its outline as rapidly as that great luminary darts its rays upon sky and mountain. I have in my head a peacock, new, magnificent, after a very different fashion, and I would only ask for an hour to beat this one." M. Sainte-Beuve's criticism is too obviously appropriate not to be recorded: "not only," he says, "had he a peacock in his head, but he was the peacock in person when he could speak like this." Frenchmen, however tolerant of vanity, have yet a limit to their endurance, and even Chênedollé was a little shocked. "I was confounded, I confess," he writes, "by the severity of the judgments, and the tone of assurance and infallibility with which they were delivered; it seemed to me out of the question that a man who talked so well could possibly be wrong." Presently, however, Rousseau fell under the lash, and Rivarol became viciously epigrammatic at his expense. "He is a grand master-sophist, who does not think a word of what he says or writes—c'est le paradoxe incarné: grand artiste d'ailleurs en fait de style . . . . . . il parle du haut de ses livres comme du haut d'une tribune; il a des cris et des gestes dans son style, et son éloquence épileptique a dû être irrésistible sur les femmes et les jeunes gens. Orateur *ambidextre*, il écrit sans conscience, ou plutôt il laisse errer sa conscience au gré de toutes ses sensations et de toutes ses affections. Aussi passionne-t-il tout ce qu'il touche." "St.-Georges de l'épigramme," as Rivarol was entitled, was now fairly astride his battle-horse, and warming with achieved success, strode right and left across the battle-field of letters, and driving all before the terror of his arms. At every word a reputation dies; scarce a contemporary had the luck to escape the discomfiture of a sarcastic thrust, impalement on a pun, or the sweep of glittering invective. The Abbé Delille was "nothing but a nightingale who had got his brain in his throat;" the luminous phrases of Cerutti were the work of a sort of literary snail leaving a silvered track—in reality, mere froth and drivel. Chabanon, a translator of Theocritus and Pindar, was said to have done it "de toute sa haine contre le Grec." Le Brun was sketched sitting on his bed with dirty sheets—a shirt a fortnight old—surrounded by Virgil, Horace, Corneille, Racine, and Rousseau, angling for a word in one or the other to compose the mosaic of his poetry. Condorcet was described as writing with opium on leaves of lead. Mirabeau as a big sponge always filled up with other people's ideas. "Il n'a eu quelque réputation," continued his assailant, "que parce qu'il a toujours écrit sur des matières palpitantes de l'intérêt du moment;—there are in his big books some happy expressions, but they are borrowed from Cerutti, Chamfort, or myself."

Three hours slipped unperceived away; the sun, regardless of the unfinished oration, went ruthlessly down; and the delighted visitors, armed with a copy of the great man's translation of Dante,—a mine of expressions, as he informed them, most valuable to a youthful poet,—heads, hearts, and mouths full of naught but Rivarol, at length took their departure.

Upon a subsequent occasion, Chênedollé was allowed to hear the beginning of the *Théorie du Corps Politique;* a work which, written unmethodically on separate slips of paper, and once suffered to fall into confusion, defied all the efforts of Rivarol's posthumous commentators to reduce it into a systematic arrangement. Part of it was stolen, and printed under another name at Hamburg, and a single chapter was published separately by the author himself many years later at Paris. Rivarol's premature death cut short the scheme half way; and we have only the conjectural decisions of friends or foes to tell us how much the world lost by its non-completion. Chênedollé, in unwavering loyalty, believes that his genius was capable of rising to the dizziest heights of political speculation; and, had time but been allowed him, of reducing the bewildering phenomena of the Revolution to lucid simplicity, and even, perhaps, of arresting its course. Catching his master's epigrammatic tone, he pronounces Beaumarchais, Mirabeau, and Rivarol the three most distinguished men of letters at the close of the 18th century: "Beaumarchais, par son *Figaro,* donna le manifeste de la Révolution; Mirabeau la fit; Rivarol la combattit et fit tout pour l'enrayer: il mourut à la peine." Calmer judges will probably have no trouble in convincing themselves that pretty analogies, nicely-balanced phrases, and fortunate retorts, though cogent in the controversies of the drawing-room, and fascinating to a coterie of fine ladies or aspiring authors, have yet the smallest possible influence on the stern facts of life, the sentiments of suffering classes, the march of a revolution; and that twenty elegant treatises, polished by easy thinkers, like Rivarol, into well-bred gracefulness, and welcomed with all the hosannas of St. Germains, would have done but little towards either explaining or impeding any social convulsion, and would have left the course of things in France very much as they found it.

For two years Chênedollé's trance of admiration lasted; every thought, every faculty, every wish seemed absorbed in the homage of his idol. "The god of conversation" exacted almost divine honours, and the young man was too busy listening to be able either to think or to write. One is hardly surprised to find that an intimacy so extravagant and foolish was broken off at last on a trifle about which two children would be ashamed to quarrel. The hero and the worshipper came to black looks and angry words, exchanged a brief fusillade of snappish notes, and resolved at once to part. Their common friends in vain attempted reconciliation: Chênedollé was immovable. "J'adore le talent de Rivarol," he said, "et j'aime sa personne; mais je ne le reverrai plus." Adoration and love, we may suspect, had sunk to a low ebb, when the first pretext for estrangement was thus readily embraced.

A curious little episode of love, which resulted in the French wit being caught by an Irish adventuress, is worth recording only for the witty language in which the victim expressed his sufferings: "Je ne suis ni Jupiter ni Socrate, et j'ai trouvé dans ma maison Xantippe et Junon." "Un jour," so runs another of his complaints, "je m'avisai de médire de l'amour, il m'envoya l'hymen pour se venger. Depuis je n'ai vecu que de regrets." At last a separation ensued, and an illiterate, but very fascinating, young lady consoled the weary husband for his late persecutions. Such a domestic régime throws a somewhat suspicious light upon Rivarol's high moral tone and the theological speculations which advanced him almost to the chair of De Maistre. His views of religion, however, as a political engine and a mainstay of the fabric of society, are sensible and well expressed; the reckless scepticism of his contemporaries affected him with sincere alarm: "C'est un terrible luxe," he said, "que l'incrédulité." "Il ne croit pas en Dieu," he wrote of one of his contemporaries, whose convictions were stronger than his piety, "mais il craint en Dieu." It is, however, with less profound topics that Rivarol's wit played most at ease, and exhibited in the most striking manner its astonishing range and pliability. With a few specimens of this we conclude a notice already, we fear, prolonged beyond the conventional limits.

His brother, whom he styled "ma montre de répétition," served as the butt for a succession of stinging pleasantries: "Il serait l'homme d'esprit d'une autre famille, c'est le sot de nôtre." He appears to have been of a melancholy temperament: "Jérémie," observed his merciless relative, "aurait été un buffon à côté de lui." Once he came to announce that he had been reading a newly-composed tragedy to M. de B—: "Hélas!" was the consoling reply, "je vous avais dit, que c'était un de nos amis." Of the Duke of Orleans' rubicund features he observed, "que la débauche l'avait dispensé de rougir." Mirabeau was equally little to his taste: "C'était l'homme du monde qui ressemblait le plus à sa réputation; il était affreux." "Ce Mirabeau est capable de tout pour l'argent, même d'une bonne action." Buffon's son, who did little credit to his illustrious parentage, was described as "the worst chapter of natural history his father ever wrote."

"C'est un terrible avantage que de n'avoir rien fait, mais il ne faut pas en abuser.

On lui demandait son sentiment sur Madame de Genlis. 'Je n'aime,' répondit-il, 'que les sexes prononcés.'

Les journalistes qui écrivent pesamment sur les poésies légères de Voltaire sont comme les commis de nos douanes qui impriment leurs plombs sur les gazes légères d'Italie.

Lorsqu'il apprit que l'archévêque de Toulouse s'était empoisonné, il dit, 'C'est qu'il aura avalé une de ses maximes.'"

ART. IV.—LIFE OF BISHOP WARBURTON.

The Life of William Warburton, D.D., Lord Bishop of Gloucester from 1760 *to* 1779; *with Remarks on his Works.* By Rev. John Selby Watson, M.A., M.R.S.L. Longman, 1863.

ABOUT fifteen years after Warburton's death, that which his friends wished to be known of his life was given to the world by his confidential disciple and admirer, Hurd, Bishop of Worcester. The same editor and literary executor left ready for press a volume of Warburton's correspondence with himself, which appeared immediately after Hurd's death in 1808. Warburton, who always expressed himself without fear or favour, softening or disguise, about friend or foe, has in these letters left a piece of self-portraiture. The correspondence is the corrective of the Life, and reveals Warburton and the Warburtonians in a thousand characteristic traits which Hurd's decorum had varnished over.

To these two primary sources, coupled with Warburton's own works, which fill thirteen volumes 8vo, Mr. Selby Watson has added a diligent search through the ephemeral literature of the period,—periodicals, pamphlets, sermons, and charges. He does not seem to have enjoyed the use of any new materials hitherto unprinted. Warburton's own letters are understood to have been almost all destroyed by his widow. One cannot help asking, Where are those which were not destroyed? Where are the letters of Warburton's correspondents? Where are the papers from which Mr. Kilvert printed a "Selection" in 1841? and where are the collections which Mr. James Crossley has been many years making? No *subsidia* from these sources are to be found in the present biography. But as this volume is already 650 pages thick, most readers will think they have too much, rather than too little. And, for a complete estimate of Warburton and his doings, we have enough. There may be many letters yet recoverable. But it is impossible that any thing can be now brought to light which could modify perceptibly the well-defined image of the man which may be traced from the materials already in our hands. All that is required for this task, beyond some skill in delineating character, is to place the man in his right relation to the social life and ideas of the time. The biographer must know his way about among religious parties in the latter half of George II.'s reign,—perhaps the least-known portion of the history of the English Church. Warburton belonged to none of these, and came athwart all of them at one period or another of his bellicose career. It is on such invisible attractions and repulsions that the main interest of a career of antagonism such as Warburton's lies. His life was a succession of battles,—battles of the pen. All Warburton's books, like those of St. Augustine, are written against some adversary. But instead of handling the great public themes of Divinity, natural and revealed, Warburton is always defending some peculiar notion of his own, to which no one attached any importance, himself as little as any. The zest lay in the fighting, of which, while he was young, he never could get enough. The most famous of Warburton's battles,—and the most serious; indeed the Waterloo of his critical empire,—was that with Lowth. In this celebrated encounter, in which the whole reading public, from the king downwards, participated with the liveliest interest, the points of sacred antiquity debated are mostly of no moment. Or where they are of moment, as, *e.g.* the date of the Book of Job, the disputants lack the requisite knowledge for throwing even the feeblest ray of light upon them. But though we can learn nothing respecting the Pentateuch and Job, we may glean much to instruct us in the inner history of the Church of England during a period in which that history is very little known to the present generation. What is wanted here, is not so much fresh materials, as the hand to reduce to order and system those which are already extant. The life of Warburton, which was passed wholly on the highways, and open to public inspection, is peculiarly calculated as a mirror of the clerical life of the eighteenth century, or at least of the literary section of it, and contrasts in this respect with the noiseless and inexpressive existence of men like Secker and Porteous.

Though Warburton inherited an ancient name, he was born (1698) to humble, or rather no fortunes. Bred to the law, his passion for literature—though Hurd pretends an early seriousness of temper—led him into the Church at the age of twenty-five. At the age of thirty he obtained from a private patron, Sir Robert Sutton, a living of some value. At this parsonage, Brant-Broughton, near Newark, he fixed himself with his mother and sisters, and spent the eighteen best years of his life in unintermitted study. An athletic frame and a vigorous constitution, seconded by abstemious habits, enabled him to support, at least without immediate injury, this severe tax on the brain. Nature, however, exacted the penalty—a penalty which may be deferred, but is never remitted—at the end of life. Though he lived to old age, his memory became impaired, and some time before death he sunk into a general torpor of the faculties. One of his sisters, Mrs. Frances Warburton, told Hurd that, even at this early period, they became apprehensive for his health, and "would sometimes invite themselves to take coffee in his library after dinner, and contrive to make their stay with him as long as possible; but that, when they retired, they always found that he returned again to his books, and continued at them till the demands of sleep obliged him to retire" (*Life*, p. 34). His absorption in his books is illustrated by a story told of his going to dine at Lord Tyrconnel's, at Bilton Hall, where a fire was raging at a house which Warburton had to pass on the road from Brant-Broughton. When he arrived at Bilton he had nothing to tell; though he had ridden close by the house, he had not noticed the fire. The company began to hope the report was not true. But it was soon confirmed by the arrival of another guest, who said he had noticed Mr. Warburton ride by without turning his head, apparently absorbed in some subject of meditation.

With these habits seconding the native energy of his mind, his knowledge of books became immense. Johnson told the king that "he had not read so much as Warburton,"—a modest admission, yet strictly true, even understood of bare quantity. But Johnson was not thinking of volumes by number. He knew that Warburton's reading ranged over whole classes of books into which he himself had barely dipped. Johnson's own stock of learning had been acquired, he once told Boswell, by eighteen, and that he had added little to it at any subsequent period. And Warburton said of himself that "he was a great reader of history, but a greater still of romances; for that nothing came amiss to a man who consulted his appetite more than his digestion." An indication, perhaps, that Bentley's sarcasm had come to his ears. The great critic, on being shown the first volume of the *Divine Legation*, about three years before his death, had remarked, "This man has a monstrous appetite, but very bad digestion." "A change in the object of his pursuit," says Whitaker, "was his only relaxation. He could pass and repass from fathers and philosophers to *Don Quixote* in the original, with perfect ease and pleasure." Of his method of reading, nothing is reported by any one who knew him during his period of acquisition. Cradock, in a conversation with Mrs. Warburton, observed that Hurd had expressed his wonder how the Bishop had acquired all the anecdotes in which he so much abounded. "I could readily have informed him," replied Mrs. Warburton. "When we passed our winters in London, he would often, after his long and severe studies, send out for a whole basketful of books from the circulating-libraries, and at times I have gone into his study and found him laughing, though alone." And he writes to Doddridge that "his melancholy habit impelled him to seek refuge from the uneasiness of thought in wild and desultory reading." He was well acquainted with the history of the Civil War, and told Hurd that "there was scarcely a memoir or a pamphlet published between 1640 and 1660 which he had not read." These are all the testimonies we can find on the subject. Beyond this we are left to the evidence his writings themselves afford of the compass and depth of his acquaintance with books.

However great Warburton's receptive capacity, his instinct to communicate thought was quite as vigorous. All this reading could not go on without a corresponding effort to write. The first direction was given to his pen, as to most men's before they have found their own vein, by the taste of those with whom he lived. Warburton had found his way, in his occasional visits to London, into a coffee-house set of fourth-rate literati,—Concanen, Dennis, James Moore, Hesiod Cooke, and Broome. The best man of the set was Theobald. When Theobald brought out his *Shakespeare* in 1733, he said that he owed Warburton "no small part of his best criticisms,"—an acknowledgment which went rather beyond than within the mark. After another emendatory attempt, of which Velleius Paterculus was the unfortunate object, Warburton forsook a track into which he had only been drawn by imitation for one proper to his own bent. He certainly did not relinquish verbal criticism because he thought he had failed in it, notwithstanding a friendly hint from Bishop Hare, intended to suggest that conclusion to him. To the last he believed in himself as a restorer of Shakespeare. Even Johnson's edition in 1765 could not open his eyes. He was very far from adopting the good-natured suggestion of the Preface that "he (Warburton) cannot now be very solicitous what is thought of notes which he ought never to have considered as a part of his serious employments, and which, I suppose, he no longer numbers among his happy effusions." But, though perfectly satisfied of his own "happy sagacity to restore an author's text" (*Letters to Hurd*, p. 367), his mind was formed with a more ambitious grasp, and impelled him to marshal ideas.

In 1736 he struck into the vein which made him famous. The *Alliance of Church and State*, brought out in that year, is widely different by its title and argument from the *Divine Legation*, which followed it in 1738. But the mould in which the thought of both works is cast is one and the same, viz. the politician's view of religion.

The immediate effect of these publications in rivetting upon themselves the attention of all the reading public is only to be accounted for by their union of two qualities: they occupied themselves with the thought with which every body was occupied, and they treated it with more force and weight than any body. The originality of Warburton's manner would not have told as it did, had it not been laid out upon a topic which was anxiously engaging the minds of practical men. His work fell at a time when the interest of the speculative part of the Deistical controversy had well-nigh exhausted itself. On the question, Does Christianity contain any supernatural elements? that generation had said on both sides nearly all it could say. The interest had merged in a new and more practical phase of inquiry, viz. What remedy could be found for the growing licentiousness of manners, and relaxation of the bonds of civil society? The title and professed thesis of the *Divine Legation* hide from us this bearing upon contemporary feeling. It was this secret bearing which recommended an otherwise barren paradox to general attention. When this engrossing subject was treated with singular force, and with a learned apparatus which had not been seen in theological controversy since Stillingfleet, the author became at once, in that frivolous world of pamphleteers, the mark for adulation and for envy. From the associate of Concanen and Theobald, he became the friend and adviser of Pope, the correspondent of Charles Yorke, received open favour from Hare, and timid encouragement from Sherlock. To the Bishop of Chichester (Hare) he owed a recommendation to the queen. Her majesty chanced one day, in the autumn of 1737, to ask the bishop if he could recommend her a person of learning and ability to be about her, to read and converse. Hare immediately named Warburton. The promised opening was closed by the queen's death in November,—an event disastrous not only to Warburton's rising fortunes, but to the whole Church of England.

His preferment was retarded by this event, but not ultimately forfeited. The intrinsic merit and ingenuity of the *Divine Legation* must ultimately have won it attention; but an immediate and exaggerated *éclat* was conferred upon it by the cloud of insect assailants who immediately fastened upon it. The liberal section of the clergy, represented by Hare, commended, but with an evident coldness. The moderate orthodox, represented by the feeble Sherlock, timidly gave in their adhesion, rather as if they feared to alienate so much power than as heartily appropriating it. But the high-church party, standing aloof in sullen opposition, felt at once, by an instinct far surer than intelligence, that the new candidate in the field of theology, however carefully he might have avoided committing himself against them, yet was not of them. They fell upon him immediately, to bury and to stifle, with the usual arms of the party—

denunciation, not argument. From the pulpit of St. Mary's, Oxford, they called for "the secular arm" to cut off the heretic. They misrepresented, twisted meanings, drew inferences, and gave a momentary interest to their malignant trash by promiscuous revilings. Warburton complains that "propositions were invented, conversations betrayed, and forged letters written." A hireling writer whom the party, though not trusting him, occasionally used, inserted, if he did not write, in a paper, *The Weekly Miscellany*, edited by him, one of the worst of these attacks. In it the "clergy who are sincere friends to Christianity" are put on their guard against this new pretended advocate of revelation, who is really a subtle enemy. The author of the *Divine Legation*, it is insinuated, denies the divinity of Christ, the merits of his death, the obligation and effects of the sacraments, and the doctrine of grace; and he "undervalues the evidence arising from miracles." The letter, signed a "Country Clergyman," winds up with a naïve disclosure of the writer's purpose in a hint that Mr. Warburton "should be hindered from any further advancement in the church." Of the imputations on Warburton's orthodoxy no proof was attempted, because none could be found. But as his friends, Sherlock included, thought he ought to take some notice of this assault, Warburton made the best defence he could. To the repeated cautions of Sherlock and Hare we must ascribe it that this "Vindication" is in a higher tone, and almost pure from that intemperate invective against assailants in which Warburton afterwards allowed himself. But that which did him most credit in it was the way in which he treated Conyers Middleton. In the *Divine Legation* he had spoken of Middleton, who was his personal friend, as a "formidable adversary to the Freethinkers." To have mentioned Middleton's name without proscribing it was enough to give a handle to cavil. Warburton's allusion was immediately transformed by the "Country Clergyman" into his being "a warmer advocate for Dr. Middleton, who denies the divine inspiration of the Scriptures, than for the Scriptures themselves." In his "Vindication" Warburton extricates himself without sacrificing his friend with a tact for which he deserved the commendation of the Bishop of Chichester, who told him that the bishops thought this part, which was the only difficult part, extremely well done. "It cannot but please every candid reader to see you do justice to yourself, and yet not do it at his (Middleton's) expense." It is to be regretted that Warburton had not always such prudent friends as Hare and Sherlock to advise him. He had probably escaped one of the worst blots upon his reputation, —the unmannerly violence towards opponents, which was the tone of his later controversy.

Meanwhile he pursued a better method of shaking off adversaries than writing against them; that of continuing at his own labour. The second volume of the *Divine Legation*, containing books 4, 5, and 6, came out in 1741. It had the fate of continuations,—of not being thought equal to the first part. But in this instance with justice. It wants the elasticity and point of the earlier books, being at once less strong and more violent. It almost seems as if the author was angry with himself at being so little able to prove the thesis he had undertaken to prove, and making so little way with so much effort. But he had no reason to be dissatisfied with its reception by the world. Any decay of interest in the argument was made up for by personalities. He had now erected the notes to *Divine Legation* into "the ordinary place of his literary executions, where offenders by the dozen were whipped at the cart's tail," to use Lowth's comparison. The stir among the pamphleteers was far greater than on the occasion of the first volume. Then, Warburton contradicted as a man who has to make his way by pulling down those above him; now, he called criminals before him as already seated on the judge's bench. He no longer reasoned; he sentenced. It was not now necessary to show that Warburton's opinion was right; the man who disputed it was, to begin with, a "scoundrel." Though here, to be sure, he is too apt to forget his own maxim that "the proving a man a scoundrel is putting him in the way to thrive" (*Letter to Doddridge*), and Charles Yorke's suggestion that the opponents were "like the spectres whom Æneas encountered, whom you cannot hurt with any weapons." And, in fact, the more heads Warburton cut off, the more the foe multiplied upon his hands. The fight waxed hotter, and promised to last. A row in the theological world did not die out so speedily in those days, when the steam-press was not yet invented. Warburton had taken the place of Hoadley. In 1746, five years after the appearance of the second volume of the *Divine Legation*, Hurd writes to Devey: "The attention of the learned world at present turns entirely almost on the author of the *Divine Legation*, who is mowing down his adversaries with as great zeal and success as ever old Bentley did before him." By this time he had become literary executor to Pope, and entered upon the inheritance of Pope's feuds in addition to his own.

Mr. Selby Watson devotes some chapters to the "Answerers" —'Answerer' is a proper term in Warburtonian history, meaning those who wrote pamphlets against the *Divine Legation*. The writers themselves were of very various capacity and position. One character is common to all, that is, the insignificance of the points they choose to dispute, and their total want of the critical knowledge necessary for settling even those points. The two parties oppose opinion to opinion; and because Warburton vociferates most loudly in defence of his, it carries the day. It is observable that the attempts to make out Warburton unorthodox gradually die away. This kind of imputation is the first weapon at which a clerical assailant grasps, and the most deadly. Warburton had succeeded in parrying it, and there was no other he had to fear. It was settled that he was orthodox, and he was therefore in a condition to hurl it back upon his assailants. He had not always magnanimity enough to abstain from doing so. For instance, on Nicholas Mann, whose provocation was that he had argued for the identity of Osiris and Sesostris after Warburton had pronounced that they were to be distinguished, he revenged himself by saying to Archbishop Potter in an abrupt way, "I suppose you know you have chosen an Arian!"

The violence of the attacks on him had no blighting effect upon his reputation. During the ten years, 1740-1750, his credit was steadily rising, his circle of connexion extending, his fortunes improving. A man who rouses opponents is not seldom found to be capable of attaching friends in the same proportion. All Warburton's friendships were formed late, and as the result of literature. They had nothing about them of early association and comradeship. His introduction into the Pope circle was perhaps the most influential event in his life. This he obtained by writing expressly for it. In his struggling days, through his relations with Theobald he had been acustomed to sneer at Pope. A very little insight into the life of the town taught him that, with a view to his own interest in literature, it would be better to propitiate Twickenham. He took the opportunity of Crousaz's critique on the *Essay on Man* to draw up an elaborate defence of the moral doctrine enforced in it. In these papers, which appeared in the *Works of the Learned* for 1739, Warburton forced his own meaning on the poet, with his usual paradox and force. "If you did not find him a philosopher, you have made him one," Middleton told him; and Pope, who was not very sure what moral doctrine he had intended to teach, was delighted to discover of himself that he was *not* a fatalist. He addressed a letter of thanks to the author, who was till then an entire stranger to him. The friendship thus begun proved more lasting and of more worth than literary friendships usually are, being cemented by the bond of mutual interest. Pope wanted a commentator and a champion against the crowd of enemies his provocative spirit had called up against himself. Warburton wanted an introduction to the great and powerful. When Pope died (1742) he left Warburton his literary executor —a legacy which was worth to him at least 4000*l.*, a considerable sum to a poor man. Pope had introduced him to Allen.

This led to his marrying Allen's favourite niece, to whom Allen left by his will the bulk of his property,—a very large fortune; and before his death he obtained for his son-in-law, first the deanery, and afterwards the bishopric, of Gloucester. All this grew from a few flimsy pages in the *Works of the Learned*, which happened to please Pope.

Pope had made a great point of introducing Warburton to Bolingbroke, and had calculated upon the certainty of "their being pleased to meet each other." After many delays a meeting was at last effected. The three dined together at Lord Mansfield's, a short time before Pope's death. Bolingbroke made a remark about the moral attributes of the Deity which did not please Warburton. He replied with some asperity, and a debate ensued, which ended in making each thoroughly detestable to the other; a very common result of such prearranged friendships! They had been forced into contact without any natural attraction: the result was a deadly animosity. Before his death, Bolingbroke scattered over his pages sarcasm by the handful against the *Divine Legation* and its author; and a whole volume of Warburton's works is devoted to tirade against Bolingbroke and Bolingbroke's philosophy.

Of the friends made by literature, the best man was Jortin, and the most intimate, Hurd. The acquaintance with Jortin was not longer-lived than literary friendships usually are; but the fault of its disruption was wholly Warburton's, and in none of his many enmities did he show to greater disadvantage. To Bishop Newton, who has left in his Memoirs a parallel between Jortin and Warburton, and to the public in common with Bishop Newton, both appeared "men of great parts, both men of uncommon learning, both able critics, both copious writers;" he adds, indeed, that Jortin "was *perhaps* the better Greek and Latin scholar." 'Better' implies comparison. The fact was that Jortin was a scholar in every sense of the word; Warburton in none: and in the matter of the disagreement between them, Jortin shows as much above Warburton in magnanimity as he is in learning. The two were exactly of an age, having been born in the same year, 1698. But the modesty, not to say reserve, of Jortin, together with what Parr calls his "unfettered opinions," kept him longer in the background, and he was in a condition to be patronised by Warburton. Warburton employed him as an occasional substitute in Lincoln's Inn Chapel, and dropt an encouraging word for him in some preface to a second edition: "The world might soon expect to be gratified with the learned Mr. Jortin's Dissertations, composed, like his life, not in the spirit of controversy, but of truth and candour." A neat compliment, but in the present case not more than strictly true.

These very Dissertations, when they came out in 1755, contained a confession of dissent from the Warburtonian hypothesis on Virgil's descent into hell. That it was indicated with the writer's habitual modesty and gentleness made no difference. Hurd was commissioned to fall upon Jortin with the sword of vengeance. This he did in a "Seventh Dissertation addressed to the Author of the Six," a long and rambling piece of irony, which, however, the contemporary world called "Attic." In spite of the "Attic irony," the public who interested themselves in all these "quarrels of authors" sided with Jortin. They translated out of the Attic irony the following rules in plain English, for the proper guidance of writers in their demeanour towards the sovereign of letters;

1. You must not write on the same subject that he does. 2. You must not write against him. 3. You must not glance at his arguments without naming him. 4. You must not oppose his principles. 7. Where you design him a compliment, you must express it in form, with all the circumstance of panegyrical approbation. 8. You must call his suggestions "discoveries," not "conjectures."

Though the public condemned Hurd, Warburton was delighted that Jortin's "mean, low, and ungrateful conduct" towards him had been properly chastised. Those who espoused Jortin's side were "dirty fellows indeed," and the compliment to Jortin was erased from the next edition of *Julian*. For all this, Jortin's revenge—neat and quiet, after his manner—was but to correct a childish mistake as to the meaning of the word *princeps*, which Warburton had committed. It was done without naming Warburton, though the application to him was made by a line from Terence, with which the correction wound up. Warburton had pretended to "prove" that *primus* meant *chief*, and had collected passages in which it has that signification. "He has omitted one," says Jortin, "which would 'suit him better' than any: 'Est genus hominum qui esse primos se omnium rerum volunt, nec sunt (Terent. *Eun.* ii. 11, 17).'" This little reproof was buried out of sight in a note to Jortin's *Life of Erasmus*. But though whispered to the reeds, it struck Warburton in his most vulnerable part,—his conceit of classical knowledge. Before his equanimity could be restored, Hurd was obliged to "prove" that *princeps*, in the passage of Cicero (*de Legg.* ii. 6), actually meant what Warburton had made it mean. This he did to Warburton's entire satisfaction; but, as Mr. Watson remarks, Hurd knew Latin enough to refrain from going before the public with these proofs, and was satisfied at having appeased his patron's wrath by a private exposure of "the poor man's criticism." Warburton sent Jortin, in an indirect way, a letter reproaching him, in return for his criticism, with the fact that, "from the first moment of my acquaintance with him to the last that he would allow me to call him friend, I had the vanity to be always recommending him to those of the first quality whom I knew." Jortin replied as follows:

"*London, October 3d*, 1758.

Rev. Sir,—I had the favour of yours, which gave me a mixture of pain and pleasure,—of pain for ever having been at variance with you; of pleasure from some prospect of seeing an end of it, unless I deceive myself.

You complain; I could complain too; but to what purpose would that serve? To irritate, perhaps; but that is not my present design.

You say that you never was concerned in the attacks made upon me. I ought to believe you; and I do believe you. But before you informed me of it, I thought otherwise; and so did many a person besides me.

That you recommended me to persons who had it in their power to do me service, I doubt not. Vouchers are needless. Your own word suffices with me, and I thank you for it.

As to the passage in Cicero, which I ought in civility to have mentioned to you; if I did not mention it, my memory deceives me egregiously. Surely, unless I am utterly mistaken, I did tell you of it, and you replied, that Bishop Hare had once said the same thing to you.

[Your correction of my translation of *apud inferos*] I would take occasion, unless you forbid it, to mention in the next volume, with respect and with thanks. 'Sit simultatis depositæ et nunquam resumendæ pignus et monumentum!' . . . .

I am, sir, your most humble servant,

J. Jortin."

When we find that this generous proffer of the right hand of reconciliation was not accepted, we are ready to welcome Parr's ebullient sentences in the preface to *Tracts by Warburton and a Warburtonian:*

"While they (Leland and Jortin) were living, no balm was poured into their wounded spirits by the hand that pierced them; and if their characters after death remain unimpaired by the rude shocks of controversy and the secret crimes of slander, their triumph is to be ascribed to their own strength, and to the conscious weakness of their antagonist, rather than to his love of justice, or his love of peace."

In the quarrel with Jortin, the public feeling was on Jortin's side. But the sense of the public was not manifested with any thing like the strength and unanimity which was shown on the next occasion,—his controversy with Lowth,—his most desperate battle, and his last. Though Lowth had on the main issue far the best of it, yet both the combatants were severely maimed in the fight,—Warburton by his enemy's spear, Lowth by his own impetuosity. As it gave a blow to Warburton's dictatorship which it never recovered, we shall give the narrative at more length.

In the year 1753 the Clarendon Press at Oxford brought out, in a splendid quarto, with all the honours of typography, the series of Lectures which Lowth had delivered during his ten years' occupancy of the chair of poetry in that University. It was not the externals only of the volume of which the University was proud. It was no less remarkable for its matter. It was the first sign of the awakening of Oxford from that torpor under which two generations had now lain, under the besotting influence of Jacobite and high-church politics. The Lectures *De Sacra Poesi Hebræorum* seemed to combine the polish of a past generation, long gone, with the learning of a new period to come. The lore of Michaelis was here dressed out in Latin as classical and more vigorous than that of Addison. Kocher has indeed shown (Laurence, *On Translations of the Bible,* 1820) that Lowth's Hebrew skill was not equal to his pretensions; and Parr has pointed out that the professor was capable of writing "*poterit*" after "*ut.*" Still the effect of the Lectures was great. The Jacobite University had at last produced a work which might vie in solidity with any thing that proceeded from Hanoverian Göttingen, and with the finished style of which Göttingen had nothing to compare. The "classic elegance of Lowth" became a standard phrase, and continued to be so till into the present century; and German Hebraists occupied themselves in refuting the temerity of his numerous emendations of the Hebrew text. In England, the monopoly of learned theology had been for nearly twenty years in the author of the *Divine Legation*—an outsider. The tyrant of clerical literature was not only sprung from the *plebs,* but had seized the Acropolis of letters over the heads of the true aristocrats of Eton and Westminster, of King's and Christ Church. Many murmurs had been heard from time to time from various parts of the usurper's realm, but they had only drawn down his vengeance upon the heads of the disaffected. The malcontents had been "hung, as they do vermin in a warren, and left to posterity, to stink and blacken in the wind" (*Warb. to Birch*), as a warning to the rest. The new rebel was sprung from the very core of orthodoxy, the inner guild of traditional discipline. Robert Lowth was the son and grandson of clergymen; his father was the well-known commentator, and Prebend of Winchester. The son was a Wykehamist, a member of that close and jealous corporation—a university within the University—which was supposed in former times to exaggerate at once the faults and the excellences of the academical training. He chose to reside on his fellowship at New College, and at thirty years of age he stood forward as the most rising academic of his day. In 1741 he was placed, by the unanimous voice of the Masters of Arts, in the chair of poetry, the only possible competitor, Townson, declining to try the strength of Magdalen and Christ Church against the Wykehamist interest. The qualifications for the poetry professorship at that day were scholastic skill of Latin versification. In this art Lowth confessedly excelled his contemporaries. But in choosing the subject of his *Prælections* he resolved not merely to be satisfied with exhibiting the graces of his Latin style, but to instruct his auditory, inviting them into an entirely new field of criticism. "Why," he asked, "should we be ever repeating our eulogies of Homer and Pindar, while Moses, David, and Isaiah, poets not inferior to them, are passed by in silence?" Lowth's audience, though no judges of Hebrew, were connoisseurs in Latin; and these Lectures, interspersed with frequent passages of tasteful Latin translation, were delivered to thronging crowds, such as professorial lecture-rooms had long ceased to hold. In the ten years (1741-1751) of Lowth's tenure of the chair, he could boast that (*Prælect.* 32) the study of Hebrew, which had been almost extinct (nimium diu neglectam et pene obsoletam), had been rekindled by his exertions. In 1755 Warburton and Lowth met on the same stage of the ladder of Church preferment, each of them obtaining in that year a stall at Durham. But Warburton was fifty-seven, Lowth only forty-five; regular breeding had been equivalent to just twelve years' start in the race. From this time Warburton began to regard Lowth as his rival for the mitre. A suppressed jealousy, embittered by the inequality of age, made him quick to suppose meanings never meant. Though Lowth's Lectures had appeared in the spring of 1753, it was only in the summer of 1756, the year after the double Durham promotion, that Warburton took it into his head to be offended with some of the criticisms in that volume, and to look upon them as aimed against himself. He accordingly desired two common friends, Dr. Chapman and Mr. Spence,—for so, we have little doubt, ought to be filled up the blanks in the published Correspondence,—to call upon Lowth at Winchester, and demand satisfaction for this constructive treason. Lowth replied to this summons by addressing a letter to the autocrat himself. What must have been Warburton's surprise and rage when, instead of the apologetic submission to which he had been accustomed, he was met with the easy courtesy of an equal, aware of his strength, and yet disguising it under a thin veil of polished indifference. Had the offender come in on his knees, with the cord round his neck, the surrender had been graciously accepted. Had he flown to arms, the conqueror would have dealt with him according to precedent. The attitude which Lowth assumed, firm without defiance, foiled Warburton. Warburton's complaint had been, that his opinion on the age of "Job" was controverted in the Lectures. Lowth replies by an intimation, that he intended to pursue his critical inquiries in any direction that might be convenient to himself, without thinking it necessary to obtain leave from the author of the *Divine Legation*. As to the opinion on the age of "Job," as Warburton was only one of many who had held the same opinion, there was no reason why he should take the refutation all to himself. And that, in fact, however surprising it might seem, in writing the criticism in question he neither had the *Divine Legation* by him, nor was thinking of it.

The correspondence extended to several letters. Warburton saw enough of his man to see that he was one whom it would be advisable to have as a friend rather than an enemy. He determined upon a bold stroke. At the end of his fourth letter, dating from Grosvenor Square, he adds a postscript:

"I am here in waiting. I mention it to you from a selfish view. Regis (*i. e.* King's chaplain) of this month is dying. What should hinder your stepping into his place?"

In the subsequent letters the tone of irritation relaxes, and from "obedient humble servant" the correspondents leave off "your most faithful and affectionate," &c. So the affair rested for a time. But Warburton's tactic had not the success expected from it. Neither threats nor favours could subdue Lowth's independence of spirit. In 1763 he brought out a second edition of the *Prælections*, in which he not only did not modify the objectionable opinion on Job, but strengthened its point by additions which seemed unmistakably to aim at the views patronised in the *Divine Legation*. Castigation for this insolence could not be withheld without direct abdication. The next edition of the *Divine Legation*, 1765, accordingly pilloried the offender in an Appendix specially devoted to him. All temporising was discarded, and Lowth was finally settled with his "business being done" in a "few strictures." This prompt execution, however, so far from crushing the foe, only put him on his mettle. Though the dictator had in the interim become Bishop of Gloucester, Lowth was not daunted. Nay, Warburton's promotion did but point his pen to give words to the long-pent-up spleen with which Oxford had regarded the gradual progress of the intruder from the attorney's office to the bench. The manifesto appeared at the close of the long vacation of 1765, in a "Letter to the Right Rev. Author of the *D. L.*,"—a pamphlet of one hundred pages, printed at "the Clarendon Printing-house." In polished dexterity of argument, tinged, and not more than tinged, with the raillery of one who knows exactly what is due both to himself and his antagonist, this short piece has perhaps never been surpassed in literary warfare. At that period of paper ruffianism, when the courtesies of legitimate warfare were unpractised and unknown, such moderate language, combined with such superiority of demeanour, was wholly new. Even the mere English composition of the "Letter" was an event which opened a new era in writing, and made the public wonder that it could ever have admired the lame sentences and clumsy English of Warburton and his followers. "It would be difficult to find in the English language of equal variety and length four such compositions as Burke's Speech to the Electors of Bristol, Johnson's Preface to Shakespeare, Parr's Dedication, and Lowth's Letter to Warburton" (*Diary of a Lover of Literature*). Nor was it in composition only that the author of the English Grammar had the advantage over his antagonist. In his knowledge of the learned languages, Lowth, though a child by the side of Bentley, was beyond his contemporaries. Learning enough to qualify him as a critic of ancient writings he had not; he had enough to expose the clumsy blunders of the *Divine Legation*. In the correspondence of 1756 Lowth appears to give Warburton credit for all the knowledge which the dictator's tone arrogated to him. The closer scrutiny to which the second provocation led him of Warburton's writings must have revealed to his astonishment that the demonstrator of the divine legation of Moses could not read the writings of Moses except in a translation,—must have awakened his suspicions that Greek was not altogether familiar to one who had talked so largely of Pythagoras and Plato and the *Tò Ἓν*; and one or two gross mistakes in the bishop's Latin, which Lowth pauses upon, might have led him to the further conclusion at which we have ourselves arrived, had not the incredible nature of that conclusion apparently closed Lowth's eyes to the inevitable inference from such mistranslations as those of which the bishop is guilty, when he has to render Lowth's Latin where he was left without an English version to guide him.

This pamphlet contains the inimitable retort which will adhere to Warburton as long as his name continues to be mentioned among men,—"one of those lucky hits," says Whitaker, "which are given to the most witty and dextrous of mankind but once in a life." The bishop had said, "The learned professor has been hardily brought up in the keen atmosphere of *wholesome severities*, and early taught to distinguish between *de facto* and *de jure*" (*Div. Leg.*, *Works*, vol. vi. p. 150). To understand the bitterness of this taunt, we must recur to Lowth's peculiar position before the world in 1765. The University of Oxford was committed by all the traditions of seventy years to the principles of High-church and Jacobitism. Convicted of scarcely disguised disaffection to the reigning dynasty, it had been treated by successive ministries with neglect and contempt. Lowth stood forward as the foremost man and representative of this disgraced and semi-outlaw society. To fasten upon him the stigma of being the champion of disloyalty and persecuting principles, the presumed atmosphere in which Lowth had been brought up, would have been a fatal bar to his prospects in the Church. Nothing, therefore, could be more malignant than Warburton's hints, while at the same time nothing could be more unjust; for though the public and the government were not yet aware of it, a great change had been working in the opinions and feelings of the University. The old High-church and High-Tory party, of which Dr. King was the representative, had been slowly losing in numbers and influence, and a new generation forming in a mould less alien from the general feeling and opinion of England. To this party, which comprehended the younger and better minds in the University, the doctrines of the old Tory, his Stuart attachments, and his passion for "wholesome severities" against Nonconformists, were already distasteful; and it was of this party that Lowth was the representative. Stung at once by the unfairness of the taunt and by its damning nature, Lowth threw all his force into his reply to it. He distinctly and emphatically repudiates, as he could with truth, the insinuation of intolerance and persecuting tenets. "I have never omitted any opportunity that fairly offered itself of bearing my testimony against these very principles, and of expressing my abhorrence of them both in public and in private." And then he turns upon the bishop:

"Pray, my lord, what is it to the purpose where I have been brought up? You charge me with principles of intolerance and disaffection to the present royal family and government. You infer these principles, it seems, from the place of my education. Is this a necessary consequence? Is it even a fair conclusion? May not one have had the good sense or the good fortune to have avoided, or to have gotten the better of, the ordinary prejudices of education? Why, then, should you think that I must still necessarily labour under the bad influence of an atmosphere which I happened to breathe in my youth?

To have made a proper use of the advantages of a good education, is a just praise; but to have overcome the disadvantages of a bad one, is a much greater. Had I not your lordship's example to justify me, I should think it a piece of extreme impertinence to inquire where *you* were bred. It is commonly said your lordship's education was of that particular kind concerning which it is a remark of that great judge of men and manners, Lord Clarendon, that it particularly disposes them to be proud, insolent, and pragmatical. 'Colonel Harrison was the son of a butcher, and had been bred up in the place of a clerk, under a lawyer of good account in those parts; which kind of education introduces men into the language and practice of business; and if it be not resisted by the great ingenuity of the person, inclines young men to more pride than any other kind of breeding, and disposes them to be pragmatical and insolent.' Now, my lord, as you have in your whole behaviour, and in all your writings, remarkably distinguished yourself by your humility, lenity, meekness, forbearance, candour, humanity, civility, decency, good manners, good temper, moderation with regard to the opinions of others, and a modest diffidence of your own, this unpromising circumstance of your education is so far from being a disgrace to you, that it highly redounds to your praise.

For myself, on the contrary, it is well if I can acquit myself of the burden of being responsible for the great advantages which I enjoyed. For, my lord, I was educated in the University of Oxford; I enjoyed all the advantages, both public and private, which that famous seat of learning so largely affords. I spent many happy years in that illustrious society, in a well-regulated course of useful discipline and studies, and in the agreeable and improving commerce of gentlemen and scholars; in a society where emulation without envy, ambition without jealousy, contention without animosity, incited industry and awakened genius; where a liberal pursuit of knowledge, and a generous freedom of thought, was raised, encouraged, and put forward by example, by commendation, and by authority. I breathed the same atmosphere that the Hookers, the Chillingworths, and the Lockes had breathed before. . . . . And do you reproach me with my education in this place, and this most respectable body, which I shall always esteem my greatest advantage and my highest honour?"

We must remark, by the way, the very significant fact which this controversy brings before us, that in 1765 the favourite alumnus of the Tory University finds it necessary to his self-preservation to declare himself an adherent of Locke, and to purge himself from the ruinous suspicion of having been poisoned by the persecuting principles of Locke's opponents—"wholesome severities" had been the cant phrase of the Tory party in the controversy on toleration in 1688.

Lowth's victory was complete. Warburton had the discretion to attempt no answer. "Whatsoever might be the merits of an insignificant controversy," says Gibbon (*Memoirs of my*

Life), "Lowth's victory was clearly established by the silent confession of Warburton and his slaves." It was, too, as public a triumph as the most ambitious man could have desired. Never had the public taken a keener interest in any literary dispute. Lowth's "Letter" went through four editions in eighteen months. It had indeed this good fortune, that it appeared precisely in the interval between the proceedings against Wilkes and the Stamp Act, and the attention was not preoccupied by greater matters. The town hailed, with the Monthly Reviewers, the fall of "the haughty and overbearing Colossus," and the "ample vengeance that had been taken upon the imperious aggressor." The newspapers teemed with squibs, parodies, and *jeux d'esprit.* Even the king participated in the interest generally felt. George III., in that celebrated interview in the Queen's Library, called for Johnson's opinion of the controversy, which "his Majesty seemed to have read" (Boswell, 1767).

But Lowth had committed one error of judgment, of so grave a nature as not only to mar his triumph, but even in some measure to compromise his character as a man of the world. At the end of his pamphlet he gave an "Appendix containing a former literary correspondence." These were the letters that had passed between himself and Warburton in 1756; thus publishing Warburton's letters without asking his permission. Lowth's general behaviour throughout his life was that of a gentleman. We are therefore compelled to think that on this occasion he was guilty only of an inadvertence. But it was an inadvertence which gave the enemy the only point of advantage he obtained in the affair. Warburton could say, with justice, "Is not this universally esteemed dishonourable conduct, to publish a man's letters without his knowledge and consent?" Mr. Watson says Warburton "affected to complain." But it is evident that public opinion justified the complaint, and that Lowth himself immediately became aware of the false step he had taken. He became angry, as a man so often does, at his own blunder. He vented his rage in some very intemperate letters to the bishop, who, as Johnson represented the affair, drew him on to expose himself, and then asked his leave to publish the correspondence, which he knew Lowth could not refuse after what he had done. After such a rencontre, and between men of such ripe age, it might have been thought the foes never could have met again. But they did do so; and the reconciliation is one among the many evidences we can cite of the goodness of heart and placability of temper which lurked beneath Warburton's coarse and rude exterior.

Lowth's victory had been won by the weapon of refined irony and scarcasm, against which the Warburtonian cudgel was a very poor defence. If any of Warburton's contemporaries could have handled this weapon against him, it might have been expected that Bolingbroke would have been the man. Between Bolingbroke and Warburton, ever since their meeting at Murray's table, there had been deadly hatred, "Ira fuit capitalis, ut ultima divideret mors." But Bolingbroke chose to use the stick instead of the rapier; and instead of setting down, as he alone could, *de haut en bas*, the insolent adventurer, has merely scattered over his pages the epithets of vulgar abuse,—"scribbler," "stupid fellow," &c.,—in which Warburton himself dealt.

It is on record that he was set down in company by Quin on more than one occasion. One of these is related, perhaps improved, by Horace Walpole. Warburton was haranguing in behalf of prerogative. Quin said, "Pray, my lord, spare me; you are not acquainted with my principles; I am a republican; and perhaps I even think that the execution of Charles I. may be justified." "Ay," said Warburton, "by what law?" Quin replied, "By all the laws that he had left them." The bishop would have got off upon judgments, and bade the player remember that all the regicides came to violent ends. "That, if I am not mistaken, was also the case of the twelve Apostles," was Quin's reply. Walpole comments on this: "There was great wit *ad hominem* in the latter reply; but I think the former equal to any thing I ever heard."

The other, though not so good as a story, was, no doubt, made very effective by Quin's acting. When Quin was staying at Prior Park, Warburton always made a point of addressing him in a way to make him feel that he was an actor. One evening he begged Quin, whom he should never see on the stage, to oblige the company with a specimen of his great powers. Quin replied, that plays were then almost out of his head, but that he would declaim a passage out of *Venice Preserved.* He stood up and gave the passage which contains the words:

> "Honest men
> Are the soft easy cushions on which knaves
> Repose and fatten."

As he pronounced the words "honest men" and "knaves," he took care that the application to Allen and Warburton should not be lost on the assembled company.

Warburton's friends were certainly not so numerous as his enemies. The first place is of course due to Hurd, whose name is as inseparably united with that of Warburton as Boswell with Johnson. Hurd was a man who, having many qualities that obtain respect, and none that attach regard, has been more hardly treated by the biographers than he deserved to be.

That he provoked a peculiar animosity among his contemporaries may well be understood. For if men ill-brooked the domineering arrogance of Warburton, they were little likely to tolerate the irritable superciliousness of Warburton's toady.

The "terse, neat, little, thin man," as one of his college contemporaries describes him, was sadly deficient in the warmth and geniality which the impetuous and choleric Warburton possessed in excess. This contrast of character promoted the intimacy which sprang up between the two. Of the origin of their acquaintance we have Hurd's own account:

"For the first years of residence at the University, when I was labouring through the usual courses of logic, mathematics, and philosophy, I heard little of your name and writings; and the little I did hear was not likely to encourage a young man that was under direction to inquire farther. In the mean time I grew up into the use of a little common-sense; my commerce with the people of the place was enlarged. . . . . When I became B.A., I was led by a spirit of perverseness to see what there was in these decried volumes that had given such offence. I wished, perhaps out of pure spite, to find the invectives I had heard unfounded.

I took the *Divine Legation* with me down into the country, where I was going to spend the summer of 1741 with my friends. I read there the three volumes at my leisure, and with an impression I shall never forget. I returned to college the winter following, not so properly your convert, as all over spleen and prejudice against your defamers. From that time I am to date my friendship with you."

He means, that he had formed a friendship for Warburton from reading his books, before making his acquaintance. Of the commencement of their personal intimacy, Hurd made the first advance in print by a compliment in his Commentary on Horace, sending Warburton, at the same time, a copy of the book. But the rosewater of dedications in those days so usually turned to vinegar, that a peculiar adaptation of the pair to each other was necessary to cement a union so fine and lasting as that which ensued between them. The equivalents in this combination of dissimilar character have been touched by the master-hand of a critic, whose genius was buried beneath genealogical parchments and the minutiæ of parochial history—Thomas Dunham Whitaker.

"It is not always true, in fact, that unequal friendships (we mean those of unequal minds) are quite as frail as they are represented. Great men, especially in the decline of life, often grow indolent conversers; they love to dictate rather than dispute; they decline the irritating and laborious collision of equal intellects; and an humble friend, just able to understand, and very willing to applaud, is a more acceptable companion than an equal, who dares to contradict, and who may chance to confute. If Warburton were a tyrant, he was a magnanimous tyrant, and, the point of unconditional submission once secured, a warm and generous friend. Over the mind of Pope himself, in his declining years, the friend and commentator enjoyed an ascendant unperceived, it may be, by the bard himself. In his intercourse with Murray and Yorke, his ferocity was blunted, not by timid assent, but by the impenetrable and unassailable polish of high breeding. Under the predominant and overbearing influence of a superior mind, Hurd, in addition to an affection as warm as his constitution was capable of, is understood to have been uniformly supple and obsequious. In all the extravagance of his wildest hypotheses, assailed by the contradiction of scholars and the laughter of wits, Warburton had one kindred bosom on which he could repose, one understanding which never questioned the legitimacy of his reasonings, or failed to perceive the validity of his conclusions."

Nothing can be added, it appears to us, to the delicate precision of this classical passage, to which Parr's laboured comparison of Hurd and Warburton is as inferior in truth as it is in expression. Parr entitled his pamphlet *Tracts by Warburton and a Warburtonian.* By "a Warburtonian" is meant Hurd. For though "the Warburtonian School" is a phrase of common occurrence in the writings of the end of the 18th century, Hurd is really the only man to whom the designation properly applies. We may perhaps include Brown and Towne. Towne was archdeacon of Stowe, and a man of considerable reading. He had studied Warburton's writings with such attention, that Warburton was wont to say that Towne understood them better than himself. He wrote a good deal, but so badly that Warburton, who revised for him, used to complain that "he had more trouble in reforming the style and method of them than it would have cost him to write the whole fresh in his own manner."

Dr. Brown was at one time an obsequious attendant on Warburton. Dr. Monsey once dined at Garrick's in company with them both. After dinner, Garrick checked Monsey, who was running on in what Garrick thought too free a style. "Oh," said Brown, "you may be sure Dr. Monsey will restrain his humour before Dr. Warburton, as he is afraid of him." Monsey retorted, "I am afraid neither of Warburton nor of his jack-pudding!" Afterwards Brown fell off from his allegiance. Two years before his melancholy end, he observed that he was sorry for having far overpainted Warburton. "I cannot bring myself," said he, "to give up the freedom of my mind to Warburton, and therefore we do not agree. Dr. Hurd will never quarrel with him."

Warburton's reputation by his writings, his controversies,

his connexions, and the confessed ascendency of his talents and temper, was already higher than that of any other clergyman in the Church of the same standing. Yet the author of the *Divine Legation*, of the *Alliance*, and of *Julian*, still remained in a country parish; and, but for his marriage with Allen's niece, he might have died rector of Brant-Broughton. Pope had shown much anxiety to bring him "in the way of some proud and powerful persons," and had actually made some application for him through Lord Granville, but without effect. But Pope died in 1744, and even had he lived, the Pelhams required other influence than such as Pope could exert. Dedications were all in vain. Edwards twitted him with this in the *Canons of Criticism*. "The first edition of the *Alliance* was presented to all the bishops; when nothing came of that, the second was addressed to both the Universities; and when nothing came of that, the third was dedicated to a noble earl; and nothing has yet come of that." His marriage, however, in 1745, which gave him a new position, a wealthy home, and a political connexion, entirely altered his prospects. From this moment the career of his preferment was uninterrupted and rapid. In 1746 he became preacher of Lincoln's Inn, through Murray, the solicitor-general. In 1753, prebend of Gloucester, from Lord Hardwicke; in 1754, king's chaplain; in 1755, prebend of Durham, through Murray, now attorney-general; in 1757, dean of Bristol, from Pitt, whom Allen had just brought in for Bath; and finally, in 1759, he was advanced to the bishopric of Gloucester.

These are the plain facts, which biographical decorum still persists in rendering into "William Warburton, whose talents and learning raised him from a humble station to the highest honours of his profession," &c.

Hurd had seen a letter of Pitt (Earl of Chatham), in which he said that "nothing of a private nature, since he had been in office, had given him so much pleasure as his bringing Dr. Warburton upon the bench." Warburton himself regarded these honours with a manly indifference, which is one of the best traits in his character. It was impossible for him to be insensible to the attractions of preferment, more especially at a period when, more than at most times, so much of a clergyman's thoughts were absorbed by them. If his mind had not turned in that direction of itself, it must have been drawn into it by the constant hints of friends and correspondents. His own letters are tinged with expectancy; but it is kept under by a real superiority of nature, and by an intellect occupied with other thoughts. Occasionally only a hint is dropped in public, as where he tells Lord Chesterfield, in the dedication of a new edition of the *Alliance*, that "of all the strange connexions which the revolutions of time bring about, the rarest and most accidental is that between merit and reward." He was well aware of what those around him were about, and his pride kept him from falling into ways of petty intrigue, which he saw through and despised. He writes to Mr. Jane:

"The general body of the clergy have been, and, I am afraid, always will be, very intent upon pushing their temporal fortunes,—a fact so apparent to government, both civil and ecclesiastical, that they have found it necessary to provide rewards and honours for such advances in learning and piety as may best enable the clergy to serve and advance the interests of the Church of Christ. . . . I endeavoured to show, that if these rewards and honours be so mis-employed, that instead of giving them to learning and merit, they were diverted upon such as can only promote the interests and flatter the passions of the great, young men, upon entrance into life, seeing how matters were carried, would be tempted rather to cultivate the sordid arts of intrigue and adulation, rather than the liberal endowments of learning and piety."

It would be difficult to find a more naked avowal of the dependence of the supply of "learning and piety" upon the demand created by endowments. He who thought thus of others shared largely, it cannot be doubted, in their motives. All that can be said is, that while inferior men were entirely dominated by such sordid views, Warburton's larger nature could never be so absorbed. We must remember, too, that before promotion came within his reach he was already in comfortable, if not affluent, circumstances. Allen left Mrs. Warburton 5000*l.*, and the reversion, on Mrs. Allen's death, of 3000*l.* a year. Warburton too had made a considerable sum by his writings,—*e.g.* for his edition of *Shakespeare* he had 560*l.* from Tonson. And besides his own books, he had the copyright of Pope's works. So that altogether, when Paul Knapton the publisher failed in 1755, Warburton was the largest creditor.

We cannot therefore wonder, when at the age of fifty-five his first preferment came to him, that he viewed it with indifference. He had been reluctant to take the preachership at Lincoln's Inn seven years before, though the society had done him the unprecedented honour of making him the offer of it. The trouble of writing the sermons, the five or six months' attendance in town, and the additional house-rent, were not compensated, to his mind, by the distinction. When the stall at Gloucester came in 1753, Dr. Birch gave him instruction as to the mode of taking possession, observing that "it was so long since he had had any preferment, that he must have forgotten all the formalities." "There was another thing," said Warburton, "he did not dream of; that it is so long since I had occasion quire about the formalities, that I am become very indifferent about the things themselves." His health too was becoming such as to detract from all enjoyment. Soon after his appointment to the bishopric we find him complaining of his "usual dizziness," in a way that implies it to be no new visitant. He made attempts to complete the *Divine Legation*, writing portions of the ninth book, Hurd says, "by snatches, and with difficulty," and unable to make any real progress with it. The ninth book remains a fragment, and has scarce any trace of the merits of the early books. It has, besides, inconsistences of expression and lapses of memory, sad indications of failing faculty, such, *e.g.*, as speaking of St. Paul as author of the Epistle to the Hebrews (*Works*, vi. p. 309), whereas in 1741 he had been careful, through a long argument, to observe the distinction (*Works*, v. p. 430 seq.). Mr. Watson says he is "generally supposed" to have held the non-Pauline origin of the epistle. We do not know on what authority this is supposed; and against his opinion in 1741 we may set his opinion in 1738, when he cites the Hebrews as St. Paul's. The inconsistency is only curious as showing the inconstant nature of his ideas, which only became fixed when they were opposed. Had any disputant challenged either the one or the other of these "opinions" on the authorship of Hebrews, we can imagine the fury with which it would have been defended, and the "folly and knavery" which would have been imputed to the alternative view.

In his 69th year we find him complaining of rheumatism in the shoulder, of a disorder of the gall-bladder, with symptoms of gravel, for which he was desired to drink the Selzer-waters, then just come into fashion. The pains he at first thought rheumatic, he afterwards suspected to be "St. Anthony's fire." More rapid than the strides of physical were those of mental decay. It showed itself as disinclination before it became incapacity. Very early in his work he required the stimulus of compulsion to rouse his mind to effort. In 1741 he had recourse to the expedient of setting the press prematurely to work, that he might be forced to supply it with copy. That part of the *Divine Legation* (viz. books iv. v. vi.) written under this artificial pressure betrays its origin in its manifest inferiority in vigour to the fresh and spontaneous offspring of his earliest thoughts. In 1766 he had lost the power of exciting himself to effort by any device, and shrunk, disheartened and disgusted, from the task of completing his great work. Looking back in 1770 upon some of his writings, he says, "The retrospect is accompanied with a mortifying conviction that the time is past when I was able to write with that force. Expect to find in my future writings the marks of intellectual decay." "You talk," says he again to Hurd, "of your golden age of study long past. For myself, I can only say I have the same appetite for knowledge and learned converse I ever had, though not the same appetite for writing and printing. It is time to begin to live for myself; I have lived for others longer than they deserved of me." Hurd, who wrote much more freely to Mrs. Warburton than to his patron, marked the rapid decline, and in 1771 took occasion to assure Mrs. Warburton that "the bishop would now write no more." She communicated this to her husband, who heard it with composure. He replied to Hurd that he had received the news "with an approving smile. I was charmed with the tenderness of friendship, which conveyed in so inoffensive a manner that fatal secret which Gil Blas was incapable of doing as he ought to the Archbishop of Granada." The seasons began to tell more on him. He had always considered the months of February and March to be his sterile season. In 1769 he writes (æt. 71):

"I think you have heard me say that my delicious season is the autumn, the season which gives most life and vigour to my mental faculties. The light mists, or, as Milton calls them, the steams, that rise from the fields in one of these mornings give the same relief to the views that the blue of the plum gives to the appetite. But I now enjoy little of this pleasure compared to what I formerly had in an autumn morning, when I used, with a book in my hand, to traverse the delightful lanes and hedgerows round about the town of Newark, the unthinking place of my nativity. Besides, my rheumatism now keeps me within in a morning, till the sun has exhaled the blue of the plum."

"Old age," he truly says, "is a losing game." Yet, with his robust frame and strictly temperate habits,—not only temperate, but abstinent, in eating and drinking, is Bishop Newton's testimony,—we should have hardly expected to find this failing from age before seventy. He speaks of himself as a "slender supper-man," and as "being obliged to old age, like Cato, for having diminished his care for eating and drinking, while it increased his desire for conversation." But excess in food is not the only excess that revenges itself on the constitution. He had discounted life in those nights of prolonged study at Brant-Broughton. A voracious appetite for reading had been indulged without restraint, for a time with impunity. But the hour was come when it had to be paid for; and, like Swift, Scott, and Southey at the same age and from the same cause, Warburton outlived himself. The death of his only son, of consumption in 1775, gave the final blow. It put an end to his labours and amusements.

"Not," says Hurd, "that his memory and faculties, though very much impaired, were ever wholly disabled. I saw him so late as October 1778, when I went into his diocese to confirm for him. On our first meeting, before his family, he expressed his concern that I should take that journey, and put myself to so much trouble on his account. . . . The evening before I left, he desired the family to withdraw, and then entered into a confidential discourse with me on some private affairs with as much pertinence as he could have done in any former part of his life. Such was the power he had over his mind when roused to exert himself by some interesting occasion. But this was an effort which could not be sustained. In less than half an hour the family returned, and he relapsed into his usual forgetfulness and inattention" (*Life*, p. 93).

The melancholy scene was closed 7th June 1779, in the 81st year of his age and the 19th of his episcopate. Just before his death a momentary rally of his faculties took place. He asked his attendant in a quiet, rational tone, "Is my son really dead or not?" The servant hesitated, and the bishop repeated the question. The attendant then answered, "As your lordship presses the question, I must say, he is dead." "I thought so," said Warburton, and soon after expired. He had been forgotten by the world long before his decease; and when he actually passed to the tomb, it was without more notice than a few lines in the *Gentleman's Magazine*. His works were not collected till 1788, and the impression then limited to 250 copies, the public having shown, as Parr insinuated, "some inauspicious symptoms of indifference about Warburton's writings." The fame, however, of the *Divine Legation* underwent a revival in the course of time; and besides taking an octavo edition of the Works in 1811, the public called for several reprints of the principal treatise.

In the performance of his episcopal duties Warburton has been censured as remiss. And Whitaker has expressed this opinion strongly. But we must not judge a bishop of the eighteenth century by what is expected of one at this day. Yet when Hurd acknowledges that though "he performed the ordinary duties of his office with regularity; further than this he could not prevail with himself to go,"—we cannot deny that there must have been some foundation for such a conclusion. Habits of study, so fixed that they cannot be thrown aside, no doubt interfere with pastoral vigilance; and Warburton himself, we are told, confessed that they did so in his case. Yet we cannot wish that theological learning should be excluded from the bench, and bishops become the tail of the paper-kite of opinion. And there were other causes, physical and moral, which made him an inactive bishop over and above that now assigned. Of these, the chief must undoubtedly be sought in failing vigour. For though the symptoms of decline do not manifest themselves as grave till 1764, yet the influence must have begun to make itself felt as an impediment to exertion some time before. It is his "*usual* dizziness for which he is going to be bled."

It was perhaps as well that he was thus disabled for diocesan activity; for his peremptory despotic temper unfitted him for dealing with men. Regarding the Church, as he did, exclusively as an institution of government, his manner with his clergy was that of an officer to the common soldier. He knew not the arts of persuasion; and if he was resisted, he could only either sulk or cajole. This is the way he writes to a clergyman of his diocese. The Rev. John Andrews was suspected of Methodism, but had also written an insignificant pamphlet against the *Divine Legation.*

"Mr. Andrews,—I have received several complaints of you. Those which concern your own curacy are on account of your frequent absence, and for not giving your parish service both morning and afternoon on a Sunday. Unless I have satisfaction on these two particulars, I shall revoke your license. I shall insist on your constant residence, not so much from the good you are likely to do there, as to prevent the mischief you may do by rambling about in other places.—Your bishop, and, though your fanatic conduct has almost made me ashamed to own it, your patron, W. Gloucester."

He tells Hurd that the effect of some directions he had issued will "depend upon the clergy's observing my direction; an attention to me which I do not expect." He was indeed little likely to obtain more attention than he could enforce at the law's point. Mr. Watson gives some passages from his Charges, which truly are not composed to the prim decorum of our day. But here again it must be remembered that bishops formerly addressed their clergy as a king did his parliament,—in much more familiar and easy tones than are now thought suitable. Bating some eccentric and truly Warburtonian metaphors, the passages produced do not strike us as remarkably differing from the pulpit style of the day. After all, he must occasionally have been carried by his impetuosity in preaching beyond the limits even then prescribed. Mr. Cradock has reported of one sermon preached at St. Lawrence's on behalf of the London Hospital, that a few passages in it were ludicrous; and that when he proceeded to describe some monks who had robbed their own begging-boxes, he excited "more than a smile" among his audience. Cradock told Hurd afterwards he was not sorry he had not been there; "for I know you would not absolutely have approved." "Approved, sir!" replied Hurd; "I should have agonised."

But his great defect as a minister of religion was his want of religious earnestness. We shall have occasion a little further on to notice this in its influence on his theological writings. We only refer to it now, because the secular and official tone which appears in all their ministerial relations is ultimately traceable to that want of personal religion common to Warburton with a large part of his contemporaries.

The slow approaches of mental infirmity will also account for his disappointing expectation in the House of Lords; if indeed any other explanation is wanting than that which Curran gave of Flood's failure in the British Parliament,—that an oak of the forest cannot be transplanted at fifty. Hurd says he had heard of a "certain minister" who dreaded Warburton's promotion, and thought he would turn out "a second Atterbury." But, as Warburton himself told the Duke of Cumberland, "haranguing is a trade, like other trades, which the bishops generally come to this bench too old to learn." His only reported appearance was in 1763, on the occasion when Lord Sandwich brought Wilkes's *Essay on Woman* before the House. The business was altogether an unlucky one, being mismanaged by the prosecutors of Wilkes from first to last. But though we may justly disregard the opinion of Horace Walpole and the men about town, that Warburton "made himself ridiculous" in it (*Letters*, i. 312), yet he had the bad taste to occupy the House with himself and his labours in "defence of revelation," and to sound his own praises in the style of his later prefaces. This, too, apropos of a ruined profligate like Wilkes! Nothing that could have been hit upon could have served that demagogue's purposes better than Lord Sandwich's attack, and Warburton's defence of himself.

Of Warburton's manner in society the notices preserved are extremely meagre. The little that is recorded goes to bear out Hurd's representation, according to which the overbearing tone of his books was not carried into company, or only showed itself as a disposition "to take a somewhat larger share of the conversation than very exact breeding is thought to allow." Malone has preserved an anecdote of his meeting with Burke. Burke sat next Warburton at dinner without knowing who he was, and at last observed, "I think it is impossible I can mistake, you must be Dr. Warburton." Johnson and Warburton appear to have met but twice. Johnson's own account of one of these meetings was: "At first he looked surlily at me; but after we had been jostled into conversation, he took me to a window, asked me some questions; and before we parted was so well pleased with me, that he patted me." Johnson always remembered with gratitude that he had been praised by Warburton at a time (1745) when, as Macaulay says, to be praised by Warburton was no light thing. And he did not know the contemptuous and brutal language in which Warburton had written of him to Hurd only two years after the "praise." "Of this Johnson, you and I, I believe, think much alike." "His remarks have in them as much folly as malignity." Dr. Kippis, who had seen Warburton once, found him "instructive and entertaining." And one more conversant in the society of the best men of the day, Charles Yorke, who had met him frequently, describes the fluency and correctness of his conversation as "beyond most men," though marred by his turn for paradox.

To his own family and connexions, where he doubtless received all the deference he exacted, he was attached and generous. He watched over, and provided for, the family of a sister, who were "the more endeared to him by their sole dependence on him." And he reckoned it a lucky year in which he married a niece to a reputable grocer at York, and got a commission in the artillery for a nephew. The commentator on Pope, who thought that "every woman is at heart a rake," may have shared in the degrading estimate of the sex common to the generation of Walpole and Chesterfield. And he spoke in theory of woman as a being "in whose capricious and variable fancy discordant and monstrous ideas are, by the force of the passions, whimsically daubed on at random." But in practice, married at the age of forty-seven, he lived happily with Mrs. Warburton for thirty-four years. This notwithstanding an irritable temper, which made the arrival of a visitor, to pour oil on the bishop's vinegar, occasionally not an unwelcome domestic incident. "Your gentleness wins," he said to Hurd, "where my roughness revolts." Mrs. Warburton is described to us as "elegant in her person, possessed of an excellent understanding, great politeness, and an engaging naïveté in conversation." Had she found married life disagreeable, she would hardly, after thirty-four years' experience of it, have entered the state a second time within two years after Warburton's death. She died in 1796.

Of the durability of his affection in friendship a touching instance is recorded by (we believe) Mr. Markland. One day in his last years, the character of Pope was being freely censured in his presence, the party not supposing the bishop capable of attending to what was passing. He suddenly woke up, and exclaimed, "Who talks against Pope? He was the best of friends, and best of men," and then relapsed into his former insensibility (*British Critic*, April 1841). Yet his friendship wit' Pope had been built on the quicksand of literary flattery;

treacherous foundation, which had given way in the cases of Middleton, Richardson, and Jortin. His placability was equal to his irritability. He patted Johnson, as we have seen, after his preface to *Shakespeare*. He was reconciled to Lowth after receiving his most signal overthrow at his hands. It is told (Barker's *Parriana*, i. 345) that for some years he had not been on speaking terms with Tucker dean of Gloucester. On a Good Friday they met at the holy table, when the bishop was administering. On giving the cup to the dean, he stooped down and said, with tremulous emotion, "Let this cup be the cup of reconciliation between us."

We have already related some of Warburton's more signal enmities. They are samples only of a whole career. Nay, the man himself is in this but the representative man of his age. Theological literature was a Babel of loud vociferation, coarse contradiction, and mean imputation. The prize in this *mêlée* was to the noisiest lungs and the foulest tongue. The Warburtonians must not bear the blame alone; nor was the disease of detraction confined to divines. In the House of Commons, Mr. Massey (*Hist. of Eng.* ii. 218) describes the men who took a foremost part as chiefly intent "on disparaging each other, and proving that neither possessed any qualification of wisdom, knowledge, or public virtue. Epithets of reproach were lavished personally on Lord North, which were applicable only to the vilest and most contemptible of mankind." The progress of refinement cannot tame the passions, but has curbed the directness with which they then vented themselves in words. Even now malignant imputation, banished from higher literature, still lingers in clerical controversy. But, after every deduction made, we still find there rests upon the Warburtonian school an extraordinary opprobrium on the score of dirt-throwing. Warburton's superiority and his generous temper ought to have exempted him from this weakness of inferior writers. Instead of that he is the worst offender. He rejoices in "chastising"—*sævo lætus negotio.* He considers it on principle "suitable to his clerical function to hunt down, as good King Edgar did his wolves, that pestilent herd of libertine scribblers with which the island is overrun." Only half a generation later, Johnson, quite as irritable, and almost as much libelled by critics as Warburton, set the noble example of taking no notice of attacks. "A hundred bad writers," says Macaulay, "misrepresented him and reviled him; but not one of the hundred could boast of having been thought by him worthy of a retort." It may be said that the mutual abuse in which Warburton and his contemporaries indulge in print is bad taste, and nothing more. It is, in fact, of a piece with the lavish compliments which friends and correspondents unblushingly offer each other,—compliments which, on the slightest offence, they were ready to exchange for savage invective; and the one had as little meaning as the other. That their rounded and fulsome compliment and their contumelious insults are gross faults in taste, is true. But they are surely something more. The manners of the ruffian here betray the morals of the savage. This prevailing license of censure is only another side of that want of depth of character which marks every product of that frivolous and superficial age. Their manners, their politics, their literature, their theology, all bear the same stamp. Never was there an age in which there was less zeal and more vehemence, less faith and more demonstration of "revelation." Knowledge and the power of weighing evidence had vanished for a time, and a talkative opinionativeness overspread the world of books. Such writers could not respect each other. Conscious of the want of solid worth, they endeavoured to supply its place by forming coteries for mutual laudation, and for setting down their enemies. Such a coterie was Pope's, and the *Dunciad* the public vehicle of its resentments and its favouritism. It was a great stroke of policy on Warburton's part by which he became legatee and proprietor of this private pillory, though he afterwards erected an independent and original scaffold of his own in the notes to the *Divine Legation.* The Warburtonians—*i. e.* Warburton and Hurd—kept each other in countenance by the same device. The more the tide of opposition ran against them, the more cloying became the mutual eulogies, the more sweeping the denunciations of every body else. We can trace the gradual strengthening of this delusion in the correspondence between the two, till they have arrived at the conviction at last that all the worth, sense, and talent in England is concentrated in themselves. Hurd says he gives the Letters "to this wretched world, to shame it into a better opinion of that excellent man, by showing the regard he had to real merit." If we except Balguy and Towne, we shall find no other single name mentioned in these letters except coupled with an expression of contempt. Hurd's favourite word is "coxcomb." "Toup is certainly well skilled in the Greek tongue, but with all this he is a piece of a coxcomb." He writes against Leland "out of pure indignation, as a coxcomb." Priestley is "a wretched coxcomb." Bishop Shipley is "a very coxcomb;" and Dr. Chapman "an insolent coxcomb." Of Dr. Richard Farmer he knows nothing; but he is "an author," and "the prince of coxcombs is the scribbling coxcomb." He may well ask in naïve astonishment, "How is it there are so many coxcombs,—indeed, so many, one hardly meets with any thing else?" Warburton, who unites in his own person "the virtues of Aristotle and Longinus," finds more variety in the characters by which this wretched world is peopled. Johnson is "this Johnson," of whom Warburton and Hurd "think much alike." Jortin is "as vain as he is dirty." Dean Tucker has "a flow of transcendent nonsense." Priestley is a "wretched fellow;" and Voltaire "a scoundrel." Young is the "finest writer of nonsense of this or any age." Rutherforth "the meanest pedant of the age." Spence is "an extreme poor creature." Smollett is "a vagabond Scot, who writes nonsense ten thousand strong." Taylor has "less understanding than the dunce Webster." Jackson is "a wretch who has spent his days in one unvaried course of begging, railing, and stealing." Romaine "has amazingly played the scoundrel." The court is an "earthly pandemonium;" and the church, "like Noah's ark, full of unclean beasts and vermin." These are not citations from angry philippics hurled against assailants under provocation; it is their settled and habitual mode of thinking and speaking of their contemporaries. One, at least, of the correspondents was so well satisfied of the justice of these opinions, that he printed them for publication, after the interval of thirty years, to show the world the regard the pair had "to real merit." And Warburton himself boasted to the House of Lords of his zeal in "defence of revelation," "services" to which he attributed all the abuse that had been heaped upon him. Though Horace Walpole found this appeal ridiculous, yet it could not have been made without the expectation of sympathy. In his own age the violence of Warburton passed for zeal on behalf of religion. The generation which thought Butler "too little vigorous" did not think Warburton's bluster out of place. A few cultivated men even then, like Charles Yorke, may have disapproved. Charles Yorke was the only friend who could address Warburton in terms other than those of submissive adulation. His station, talents, tact, and power of serving Warburton retained for him a superior influence over a temper to which all others gave way. He ventured to hint to Warburton that "the unguarded sallies of a generous mind" might be sometimes "too warm," and were "scarce forgiven" him (Sept. 30, 1746). This is the solitary protest against vindicating religion by foul language which proceeded from a contemporary.

Their contemptuous violence towards others argues a defect of moral breadth in themselves. It is, further, an indication of want of intellectual breadth. The greatest minds, fully possessed by great objects, are never controversial. In contrasting himself with Lessing, Goethe drew two contrasted types of men. "Lessing's polemical instincts make him at home in the region of contradictions; he is great in distinctions. I am different; I never dealt in contradictions; I have given utterance only to results." If this contrast be true of life, it holds good equally of religious life. By an intellect which is habitually filled with the wisdom which is from heaven in all its length and breadth, "objections" against religion are perceived at once to proceed from imperfect apprehension. Such an intellect cannot rage against those who give words to such objections. It sees that the objectors do but intimate the partial character of their own knowledge. Warburton, like his contemporaries, approached religion from the outside. They never got beyond the scaffolding. They added demonstration to demonstration, till the thing to be proved grew more and more obscure behind the forest of arguments. Warburton was essentially one of these demonstrators. He had no real grasp of the essence of religion, or he would have understood that it did not possess that character of certainty which he attributed to his own reasonings. What Mr. Gladstone has said of his *Alliance* is equally applicable to all his writings:

"The greatest intellectual defect of [the *Alliance*, &c.] appears to be the absolute and rigid form of its propositions in indeterminate subject-matter. The writer argues for his particular scheme of the support of an establishment with full toleration of dissent, and the maintenance of an exclusive test, as though it were the single and mathematically necessary result of all general arguments from the nature of the State and the Church, whereas his is, in fact, only *one* mode of constructing the social equation; adapted perhaps to one particular stage of the progression of religious freedom, but not distinguished by any inherent properties of truth from other modes, which may be equally suitable to the preceding or the following stages" (*Gladstone on Church and State*, i. p. 20).

Warburton offers nothing to his readers that is short of moral certainty. His pages are full of the language of proof. It is evident; it necessarily follows. The *Divine Legation* is laid out on a syllogism, with a major and a minor premiss, separately established, and then the conclusion drawn. That all this logical array should fail to carry conviction on the instant, seemed to him a thing incredible. Those who withstood it must be men of perverse minds, and must be "chastised" into submission. Nor does he only offer his readers certainties. He sees nothing but certainties all around him; he is thoroughly convinced himself. There is no laborious groping after truth amid doubts and perplexities, to arrive, after all, at a qualified and provisional judgment. He catches from the first at some view of the case, and proceeds to make all the evidence support that view.

He has himself said of Bayle, that he "struck into the province of daradox as an exercise for the unwearied vigour of his mind." What he said of Bayle was applied to himself by Charles Yorke; and the application has been repeated since by all the critics who have ever sat in judgment upon Warburton. That the desire of originality influenced what he wrote is undeniable. He says arrogantly, "It is not my manner to say what others have said before me." And that the love of contradiction was strong in him, we have already seen abundantly. But the paradoxical taint which pervades all that Warburton has written has its cause in an intellectual foible still more vicious than the spirit of contradiction, or the ambition of originality. His so-called paradox is really a capriciousness of opinion. It is a want of judgment in the subject on which he writes. He is under the imperious necessity of adopting an opinion on every subject, without the power of forming one. His mind plunges into the bewildering chaos of fact and opinion, like the Irishman into the fight, with a "God grant I may take the right side!" To take his side is at the beginning, and not at the end of his intellectual process. To follow the evidence up to its edge, and not beyond it, to suspend the judgment, to balance probabilities, to wait upon the slow discoveries of time and experience,—these are not Warburton's arts. He must start at once with a proposition, and then ransack libraries for material out of which to forge the proof of it. It is an injustice to Bayle to compare his paradoxes with those of Warburton. Bayle is not seldom right. Where Bayle runs counter to the prevailing opinion of his time, he does so because he saw further; and posterity has vindicated the correctness of his view by coming round to it. Warburton, where he differs from the received opinion, is always wrong. His paradoxes will never make a convert. The more copious his citation, the more dexterous his ingenuity, the more irrefragable his logic, the more vehement his determination to make us think so, the more the reason revolts from the demonstration. The intellectual character exemplified by Warburton is common enough in life. But it only attracts wonder when it is coupled with powers and industry like Warburton's, and dedicated to some literary theme of widely-extended interest. In reviewing the *Divine Legation*, we cannot help being forcibly reminded of the *Homeric Studies* of Mr. Gladstone. The differences between the two men are many and radical; the intellectual character of the two works is the same. A comprehensive general reading; an heroic industry in marshalling the particulars of the proof; a dialectical force of arm which would twist a bar of iron to its purposes; and all brought to bear to prove a perverse and preposterous proposition. The mischief done by such powerful efforts of human reason is not in the diffusion of erroneous opinion on the subjects of which they treat, but in setting brilliant examples of a false method. A visionary projector carries his own refutation with him; but when a first-rate calculator devotes his powers to squaring the circle, there is so much method in his madness, that his example is sure to be influential on similarly constituted minds.

In Warburton's famous work the paradox so commonly imputed is to be found, we conceive, not in the main positions proposed to be proved, but in the connexion or inference attempted to be established between the positions; in the absolute statement of those positions without any qualification; and lastly, in the supposition that this connexion or inference could be shown by proof of demonstrative cogency. Bishop Bull had remarked (*Harmon. Apost.* ii. 10. 8), that in reference to the doctrine of a future state, the Old Testament must be separated into an earlier and a later part; and that while the Law contained no promise of eternal life, in the Prophetic books a distinct and direct promise could hardly be said to be found ("clarum ac disertum promissum vix ac ne vix quidem reperias"). This guarded statement probably meets, as nearly as possible, the exact requirements of the language of the Jewish canon. But it is a point of critical judgment, to be founded on a consideration of all the passages, not admitting of being either proved or disproved. The constant opinion of all moderate and impartial persons has been, as Mr. Lancaster (*Harmony of Law and Gospel*, p. 409) puts it, that "this doctrine was both recognised and countenanced, but not explicitly and directly taught, in the Pentateuch." In Warburton's hands this opinion becomes the affirmation that future rewards and punishments were not taught in the Mosaic dispensation at all, and that the Israelites, from the time of Moses to the time of the Captivity, had not the doctrine of a future state. This he declares that he shows by the clearest and most incontestable arguments. Then he proceeds to draw the inference, that a people who could have been placed under such a system must have had an immediate providential superintendence to replace a doctrine which is found to be the very bond and cement of human society. Finally, the propositions here involved, and the inference from one to the other, are put forward, not with the modest diffidence of an inquirer, but with the arrogant swagger of a demonstration, and an insulting challenge to all the world to yield an immediate assent. Gibbon, speaking of one of his later productions, says: "The secret intentions of Julian are revealed by the late Bishop of Gloucester, the learned and dogmatic Warburton, who, with the authority of a theologian, prescribes the motives and conduct of the Supreme Being."

We cannot help thinking that in the epithet "learned" in this quotation lurks a Gibbonian sneer. No one knew better than the historian, that to have read many books and remembered their contents, is "learning" only in a very popular acceptation of the word. But in no other sense was Warburton entitled to be called a "learned" man. His temper was too arrogant to "learn," too impatient to inquire. He went the *à priori* road, and, having formed a very decided opinion, searched books to find arguments with which to support it. For some employments, for metaphysical speculation, for arbitrating between predestination and free-will, for framing an ideal polity, or for any theorising where the facts are few and obvious, such an intellect is well fitted. But it was Warburton's ill fortune that his own bent no less than that of his age determined his pen to social and historical topics. The crying evils of society, both in France and England, were forcing the minds of men upon the consideration of their causes and their remedies. Political institutions appeared to them the most influential of these causes. The great work of Montesquieu, the *Esprit des Lois*, is the epochal book of this phase of speculation, which was only closed by the revolution of '88. To the same mode of thought must be referred Warburton's speculations, however deficient in those qualities of judgment, profound observation of human character, and attentive induction of fact, which made the *Esprit des Lois* overlive the epoch which produced it. The idea of a future state of reward and punishment employed as a restraining force over human passion and appetite in aid of civil sanctions, this view of religion, which belongs entirely to his age, Warburton took up, and the greater part of what he wrote turns on it. To detect the presence or absence of this idea through past times, and the amount of its influence at various periods, is by no means an uninteresting inquiry. But it is an inquiry which demands not only the most extensive survey of ancient literature, but a delicate appreciation of modes of thought, and an exact knowledge of the ancient languages. Of "learning" in this sense Warburton was hopelessly destitute. That he was not a philologian of the calibre of Bentley, every one is prepared to admit. That he was not as a classical scholar equal to many of his own generation—Jortin or Markland, Lowth or Parr—may perhaps surprise no one to hear. But the truth goes far beyond even this. Warburton was wholly without any tincture of what we understand by scholarship. Of the Greek language he had scarcely any knowledge. Latin he knew very badly. He was not competent to decide upon the sense of any difficult passage in a classical author, and was wholly at the mercy of translators and commentators. Yet so impudently did he assume the privileges of a scholar, and so cleverly did he disguise his amazing ignorance, that he succeeded in imposing his opinion on the world, as one that was at least entitled to a refutation. Even his professed biographers have not sounded the depths of his deficiencies. All that Dr. Whitaker says is, "In the mind of Warburton the foundation of classical literature had been well laid, yet not so as to pursue the science of ancient criticism with an exactness equal to the extent in which he grasped it." And the present biographer only speaks of his "imperfect acquaintance with Greek," and "unskilfulness in the niceties of Latin;" phrases far too lenient for the imposture in this respect actually practised by Warburton. The secret was divined by more than one of his contemporaries, though even by them hardly in its full extent. If we compare the correspondence with Lowth in 1756 with Lowth's letter of Sept. 1765, we see that in the interim Lowth's eyes had been opened to the fact he had not suspected,—that one who undertook in such dogmatic tone to settle the age of the book of Job, had not, and could not, read it, and that the demonstrator of Moses' legation never read the Hebrew Pentateuch! This discovery may have led him to surmise that similar dogmatism in the use of Greek and Latin concealed similar ignorance. He accordingly concludes his letter with the threat that he would take in hand the *Divine Legation*, as he had demolished the Appendix. As this threat was never executed, we have no means of knowing how far Lowth was in the secret. Upton, referring to Warburton having cited Homer in this fashion, *δ' ἔνδυνε χιτῶνα καλόν*, remarked that as *νῦν* and *καὶ* begin sentences, so might δὲ for aught Warburton knew to the contrary. The Rev. Henry Taylor detected him, in citing the *Phœnissæ*, copying Brumoy's French (very French) version. Dr. John Taylor had denounced him in Cambridge combination-rooms as "no scholar." The story bears marks of having been improved, but is perhaps not untrue in the main point. It is, that Warburton sent a friend to ask Taylor, if he had really used the words? And that Taylor replied, "He did not remember ever having said that Warburton was no scholar, but he had certainly always thought so." Edwards, the author of the *Canons of Criticism*, is the subject of another anecdote. Edwards was a frequent guest at Prior Park in Allen's time. During their conversations, Warburton was fond of showing a knowledge of Greek, assuming that Edwards, who was, or had been, in the army, knew nothing of the language. One day, a dispute arising in the library, Edwards took down the book, and explained the passage in a sense quite contrary to that which Warburton had given it. Warburton, of course, maintained his own opinion, till Edwards was obliged to show him that his misconception arose from his having trusted to the French translation. Jortin's gentle admonition in his correction of Warburton's translation of "princeps" has been already mentioned.

Forearmed with these hints, we approach Warburton's writings with the distrust they are calculated to create. Recollecting the case of Gibbon, and considering that want of the language of the Greeks does not absolutely exclude a critic from *all* use of the wisdom of the Greeks, we could not say beforehand that Warburton might not have ascertained correctly some of the forms of Greek life and opinion, and reasoned soundly upon them. A cautious man, conscious of labouring under one heavy disqualification for the task he had undertaken, might have done this. But Warburton was not conscious of the limited range of his aquirements in Greek and Latin, and was the reverse of cautious. He thought he could refute Bentley; he had "a very poor opinion of both Markland and Taylor's critical abilities" (*Letter to Birch*); and he confidently undertook to amend the text, not only of Shakespeare, but of Cicero and Velleius Paterculus. The emendations of Paterculus which he sent to the *Bibliothèque Britannique* in 1736 were specimens of an edition which he contemplated. Of the loss that letters have sustained by the non-execution of this scheme, one example may enable the reader to judge. Speaking of Cumæ and Neapolis, two Greek settlements in Italy, the text of Velleius had "Utriusque urbis semper eximia in Romanos fides. Sed aliis diligentior ritus patrii mansit custodia. Cumanos Osca mutavit vicinia." "Aliis" in this passage is certainly not above suspicion, and Ruhnken printed "illis;" a neat conjecture, which has been received with the favour it deserved. Warburton's note is: "I read, sed *Neapolis* diligentior ritus patrii mansit custodia; which makes it a pertinent observation, and worthy the notice of an exact historian. And it is not difficult to conceive *Neapolis* being corrupted to *aliis* by a stupid copier." We cannot help Mr. Selby Watson in his grave perplexity, whether "he means Neapolis for Neapolitanis, or for the genitive case of Neapolis." But the critic who could turn Shakespeare's "past the *infinite* of thought" (*Much Ado,* ii. 3) into "past the *definite* of thought;" who could explain "prayers from preserved souls" (*Measure for Measure,* ii. 2) as a metaphor taken from fruit *preserved* in sugar, will scarcely be thought to have more skill in his own language than in Latin. We could fill a page with his verbal mistakes; show him restricting ἀθάνατος to the immortality of gods; explaining δεισιδαιμονία as the fear of demons or inferior gods; and misconstruing his own citations so frequently, that at last we cannot avoid thinking that he does not apprehend the meaning of Virgil's "sub luce maligna" (*Works*, iv. 416), or understand "testari" in its sense of "to cite" (*Works*, iii. 203); though we should be disposed to give any one else the benefit of the doubt, which the reader, who chooses to turn to the references, will see exists in these two cases.

Such verbal mistakes might be but slight deformities on the surface of a grand and noble work. To make much of them would then be only worthy of those "little grammarians," for whom Warburton so habitually expressed his contempt, including therein, as Jortin slyly suggested (*Life*, p. 446), a contempt for grammar. But the truth is, they are not flaws in the fabric; they are of its texture. When he is writing of "the ancients," —Warburton always speaks of "the ancients" or "pagan antiquity" in the lump, and this when he is investigating the history of opinion:—his notions are one mass of misconception from beginning to end; a misconception in which his misunderstanding of single passages is but a subordinate element. His reasoning is such, that any thing whatever might be proved in the same way of argumentation, as Mosheim told him, while at the same time doing ample homage to his talents,* in a compliment which Warburton himself transcribed into his own pages. Of all the tasks which have exercised the ingenuity of scholars, that of reproducing the religious and philosophical opinion of the Greek schools from the fragmentary and contradictory accounts which remain to us, is the most delicate and precarious. Warburton is hampered by no doubts; he rushes in where Wolf or Heyne fear to tread, and "presumes to enter the very penetralia of antiquity" (*Works*, iii. 215). Entering these dark recesses under the conduct of our self-confident guide, we are surprised to find how plainly and clearly all objects are visible there; the "double doctrine" and *Tò "Eν* are every where round us; Aristotle is cleared up by "his best interpreter, Bossu" (*Works*, ii. 80); "Lucian of all the ancients best understood the intrigues and intricacies of ancient philosophy" (iii. 105); and Socrates "was in morals a dogmatist, as appears largely by Xenophon and the less fabulous parts of Plato" (iii. 52). If there is any "obscurity in Plato's writings, it is caused by the double doctrine, and by the joint profession of two such contrary philosophies as the Pythagorean and the Socratic" (iii. 87). But it need not give us much concern if there be; for "all the Greek philosophers are shown for knaves

* "Ego quidem mediocris ingenii homo, et tanto viro quantus est Warburtonus longe inferior, omnes Theologos nihil eorum quæ publice tradunt credere, et callide hominum mentibus impietatis venenum afflare velle convincam, si mihi eadem eos via invadendi potestas concedatur, qua Philosophos vir doctissimus aggressus est."

in practice and fools in theory" (iii. 201); unless perhaps it be Socrates, who "being perpetually ironical, take him in the reverse, and he is in his right senses" (xi. 161); or Zeno, who seems to have been only a fool, for "the man had forgot sure that he was writing laws for a community, while he thus impertinently philosophises to the Stoical sage" (iii. 102, so in 1st ed.). Socrates might have been witty as well as ironical, had Simmias anticipated the suggestion of the *Divine Legation*, that to his cock he should add a bull (iii. 357). That of all philosophic tenets the Pantheistical are "the most absurd" (iii. 209), we might have scored down as one of Warburton's random shots, but that Bayle appears to have said the same before him. And that Homer's invocation to the Muses "is an intimation that he took his account from authentic records, and not from uncertain tradition" (iv. 434), is an opinion which, whatever else it may be, must at least be orthodox, since it is sanctioned by the authority of Mr. Gladstone and of the University of Oxford.

Notwithstanding the preposterous nature of his argument, the coarse vulgarity of his style, the supercilious dogmatism of his manner, most dictatorial when he is most wrong, there is still some quality latent in Warburton's writings which will make them "ever be read with delight, even by those who are indifferent to their subject." Perhaps we ought to restrict this to the three first books of the *Divine Legation*; for neither the later books of that work, nor any thing else that he has written, appear to us to stand on the same level with that effort. This quality is intellectual vigour; a quality so rare in literature, and above all in theological literature, that its exhibition, even in its most undisciplined state, always commands respect. "His rants are amazing, and so are his parts," said Horace Walpole of Lord Chatham; and the rant and fustian of his speeches was forgiven the orator, in consideration of the moral vigour of the man. The causes which concur to break down vigour in a writer are so many, that before the thought comes to the birth it has mostly lost all the raciness of the soil from which it springs. Of these causes, classical education and a nice and conscientious sense of truth are among the more powerful. He who can set at nought the traditions of taste, and take up an opinion irrespective of the facts, can employ the whole unimpeded energies of his mind in giving momentum to the view he happens to have espoused. "The manners of a gentleman," says Whitaker, "the formalities of argument, and the niceties of composition, would have been unwillingly accepted in exchange for that glorious extravagance, which dazzles while it is unable to convince, and that haughty defiance of form and decorum, which, in its rudest transgressions against charity and manners, never failed to combine the powers of a giant with the temper of a ruffian."

It would be unjust to quit Warburton without drawing attention to one or two instances in which his vigour was not employed in the maintenance of paradox. At a time when copyright was generally regarded as a legal monopoly, he argued the natural right of an author in the produce of his mind (*Works*, xii. 406). He had the courage to denounce the slave-trade in indignant terms from the pulpit (x. 57). A poor-law he declares to be a "beneficent but ill-judged policy" (x. 253). He had formed from his own observation a just estimate of the effect of mathematics on the mental faculties (viii. 14). He dismisses the sophism, which has imposed on many besides Akenside, that "ridicule is a test of truth" (i. 181). Dr. Whewell has bestowed approbation on his discriminating the power of reason as sufficient to *perceive* truth when proposed to it, but not to *discover* it (*Moral Phil.* p. 145). And Dugald Stewart (*Dissert.* p. 161) has noticed that Malebranche's extraordinary merit has been recognised by few English writers except Warburton, "who even where he thinks the most unsoundly, has always the rare merit of thinking for himself." Of his solid good sense we cannot give a better instance than his remarks on the Lauder forgery. He writes to Jortin:

> "Lauder has offered much amusement to the public, and they are obliged to him. What the public wants or subsists on is news. Milton was their reigning favourite; yet they took it well of a man they never heard of before to tell them the news of Milton's being a thief and a plagiary. Had he been proved a ——, it had pleased them better. When this was no longer news, they were equally delighted with another [Dr. Douglas], as much a stranger to them, who entertained them with another piece of news,—that Lauder was an impostor. Had he proved him to be a Jesuit in disguise, nothing had equalled the satisfaction" (*Life*, p. 368).

The vigour of his thought does not concentrate itself in telling paragraphs. It is a rude—we had almost said brute—force penetrating the whole. And his English style is so slipslop, that it would be difficult to find in all the thirteen volumes of his works half a dozen passages which might be taken as fair specimens of his peculiar powers. We will conclude our notice with one of the best of these:

> "Those who are upon the records of history for having failed [in their projects] were either mere enthusiasts, who knew not how to push their projects when they had disposed the people to support them; or else mere politicians, who could never advance their wise schemes so far as to engage a fanatic populace to support them; or

lastly, which most deserves our observation, such as had the two qualities in conjunction, but in a reverted order.

Of each of these defects we have domestic examples in the three great companions of the last successful imposture; I mean Fleetwood, Lambert, and Vane. Cromwell had prepared the way for their succession to his power as thoroughly as Mahomet had done for that of Abubeker, Omar, and Othman. Yet these various wants rendered all his preparations fruitless. Fleetwood was a fervent enthusiast without parts or capacity; Lambert, a cool contriver without fanaticism; and Sir Harry Vane, who had great parts and as great enthusiasm, yet had them and used them in so preposterous an order as to do him no kind of service. He began a sober plotter. But when come in view of the goal, he started out the wildest and most extravagant of fanatics. He ended where his master began; so that we need not wonder his fortune proved so different. But this was a course as rare as it was retrograde. The affections naturally keep another order. The most successful impostors have set out in all the blaze of fanaticism, and completed their schemes amid the cool depth and stillness of politics. Though this be common to them all, yet I don't know any who exemplifies it so strongly as the famous Ignatius Loyola. This illustrious personage—who confirms the observation of one who came after him, and almost equalled him in his trade, 'that a man never rises so high as when he does not know whither he is going'—began his ecstasies in the mire, and completed his schemes with the direction of Councils that, even in his own lifetime, were ready to give the law to Christendom. The same spirit built up old and new Rome. When the city had not six miles of dominion beyond its walls, it indulged the dream of universal monarchy. When the jurisdiction of the bishops of Rome extended not beyond a small diocese, they entertained the celestial vision of a popedom. And it was this spirit which, in defiance and to the destruction of civil policy and religion, made the fortune of both."

Art. V.—THE ART OF TRAVEL IN EUROPE.

Handbook of France (1861); *of the Continent, Belgium and North Germany* (1852); *of Southern Germany* (1858); *of Denmark, Norway, Sweden, and Iceland* (1858); *of Russia* (1840); *of Rome* (1862); *of Florence* (1861). John Murray, Albemarle Street.

Guides de Paris à Havre; de Paris à Bordeaux; de Paris à Strasbourg et à Bâle; de Paris à Genève et à Chamounix. Hachette: Paris.

Guida dell' Italia Superiore di Massimo Fabi. Ronchi: Milano.

Caen: Guide portatif et complet, par G. S. Trébutien. Hardel: Caen.

Handbook of Travel-Talk. John Murray.

Bradshaw's Continental Railway Guide.

The art of travel is rapidly becoming so vast a subject that no single professor will be able to expound it. Mr. Galton and Captain Burton have gone far to exhaust the science of life among wild-beasts and savages; and either of them could probably act as master of the ceremonies to the king of Dahomey. But they would, we suspect, be the first to disclaim any like acquaintance with the mysteries of the *haute volée* in Viennese society, or with mountain travelling in Switzerland. It must be a great chance at least if a hero of the Alpine Club would be as good a guide about Rome as many a shy scholar who has not the strength to scale ice-encrusted cliffs, or the peculiar knack of walking up perpendicular rocks. The East is a field in itself, and something more than mere going over the ground is wanted to make it intelligible. But for one traveller who has the leisure or the opportunity to explore the Zambesi river or to wander out towards Palmyra, there are at least a hundred who find every summer that six weeks in Germany or France do more to refresh the brain and turn the mind into a new track, than even the sea-side or the moors in their own country could do. It is a long time before the most cosmopolitan Englishman gets to feel as thoroughly at home in a foreign railway carriage as on the Great Western. In spite of all that has been done to Anglicise the Continent, where English churches, *bifsteaks saignants* and bottled beer, large basons, shooting-coats and wide-awakes, have sprung up sporadically in the track of the locomotive, the differences of language and manner, if not of opinion, are still in all material respects unaffected by our superficial intercourse with our neighbours. One chief cause of this, no doubt, lies in the strong objection a highly educated man feels to express himself in a language he can only speak imperfectly. He is painfully conscious of every blunder he makes, the moment after it is made, and the subjects he cares to talk about are precisely those which require a large vocabulary and a ready power of translating ideas by their foreign equivalents. Accordingly a bagman will go over half the Continent, joking, chattering, and making friends, with fewer words than enable a scholar to stumble through his wants in the railway terminus or the inn. But the chief reason no doubt is, that no man can catch the tone of a new society in a moment. All that difficult family history, which we learn half unconsciously in our own country, the distinction of great and small requirements in etiquette, and the chief political and religious shades of feeling, are a shibboleth that cannot be hastily mastered. Mr. Grattan mentions in his last book, that he once gave great offence in a country district of France because, in entire ignorance of days and seasons, he invited a large party on the anniversary of the death of Louis XVI. In the same way, we have heard of English people electrifying the residents of a foreign town by making promiscuous visits without letters of introduction. Our countrymen had no doubt been told that the custom abroad was for the last arrival to call first, and did not understand that the custom only warrants visits where there is some excuse for acquaintance. Every man who has lived out of England will probably remember some circumstances where he has acted awkwardly or given offence, in spite of the very best intentions to the contrary.

An excellent article on "Companions of Travel," that appeared rather more than two years ago in the *Saturday Review* (Nov. 2, 1861), among other hints to which we shall have occasion to refer, suggested that pictures of society and manners should form part of a future series of Handbooks. We should like to see the task attempted, but we confess to a grave doubt if it could be achieved to any thing like the extent the writer seems to contemplate. Take, for instance, the wonderful descriptions of German manners in the works of Baroness von Tautphoeus, to which the article referred, among other instances, as examples of what was possible. No one can read *The Initials* without instinctively feeling that it is true to life; but a German, while he admitted this, would say, and would say rightly, that it was true only of life under very exceptional circumstances. The interest of the plot turns mainly on the character of a young girl whose father has made a *mésalliance*, and whose stepmother takes a handsome young Englishman into her family as a boarder. In a three-volume novel all this is gradually explained away and becomes natural; but a selection of passages would give a very unfair idea of German habits and homes. Of course books may be mentioned where the plot is less exceptional, but the difficulty of epitomising a highly complex society, such as that of the upper classes always is, remains extremely great. Let an Englishman take the writings of Washington Irving, of Emerson, and of Esquiros, all excellent in their way and written by men who cordially appreciated our country, and ask himself if any alchemy could distil the perfume of these half-dozen volumes into one. Peasant life is to a certain extent simpler than the life of the *salons*. But the Lancashire peasants of Mrs. Gaskell are quite a different race to the Yorkshiremen of Miss Brontë and to Mr. Kingsley's Hampshire clowns. In fact, there is no royal road to the knowledge of society. A traveller must work it out for himself; and for every reason he had better read first-hand the novels and sketches of manners that contain matter to assist him.

In saying this, however, we do not mean that a few hints on little points of difference between English and foreign manners may not save the traveller some annoyance. There are two or three pages in the introduction to Murray's *Handbook of Northern Germany* which go directly to the point, but which, unfortunately, are so offensive and absurd as to be useless. The writer assumes that a large number of his countrymen are purse-proud, underbred, and swaggering, and lectures them gravely on faults which mostly do not exist, but which, if they do, are incurable. No doubt there is still here and there a rowdy Englishman to be found who scatters oaths and insults and gold over the Continent; but the type will soon be numbered with the dinotherium, and retains its place on the foreign stage only in the same unreal way as harlequin and columbine figure on our own. The real offences that make our countrymen unpopular are of a slighter kind: a habitual want of deference to foreign *convenances*, a custom of free speech, and an unlicensed sense of the ridiculous. We do not seek to extenuate these offences, in which our young men are naturally the worst sinners; but wearing a wide-awake in Paris, or chaffing a sergeant of police, are not, after all, very grave international crimes, and would scarcely be remembered against the offenders, if their country were not the first power in the world and the most jealously watched. Besides, those who rail at Englishmen for carrying England with them, should remember that soap and clean sheets have been introduced in this way into numberless districts which only know of them in the dictionary. Nor would it be difficult to retort the charge. There are quarters in London, neither small nor obscure, where the cockneyism of foreign capitals has been reproduced even in its most trifling details. To add a very small matter, it seems curiously difficult for strangers to learn, that it is not the custom in England to call on a new acquaintance in evening or half dress between ten and twelve in the morning.

Quite as often as not the mistakes of Englishmen arise from a misappreciation of the structure and tone of foreign society at the very time when they are striving to conform to it. There is a common idea that people make acquaintance abroad more readily than in England. Admitting this to be, to a slight extent, a feature of the foreign bathing-places, it remains none the less certain that a well-bred and highly-cultivated man is pretty equally reserved and shy of chance comers on both sides the Channel. What has caused the mistake is, that the upper class is comparatively limited on the Continent, and the middle class comparatively large. An average English gentleman, if he go abroad without introductions, must therefore make up his mind that his chance of making friends, on a level with himself in refinement and education, will be decidedly less than in any part of his own country where he is equally unknown. With ladies the danger is of a different kind: they will meet with more intelligent deference in France than in their own country, and whatever mistakes they may commit, the courtesy of those around them will secure them from all unpleasantness. But the conventions of foreign society are far more rigid than our own for women; and the tone of that large and idle society for which French novelists write is painfully low. In the French provinces an unmarried lady is a little compromised if she is seen twenty yards behind her party with an unmarried man; and the freedom of an English country-house is regarded with wonder, and, we regret to say, with a feeling very like disgust. That this feeling is unhealthy and bad we do not pretend to deny; but, so long as it exists, our countrywomen will do well not to part with any portion of their native reserve in travelling. Nor is there any great difference between different parts of the Continent in this respect; the mere fact that no reputations are so safely demolished any where as those of foreigners, marks the Englishwoman from the first as the theme of idle gossip, which may easily become scandal. Lastly, on few points are foreigners so sensitive as on any thing that wounds their exaggerated *amour-propre*. A German is driven wild by the serene superciliousness of the chance Englishmen whom he meets, regards their morning-dress as a national outrage, and suspects that every sentence he does not understand is a sneer at the country. A Frenchman is commonly too certain of himself to suspect that he can be thought ridiculous, and quietly shrugs his shoulders at eccentricities that are not his own. But even a Frenchman cannot understand irony. His own wit is *badinage*, a shuttlecock tossed between opposite players, who have no other thought than to keep it up skilfully. The heavy English irony, with its under-current of earnest, seems to him spiteful and cruel; he cannot comprehend men who hit one another so hard in jest. Before all things, we would recommend a man who wishes to be understood or to succeed in foreign society, to say nothing that is not absolutely transparent.

Perhaps the best suggestion of the Saturday Reviewer—as in fact it was his first—was in recommending that the recent history of the country should be given. Some of Mr. Murray's handbooks—as, for instance, those on Northern Europe—give a meagre and very dull outline of the country's general history. Now Michelet himself, whom we take to be the most fascinating of précis writers, and who is certainly the most unscrupulous, would infallibly break down in the task of such an abridgment. What we want for every country is the philosophical outline and the more picturesque details—every thing, in a word, that gives local colouring. A sensible man wanting to enjoy Norway, would read the Sagas and one or two modern novels; for Russia, he would take especially the Lives of Ivan the Terrible, Peter the Great, and Catherine II., with the History of the French Campaign, and Stanley's *Eastern Church*, and Tourguénef's or Tolstoi's novels. Conceive all this condensed under the hydraulic press of a gentleman whose chief business is to write about inns, roads, signs, and scenery. In fact, Mr. Murray's editors have wisely abstained from any similar attempt for France or Germany. In these matters every man must compile his own history, and the most a handbook can do is to point out the best sources of information in a *catalogue raisonné*. But the history of the last generation is something quite different. The state of parties, the history of different ministries, the court cliques that exist or are believed in, the biographies of the more notable men, the private history of the press, are all matters on which an intelligent man likes to have some knowledge before he visits a country. A chapter like Mr. Kinglake's episode on the *Coup-d'Etat*, but written from the point of view of historical fidelity, would be inappreciable to a tourist in France. It would be more difficult to give a *résumé* of Continental literature in such countries as France and Germany. The Saturday Reviewer, indeed, suggests two rules which he thinks would simplify the matter. First, that our writers mentioned should be well known; and secondly, that they should be typical. But this, after all, is a little like the old school discussion, whether logic was a science or an art, and turns entirely on your first definition. When the first five or the first ten names in the literature of any country are written down, it becomes matter of very careful weighing to decide who are and who are not worth writing about. Is a man like Jasmin, the patois poet of Gascony, to be admitted as typical, or rejected as insignificant? Again, is any mention to be made of theologians like Lacordaire and Dupanloup; or of men of science like Boucher de Perthes and Milne Edwards or Quatrefages. The difficulty is the greater as the traveller may be an antiquarian or a naturalist, and in either capacity has a fair claim on a few pages in the handbook. We incline to think we should solve this difficulty by treating of the literature of natural science in connexion with a general chapter on the physical geography of the country; throwing Thiers, Béranger, and Courier into the political section, and leaving Lamennais and Montalembert to the chapter on church history. Such books as the *Life of Madame Récamier*, and the *Journal and Letters of Eugénie de Guérin*, would go far to make a description of the higher French society among women possible. So many names worth knowing would be disposed of naturally in this way, that poetry proper, history, and novels would be almost the only topics that would require a chapter to themselves.

Whatever modifications some plan of this sort might admit of, there can be little doubt, we think, that it ought to produce books as far superior to Mr. Murray's present handbooks as those were to any thing that preceded them. We do not wish to be unjust to a pioneer in travelling and an old friend; and though, with one or two exceptions, we have never thought the famous red manuals satisfactory even for what they attempt, we freely admit that ten years ago they were the best in existence. But the old order has changed, and Mr. Murray's only recognition of the new world is in making his new editions a little bulkier than his old. His conception still is of a literary road-book, which is to tell the traveller on what roads he can get from point to point, what are the chief inns, what he will see on the road, and what he is to admire. Now, as regards routes, the great lines of railway that at present branch over the Continent practically determine the routes of ninety-nine in a hundred Englishmen, and the days of posting-carriages are gone by. Let the editor of a handbook tell us, by all means, what towns are worth seeing, and what lines of country are interesting; but he need not take us over the track in leading-strings. Every one, in fact, disregards these absurd itineraries, and finds a good map the best *ductor dubitantium*. Next, a handbook that is only published from once in three years to once in fourteen cannot possibly compete for small local knowledge with minor publications such as *Bradshaw's Railway Guide*, and had better not attempt what it does ill. New hotels are springing up every day in the place of worn-out veterans; and we have painful reminiscences of searching in the small hours of the morning in a well-known Austrian town for a non-existent hotel, which was first on Murray's list. If Mr. Murray would separate these matters altogether from his handbooks, and publish once a season a general list of Continental hotels, with notices where new routes have been opened, or old ones stopped, he would be conferring a real service on the community, while he improved his own works. The character of hotels which his editors give are the only ones thoroughly reliable; and there is no reason whatever that they should be published in a form which exposes them to become antiquated and inaccurate. It is a smaller point, but we will just notice that there are limits beyond which the badness of a map becomes unendurable; and we know no exception to the badness of those of countries in Mr. Murray's editions. The printing is bad, the execution is slovenly, the places marked are few, and the outlines of departments and kingdoms are so faintly indicated as to be useless. In these respects the whole series contrasts markedly with the less ambitious and more satisfactory performances of the *Bibliothèque des Chemins de Fer.*

Another general fault in the present handbooks is, that too much is said on trifling matters, or on points which the tourist is certain to attend to and to have an opinion on. It is mere book-making to transcribe from the catalogues of small museums; and pictures had probably better be left to a special *catalogue raisonné.* In the handbook for Norway remarks about the scenery are constantly interspersed, the truth being that there is nothing else to write about; but, as the traveller has literally no choice of roads, nine times out of ten, in that country, it would surely be sufficient to say generally that the road from Gjövig to Leirdalsören is romantically beautiful, and leave details to the tourist. It is very doubtful, indeed, whether any handbook for Norway is wanted beyond the little road-book (Bennett's) published in Christiania. Mr. Murray's, though well written, not unfrequently describes stations which no longer exist, as there is great activity in road-making throughout the country. The five years that have elapsed since the last edition was published have already gone far to make it obsolete; and, out of twenty-eight stations which the handbook enumerates between Lillehamner and Drontheim, nine are no longer to be found. But the most faulty of Mr. Murray's handbooks in this respect is the one for Russia. Considering that the last edition dates from 1849, and was merely a revision of an older one, it will be understood that, for this reason alone, it has no great claims upon the traveller. But the book was bad from the first. It was evidently written by some one who knew many thousand miles of post-road, but had only stayed in three, or at most four, towns beyond the Baltic provinces, Odessa, St. Petersburg, Moscow, and perhaps Nijni Novgorod. Plunder from Kohl, and hasty impressions from a drive in a diligence through the streets, make up what is communicated about the other towns of the empire; while some of the most important and interesting places, like Uglitsch, where the young Demetrius was killed, and the beautiful town of Jarosloff, with, in fact, the whole course of the Volga, between Tver and Astrakan, except Nijni Novgorod, are altogether omitted. The writer has not even compiled carefully. His description of Great Novgorod, for instance, is a triumph of inaccuracy. He speaks of it as a desolate town, with "mouldering walls, ruined churches, and grass-grown streets," with only seven thousand inhabitants, and with nothing but the old Kremlin and the brass gates of the church to attract attention. The facts are, that, although traffic has been diverted from it by the absurd whim of the late czar, who made his first railway, between St. Petersburg and Moscow, as straight as the crow flies, through morasses and uninhabited wilds, instead of taking it by the old route through towns, Novgorod is still a thriving country town with a good corn and timber trade, and with at least seventeen thousand inhabitants; the battlements are no more ruined than the walls of York or Chester; the streets are open and cheerful; and the wealth of the old churches is talked of with astonishment even in Russia. Two of them alone, St. Sophia's in the Kremlin and one on the other side of the river, would well repay a visit to the place. Probably some parts of the editor's description were true a hundred years ago, when some book which he has consulted was written, and the remainder is due to conjecture and to the confused memories of rapid travel. But faults of this kind are serious; and as the general hints on Russian travel at the beginning are by this time obsolete, we counsel the intending traveller to consult the imperishable *Letters from the Baltic*, or Mr. Spottiswoode's *Tarantasse Journey*, or Professor P. Smyth's *Three Cities in Russia*, and to trust the red manual for nothing but the sights of Moscow and St. Petersburg, and very sparingly for those.

Of course there are good as well as bad exceptions to the general cumbrous mediocrity of the handbooks. That for Rome is the best instance we know of, having been carefully compiled by one who is evidently a man of taste, a scholar, and a resident. But we know none which, for antiquarian completeness and charm of style, can compare with the little book on Caen by M. Trébutien which we have mentioned at the head of our article. It is true, no doubt, that Caen is a small town, and that it is easier to know and describe such a place than a great kingdom. But M. Trébutien's book is small also in proportion to his subject, and yet contrives to exhaust it. The whole growth of the town is traced; the names given at the Revolution are recorded; the most remarkable houses for architecture or local association are pointed out; and the art criticisms evince singular judgment. If such books by local antiquaries were more common than, we fear, they ever can be, we should recommend every tourist to travel only with a railway time-table and list of hotels, and purchase his information on the spot he visits. For those who confine their wanderings to the great French lines of railway, the *Bibliothèque des Chemins de Fer* will be found amply sufficient. Its little manuals are so cleverly written as to be more a narrative than a text-book, and the information about hotels and tradesmen is given compendiously and unobtrusively in an appendix. Otherwise, foreign guide-books, such as those of Ronchi and Baedeker, are only recasts of Murray's handbooks, with the advantage of being shorter and more practical, and the disadvantage of being less reliable for Englishmen. Almost every German town has its local guide-book; but these, with few exceptions, are badly printed and prolix, beginning, like American oratory, from creation or a little earlier, and travelling by slow stages—as suits the Teutonic mind—through the succeeding centuries.

We believe a few slight changes and a little arrangement would remove most of the faults we complain of in Mr. Murray's present series. The manuals we spoke of at starting—of actual history, manners, and literature—must of course form a perfectly distinct series. Only in this way could they be well done. The hotel-guide, and the hints about roads and conveyances, would form a separate pamphlet of a few pages, to be corrected every season, and bound up with the copies of the handbooks sold during the year. The art-manual might perfectly well be printed in the same manner, in detached parts, so that a traveller could either buy a guide to the collections of the country, or a fairly exhaustive book for the whole Continent. It would in every sense be more satisfactory if this department were conducted by a single man trained professionally, than if art criticism, one of the last achievements of education and taste, were carelessly thrown in among the chance duties of Mr. Murray's encyclopædical staff. Cleared of all irrelevant matter, the handbook proper would then give a description of the country and cities travelled in, and would be reduced to a volume of half, or less than half, its present bulk, except where the tourist preferred to have the art-manual and hotel-guide bound up with it. If he were of our opinion, that a big book is a great nuisance in the pocket or portmanteau, he would commonly not do this; and we believe the mere reduction of size would largely promote the sale of the series generally. At the same time, we are quite aware that these alterations would add something to the expense of production. Several small books are always more costly than a single large one. But Mr. Murray's profits by the whole series must have been very large, and success, like nobility, has its obligations. Besides, any real improvement is always remunerative in the long-run. Anyhow, if some change be not speedily made, he must be prepared to see the sceptre pass from Albemarle Street.

We desire to add a few words upon handbooks of travel-talk generally. Here, again, Mr. Murray's is the best we know of, and is most imperfect. The faults common to almost all this kind of literature are, a glut of useless phrases, scarcely-used words, and inappropriate idioms. With all deference to Mr. Murray's eminent translators, the German is not always reliable; such a phrase, for instance, as "gefälligst," for "if you please," being unused in good society; and the Tuscan style of address (in the third person) ought, we think, to be more generally given than it is in the Italian. These, however, are slight faults. The prolixity of the book is much less pardonable. A hundred and forty columns of conversation and vocabulary are proof in themselves that a wrong system has been adopted. In fact, the editors have confounded the functions of a vocabulary and a dictionary. What tourist can possibly wish to commit to memory a list of more than seventy terms relating to railroads and steamboats, which is still so far from being exhaustive that the words "return-ticket" and "fare" are omitted, while "guard" is transmuted into "conductor"? Again, the vocabularies are kept distinct for different subjects; the consequence of which is, that there are frequent cross-divisions, and that, while the word "waiter," for instance, occurs in no list, the chief articles of dress occur in two, the toilette and the laundry list. Half the number of words, in a single list at the end, would save endless trouble in making references. Above all, it ought to be remembered that the indifferent linguists for whom these manuals are intended are only puzzled by variety and confusion. It is astonishing how few words are really required to carry on small talk of any kind. It has been said that the vocabulary of a French lady of fashion consists of five hundred common words, mostly adjectives, and of five hundred proper names. It has been said, more seriously, that an

English ploughman in some districts does not know more than three hundred words. Any one may convince himself that this is an exaggeration, but it is based on the real fact that half the words we use are philological superfluities, which might easily be retrenched from conversation. Much more does this apply to the wants of a traveller, who is not expected to talk politics or philosophy. The true art of language can only be acquired from studying a learner, be it child or foreigner. Twenty or thirty verbs expressing broad primary ideas, like necessity or liking, without regard to little shades of meaning,—as many adjectives, adverbs, and prepositions severally,—and the framework is made, which only requires to be filled up with substantives, the most easily learnt of any part of speech, and the number of which must of course vary with occasion. Let the young linguist only add to this a rigid care to avoid conditional moods and complex constructions generally, and he will be astonished himself at the ease with which he makes himself understood. In speaking, as in swimming, beginners are always prone to expend their strength superfluously. But there is no excuse for their instructor in Murray if he confirms them in this vicious habit. A single example will at once show what we mean. Nothing can seem more simple than to ask for tickets at a railway-office. The handbook gives the following as its German sentence: "Ich wünsche vier Billete nach M—; drei für die erste und eins für die zweite Classe." Practically, a traveller would say, "M—; drei, erste—eins, zweite;" and the abridged form would not only save breath to the speaker, but make his meaning easier to the clerk.

We pass from handbooks of travel to the subject of travel itself, on which alone a long article might be written. It is hardly too much to assume that three tourists out of five set out without any very definite aim beyond that of locomotion, and are guided quite as much by advertisements of easy routes as by their own forethought, or knowledge. A certain number of miles are to be travelled over, so many cities lionised, and so much time spent in change of scene. The result of this *recherche de l'imprévu* is no doubt often better than might be expected; but the plan is none the less a bad one, and the traveller sometimes returns disgusted for ever with first impressions foolishly collected. The first wisdom is for every man to know his own tastes, and to decide beforehand whether he means to see landscapes, or churches, or picture-galleries. Of course this rule need not be pedantically carried out, and a man travelling towards the Saxon Switzerland may yet stop and admire the Madonna di San Sisto; but, generally speaking, it is wise not to aim at too many effects. The next rule we are inclined to give may sound a little inconsistent with the first, though it is not really so. It is, that every one should take up some specialty as an amusement on his tour, and collect ferns or geological specimens; study a *patois*, or visit hospitals or courts of justice, by way of attaching some particular reminiscence to his tour. The work of six weeks or three months will not be worth much for reproduction, but it will leave durable traces on the man's own mind. Perhaps one of the pleasantest ways in which this can be done, is by taking some favourite author, and working out his local allusions on the spot. A scholar of that old school which is now unluckily becoming not only old but obsolete, will light up all the Roman and Sabine districts with sunny memories from Horace. Northern and Central Italy are thronged with associations of a deeper interest from the *Divina Commedia.* For those who are careless of other languages than their own, Byron, and in North Italy Shakespeare, are the natural companions. To every educated man Shylock is still visible on the Rialto, and the garden of the Capulets at Verona is consecrated by a legend that it would be impiety to doubt.

Still, even these methods of making a tour something more than a string of railway distances and hotels, are imperfect compared with the serious interest that a more systematic study of any kind gives. Suppose a traveller to take either a single great book like the European chapters of Gibbon, or an episode of national life like the story of Joan of Arc, and to resolve to work it out. In the first case, he would begin with Imperial Rome in the palace of Nero, the baths of Diocletian, and the Coliseum, and would fill his mind with the barbaric greatness that piled masses of peperino for a lady's tomb or the basement of a patrician's garden, compared with which our vaunted railway-works are flimsy and unsubstantial. He would trace the growth of that new life which rose above the rotting Roman civilisation in the myriad-celled Catacombs, and in the marvellous monuments of Christian hope and endurance that have been taken out of them. In provincial towns like Verona and Arles he would visit perhaps with even greater wonder the second-rate monuments of the old world, unsurpassed and unsurpassable at this day. He would understand more vividly than from any book the adamantine solidity of those municipal institutions which survived the Hun and the Goth, and which gradually became the symbols of law to freemen as they had been the instrument of oppression to slaves. In all this, and in the very network of Roman names and Roman roads to be traced along the Danube and to the Clyde, he would read the secret of that marvellous vitality by which Rome, shorn of all its conquests, repeatedly stormed and ravaged, plague-stricken and helpless, retained its dominion over men's thoughts as the only legitimate centre of civilisation, and became the throne of a new power more durable and more august than the Cæsars. For any man wanting to understand the inner life of the Empire, Suetonius and Tacitus are scarcely more pregnant and life-like than the statues of the Vatican, the vases and ornaments of the Etruscan Museum under the same roof, or the remains at Pompeii. No influences of Greek art, no divinizing of Imperial features, disguise the main traits of character in the world-rulers,—the unspiritual common sense, the relentlessness of purpose, and the vulgar animalism that stamped the men who were born to wrestle with facts, and who valued victory for its plunder, not for its laurels. There is scarcely a face of real life in all Roman art that a child would instinctively trust. The Dacian and German features interspersed, and growing steadily in number and importance, tell their own tale of the fall of the Empire. But our space forbids us even to indicate the splendid outlines of Roman antiquarianism in its capital alone, or in Western Europe, for the period between the Flavian Cæsars and Theodosius. Take the second case, which a few days would exhaust. The village of Domremi and its neighbourhood, in which Joan of Arc grew up; the Castle of Chinon, where she first saw the Dauphin; Poitiers and Blois, where she lodged; Orleans, which she relieved, and where the house in which she stayed is still shown; Rheims, where her true mission was accomplished; St. Denys, where she first failed; Compiègne, where she was taken, and Rouen, where she was burned,—are mostly places which might well be visited for themselves, and which become doubly interesting in connexion with a single heroic life. The advantage of this second plan is, that it requires no particular knowledge in the traveller. Let him simply take Michelet's little book with him, and remember so to arrange his route as to visit all or the chief places mentioned in it.

Instead of a tour, which it is not always easy to arrange, the traveller will sometimes do well to take a city and work it out. Mr. Ruskin once suggested that the rich men of Manchester ought to buy some old city like Verona, and keep it as it were like a fly in amber enshrined to all perpetuity in its own memories. The thought was of course wrought out with that profusion of fanciful argument which has made Mr. Ruskin mistake his poems for philosophy, and carried him out of the regions where he reigns supreme to those in which Cocker and Mrs. Marcet are more worthy. But setting aside the economical objections to turning the capital of a province into an art museum, it has always struck us that Mr. Ruskin, like many artists when they come to reason, was untrue in this instance, at least to his own better nature. No one has spoken more forcibly than he against so-called "restorations," and it is at least as unnatural to conserve a great city in its entirety as to *restore* a church or a hôtel-de-ville. A single building may be, and sometimes is, the expression of a single thought; but the true being of a city is in its many-thoughtedness, so to speak; in the fact that it has summed up the lives of nameless generations, and recorded the beauty or worthlessness of their highest purposes in stone. If any fortune arrest their development, so that human faces die out from the streets, the buildings ought to express the incompleteness or failure in which their makers' life has culminated. Time, the great beautifier, will cast down what was vulgar and common from its high places, and inform the ruins with that serene spiritual charm which mellows all the masterpieces of man's hand in their gradual decay. But the more common case is of a city that has held its own through all changes of fortune, and can number half-a-dozen alternations of pure and degraded taste, as one or another influence swayed the century. Its noblest monuments are probably impaired by some change or ornament that is unsuited to them: a Gothic baptistery is fitted with a Corinthian porch, or a gaudy, loaded, meretricious Jesuit church elbows a fourteenth-century hôtel-de-ville. We say deliberately that even these mutilations and deformities are to be respected up to a certain point as a part of national history. They express facts of which it is sometimes difficult to say whether the bad or good have the higher significance. A city like Munich, where the work of several generations has been crowded into one, has a certain thinness and monotony of expression in consequence; the architects all seem to have been wire-drawing a single inspiration. Lastly, it is obvious that if the principle of changing for the better be once allowed, without any respect to the work of other men, the noblest art will take its turn of suffering when a generation sinks below its meaning. All these arguments apply equally to allowing growth to continue. Its processes may sometimes have a rude vigour almost akin to destruction, and the superfluities of the old city's work, and sometimes much that expressed its highest meaning, will be swept away to make room for a factory or a gaol. It is well to protest against this Jacobinism, and to enforce a due reverence for antiquity whenever antiquity does not encroach on actual life. But, after all, cities were made for men, not men for cities; and the art that cannot adapt itself to facts is morbid and unreal. Unless we can restore the conditions of medieval society, a city like Nuremberg is an artistic anachronism. The permanent elements of medieval-ism, its Christianity and its municipal and feudal life, will pretty certainly hold their own, in proportion to their respective vitalities, in all places and to all time.

For a man who determines to work up the historical growth of one or two cities during his holiday, the first difficulty of selection will be the *embarras des richesses.* Italian cities generally possess one great advantage over all others in their pre-Christian remains. The definite history or historical legend that attaches to the Tarpeian rock, and the Cloaca Maxima, can never be balanced by the shadowy forms of Ossianic heroes, or by the nameless records of the Lake cities in Switzerland. When all criticism has done its worst or its best, the bridge which Horatius Cocles kept will remain a memory among men, and its dismantled piers be visited. On the other hand, Rome, the true world's capital for continuous historical life, is a little wanting in medieval associations. The popes stamped themselves upon Europe much more indelibly than on their own city, till Catholicism, at the last moment of its undisputed supremacy, found an adequate expression in St. Peter's. But Rome altogether is too vast a subject to be even touched upon in a short article. Perhaps Florence and its neighbourhood afford as good instances as can be named of the various generations that have written their own epitaph in their works. In Fiesole we find the suggestive remains at least of the old Etruscan walls, and there is reason to hope that the local amphitheatre will soon be partially disinterred. With the thirteenth and fourteenth centuries we come to Brunelleschi's dome, Dante's house and seat, the gates of the baptistery, "like the gates of Paradise," and the towers which Villani raised. The period of the Renaissance and of the Medici is crowded with recollections of Lorenzo the Magnificent, of Pico di Mirandola, of Savonarola, and of Michael Angelo. St. Mark's, where Fra Angelico painted, and with which Savonarola's name is associated; the Palazzo Vecchio, or city parliament-house, which witnessed all the constitutional struggles, and the great square in which the Reformer attempted to consume the unchristian art and learning of his times,—are a part only of that marvellous stone-setting to Florentine history. The Pitti and Strozzi palaces alone are monumental for the fortunes of their founders. A little later and the batteries of San Miniato, superintended by Michael Angelo in the last struggle of freedom, absorb every other interest; while the sorrow that succeeds defeat expresses itself in the statues of Sleep and Death. Then we pass into the sumptuous tyranny of the Medicis, with the Pitti and Uffizi collections. The absence of all monuments attests the absence of all national life during the last century; and the new buildings that are now springing up, not always in the most perfect taste, are at least signs of the resurrection of Italy. Every one who knows Florence will know how meagre this sketch of its history is, but it surely gives the outlines of a week or a month's study well spent. There is no French town that will repay the tourist as well. But a man must be hard to please indeed if the Roman antiquities of Arles and Nismes do not satisfy him till he has crossed the Alps. For the Middle Ages Caen is a perfect compendium of history. For the sixteenth century, Blois—with its old houses, and the palace where the court lived, where the estates met, and where the Duke de Guise was murdered—exceeds even Paris in richness of material; and the castles near it—Chambord, Amboise, Chaumont, and Chénonceaux—are as full of story and interest as French memoirs. Of Paris itself we can only speak regretfully. The barbarous policy of its present ruler has completed the havoc which the Revolution began; and in the unhappy attempt to destroy all memories of the old *régime*, the very *Temple* which Marie Antoinette's sufferings consecrated has not been spared. Broad boulevards each the image of its neighbour, monotonous stone façades of bastard architecture, and an occasional *réchauffé* of bad Gothic, give the measure of Imperial taste, and constitute the improvements to which Englishmen often refer as a justification of the December massacres. If art be any measure of statesmanship, the second Empire has no element of vitality.

It is from no indifference to the claims of Germany upon the tourist that we have neglected to speak of it. But as its history, except at two or three epochs like the Reformation and the War of Liberation, has no steady European interest, while its literature, for all practical purposes, dates no further back than Lessing, it wants the large human associations which make France and Italy the second fatherlands of civilised and educated men. The traveller in Germany had better confine himself to landscapes and art. To enjoy the former, he must go well armed against the uncleanly habits of the dirtiest race in Europe, and prepared to endure the manners of the rudest. If he is proof against the spitting of a Yankee bar, against the smoking of bad tobacco in close carriages before ladies, and against the manners of third-rate cockneydom in England, he is then in the right frame of mind to begin a journey in the Fatherland; though he must not consider himself perfect till he can listen without a smile to the common talk of German civilisation, German cleanliness, and German morality (*Deutsche Bildung, Deutsche Reinheit, Deutsche Sittlichkeit*). In fact, the virtues which the Germans no doubt possess are those of a patient, speculative, and coarse-fibred race, who want the education of a powerful and respectable aristocracy, and who are just now in a fever-fit of material progress, which has impaired the scholarly element without perceptibly increasing self-reliance or self-respect. Probably self-government and consolidation, if they come soon enough to save the country from being dismembered by its powerful neighbours, will do much to bring the natives up to the level of the rest of Europe. Meanwhile it is a great misfortune for them that they have never attracted sufficient attention out of their own country to be seriously satirised. A French—or, better still, an English—Mrs. Trollope or Dickens would lash them out of that inveterate conceit of perfection which is at present the great obstacle to their improvement. We regard Victor Cousin's report on Prussian education as having done more to retard political and social development in Germany than any single book ever yet did any where. It analysed an excellent paper system, of which the writer had no practical knowledge, and, perhaps unavoidably, confounded the theory with the expected results. Since then the resources of English primary instruction have been more than trebled; France has added largely to her schools and colleges; Germany has stagnated, or gone back, as in Bohemia; and the people none the less believe, with a Chinese self-sufficiency, that Europe looks up to them as its models in all intellectual progress.

Nevertheless, if a traveller will eschew Murray's hints and Bradshaw's positive statements, and will steadily travel first class, as the more respectable natives and experienced foreigners do, and will take a little more than ordinary care not to offend very irritable susceptibilities, he may traverse North Germany in its least civilised parts without any great discomfort. On the great highway of travel, the Rhine, he is more likely to be annoyed at finding that England somewhat changed for the worse has followed him, than by any flagrant deficiencies in the essentials of decent comfort in the hotels. In Austria, the accommodation and fare are often a little rough; but the people are genial and good-natured to an extent that covers a multitude of sins. After all, something may well be ventured and endured for the sake of what is to be seen. Among art-collections, those of Dresden, Munich, and Vienna, have no rivals north of the Alps, except in the Louvre. But the true life of the country, artistic and political, has always been in its cities. The most peculiar interest, no doubt, attaches to Hanseatic towns like Lubeck, whose gate and cathedral are almost unmatched of their kind; and to old imperial cities like Nuremberg, where the burghers pushed German individuality to its last extreme, and having maintained a peculiar religion, a distinct civic aristocracy, and an intolerance that went the length of excluding Jews from the walls, have at last immured themselves as it were in their own past, and resolved that every house shall be rebuilt as it was in the sixteenth century. Cologne, Ratisbon, Augsburg, Dantzig, and Frankfort, are a few in the long list of memorable towns; places that have a distinct individuality, and are not mere creations of the *valet de place* and of the handbook. We scarcely know whether Prague is properly to be called a German city; but it is so entirely bound up with the fortunes of Austria, and from the fourteenth century downwards has been so largely peopled by Germans, that it belongs, one-half at least, to the Empire. It is the meeting-point of the two great races of the East, Slave and German, and reflects their different civilisations. An amphitheatre of hills round it, an acropolis covered with churches and palaces rising on one side the river, the Moldau spanned by a splendid bridge in the midst; and on the other side the old city, with its Jews' quarter a thousand and odd years old, and with the third University of the North, in which Englishmen kindled the flame that consumed Huss at Constance, and the Pope's bulls a century later at Wittenberg. Pass from city to country, and we know not what fairer land heart could wish for than the "Kettle-land" of Bohemia, bowl-shaped and mountainous, every hill instinct with memories of the time when Zisca drove the armies of the Empire, with their chivalry and wealth, before a few peasants armed with flails. To the south-west of Bohemia lies an even lovelier country, the true Garden of Germany. Perhaps more beauty could hardly be crowded into a few days any where, than by a man who should take the route of Salzburg and Ischl to Linz, exploring a little right and left by the way, and should then start down the Danube to Vienna. There is a wealth of unexplored beauty throughout Austria. Probably not one traveller in a hundred ever thinks of tracing the Save from Laibach to Agram, yet a better day's work scarcely exists for a genuine lover of the picturesque. We have not cared to allude to the Mosel and the Rhine, which every one knows,—hotels, companies, touts, and tourists have made them populous, and done their best to vulgarise them; and they are still beautiful. The views from Johannisberg, from Ehrenbreitstein, or from Remagen, defy time and man's hand.

To many there is a strange interest in wandering into countries where civilisation is still only a distant name and a whisper. A weariness of ceiled houses and London tailoring, of lower classes who know the gradations of rank instinctively, and of a whole society that seems to move steadily in the groove it first slid into, is very apt to overtake the dwellers in great cities. To such, in default of more distant regions, a tour in Hungary, in Russia, or in Servia—but especially in the latter—may be recommended. It is only this summer that the Piedmont of Turkey has attracted any general attention, and perhaps the wrongs of the Christians have done less for Belgrade than the presence in London of a pretty woman claiming to represent their interests. Yet those who value a unique phase of society should hasten to photograph it before it disappears. There is not such a being in the whole country as a man whose ancestors fifty years ago were wealthy, independent, or educated. The father of the present prince was a cowherd. The ministers, though their wonderful Slavonic versatility enables them to learn the languages and catch the tone of Western society, have risen by dint of ability or by favour from the ranks. Titles, except as derived from office, do not exist. All the problems of woman's education and woman's rights, which we in Europe have been discussing for some centuries past, are still unknown to the primitive people, who rule their families in patriarchal fashion, and have not altogether unlearned the trick of Oriental seclusion. A woman's best right in Servia is to her husband's fidelity, and, if native stories may be trusted, she is apt to enforce it with the dagger. Then, too, there is a certain romance of travel in a land where every man goes armed, and where the picturesque costume recalls legends of the Klephts and of Albanian brigands. The much-enduring Ulysses would find himself more at home at a Servian hearth, the peasants telling stories round a wood-fire, in rooms without chimneys, glass windows, chairs, beds, or carpets, than in Ithaca itself under modern influences, or than in the country of Polyphemus. A recent English traveller in Servia, Mr. Denton, has opened up a vein of new interest in the ecclesiastical architecture. Our own impressions were, that it could not rival the Russian in effect any more than in extent; and of the secular buildings out of Belgrade, we can only quote the famous chapter in Henderson's *Iceland*, "on Snakes." There are literally none that deserve the name. The country, however, is very interesting, hill, glen, and forest, like the best parts of Normandy, and with a better climate. It would be a noble land for English emigrants, if they went out in sufficient numbers to secure an educated society, and the protection of the Foreign Office from our unchristian friends the Turks. Land may be bought as cheap as in the Backwoods; labour is more abundant; and the colonist would be within five days' journey of London, and if he lived within a fair distance of Belgrade, could have the *Times* laid regularly on his breakfast-table.

Railways are doing so much for Russia, that before five years are over, the great roads of the country will probably be as well known as the highways of Germany now are. There is no reason even now why a man of moderate strength should not travel in the empire. The residents in St. Petersburg affect, it is true, to speak of the whole country beyond its two capitals as barbarous; but to an educated foreigner there is infinitely more of true barbarism in St. Petersburg itself, with its tasteless public buildings, like palatial barracks, its dirty, comfortless hotels, and its monotonous life drilled into Western respectability, than in the provincial cities which have been allowed to grow up naturally. The only real difficulty in visiting the interior is the language; and although this will well repay learning, and is not as impracticable as it seems, a tourist may be excused if he shrinks from acquiring it. In this case he must make up his mind to the expense and discomfort of a native servant. But the mere work of locomotion is easy. The track of Russian colonisation has mostly been along the lines of the great rivers, and the most important of all, the Volga, is now as well supplied with steamers as the Danube. The swamps and pine-forests of the north and the prairie-land of the south are beginning to be traversed with railways; and the line joining Moscow with Nijni Novgorod makes it possible to get from St. Petersburg to the two most interesting places in North Russia with only some thirty hours' travel in a railway carriage. A day and a half's easy work in a steamer will take the traveller on to the Tartar capital, Kazan, and a dash into the limits of Siberia is no very difficult matter from that starting-point. As for inns, the traveller will do well to follow the custom of the natives, and take his own sheets and tea with him. But clean beds can be procured at all towns, and the general accommodation of Russian inns is quite equal to that of German or French, in parts little visited. The food is commonly good, and Sauterne does duty for *vin ordinaire*. It is true that the upper classes, being a small minority, have to pay rather disproportionately for their comforts; but less than two pounds a day ought, after all, to defray all expenses.

The interest of Russia is, that it is unique. In no other great country has a Christian and Indo-Germanic race developed itself without aid from Roman law, from feudalism, or from chivalry. From this, and from a few vestiges of the Tartar conquest, has come the utterly groundless idea that the Russians are an Asiatic people. The truth is that, like the old Greeks, they are the outpost of Europe against Asia, and have all the burning hatred of a frontier people for their antagonists. It would be truer to say that their civilisation is Byzantine. Their whole history has been moulded by a faith derived from Constantinople; their official organisation is a strange reproduction of the Lower Empire; and their policy looks steadily to Stamboul as their future capital. Their architecture and sacred art are on the models which Vladimir or Alexander Nevsky may have witnessed. With all this antiquity of type, there is a strange air of novelty about the empire. The bitter winters disintegrate brick and mortar pitilessly; the frequent fires in towns consume wood. Every thing seems as new as in an American clearing; and, in fact, the Russians are as great colonists as the Anglo-Saxons, only that they migrate within the limits of their empire, not beyond it. But no one could mistake the Russian church, with its gaudy cupolas of blue and gold, for any thing but the fresh form of an immemorial faith. Our own Gothic cathedrals are scarcely more instinct with the life that is beyond time. The kremlins or fortresses, from their massive construction, are commonly older in actual date than the churches; and the white conical towers, enclosing the lowest and highest parts of the town, with palace and cathedral, are indescribably picturesque. It is a curious tribute to the permanence of type in Russian edifices, that no visitor to Moscow ever thinks of it as a new city, though most of it of course dates from within sixty years. One great advantage of Moscow over its rivals in the empire lies in the fact, that it has been laid out irregularly. After the fire, which burned away the stain of French occupation, every one was allowed to build pretty much as he liked: palaces and gardens were clustered in unsymmetrical lines without interference from imperial edicts. Then the architects of the two greatest buildings—the Cathedral of St. Basil and St. George's Palace—have been men of the highest capacity in their respective ways. Add to this the unrivalled natural position; and it will be understood that the whole effect is rather that of an Arabian Night's story than of an ordinary second capital. Nijni Novgorod is scarcely less remarkable. The old town, with its kremlin and cathedral, on a cliff that overhangs the junction of two imperial rivers—the Volga and the Oka; on the other side, an illimitable plain fringed with many thousand booths, interspersed with mosques and pagodas; and the river between gay with decorated junks, which alone contain the population of a city; Cossack, Armenian, and Chinaman here confronting the bagman from Manchester or Lyons,—never surely had commerce a more fantastic metropolis. This generation will probably look upon its last. There is talk already of telegraph lines in Siberia; road and rail have made Moscow as accessible as Nijni Novgorod; and the days of fairs are numbered.

There is still one class of traveller whose interests we have not considered,—the man who wishes simply to lie fallow, and rejects all idea of self-improvement. To such a one we recommend Norway. It has lain idly looking on at the world round it since its heroic age some eight centuries ago, and has no manufactures, no art, no history, and almost no literature. The common mode of travelling in carriole, a sort of low chair upon two wheels, with a place behind for luggage, saves the tourist from some of the common and most annoying incidents of a journey,—the hurry to catch a train, the waiting-room, and the temporary loss of *impedimenta.* To be quite independent, however, and enjoy the country leisurely, he had better travel with his own horse: the loss, if any, on this will be slight in a country where fifteen or twenty pounds is a large sum for the best. The great conveniences of Norwegian travelling are, that the light lasts far into the night, that mists are unknown, and that, as a general rule, the best views may be seen without climbing. The waterfalls are perhaps superior to the Swiss; the fiords are longer and with more reaches than the lakes; and the frequent changes of scenery along the roadside are indescribable. But the country is not one for a delicate man, nor for any but a very adventurous lady to travel in. Oat-cakes and milk are in many parts the only food that can be counted on; and the doctor may have to be summoned from many miles' distance. On the other hand, clean sheets are the rule. It is needless to describe cottage interiors for any one who has seen Tidemann's pictures. It must be well borne in mind that such rooms as he paints are the only ones that await the traveller, except in the three or four towns where there are hotels.

What we have said is addressed, not to the learned in travelling, but to those who are beginning it, or who have never had time and occasion to master its first principles. Of the traveller, as of the poet, it may be said that he is born, not made. There is an irresistible impulse in certain races and families to go out into the unknown world about them; and few instincts bring a richer reward with them, or are more durable. Yet we hold a sort of Hegelian doctrine, that the feeling for home is nowhere stronger than in the wanderer. Probably no nation has better proved its credentials in this respect than the Scotch, and in none is there heartier local patriotism or a stronger family pride. The men who really renounce England for the Continent and sink contentedly into the second-rate circles of a provincial German town, are not travellers, or to be so accounted, because they have given up one form of cockneydom for another. They are also the last men who ever understand the society into which they have thrown themselves. They catch, perhaps, its tricks of manner or vice; but the same want of individuality that hindered them from taking their proper place at home unfits them to learn the more difficult lesson—what the highest aspirations of a strange people are. It is only the artist in travel, "always roaming with a hungry heart to follow knowledge like a sinking star," who is also "a part of all he meets." To those who understand this instinctively it will not seem strange if we have dwelt even to weariness on the uses to which a journey in the most hackneyed parts of Europe may be turned.

Art. VI.—EWALD ON THE JOHANNINE WRITINGS.

Die Johanneischen Schriften übersetzt und erklärt. Von Heinrich Ewald. Göttingen, 1862.

Geschichte des Volkes Israel. Von H. Ewald. Siebenter Band. Göttingen, 1859.

Zehntes Jahrbuch der Biblischen Wissenschaft. 1859-1860.

[The following Article is intended to furnish a digest of Ewald's views, and does not aim at giving an estimate of the questions connected with St. John's Gospel generally.]

Few readers can study the Johannine writings of the New Testament with merely ordinary feelings of curiosity and interest. To the devout and thoughtful, the Gospel of St. John has ever been the revelation of the highest spiritual truth given to man, and the setting forth of the divine character with a glory which is found nowhere else in human letters. Readers of this class know that their own apprehension of the book depends upon the love and the light which are in them, upon the hold which the unseen realities, the subject-matter of the book, have upon them. And the critical student, who engages in the study out of the resolve to let no writing of the ancient world escape his inquiry, whose aim it is to discover the authorship, design, and history of every book which has told powerfully upon the course of human thought, and who will not be deterred from this task because any such writings are clothed with a sacred character, or because many will consider the inquiry over bold, if not profane,—he, we dare say it, does not long study the Gospel of St. John as he would another work. He meets in it with thoughts, words, and deeds which the critical faculty is inadequate to explain. He finds the mere historical insight fail him. He learns that this Gospel speaks less to his intellect than to his affections; that he must find its meaning and explanation in the experiences of his daily working life with and among men, as well as by the aid of the understanding. And he acknowledges at last that, to know the Gospel as he would wish to know another book, he must be in relation with the mind of the writer. We think that both the critical and the devout reader, like-minded and sincere in their aim, arrive at the same conclusion.

With the Gospel we class the three Epistles, which bear indisputable marks of the same handwriting. Indeed, the longest of the three, which may be entitled *the* Epistle of St. John, is but the expanding and applying to immediate wants of the church the discourses narrated in the last chapters of the Gospel, and stands or falls with the Gospel as the work of the apostle.

The remaining book of the series awakens its own interest, though of a different kind. The dramatic form of the Apocalypse, "the majestic image of a high and stately tragedy, shutting up and intermingling her solemn scenes and acts with a reverential chorus of hallelujas and harping symphonies;" the passionate glow of devotion which pervades it; the vivid character of its symbolism, at once so real and so strange, making us feel that the book is treating of actual things under a form and dress altogether foreign to present modes of thought; and again, the fact of its being the one prophetic book of the New Testament, and that the old Hebrew spirit appears in it anew, clothed in still more fiery language,—combine powerfully to attract students to the study of it. Rarely does the study prove satisfactory. On the very threshold the want of some guide is felt, and not a few offer themselves. No other book has been more frequently commented upon,* to the bewilderment rather than to the help of the student. The largest class of expositors with all the confidence of dogmatism hammer out of the book their own theories of the divine government of the world since Christ came till now, which bear the *odium theologicum* upon their front, and are too plainly the issue of that mother of monstrous fables and fancies. The student who is told to believe the Apocalypse a catalogue of unfulfilled predictions which contain the history of Christendom written out in enigma, and who finds that the different theories of interpretation, even when based on the same principles, are mutually destructive, gives up the study as hopeless. The book becomes to him the name for what is past finding out. The neglect into which the book has fallen, and the low esteem in which the study of it is held, even as a weakness, lie heavily at the door of the expositors. We would not seem unmindful that the book retains its place among writings which are the spiritual food of men. We know how children and untaught peasants pore over it with delight and wonder.

* "Si quâ in re libera esse debet sententia, certè in vaticiniis, præsertim cum jam Protestantium libri prodierint fermè centum (in his *octoginta* in Angliâ solâ, ut mihi Anglici legati dixere) super illis rebus, inter se plurimum discordes." Grot. Epist. 895, quoted by Hallam, *Literature of Europe*, 5th edition, vol. ii. p. 455, n.

But the simple faith that the book bespeaks the ultimate triumph of the cause of God and his saints over the oppression and injustice of the world, that he hears the prayer of the poor destitute, and will yet cause right to be done, renders it a living book and prized possession to many a wayfarer. The fortitude and patience with which its pages have inspired the afflicted and distressed, the betrayed and persecuted, the confessor hiding to pray in the catacomb, or fleeing to the caves and dens of the earth for shelter, from the first age of Christianity till now, more than justify its place in the canon. The book has a special meaning for special times, and is then most felt to be true when most needed. While we recognise these facts, we cannot withhold the inquiry what the book means, whether the symbolism which is its most distinguishing feature may not have been most intelligible to its first readers deeply read in Old-Testament prophecy; and whether the time of its composition, once clearly established, will not clear away many difficulties, by showing how earnestly the events which were happening and just about to happen, the strong fears and cries of Christendom, called for a revelation of the kind. The historian, the scholar, the critic, who should furnish this key, would open a storehouse of truth hitherto well nigh closed. It is equally in their province to make the study of the Gospel more fruitful. We have expressed our conviction of the one essential condition, without which no appliances of learning will avail. Deeply as we feel the need of that,—the fear of God in our hearts and good-will towards men in our lives,—we shall eagerly seek for every gleam of light that knowledge can shed upon the least letter of the text. This Gospel differs in one respect from the earlier Gospels. It has a more evident reference to the time and circumstances when it was written, to the thoughts and beliefs which stirred the first Christian communities. The historian who should reproduce this environment of the apostle, who should set us in the midst of one Christian congregation and acquaint us with the minds of its elders and members, would make the form, yes, and the spirit of the Gospel more easily understood, and he would deserve well of the student. We want to stand near the men who were the first to read this book, to know how they understood the language which came to them fresh from the lips of the beloved disciple; how it became, as far as any even the most sacred book is capable of this, their guide and counsellor. Who is sufficient for such a task? On the brief roll of those who can without presumption undertake it, we place among the foremost Heinrich Ewald. It is unnecessary to mention the great works which have earned him the high place he holds among biblical scholars. Those of us who know nothing of foreign theological literature, who look with suspicion upon every German school and author, cannot be ignorant how very much the ablest writers of the most recent work of English biblical scholarship, Smith's *Dictionary of the Bible*, even when widely dissenting from his points of view, are yet indebted to him. We will add, that only such as have studied the *Geschichte des Volkes Israel*, the work of twenty years' unceasing study and thought, and *Die Propheten des Alten Bundes*, and compared them with the most valuable papers in Smith's Dictionary, can estimate the extent of the obligations of our own best writers to Ewald.* We are glad that it is so. The letter of Scripture needed to be read anew, that the spirit which underlies it might no longer be hid. It was time for traditional comments and glosses to be tried and sifted; for the date, authorship, and composition of the most sacred books in the world to be examined by the plain rules of criticism, and to be judged in the same court of inquiry as all other ancient books, that their true place in the realm of literature might be assigned. It was time for acquiescence to be disturbed, for genuine belief to be strengthened by the conviction of unbelief, by the satisfaction of every honest doubt, by the refutation and overthrow of every false one. Only those who mistrusted their own belief in the sacred books, or who in their hearts feared that the nation's faith stood on no surer ground than props of unquestioned testimony, or who "cared for none of these things," could fear the inquiries of our time, whether on the part of Germans or Englishmen. The works of H. Ewald, more perhaps than of any one single writer, are typical, and have set a mark upon our century. He has given his life to the study of sacred literature, and of all other literature that could illustrate it; his abilities and acquirements, *more humano*, are vast enough for the task. He seems to converse with the great minds of the ancients as though the men themselves were present; to possess in an uncommon degree that rare gift, not only of imagination, but of intuition, by which the history of the past is recalled to life as the history of actual men. We might suppose Ewald to have seen and heard the kings and prophets of the old dispensation, the apostles and disciples of the new, and to have escaped the waters of Lethe in his passage to the midst of us.

It is unfortunate that our author's language, in which sure historical facts are told clearly and with photographic minuteness, but ideas and reasons too often loom through the mist, render it unlikely that his works will be soon accessible to English readers.

* Since this was written, Canon Stanley, in the preface to his *Lectures on the Jewish Church*, has warmly expressed his own high estimate of Ewald's studies, and adequately acknowledged the help they have been to him.

Seeing how much there is in his last published work on the Johannine writings of the greatest value for a right understanding of them, and how many difficult points connected with their date, authorship, and design are to our mind decidedly cleared up, we propose to lay before our readers some account of Ewald's studies, such especially as bear upon the aims and composition of the Gospel. We premise that, while we estimate most highly, and gratefully acknowledge, the help which this book affords us, there is an absence in it of much that we would wish to find; most of all do we miss sufficient reference to the guiding, informing Spirit of him, for whom and by whose aid these works were written. And we find much affirmed positively, as it seems to us, on insufficient grounds. But we are in the hands of a critic and historian whose constructive power is the marvel of every reader, whose conclusions are never hastily formed, and who is frequently careless of stating all the reasons which lead to them. The longer and the better we are acquainted with him, the deeper becomes our respect for his judgment, the less confidence we feel in our own when at variance with it.

Ewald thinks that the doubt as to the authorship of the Gospel is wholly unscientific and baseless. The doubt cannot be regretted in presence of the diligent inquiry it has awakened, and the very able reply it has found. Reasons for our author's strongly expressed belief, as well as the relation between the Gospel and the life of the apostle, will be best examined after the Gospel itself. Our author assigns its date to the year 80. From the description of localities, it is plain that Jerusalem had already fallen (xi. 18, xviii. 1, xix. 41). Why the apostle came to the task so late in life, and so late in the history of evangelical literature, will appear from a review of the opinions and state of the church at the time.

His *main* design was undoubtedly to compose a true gospel, one of those books which gave briefly or at length the true historical outline of Christ's earthly appearance. There were already many gospels in existence; his own, from the fact of its being the last, could not but serve as their complement and correction. Each of these had set forth some one side in particular of Christ's earthly appearance. The apostle's design was to bring all the sides of that appearance into one great connected image, to unite the divine and the human side, the works and the words of Christ's earthly life, in one perfect history; and in this lay the peculiarity, as well as the glory and independence, of his work.

Another aim of the apostle was to present a complete chronological arrangement of our Lord's life, which was wanting to the earlier gospels. St. Luke, who wrote about the same time as the apostle, had more carefully defined the chronology, and inserted it into the framework of the world's history. St. John observes the chronology only with reference to the life of Christ. He confines himself to the history of that life without reference to the contemporaneous events of the history of the world.

Besides this main design of the apostle,—to give a faithful and true life of Christ, supplying every omission of former writers, —there were subordinate aims arising out of questions which stirred Christendom when he wrote, and which exercised their own influence upon his work. Three such may be distinguished. The relation of the church towards the old Jewish community and the heathen world was completely changed; it had separated itself from the former, and spread widely among the latter. Had the words of Christ anticipated this change of relation? Could it be justified by them? Was it his intention that such change should take place? St. John brings prominently forward whatever is most pertinent to these questions. Christ had not spoken often to the heathen; he had not on many occasions come into contact with them. All the more carefully does the apostle report these words and occasions. He narrates at length the intercourse between Christ and the Samaritans; for these latter were considered in some respects as a heathen people, and his intercourse with them had not been fruitless (iv. 4-42, viii. 48).

Another aim of the apostle is connected with the preceding. The separation between the old congregation and the new, the church and the synagogue, since the destruction of Jerusalem, had been completed. The new Christian generation felt itself as widely removed from Jews as from Samaritans and heathens. The apostle's language throughout witnesses to this feeling. He speaks of the Jews very much as we speak of them to-day (i. 19, ii. 6, 13, 20, and throughout). In proportion as this separation deepened, and the Gospel spread more widely among the heathen, the Jews were the more eager to render Christians suspected, and throw doubt upon their teaching. Such questions as these would be raised: Why was it that Christ, living in the midst of his own people, found so little credence? that so few, and those only unlearned and obscure Galileans, became his disciples? These questions could not be satisfactorily answered out of the earlier evangelists. The apostle supplied what was wanting in them. They had named only one of the chief council as Christ's friend, though a hesitating one, and that only because of his part in the burial of the body of Jesus. The apostle brings forward another such councillor, who from the beginning to the end of Christ's earthly life had been interested in him. He reports the confidential interview which this councillor sought with Christ. He is careful to mention that many of the rulers of the people believed in him, and only held back through fear of the powerful Pharisees from confessing him openly. He describes the journeys to Jerusalem, in reply to the false charge that Christ had remained hidden in one corner of Galilee. From the same point of view we understand why he lays such stress on the favourable and unfavourable dispositions of the Jews towards him on his last journey.

Soon after the destruction of Jerusalem, the disciples of John the Baptist formed themselves into new congregations, vehemently disputed with the disciples of Christ, and maintained that John had never acknowledged Christ to be the higher one sent by God. Ewald's exposition of the opinions of this sect forms a most interesting section of the seventh volume of his *Geschichte des Volkes Israel.* He treads here on firm historical ground; and his constructive power is happily employed in piecing together the scattered fragments and notices of these early Baptists contained in works little known to the general reader. Certainly this page of church history, which nowhere else is so fully and carefully written, throws much light on one portion of the Gospel before us.

It was after the destruction of Jerusalem that the disciples of the Baptist awoke to fresh life. The second Sibylline book, written about A.D. 80 in Asia Minor, in the neighbourhood of the apostle, and where the new impetus was given to the movement, assists us in discovering the main tenets of the sect. The whole of this short poem was composed by a Baptist. We learn from it that the Baptists and Essenes had united, and that from this union had sprung up a new and active congregation. From the first, the two sects had held much in common. The Baptist sect claimed to be the mother of Christianity, and even to excel it in deeper earnestness and purity of life. The Essenes sect easily came to an understanding with the Baptist, which was its own scion. Both sects interchanged their most characteristic teaching. The constant bath, as the means of purification, took the place of the temple; penitential exercises, springing out of and joined with strong fear of the judgment soon about to come upon all the world, were insisted on. The Essenes relaxed their prohibition of marriage and active life, and allowed the name "religious" to all within the congregation. Those outside it were "profane." The Sibylline books witness to the bitter hatred which they met with,—to the deep feelings and earnest zeal which existed among them,—to the bold thoughts and words which they did not hesitate to speak aloud to the whole contemporary world. In the year 80 this sect does not seem to have outstepped the limits of Asia Minor. We can recall the name by which its members were known, and under which they were classed among the opponents to Christianity by church fathers and historians,* Hemero-baptists, *i.e.* day-baptists, a name which sufficiently marks their separation from Christians.

It would lead us beyond the limits of our subject, which is to collect the main features in the history of religious opinion when St. John wrote, were we to follow our author farther in his most interesting inquiries into the doctrines of the powerful sect of the Elcesaites, which grew out of the fusion of these earlier sects. Since the publication of Chaolson's *Sabies,* more complete information on this subject has been given to the student. It will suffice to add, that Elcesai pushed to the farthest extreme, whilst he incorporated in his system, the prevailing notions concerning baptism of the Hemero-baptists. Baptism was asserted to be the highest medicine for the salvation of the world,—not only a means of grace, a sacrament in the later language of the church, or the initiatory rite and act of dedication, but the very medicine and cure for all possible evils of soul and body; and not once only to be administered, but to be repeated as often as the recipient felt himself and was judged by others to have sinned. The rest of his doctrine appears to have been a blending of Chaldæo-Jewish notions concerning lucky and unlucky days, times, and things, the application of the one for the healing or neutralising of the other, and the hidden significance of numbers. The sect never spread far westward, but in the east the scanty remnants of the Sabeans still witness to the hold which it once had upon the minds of men.

St. John lived amongst men who had thus exaggerated the Baptist's teaching. The care and the detail with which he sets forth the actual relations between the Baptist and Christ; the acknowledged inferiority and submission of the one to the other; the witness of John to Jesus as the Christ, and his statement of the transitory nature of his own work in comparison with that of the bridegroom whose friend he was,—acquire fresh meaning when read in connexion with the history of the apostle's time.

One other, and a very different, class of opinions may not be overlooked, though perhaps too much rather than too little prominence was once given to it by many respected writers of the English church, in their interpretation of the New Testament. At the very name of Gnosticism some of us will recoil from the memory of dreary pages which started from that text. There is at least one exception to the ordinary treatment of the subject. In Mr. Maurice's admirable and only too brief *Lectures*

* Eus. Eccl. H. iv. 22; Epiph. Hær. 17.

on the Ecclesiastical History of the First and Second Centuries, the Gnostics are fairly dealt with, and speak to us as living and thinking men, not as mere holders of a certain set of wild opinions. The reader cannot but regret that the author contented himself with drawing the rough outlines of church history, the deeper problems of which no living writer among us could so well explain.

Ewald's review of the rise and growth of these opinions, which come generally under the name of Gnosticism, deserves careful study. We can here only convey the substance of it. Christianity presented itself as a new subject of inquiry to the most active minds of the apostle's time. These were eager to assist in the task of forming and developing Christian doctrine, of which the first and most influential teachers were no longer living, and which was known to many only through a few short writings. The great weakness of their attempts, as well as of all knowledge of divine and human things, in the ancient world, was the want of the historical temper. Instead of taking pains carefully to investigate every particular fact, men gave themselves over to the mere exercise of the imagination, which sought to bring every conception into equal proportions and round numbers. Had the scholars of those days, who made Christian doctrine the material of their speculations, been willing to become Christians in science itself, *i.e.* to accept nothing but in the calmness and certainty of divine knowledge, they would have produced something more enduring. But whilst they took the words of Christ in the Gospels, and of St. Paul in the Epistles, as the subject-matter of their science, they followed the method of Philo or the heathen philosophers. There grew up with surprising quickness an almost endless number of schools and theories, differing in their main principles according to the countries in which they arose and the doctrines which they followed, one seeking to outstrip and correct the other, yet agreeing in this, that they issued from Christianity itself, and laboured to attain a new and deeper insight into divine and human things. The zeal once set in motion soon passed all bounds. The search for fragmentary and one-sided truths became the mere play of fancy. Minds which were content with thinking out mere possibilities, or following up single unconnected thoughts, soon forgot the plainest Christian duties, and came at last, through the specious depth and results of pure speculation, or through the attraction of ingenious words, to introduce into their belief and practice what was half, if not wholly, unchristian.

Gnosis was in itself, from the Christian point of view, not only quite blameless, but, in opposition to heathen philosophy, something peculiar to and necessary in Christianity,—a true ornament of it. The manifestation of Christ, and the results of it, suggested many fresh and hitherto unknown subjects of meditation to the reflecting mind. The word received in the apostle's days its genuine Christian meaning, as is plain from 1 Cor. i. 5, and many other passages of the Epistle; from Rom. xi. 33, xv. 14; Phil. iii. 8; Col. ii. 3. Originally it was the common possession of all Christians who had the mind and disposition to seek it,—of Jewish as well as Gentile Christians, especially, indeed, of the former; for Philo, and men like him, had long sought for a deeper wisdom in Judaism itself; until at last, on account of its evil fruits, it was universally suspected and combated. From the end of its full development the word acquired that bad second meaning which it has since retained. Careful inquiry proves that Gnosticism arose and gave indication of its errors before the destruction of Jerusalem, though it was not till afterwards that it developed itself with full freedom. The difficulty of tracing this long growth is very great. The first of the three Gnostic movements is overshadowed and obscured by the much greater and more important which followed. But although the works of Basileides, Valentinus, and others who belonged to the flourishing period of Gnosticism, are as good as destroyed, and only some few passages of Gnostic writing survive, yet are their works fairly well known to us from the elaborate refutations which they met with, and which in part remain. Unfortunately it is just the earliest and most imperfect attempt of Gnosticism which is the most obscure, for it is this which we most want to learn. The truth holds here as in every other long-continued spiritual movement, that the later development depends upon the beginning and the way in which that beginning is received. The allegorical interpretation of Scripture in the end gave a great impulse to Gnosticism. The Corinthian teachers who thought that the resurrection was already past did not deny the resurrection of Christ, nor were they probably in other respects bad Christians. They appealed to certain truths which seemed to them to lie nearer home, and to be undeniable; starting from the truth (to which no one had given greater prominence than Paul) that Christians had suffered with Christ and been raised together with him. Resurrection in this sense could be understood as already past. They were probably the same men who, appealing to the judgment of Christian Gnosis, misused their Christian freedom to partake of heathen sacrificial meats. These men issued from St. Paul's own school, as far as one can speak of his school, and exaggerated their freedom under the pretence of Gnosis. Evidently Gnosticism, in its darker aspect, was, in St. Paul's own time, in full swing, although we know little or nothing of the names of its first advocates. One name, however, has been preserved from its place in the Apocalypse—the name of the Nicolaitans. These men belonged to the first Gnostic movement anterior to the destruction of Jerusalem; they based their theories on genuine Christian truths, boasted of greater depth of wisdom than ordinary Christians, and had their own inspired apostles and prophets (Apoc. ii. 24, cf. ii. 2, 13-15, 20). Their new teachers in and around Ephesus taught the same doctrine as the too liberal Christians in Corinth had willingly heard, and against whose tendencies Paul had raised his warning voice. Their doctrine was that a Christian might, without endangering his faith, take part in heathen rites and sacrifices, that he ought to misuse the flesh, and indulge himself even in what the universal laws of morality forbad, in order to prove how superior the spirit was to mere things of sense, and how little it could suffer from them. This was what they meant by Christian freedom from law. If we ask through what supposed deeper knowledge they sought to establish such dangerous theories, we must refer back to the two natures in the historical Christ, the lower sensitive and the purely spiritual, which had come from the invisible heaven, and to the distinction which they drew between the Creator of the world and the purely spiritual and Invisible One. This severe distinction between the God who reveals himself in the sensitive faculties and him who is purely invisible, apparently so scientific and yet so utterly erroneous, lay at the root of all their theories, and is the key to the understanding of Gnosticism. We find it in Philo and in other much-read writings of the time. The Gospel narrative of the descent of the Holy Ghost upon Christ at his baptism most powerfully stirred the imagination: hence arose a multitude of strange conceptions, how that the human nature in Jesus was quite withdrawn from that moment, and became a mere appearance. Now when this distinction was thus sharply defined in the historical Christ,—when the human and visible in him was dishonoured, and the purely spiritual so exaggerated that his body became a mere appearance,—men soon began to maintain that it was the duty of every sincere Christian also in himself to esteem only the spiritual, to despise his body as being something indifferent, to use it according to his pleasure, though such using were, in the opinion of the carnal and less spiritual-minded, a misuse. We can thus form to ourselves some corresponding idea of what these earliest Gnostics and advocates of unrestricted Christian freedom really meant, and confidently accept the tradition that Nicolaus was the author of this movement, which had spread widely in Corinth and Asia Minor before the overthrow of Jerusalem. The storm of that overthrow—the first great shock given to Christendom—laid low this great corruption of Christian freedom. The second Christian generation grew up in the midst of heathen persecutions, and shrunk back with abhorrence from every thing heathen. The Nicolaitans disappear from history under the severe condemnation of the writer of the Apocalypse. But the passion for building up similar vague theories remained, although the object sought for, and the means followed to attain it, were different. Cerinthus owes his place in history to the fact of his having been the apostle John's contemporary at Ephesus. He was a Jewish Christian, educated in Egypt, who afterwards taught at Ephesus. Early Gnosticism found in him its successor and continuator. The Gospel narrative of the descent of the Holy Spirit upon Jesus made a deep impression upon him; and since he could not explain from the human side all that the Gospel recorded of Christ, he lost himself in the dualism which Philo imagined of a twofold God, and a ruling intermediate being. He conceived the Creator of the world not as the first pure Almighty God, but as a power widely removed from, and even misapprehending him, and his creative work as imperfect and needing correction. He conceived Christ to be Joseph and Mary's son, juster and wiser than all other men, but first at his baptism, and then only, to have become Christ by the descent of a purely spiritual power upon him from the Almighty God, who had been hitherto unknown to the world. By virtue of this spiritual power he had preached the unknown God, and done his wonderful works. On the cross the man had suffered, and not Christ; for Christ was incapable of suffering, and had left the man Jesus, who had been crucified, had died, and had risen again by virtue of the momentary union with him once again of that pure spirit. Cerinthus was the first who worked out the notion of a purely spiritual power descending upon Jesus, and again at times leaving him, and made this a new gospel.

These thoughts of men who in the apostle's days wanted to fathom all human and divine knowledge, and clearly to lay down the border-lines of both, seem to us idle and dreamy images, altogether inadequate to satisfy the desire of men for the knowledge of God. The reader of Neander will know their great historical importance for understanding the later history of the church; and these errors may have another interest for us. They are but the logical consequences of half-truths possessing earnest and onesided minds. Those who have reflected most thoughtfully upon the character of the popular theology dealt out to a warm-hearted, half-educated people, singularly docile to the religious teachers of its choice, tell us that stranger forms of error, and more monstrous conceptions of spiritual truth, than Gnosticism ever dreamed may at any time flourish among us.

We have given this account of our author's inquiries into early Gnosticism because they tend to throw light upon the language and method of the apostle, who, we must not forget, lived in the midst and witnessed the activity of these half Jewish, half Christian, half heathen thinkers. His treatment of the great subject tells us more convincingly than the most elaborate *Aids to Faith* that the spirit which filled his thoughts and aided his pen was indeed from God. The Gnostics strove to attain to a higher conception of Christ and his work than the most part of Jewish Christians. So far is the apostle from avoiding the subject as beyond human intelligence, that he begins his narrative with the highest conception possible of Christ. He brings forth such wisdom concerning him as could not but disprove the errors of the Gnostics by the simple statement. He asserts that idea of Christ's appearance which most plainly represented the divine side in him, and which, though long before given, had not been yet sufficiently referred to him. This idea is the Logos, the name which preceded the appearance of Christ, which had served to designate him (Apoc. xix. 13, as also in the book of Enoch), which since Philo's time had engaged the more serious thoughts of men, and which now the apostle most thoroughly and strikingly coupled with his own clear recollection of Christ's actual manifestation. That divine love and truth had first revealed itself in Christ, enlightening every man; that, since his manifestation, this could be applied to every human action and effort; that the same hidden divine love and truth, which was before all worlds and will be the same in all the future, shone forth in him speaking and acting humanly, and so through him spoke and acted for all men,—this is the essential in the idea of the Logos which John refers to Christ; and such a union between the eternal and the temporal, the hidden and the revealed in divine and human things, no conception which had yet been given could so strikingly and plainly express. Further, if the Gnostics conceived Christ to be a mere angel or phantom, the apostle asserts the truth by a statement only intelligible through its opposite, "the Word was made flesh." If in the height of his great argument of the divinity of Christ he seems to abandon the ground of the earthly manifestation, the more strictly does he observe the subtle limits between the divine and human, so that, according to the old true religion, God remains in his purest height.

Whether the partial views and errors of Jewish Christians, or of the disciples of the Baptist, or of the Gnostics prevail, the answer to each and all is found in the Gospel; and it is just in those parts where these opinions are evidently touched upon, that the apostle's recollections are coloured with greater life. The true relation between Christ and the Jews, between him and the Baptist, is established by the historical fact of what it was during his life on earth. The truths which underlie some Gnostic conceptions are asserted; the fatal and corrupting errors of others are corrected. The words of our author in reviewing the position of this Gospel in the first century are true: "This is the writing which, no less on account of the creative power and the historical character of its author than on account of its elevated contents, is the most sublime of the writings of the New Testament."

II. How did the apostle accomplish his great task in respect to the composition and arrangement of his work? He needed a large frame in which to insert not every particular, but the great features of the life of Christ. Chronology supplied this frame; not indeed a chronology of days and years and of every single event, for such a one in a life like that of Christ was needless and impossible. Even St. Mark had not thought this necessary; and since his Gospel was written, the revolution which the overthrow of Jerusalem had brought about rendered many particulars of less importance. Christ's earthly life is the frame of the Gospel, which starts from the mysterious beginning of all history in order to set forth the inseparable connexion between his earthly appearance and his eternal and divine existence before the worlds. That Christ was a Galilean, and spent the greatest part of his public life in Galilee, the apostle states as plainly as the earlier evangelists; but Jerusalem, and not Galilee, was the place where his cause, in its earthly aspect, was finally tried, where the real commencement and the unfolding of his earthly life was to take place. The journeys to and from Jerusalem are therefore the critical times in his life: and north and south are the two poles around which its movement turns. These journeys from north to south are five, differing in some respects from one another (the first did not reach as far as Jerusalem, and the last might be called a double journey), yet similar in their decisive results. These five journeys, mostly depending upon Jewish festivals, supply the chronological data and correspond to the five progressive steps of the history: 1. the beginning of the Gospel movement (i.-ii. 11); 2. the progress of that movement (ii. 12—iv. 54); 3. to the highest point where the first traces of its earthly fall appear (v. f.); 4. the beginning of that fall (vii.-xii.); and 5. the fall itself (xiii.-xx.). These are the five main acts of a tragedy, the most sublime which actual history presents, and which passes over to the most divine victory which is possible. The victory at the close of the history answers to the purely divine character of its beginning. The Gospel contains in its perfect frame this supernatural beginning as well as that supernatural close.

In studying the life of Christ, as it was passed in presence of an opposing world, the wide-reaching questions occur,—What was the work of Christ? in what did it consist? what was its aim? The activity of his earthly life consisted in words and deeds; and as the object of the apostle is to produce the complete image of this activity, he narrates in the Gospel with equal earnestness and equal care both words and deeds. He raised the question, in what relation these two stood to one another. Every word which Christ had spoken had its own inestimable worth, and therefore his dearest wish is to recall all his words (especially such as had been omitted in the previous Gospels) in their mutual connexion. Hence, in this series of Christ's great discourses, we are able to follow the historical development of the main thoughts of his doctrine. The apostle does not bring forward the mere number and variety of Christ's mighty works; these could be read in St. Mark's Gospel; his object is rather to select from them such as were typical. There are seven signs recorded by him, and each one is representative and a work of its own kind: 1. the change of water into wine, ii. 1-10; 2. the fever-cure from a distance, iv. 47-54; 3. the healing of a lame man, v. 1-9; 4. the feeding the multitude with bread, vi. 4-13; 5. the walking on the stormy lake, vi. 16-21; 6. the cure of a blind man, ix. 1-7; 7. the raising-up of one dead, xi. Now, if for the fifth of these signs, which Ewald thinks is less connected with the narrative, we substitute the healing of a demoniac, we have in these seven diverse and wonderful signs of Christ examples of almost every kind of work which he wrought for the removal of human want, misery, and sin. There is seen in them also an inner progress, the raising from the dead being their close and completion. Each one of these works left its own impression upon the spectators, and has its necessary place in the history; but not on that account, and merely as works, do they prove the truth of him who wrought them. Their result is different. They strike the minds and arrest the attention of men more readily than the divinest words and doctrine, and cannot be so easily mistaken or overlooked. This is their great purpose. Christ's works lead necessarily to the inquiry, what it was in him which wrought them, and what he wished to effect; hence indifference to him became impossible. All who came in contact with him could not but either believe or disbelieve, and, in the latter case, deny the truth and the light of his manifest and enlightening works. This is the ground-thought of the relation between

Christ's words and works which the apostle sets forth. His aim is not merely to reproduce a series (and in their true historical place) of Christ's works, what he did and suffered; but much rather to show the effect of these upon men, the belief or unbelief to which they led, the means whereby those who believed came to believe, if not at once through his words yet through his deeds, and the necessary end of unbelief, the denial of the light and truth of those deeds. At the commencement of Ewald's essay on the reproduction of the very words and discourses of Christ in this Gospel, a grave question arises, which to many will seem needless. Those who understand by inspiration "an infallible Intelligence" overpowering the mind of the sacred author, and dictating to him the thoughts and the words to write, will feel no difficulty or interest in the inquiry, how the apostle was enabled to reproduce his Lord's words. It appears to others that this doctrine of inspiration is not in harmony with the ordinary method of divine assistance and interference for the education of men, or one which we should expect *à priori*, or one which the written documents themselves appeal to. We think it to be the more reverent as well as the more rational of the two theories, that the Holy Spirit purified and strengthened, according to the measure of the need, the natural faculties of each writer, whose personality, far from being overlaid, came forth with greater prominence in his work. Now the apostle repeats the words of Christ, not in scattered and fragmentary portions, but as he had repeated his deeds, in the same great *ensemble*. He is the same writer whose careful and accurate memory was evident in the narrative of every incident. And could he, who remembered so well the minute details of each event, and so truly described them, who had stood in closer intimacy with Christ, and loved him more deeply, than any other man, have failed to treasure up in his mind most carefully, most lovingly, the discourses of Christ, or have wanted the strong will to recall the memory of them? This is no mere supposition. The apostle distinguishes clearly between the original statement and the later interpretation given to it, between what Christ had certainly said and men had heard from him, and the later belief concerning it, either because the belief was subsequent (ii. 19-22, xiii. 27 f.), or because the apostle wished to lay greater stress upon the actual words of his beloved Lord (vi. 6, vi. 70 f., vii. 37-39, xii. 33: cf. xviii. 9, 32). This manner is peculiar to the apostle. He introduces with it a kind of literary criticism on some passages of the gospel history with a simplicity and skill which no other could use, and with a marvellous confidence and certainty which only an eye-witness and hearer could feel. Indeed, we are made conscious that every word which he had heard from Christ was sacred to him, and moreover in the very form and manner in which he had heard it; and we have every reason to expect that, in the repetition of the discourses of Christ, he will recollect every word as carefully and accurately as was possible, and, just as in single details he had completed and here and there corrected the earlier Gospels, he will do the same in collecting and restoring the discourses of Christ, in all that pertained to their fulness and richness, and to their colouring and forms of expression. Hence the apostle alone of the evangelists repeats the Amen in the words, "Verily, verily, I say unto you," from his recollection of Christ's custom; he alone recalls the word *ὑψοῦν*, by which Christ had referred to the close of his earthly life (iii. 14, viii. 28, xii. 32-34). He remembers Christ's manner of leading the conversation, and of founding convictions by sudden turns of thought (vi. 51), or by sharp setting of his words (viii. 26 f.); and, again, of inserting parables into the flow of his discourse (xv. 1-10, x. 1-6).

The difficulty is not removed by these traits of the apostle's work, but rather heightened. We know how much more difficult it is to remember discourses and conversations than mere events. And how could the apostle remember so accurately these discourses and conversations, and bring them back to life? The most tenacious memory is unequal to that. We cannot doubt that he read and used the earlier Gospels, and thereby freshened his own memory; but these could not suffice him; the less, as his aim was not to repeat what had already been written, but to compose a larger and living whole. What else remained to him but to attempt, by the use of every help within his reach, as vividly and as perfectly as possible to recall such words and conversations in the passages of the history where they seemed most necessary?

We think Ewald over-estimates the difficulty of reproducing by the ordinary human memory the words and conversations of another. The force of recollection depends rather upon sympathy than upon nearness of time. Words which we heard long ago will lie forgotten till the string is touched which recalls them not only vividly, but with a meaning unknown before. Christ's words had reference to events and circumstances in which the apostle was hereafter to be concerned, and which would be the key to their interpretation. We think this correct from the human side; but he who believes in Christ's promise of the Comforter and his work feels no surprise at the marvellous memory of the beloved disciple. Ewald reminds us of the art which was so much practised by the historians of Greece and Rome, manifest in all their great works,—the art of recalling the words of great men, and important events of the past; and he finds little comparison between the excessive freedom which these ancient writers allowed themselves and the art of the apostle. The apostle had heard Christ's words as also the Baptist's, and the words of the former had stamped themselves indelibly within him. He lived in these words of his Lord as his holiest thoughts. He retained the most perfect recollection of the manner and circumstance with which they had been spoken. He made use, moreover, of the treasure of rich memories which the earlier evangelists gave him. And when he earnestly applied all these aids to reinstate the words of Christ in their majesty, and in nearer connexion and agreement with their original life, he could not but succeed. It is here that Ewald thinks the art of the apostle is dominant, and that without it such reproduction and revivifying of his Master's words would have been impossible.

Nor is it only the reproducing of the very words of the discourses which is so wonderful; the manner in which it is done is no less wonderful. The language of the apostle is outwardly calm and even, clear and penetrating, like that of an old man who is lifted far above the storms and passions of this world, but in whom the fire of his youth is unquenched, and never fails long to burn up with clearer light. The language is for the most part uniform; but where the subject requires a change of style, there it will be found. Hence every greater section of the work has its own appropriate and perfect manner of representation. We can distinguish three such manners in those passages which describe how Christ bore himself in the different circumstances of his life. (*a*) The section iii. 1-21 shows how Christ conversed with the most learned and esteemed man in Israel; the following, iv. 5-12, how he condescended to the most simple and despised of every class, and sought to raise them to his own height. If c. v. informs us how Christ discussed one of the most difficult questions on all its sides, in c. vi. we wonder at the manner in which he maintains a truth which the world would not comprehend against every and the most different kind of objection. But nothing seems comparable to the perfect art with which the large section vii.-x. 39 presents a very varied but most true picture of the public life of the people in Jerusalem as it was when the temple stood; how Christ behaved in the midst of those noisy crowds; of that excitable multitude, with its quickly passing favour and disfavour, in the midst of wily Pharisees, of friends and enemies of every class. Nowhere else can we find so living and so true a picture of the ordinary life of the Jewish people, with all its light and shades, as it was in comparatively quiet and peaceful times. Yet even this great picture falls into the background as soon as the eye opens on one still more wonderful—the last acts and conversations of our Lord with his own (c. xiii.-xvi.). In these sections of the Gospel we learn Christ's conduct towards men, how he maintained his truth against them and for them.

(*b*) The language and manner of representation altogether changes when the apostle, in c. xvii., makes known the language of Christ to God himself. Here there burns forth a glow of discourse than which nothing can be more ardent; and here, too, is given the most perfect pattern of prayer in its sublime inward strength and certainty of victory.

(*c*) On a line with this, and equally claiming our wonder, is the section c. i. 1-18, which, at the beginning of the Gospel, in setting forth the eternal existence of the Word and his advent in the flesh, passes involuntarily as it were into a hymn; just as the history of the creation at the beginning of the Old Testament. This section has been incorrectly called a preface, as though it could be omitted, or formed a less substantive part of the work than other sections. It is indispensable to the Gospel, in respect to the main and secondary aims which its author had in view. Ewald concludes his careful examination of the literary structure and composition of this Gospel with the statement, that the variety, warmth, and energy of its description give to it an ever-fresh grace; and that the work, from the sublimity of its contents, the harmony and connectedness of its parts, the constant, clear, and gentle light shed over all, possesses an indescribable attraction which is found to an equal degree in no other writing of the Old or New Testament.

The Gospel is not only important in itself as a literary work, and from its place in the history of Christianity, but important also as being the work of St. John the beloved disciple, who, although not educated for literature, and accustomed, in spite of the fiery zeal of his spirit, to live a life of retreat and meditation, yet in his old age undertook and accomplished the great task of writing the Gospel. That the apostle John is the author, and that no one else could have composed it but he who has always been considered its author, admits, Ewald boldly affirms, of no reasonable doubt or denial; rather, whichever way we examine the question, every reason and evidence concur in decidedly rejecting such doubt.

It is possible that the many among us who are most nervous at the results of our author's criticisms upon the Old Testament, and by whom, in consequence, he is more than "suspect," will yet not refuse the aid which his studies afford them in regard to the authorship of this Gospel. Indeed, the importance of the question is great. The work stands sufficiently sure to the Christian believer on its own evidence, and *proves* itself true to him; for it speaks to him, in the midst of the toil and weariness, the joys and sorrows of his life, of the unseen Friend and Brother whom he knows and feels to be present. No criticism which should remove this great Gospel of the love of God from the apostolic age, or divest it of the authority of an eye-witness to the facts recorded in it, would destroy the faith which is part of himself. But it were idle to forget that the multitude of earnest inquirers ask anxiously for an historical basis of evidence, and are not satisfied that the work is true because devout believers affirm that they know it to be true. The Gospel literature belongs to the domain of ancient literature; all are interested that its right place should be, on the surest grounds, assigned to it; many of us are more than interested that the place for ages assigned to it in the Christian church should not be taken away.

If we did not know the name of the author of the Gospel, we could not doubt that he was one of the twelve. He clearly designates himself as such; and throughout the work the historical spirit (taken in its best and simplest meaning) is so manifest, every assertion is made with the confidence and certainty which history alone can give, that it is impossible not to believe the author when he intimates that he is one of the twelve. This confidence runs through the work. The author can relate all that he thinks necessary, because he knows that he will be believed. Hence it is that no one who has been accustomed to distinguish between books of simple true narrative and books of a different character, can hesitate in regarding the author of this Gospel as a man who tells the whole truth, because he had been himself an eye-witness, and because, from a perfect knowledge of the facts, he was in a position to tell the truth. Now, in the late period when the book was written, no other of the twelve survived who could have written it but John.

Again, in the artistic arrangement and execution of the work, the author proves himself a genuine Hebrew historian. His Greek wears all the marks of a Hebrew who had been born and brought up among Jews in the Holy Land, who had been unaccustomed to speak Greek, and who in the Greek dress, which late in life he learnt to put on, never laid aside the spirit of his mother-tongue, or ceased to be guided by it. His Greek, indeed, is less strongly coloured with Hebrew than that of the older Gospels; rather it has adopted much of the genuine Greek manner. But in its life and breath no language can be more really Hebraic than that of this author. And only the age, the character, the personality of the disciple John can account for such a language. It cannot be explained as a composition from different materials, or as an imitation of Old-Testament and Hebrew phraseology, still less as having been formed within the Christian congregation after the death of the long-lived and most aged apostle. Indeed, the language is as thoroughly original and single in its kind as the apostle himself in his life and work. He knows that he is writing for Greek, *i.e.* educated Roman citizens, whether Jewish or Christian, but he does not care artistically to imitate pure Greek; and although he was completely separated from the Jews of that time, he does not hide his own intimate acquaintance with their language. He gives *e.g.* the genuine Hebrew names which were unused in Greek (the name *Μεσσίας*, i. 42, iv. 25; *Κηφᾶς*, i. 45; *Βηθεσδά*, v. 2), or the Greek interpretation of such Hebrew proper names as were used in Greek books (as i. 38, 42, ix. 7, xix. 13, 17, 20: cf. xxi. 2). It is not unimportant that all these Hebrew interpretations are correct; whereas soon after the apostle's death all knowledge of the kind was lost among Christians. It is remarkable also that St. Luke, who, as Ewald thinks, wrote nearly at the same time as the apostle, avoided all such Hebraisms.

Again, if we compare ancient books which were written under foreign names with this Gospel, we find that there is no similarity between them. Ordinarily, such books were written under the name of some celebrated deceased writer or saint. This Gospel, on the hypothesis of its not being the work of St. John, would be written under the name of an apostle who still lived, who had never before composed a work, and who, as far as his activity in the world went, was not to be compared with Peter or Paul, or even with James. Moreover, such books had a particular object in view, for the sake of which some great name was used, so that it is not difficult to discover why that name was chosen under the shadow of which they sought to attain their object; whereas this Gospel would be ascribed to the name of an apostle, to whom (if he be not the author of the four works) there would be no reason why they should be ascribed, since in the earlier Gospels, in the Epistles of St. Paul, in the Acts of the Apostles, John nowhere appears so prominent as Peter. Again, such books bear on their title-page the names of those to whom they are imputed, and artistically conform to that character, in order to gain credence as being what they wish to be thought; now this Gospel bears no such marks upon it, does not once name its author, so that no reader would suppose it to be the apostle's if he did not on other grounds know it to be his. Again, such books imitate the language and standing of the men whose they are said to be, and are forced to submit to this severe artistic rule; now in this Gospel there is no imitation of any work, not even of the Apocalypse; it is, on the contrary, as natural and as original as possible. All the later fame of St. John (apart from the Apocalypse, which was afterwards ascribed to him) refers back to, and agrees with the spirit of, the Gospel and the first Epistle; indeed, if any genuine writings have ever been published to the world free from the least suspicion of spuriousness, they are the Gospel and the first Epistle of St. John. This is Ewald's conclusion as to the authorship of this portion of the Johannine writings. He states and satisfactorily answers the question, whether the apostle wrote the Gospel in its present form quite alone or with the aid of friends. The fact that St. John and the rest of the twelve (the single exception of Matthew does not come into consideration) were not during Christ's earthly life literati provokes the question. Many remarkable phenomena in the book itself invite us to consider it.

Some readers in our time are inclined to think that if the apostle had been an eye-witness, and had taken part in the history, he would have declared himself plainly and openly as the author of it. It is partly from this supposition that doubts as to the authorship have arisen. But the very omission complained of is just what we ought to expect, and could not be otherwise: that it appears surprising, is owing to ignorance and mistake. For the Apostle, in this like the other evangelists, adheres to the old Hebrew custom of publishing historical works purely for themselves, and without mention of authorship. This custom had been interrupted by the influences of Persian and Hellenistic culture; at no time could it be more fittingly revived than in the literature of the Gospels. If ever, indeed, a writer should be silent, and that willingly, in presence of his subject, surely it would be here in presence of the most sublime and unparalleled subject which had entered the domain of history, which lived still fresh in the memories of the faithful, and called out their reverence all the more deeply in proportion as the world was insensible to it. Of these faithful, even of the twelve, not one would gaze upon him with deeper reverence than John his beloved disciple; not one would feel more deeply his own nothingness in his sight than he who had long served him in retirement and meditation, rather than in conflict with the world, and in the circle of a few trusted friends rather than in public life. Had there been no other causes which exercised their own decided influence upon the outward form and execution of the work, the reasons just given would suffice to explain why John did not name himself as author of it. According to an ancient tradition,* it was late at Ephesus, and only on the advice and at the request of near friends, that the apostle composed the Gospel. The tradition agrees so plainly with all other traits, that we undoubtedly read in it the fragment of an historical truth. If we compare it with what we know of the apostle, and learn about him in the Gospel, we may well believe, in the darkness in which we are, that it was to the wishes of his friends that the apostle yielded, and that he made use of their help.† Those who learned Greek late in life availed themselves of the aid of the learned in that language. St. John had made Greek his own since his youth, and we cannot doubt had already formed his peculiar Greek style; yet in his old age he would be less able to dispense with the aid of literary friends, as he had been less practised in literary composition in his early life. There was no lack of younger friends in the large congregation at Ephesus who could assist him. Again, the style of his sentences bears all the marks of having been dictated to one or more writers. They are briefly expressed, and not unfrequently correct, repeat, and complete one another (iii. 22-24, iv. 1-3, or iv. 43-45, are instances). This is just the style of one who dictates to another his words, thoughts, and assertions, and very different from that of St. Paul, who sketched his thoughts in writing, and left them to be clearly written out by a good penman. And if this be so, it is easy to suppose that the friends, maybe presbyters of the church in Ephesus, whose help the apostle used, might in one or two passages come forth, and from their own point of view assert what they had to say better than the apostle. And if this according to unmistakable signs actually happened, it furnishes a proof of the correctness of this view of the literary composition of the Gospel.‡

We are thus enabled to understand the relation of the apostle to his work. He did not wish to name himself as its author, either in the beginning or the end or the course of his Gospel. He used no opportunity of speaking of himself and of his relation to Christ and the rest of the twelve; and this is just what we should expect from the tenderness and elevation of his mind. His own name does not pass his lips; the more easily can he designate the Baptist (differing in this from the other evangelists) plainly as John. And yet there were passages in which it was unavoidable that he should speak of himself; to

* Euseb. Hist. Eccles. vi. 14. Ἰωάννην . . . . προτραπέντα ὑπὸ τῶν γνωρίμων πνεύματι θεοφορηθέντα, πνευματικὸν ποιῆσαι εὐαγγέλιον.

† Compare the case of Josephus κατὰ Ἀπίωνος, i. 9: χρησάμενός τισι πρὸς τὴν Ἑλληνίδα φωνὴν συνεργοῖς.

‡ Ewald thinks that in the work itself there is only one such passage, c. xix. 35, which cannot be otherwise understood. At the close of the appendix, xxi. 24 f., is another; so that these two passages explain one another.

have refrained from doing so would have been false modesty. His memory could not but dwell on that Day, and on the bond of love between himself, Christ, and his mother; and how could he refrain from speaking of it? With the gentlest hint at the beginning of his work (i. 35-41) did he allude to himself and his brother; such a hint as only attentive and sympathising readers would understand; and now at the close of Christ's earthly life, when the relation of love between them was perfected, and had been manifested by two most memorable tokens, he designates himself as "the disciple whom Jesus loved" (xiii. 23, xix. 26 f., repeated in the appendix, xxi. 7, 20), or, where he has to name himself together with Peter, as the "other disciple" (xviii. 15, xx. 2-9). Once, where his attestation had to be recorded to something quite special as having been seen by him, he does not bring forth his own witness, but the friends who were ever at his side and guided the pen for him report his attestation to the truth of what had been written (xix. 35). This is the only passage where the friend's hand who helped him plainly appears.

Ewald thinks that the Gospel was not designed for immediate publication, but only for the use of a few friends, and that the apostle rather intended it as a legacy of his love to be published after his death. His views and the grounds of them are as follow. That the book closed with c. xx. is inferred from the words xx. 31, and xix. 35. The words are plainly spoken to trusted readers whom the apostle knows, and who know him, and for whom, and not for others, he writes. A more certain proof is found in c. xxi. This appendix was clearly added some time later. For though the language rings with the voice of the aged apostle, and though the same hands which helped the apostle before appear again, yet there is a sufficient change from the earlier language to show that some time elapsed before the chapter was added;* and while the same hands appear, there are signs that they move more freely than in the book itself. (The designation of the apostle in xxi. 20 betrays this. There is a perceptible difference between this and similar passages in the book.)

If we consider the aim and meaning of the appendix, we come to the same conclusion. It was evidently written to correct the false opinion which had spread among Christians on account of the unusually long life of the apostle. The right time to do this was before the apostle's death; and hence the apostle

* *φανεροῦν* is twice used with a meaning which in the book itself (and where also the subject is the same) is expressed by other words, xiv. 21 f., and the whole of c. xx. This difference is more striking because c. xxi. 1 follows c. xx.; and had that passage been written immediately after, the same word would certainly have been repeated.

so far deviated from his original intention that he allowed the Gospel to be published in his own lifetime.

This Gospel won its way to universal acceptance because of its own priceless worth; and because the one mind of Christendom was sound and vigorous enough, in spite of inner controversies, to recognise it as the work of the apostle,—as the most sublime work of evangelical literature. The objections which have been raised in our time are founded on the fact that it was less often quoted in the second century than the earlier Gospels, and that some time elapsed before it took its place beside them. This fact becomes intelligible when we remember that it was at first designed rather for the apostle's friends and disciples, for the inner circle of Christian believers advanced in true Christian gnosis and culture, than for common use. Indeed, the difference between this and the earlier Gospels is not to be explained away; it is a difference which may be little felt by us who have received them together in one volume, and who have been always accustomed to read them as parts of one book; but the difference must have been felt by those who read it for the first time. And this is one cause why the Gospel was less quoted; though it would be an insufficient explanation if there were no traces of it in the literature of the second century. Happily the more carefully the writings of that period are studied, especially those which have come to light within the last twenty years, the more numerous and undeniable are the traces of this Gospel found in them.* Epiphanius took the trouble to refute the objections of those who set it aside on account of the misuse which the Montanists made of it. But there was no question of the authorship; the controversy did not in the least turn upon that issue. Antiquity never doubted that St. John the apostle wrote the work; modern writers of the Tübingen school initiated the doubt which their own able countryman and critic, after a searching inquiry, pronounces to be both unscientific and groundless.

Besides universal tradition, internal evidence proves that the Epistle is the apostle's. The language wears the same colour; here and there a word is found which was not used in the Gospel, or which has received a new shade of meaning, but not more so than the subject-matter would lead us to expect. The difference of language is not greater than that between the original Gospel and the appendix, c. xxi. The same Hebrew breath has passed over the Greek of the Epistle as over the Gospel, and indeed over all the writings of the New Testament which are of Palestinian origin. The spirit of the writer in the

* Ewald refers to the clear references to St. John in the earlier Gnostics, quoted by Hippolytus c. Hæreses.

arrangement of the whole and the subdivision of the parts, in the very words and images, in the main thoughts and intuitions of the Epistle, is the same. We recognise the handwriting, but no copy or imitation. The writer's character is the same. As in the Gospel he stands back hidden beneath the greatness of his theme, so in the Epistle he is reticent of himself; although he is no longer the calm historian, but a letter-writer, the mentor, teacher, apostle, the one surviving apostle to the Christian church, he upholds no statement by the mere weight of personal authority. There is throughout the same calmness and confidence, the same holy and elevated mind, as in the Gospel. And though he will not bend his readers to his words by command, or by the weight of his name, we never forget who he is; we feel that no other could so write; nor, when the subject requires it, does he conceal from us that he had once stood as near to Christ as possible, or refrain from telling us his own experience then, with a naturalness and sincerity which leave no room for doubting that the writer of the Epistle is the same as the writer of the Gospel,—St. John the apostle.

The immediate cause of its being written must be sought in the Epistle itself. Christendom was tried less by persecutions from without than by false teachers within. What the special errors were, and the date of the Epistle, are less easy to determine, because it contains no reference to the state of the contemporary world, and no systematic exposition of the errors themselves. "This is he that came by water and blood, Jesus Christ; not by water only, but by water and blood" (v. 6), plainly alludes to the opinions of the Baptist's disciples; but it is the single passage of the kind. The danger, therefore, was not from that quarter. It came rather from those who taught within the church those Gnostic theories which have been already mentioned, and of which the ground-thought was, that Christ was merely an apparition, and something more than an angel (a philosophically embellished theory to avoid the scandal of the cross): and the same notions concerning unrestricted Christian freedom and the consequent sinlessness of Christian men. These men—the troublers of Christendom—had come into the apostle's near neighbourhood. No wonder that out of zeal to maintain Christian truth, to overthrow error, to save all who would be saved, to assert afresh the teaching of the Gospel, the voice of the aged man was raised. The language is that of a calm and elevated spirit which has experienced the highest spiritual blessing of which men are capable on earth, uttered with a simplicity and naturalness than which nothing can be more sublime. It is clear and brief without the least ornament and effort: intimating what has to be said rather than describing it; and indicating the advanced age of the writer. It must not, however, be forgotten that there is a strict sequence of thought; that nothing is said too much or out of place.

The Epistle addresses itself to the inner wants of Christendom, and refers to no outward persecutions. In this it is like the Epistles of Jude, 2d Peter, 2d and 3d John; and it differs from the Epistles of James, 1st Peter, and Hebrews. With the destruction of Jerusalem and the complete overthrow of the Jewish nation, the heaviest persecution of Christians had passed away, and the rest which followed allowed of the freer growth of errors within the church. Hence we shall not widely err if we place the Epistle about A.D. 90, under Domitian, and ten years later than the Gospel.

The evidence that the apostle is the author of the two shorter Epistles is similar to that which proves him the author of the longer. The circumstances which called them forth have passed away, and yet do those Epistles remain of lasting interest, as explanatory of the position of the apostle towards single churches and individuals, and of his manner of addressing them. Every word, every thought, every turn of expression, point back to the apostle as their author. In one respect they have a special historical interest. They show that though Christians were enjoying comparative rest, yet that a thousand dangers were near, and that extreme caution was necessary. The language is allusive rather than direct. The Epistle to Gaius avoids the name of Christ: Christianity is called "the Truth;" Christ himself "the Name;" and in the second Epistle the church is designated by the title, only intelligible to the faithful, of the "Elect Sister."

Here we close our *résumé* of Ewald's valuable introduction to the Johannine writings. We have purposely omitted any comparison of his views, with those of other writers, because these last can be found in the prolegomena of late commentaries, and Ewald's will long (we fear) be inaccessible to the English reader. Whatever may be our opinions of his views, whether we consider him rash or needlessly conservative, there can be no question that he is most suggestive and helpful. And those who are indifferent to analysis of style and language, or to inquiry into the prevailing thoughts of the apostle's time which may have affected the apostle's language—who are only anxious to know the mind of their Lord, and to read the very words of Christ, written down by the beloved disciple—can be told that the critic who is most rarely gifted to appreciate every work of ancient, and especially of Hebrew, literature comes from the study of St. John with no less wonder and reverence than the simple-minded and devout.

Art. VII.—ACCLIMATIZATION AND PRESERVATION OF ANIMALS.

Catalogue of the Menagerie and Aviary at Knowsley formed by the late Earl of Derby, K.G., P.Z.S. Liverpool, August 1851.

List of Vertebrated Animals living in the Gardens of the Zoological Society of London. London, 1862.

Bulletin de la Société Impériale Zoologique d'Acclimatation. Tomes I-VIII. Paris, 1854-1861.

Jaarboekje van het Koninklijk Zoologisch Genootschap "Natura Artis Magistra." Amsterdam, 1860.

Der Zoologische Garten. Organ der Zoologischen Gesellschaft in Frankfurt am Main. Frankfurt am Main, 1860.

First, Second, and Third Annual Reports of the Society for the Acclimatisation of Animals, Birds, Fishes, Insects, and Vegetables within the United Kingdom. London, 1860-63.

First Annual Report of the Acclimatisation Society of Victoria. Melbourne, 1862.

Journal of the Royal Agricultural Society of England. Vol. XXIII. Article on "Destructive Insects, and the immense Utility of Birds." By Frederic de Tschudi. London, 1862.

As generally accepted, the term 'acclimatization' means the colonization of one country by the natural products—be they animal or vegetable—of another, with the view of rendering them subservient to the purposes, whether necessary or luxurious, of mankind. Acclimatization may therefore be justly considered the utilized application of the sciences of zoology and botany; and it follows almost as a natural consequence that what is to be learned from their study cannot be safely disregarded by those who wish to advance its objects and realize the expectations it holds out.

Bennet Langton tells us, that when Goldsmith announced his intention of going to Jericho, Aleppo, or some place still further in the direction from which the wise men came, Johnson exclaimed, "Sir, he would bring home a grinding-barrow, and think he had furnished a wonderful improvement." It seems to us that some of the advocates of the various schemes for acclimatization might take the hint which this anecdote conveys. Bacon, in a passage which has been often quoted, speaks of "tryall places of beastes and birdes" among the institutions of the New Atlantis, considering the experience to be derived from them as a necessary means of complying with the ancient behest to mankind, to "replenish the earth and subdue it." And, indeed, a very small amount of reflection will show that acclimatization entails on the part of its promoters some knowledge of natural history. To take some extreme cases: it would be manifestly absurd to attempt the introduction of the musk-ox to the plains of India, or the camel to the tundras of Siberia; of the Scotch-fir to the llanos of South America, or the bread-fruit to our English forests. The definition we have above given of the term also limits its application to those species which are really of service to man, either directly as affording him food, clothing, and the like, or indirectly, by assisting him in obtaining these benefits from other species. It could, therefore, scarcely with consistency be said to comprehend the naturalization of the fox in Australia, even for purposes of sport, still less that of the tiger in the forests of Europe, or the nettle in the West-Indian sugar-islands; though all these may have their proper functions to perform in the countries of their birth. Further, acclimatization is not limited to those species only which seem to be capable of complete domestication, any more than it could be correctly extended to those which are induced to thrive and propagate their kind in an undoubtedly artificial mode of life. It is a sort of probationary process, which may possibly result in actual domestication, but more probably in the introduction of certain exotic species into a country, which, after a period of modified reclamation, will become as it were *feræ naturâ*, share with its original inhabitants the same risks to which they are exposed, and yet finally increase and multiply without the immediate protection of man.

As our present object is to assist, if possible, the labours of acclimatizers, we think it advisable, before proceeding further, to consider our present position as regards the kinds of animals which have already been more or less subdued.

Easy as it might at first sight appear, it is in reality rather the reverse to enumerate with accuracy the different races which have been domesticated by man in one part of the world or another, even without taking account of the many isolated cases on record wherein certain individuals have been wholly reclaimed, but have not perpetuated a domesticated breed. We shall find, on looking into the subject more closely, so many different degrees of mansuetude, that it is difficult to draw the line between those species which seem to have succumbed to the influence of domestication, and those of which the conquest has not been entirely effected. Some there are known to us only as the obedient slaves of mankind: either the wild races from which they have sprung have been entirely extirpated, or else it is now impossible for us to trace from what source they have been derived. These, of course, comprise some of the animals whose reduction to servitude is the most complete, and probably of the oldest standing. We need not dwell on the remote antiquity of the Arabian camel's domestication, for that is every where admitted. The pictured walls of Egyptian tombs and temples show us that the tame geese of the time of the Pharaohs were subject to the same variations in plumage,—evidence of a long period of antecedent domesticity,—as the unhappy captives of Alsace who at the present day furnish the immortal *pâtés de foie gras,* or as their less cruelly used English brethren who are yearly offered at the shrine of St. Michael. We find bones of the dog in the oldest Danish "kitchen-middens," those interesting monuments of a period when probably the most civilized inhabitants of Europe were not more advanced than the present limpet-eating savages of Tierra del Fuego. The curious relics of the ancient "pile-buildings" of Switzerland reveal the fact that the dog, sheep, goat, ox, hog, ass, and horse were domesticated by their builders; and even at one place, though belonging to a later epoch, a single bone of the barn-door fowl has been recognized.* The vast remoteness of the periods at which the subjection of these animals took place prevents our even conjecturing the process by which it was brought about; and we are consequently unable to test the truth of the supposition, very strongly advanced by many naturalists, from Pallas to Professor Agassiz, that, probably in several instances, more than one wild species has contributed to the formation of our modern breeds; or, in other words, that these may be the result of a cross between two or more original species; and this adds to the difficulty of enumerating the latter accurately. But the following lists seem to be as comprehensive, with regard to the two highest classes of animals, as, in our opinion, any correct meaning of the term 'domestication' will permit:

BEASTS.

Dog.	Reindeer.	Hog.
Cat.	Sheep.	Ass.
Ferret.	Goat.	Horse.
Alpaca.	Yak.	Indian elephant.
Llama.	Ox.	Guinea-pig.
Arabian camel.	Buffalo.	Rabbit.
Bactrian camel.		

* In the summer of 1856, a friend of ours found a bone of this bird in an ancient burial-place in the island of Œland, in the Baltic; but we are not able to state what age may be, even approximately, assigned to it.

BIRDS.

Canary-finch.	Guinea fowl.	Chinese goose.
Rock-dove.	Peacock.	Mute swan.
Barbary turtle-dove.	Barn-door fowl.	Tame duck.
Mexican turkey.	Tame goose.	Muscovy duck.

We must confess that some objection may be not unnaturally taken to the exclusion from the above catalogue of several other names. For instance, the grounds on which the zebu (the humped ox of India and parts of Africa) is believed by some to be of totally distinct origin from the common ox, are very different in their nature from the considerations which tend to the persuasion that this last is compounded of more than one specific element. Indeed, were it not that we are acquainted with the wild originals of the common and the Chinese geese,—while we are left to guess at the primitive sources of the common ox and the zebu,—the two cases would be almost exactly parallel. By far the greatest number of investigators declare in favour of the belief that two, if not three, species of wild ox have combined to form our domesticated breeds of cattle; and all are agreed that the cross between these and the zebu is a perfectly fertile one. The late Mr. Yarrell, in his invaluable and well-known work on British Birds, stated his reasons—and very good reasons they are—for thinking "that one other species at least" besides the grey goose "has had some share in establishing our domestic race;" while it appears from what Mr. Blyth—confessedly the highest authority on Indian, or, perhaps we may say, even Asiatic zoology—says that though a thorough-bred goose may not be exactly a rarity in Hindostan, yet that in various parts of the country whole flocks of hybrids between the common and the Chinese species are profitably kept.

Furthermore, to the above lists might almost be added, among beasts, the cheetah, or hunting leopard, and the otter; and among birds, all the species which are used in falconry,—probably not less than a dozen in number,—as well as the cormorants of Europe and China, which, especially the latter, have constantly been thoroughly reclaimed and employed in taking fish; but we do not know of any instances of their breeding in a domesticated state (though it is very possible that, were due facilities granted them, they would do so); we therefore deem it advisable to omit them.

Of reptiles, not one species has suffered domestication; and of fishes, as far as known, only the golden carp. Among the articulata, there are several kinds of silk-worm,—of which we shall have more to say presently,—two species of honey-bee, and the cochineal insect. Lower in the scale we do not propose to descend.

Now as regards animals which may be said to have undergone acclimatization as distinguished from domestication, it would be utterly impossible to furnish full lists, for the materials to form them do not yet exist. Even if we were to search through the whole range of zoological literature, the extent of which few but the initiated are aware of, we could not do more than hope to arrive at an approximation; while how near such an approximation would be to the truth, we should, at the end of our task, have no means of ascertaining. Here we will only venture upon safe ground, and mention the species of vertebrates the acclimatization of which in the British Islands may, we think, be looked on as well established. They are the following:

Wapiti.
Fallow-deer.
Eland.
Silver pheasant.
Golden pheasant.
Ring-necked pheasant.
Colchican pheasant.
Japan pheasant.
Capercally.
French partridge.
Californian quail.
Wood-duck.
Canada goose.
Egyptian goose.
Edible frog.
Common carp.
Crucian carp.

We particularly wish, however, to guard any of our readers from supposing we give the above list as infallible. It is a mere matter of opinion almost whether it might not be twice as large. Among birds alone there are some five species of Indian pheasants, and as many of the duck tribe, which have almost as much right to be included in it. Our principal reason for excluding them is, that their introduction to this country is of comparatively recent date; and though there is little doubt of their succeeding, it yet remains to be proved whether they will eventually establish themselves here. Man has nearly done his part in their naturalization, and it will soon rest with themselves alone. Some of our readers may object that we have not also included the Virginian as well as the Californian quail. The former bird had a place in the British fauna assigned to it by the late Mr. Yarrell; but it is indubitable that he did so prematurely, and that the numerous examples which have been liberated in this country have, from some cause or other, failed to maintain their position. Again, others may urge that we have improperly reckoned the edible frog, seeing that Professor Bell gives it rank as an undoubted native; but having equal regard to his high authority and to the circumstances of the case, we consider that the scruples entertained by the late Mr. John Wolley, and the reasons which he brought forward against the Professor's view,* justify us in our opinion.

* See *The Zoologist* for 1859, p. 6606.

It may be asked, too, on the strength of the old doggerel,—

> "Hoppes and turkies, carpes, pickerel and bere
> Came into England alle in one yeare,"—

why we have excluded the pike from among the introduced fishes. To this we have to say, that the British Museum and other collections contain undeniable bones of this species from the peat of the eastern counties; and we see no reason to suppose that, as in the case of the capercally, our native race has ever become extinct and been restored.

But it is now time to have done for the present with the acclimatized, and to say a few words of the acclimatizers.

The early prosecutors of maritime research, the Spaniards and Portuguese, seem to have soon commenced the practice of stocking their new discoveries with domestic animals, especially in the case of oceanic islands, which they almost invariably found deficient in products supplying fresh meat, that great want of ancient mariners. This was done no doubt with the triple motive of adding to the value of the new countries as places of call for future explorers, of creating natural storehouses, as it were, for the expedition to fall back upon in cases of difficulty, and also of affording a means of subsistence to cast-away sailors. Their prudent example was soon followed by the English, the Dutch, and indeed by all nations who occupied their business on the great waters; and the benefits thus provided have been reaped by many a distressed seafarer besides our childhood's favourite, Mr. Robinson Crusoe. Hogs, goats, and cats were the beasts chiefly used in planting these colonies; of course because they were the species most easily kept on board the confined and inconvenient ships of that period. But presently larger animals were tried; and the Cape of Good Hope, the Falkland Islands, and the vast continent of South America, owe to these pristine navigators the innumerable herds of horned cattle and horses which nowadays form such an abundant source of their wealth. The practice was continued long after the dominion of the seas had fallen out of the hands of the natives of the European peninsula; and on Cook's voyages useful animals of one sort or another were left at nearly all the places visited, where the chance of their thriving seemed a good one.* The French navigators appear to have been much more

* Though not a case of attempted animal acclimatization, we may perhaps be excused for here reminding our readers that the celebrated voyage of the *Bounty* was undertaken for the express purpose of introducing the bread-fruit tree to the West-Indian Archipelago. Captain Bligh had the satisfaction of at last succeeding in landing a cargo of healthy plants at St. Vincent and Jamaica in 1793. The most sanguine anticipations of the benefits to be derived from it were indulged in, but they can scarcely be said to have been at all realized.

far-seeing; for they by no means confined themselves to stocking their settlements with the most obviously useful animals, but they were fond of introducing any thing they could lay their hands upon, and some even of very questionable utility. Indeed, the success which has, even to the present day, attended their efforts in this respect, entitles the *grande nation* to be regarded as the great acclimatizing—just as England is the great colonizing—power of the earth.

However, among those who have done most for acclimatization, we must award the palm to a fellow-countrymen. Not one can be ranked, in our opinion, higher than the late Earl of Derby. To most persons, no doubt, the extraordinary menagerie which he formed at Knowsley seemed to be but the hobby of a man who spent an enormous rent-roll in this manner rather than on the turf or in electioneering. Few were surprised that his successor, the present leader of "Her Majesty's Opposition," declined the maintenance of such a costly and apparently unprofitable establishment. But we believe the motive which prompted its founder, was far from being the mere indulgence of a whim. Lord Derby really intended to benefit his fellow-men by applying his own natural taste for, and knowledge of, zoology to the reclaiming of new species that might be useful to them. For more than a quarter of a century he worked on with this object in view; but even with his princely fortune to aid him the progress was slow. A few years longer would have seen important results follow: experiment would have produced its usual consequences; theory would have been reduced to practice. He had already succeeded in breeding the eland in confinement—probably of all wild quadrupeds the one that could be most advantageously domesticated—when death put an end to his aspirations. Unfortunately, of the experience he had so dearly bought, nearly all perished with him. The services of his head-keeper, who was supposed to embody all that hardly acquired knowledge, were secured by the Zoological Society of London; but scarce a recorded observation remains to furnish a guide for those who would follow in his footsteps. By his will he empowered the same Society, of which he was the president, to choose from his menagerie some one group of animals as a bequest, and they wisely selected the newly-founded herd of elands; but all the rest of the collection, brought together with so much trouble, and at an expense so great, was sent to the hammer and dispersed. First in the list of works which head this article we have placed the catalogue drawn up for the sale; it is the most complete, we might say the only, permanent memorial of the magnitude of this wonderful repository of living beings, the extent of which is shown by the summary which we here extract from its last page:

	Species.	Individuals.	Of which are Knowsley-bred.	
			Species.	Individuals.
Total number of MAMMALIA . . .	94	345	39	207
Total number of BIRDS, exclusive of POULTRY	318	1272	45	549
Total . .	412	1617	84	756

Of the labours of other private persons in this country or abroad, though some are undeniably great, we do not feel called upon to say much here. The late Marquis of Breadalbane is understood to have attained a fair share of success in acclimatizing several likely species, but we are not acquainted with the particular cases. Certainly it is to him we chiefly owe the successful re-introduction of our extinct race of capercailzies. The exact date when this noble bird ceased to exist in the British islands is not quite clear. Pennant says that a few were still found about 1760 in Ireland, around Thomastown, county of Tipperary; he also adds that he saw a male bird at Inverness which had been killed in the Chisholm's country; and his *Tour in Scotland* was published in 1769. We do not know that a single indigenous specimen has been preserved in any of our numerous collections.*

About five-and-thirty years ago Lord Fyfe tried to restore this grand species to its former home in the forests of Braemar, but nothing seems to have come of his endeavours. Some ten years afterwards the Duchess of Athol renewed the attempt at Blair; and almost at the same time Lord Breadalbane, through the intervention of Sir T. Fowell Buxton and Mr. Ll. Lloyd, the well-known Scandinavian sportsman, imported from Sweden a large number of capercally, which were subsequently libe-

* In the Catalogue of British Birds in the British Museum, published in 1850 by Mr. G. R. Gray, we find a hen-bird entered with the remark, "Scotland: from Col. Montagu's collection." We imagine this statement to be erroneous; at least, the careful naturalist last mentioned makes no allusion to such a specimen in his *Ornithological Dictionary*, published in 1813; while he specifies his having received birds from Norway in a manner which leads us to suppose that they were the only ones he ever examined. Mr. G. T. Fox, in the *Synopsis of the Newcastle Museum*, asserts (p. 78) that the example in the National Collection was formerly in Mr. Bullock's Museum: this we think possible; but if so, the probability of its having been obtained in Scotland is thereby diminished. The same author says he is unable to make out if the specimen from Mr. Tunstall's cabinet, now preserved at Newcastle-on-Tyne, was really of British capture.

rated at Taymouth, where they have thriven so well, that now we are told all the old woods in the neighbourhood are full of them. They have also thence been disseminated throughout many other forests,—to Dunkeld, Blair-Athol, and Balmoral,—meeting with encouragement from all the proprietors, and from no one more than the late Prince Consort. We are also informed that Lord Orkney has more recently tried them in Ayrshire, with a good prospect of success; but, in Ireland, Lord Bantry has failed at Glengariff. However, it is not only as having brought about the restoration of the ancient monarch of British game-birds that Lord Breadalbane's memory will ever be grateful to the lovers of zoology, whether pure or applied; his efforts for the protection of the very king of birds itself demand equal praise. On his unrivalled deer-forest of Black Mount, the eagles—elsewhere persecuted to the death—were ordered to be unmolested, so long as they were not numerous enough to cause considerable depredations on the farmers' flocks. He thought, and all who have an eye for the harmonies of nature must agree with him, that the spectacle of a soaring eagle was a fitting adjunct to the grandeur of his Argyllshire mountain scenery, and a good equivalent for the occasional loss of a lamb, or the slight deduction of the rent paid by his tenantry in consequence. Those who remember in the International Exhibition last year Sir Edwin's glorious picture of "The Defeat," —the scene of which was laid in the Breadalbane principality,—know the effect of this feature in a Highland landscape. Whichever of the claimants may be "served heir" to those magnificent estates, we can only hope that the future lord of Taymouth and Mona-Dhu will not be forgetful of his predecessor's partialities.

From the very small number of animals that have been acclimatized in this or other countries as compared with that of plants, it may be rightly inferred that the former operation requires far greater resources than the latter. Indeed, the introduction and naturalization of exotic trees, shrubs, and flowers, has long been a regular trade, and in England has been carried on with much intelligence, and a corresponding degree of success, by a large number of professional persons. But it is otherwise with the acclimatization of animals. This is a business entailing a large expenditure of money, not only as capital at the outset, but continued throughout the whole process. Except, therefore, in the case of those who are blessed with a superabundance of worldly wealth, its advancement can hardly be expected from the efforts of private individuals; and hence we look mainly to the various associations now established in different parts of the globe for the future progress that can be made in the undertaking.

The oldest of these associations is the Zoological Society of London. The intention of its founder, Sir Thomas Stamford Raffles,—that great man whose early death was one of the severest blows ever dealt to England's colonial empire,—and his colleagues, was not more the exhibition of all that is rare and interesting from a purely zoological point of view, than that useful application of zoology which has since received the name of acclimatization. We have now before us a copy of a "Prospectus of a Society for introducing and domesticating new breeds or varieties of animals, such as quadrupeds, birds, and fishes *likely to be useful in common life*, and for forming a general collection in zoology."* The result of this paper was the establishment of the now flourishing body which has its chief seat on the banks of the Regent's Canal; and in the Society's charter of incorporation, granted in the last year of King George IV., its objects are declared to be "the advancement of zoology and animal physiology, and the *introduction of new and curious subjects of the animal kingdom*" to this country. Nor has the Society been unmindful of its original aim, though in the course of its chequered career the scientific may, on the whole, have prevailed over the utilitarian element. When the Knowsley menagerie was broken up, the Society's finances (thanks to the attractiveness of our old friend Hippo, and the full London season of the Great Exhibition year), were most prosperous, and large and important purchases were made from Lord Derby's collection, most of the animals which formed these additions being selected expressly with regard to their capabilities for naturalization. Passing over here the more important publications of the Zoological Society, notwithstanding the splendid scale on which they are conducted, the modest little pamphlet, whose title stands second in our list, shows a good amount of solid work done in the way of acclimatization. At the time the "List of Living Vertebrated Animals" was printed—namely, May 1862—the society possessed examples of no less than thirty-three species of beasts and thirty-nine of birds bred in their gardens, and in some cases a very large series of examples. We know besides that this bede-roll, long as it is, does not contain a record of all the Society's exploits in this branch of their duties. No small number of other species have been propagated in the Zoological Gardens; but the breeds have subsequently been lost, owing to various unfavourable causes, chief among which must be set down the insalubrity of the locality (now in some measure lessened by improved drainage), and the want of space—in acclimatization perhaps the most necessary requirement of all;—to

* Reprinted in the *Zoological Journal*, vol. ii. p. 285.

which the Society is subjected. When first established, a farm was taken at Kingston for the especial purpose of breeding animals; but various circumstances, on which we need not here dwell, brought about the abandonment of the design after a few years' trial. Not to mention more than a few instances, it is believed that at the present moment all the wapiti deer—which we have already mentioned as a fully acclimatized species—in Europe have descended from the stock introduced by the Zoological Society. In 1857, with the coöperation of the late Lord Canning and several other gentlemen in India, examples of five fine species of Himalayan pheasants* were imported, from which upwards of three hundred birds have been bred and dispersed among public bodies or private persons in Great Britain or the Continent. In like manner, the black-necked swans of Chili, which Lord Derby first introduced, but could not succeed in propagating, have, since 1857, almost annually reared cygnets, for the possession of which the demand has been practically unlimited; and through the Society's means this beautiful bird is in a fair way of being perfectly acclimatized in Europe.

We have already spoken of the French as a nation of acclimatizers; our readers will not, therefore, be unprepared to hear of the prosperity which has attended the Société Impériale d'Acclimatation, and of the satisfactory success which has crowned some of its efforts. Those who wish to become fully acquainted with the remarkable results which have followed from its establishment we must refer to the series of *Bulletins* named at the head of this article. Here we shall only have space to glance at the constitution of the Society, which to us seems a model in every way deserving of imitation, and briefly to recapitulate its achievements in one direction which have enlisted in its favour all classes of French men and French women.

The Society was started in 1854, the idea of forming it emanating from the fertile brain of Isidore Geoffroy-St.-Hilaire, the great zoologist, who eclipsed his celebrated father's fame, and whose recent death is mourned throughout the world, wherever natural history is appreciated. He was its first president; and it began its labours by creating, through the means of affiliated societies in the provinces, several establishments in various parts of France. A capital of one million of francs was soon subscribed to carry on its operations, which were favourably regarded by the Emperor. In 1858 a piece of ground, nearly sixteen hectares, or almost forty acres, in extent, situated in the Bois de Boulogne, was conceded by the city of Paris to form a Jardin

* These are the white-crested, purple, and black-backed kaleege, the cheer, and the monaul or Impeyan pheasant.

d'Acclimatation, which was placed under the direction of the late Mr. D. W. Mitchell, then secretary of the Zoological Society of London. The next year this unfortunate gentleman met his death, whereupon a committee was appointed to superintend the laying out of the ground and the erection of the necessary buildings. Subsequently MM. Rufz de Lavison and Albert Geoffroy-St.-Hilaire were named joint directors of the gardens, which in October 1860 were opened to the public, after being "inaugurated" by the Emperor in person. The excellent taste of our neighbours, aided by the experience obtained in the formation of other zoological gardens, has produced an *ensemble* which is as agreeable to the eye of the mere lounger as it is strictly in accordance with the required objects of the undertaking. Meanwhile the Society was busily employed in extending its influence and collecting information of every description bearing on acclimatization. Nearly all the great ladies of Paris were induced to become its patronesses, and nearly all the sovereigns of Europe its patrons, while it soon counted its ordinary members by the thousand. The proceedings of its meetings were fully reported and published in monthly *Bulletins*, which contain papers by various authors, most valuable to all interested in acclimatization. Of course the importance and worth of these articles vary greatly, but it is noticeable how closely all the different contributors keep to the main objects of the Society, and what a very small proportion of them recommend impracticable projects. Herein we see the wisdom of its founder in taking care that its Conseil d'Administration should include a sufficient number of the most eminent men of science in France. Numerous branch societies have now sprung up under its auspices throughout the empire, and every facility has been given by the Imperial Government to promote its objects. At the present moment, then, we may not unreasonably indulge in the most sanguine expectations for its future progress. It has abundant space at command for its operations,—in this respect unlike our own Zoological Society,—excellent accommodation for its animals, a large invested capital, and an almost remunerative revenue arising from annual subscriptions, the entrance money taken at its garden-gates, and the proceeds of the sale of its duplicate specimens.

It is well known how deeply the prosperity of France is concerned in the silk trade. For some years past, however, this branch of industry has been in a languishing condition, proving a source of great anxiety to the government of the country, the more so that its real cause was not understood. M. Guérin-Méneville, one of the secretaries of the Imperial Society, and long known as a scientific entomologist, began to take up the matter. It soon appeared to him that a deterioration in the average quality of the silk grown in Europe (chiefly in Lombardy and the south of France) was the immediate cause; but proceeding further, he found that this was produced by the prevalence of an epidemic—generally known to sericiculturists as the "*gattine*"—amongst the silk-worms. It was not long before he ascertained that this in turn took its rise from a disease to which the mulberry-trees all over Europe had been for many years more or less subject. Now, both silk-worms and mulberry-trees were beyond the reach of his therapeutic art; but it occurred to him that a complete remedy would be provided for the disastrous state of things if he could only find some other species of silk-worm of industrious and domestic habits, spinning silk of a good quality, and which would yet bear the climate of France, and not be so particular in its tastes as to require a mulberry-leaf diet. It would take many pages to detail how he set about making his researches. Though his entomological knowledge led him at once to conclude that China was the most likely quarter to look to for what he wanted, M. Guérin-Méneville wisely determined to give every kind of silk-worm that he could get hold of a chance; and in consequence we have a long series of most valuable observations,—not only from a utilitarian, but even a scientific point of view,—which are recorded by him in the *Bulletins* of the Imperial Society, and in the *Revue et Magasin de Zoologie pure et appliquée*, of which he has for many years been the able conductor. The upshot of the whole business is, that he has proved the existence of at least four species, and a fertile hybrid between two of them, which seem destined to play an important part in the world's industry. Three of them certainly produce a very valuable commodity, but there are at present certain difficulties in the way of making use of the silk spun by the fourth. This is an insect whose native country is somewhat doubtful; but its cocoons have long been employed in China, Assam, North-eastern India, and Thibet, to produce a coarse though durable material. The caterpillar feeds on the leaves of a species of Ailanthus, often called the Japanese varnish-tree, which is not only of a hardy nature, but of easy propagation and quick growth, flourishing also on very poor soils. Among other properties, it will endure the smoke and the thorough surface-draining of large cities; and it may be seen growing luxuriantly in the avenues of New York, the boulevards of Paris, and the squares of London. The insect, which is known to naturalists as *Attacus cynthia*, is really a magnificent thing. It belongs to a group which contains the largest of known *Lepidoptera*, and whether in its perfect or its immature stage is equally remarkable for its beauty. As a caterpillar, it is about the size of a man's fourth finger, of a lively apple-green, studded with velvetty black spots, and tubercles that look like so many turquoises. When full-fed, it spins an elongated cocoon of a reddish colour. From this in due time emerges a moth, measuring some five inches across the wings, which are of a particularly graceful shape, and though not brilliantly coloured, yet the various shades of rich brown, harmoniously blended together, and boldly picked out with white tracery, justify what we have above said of its appearance. This creature was sent by the Abbé Fantoni from China to Turin in 1857; the year after, M. Guérin received it, and has since bred it to a great extent, both in the gardens of the society in the Bois de Boulogne, and also on a farm at Vincennes, where he has, with the Emperor's sanction, established a large plantation of the Ailanthus. It has besides been introduced to many parts of France, especially the Landes, where its food-plant is found to grow well, to Algeria, to England, and more recently to South America. In April 1861 M. Guérin exhibited to the Imperial Society 10,000 living cocoons, being about a tenth part of the number which had been grown in the open air the preceding year, notwithstanding the unfavourable season, by the Comte de Lamotte-Baracé, near Chinon. We are not able to state what the increase since has been; but it is clear that this species at least is perfectly well established in France. A serious drawback remains to be told: it is not only that the silk, as before mentioned, is of an inferior quality, but the caterpillar has a slovenly habit of spinning its cocoons in such a manner as to make it a hard matter to unwind them in the form of a skein. But it is stated that quite recently machines have been invented which are expected entirely to get over this difficulty; and in this case M. Guérin's work may be looked upon as crowned with success.

Very nearly allied to this species of silk-worm is one that has been long employed to a very great profit in India, where it is commonly known as the "Eria," and called by naturalists *Attacus ricini*, from the Ricinus or castor-oil plant, on which it principally feeds. This also has been largely introduced by M. Guérin, and is found to flourish in the open air in France. Its silk is of a finer quality than that of its neighbour; but the Ricinus is of a somewhat delicate nature, and too tender at present for the climate of most parts of France. In time it will probably grow hardier, as so many plants have done, and then this insect is likely to become of valuable use in Europe. M. Guérin has succeeded in breeding a cross between this and the former species, which, as we before stated, is perfectly fertile, and it seems to unite many of the good qualities of each. We have now to notice the two remaining species. One was sent from China in 1855 by Mgr. Perny, now Bishop of Canton.

Its silk is available for the finer sorts of fabrics, and its food-plant is an oak (*Quercus montignii*). This will probably be completely naturalized in France before long; but hitherto it does not appear to have been so successfully treated as those we have spoken of. The fourth, and last, has been but recently received in Europe, where it was not known before, and its acclimatization is far from being perfected, though we may with confidence predict its future establishment, if all we hear about it be true. In 1861 a small stock was sent to Paris by M. Duchesne de Bellecour, the French consul at Jeddo, and this stock has unfortunately been further diminished, as is asserted, by improper treatment. The squabbles of scientific men not being agreeable subjects of contemplation, we shall say no more on the subject. We only hope that M. Guérin will eventually accomplish the successful *education* of the "Yama-maï," by which euphonious name it is known to the Japanese. Its silk is stated to be of excellent quality, and the caterpillar, like Mgr. Perny's, feeds on oak-leaves. By the latest accounts, we learn that a M. Mazade has been despatched by the French Government on an *expédition séricicole* to Japan; and we trust some day to congratulate M. Guérin, whose indefatigable industry in this important branch of acclimatization is worthy of the highest recompense his country can bestow, on the full accomplishment of his patriotic aspirations.

"The worm that spins a queen's most costly robe," and furnishes millions with the means of obtaining their daily bread, will, we hope, be thought by our readers worthy the attention we have accorded it. But we must hasten towards an end; and though the systematic efforts for acclimatization made in some foreign countries should by rights receive ampler recognition at our hands, we can here do no more than indicate the sources from which further information can be derived, by prefixing to this article the names of two works chronicling the progress effected.* We pass on, accordingly, to mention the chief schemes for acclimatization planned in England and her colonies.

We are sorry to say, we cannot regard the London Acclimatization Society as having yet proved itself worthy of this metropolis. Whether it is that people look upon the ground as already in a great measure preoccupied by the Zoological Society we do not know; but it is certain that the general public have not rallied as readily as might have been expected to the standard recently set up. On the part of the older body, we believe that not the slightest jealousy has been evinced, but its more active members seem to stand aloof from their younger

* Several of the Continental Zoological Societies do not, we believe, publish any account of their performances. This is especially to be regretted in the case of the well-conducted Gardens at Rotterdam, Antwerp, Brussells, and Cologne.

brethren. The not inconsiderable list of patrons of the newer association contains the names of but five who are looked upon as first-class men of science, and of these only one also appears as subscriber. The Council does not include a single zoologist or botanist of eminence; nor do we find admitted there more than two or three (since the great loss sustained by the Marquis of Breadalbane's death) of those gentlemen who are known to have had special experience of the subject. Now we are far from imputing blame in any particular quarter, but surely this is not as it should be. We have before instanced the necessity of applying a knowledge of natural history to the practice of acclimatization and the most prosperous results of the latter we have mentioned have been obtained by those who possessed the former. One of the Society's secretaries—the heir of a great scientific name—has justly achieved much popularity from his writings; but we fear that Mr. Buckland must often find himself the sole member of the executive enjoying a knowledge of natural-history facts most important in their bearing on particular cases, and the want of which cannot be supplied either by zeal or practical common sense,—for both of which we readily give the Council all credit. This absence of the scientific element betrays itself in several ways, sometimes rather curiously. For instance, the very redundant title the association assumes of being "The Society for the Acclimatisation of Animals, Birds, Fishes, Insects, and Vegetables within the United Kingdom," would never have met with the concurrence of any naturalist, scarcely of any man of education; for who of these requires to be told that the word 'animals' includes birds, fishes, and insects?* It may be said that this is only a trifling oversight; but the want of zoological assessors becomes more seriously apparent when, in the Second Annual Report, for 1862, we read that an experiment "to obtain a hybrid between the common cow and the eland was thought desirable" by the Council; and we must protest against the implied assertion, that the Zoological Society ever expected success from such an attempt; or, further on, in the statement that "the finest poultry known at Rio Grande is a cross between the male guan and the common domestic fowl." This last, it is true, rests on anonymous authority, which in natural history is very properly regarded as no authority at all; but the Council, we consider, by permitting it to appear unchallenged in their report, virtually endorse it. Now, we do not go as far as some naturalists do in our belief respecting the sterility

* We must mention, however, that there appears a disposition to correct this vulgar error; for though the unnecessarily long designation is retained on the title-page, the outer cover of the Second and Third Annual Reports bears the imprint of "Acclimatisation Society of Great Britain, Ireland, and the Colonies,"—a far more preferable title, if the word Acclimatization were but spelt right.

of all hybrids; but we look upon it as a well-ascertained fact, that the mules between species of groups naturally distinct—as are the Bovine and Antilopine, the Cracine and Galline—are unprolific, and therefore, except as the production of a mere matter of curiosity, we cannot imagine what useful end would be reached by obtaining such crosses. These objections we make in no cavilling spirit; we are earnestly anxious to promote the practice of acclimatization in England, and desirous of seeing the practice elevated into a science; but we hold it to be impossible for these results to follow save by an infusion of scientific blood into the Society's directorial staff. We are greatly pleased to observe, by the last report, which has only come into our hands since we commenced this article, that there has been during the past year a clear increase of 135 per cent in the number of subscribing members, and of course a corresponding augmentation of its funds; it is therefore all the more important that these should be judiciously expended, and this we are confident can only be ensured in the manner we have suggested.

The formation of the London Acclimatization Society originated in June 1860 with the proprietors of the *Field* newspaper; and the valuable privilege of having thus an energetic advocate ready found for it in a popular sporting organ—for the assistance which sportsmen can afford to acclimatization is as great as that they do afford to zoology—has not been neglected. But the progress made in this sort of attempt must of necessity be slow. The main thing to be looked to is, that it be sure. At present we are content to live in hopes. It is not to be expected that in three years any new species could be acclimatized, nor has such been the case; and we cordially support a statement, made last year by the Council, that in all experiments of acclimatization, "no amount of failure should destroy the effect of a single instance of success; and that, when one experiment has succeeded, there is every reason to believe that further investigation must lead to the discovery of the elements which will render success invariable." With these words of promise, we recommend to all persons interested in the objects it is intended to promote that they should at once join the Acclimatization Society.

Most of our readers will be aware that for some time past the question of acclimatization has been much discussed in the Australian colonies, and many of them may know that several animals, beside the common domestic races of Europe, have already been successfully introduced to the lands of the Southern Cross. Some of these—as witness the camels on the glorious expedition of the ill-fated Burke—have even yet begun to play an important part in their new country's history. Most of them are due to the enterprise of private persons, at the instigation of Mr. Edward Wilson; but of late the Government of Victoria—

and we believe also of some of the sister colonies—has taken the matter in hand. Nearly 4,000*l.* has been voted by the Parliament at Melbourne for this especial purpose, and an Acclimatization Society has been established in that city under the most favourable auspices, with the Governor, Sir Henry Barkly, as its patron, while Dr. Ferdinand Müller and Professor M'Coy, naturalists of great scientific attainments, hold office in it. The camels which have been imported to the colony are said to be thriving admirably. A large number have now been bred there, and several, escaped from exploring parties, have adapted themselves perfectly to the country, and have been seen in various parts of New South Wales, Queensland, and South Australia. The naturalization of the llama, undertaken at a great cost by Mr. Ledger, may be considered as accomplished; and a contract has been entered into for the introduction of no less than 1500 alpacas, of which a third part has already arrived, notwithstanding the hindrances caused by the jealousy of some of the South American Governments—hindrances so great as to entitle Mr. Duffield, the gentleman charged with the execution of the commission, to the highest praise in overcoming them. These animals are all intended for the high cold mountains of Gippsland, where, in a climate like their own and with suitable plants for food, there can be little doubt that all their best qualities will be preserved, if not improved. Not satisfied, however, with stocking the colony with the fleecy staple of the Cordilleras, the society has introduced the fine-haired Angora goat, and has taken steps to procure that of Thibet, bearing the beautiful wool from which the costly Cachmere shawls are made. The acclimatization of the eland is another object for which special arrangements have been made; and this stately and gentle beast has in England shown itself so apt for domestication, that it requires no prophetic foresight to predict its speedy and thorough naturalization in a country so much more resembling its own, while the surpassing excellence of its flesh makes its introduction there a consummation as devoutly to be wished for as it is probable.

We have been striving to maintain that every where the acclimatization of animals, to be successful, requires the aid of zoological knowledge. We have now to point out another, and, in our opinion, a more serious, class of errors into which its promoters, without the help of that knowledge, are likely to fall.

Botanists, we believe, are unanimously of opinion that in several countries many of the native plants have been extirpated by the introduction of foreign species. The "struggle for life," of which we have all lately heard so much, has gone against them when stronger and hardier kinds have been set by their side. To take one instance as an example among many others that have been discovered: "in St. Helena," according to Mr.

Darwin, and we are not aware that the assertion is disputed, "there is reason to believe that the naturalised plants and animals have nearly or quite exterminated many native productions" (*Origin of Species*, p. 390). The same may be said of another African island, the Mauritius. The narratives of the earlier voyagers thither mention many birds, besides the dodo and its kindred species, which are now no longer to be found there; and it is an equally well-ascertained fact that numerous foreign species, mostly during the French occupation, have been introduced into that island. Now, if we are not misinformed, a considerable tract of virgin forest still exists there, and therefore the absence of all these aborigines cannot be entirely ascribed to the alteration of its physical features consequent on the colonization of the island,—nor were most of the missing members of its fauna of a class that would be warred against by man. It seems only reasonable, then, to account for their extirpation on the supposition that the introduction of other species has deprived them of the means of living.

Now we would desire to bring these facts specially to the notice of those well-intentioned gentlemen who are making such strenuous efforts to introduce exotic, and particularly European, animals to the Southern Continent. We should be the last persons to demur to the Australian colonist carrying with him among his household gods all that can with reason make his new-found home dear to him; but we must warn him against the probable results of importing robin-redbreasts, blackbirds, mavises, skylarks, and the like. It is not that we dread the adoption of blood-thirsty advice such as that tendered by a gentleman at the last meeting of the Victorian Society, who stated that the English song-birds which had been introduced to the colony were "much persecuted by the native hawks, whose extirpation would therefore be an advantage;" but we may depend upon it, that if any of the imported species becomes established, it will be at the expense of the original dwellers in the land, which, at any rate, have not been proved to be less valuable in an economical point of view. How great a nuisance a not very noxious weed in Europe may turn out when transported to Australia, is abundantly shown by the acts of the colonial legistures for the prevention of thistles, all originating, it is said from a single plant carried out by a too patriotic Scotchman. Indeed, the flora of Australasia, particularly in New Zealand, has already sustained a dire defeat from the European interlopers. So will it undoubtedly be with the Australasian fauna. Even now some of its members are undergoing a fearful conflict for existence against the few foreign animals that have been introduced. Dogs, cats, and hogs run wild in many places, and commit dire ravages. The native rat of New Zealand—a comparatively harmless animal—is more easily and more fatally conquered by the invading species, than the Maori by the Armstrong gun and Enfield rifle. And what a conquest it is! Extirpation is its natural, its only consequence. The apteryx, like a ghost, vanishes at the crow of the settler's cock. The emeu and kangaroo retire before his sheep and horned cattle; and retirement is but the incipient stage of extinction. What, then, will be the result if the schemes of naturalizing new beasts, new birds, and new fishes in their wild state succeed? The endemic species must be worsted in the encounter, and then *Væ victis!* It is not as among the more highly developed forms of Europe—for surely we must so call those whose constitution enables them to do battle victoriously against their fellow-creatures. In England or in France acclimatization does not in most cases carry with it the penalty of death to other species; but in Australasia, unless care be taken, it will simply be another word for extirpation.

These reflections lead us to offer another suggestion to acclimatization societies, and one which they seem to have in their power to carry out.

While endeavouring to introduce new species, why should we neglect to retain the old? If charity begins at home, surely our native animals deserve some of the care that there is such an inclination to bestow on distinguished foreigners? We have shown how Lord Breadalbane saved the eagles in his deer-forest from extermination, and how he was the chief agent in restoring the capercally to its former domain. There are many other animals on the verge of extinction in the British islands. Some of them are really useful in their way; others merely gladden the eye, or are interesting from their historical or poetical associations. Their fate is trembling in the balance: can we not make a slight effort to turn the scale in their favour? We are glad to see in a recent number of the *Journal of the Royal Agricultural Society* a translation of Professor von Tschudi's eloquent appeal on behalf of the protection of small birds from a strictly economical point of view, and trust that farmers in this country will profit by its study; but we would rather devote the remainder of our space to a few remarks on some birds not indispensable to the agriculturist, and therefore not alluded to by him. There was a time, not many years ago, when the great skua was all but destroyed from its two or three nesting-places in Great Britain. It is stated that the stock on the island of Unst, the most northern of the Shetland group, was reduced to three pairs. One gentleman, Mr. Edmonstone, whose name deserves to be recorded with honour, interfered, affording the bird his protection, and it now resorts in no inconsiderable numbers to breed upon his property. During several years previous to 1838, when the last British-born bustard was killed in Norfolk, it would have probably been in the power of any of the great landowners in that county to have kept up the native breed; and many we know would have gladly done so, had they known how. Yet we believe the end would have been effectually gained had some two or three cock-birds—easily enough procured from Germany—been liberated on the East-Anglian "brecks" early in the spring: for it appears that the males of this noble species had been all killed down, while several females yet remained, mourning their lost lords, and annually dropping unfertilized eggs in the waving corn-fields, "when the bloom was on the rye." All experiments to induce this noble fowl to breed in captivity have failed, and probably not even the most stringent Act of Parliament could now restore it to a station among England's denizens, when thirty years since the outlay of a few guineas, and a good understanding between a few country gentlemen, would have sufficed to retain it. But ten years ago the osprey still bred on some of the Sutherlandshire lochs. Now all we know of it as a British bird is, that every spring and autumn, most commonly the latter, a stray example or two, of unquestionably foreign origin, falls a victim to some professional punt-shooter on one or other of our great rivers. We understand that more than one Highland proprietor issued orders in its favour, but we doubt if any one ever took care to see they were carried out; for had the birds been left unmolested in their breeding-places, there would they still be found.* Then, again, how many of our constant feathered visitors have the misfortune to be accounted wonderful rarities, and when they appear have every gun in the neighbourhood levelled at them, until chance lays the unhappy hoopoe or oriole bleeding at the feet of some Mr. Winkle, who forthwith obtains an apotheosis as an ornithological hero in the county paper. The *Times*, much to its credit, occasionally finds room for a remonstrance against this silly practice, and we are sure that all the best naturalists view it with extreme disgust. In ninety-nine such cases out of a hundred nothing is ever gained to science: the "specimen" is rudely stuffed by the nearest "taxidermist," and is displayed in a glazed box to his admiring friends by the exultant bird-murderer as the "*Poluphloisboio thalasses* of naturalists," which he had the good fortune to shoot on such a day at such a place. But still greater is the abhorrence which not only naturalists, but all persons with any humanity in their disposition, feel at the wanton and savage slaughter

* A very singular and almost unaccountable case of the recent extinction of a European bird—the francolin—was noticed by Lord Lilford in *The Ibis* for October 1862 (p. 352). See also the remarks made in the succeeding number of the same excellent ornithological magazine for January 1863 (pp. 113-116).

which yearly takes place at the few remaining spots around our coasts where sea-birds yet throng to build.* It is sickening to think of heaps (we are speaking literally) of winged kittiwakes and body-struck guillemots drifting out with the ebbing tide to be nibbled to death by fishes, while their callow young are perishing miserably on the cliffs above for want of the food which their parents met their fate in bringing. And all that a train-ful of sea-side excursionists may enjoy (save the mark!) a holiday. Surely it is but a step from acclimatization to preservation, and a society formed for the promotion of the one object hardly exceeds its functions if it extends them to embrace the other. Only bring it home to the public mind that the destruction of an animal at its breeding place, or when it is seeking for its breeding-place, is a cruel, and consequently an unsportsman-like act, and the practice will cease; for the English people are, of all nations, at once the most prone to humanity and the most addicted to sport. We certainly think that the Acclimatization Society might work this change of opinion, and obtain strength for their other objects by the attempt.

The acclimatization of animals, then, on sound principles, and thus extended, we believe, deserves the utmost encouragement it can receive at the hands of every one, for to all classes do its results appeal. The high-born dame may derive from her silk-worms or her aviary constant occupation and excitement of the most harmless description, even if no more practical results wait upon her ministrations. The humble cottager may in like manner form one more tie to his own home by attending to his modest poultry-yard. The mechanic solace himself in his hours of rest by the care which his dove-cote will demand. The sportsman will be better pleased with the day's shooting that affords him greater variety of game than with one of prolonged sameness, even though the *bouquets* of pheasants be unceasing, and each bird a "rocketter." The farmer add to his substance from cattle newly introduced to his flocks and herds; and the manufacturer may gain by new kinds of raw material out of which to produce his fabrics. The philosopher, the painter, and the poet draw fresh ideas to illustrate never-dying works; while the political economist thus will see the wealth, the health, and the happiness of his fellow-men augmented. It is an old saying, that "he who makes two blades of grass grow where only one grew before, deserves well of his country," and the truth of the proverb is not confined to the improved cultivation of plants.

* The Farn islands off the Northumberland coast must be mentioned as a creditable exception. The protection to the birds nesting there is due to the efforts of the late Archdeacon Thorp.

Art. VIII.—THE POETRY OF OWEN MEREDITH.

Clytemnestra, the Earl's Return, the Artist, and other Poems. By Owen Meredith. Chapman and Hall. 1855.

The Wanderer. By Owen Meredith. Second edition. Chapman and Hall. 1859.

Lucile. By Owen Meredith. Chapman and Hall. 1860.

Mr. Owen Meredith's poetry has won a considerable share of general popularity. Two of the books at the head of this article are already out of print, and he himself refers in his last long poem, with modest self-congratulation, to the gratifying fact that several of his early poems have been set to music, and are favourites with the young ladies of the present day. He has established a certain position, therefore, in the world which entitles him to the benefit of serious criticism at the hands of all who are jealous of the fame of English literature.

Mr. Matthew Arnold has recently invented a new name for the quality which characterises permanent as contrasted with ephemeral fame, that fine clear-cut individuality of touch which does not merely stimulate the mind with transient little shocks of interest, but engraves the form of a poet's thought on the memory, as distant hills are chiselled out against a sunset sky; —he calls it "distinction." "Of this quality," he says, "the world is impatient; it chafes against it, rails at it, insults it, hates it; it ends by receiving its influence and by undergoing its law. This quality at last invariably corrects the world's blunders and fixes the world's ideals. It procures that the popular poet shall not finally pass for a Pindar, nor the popular preacher for a Bossuet." And it will, we feel no doubt, convince the readers of English poetry, after careful study, that the clever writer who composes under the name of Owen Meredith has no part or share in the true poetic faculty.

Mr. Owen Meredith is by no means what would generally be called a dull writer. His verses shimmer like shot-silk with antithesis, sentiment, and similes. There are smart hits at times, that show a considerable knowledge of the world. He admires nature, and analyses character, and versifies with a fatal fluency. But the more you read of him, the more clear it becomes that he is a poet of what we may call the decorative school, and that even his decorative art is essentially meretricious. His poems remind us of the judgment passed by Eckermann (or shall we rather say by Goethe's mind speaking through

Eckermann), and approved by the great poet, on a certain German poem: "They are the impressions of a dilettante who has more good intention than power, and to whom the highly-developed state of our literature has lent a ready-made language which sings and rhymes for him, while he imagines himself speaking." And this seems to hit exactly the sort of talent displayed by Mr. Owen Meredith. He plays on what Coleridge calls the ready-made barrel-organ of our poetic phraseology with a facility that pleases the ear unaccustomed to true and individually elaborated poems. But the more you read the less you admire him; the colours with which his poetry is so liberally heightened seem all hot and glaring, and put on in patches, like rouge; the artificial tone of the pleasantry jars more and more; the sentiment is thick and blurred, and over-luscious, like Tokay; and, on the whole, you feel that this poetry is a gaudy artificial costume for life, which catches the eye at first as striking, but the enjoyment of which is soon exhausted. We are sorry to pass so severe a judgment on a poet who has no doubt attained a certain level of popularity; but we are convinced that it is a true one by many concurrent evidences, and fear that we can only too easily convince our readers also.

When we attempt to compare Mr. Owen Meredith's poems, or any poems of the same class, with a high poetical standard, we are vividly reminded of the fine passage in Plato's *Gorgias* in which he compares with the four genuine Arts that concern themselves with preserving or restoring the well-being of the body and the mind,—namely, Gymnastics, Medicine, Law, and Justice,—the four imitative counterfeits which concern themselves not with the well-being but the temporary gratification of the body and the mind;—the trick of dressing up the body so as to counterfeit the symmetry and beauty produced by gymnastic training, the trick of dressing up food so as to make it gratify the palate instead of imparting nourishment, the trick of recommending false measures to the people which salve over the public disorders instead of ensuring the well-being of the commonwealth, and finally the trick of persuading the judges so as to gain for the criminal not justice but impunity. This last spurious or counterfeit "dexterity,"—namely Rhetoric,—which is concerned not with procuring the true well-being of the soul, but its immunity from temporary pain, is defined by Socrates as "a state not belonging to true Art at all, but the quality of a soul ready in taking aim, and bold and clever by nature in its intercourse with men." It is impossible for a modern critic not to add to this enumeration of genuine Arts, and the corresponding parasitical dexterities which aim at a temporary gratification instead of true artistic standards,—on the one hand the genuine poetry which aims at taking the veil from life, whether the life of nature or of men, and showing us, on however modest a scale, the impressions made by men and things on the creative imagination,—and, on the other hand, that merely decorative talent which seems to aim at giving the pleasure and surprises which poetry gives, but without the labour, without the fidelity, without the spontaneous simplicity of true poetry. While true poetry unveils through the imagination the secrets of natural and of human expression, the decorative poetry of which we speak paints for it a new, and at first sight pleasing, external veil, which bears the same relation to the transparent medium of the poet which the patterns drawn on ground glass to prevent vision bear to the images of living forms in a perfect mirror. This decorative trick of false poetry seems to be exactly described in Plato's words as "a state not belonging to true Art at all, but the quality of a soul ready in taking aim, and bold and clever by nature in its intercourse with men.". Socrates adds that he considers the sum and substance of these pleasure-seeking parasites of true art to be a species of flattery,*—a dexterity, that is, in selecting the weak place in human nature, where a very little tickling with plausible falsehoods will win a great deal of temporary power. And this is, though of course without any of the dishonourable character of *personal* flattery, exactly the characteristic of the kind of poetry we wish to discuss. It is the instrument of minds "ready in aim, and bold and clever by nature in their intercourse with men," and its method of procedure seems to be just that amount of plausible deception which is certain to follow from taking the superficial tickling of the fancy as the aim of poetry, instead of the effort to grasp truly in the imagination, the life within and the life without.

In the first place you may see this false aim at the plausibly agreeable, instead of at the true, in Mr. Owen Meredith's occasionally clever but always over-emphatic descriptive poetry. True poetic descriptions are of many kinds, following the law of the poet's own mind. There is the careless school of description, which succeeds like Byron's later genius by the mere audacity with which he thrusts into his verse accidental and miscellaneous objects in the arbitrary kind of way in which they would arrest the eye of an absent-minded spectator,—"a sail peeping out here and there, so full of life that you seem to feel the sea-breeze blowing;"† and here again London sights

* *κολακεία.*

† Goethe's conversation on Byron with Eckermann.

and sounds tumbled in pell-mell upon the imagination, "the wigs in a hair-cutter's window and the passing lamplighters" jostling one another in the memory. Or there is the tranquil German school of description, which Goethe adorned, a school that aims at realising in due perspective, moral as well as physical, the whole picture before the eye, choosing your point of sight at some defined personal centre,—as for instance in the mind of the good old hostess of the Golden Lion in *Hermann and Dorothea*,—and then painting the scene traversed by her exactly as it would seem to her eye, looking at the kitchen garden with a gardener's vigilance for the caterpillars on the leaves, or scarlet runners that need new staking, and so forth. Or there is the meditative school of description, like Wordsworth's, which describes not so much the outward reality as the trains of reverie it set moving in his breast. But whatever the school be, so long as it is a true poetic description, there is always some one point of view which reconciles all that is noted down into a distinct harmony of intellectual effect. Nothing of the kind is discernible in Mr. Owen Meredith's descriptions, which sometimes remind us of a lady's letter, with dashes under all the non-emphatic words, and notes of admiration after all the least significant sentences. Take for instance the following description of the Pyrenees by moonlight, in *Lucile*:

"The moon of September, now half at the full,
Was unfolding from darkness and dreamland the lull
Of the quiet blue air, where the many-faced hills
Watch'd, well-pleased, their fair slaves, the light, foam-footed rills,
Dance and sing down the steep marble stairs of their courts,
And gracefully fashion a thousand sweet sports.
Like ogres in council those mountains look'd down,
Impassive, each king in his purple and crown."

For the moon to unfold "the lull of the quiet blue air" must, we suppose, mean that it was unfolding the quiet of the quiet blue air, a difficult thing for moonlight to effect, though it may well indeed make stillness more emphatic, the silence being much more striking when the air is luminous than when it is dark. Whether that were Mr. Owen Meredith's meaning we do not know; but what we care to point out is not the mere clumsiness, which may have been the result of random rhyme, but the incongruity of emphasis, the absolute want of keeping, in the whole passage. The moon is just gaining power to conquer out of "darkness and dreamland" the blue air of night, when we discover "the many-faced hills" "watching well pleased the light foam-footed rills," and find that the latter remind us of dancing slaves singing and leaping in the marble courts of a palace, and the former, who were a moment ago "well pleased" at watching their graceful movements, are suddenly changed to "impassive" ogres in council. Why ogres? and why impassive? If they look cruel and hungry, and disposed to eat somebody up, they can't look especially "impassive," and still less at the same time "well pleased." Here are three expressions all fastened on the mountains in one breath which are inconsistent with each other, and still more inconsistent with the tranquil partially moonlit scene described in the first two lines. A soft summer moonlight, just catching the snow and the gleaming water of the torrents here and there, could suggest nothing less than dancing-girls and either smiling or impassive ogres. The criticism may seem trivial, but not when we consider how much this continuously false stress of metaphor really implies in a poet,—how little he can have studied the truth of either nature or his own impressions to conceive such lines at all, much more to tolerate them as a true delineation of nature when he has conceived them. It is like the child's effort to find as many and as glaring colours as he can when he is painting the dress of his favourite hero. Mr. Meredith's lines represent nothing either in nature or the mind of man; but they seem to promise a succession of impressions on the retina, at short intervals, that will make the eye swim with colour and feel that it has been excited,—which is exactly what we mean by the vice of that meretricious school of poetry which aims at tickling the fancy with superficial impressions rather than delineating the truth of either nature or feeling.

Mr. Meredith's descriptive powers seem, indeed, to have rather degenerated since his first volume was published in 1855. Even then we noted the same tendency to a profusion of colour and arbitrary spangles, which dazzle the eye, spoil the picture, and prove that the artist did not realise what he described. But there were passages here and there of somewhat greater promise, in which he had embodied some Tennysonian studies of landscape intended to harmonise exactly with the mood of mind which they framed. Thus, where Tennyson has "Mariana in the moated grange," and describes a desolate house in a desolate fen country, with a single poplar near it, and a lady waiting in vain for somebody's return, Mr. Meredith had a desolate castle on a desolate sea-shore, and a single blasted thorn near it, with a lady waiting, not eventually in vain, but with feelings the reverse of impatient, her earl's return. The study was much cleverer than most of his recent descriptions; but even there it was easy to discern the faults,—the want of real *eye*, and the tendency to accumulate telling touches, often inconsistent with each other, that have developed into a thoroughly spurious style in his later works. One of the most ingenious efforts of his descriptive power, however, this desolate castle certainly is:

"The land about was barren and blue,
And swept by the wing of the wet sea-mew;
Seven fishermen's huts on a shelly shore,
Sand-heaps behind and sand-banks before;
And a black champaign streaked white all through
To a great salt pool which the ocean drew,
Sucked into itself, and disgorged it again
To stagnate and steam on the mineral plain.
Not a tree or a bush in the circle of sight
But a bare black thorn which the sea-winds had withered
With the drifting scum of the surf and blight,
And some patches of gray grass-land to the right,
Where the lean red-hided cattle were tethered.
A reef of rocks wedged the water in twain,
And a stout stone tower stood square to the main.
And the flakes of the spray that were jerked away
From the froth on the lip of the bleak blue sea
Were sometimes flung by the wind as it swung
Over turret and terrace and balcony
To the garden below, where in desolate corners
Under the mossy-green parapet, there
The lilies crouched, rocking their white heads like mourners;
And burned off the heads of the flowers that were
Pining and pale in their comfortless bowers,
Dry-bushed with the sharp stubborn lavender,
And paven with discs of the torn sun-flowers,—
Which day by day were strangled and stripped
Of their ravelling fringes and brazen bosses,
And the hardy Mary-buds ripped and nipped
Into shreds for the beetles that lurked in the mosses.
Here she lived alone, and from year to year
She saw the black belt of the ocean appear
At her casement each morn as she rose, and each morn
Her eye fell first on the bare black thorn.
This was all, nothing more; or sometimes on the shore
The fishermen sang when the fishing was o'er;
Or the lowing of oxen fell dreamily
Close on the skirt of the glimmering eves,
Through some gusty pause in the moaning sea,
When the pools were splashed pink by the thirsty beeves,
Or sometimes when the pearl-lighted morns drew the tinges
Of the cold sun-rise up their amber fringes,—
A white sail peered over the rim of the main,
Peered all about o'er the empty sea,
Staggered back from the fine line of white light again,
And dropped down to another world silently.
Then she breathed freer."

No doubt this is pains-taking and to some extent striking, and far more laborious and true than any of Mr. Meredith's recent studies in the same way. We have quoted it at such length because it is, we think, his most elaborate effort of this kind. Still it is marked by the ingrained taste for external decoration which is the essence of his talent. For example as to truth of feeling: "the froth on the lip of the bleak blue sea" attempts to crowd into a single line touches entirely inconsistent with each other. The sea often looks bleak, but least so when it looks blue; and to draw attention to its blueness at all just when you are speaking of the spray as the froth on its lip renders the image false, disagreeable, and confusing, instead of graphic. Blue lips and froth suggest, if any thing, convulsion fits, and are wholly inconsistent with the image of the ocean. Again, though lilies rock in the wind, they literally *can't* "crouch" under a wall, and the word is put in only to aid the funereal metaphor of the mourners which Mr. Meredith wants. Nor is it at all possible for the lady to have seen the sea every morning as a "black belt." There is nothing which first strikes the eye so much on looking out to the sea in the morning as the glare of light upon it, and even on the most clouded days the glancing of the waves entirely prevents any effect like a black belt. The expression is used only to heighten artificially the melancholy of the patient. Then as to the point of sight: as the whole landscape is meant to mirror the lady's melancholy,—just as Tennyson notes in the neighbourhood of the Moated Grange only that which reflects back Mariana's desolation,—the true perspective requires him to delineate what the lady would see, and the impression it would make on her sick mood of mind. Mr. Meredith goes far beyond this in his anxiety for more local colour. She might hear the oxen lowing "through the gusty pause in the moaning sea;" but the idea immediately suggests to Mr. Meredith to transport us to where the oxen are drinking, and make a fresh little point of colour of it,—so he adds, "when the pools were splashed pink by the thirsty beeves," which is clearly Chinese perspective. Moreover, we suspect he has put in this touch from a wholly different landscape. If the pools were splashed "pink," the soil must have been a reddish one, and the whole of his description harps continually on a blue-black mineral plain, which implies a quite different ground-colour; nor can they be the salt-water pools in the sand, as the epithet "thirsty" seems expressly to shut this out. It is another great error of perspective to make the lady watching a sail in the offing see it "*stagger* back from the fine line of white light again." It is impossible to see a sail stagger in the offing. A similar and worse artistic blunder is made in *Lucile*, where he speaks of a young lady's full heart beating "*loud in her small rosy ears.*" She who alone heard her heart beat could not see her own ears, and certainly could not then be thinking of them; the sentence is in fact a horrid medley between the analysis of a young lady's own feelings, and the gourmand sort of admiration felt by a spectator for her pretty ears. All this may seem hypercriticism, but these faults are sown thick through the poems, and indicate just the sort of disposition to stick on stucco ornament from the outside which has got almost complete possession of the writer. Its worst result is, that it destroys the true artist's sense of vision. Wherever you try to realise Mr. Meredith's pictures, even when they look most tempting and picturesque, you find something wrong. Here, for example, is a pretty picture, drawn by a lover of happy travels:

> "We will see the shores of Greece,
> And the temples of the Nile;
> Sail where summer suns increase,
> Toward the south, from isle to isle,
>
> Track the first star that swims on
> Glowing depths toward night and us,
> While the heats of sunset crimson
> All the purple Bosphorus,—
>
> Leaning o'er some dark ship-side,
> Watch the wane of mighty moons;
> Or through star-lit Venice glide,
> Singing down the blue lagoons."

This sounds musical and picturesque enough at the first reading; but when you come to look into its structure, it is like a mosaic of which every item is false, though at a certain distance it gives a pleasing effect. True poetry, though it must often be vague, need never be false even in its minutest features to the artist's point of view; for you can never really get closer to his subject than the attitude of mind in which he chooses to place you. Now put yourself in the place of the lover who is dilating on the pleasure of seeing beautiful southern scenes with his mistress,—could he either from experience or natural prejudice expect to see the "southern suns increase" as he went southwards? If he did, he was very much mistaken in fact, since of course nothing of the kind happens;—indeed, *ceteris paribus*, the more obliquely the sun is seen the larger it appears; nor is there any kind of popular fancy or prejudice in the image. One expects hotter suns but certainly not larger in the south. Then, again, to propose to track a star that is coming *towards* you is as unnatural a mode of speech as the feat is difficult which it suggests. Moreover, it is swimming "on glowing depths towards *night* and us," which is either unmeaning, or would imply that the stars rise in the glow of sunset and revolve eastwards,—a curious astronomical phenomenon; for wherever the spectator of a sunset may be, he and night must clearly be east of it. Once more: to make sunset "crimson" a "purple" sea is childish profusion of colour. If the sea is purple, it must be the sky which makes it so, it is not its intrinsic colour; and if the sky is making it crimson and not purple, the adjective 'purple' is a false dye put in for the sake of a more gorgeous variety of colour. Finally, if the gentleman was thinking of the lagoons in *star-lit* Venice, they would certainly *not* present themselves to him as blue, which requires daylight. These verses are the best specimens one could find of the abuse of a ready-made poetical language by a writer skilled in selecting words that have what we may call a poetical smell or *bouquet*, but careless of the real meaning they convey. In a passage of some cleverness in *Lucile*, we have a similar shipwreck of artistic effect from a similar blunder. One of the heroes, Lord Alfred Vargrave, has just seen his rival enter Lucile's room, and has left it angrily through the window, and stands in the garden, where we are told,—

> "When left to his thoughts in the garden alone,
> Alfred Vargrave stood, strange to himself. With dull tone
> Of importance, thro' cities of rose and carnation,
> Went the bee on his business from station to station.
> The minute mirth of summer was shrill all around;
> Its incessant small voices like stings seem'd to sound
> On his sore angry sense. He stood grieving the hot
> Solid sun with his shadow, nor stirr'd from the spot."

The important business character of the bee's droning hum,—the effect of it and of the "minute mirth of summer" on Lord Alfred's "sore angry sense," is perhaps truly and at all events cleverly imagined; but just as we are yielding to the impression that here for a moment the author has imagined accurately a real situation, comes the foolish and senseless bit of bombastic imagery, "he stood grieving the hot solid sun with his shadow," which is not only shifting the point of view very abruptly indeed from a geocentric to a heliocentric position,—passing rather hastily from Lord Alfred's grief to the sun's grief,—but is a very quaint piece of emotion indeed for the "solid sun" to feel. Moreover, it appears to be not the *light* of the sun which is grieved at Lord Alfred's shadow, but the "hot solid" mass; in other words, the emotion of grief broke out in that substantial orb itself,—evincing itself, we suppose, as soon after Lord Alfred had taken his sultry station as the fact became visible there,—say in about eight minutes' time:—a nonsensical criticism no doubt, but only nonsensical because the rhetorical phrase criticised is so absolutely destitute of meaning, that directly you come to think of it, you fall into an abyss of nonsense. That we may not be thought to be cavilling at an accidental blot, here is another instance of the meaningless use of well-sounding words in *Lucile:*

> "And so, as alone now she stood, in the sight
> Of the sunset of youth, with her face toward the light,
> And watch'd her own shadow grow long at her feet,
> As though stretch'd out, the shade of some *other* to meet,
> The woman felt homeless and childless: in scorn
> She seem'd mock'd by the voices of children unborn,"—

which involves certainly, as it stands in the text, one of the most wonderful pieces of optics we have ever met with. We may, perhaps, in common charity suppose that either "toward" is a misprint for "from," or "face" for "back;" but the whole image is so mere a draft on the conventional verbiage of poetry, —in which suns are always obliged to set whenever any thing pleasant is ceasing,—that we don't know how far the mending of the optics will mend the poetry. For any real vision the passage arouses in the reader's mind, the "sunset of youth" might just as well draw the shadows towards itself instead of throwing them off in the opposite direction. To follow out the idea at all is only to be landed in nonsense; for we are told that this shadow seems to be in search of another shadow which ought to be there to *meet* it, and, if it did, would come, we conclude, from the opposite point of the horizon; and therefore—may we infer?—be cast by the sunrise of youth, and, therefore, perhaps be the shadow of a baby; to which doubtless reference is made in the last line we have quoted about the babies that would not come. What a jumble of conventional images the whole thing is! And these are the sort of images which stud the whole surface of Mr. Meredith's poetry; not always so ludicrous, but almost always as little really expressive. Here, for instance, is another tune on the barrel-organ of conventional poetic phrases. The Duc de Luvois is recounting how he tried to convince himself that he ought to forget Lucile and get on cheerfully without her, which he did by grinding for himself on the said organ the following unsatisfactory but extremely commonplace strain:

> "Hast thou loved, O my heart? to thy love yet remains
> All the wide loving-kindness of nature. The plains
> And the hills with each summer their verdure renew:
> Wouldst thou be as they are? do thou then as they do.
> Let the dead sleep in peace. Would the living divine
> Where they slumber? Let only new flowers be the sign!
>
> Since the bird of the wood flits and sings round the nest
> Where lie broken the eggs she once warm'd with her breast;
> Since the flower of the field, newly born yesterday,
> When to-morrow a new bud hath burst on the spray,

Folds, and falls in the night, unrepining, unseen;
Since aloof in the forests, when forests are green,
You may hear through the silence the dead wood that cracks,
Since man, where his course throughout nature he tracks,
In all things one science to soothe him may find,
To walk on, and look forward, and never behind,
—What to me, O my heart, is thy joy or thy sorrow?
What the tears of to-day or the sneers of to-morrow?
What is life? what is death? what the false? what the true?
And what is the harm that one woman can do?"

That the broken egg-shells litter the nest, and perhaps render it a prickly seat when the hatching is over, is no doubt a grievance which the wise fowl would do well to remove; but this circumstance does not seem to be capable of yielding much encouragement to a gentleman who has *failed* to hatch his pet egg. The flower that fades unrepining, and the dead-wood that cracks in the forest, would teach him a melancholy lesson of resignation, but hardly to look forwards and neglect the things which are behind, which is the lesson he tried, and we are not surprised to find vainly, to learn from them. This last passage is as good a specimen as we could have of the average stuff of the poem, and shows the utter rootlessness of the poetic imagery of the writer, whose similes and metaphors, instead of growing out of the subject, are stuck into it like the stalks of cut flowers plunged into the ground. His ornaments have usually no sort of living connexion with the feelings, which his verse, instead of expressing, only varnishes over, or, we might perhaps say, to use an expressive house-painter's term, distempers.

But though poetical description is, on the whole, a fair test of the veracity and strength of a poet's apprehension, as it is also in some sense the lowest department of his art, and certainly that which it is most easy for the critic carefully to check, it is scarcely fair, on this ground alone, to speak of any poet as a dealer in plausible effects,—one who tickles the fancy with kaleidoscopic combinations of poetic phrases instead of drawing the veil from life and nature,—unless there be the same conventional plausibility about his higher artistic *aims*, so far as we have the power of discriminating them. Does it seem to be the animating effort of Mr. Owen Meredith's poems to delineate, by the aid of the imagination, the *truth* of human character, or thought, or emotion? or is it rather his function to paint fanciful shadows which amuse the mind of the public more, at much less cost to the author, than any truth of delineation would do? We have of course no means of judging this cardinal question as to the author's effort or aim except from the literary result. But the total effect left upon us certainly is, that while the best gleams of purpose and feeling in these books are those which Meredith shares with his time, there is a very large proportion of his poetry spurious in aim as well as in method, for which our own day is not at all accountable. "We live in a time," said Goethe, "when culture is so diffused that it has become the atmosphere which a young man breathes; poetical and philosophical thoughts live and stir in him; he has sucked them in with the very air about him; but he imagines them his property, and so expresses them as if they belonged to him individually. But after he has given back to the time what he had received from it, he is poor. He is like a fountain which for a few moments spouts forth the water which had been carried to it, and which ceases to give a drop when the borrowed supply is exhausted." Thus the drift of *Lucile,* if it is intended to have one, is, we suppose, that gospel of earnest work which Mr. Carlyle has preached into the age, without having taught us any very definite object for it, and having unfortunately *un*-taught us some few rather important ones which he has made it his amusement to ridicule. The two heroes in *Lucile,* the English and the French, both lead lives wasted by want of purpose: the former being led astray, we are told, by natural indolence, the latter excluded from his fit political work by the political condition of France, which left no room for the coöperation of a legitimist noble. The heroine again, Lucile, is delineated as a woman of genius with no adequate outlet for her powers, and a natural yearning for domestic life which she does not succeed in attaining. All these three fruitless young people are conducted by the path of calamity, and one of them at least by a very short cut, to a nobler state of mind and purpose, and consequently a more earnest mode of life. The idea of the character which Mr. Meredith has sketched at the greatest length, and perhaps with most satisfaction to himself, that of his French hero the Duc de Luvois, will be gathered from the following lines, which are some of the most simple, perhaps the most carefully thought-out, and, on the whole, certainly some of the best in the book:

"His life was of trifles made up, and he lived
In a world of frivolities. Still he contrived
The trifles, to which he was wedded, to dower
With so much of his own individual power
(And mere pastime to him was so keen a pursuit),
That these trifles seem'd such as you scarce could impute
To a trifler.

* * * * *

Nevertheless,
What in him gave to vice, from its pathos and stress,
A sort of malignity, might have perchance
Had the object been changed by transposed circumstance,
Given vigour to virtue. And therefore, indeed,
Had his life been allied to some fix'd moral creed,

In the practice and forms of a rigid, severe,
And ascetic religion, he might have come near
To each saint in that calendar which he now spurn'd.
In its orbit, however, his intellect turn'd
On a circle so narrow'd as quite to exclude
A spacious humanity. Therefore, both crude
And harsh his religion would ever have been,
As shallow, presumptuous, narrow, and keen,
Was the trite irreligion which now he display'd.
It depended alone upon chance to have made
Persecutor of this man, or martyr. For, closed
In the man, lurk'd two natures the world deems opposed,
A Savonarola's, a Calvin's, alike
Unperceived by himself. It was in him to strike
At whatever the object he sought to attain,
Bold as Brutus, relentless as Philip of Spain,
And undaunted to march, in behalf of his brothers,
To the stake, or to light it, remorseless, for others.

* * * * * *

Thus, he appear'd
Neither Brutus nor Philip in action and deed,
Neither Calvin nor Savonarola in creed,
But that which the world chose to have him appear,—
The frivolous tyrant of Fashion, a mere
Reformer in coats, cards, and carriages! Still
'Twas this vigour of nature, and tension of will,
Whence his love for Lucile to such passion had grown."

So far as the gospel of work is inculcated with any earnestness by the author, it is done in the character of this French nobleman, who was a reality, we imagine, to Mr. Meredith, and is conceived, in his frivolous earnestness and theatrical passion, much less indistinctly than any other character in the book. The Duc de Luvois is the one present which Mr. Owen Meredith has to give to "his time," in return for the Carlylian ideas which his time has bestowed upon him. We cannot say it is a rich one, for it is so disfigured by the essentially poor and often base material in which the whole work is executed, that even in relation to this character we only here and there come across a line or two which convince us that the author was painting from individual apprehensions of his own, and not from ornamental fancies. However, this, if any, is the character which seized upon Mr. Owen Meredith's own imagination, and we believe that it did really in some sense occupy *him*, and not merely his fancy. One may perceive even through the turbid and muddy rhetoric of *Lucile* a certain fascination of the author's mind with this Frenchman, a word here and there that seems to say he was touching something real in modelling it, and not merely wreathing the vapours of his own fancy. If there are any lines that deserve the name of poetry in the book, they are those which on two occasions delineate a crisis in the duke's turbulent passions. Once when he is roaming about at night in a forest, rejected by Lucile, in rather a fiendish state of mind, he sees the moon break through a cloud-structure that has been somewhat theatrically painted,—representing it, we suppose, as it might seem to a theatrical mind in genuine excitement,—and the verse runs on:

> "While he gazed, that cloud-city invisible hands
> Dismantled and rent; and reveal'd, through a loop
> In the breach'd dark, the blemish'd and half-broken hoop
> Of the moon, which soon silently sank; and anon
> The whole supernatural pageant was gone.
> *The wide night, discomforted, conscious of loss,*
> *Darken'd round him.* One object alone—that gray cross—
> Glimmer'd faint on the dark. Gazing up, he descried
> Through the void air, its desolate arms outstretch'd wide,
> As though to embrace him. He turn'd from the sight,
> Set his face to the darkness, and fled."

The line we have italicised seems to us a breaking of the light of genuine poetry through the clouds of Mr. Meredith's stilted fancy. And we imagine we discern the same rather rare event towards the conclusion, when the Duc de Luvois, having meditated something rather more wicked than usual, is brought to his right mind in a long-winded midnight interview with Lucile in the garden of the hotel at Ems;—it is French, and somewhat theatrical, but also we think something more:

> "Then, by solemn degrees,
> There crept on the midnight within him a cold
> Keen gleam of spiritual light. Fold by fold,
> The films of his self-gathered blindness, in part
> Were breath'd bare, and the dawn shuddered into his heart."

But even in this, as in a much greater degree in every other attempt to delineate passion that we could pick out, there is the detestable spirit of rhetorical grandiloquence which Mr. Meredith identifies with poetry. In any genuine poem we should point to the priggish words "by solemn degrees" as giving indications of base alloy; but when the substance which the artist models is almost entirely composed of this alloy, we must be thankful for any indications of an admixture of higher material.

The true dramatic test of a poet is in his feminine characters. Every great critic has remarked that a genuine poet's mind differs most remarkably from other men's by the intuitive sort of sympathy with the feminine nature which it holds easily and gracefully, within the hollow, as it were, of a large masculine experience. "Women," said Goethe, "are silver saucers, into which we put golden apples. My idea of women is not one abstracted from the phenomena of actual life at all, but it is innate in me, or has sprung up in me, God knows how.

My feminine portraitures have therefore all come away successfully from the mould; they are all better than you could find in the real world." And it is a law, we think, almost without exception, that the feminine nature lies within the poetic like the pistil within the calyx of a flower. In Lucile Mr. Owen Meredith has made a very elaborate effort to paint his conception of a woman of genius, and of the conflict between the masculine vigour which genius gives her and the yearnings of a feminine nature for support. With a dash of Oriental blood in her, Lucile is meant to have a dash of Oriental imagination and tenderness combined with the lucid self-possessed intellect of Europe. This, again, is an idea which, were it worked out with any fidelity, would be worthy of a poet's endeavour. There are glimpses throughout the character that the intention was sincerely artistic, but the execution is as much more inadequate than in the case of the French duke as the aim is higher. Lucile's portrait is not defined at all: she begins and ends in the abstract; her genius is mere declamation, and no distinctively feminine impression is produced at all. We are told upon her first introduction, in lines that are of Mr. Meredith's best, of Lucile,

> "The woman that now met, unshrinking, his gaze,
> Seem'd to bask in the silent but sumptuous blaze
> Of that soft second summer, more ripe than the first,
> Which returns when the bud to the blossom hath burst
> In despite of the stormiest April. Lucile
> Had acquired that matchless unconscious appeal
> To the homage which none but a churl would withhold,—
> That caressing and exquisite grace—never bold,
> Ever present—which just a few women possess."

This is prettily described, and we expect to have Lucile acting up to it; but the impression produced by her least restrained language, when you come to hear it, is of a rhetorical and windy cast, ornate and grandiloquent, without any touch of the real woman in it. For example, after the crisis of the first part, when Lucile has failed to win back her old lover, she pours out her labouring feelings to a friend in the East, whom she proposes to visit, and her letter ends thus:

> "My friend, ask me nothing.
> Receive me alone
> As a Santon receives to his dwelling of stone
> In silence some pilgrim the midnight may bring:
> It may be an angel that, weary of wing,
> Hath paused in his flight from some city of doom,
> Or only a wayfarer stray'd in the gloom.
> This only I know: that in Europe at least
> Lives the craft or the power that must master our East.
> Wherefore strive where the gods must themselves yield at last!

Both they and their altars pass by with the Past.
The gods of the household Time thrusts from the shelf;
And I seem as unreal and weird to myself
As those idols of old.
Other times, other men,
Other men, other passions!
So be it! yet again
I turn to my birthplace, the birthplace of morn,
And the light of those lands where the great sun is born!
Spread your arms, O my friend! on your breast let me feel
The repose which hath fled from my own.
Your LUCILE."

We venture to say that no woman overflowing with either genius or feminine tenderness (and Lucile is meant to be rich in both) ever wrote in that inflated style, unless she were half acting the desolation she expresses. Still more unfortunately is she delineated when in the second part she starts on her higher career of raising the fallen and rebuking the impenitent. There is a stony sort of grandiloquence about her then which gives the notion of a rhetorical strong-minded woman. Here, for example, she is lecturing her former lover, Lord Alfred Vargrave, on the danger of making his wife jealous of him, and then throwing her in the way of another's admiration, which she does in the following dreadful style, that reminds one of a reformatory chaplain who has not forgotten his classical education :—

"I know that your wife is as spotless as snow;
But I know not how far your continued neglect
Her nature, as well as her heart, might affect,
Till at last, by degrees, that serene atmosphere
Of her unconscious purity, faint and yet clear,
Like the indistinct golden and vaporous fleece
Which surrounded and hid the celestials in Greece
From the glances of men, would disperse and depart
At the sighs of a sick and delirious heart,—
For jealousy is to a woman, be sure,
A disease heal'd too oft by a criminal cure;
And the heart left too long to its ravage, in time
May find weakness in virtue, reprisal in crime."

We need give little further evidence, we think, that though Mr. Meredith began *Lucile* with an aim not unworthy of an artist, he soon plunged again into that blue-and-gold papier-mâché style of art which is the general characteristic of his poetry.

On the whole, *Lucile* must be called a third-rate novel, rendered disagreeable by very poor and monotonous rhyme. Indeed, the versification is a real mischief, and has no doubt misled Mr. Owen Meredith into many of his monstrous conceits. It bears almost the same relation to the natural language of prose expression as snoring bears to natural breathing, and creates exactly the same kind of nervous annoyance in the reader when the snore (which you cannot avert) is at hand. Only a diseased appetite for the petty surprises of rhyme could endure such rhyme as this, which frequently distracts attention from the false composition without answering one of the purposes that the rhythm and rhyme of a true poem should serve. A long epic poem in couplets is always bad. It suits Pope's epigrammatic style, which always seems to clinch the thought as with the sharp snap of a steel clasp; but in Mr. Owen Meredith's hands it has no possible relation to the flow of the thought, and produces, as we said, only the periodic pang of stertorous breathing. Then, again, the metre is very bad. It is written usually in the metre of Byron's

"The Assyrian came down like a wolf on the fold,
And his cohorts were gleaming in purple and gold;"

which, though grandiose, is well adapted to the flashing splendour of a picture of that kind; and this Mr. Meredith occasionally varies with the metre Goldsmith chose for his "Venison Pasty"—

"Thanks, my lórd, for your vénison, for finer nor fátter
Ne'er ránged in the fórest nor smóked on the plátter."

The first metre Mr. Meredith has in such lines as these,—

"Listen tó me, my friénd. What I wísh to expláin
Is so hárd to shape fórth, I could álmost refraín;"

while Goldsmith's is chosen in the couplet next following:

"From toúching a súbject so frágile. Howéver,
Bear wíth me a whíle if I fránkly endeávour."

Slight as the difference between them is, the first is grandiose, and the second mock-grandiose. And when a long epic poem runs from one into the other, the hero passes as it were from a slightly ostentatious march into the mocking trip with which naughty boys imitate him. However, it is the former metre in which by far the greatest part of the poem is written: and this grandiose rhythm naturally often makes Mr. Owen Meredith ashamed of a plain sentence, and induces him to dress up his impressions in a uniform worthy of so stately a marching-step. We scarcely know whether this, though the worst intellectual result of the rhythm chosen, produces so lamentable an artistic effect as presents itself when the poet omits to put this full costume on his thought, and orders it into this grand march in a slovenly flannel dressing-gown like the following:

"I foresaw you would conquer; you have conquered much,
Much indeed that is noble! *I hail it as such!*"

—a climax so grand as almost to suggest to us Mrs. Gamp coming down "like a wolf on the fold." In general, however, you see that the metre stimulates the rush of the words into something at least equally grand in their swing, even when, as in the following lines, we hunt in vain for any similar march in the thought:

> "What then,
> If earth in itself were sufficient for men,
> Would be man's claim to that glorious promise which arches
> With Hope's fourfold bow the black path where he marches
> Triumphant to death, chanting boldly, 'Beyond!'
> Whilst invisible witnesses round him respond
> From the Infinite, till the great Pæan is caught
> By the echoes of heaven, and the chariot of Thought
> Rolls forth from the world's ringing walls to its goal,
> Urged by Faith, the bright-eyed charioteer of the soul?"

How infinitely wearisome this pomp of movement, continued through three hundred and sixty-one pages, becomes, accompanied as it is by the perpetually recurring clack of the rhyme, —the metre meantime frequently disarranging the accent, or the rhyme compelling words like "liberty" to be rhymed with "free,"—the conscientious reader of this poem alone can know. Sydney Smith once said that his idea of heaven was consuming *pâtés de foie gras* to the sound of trumpets. Reading *Lucile* is like consuming an intellectual delicacy, if not quite so rare, still in several respects analogous, to the sound of hurdy-gurdies, and supplies only too vivid a foretaste of the opposite state.

There are many poets, however, whom it would be exceedingly unfair to judge, either by their longer poems or their directly visionary faculty; many who have neither the sustained narrative vigour for an epic poem nor the visionary eye which realises the details of an invisible scene. In fact, the forms of true poetry are quite as numerous as the forms of full personal life; and the man who fails to expand his apprehensions of the world into an epic may often succeed in precipitating the solid thought into a sonnet, or setting free from his materials the airy sentiment of a song. Moore, for instance, whose longer poems are heavily charged with gaudy and grandiloquent sentimentalism, wrote many a little poem which just caught the momentary sparkle of social feeling, or gave the feathery wings of melodious verse to satire with barbs as cruel as wit could make them. Again, Wordsworth, who had in him far too much weight of meditative thought to rise successfully on the light wings of song, and made his longer poems, fine as they are, rather too solid for ordinary taste, gave a grandeur to the sonnet, and a fervour to the homely grief or gladness of his ballads, which no other poet has reached. A true poet, though he may miss his way often into compositions quite unsuitable to his genius, will blossom somewhere into the poetry which is really his natural life. Can Mr. Owen Meredith take a higher rank by virtue of song, or sonnet, or ballad, or lyric of any kind, than we have been able to assign him in his pictorial scenes and versified drama? The sonnet is clearly a form of verse not suitable to him at all. The strong, deep, meditative note which should vibrate through it from first to last and give it reflective unity is not at all in his way. Such of his poems as profess to be meditative are exceedingly diffuse and meandering, without any single focus of thought. They wander from a pictured love-scene to general and vague reflections, and back again to young ladies, in a very vagrant fashion. After much search among Mr. Meredith's meditative productions, we can find nothing else so good as the following verses, which are two among a considerable number devoted to illustration of the same not very real idea, —that desire is better than possession, and even, as he seems to express it in the second of the two, the unknown than the known, which is a strong thing to say:

> "How little know they life's divinest bliss,
> That know not to possess and yet refrain!
> Let the young Psyche roam, a fleeting kiss:—
> Grasp it—a few poor grains of dust remain.
> See how those floating flowers, the butterflies,
> Hover the garden thro', and take no root!
> Desire forever hath a flying foot.
> Free pleasure comes and goes beneath the skies."
>
> * * * * * * * * *
>
> "Chase not too close the fading rapture. Leave
> To Love his long auroras, slowly seen.
> Be ready to release, as to receive.
> Deem those the nearest, soul to soul, between
> Whose lips yet lingers reverence on a sigh.
> Judge what thy sense can reach not, most thine own,
> If once thy soul hath seized it. The unknown
> Is life to love, religion, poetry."

But in Mr. Meredith's meditative, as in his other poems, we cannot find any genuine or personal reality. These, if any, are the kind of poems in which the mind should be true to itself. When you are honestly looking into your own past and present, it may be natural to find the fancy or imagination kindle; but neither fancy nor imagination, kindling in order to express real thoughts about oneself, give rise to what De Quincey calls "a jewelly hæmorrhage of words." Now there is no kind of poem in Mr. Meredith's volumes which seems to be written more for ornamental purposes, and less to satisfy the craving for true insight, than these long meandering meditations. To us they read, not at all like what a man really thinks to himself, even in the most excited moods, but plausible meditations—the sort of thing a young man might (injudiciously) *like* to think. We have given two of the simplest and best verses of this kind we can discover, expressing rather vividly the sensuous awe of grasping the very thing you seek, and trying to exaggerate that awe into a divine veto. But the following is a more common specimen of the way in which Mr. Owen Meredith philosophises on these occasions, which, we trust, is only a theatrical fiction; for if a man really rants thus to himself alone, the most solitary exercise of his intellect must be taken on stilts. It is from a piece called "Condemned Ones," in which, after reproaching himself and some lady, who appears to have deserted him, he goes on:

> "Yet is there much for grateful tears, if sad ones!
> And Hope's young orphans Memory mothers yet;
> So let them go, the sunny days we had once,
> Our night hath stars that will not ever set.
> And in our hearts are harps, albeit not glad ones,
> Yet not all unmelodious, thro' whose strings
> The night-winds murmur their familiar things,
> Unto a kindred sadness: the sea brings
> The spirits of its solitude, with wings
> Folden about the music of each lyre,
> Thrilled with deep duals by sublime desire,
> Which never can attain, yet ever must aspire,
> And glorify regret."

By very careful reflection it is possible to make out that Memory playing the mother to "Hope's young orphans" is a paraphrase for saying that the writer still cherishes the memory of the wishes which he once hoped for. But neither a poet nor any other man ever really conceived that very simple idea in the form of a Foundling Hospital or Orphan Asylum for Hope's babies, in which Memory has the post of matron. A man must go a very long way for such a metaphor as that to express one of the simplest of all thoughts. Then the last simile no ordinary mind is equal to. The duals thrilled by sublime desire must have of course some reference to the lady, and perhaps to some form of moral duet with her; but the sea and the spirits and the lyre, and the wings that are folded about its music, are a problem far beyond a simple person's mind, and can never have been the imaginative form of any man's genuine thoughts. These are the bright glass beads and bugles which Mr. Meredith hangs about his ideas to make them look poetical, but which really destroy Truth, and substitute showy glitter in its place.

As a song-writer Mr. Meredith would have more chance of

attaining a moderate excellence, if he would attend a little more carefully to the duty of having something distinct to say. His one qualification as a verse-writer is a keen sense of what we may call the *physical* atmosphere which belongs to words, and which often overpowers for him their intellectual significance. Still this is one of the most important qualifications of a song-writer. Moore had this sensuous feeling for words, and an infinitely greater poet, Tennyson, has it in a very high degree; but neither of them sacrifice a clear drift and image to the mere vapour or scent which words give off, as Mr. Owen Meredith often does. Take for example the following verses in the poem called "Once:"

> "O happy hush of heart to heart,
> O moment molten through with bliss,
> O Love delaying long to part,
> That first, fast, individual kiss!
>
> Whereon two lives on glowing lips
> Hung claspt, each feeling fold in fold,
> Like daisies closed with crimson tips,
> That sleep about a heart of gold."

We defy any one to get a clear notion out of the latter verse, though it sounds the *kind* of thing which Moore would have put into a song. Are we to conceive *two* crimson daisies, closed and placed cup to cup, as there are clearly two hearts, and the "deep duals" are, we suppose, the essence of the conception? And more, what is the force which the simile adds to the previous verse? Surely in fact it very much weakens the strength of it. If "the moment molten through with bliss" can be expressed by crimson daisies closed for the night, and, as we infer, somehow looped into each other, it cannot have been a very exalted moment after all. The capacity for an effective sensuous use of language is a very dangerous one, and requires a much stronger intellectual control over it than Mr. Owen Meredith thinks of wielding. Still it is a qualification for a song-writer; for a song should generally effervesce with airy sentiment that rises up lightly to the very surface of the mind without absorbing much attention, and should therefore carry its whole effect with it on its very first contact with the ear of the hearer. And in order that this may be the case, the mere *physique* of the words should be in some sense almost as important as the ideas they contain. We think, for instance, that in three other verses of the same piece Mr. Meredith has fairly succeeded in combining this effective sensuous organisation of words with thought clear enough and telling enough for a very effective song; though that would not, we suppose, be his name for the piece in which we find it:

"As some idea, half divined,
With tumult works within the brain
Of desolate genius, and the mind
Is vassal to imperious pain,

For toil by day, for tears by night,
Till, in the sphere of vision brought,
Rises the beautiful and bright
Predestined but relentless Thought;

So, gathering up the dreams of years,
Thy love doth to its destined seat
Rise sovran, thro' the light of tears—
Achieved, accomplisht, and complete!"

And there is a song in *Lucile* with the peculiar muscatel flavour of Moore's songs, though the idea it tries to embody is not worked out with any distinctness,—the song about the ship and the bird-of-paradise. Its metre has the peculiar swing of a skipping-rope, in which Moore's sentimental tenderness so often expresses itself, and its language has Moore's luscious effects, but its meaning is not brought out with any of Moore's point, and leaves but a faint glimmer of suspicion on the mind as to its true drift. Again, there is a song called a "Canticle of Love," that reminds us somewhat of the same poet, who would not, however, have allowed the last verse to descend into so deep a bathos. On the whole, Mr. Owen Meredith shows more qualification for writing a certain kind of sentimental song than for any other species of poem,—chiefly, we fear, because the need of an intellectual drift is then at its minimum, and the importance of the physical effect of words at its maximum. He tells us as a fact in *Lucile* that there are "Miss Tilburinas" who "sing, and not badly," his earlier verse. This is one of the few poetic distinctions which Mr. Meredith is likely to attain.

But if Mr. Owen Meredith's sentimental songs are decidedly above his average poetic level, we are sorry to add that his would-be comic effusions are very decidedly below them, and about as vulgar and weak as it is possible for a cultivated man to write. The light social chat in *Lucile*, so far as it does not strive after humour, certainly shows a knowledge of society that might be turned to good account in a novel; but he is absolutely without humour, and unfortunately deeply convinced that he possesses it in large measure; and the result is the disagreeable trash of such pieces as "Matrimonial Councils," "See-Saw," "The Midges," "Small People," and others,—pieces that it is marvellous his friends should have allowed him to reprint in a second edition. The raillery which Mr. Meredith speaks of in one quiet and smooth copy of verses as a result of

"The pride which prompts the bitter jest,
Sharp styptic of a bleeding heart,"

has often a certain literary value as an indirect measure of the force of a repressed intensity of feeling. But Mr. Meredith's jokes, while they have none of the brightness of natural gaiety, have also none of the genuine caustic which gives irony its flavour; they are simply forced jokes, and nothing more; and we know of no species of literary product more intolerable than this.

It would, however, be unfair to Mr. Meredith to omit from our criticism a class of poems to which he has evidently devoted more time than to most others, and which are perhaps distantly related to these *manqués* levities of his. There are a considerable class of—lyrical ballads we cannot call them, for there is little or nothing of lyrical feeling in them,—but ballads with an Edgar Poe-ish flavour, the essence of the poem being a sudden horror, generally reaching a climax at the close. Of these we find a large number in the *Wanderer*, containing, with many others, the "Castle of King Macbeth," which, like the tale of the Hunchback in the *Arabian Nights*, throws down a solitary corpse upon us, and leaves us with it,—"King Limos," which begins with physical and ends with suggesting moral cannibalism,—"The Pedlar," a tale of permanent nightmare,—"Mystery," the dream of a delirious man whom the surgeons have bled,—"Misanthropos," intended, we fancy, as a kind of pendant to Tennyson's "Vision of Sin,"—the lines in a French *café*, which are an attempt to intrude the shadow of supernatural remorse into the life of pleasant sin,—"Going back again," which delineates a soft moonlight picture of a beauty sitting with her throat cut,—"The Ghost," and finally "The Portrait," which is, we take it, meant to contain the climax of the morally monstrous. This enumeration—and we might add some others of the same class—will be sufficient to show that Mr. Owen Meredith has made a special study of horrible situations. He has tried too, in most of these cases, to give piquancy to the horror by a certain dash of levity such as Edgar Poe throws into his "Raven;" and this was what we meant by saying that there is a certain connexion between these poems and the atrocious comic poems of which we spoke last. They are not, however, open to the same kind of criticism; for the touch of levity is seldom obtruded, and is always secondary to the touch of horror. The writer's notion evidently is that the poetical effect consists in the thrill with which the scene pictured inspires you; that if his picture can startle you in any thing like the same degree as the actual discovery of a beauty sitting at her window in the moonlight with her throat cut, or of a man carousing at night with the ghost of his dead mistress, he has attained the highest triumph of poetical art. Accordingly touches are sedulously introduced which in any way tend to enhance the thrill of horror;—but we do not think that this is a path by which any one could reach a true poetical effect. Poetry has something better to do than to imitate humbly the influence of ghost-stories and murders on the nervous system. It should, if it touches such matters at all, attempt to draw away the veil of shuddering sense with which horrible catastrophes preoccupy and blind us, and present in its place the realities of human feeling or passion which have led to tragedy as their result. Edgar Poe certainly does not do this. He rests on the merely morbid, as if the morbid were a final and universal root of human nature instead of a result of some deeper mental or moral distortion, the secret of which the poet ought to be able partially to fathom. Hence the exceedingly low level of Edgar Poe's power,—certainly marvellous of its kind. But Mr. Owen Meredith, without any of Edgar Poe's wonderful capacity for inspiring a hypochondriac mood in his readers, insists very unfortunately on pursuing the same course. And he succeeds in producing one or two disagreeable qualms of the same kind, though less acute than an actual ghost or an actual murder would produce. Now this seems to us to show that Mr. Owen Meredith has entirely mistaken the true field of poetry in relation to this species of tragic effect. The part of poetry in tragedy can never be the mere statement of a horrid moral riddle, to which the reader is left to find the answer. This is to put poetry below even the sensation drama. That aims no doubt at producing *coups de théâtre*, but at least it leads up to them and puts in the hands of the audience all the moral clues by which they are apparently explained. It relies on thrilling situations, but at least on thrilling situations which are intelligibly evolved out of known causes, and which intelligibly contribute to visible effects. And none but the very lowest art relies even on the great scenes for its "surprises" at all, but only for the greater scale of action and passion for which these great scenes make room. It is not the thrill which the audience feels in the suffocation of Desdemona, but the gradual maturing of Othello's jealousy and its consummation in its natural fruit, which lends the interest to that last scene,—not the surprise, but the fulfilment of the growing dread, in some sense the very absence of all room for surprise. True poetry may sometimes, though rarely, *begin* with an enigma, as in the case of *Hamlet*, for instance, where the suspicion of murder does not dawn even on Hamlet's own mind till the ghost has appeared. But it can never end with one without ceasing to conform to all the laws of art. It is of the very essence of all art—poetical no less than that of the sculptor or the painter—to satisfy the mind, not to perplex it,

—to offer a coherent vision; to help us to understand something we did not understand before, if the subject is old; to give us a new object of imaginative perception which exemplifies known principles of human life, even if the subject is original. The situation in which the mind *cannot* rest, but which simply sets it speculating, is *ipso facto* inartistic. When, indeed, a poet or an imaginative writer has fashioned for us a whole narrative, then the painter may single out any momentary crisis in it and try to work out his conception; and this may be true art. But then the mind rests upon the known story, and looks to the painter for some fresh commentary on it, some fresh insight into it by which we may be able to appreciate more fully the conception in the creative mind of the dramatist. All true art extends our vision; and so far as it does not, but simply excites our curiosity or dread, it is not art. If the artist deals with a horrible subject, he must treat horror as a result of crime, sin, ignorance, or some other evil, and satisfy us that it is in its right place, however wrong the cause. Thus Shelley's *Cenci*, which is a study of the most fearful of human horrors, is a work of high art so far at least as the character of Beatrice is concerned, because Shelley helps us to understand the secret of her childlike vindictiveness, the impersonality of her unscrupulous passion to rid the earth of her destroyer. But it is not a work of high art as regards Count Cenci, because it leaves him the same riddle that it found him. Nor can poetry be absolved from this universal condition of all art. Even Mr. Owen Meredith's own poems sufficiently show this; for wherever we find one rising above the level of his ordinary verse, there also we find one which, instead of merely piquing curiosity, gives us a somewhat fuller insight into some corner of creation or some recess in the heart of man. If his sketch of the Duc de Luvois in *Lucile* is worth any thing, it is for this reason; if his picture of the desolate sea-side country in which the scene of "the earl's return" is laid is worth any thing, it is for this reason; and just so far as he puts forward an insoluble terror, simply for the thrill it excites in the nerves, so far he abjures his function of an artist, and does what the sensation paragraphs of an American newspaper effect better, instead.

We have said that Mr. Owen Meredith's "Misanthropos" is a kind of pendant to Tennyson's "Vision of Sin,"—not, we need scarcely say, comparable to it in any way, though the "Vision of Sin" is one of Tennyson's least successful pieces, but apparently allied with it in the form of conception. "Misanthropos," if, as we think, it does exemplify, does not exemplify strikingly, the fault we have just spoken of. It is comparatively a connected and rational piece, striving to delineate the state of mind of a dying misanthrope disgusted with life and all that it contains. But for this very reason it illustrates in the germ the poetical vice which such poems as "The Portrait" present in full bloom. The misanthropic state is not a subject for Art without some delineation of how a man has grown into misanthropy. It is essentially the fruit of a peculiar history and career. If delineated alone, it is like a shadow without any visible substance to cast it, or an image of revenge without the wrong which gave birth to it. Now Tennyson is clearly aware of this. He does not introduce his jaded sensualist, jeering at every semblance of good, till he has given us a glimpse into his history. The youth "who rode a horse with wings that would have flown, but that his heavy rider kept him down," and who had been led by a child of sin into the company "with heated eyes" and "sleepy light upon their brows and lips," is already printed on the imagination before the "gray and gap-toothed man, as lean as death," crosses the horizon again, and launches out into that bitter satire against even the name of virtue:

> "Virtue!—to be good and just—
> Every heart, when sifted well,
> Is a clot of warmer dust
> Mixed with cunning sparks of hell!"

And without the prologue the long philippic would have little or no artistic meaning. But Mr. Owen Meredith characteristically gives us the misanthropical declamation without a hint as to its birth. He opens with the waters of bitterness. The speaker introduces himself first in the caricaturing verse:

> "Not a light in yonder sky,
> Save that single wicked star,
> Leering with its wanton eye
> Thro' the shatter'd window-bar;
> Come to see me die!"

Now, not to speak of the absurd straining of the misanthropic mood implied in attributing wickedness to a star, the whole picture is utterly *unmotived*,—an eclipse without a vestige of the body which casts the eclipse, a collapse without a paralysing stroke, a passion of hatred without either a crime or a wrong. This cannot be good art; and when we are reminded from verse to verse, now, of the poem of Mr. Tennyson's we have mentioned, now, again, of Faust's curse, and now of Timon's just resentment, and yet find no root for any of these phases of misanthropy,—we see how completely Mr. Owen Meredith's notion of poetic effect is not artistic, but sensational. The Misanthrope too occasionally lapses into rather inconsistent apologies for sinners:

"O the vice within the blood!
  And the sin within the sense;
And the fallen angelhood
  With its yearnings too immense
To be understood!"

—a form of apology the last lines of which Mr. Owen Meredith might fairly adopt in his character of poet; but whether the immensity of his yearnings is sufficient excuse for the curiously torso character of his art, we are not quite sure.

But "Misanthropos" is, as we said, not only not the worst, but one of the least tricky of these sensational minor poems; for it does attempt to expound the intellectual attitude of the Misanthrope, though not to explain it. The real climax of poetical vice is reached in such pieces as "The Vampyre" or "The Portrait." In the latter poem a gentleman is introduced listening on a gusty night to the "wind at his prayers," whatever that meteorological phenomenon may be, and thinking by the dying fire of "the dear dead woman up-stairs." He explains to us that only two persons know any thing about his trouble, —one "the friend of his bosom, the man I love," whom grief has "sent fast asleep" in the chamber up above; the other is the Raphael-faced young priest who confessed her when she died, a man "of gentle nerve," whom this grief of another man had moved beyond measure, for his lip had grown white as he speeded "her parting soul." In this desolate situation he recalls to mind that he has left a portrait of himself on the bosom of the corpse:

"On her cold dead bosom my portrait lies
  Which next to her heart she used to wear;
Haunting it o'er with her tender eyes
  When my own face was not there.

It is set all round with rubies red,
  And pearls which a Peri might have kept.
For each ruby there my heart hath bled;
  For each pearl my eyes have wept!"

What this last statement may amount to as a measure of tenderness is not apparent; but he decides to reclaim his portrait before it is buried with her: and on going up-stairs to feel for it in the moonlight, he encounters another hand on the breast of the corpse, which turns out to be that of the "friend of my bosom, the man I loved," on the same errand; and a dispute very like that about the colour of the chameleon occurs:

"Said the friend of my bosom, 'Yours, no doubt,
  The portrait was, till a month ago,
When this suffering angel took that out,
  And placed mine there, I know.'

'This woman, she loved me well,' said I.
'A month ago,' said my friend to me:
'And in your throat,' I groan'd, 'you lie!'
He answer'd . . . 'let us see.'

'Enough!' I return'd, 'let the dead decide:
And whose soever the portrait prove,
His shall it be, when the cause is tried,
Where Death is arraign'd by Love.'

We found the portrait there, in its place:
We open'd it by the tapers' shine:
The gems were all unchanged: the face
Was—neither his nor mine.

'One nail drives out another, at least!
The face of the portrait there,' I cried,
'Is our friend's, the Raphael-faced young Priest,
Who confess'd her when she died.'

The setting is all of rubies red,
And pearls which a Peri might have kept.
For each ruby there my heart hath bled;
For each pearl my eyes have wept!"—

with which the poem concludes, without any speech from the dead woman, like that addressed by the chameleon to the positive travellers, concerning the folly of judging by so limited an experience. The cold comment that "one nail drives out another, at least," with which the discovery of this harlot's elaborate double prostitution in the very face of death is received, is scarcely any addition to the very obscure testimony to the hero's tenderness, which appears to be typically set forth by the setting of the portrait in rubies and pearls. You are left with the raw horror on your mind of this frightful network of sensuality, duplicity, and death, and without any touch, however slight, which can serve to mitigate this horror by throwing the fine light of art over the scene. It is like an exceedingly detestable police-case thrown into rhyme. Owen Meredith may say, with great justice, that the plot of Shelley's *Cenci* is infinitely more frightful, and so it is; but, as we have said, Shelley has cast so bright an artistic beauty over the conception, has taken it up so completely into his imagination, that we can see nothing beyond the terrible intellectual and moral problem under which Beatrice Cenci's mind laboured, and by which it was so fearfully warped. But Mr. Owen Meredith does not throw this horror into any intellectual form at all. He does not even delineate it, if he is fully aware of it,—he only tells us what he expects will make us shudder, and imagines that that shudder is due to his poetry. Why, if you were to translate the thing into prose, you would lend it a much stronger effect. The only influence of the verse is to give a certain dilettante sort of ornament to the story, without once rousing the imagination. You wonder what the rubies and pearls mean, and what sort of troubles he alludes to in the many bleedings of the heart to which he has been subject, and the tears he has shed, —whether they were all for this woman or not, and so forth. But the only intellectual kernel of the piece, if the incident be possible at all,—the state of mind of this dying prostitute,— is not even touched. The story is pitched down before us in naked loathsomeness, a kind of monstrous nut to crack; and not a particle of artistic assistance is rendered towards solving the mystery of evil which the poet has indicated. No artistic crime could be more heinous.

We have now attempted to show that in almost all the departments of his art which he has attempted at all, Mr. Owen Meredith, or the gentleman who writes under that name, has substituted, for the genuine poetic art, which tries to reveal through the imaginative world, as fully as possible, the true spirit of human life and nature,—the spurious poetic art, which invents decorative artifices to hide the emptiness of its form. The latter is to the former what dress and ornament are to the culture of perfect beauty. Indeed, Mr. Owen Meredith's skill is mainly, as it seems to us, a branch of literary cosmetics, through which signs of healthy, earnest, and rounded purpose only shine in glimpses here and there. If we have been too severe, it is not at least from any personal motive; for we have never heard any thing of the writer except that his poems are popular, and that he stands socially far above the need of any thing like literary compassion. At a time when poetry has to do, for the cultivated world, much, not only of its own proper work, but of that of faith also,—when the true poets know intimately how infinitely difficult it is to find for their delineations but "one feeling based on truth"—on the absolute solid rock of truth, it is in our mind a serious duty to sound the artifices of the mere decorators of human life, who put a chain round its neck, and earrings in its ears, and fine raiment on its back, and beautify its complexion, and teach it the graceful attitudes of movement and repose, and call the result—poetry. We shall be grieved if we have done this gentleman any injustice. We have anxiously noted almost any sign of imaginative sincerity and vigour that a very careful study of him has discovered; but with every fresh reading we have gained fresh certainty that his models are bad, his method spurious, and his own feeling for nature either dull or blunted. His art is typified by the fair ghost whom he describes in one of his pointlessly thrilling poems. A woman "pale and fair," who seems a monarch's daughter "by the red gold round her hair," comes to him towards dawn, lifts up her head "from her white shoulders," and says,

> "Look in! you'll find I'm hollow;
> Pray do not be afraid."

That must have been Mr. Owen Meredith's Muse. She is a well and even ornately-dressed ghost, who habitually proclaims the gospel of her hollowness to any critic who will allow himself to be haunted by her for a season. We have looked in, we have found her very hollow, and we are not at all afraid; but we are very much fatigued, and, as the beaten soldiers say, "demoralised" by the process. "Earth is sick and heaven is weary" of this tawdry finery affecting the grandeur of an art which of all arts is the most real to the very few to whom has been given the vision and the power to discern, and live by, the truth of life. Mr. Owen Meredith has cleverness, and is not incapable of higher aims. He will one day cast off with a sigh of relief the meretricious and dilettante costume which has so long disguised him from his true self, as well as from the world which has applauded and misled him.

Art. IX.—CHURCH REFORM.

A Letter to the Lord Bishop of London on the State of Subscription in the Church of England and in the University of Oxford. By Arthur Penrhyn Stanley, D.D., Regius Professor of Ecclesiastical History and Canon of Christ Church, Oxford; Examining Chaplain to the Bishop of London. Oxford and London: John Henry and James Parker.

Lord Eldon would never have understood the present position of the Church of England. He firmly believed that the first effect of the Reform Bill, of Catholic Emancipation, and all the thousand changes which harassed his old age, would be the "demolition" of the Church of England. He had seen a new world of thought arise around the old and sacred fabric. For years he had striven to keep down the new world; for years he succeeded; at length he had been vanquished. He could not doubt what the effect would be. The Church would be attacked "from without," its external enemies would close in upon it day by day: day by day their strength would increase, and its strength would decrease; in no long time it would fall, amid the jeers of its assailants, and in a storm of revolution. Thirty years have passed on, and we see the reality before us. It is the reverse of the anticipation. The assailants of the Church from without are less powerful, less formidable, less hopeful, than they were thirty years ago. A small section of the orthodox Dissenters excepted, no one attacks the "Establishment" as such. The very phrase has died out of our controversies. The abolition of church-rates seemed a short time since probable; but an injudicious advocate, the authorised agent of an influential society, happened to say that it was only a step towards "further changes,"—towards the destruction of the Church: and then immediately public feeling changed; the English people were alarmed, and church-rates were preserved. Thirty years ago, Liberals were not only wrath but loud at the position of the Bishops in the House of Lords; who is either loud or angry now? Who cares at all about the matter? The Irish Church is as bad as ever; it is, as formerly, the Church of a minority. The Scottish Church, which old reformers hardly ventured to attack, which had cast its roots deep and wide in the whole Scottish people, has become the Church of a minority too. The *case* of the assailants of ecclesiastical establishments has improved, and yet they assail no longer.

But the existing Church is not safe; it has never *felt* so unsafe. It is attacked *from within*. In the old times—in Lord Eldon's times—there was at least a demarcation between friends and foes. The assailants might be eager, but there was no treachery in the interior. Now the clergy attack the formularies of the Church, some one and some another; others attack the Bible itself. Courts of law are harassed with arguments to prove how many heresies beneficed clergymen may safely and consistently hold. Many of the best churchmen write pamphlets in favour of change: they would relax something or they would alter something. Now most educated people are for *a* Church, though few are satisfied with *the* Church; thirty years ago the issue was different and simpler,—every one was either for *the* Church or else for *no* Church.

The causes of so remarkable a change are well worth a little consideration, though they cannot be fully understood without a little theory.

There are three courses which the State may adopt with religion. First, it may leave it alone altogether; it may affect to say or think, "Religion is of so high a sphere that I decline to have any thing to do with it;" it may really think, "Religion is a thing so intangible, so curious, so affected by the various idiosyncrasies of different minds, so sure to breed quarrels and contention, that I *will* have nothing to do with it. To do the plain political work of this world is the business of the

State, and it will only augment the difficulties of that work to connect it with any thing so obscure, so impalpable, so incapable of effectual proof, as religion." The high aspect of the voluntary principle has appealed to a few men out of the way of the world; it has induced sincere and pious Christians in quiet places to be unwilling that their creed, their hope, their trust, their real being here, and their expected being hereafter, should be identified with what they think the coarse, the crude, the ungodly work of the State. The low aspect of the voluntary principle has moved, and is daily moving, the natural instincts of many a statesman. He sees his work, he believes, plain and easy before him, if "the clergy of all persuasions" will leave him alone; he can keep peace in streets and conquer the king's enemies, or at least contend with them manfully and well; but he cannot predict what will be the result if he introduces into his simple formula the great "unknown quantity" religion. From the combined force of these two extreme classes—the most Christian and the least Christian in every country—the voluntary principle will always retain much strength. But in England neither of these classes is the ruling class, or is even a very powerful class. The *mere* Christian and the *mere* politician do not much influence the sluggish mass of vague judgments which we term public opinion. Their voices are various in sound, but they are alike in origin. They are the anomalous utterings of eccentric minorities, and are unheard more than unheeded, are drowned even more than disregarded. The plain judgment of the English people is, that "the State ought not to separate itself from religion; on the contrary, it ought to knit itself to religion." Religion, they hold, "is the real producer of that order, that peace, that harmony, that justice, which the State only strives to produce. It is the greater power where the State is the lesser power; it is the greatest ally which the State can hope for, and statesmen are foolish, if not wicked, if they do not avail themselves of it."

The English people do not like the opposite way any better. Many speculators have proposed, and some countries have enacted, that out of the taxation all sects should be paid a certain annual sum proportionate to their real influence. The State on this system declines to answer the question, What is religious truth? It neglects and passes it by; it only attempts to answer the practical problem, How shall religion be made politically useful? It replies to that question by paying each form of religious sect which inculcates political morality, which teaches obedience to the magistrate, respect for property and for plain social duties, in some proportion to the degree of morality which they have the means of creating. A large sect is paid much, because it can make many men moral; a small sect little, because it can make few men so. The preacher is paid in proportion to his congregation, because that is the best test of his social influence and his political utility. A theorist may easily make an adroit case for this system; but as respects a deeply religious people such as the English, it has an inherent defect which will always prevent its being applied, and which makes it clear that it ought not to be applied. The object of the plan is to make religion politically useful by the patronage and hire of all religions favourable to politics; but that diffused patronage and that indiscriminate hire have an influence deeply unfavourable to religion. The State seems to say, "We, the embodiment and representative of the sense and the practicality of the community, care nothing for religious truth; we do not think about, or regard it, or heed it; we treat all religious creeds as useful *employés*, as inferior servants, but we acknowledge ourselves no fealty to any of them." The spectacle of this indifference to the unseen world, this systematic adoption upon principle of religious "know-nothingness" by the State, which is the greatest human institution, which is the most visible human institution, which overawes more than any other the human heart, which attracts more than any other the human imagination, is unfavourable to religion. No deeply religious people would ever endure it, or admit of it. No English parliament would ever entertain an annual series of "religious estimates" to be divided among all sects in proportion to their power. Every English parliament would feel that such a system, by exhibiting a conspicuous indifference to religion, by annually making it a political engine, injured the sources of its best influence, and impaired that very political morality which the whole scheme was intended to strengthen and to aid.

The third scheme is the old and simple one, that the State should publicly make a selection of a religious creed; that it should assume to distinguish for itself and its own actions, if not for its subjects and their actions, what is religious truth. The plan was called formerly the plan of the "State conscience." The duty of the State, or at least one of its principal duties, is, on this theory, the discrimination between religious truth and religious falsehood—the arriving at right conclusions and opinions concerning the unseen world. But, as far as respects the present English State, and especially the English parliament, which is its ruling organ, no one could imagine an annual selection of a religious creed by the English House of Commons on the production by the "Minister for Public Worship" of a religious "estimate." The House of Commons would not vote away millions of public money for any one religion, would not undertake an annual investigation which was the true religion, any more than it would vote those millions as a subsidy for all religions. The plan of selection suits a popular assembly of mixed opinions, even as ill as the plan of indiscriminate payment suits a nation which, amid whatever superficial secularity, is at heart passionately religious.

We then seem to be landed in a great perplexity. On the one hand, the State cannot leave religion alone without relinquishing the most valuable aid and help in its own functions; on the other hand, it cannot in England now—out of its own resources—out of the annual revenue which is its sole property—support all religions, or choose any one to support. There seems at first no help for a difficulty like this.

In an old community like the English, however, the existence of a vast ecclesiastical *property*, which was given for religious objects, which is even now indefinitely useful in religious concerns, which cannot be diverted from those concerns without palpable and plain evil, not only aids our difficulty, but extricates us from our difficulty. The State finds a vast property, not for the most part granted by itself; which was never State revenue; which was given by its owners to religion when there was but one religion in the country; which was given by those owners to a religion which was once ours, which is not now ours, which is hateful to the English nation. The State finds itself *trustee* of a great estate destined by its donors for *national* religious purposes; but, in the progress of time and the changes of opinion, in fact never devoted now to the support of the Church to which those givers adhered, but always devoted to the support of those beyond its pale, and often devoted to the support of those who furiously and fanatically denounce it.

What is the State to do with this large property? In the first place, it would not practically be endured that the funds heretofore devoted to the support of religious worship should be devoted to any object but religious worship. In nine-tenths of the parishes of England such a change of employment would be alien to the opinions and feelings,—the most confident opinions and the deepest feelings,—of the mass of the population. It might be possible, if it were enforced by law and by the sword, but it would not otherwise be possible. Again, if the State proposed to confiscate the church property, and to devote it to other uses, it would have at the very outset to deal with a most delicate question of *individual property*. The right of appointing a beneficed clergyman is a legal, valuable, and saleable property; and if we say there are to be no longer beneficed clergyman, we must compensate those who have the right of appointing them. *Advowsons* are as good property as fee-simples; and we must first buy the *advowsons,*—a costly matter, for they are most valuable,—ere we could set apart the present ecclesiastical property to a *non*-ecclesiastical use.

The difficulty of diverting the yearly income of the English Church property to secular uses would be as great as any political difficulty ever was or can be. The secular passions and the religious passions would both be against it. Religious people would hate it as sacrilege; all people with any thing to lose would hate it as confiscation, and very many would hate it as both. And if the advowsons were bought up first, the applicable money—the tempting money, the money to *spend*—would be much less than, at a first glance, would be anticipated.

Nor should the income be so diverted. The arguments which show that the English State could not, out of its annual taxation, set apart a conspicuous sum—a sum of millions—either for the support of one religion or for the support of all religions, do not withhold it from acting as trustee, for the national benefit, of this vast inherited property. An annual vote, whether of distinctive selection or of indiscriminate gift, would be unsuitable to our habits: the first would be too *religious* for our Parliament,—it cannot pretend to be an exceptionally good judge of religious truth; the second would be too *irreligious,*—it dared not in the face of the nation, it does not itself wish, to avow an indiscriminate support of all useful religions, whether they be true or false. But the English Parliament, though an exceedingly bad judge of abstract religious truth, is well qualified to decide what sort of administration of this great ecclesiastical estate would most conduce to the religious welfare of the English nation. They are Englishmen predominantly of the predominant creed, exceptionally of the exceptional creed; they are most of them men of some sense; they are most of them men of some education; they are most of them men of some ability; as an assembly they, by the admission of the world, excel every other in testing taste and discriminating ability. They will therefore be well able to act as trustees on behalf of England. They need not make an annual vote, which would be a glaring exercise of supreme authority; they have only to exercise a general, an occasional, a hidden trusteeship over these large ecclesiastical domains.

The exact dilemma applying to religious votes is this—either you must annually choose the creed you pay, because it is the one sole religious truth, or you must annually choose to pay what you admit may not be the religious truth. You have either to tax men for your selected creed as the one truth, or for some other religion, or for all religions. In this case, as in the far less objectionable, the comparatively imperceptible case of church-rates, the dissidents from the paid religion will say, "We *will* not pay, we *may* not pay; we risk our salvation *if* we pay to the support of creeds which are the antithesis and opposite of all we believe, which at the least endanger the future happiness, and perhaps ensure the future misery of those who believe them." But no one can say that his conscience is aggrieved because the produce of certain acres which never belonged to him, on which he has no claim, are devoted to the support of a religion of which the vast majority of the nation approves, even though he may not approve of it himself. The human imagination, in fact, not only recognises and admits, but aggravates and intensifies the difference between payments by the individual,—payments "out of pocket," as the feeling phrase goes, and payments *not* by the individual. Few consciences could be aggrieved at the use by the nation of an old ecclesiastical estate in the manner that the nation, speaking by the State, declares that it thinks desirable.

Nor is this the only advantage which the maintenance of a proprietary Church secures to us. As we have explained, it enables the State, in such an age as this, and such a country as this, to connect itself with religion without violating what any one can even fancy to be the claim of the individual citizen—the right of the tax-payer's conscience. But it does more than this. It supports in independence an educated clergy. We are not disposed at present to set forth an elaborate theory on the relation of the clergy to their congregations. But we venture to assume that an entire dependence of the instructor upon the instructed is by no means desirable. In the Church as it now exists the clergyman is entirely independent of his congregation. He may set them at defiance; he may disregard their wishes; he may pay no respect to their opinions, so long as he keeps within the limits of the law. This entire *in*dependence is perhaps faulty. In an ideal state of things, the minister would probably be dependent on his congregation for some part of his income, and independent for the other part; he would be obliged to them for non-essentials, and not be obliged to them for essentials. But however this may be, no one can have watched the real working, and no one can have considered the true theory of ecclesiastical relations, without perceiving that *some* independence of the teacher on the taught, a certain secure *status* in the preacher, which no deviation from the opinion of the hearers can impair or weaken, is an essential ingredient of a desirable organisation. The duty of "making things pleasant" is a great duty in a religious teacher, but it is not the sole duty. A proprietary Church naturally, if not necessarily, vests a freehold in

P

the clergyman; and it is the second of its great excellences. It not only enables the State, in an age of divided opinion, to identify itself with religion, and religion with itself, but it improves the *communicated* religion itself, by giving to the teacher a fixed dignity and free reflection such as can hardly be found elsewhere.

Such is the sort of reasoning which has satisfied even the classes most opposed by inherited tradition to the Church of England that its maintenance is desirable. It would be idle to say that these abstract reasons are those which have convinced the English people. As a people they have never inquired into the subject; they have never doubted about it. They see that in almost every parish the abolition of the Church would do obvious harm, that in almost every parish its continuance does obvious good; and they are contented with this practical test, which, indeed, suits most of them better than difficult arguments, which they could hardly understand, and would never remember. Nevertheless, a quiet person, searching calmly for mere truth, will perceive that these arguments are very valuable, because on so great a subject they are critically decisive.

The reason why the educated classes, though desirous of *a* Church, are not satisfied with *the* Church are better known and more obvious. The English Church was founded in an age utterly different from ours in genius and character and spirit. Between the England of Queen Elizabeth and the England of Queen Victoria there are differences not of detail but of essence, —differences which could not be removed from either age without changing its identity. The English Church was framed in what was then thought a spirit of compromise. Its founders intended that there should be only one form of religious worship, and one creed of professed religion, in England; and they were fairly and naturally anxious that this one creed should be one professed by very many persons, and this form of worship should be one in which many persons could join. They were ready, as Englishmen in authority generally are, to sacrifice something of consistency and system for an equivalent in convenience and expediency. But there were limits to their moderation. They intended that the English Church should be a mean between the Roman Catholic Church and the extreme Protestant sectaries; they wished it to be a tolerant and comprehensive mean, but still a mean. They did not wish it to include either extreme; they advisedly wished to condemn the doctrines of the consistent Papists and the doctrines of the consistent Puritans.

In the present age, pernicious effects arise both from their wish to include and their wish to exclude. Their wish to exclude has given rise to the Thirty-nine Articles. Speaking generally, it is the object of these propositions to keep out the two extremes of conflicting opinion of the age in which they were composed; their whole scope is explicable only by long past controversies; many of their minuter points remain grotesque even after every explanation has been given to them. It is idle now-a-days for any educated man to fancy that he believes those articles as a whole and in their spirit. By a mental contortion he may be able for a moment to force, or to fancy that he forces, his mind into a temporary reconcilement with most of the propositions taken separately. He may enforce on his intellect an occasional conformity with sentence A and sentence B and sentence C; but no energy of effort, no illusion of imagination, no fond emotion, can make a sincere man say that these obsolete dogmas really represent his *mind*. If he had to write a creed for himself, he would not write *that* creed. They have been called "Articles of Peace," and so they may have been; but now they are "Articles of Perplexity." They contain many propositions which few can more than half believe; and their spirit, their language, and their tone, are alien to the present times.

Such has been the effect of the exclusive efforts of the first Anglicans, and they have aggravated it by their efforts in the way of inclusion and comprehension. They wished, rightly and wisely and naturally, to write anew as little of the real Prayer-book, as little of the ordinary and vital Church Services, as they dared. They wished to use as much of the immemorial prayers of the Church as they by possibility were able. They wished to use as many of the old words—of the words familiar to their youth, and remembered from their childhood—as they possibly could. Such was their real inclination; and even if they had not been so inclined, the statesmanlike and conservative instinct which has nearly always been the critical and determining force in English politics, would have compelled them to choose that course. They were making great changes; they were altering the language of the prayers; they were abandoning the mystic unknown tongue for the vulgar tongue; they were substituting a new and homely ceremonial for an old and attractive ceremonial; they were making great changes in doctrine, of which these changes in gesture and ceremonial were the symbols and effects. Common sense and plain statesmanship were therefore imperative. They said, "As you must change so much, do not change an iota more than you must, especially in the familiar part of religion; in the common public worship leave what you can unchanged. As the words and gestures are to be new, let the substance of what is said be as old as possible."

Coming to the formation of a new English Liturgy in this spirit, the reformers have kept as much of the old Latin prayers as they were able. And it is fair to believe that they did not always know the precise meaning of what they were keeping. These old words were so familiar to them, as many old words are to us, that they hardly knew their meaning. They went on uttering many old phrases wholly unconscious how little these phrases represented their own belief,—how much more in harmony they were with the creed from which they revolted. In ages of transition such is always the case: the old formulæ linger over the new doctrines; they are like the proverbs of an old period; they are cited as confirmation of practices and habits utterly alien from their original meaning, and almost from any possible meaning. The reformers were in the worst position to estimate the meaning of the old prayers; their minds had gradually ebbed away from much of their spirit, though they retained an attachment to almost all their words.

The result is the singular structure of the English Prayer-book. It is made up of prayers written mostly by Catholics and in a Catholic spirit, and of Articles entirely written by Protestants and in a Protestant spirit. The services are favourable to one creed, the Articles enjoin another creed; and to fresh readers, such as are common among the educated classes of the present day, the result is strange and peculiar. It is to no purpose that a refined argumentation is put before men to show that these two documents may be rendered consistent; that there is no absolute inconsistency in them; that by some clippings of inconvenient words, and some enlargement of convenient words, they may be "held together." An educated mind does not like two "lobes" of belief; it hates to be always twisting words into senses which, if they really bear, they will not well bear, which it is certain the writer did not mean them to bear.

The notion of many minds is, that there is a sort of compromise to be struck between the tone of the Articles and the tone of the Liturgy, and that the legal creed of the English Church is some way and somewhere between them. Such was doubtless Lord Chatham's notion when he spoke of the English Church as having Calvinistic Articles, a Popish Liturgy, and an Arminian clergy. But though, as a rough practical compromise, such a combination of inconsistent elements may be possible,—though it may be congenial to the ruder species of the active mind, it will not be suitable to or accepted by the learned and logical intellect. For a Church to issue two documents, in spirit, if not in terms, inconsistent, and then say to its disciples, "Go to, now reconcile these," is at once a dangerous temptation to speculative disputants, and a severe trial to simple and pious minds. thinker who is bound to accept the English Prayer-book, is bound to accept many hundreds of propositions, written by very many persons, and in very many ages; he is bound both to accept the lyrical semi-Catholicism of the services, and the wholly Protestant prose dogmatism of the Articles. A really logical mind cannot do this. Father Newman says, and justly says, that it is impossible to hold *any system* of theology without putting some violence on some propositions in some part of the Prayer-book. The High Church have to manipulate the Articles; the Low Church to manipulate the Liturgy; the Broad Church have to manipulate both. Free thought is inevitably weighed down by such a number of imposed propositions; and if it had been intended to aggravate the certain hardship, it could not have been more effectually accomplished than by compiling these propositions from two dissimilar and hostile schools of theology.

Such is the evil in a word in which the Church of England now labours. It has formularies which are so long that nothing short of inspiration could exempt them from error,—that scarcely any known human intellect could have made them consistent; and yet these formularies are not inspired, and are compiled of the various expressions of various minds in various ages. In consequence they often at least *seem* to be untrue, they often at least *seem* to be inconsistent.

The laity, indeed, of the Church do not practically feel this evil much. They are not obliged to believe all these services, or any of these Articles; they are subject to no severe penalty for impugning them. But this liberty is only a result of social laxity. The laity are subject to a prosecution for heresy, and if convicted, to excommunication for heresy; but no one is convicted, because no one prosecutes, and no one prosecutes because no one would care for the punishment. In an age in which there is a real social toleration, excommunication, which does not affect property, which does not (as in the case of a layman it could not) affect the right to perform public worship, is a nullity. It cuts a man off from no communion. He can do as much and can possess as much as ever.

The position of the clergy is very different. They are bound by most stringent obligations to conform to the Liturgy and to believe the Articles. It is therefore the clergy who complain. The anomalous nature of the Prayer-book—its division into dissimilar halves, the vast number of propositions which it lays down—affects the laity little, but the clergy much. It only affects the laity through the clergy. The fetters on the teachers are indirectly fetters on those whom they teach. The precise position of the clergy is this:

They are subject to four species of legal obligation.

1st. They are required to subscribe the Articles.

2d. They are required to conform to the Liturgy.

3d. They are bound in *some* sense by the Ordination Service to believe all the canonical Scriptures. We say in *some* sense, because, after Dr. Lushington's decision in the case of *Essays and Reviews,* it is not easy to say very shortly *how far* the clergy are so bound. A few words will explain this.

The Ordination Service contains two passages as to the belief of the person ordained in Scripture. The first is in the Service for the Ordination of Deacons, and is as follows:

"*Bishop.* Do you unfeignedly believe all the Canonical Scriptures of the Old and New Testament?

"*Answer.* I do believe them."

The second passage is in the Form for the Ordination of Priests, and is as follows:

"*Bp.* Are you persuaded that the Holy Scriptures contain sufficiently all doctrine required of necessity for eternal salvation through faith in Jesus Christ? and are you determined out of the said Scriptures to instruct the people committed to your charge, and to teach nothing, as required of necessity to eternal salvation, but that which you shall be persuaded may be concluded and proved by the Scripture?

"*A.* I am so persuaded, and have so determined by God's grace."

These two passages obviously relate to different doctrines: the first relates to the *truth* of Scripture, the second to its *sufficiency.* These two doctrines are manifestly different, and a large part of the Christian world believe the first, but do not accept the second. The Roman Catholic Church and the Greek Church would not admit that the Scripture is sufficient, though they would not only admit, but maintain that it was true. The supplemental revelation of the Church is, in their judgment, as necessary as the primary revelation of the Scriptures. The English clergy are bound to believe that the Scriptures are true, and they are bound also to believe that nothing that cannot be found there need be believed in order to salvation.

It is very remarkable that Dr. Lushington regards these two seemingly distinct obligations as identical. He almost confounds them. "I think," he says, "that the declaration, 'I do believe,' must be considered with reference to the subject-matter, and that is the whole Bible, the Old and New Testament. The great number of these books; the extreme antiquity of some; that our Scriptures must necessarily consist of copies and translations; that they embrace almost every possible variety of subject, parts being all-important to the salvation of mankind, and parts being historical and of a less sacred character, certainly not without some element of allegory and figures,—all these circumstances, I say, must be borne in mind when the extent of the obligation imposed by the words 'I do believe' has to be determined.

"Influenced by these views, I, for the purpose of this cause, must hold that the generality of this expression, 'I do believe' must be modified by the subject-matter; that there must be a *bonâ fide* belief that the Holy Scriptures contain every thing necessary to salvation, and that to that extent they have the *direct* sanction of the Almighty."

It is, at the least, exceedingly difficult to say, that this interpretation is a very natural one. Dr. Lushington interprets an unfeigned belief in all Scripture to mean a restricted belief in *such parts* of Scripture as contain matter essential to salvation. Take a single book, say the first book of Kings: it is a canonical book; it is an historical book; for the most part it is a very simple book; for the most part of it no one can accuse it of poetry. Would it be possible for a clergyman to say, "I do not believe any part of the narrative in the first book of Kings; I do not believe there ever was such a person as Rehoboam or as Jeroboam, as Jehu or Jehosaphat; I do not believe that any one of the series of kings of Judah ever lived, or any one of the kings of Israel ever lived"? Can this in any fair sense be called "believing" the Scripture? Certainly not; and yet it is equally certain that no doctrine essential to salvation is contained in this long list of monarchs. It is not a spiritual truth that there was such a person as Ahaz, or as Jehoiada, or as Naboth. Would it be competent to an English clergyman to say, "I know that the Scripture says there was such a person as Solomon, but I do not agree with Scripture. I think there never was such a person; and I am free to think so, for the existence of Solomon is not a truth essential to salvation"? We do not believe the common sense of the English people will ever call *that* "believing the Bible."

We confess we do not see why the word "true" should not be construed in its plain and moral sense. If a man says, "I believe Saturday's *Times* to be true," he does not mean "I believe such parts of Saturday's *Times* to be true as are essential to salvation." He means that the events there set down did happen, that the world as described in the *Times* corresponds with the world which exists in reality. It is quite true that much of the Bible is very difficult of interpretation. We often cannot say with any confidence what meaning the writer intended to convey; but we cannot help thinking that those who declare the Bible to be true are not at liberty to say the writer of the Bible "said this, and meant to say this, but I think he meant wrong and was in error." Whether the writer was inculcating an eternal truth, or whether he was saying that Jeroboam was king in Israel, is, according to every natural and simple explanation, for this purpose immaterial.

The entire bearing of Dr. Lushington's interpretation of the part of the Ordination Service which refers to the Scripture, and the monstrous state in which it leaves the subject, cannot be fully understood unless it is considered in connexion with his interpretation of that part of the Articles which relates to Scripture. The material Articles are these:

Article VI. *Of the sufficiency of the Holy Scriptures for salvation.*

"Holy Scripture containeth all things necessary to salvation: so that whatsoever is not read therein, nor may be proved thereby, is not to be required of any man, that it should be believed as an Article of the Faith, or be thought requisite or necessary to salvation. In the name of the Holy Scripture we do understand those Canonical Books of the Old and New Testament, of whose authority was never any doubt in the Church.

"Of the names and number of the Canonical Books: Genesis, &c. &c.

"And the other Books (as Hierome saith) the Church doth read for example of life, and instruction of manners; but yet doth it not apply them to establish any doctrines; such are these following: The Third Book of Esdras, &c. &c.

"All the Books of the New Testament, as they are commonly received, we do receive, and account them canonical."

Article VII. *Of the Old Testament.*

"The Old Testament is not contrary to the New: for both in the Old and New Testament everlasting life is offered to mankind by Christ, who is the only mediator between God and man, being both God and Man. Wherefore they are not to be heard, which feign that the old fathers did look only for transitory promises. Although the law given from God by Moses, as touching ceremonies and rites, do not bind Christian men, nor the civil precepts thereof ought, of necessity, to be received in any commonwealth; yet, notwithstanding, no Christian man whatsoever is free from the obedience of the commandments which are called moral."

Article XX. *Of the authority of the Church.*

"The Church hath power to decree rites or ceremonies, and authority in controversies of faith: and yet it is not lawful for the Church to ordain any thing that is contrary to God's

Word written, neither may it so expound one place of Scripture that it be repugnant to another. Wherefore, although the Church be a witness and a keeper of Holy Writ, yet, as it ought not to decree any thing as against the same, so besides the same ought it not to enforce any thing to be believed for necessity of salvation."

On these Dr. Lushington observes:

"It becomes, then, of the last importance to ascertain what is meant by 'Holy Scripture,' and by that which 'containeth all things necessary for salvation.' The Article declares that Holy Scripture is contained in the Canonical Books enumerated, and in the New Testament. But that is no explanation of what is meant by 'Holy Scripture,' or by the word 'Canonical.'

"I am not at all surprised at this silence, because I apprehend that the meaning of both expressions was fully understood at the time, and that explanation was deemed wholly unnecessary. I think that the expression 'Holy Scripture,' well understood by all, meant Scripture contradistinguished from all other writings, and that the adjective 'Holy' denoted Divine origin. I think that the meaning of the word 'Canonical' clearly appears upon the face of the Article itself, namely, books whose authority was never doubted in the Church; and by 'authority' I mean divine authority, for there is no other authority which by possibility could cause them to contain all things necessary for salvation. This doctrine is, moreover, distinctly stated in the Twentieth Article, which declares that 'it is not lawful for the Church to ordain any thing that is contrary to God's Word written, neither may it so expound one place of Scripture that it be repugnant to another.' The expressions 'God's Word written' and 'Scripture' are in this Article plainly identical.

"It has been said that the Church has not in these Articles or elsewhere defined inspiration. It is no part of my duty to define it, and I shall not attempt to do so; but I must put a construction upon the Articles, and I hold that in the phrases 'God's Word written' and 'the Holy Scripture containeth all things necessary to salvation,' is necessarily implied the doctrine that in all matters necessary for salvation the Holy Scriptures emanated from the extraordinary and preternatural interposition of the Almighty,—the special mode and limit unknown to man. It is true that all good gifts spring from the same source—from the power and will of the Almighty; but the gifts of genius or of mental power, even in a greater degree than is common, the gifts of any faculty of mind or body in unusual excellence, the existence of these qualities in the highest perfection, overleap not the ordinary course of human affairs, and are plainly to be distinguished from the special interposition of God, which is necessarily implied in these Articles as the cause and origin of the Scriptures. I must hold, therefore, that any clergyman who advisedly maintains, whether in direct or indirect language, that the Holy Scriptures proceed from the same mental powers as have produced other works, or *vice versâ*, even with the qualification that these powers in the one case and the other differ in degree, impairs the Divine authority of the Holy Scriptures, does in fact maintain that the Bible is not God's Word written, but is the work of man, and thereby contravenes the Sixth and Twentieth Articles of Religion. I think it expedient to repeat, that when, in my judgment, the plain grammatical sense of an Article has been violated, it is not competent to this Court to refer to any of the numerous authorities which the learning and diligence of counsel have brought before me.

"Another question raised is the right of criticism. By criticism, as distinguished from interpretation, I mean examining and determining the text of Scripture. Here I am wholly without legal authority or precedent of any kind to guide me. All I know is, that, as a matter of fact, learned divines, of whose orthodoxy I believe there is no reason to doubt, have come to the conclusion that certain verses or parts have been erroneously introduced, and are not really entitled to keep their place in Scripture. I am of opinion that, under such circumstances, the law would not require me to hold persons coming to similar conclusions guilty of any ecclesiastical offence. I exceedingly doubt, however, if this liberty can be extended beyond the limits I have mentioned, viz. certain verses or parts of Scripture: I think it could not be permitted to clergymen to reject the whole of one of the Books of Scripture. I could not go that length, though I have certainly no disposition to draw the limits closer than the law requires; but the Sixth Article having declared that all the enumerated books are canonical, to reject one altogether as spurious is to deny its canonicity, and constitutes a violation of the Article."

Now the effect of this in brief is, that every clergyman must believe that every book in Scripture contains some part which was not produced by the unassisted agency of the ordinary human faculties. Taking this, therefore, in connexion with what went before, we have this result: no clergyman need believe all of any book of the Bible to be true; no clergyman need believe all of any book to be inspired; but every clergyman must believe some bit in every book to be true, and some bit in every book to be inspired.

Apply this to a case or two. Suppose a person who believes all the New Testament to be inspired, and most of the Old, but who does not believe any part of the book of Jonah to be inspired,—he is to be excluded from the Church. He believes all the main doctrines, and the really important narratives in the Bible, but he cannot satisfy himself as to Jonah and his gourd, and out he goes. Suppose a divine believes the Second Epistle of St. Peter to be of late origin, and that he does not see any evidence that it could not have been produced in the usual way by the human mind. He must go out: he may believe all the rest of the New Testament, but the law is imperative; he cannot remain. These are no improbable cases; on the contrary, these, or something like them, are very common.

In his interpretation of the Ordination Service, Dr. Lushington has permitted great laxity, greater laxity than we think the words of that service can fairly and rationally be stretched to mean; but in his interpretation of the Articles he has made ample compensation. By requiring a belief not only in the truth, but in the "divine authority"—the supernatural origin of some part of every book, he has imposed a restriction which, if it were pressed with vigour and consistency, would soon exclude from orders the greater number of reflecting and studious men.

Whether Dr. Lushington's judgment will be in all points confirmed and followed by subsequent decisions is perhaps doubtful; but it is *not* doubtful that it leaves the relation between the English clergy and the Bible in a very unsatisfactory state, and that it will puzzle subsequent judges to place it in a satisfactory state.

4th. Independently of the subscription to the Articles, the clergy are bound by statute not deliberately or "advisedly to maintain any doctrine directly repugnant" to any of the Thirty-nine Articles. This enactment was passed in Queen Elizabeth's time, and is much earlier than the subscriptions to the Articles, which were only enacted in the subsequent reigns.

Such are the heavy and stringent obligations which the law imposes on the English clergy. It is generally thought that the course of judicial discussion has been favourable to a lax interpretation of these obligations. But in most respects this is a mistake; and in one most material respect the chain of obligation is clearer, is more stringent, is more galling than it formerly was. If Dr. Lushington's judgment in the case of *Essays and Reviews* should be followed and confirmed, the clergy may have in some respects a greater freedom as to the Bible than used to be believed; but as to the Prayer-book, the notoriety of the stringency of the law, if not its real stringency, has been augmented. The Articles and the Liturgy have the force of an Act of Parliament: though known not to be inspired, the clergy are more bound to believe them than to believe the Bible, which, to say the least of it, *may* be inspired. The Articles and the formularies have been enacted, and these we now know the clergy must believe in their "plain and grammatical sense," notwithstanding the number of propositions which they contain, notwithstanding their various origin, notwithstanding their frequent apparent discrepancy, notwithstanding their almost accidental character, notwithstanding their conspicuous complexity.

The effect of such an accumulation of obligation is much more considerable, because it is an obligation which *young* men are asked voluntarily to undergo. The Church of England at this moment takes the best possible means of excluding able, educated, and active men from her pulpits. At the time of life when a profession is chosen, zealous and religious men, as a rule, set a peculiar value on religious system. They are young, they are intellectual, they are educated; they are proud of the intellectual tools which their education has given them; they wish to use these tools on the highest possible subject-matter. They are scarcely content unless they can *see* their faith as an intellectual vision; unless they can set it forth in distinct consecutive propositions as a pure theory. In later life men learn to take their creed in fragments; one part has but a slight relation to the other parts; each is in some sort half a whole. But in intellectual youth this belief by *compartments* is impossible. The eager argument of sanguine youth rushes in and *will* have every thing in its whole creed distinctly related and obviously joined. Now as the formularies of the Church of England can scarcely be held on *any* system, as they were written in different ages and instinct with the spirit of contracted beliefs, they will never *seem* to the eager and simple mind of youth to be consistent. Intellectual young men, interested in religion and employing their minds in their religion, are reluctant to conform to them. A world of apparently discrepant propositions is exhibited to the very persons at the very age when consistency is most idolised, and discrepancy most abhorred: who can wonder that the result is dislike, if not disgust—hesitation, if not avoidance? Some years since, too, the Church of England tempted secular ability into the Church, but now it tempts no longer. Mere scholarship no longer is a sure road to eminence in the Church, or rather it is a road no longer. "The bad edition of a useless classic," which Sydney Smith described as being a principal step to the episcopal bench, is now a step away from it. A serious age thinks perhaps less of pure scholarship than it ought. Nor can such men as Philpotts, or Warburton, or Horsley, who are strong-brained and logical, who are bold and daring, hope or a place now. They become eminent by expressing a view, by elaborating a system; but a distinct view is exactly what our dispensers of High-Church patronage do not like. They love an indistinct mediocrity, which is safe because it is timid, which is intangible because it is illogical; they do not love a system-making mind, which must be odious to many, which must be in controversies with many. A favour to safe mediocrity will excite no political censure; a favour to eager and consecutive genius is sure to do so.

The Church of England in this manner repels from her orders both the clever and pious youth and the clever and secular youth. The result is what we see,—many quiet and ordinary men usefully doing ordinary work; tiresome bishops conscientiously delivering commonplace charges; a few clever eager men who have entangled themselves in the net, who cannot get free from it, who are puzzled and harassed, who are neither satisfied to be in it nor satisfied to be out of it.

It is to be observed that some written and obligatory creed is essential to—is almost implied in the idea of—a proprietary church. It is not possible that large masses of property should be held for religious purposes, and yet that that religion should not be in some manner prescribed. It is true that the property might be bequeathed to follow the sentiments and support the opinions of a particular congregation, of a specific body of ascertainable persons. But this is in substance placing the clergy in subjection to the will and pleasure of their hearers, is making it essential that they should please in order that they should live, is securing in fact that they should repeat the familiar commonplace which the average mind loves and knows, rather than that they should try to raise that low and common mind to the perception and the reception of some new, some high, some unfamiliar truth. One principal advantage in a proprietary church is, that it fixes the dignity and secures the status of the preacher; and to this a written creed, a statutory creed, is essential.

Where there is lay patronage, as there is in England, the necessity of a compulsory creed of some sort is yet more imperative. Lay patronage means that one layman has a *saleable* right of property in the appointment of the paid religious teacher of other laymen. Z, perhaps a Jew, appoints the Christian instructor of A, B, C—humble, pious, but not very wise Christians. Unless the law defines, and defines with some exactness, what sort of person may be chosen, what kind of religious teacher may be imposed on the unconsulted congregation, the tyranny is monstrous in theory, and would be intolerable in practice. The hearers would be bound to hear any thing that the owner of the living or his assignees—for he may be a bankrupt—might choose to say: their religious teaching, and that of their children, would be absolutely chosen for them without restriction by a person whom they never saw, and whom they cannot control. Such tyranny as this would surpass the acquiescent submissiveness of the most patient Orientals. Even they *will* have their religion to themselves.

The specific evil which we now suffer from, is not the existence of *a* creed in the national Church, but the nature of *the* creed. It is not an evil, but a good, that the clergy are bound to teach something definite. The evil is, that what they are bound to believe is so complicated, and so accidental an accumulation of inconsistent propositions.

What then, again, is the remedy? At first it might seem obvious; it might seem that we should at once revise the Liturgy—revise the Articles; in a word, alter the Prayer-book from what it is to what we would wish it to be. But deep evils are seldom cured by simple suggestions. No such simple and effectual remedy as this is in fact possible. Parliament would never agree on another Prayer-book, on another set of Articles, on another Liturgy; it would be incapable of discussing such a subject. It would be impossible to induce many most estimable members not to mix up the various discrepant opinions which they may themselves hold with the subject in hand. Low-Church people would wish a Low-Church creed; High-Church people a High-Church creed; and so on through all the various shades of theological belief. In an assembly containing Jews, containing Catholics, containing Quakers, containing Unitarians, there would be an unseemly conflict of theological dogma. What the English people ought to be taught would be confounded with the question what Mr. Newdegate thought, and what Sir Roundell Palmer thought he should not think.

It would be impossible, too, to induce the House of Commons—though it calls itself, and though it is the Imperial Parliament—to take an imperial view of this question. It maintains the Scotch Church because it is, or was, or is believed to be, suitable to the Scottish people,—the most effective teaching apparatus they could have: it endows Maynooth, because it believes it can usefully aid real morality, real peace and order, by aiding to teach Catholicism. But if the English Church were a substantial subject of practical debate, if in a simple issue it were discussed what should be the doctrine of the Church of England, and what should not be its doctrine, there would be no political calmness. The same doctrines which determine the maintenance of the Scotch Kirk, which enjoin the endowment to Maynooth, would not be permitted to have their legitimate influence. It would not be possible to say, "In that part of the English empire called England the doctrine which it is most *advantageous* to teach is so and so." England would not be looked upon as only a component of the

English empire, it would be contended that in England we must teach the *truth;* and what the truth was we should never settle.

Again, the English Parliament will not for many years undertake to revise the Articles, or to revise the Liturgy, still less to revise them both. It is not easy to lay down general rules as to the policy of the House of Commons. Like all popular assemblies, though less than most, its policy is fluctuating, is mutable, is variable. But if any principle is true of it, perhaps it is this: when the instincts of the House coincide with the convenience of its leaders, the result is sure. The course on which the two coincide will be adopted. Now the instincts of Englishmen are opposed to the commencement of a vague, boundless, endless theological discussion. They think it rather irreverent to talk freely on such matters. They do not *like* to talk freely about them, for they do not know where they stand. They know that there is no short conclusive test, no incisive applicable argument, which will put an end to the interminable discussions (as men of the world call them) on religion. Even on so easy a subject, in comparison, as the currency there is the same feeling. The English people support "Peel's Act" because they think "there was only one person who understood the currency, and he is dead; if we consent to alter it, we shall be a prey to countless and inconsistent arguments,—to people who say that the world is being ruined by too many bank-notes, by too few bank-notes,—to people who say what no one can understand,—to screaming individuals who say that they alone have the one truth; and unless you listen you are lost." The same arguments apply to religion, and the convenience of statesmen supports them. Whoever brings forward a motion to revise the Liturgy must be prepared with a bill with clauses, must fix what words he will put in, and what words he will leave out. It is not easy to fancy what kind of mind a premier who thinks it an *admitted* principle that "all babies are born good" would apply to a revision of the Baptismal Service. Probably men long battered in London life, and such are most English statesmen, are more unfit to deal with these matters than any other Englishmen their equals in ability and their equals in instruction.

In truth, no one proposes that the House of Commons should revise the Prayer-book: it is only useful to dwell upon it because we best see the true nature of a difficult subject when we examine the real reasons for conclusions which every one adopts.

The second remedy, and a much more practical one as far as it goes, is the abolition of subscription. Dr. Stanley has just proposed this remedy in a most excellent pamphlet, and the House of Commons has discussed it in a very practical spirit.

And there is the best of practical reasons for selecting this remedy. It is easy, in comparison with every other remedy very easy, and it would be of very considerable use. The English clergy would not then be bound to *believe* the Articles. They would never have promised to do so.

It is impossible not to know that this alteration would of itself bring quiet to many anxious intellects and half-agonised consciences. It would be a material and most useful help in the extremity of our difficulty; it would do much of itself: and being in itself a considerable change, it would be an instalment and a pledge of further changes.

But these great advantages must not blind us to the fact that the mere abolition of the subscription to the Articles would not of itself be an effectual medicine for the present maladies of the English Church. Though excellent as a palliative, it is imperfect as a cure. A mere reference to the position of the clergy as we just now described it will make this apparent.

First, the clergy will not be any more able than they are now to teach or publish any thing contrary to the Articles. The Act of Elizabeth that we cited, which regulates their teaching, which hedges them in as effectually as words can hedge them in, which was intended to define their teaching rigidly, which does define their teaching rigidly, would remain. It is certain that this sharp restriction must tend to cramp theological thought and to deteriorate theological instruction. The dogmatic document which the first Protestant age imposed on succeeding ages would remain; it would be a series of dogmas *undeniable even though incredible.*

It is said, that if the practice of subscription were abolished, the law which forbids the clergy at all to contravene the Articles would gradually fall into desuetude; and so it might turn out. There is a precedent for it. Acts 9 and 10 William III., c. 32, —a statute in this respect still unrepealed,—enact "That if any person or persons having been educated in, or at any time having made profession of, the Christian religion within this realm, should by writing, preaching, teaching, or advised speaking, assert that there were more Gods than one, or shall deny the Christian religion to be true, or the Holy Scriptures of the Old and New Testament to be of Divine authority," he shall be for the first offence incapacitated for holding any office under Government, lay or ecclesiastical; and for the second be unable "to plead or sue any action or information in any court of law or equity, or to be guardian of any child, or executor, or administrator of any person, or capable of any legacy or deed of gift," and shall also suffer imprisonment for three years. Under this law many authors of popular heretical works would be incapable of most civil rights. They could not get in their debts; they could not be guardians to their own children. Under this statute the public offices ought to be perfectly pure from the most eminent heresies of the day, to contain no person who has questioned the inspiration of any book in Scripture. But we all know that the enactment is obsolete. The most heretical authors sue and are sued daily; no one questions their legacies; they have as much power over their own children as any one. No one ever thinks of indicting lords of the treasury or commissioners of customs, or any lay official, for any theological tenets they may profess, or for any books they may write. The law which enforces on secular *employés* a sort of theological obligation is practically useless, is ineffective and unknown. Its repeal would make no alteration, and its existence produces no result.

If such be the case with the laity just lately, why may not something similar happen with the clergy in times that are now to come? We do not say that it may not happen, but there are two very material differences on such a matter between clergy and laity. A theological obligation affecting the clergy is a matter affecting their daily business; a theological obligation affecting the laity is a matter *not* affecting their business. It is much easier to suppose that a commissioner of inland revenue, who is occupied with the collection of the income-tax and the adjudication on stamps, who has to produce money at a certain day, will not busy himself in theological discussion, will not kick against theological pricks, shall not fall into a theological snare, than that the same luck should happen to a clergyman, who is bound to think of theology; who is nothing unless he does think of it; who has every motive, both good and bad, to write on theology; who if he write an adroit book may become a bishop by it; who if he write a good book may advance the truth by it. The clergy are bound to teach religion; the intellectual clergy must think of religion. If they would guide their age, they must take a part, a principal and important part, in its religious discussions. It is hardly to be supposed that an active-minded clergy could for years discuss the subjects of the formularies without contradicting them more or less. The religious freedom of the clergy will be secured at the expense of their religious silence, if they only cease to subscribe the Articles, and do not cease to be obliged never to impugn them.

It may be said that if the clergy did contradict the Articles which they no longer subscribe, this would be immaterial; no one would prosecute them. The expense would be too great, and the doubt of success too certain. And if they were not prosecuted, they would be free. But on this matter we have a keen conscience. The clergy are set apart from other men; they take no share in active life; they are excluded from all its cares, its hopes, and its temptations. They are confined to a few duties; they are intended to exhibit to men a type of goodness not higher than that of the laity, not more simple, less complicated, certainly more intelligible, perhaps more winning. But so peculiar a calling exacts peculiar conditions. As the clergy have few duties, they must be scrupulous in performing them; leading a life of meditation and thought, or having the means of so doing, and having but simple moral problems, they have no excuse for that *slovenliness* of conscience which grows insensibly on those involved in the rapid business of life, who must act at once, who must act before they have thought, who must act among shifting and multifarious data with but slender means of foreseeing the result. If these busy men can be "about right" in the rough and in the main, they must be satisfied; the wisest of them and the most thoughtful dare not hope for so much. But the clergy should preserve an exacter aim in their simpler duties. They should at least teach the creed which they were *intended* to teach.

Now it is certain that when the legislature required the clergy not to contravene the Thirty-nine Articles, it did so as a means of securing a belief in them. The habit of English thought and the genius of English law forbad any inquisition into opinion as opinion. But the legislature did as much as it could. It said, We judge of felt belief by expressed belief; if we forbid the expression of an opinion, we do so in the hope that we shall prevent the holding of that opinion; not only, therefore, would the mere prohibition of the clergy to deny the Articles be unfavourable to the freedom and thoroughness of theological discussion, not only would it place them in an inconvenient and in part ridiculous position, but it would place those who did not believe them in a nearly dishonourable position. They would, after all, be holding the precise opinions which the legislature endeavoured to prevent their holding.

The abolition of subscription would not remove the necessity of conforming to the Liturgy; nor would it improve the unsatisfactory position of the clergy towards the Bible, which we have explained, as far as that position is consequent on the ordination service. The whole real litigation as to *Essays and Reviews,* the whole threatened litigation as to Bishop Colenso, would be entirely unaffected by the abolition of subscription. The clergy would still declare that they "believe all the canonical Scriptures to be true;" and it would be for a court of law to say whether such belief is compatible with a denial of what the writers of these Scriptures intended. But if the abolition of subscription is only a partial and an incomplete remedy, how shall we add to it and supplement it?

No remedy can be complete which does not remove all needless burdens from the clergy. We have shown what those burdens are, and what the true design of a national establishment is. We have shown that some creed is essential to it,—that the whole notion of a proprietary church requires it. But the very design of a national establishment implies that that creed should not be over-complicated. In a politician's view, the use of the establishment is to inculcate those stable and ordinary, those uninteresting but most essential virtues on which the well-being of a nation, the power of a nation, almost the existence of a nation, depends. The extensiveness of an establishment is therefore what a politician would desire; he would wish that it should influence as many persons as possible, that it should spread the blessings he wishes to spread as widely as possible.

The greatest number of persons can be influenced only by the reduction of the creed of the Church to the creed upon which the greatest number of persons agreed, in the choice of a form of worship which shall suit the greatest number of persons. The choice of a form of worship is in fact the choice of a creed, for in every prayer many doctrines are implied; and in almost all forms of worship certain declarations of belief are to be found which may be called creeds and not called creeds, but are in fact distinct declarations in appropriate language of the belief of the worshiper. The statesman wishes to choose that creed for the Church over which he watches which shall be most useful and suitable,—that creed which shall really exercise the greatest and best influence over the greatest number of his fellow-subjects.

In the present state of England these principles require the following changes:

1st. The abolition of the practice of subscription.

2dly. The repeal of the Act of Elizabeth which forbids the clergy to contradict the Articles.

These two alterations, if they could be made, would entirely set the clergy free from one class of restrictions, and that the heaviest,—from the restrictions imposed by the Thirty-nine Articles, in one form or in another.

3dly. The declaration of "unfeigned belief that the canonical Scriptures are true," might be altered to a declaration that these Scriptures "contain the record of a revelation from God." This would not imply that they contain nothing else; and while preserving all that is beneficial and vital in the present test, would leave all minor matters open to argument, criticism, and investigation.

4thly. Each clergyman should be permitted to omit a certain prescribed number of passages from the ordinary forms of common prayer. Most or many clergymen feel some objection, are conscious of some hesitation, more or less strong, in using some portions, often very trivial portions, of the many enacted services which they are now obliged to use without alteration or omission. A remarkable instance of this has just been made known. The most cautious of English prelates, the Bishop of St. David's, wrote to one of the ablest of English newspapers, the *Spectator*, to say that though he did not share in the hesitation and disinclination to use certain passages in the Burial Service, he nevertheless did feel a dislike to a passage which is much less known, which has been little controverted, to which no one, so far as we know, ever objected before. The Bishop observes: "I am, perhaps, unfortunately singular in my view of the subject; but, while I am more than satisfied with those portions of the service to which alone any exception appears to have been taken, and heartily agree with you in your excellent and timely remarks on its general merits, I must own that it contains some expressions which grate upon my ear, probably not less than others are offended by those which gave rise to Lord Ebury's motion. I may be over-fastidious, but I cannot help questioning the propriety of language which sounds as if we desired that the All-wise should bend his decrees as to 'times and seasons,' which 'he has put in his own power,' to the impatience of our wishes."

Many clergymen, too, who have no substantial disagreement from the most important part of the accepted Church doctrine, at the same time cannot satisfy their minds as to many casual allusions to incidental narratives in Scripture scattered through the Prayer-book, which seem to them to imply an assertion that certain narratives which they believe to be mythical are historical,—that certain facts did happen which they believe did not happen. If a good opportunity were given for the explanation of such minute objections, a very great number of them now unknown would soon be intelligibly and distinctly suppressed.

For the ascertainment of such objections a commission might issue from the Crown, which should report to what parts of the services they were applicable, and whether each objection seemed to be felt by few clergymen or by many. Such commission should report also to which parts of the service no objection was made, and to which parts, in their opinion, no objection ought to be made.

If all the clergy were obliged to use substantially the same religious services, though each clergyman might be allowed to omit some little; if there were certain passages which no one could omit; if no one could omit more than a prescribed maximum, —the essential *quæsitum* of a proprietary Church—a creed and worship in which the greatest number of persons could heartily believe, and would voluntarily join—would be attained. The present services in the main correspond now with the general feeling of the country; and, if each clergyman were allowed a small license of omission, would cease to cause, what they now cause, a suppressed dissatisfaction in many clerical consciences, and a wavering unreality in yet more clerical intellects. Each clergyman would of course always read the same service, and would be required on stated occasions to give due notice to his ecclesiastical superiors what portions of the Liturgy he in future intended to omit; and, as we have before observed, certain vital portions should be fixed which he could not omit. The limits of this optional emancipation should be investigated by a commission, and it would be for Parliament to confirm what such commission reported. As it would be the simple concession of a regulated license, it need entail no long theological debate, and need excite no religious strife or angry contention.

If it were wished, the same license of omission and exception might be extended to the Thirty-nine Articles. The clergy might be required to sign the Articles, subject to certain omissions, which they should select and specify. The abolition of subscription would then be unnecessary, because its object would have been attained; and the indirect manner of attaining that end is scarcely an objection according to English habits of thought and practice, for in England we rarely reform any thing or create any thing in the most obvious and simple manner. The critical point is, that the clergy should be freed from the necessity of believing every word of the Articles and every word of the Liturgy; whether all subscription to either be abolished is, in comparison, immaterial. If the clergy subscribe, subject to certain omissions and exceptions to be selected by themselves, subscription ceases to be formidable. Either way, the necessary freedom is inevitably secured

To some these reforms may appear unpractical. They could not be carried at this moment, and they would be opposed by much intellectual prejudice and much unintellectual conservatism. But year by year the controversies of our time will augment till they render some such changes necessary. To others, such alterations may appear trivial, because they would not open the Church to every extreme heresy, or any very new form of belief. But it should be remembered that they are wholly based on the present creed of England. If that creed should change, further alteration in the Church would be necessary. But while that creed is what it is, these changes would, we believe, be sufficient and satisfactory. At any rate, in the expectation of many similar discussions for years to come, we offer them as contributions to the "Church of the future."

CURRENT LITERATURE.

I. *History of England from the Accession of James I. to the Disgrace of Chief-Justice Coke*, 1603-1616. By Samuel Rawson Gardiner, late Student of Christ Church. 2 vols. Hurst and Blackett.

THIS is the most important historical work of the quarter. "It is only," says Mr. Gardiner in his preface, "after investigating the circumstances under which certain dominant ideas have arisen, that it becomes possible to enter into the feelings of those who entertained them, and even approximately to draw the line which separates a blunder from a crime. It is for this reason that the first fourteen years of James I. are especially worthy of study. At the end of 1616 the Constitution, at least in the minds of the supporters of the Crown, had assumed that form which was always defended by them, in the course of the ensuing conflict, as the true Constitution of the country. The prerogative had established its claim to be considered as the regulating part of the machinery. The sittings of parliament had been suspended without any immediate prospect of their renewal. The judges had been taught, by a practical example, that they held their offices only at the good pleasure of the sovereign. In short, these thirteen years and a half were years of constitutional change, no less real because it was carried on within the letter of the Constitution. It was in them that the weapons were forged which were to be used by James and his son, with such unfortunate results for themselves."

It will be seen by these words that Mr. Gardiner considers the period he has chosen for his historical studies as the momentous era in which all those arbitrary principles were framed and developed, against which the popular and constitutional party in England were constrained to protest, and eventually have recourse to arms. This is his answer to the assertion of Hume, that in the maintenance of their prerogative the Stuarts never exceeded the Tudors; though the spirit of the nation had changed, yet, judged by the letter of the Constitution, the measures of James I., or at least of Charles I., were no more illegal than those of Henry VIII. or Elizabeth. For those supposed aggressions on the liberties of the subject which led to a civil war, and developed the energies and opposition of Hampden, Pym, Selden, and Elliot, abundant precedent could be found. The difference of the two eras consisted only in this: under Elizabeth all parts of the Constitution equally and progressively developed themselves, and so one part counterbalanced the other; under the Stuarts the royal prerogative had assumed dimensions incompatible with those rights and liberties which had descended to the people undiminished, yet unprogressive, from the last reign. The political monster-births of the seventeenth century were not, according to Mr. Gardiner, a fungus or an excrescence caused by some adventitious matter not natural to the body politic, but an undue development of one organ, which in its overgrowth threatened destruction to the rest, and ultimately to itself. The kingcraft of James, the cunning of Salisbury, the brilliant genius and profound philosophical abilities of Bacon, all lent their aid to this disastrous object; and like the Cyclops, though of unequal size, they all equally helped to forge those chains by which the liberties of the people should be kept within due bounds, whilst the royal prerogative ranged and roamed at large.

Undoubtedly this theory of Mr. Gardiner's, worked out by great research, by a most honest and conscientious inquiry into the state-papers and correspondence of this reign, will prove very attractive. Unjustifiable as might be the motives and purposes of James and his courtiers, they are redeemed from that insignificance and even meanness thrown over them by popular historians. It sorts better with our notions of the genius of Bacon, and even the talents and experience of Salisbury, to be told that they were not merely led by the caprices of the moment, or ministering to the idle tastes and pedantic follies of a shambling and irresolute king. There is something in Mr. Gardiner's view to justify the oft-repeated compliment of Bacon, hitherto regarded as gross flattery, when he compares James I. to Henry VII., and indorses the epithet of the Second Solomon. It may not be a grandeur without alloy, but it is a grandeur strangely at variance with the popular conceptions of this reign, to learn that the thoughts and measures of James I., not unlike those of Henry VII., were steadily turned to the purpose of fortifying the monarchy against popular aggressions, and developing the prerogative within the letter, and therefore within the limits, of the Constitution.

But though we might be tempted to admit such consistency of purpose in the politic mind of Bacon, and of some others, the greatest difficulty against this admission will be found in the character of James himself. Popular belief guided by popular instincts, and still more confirmed in these impressions by the great novelist, will hardly be induced to attribute so profound and consistent a design to James I.; it will hardly confound him with his grandson James II. Undoubtedly he was desirous that the House of Commons should be kept in good order; that it should listen, like "beardless boys," to his speeches, and be profoundly impressed by his wisdom and his eloquence. He hated to be bothered; he disliked business. He had come from Scotland with no pleasant reminiscences of Buchanan, Knox, Presbyterianism, and the Gowries. England was the *promised land*. He had expected to sit down in quietness and enjoy himself at the banquet which the frugality and stern administration of Elizabeth had prepared for him. His notions of the English Constitution, in church and state, were measured by these feelings. He had seen under Elizabeth a submissive parliament and very obedient bishops,—a striking contrast to his rougher experience of Scotland,—and he anticipated the same. He thought he had found the secret of her plenty, peace, and prosperity; and he formalised the thought, to which all his former suffering at home seemed to bear evidence, by his favourite maxim, "No bishop, no king." Long before his arrival, every statesman of any account had paid him the utmost deference; all parties had sought his favour,—Church of England, Puritan, Catholic; Essex and Cecil, Northampton and Raleigh. On his arrival, Bacon was just ready to welcome him with his *Advancement of Learning*. "Beholding you not with the inquisitive eye of presumption, to discover that which the eye telleth me is inscrutable, but with the observant eye of duty and admiration, leaving aside the other parts of your virtue and fortune, I have been touched, yea and possessed, with an extreme wonder at those your virtues and faculties which the philosophers call intellectual." With such language, such submissiveness, reflected in every part of England, we can see no reason, even if the character of James encouraged such an hypothesis, for supposing that James had so deep a design as is attributed to him by Mr. Gardiner. It seems to us a much more probable supposition, that he had miscalculated the temper of the people of England; he had expected to find them compliant and submissive. Their long and patient reluctance to oppose his measures he construed into a general admiration of his wisdom and of the moderation of his rule. This is evident from his public behaviour on all occasions. He talked to the House of Commons like a parcel of schoolboys; and to the Puritan divines at the Hampton-Court Conference as if, in his own words, they were truants and deserved the rod. "We have kept such a revel with the Puritans here this two days," he tells one of his correspondents, "as was never heard the like; quhaire I have peppered thaime as soundlie as ye have done the Papists thaire." Such self-complacency is incompatible with a deep-laid design of systematically subverting the constitutional liberties of his subjects,—if, indeed, such a phrase could convey any distinct meaning to Englishmen in the first half of the seventeenth century,—and of developing the prerogative in the way Mr. Gardiner apprehends. That is attributing a degree of caution, consistency, and prudence to James utterly foreign to his habits. Mr. Gardiner has produced instances of arbitrary and unjustifiable acts, on the part of the king and his advisers, which seem to fortify his hypothesis. He can appeal to the opinions of those who have carefully studied the constitutional history of the reign, and, better still, to the evidence afforded by the state correspondence of the time in support of his theory. But such evidence is not sufficient; it can be explained on better grounds than the assumption of a purpose foreign to the temper and inconsistent with the general character of James. That in succeeding to the throne of Elizabeth he should have imagined he more than inherited her authority and her claims on the obedience of her subjects; that he should have visited with severe and arbitrary penalties instances of disobedience to his wishes; that with his own special ignorance, and in the general uncertainty of constitutional rights, he should have overstepped the limits of the prerogative, was natural enough; any opposition seemed to him to exaggerate itself into the crime of disaffection. We admit that the royal prerogative was brought more frequently into play as part of the state machinery under the Stuarts than under the Tudors, but not in the way which Mr. Gardiner apprehends. The Tudors wielded that strongly, and without conscious effort, which James exercised feebly and inconsistently. They persuaded the people that the royal supremacy was identical with popular liberty and national independence. James, like all weak people, by talking so much of his prerogative, anticipated and provoked opposition.

That Mr. Gardiner has done wisely in rejecting the absurd stories propagated "by the great mass of anecdote-mongers,"—that he is perfectly right in stigmatising their narratives as thoroughly untrustworthy,—no one who has ever been at the pains to examine these subjects will question. "Of all these offenders," he remarks, "Weldon is incomparably the worst. I believe there is not a single instance in which his assertions can be in any way tested, in which they cannot be shown to be, if not downright lies, at least recollections so distorted as to be utterly worthless for the purposes of history." Yet so carelessly has the history of England been written, that Weldon and Wilson and other equally unveracious writers have been the chief, in some instances the only, source from which the popular notions of this reign have been derived, and continued, almost unchallenged and unquestioned, to the present day. Most of the scandalous stories—all the grosser ones—connected with the reign of James I. rest on no better authority. Even the scepticism of Hume, though shocked more than once by the inconsistency and effrontery of these writers, was not sufficient to break through their trammels. He retained their falsehoods probably for no better reason than that he was too indolent to undertake the necessary labour for discovering the truth. English readers are under great obligations to Mr. Gardiner for having done that which all his predecessors neglected to do. He has gone for his information to the fountain head. He has examined every statement by the light of original and contemporary authority. He has at once thrown off the superincumbent mass of idle traditions and unauthenticated anecdotes, and the result is, that he has produced two volumes, on the most important period of this reign, replete with accurate and well-digested information. If the reader do not agree on all occasions with Mr. Gardiner's conclusions, if he feel inclined to dissent from his historical theories, he can have no reason to doubt the accuracy of Mr. Gardiner's facts. Indeed, with a singular and fearless honesty, Mr. Gardiner more than once furnishes reasons in his notes for dissenting from the opinions he has propounded in his text. It appears to us that his views are more advanced than he is perhaps willing himself to acknowledge, or dares trust himself openly to enunciate to his readers. He has seen the baselessness of many favourite notions, of the popular impressions, of the long-established conclusions respecting the most momentous events of the reign. But either he has not dared openly to contradict prejudices fortified by so much authority, or has not succeeded in emancipating himself from the influence of those writers, of whose worthlessness and untrustworthiness he is fully convinced. Does he believe in the patriotism of Salisbury? Was Raleigh the innocent victim he is fondly represented? Was the Gunpowder Plot really intended to blow up the Parliament and reëstablish popery? Was the letter to Monteagle a forgery or not, to crown his own perfidy? Was Overbury poisoned by Rochester, or poisoned at all? Was the humiliation of the judges the act of James or the officious policy of Bacon? When we consult Mr. Gardiner's text for an explanation he gives us one answer, but he seems to suggest another and more correct one in his notes. In fact, though Mr. Gardiner has done much towards clearing away the popular misconceptions relating to this period of history, more yet remains to be done. His mind is yet in a transition state, lingering half way between the old prejudices of earlier impressions and the new conclusions continually forcing themselves upon his mind by the evidence he has brought to bear on his subject. He cannot stay where he is, and we shall watch with considerable interest his future labours. One or two things we would suggest to him: that he should devote himself to a history of the whole reign, and break through the arbitrary and artificial limits he has imposed upon himself. Let him keep his narrative more together, and reduce his digressions from the main subject, as in chapters i. vii. and ix., to more reasonable dimensions. In a history of James I. there is no need to straggle back to the Norman Conquest or even the Spanish Armada; still less, if he must allude to the condition of Ireland, to begin with the victories of Henry II. This is a tedious impertinence of modern historians which Mr. Gardiner may well afford to avoid, without injury to the completeness of his work, and with much advantage to his readers.

II. *Six Months in the Federal States.* By Edward Dicey. Macmillan.

Mr. Dicey visited New York, the Empire City, and Washington, the official capital, of the United States, traversed the railways which cross the garden-like country of Kentucky and Tennessee, went northwards by St. Louis, the point of departure for the Western provinces, through the corn-land of Illinois to the emporium of Chicago, and after a voyage on the Mississippi turned eastwards, and completed his travels at Boston. He thus had ample opportunity of contrasting the sentiments and polities of New England, which have had time to become in some degree historical, with those of the Western free-states on the one hand, where material interests are little counteracted by habit and tradition, and with those of the border slave-states on the other, where a dubious loyalty indicates a balance rather than a predominance of motives.

One peculiar charm of all Mr. Dicey's writing is a style of singular grace and simplicity. He has the art of speaking unaffectedly without garrulousness, and of expressing strong opinions in the moderate language of a man of the world. But the higher merits of his present book, which leave it we think unsurpassed by any English travels in America except Mr. Stirling's, are the instinct of an observer who knows what to see and what to pass by, and a thoughtfulness which rises to the level of the highest common sense, though perhaps it never goes beyond it. With much European experience, which often serves him in good stead, Mr. Dicey a little wants the European or cosmopolitan point of view; and having divested himself of English prejudices, writes like a New-Englander of high culture. His strength and his weaknesses are those of society in Boston or Harvard, with a little less passion and a little more philosophy. He has the democratic fibre, the belief in the equality of men, and the sympathy with popular institutions because they are popular. He follows his principles out unreservedly, and, as an Abolitionist, would destroy the society he admires sooner than see its existence rest upon slavery. But he has also the want of reverence for men and things which stamps a new society, and his descriptions of the leading statesmen he met have all the fidelity and the unpleasant hardness of photographs. Probably scarcely one reader will derive the favourable impression Mr. Dicey wishes to convey. To the main causes of rottenness in American society,—the worship of material success, and that incapacity for all idealism which has made the nation confound vastness with greatness,—Mr. Dicey seems to be insensible. He forgets the want of moral elevation in his admiration of the nation's energy and resources, and in his just advocacy of their temperate order and institutions.

In a certain sense this horror of all transcendental views makes the book all the more reliable. Mr. Dicey does not affect to find in the North a principle of action clearly announced and maintained, but grounds his whole advocacy of the Northern cause upon the "logic of facts," which half-insensibly determines the upholders of the Union more and more in a direction of simple antagonism to slavery. Nor does this point of view weaken his argument. The Union was in its commencement a compromise, in which the smallest possible powers were conferred upon the central government, and the largest possible rights reserved to the separate states. It was a government without the means of coercing its subjects, and those means, when the occasion came, it must find upon pain of annihilation. It was provisionally maintained by compromises which revealed more and more clearly the original fault of its composition. The Missouri compromise in 1830, the Clay compromise in 1849, the Douglas compromise in 1854, were so many attempts to maintain it together with the continued development of slavery. It is not wonderful that the adherents of a Federation with these antecedents should be slow to recognise the necessity of a change in its very nature. This is implied in the speech of the great abolitionist orator Wendell Phillips: "The South comes up to the southern bank of the Potomac without either men, munitions, or money —nothing but an idea; and the North goes up with men, munitions, money, and major-generals, and the only thing she lacks is an idea." Probably the emancipation proclamation of President Lincoln marks the first stage in the substitution of a real principle for a mere conservative instinct. The proclamation secures slave property in the loyal and destroys it in the rebel states. There is still a halting between two opinions; but there is a direct attack upon the "peculiar institution," and an assumption of a paramount authority in the constitution to deal with unforeseen accidents. That the real reason of the war was the necessity felt by the Confederate States of providing for the maintenance and extension of slavery is evident alike from past history, and from the fact that whereas every free state is loyal to the Union, every slave state, with the single exception of Delaware, where slavery has been nominal, has been disloyal openly or covertly.

If these views are correct, it becomes of little importance whether the South was really aggrieved by the protective tariff, or whether she was technically warranted in seceding. None can suppose that the tariff alone would have produced the war, or that what is technically right is therefore morally right. The grave and difficult questions of the government of the recovered slave states, and of the position of the emancipated Negro, cannot certainly be easily answered or evaded by the North. But whatever solution may be found, it cannot be so great a blot upon civilisation and humanity as the existence and development of the institution for which the Confederates are fighting. No chivalry or generalship should blind Englishmen to the real issues at stake. We have to thank Mr. Dicey for contributing to point them out.

III. *At Odds: a Novel.* By the Baroness Tautphoeus. 2 vols. London: Bentley, 1863.

Novelists may be divided into two great schools, the natural and the poetical,—those who depict human nature in its every-day aspect, and represent people as subordinating the imagination to the reason; and those who, taking a higher artistic stand-point, make at all events their leading characters act from more ideal or at least more passionate motives. This latter school, however, in answer to the incessant demand for novelty from readers whose attention is too languid and fancy too jaded to be moved by any but the strongest literary stimulants, has of late resorted almost exclusively for its subjects to what may be called morbid mental anatomy. Exceptional character and irregular desires acting so as to produce startling situations are become its staple wares, until what was the poetical school has degenerated into the sensational. Nevertheless, it has maintained its popularity in spite of the protests of the judicious, until at last the publication of a novel by a writer of the natural school—of the school of which Miss Austen is the great example—is a rare event. Although, however, the Baroness Tautphoeus is perhaps its best living disciple, her present book is hardly of a kind to restore its lost popularity. Indeed, her first novel, *The Initials*, still continues by far her best; a result which must, we think, be attributed to the strange want of invention that her writings display. Thus the motive—to borrow a word from the art-critics—of all her novels, has always been the same,—the conversion of dislike into love. In *The Initials* two people who dislike each other become lovers. In *Cyrilla* and *Quits* the heroine is gradually won over by a lover to whom she was originally indifferent, or one against whom she was prejudiced. The subject of *At Odds* is the gradual growth of passion in the heart of the hero for one whom he has been compelled to marry by "circumstances over which he had no control," at the very time that he was in love with her sister. It is a subject of which the author is no doubt mistress; but we think far too highly of her powers to be content, while they are always devoted to the consideration of human nature in a single attitude.

Another indication of this poverty of invention is a certain tendency in the author to resort for incident to the results of her reading. It has been pointed out by a weekly contemporary that large portions of *Cyrilla* are actual translations of the printed report of a remarkable German trial. In this work, the author informs us that she is merely narrating things which actually occurred at the period in which she places her characters. But the stirring events of the wars between France and Austria, in the early part of this century—the complications produced by the siding of Bavaria first with Austria and afterwards with France—are not merely no assistance, but an actual hindrance to a writer of her school. Men like Andrew Hofer and Napoleon are above or below her range of sympathies. Indeed, of all the historical characters whom she has occasion to mention, and of whom Scott would have given us life-like, though perhaps not very accurate portraits, Hofer is the only one she ventures to bring on the actual stage, and even he plays no very important part in the development of the story. Thus the historical incidents always wear the aspect of an excrescence, or at least an unnecessary setting; for it is the business of an artist to unfold the characters whom he has imagined; and mere historical incidents which are not introduced with this object control the characters instead of unfolding them. We hope it will not be thought hypercritical if we say that the same want of invention may be also seen in the clinging, in all her novels, to the local scenery, which she best knows, namely, the Bavarian highlands and adjacent countries.

Want of invention, however, is not want of imagination; and there is perhaps no novelist of the present day, except, perhaps, George Eliot who has the same power of conceiving character,—of giving us, not a mere walking embodiment of some one emotion or passion,—not a perfect angel or a perfect devil, but human beings not so bad as to have no good in them, nor so good as to be quite without a fault. And this is brought out so forcibly by the means of the dialogue—which, nevertheless, is always kept strictly in the key of every-day life—that the author never has to resort to the usual expedient of ordinary writers and tell us by narrative what is the kind of character she wants to portray. In this book there are four principal personages,—Hilda, Doris, Emmeran, and Frank,—all thoroughly amiable and engaging. We are never told a word about them, and yet we see plainly the self-will of Hilda, the coldness of Doris, the indolence of Emmeran, and the levity of Frank; and we feel, moreover, that though these bad qualities are quite subordinate elements in their respective characters, yet without them they would have acted very differently in the circumstances in which they are placed. Even Sigmund, the villain of the story, has at least courage, and sacrifices his own life in saving his brother's.

As a composition, the book is sketchy. Mina Pallersberg is never brought out half enough, considering the very important part she plays in the story, and how much is made to depend on her interested intrigues. Doris, again, is made too prominent at first; one mistakes her for the heroine; but this, probably, is part of the framework of fact, by a too strict adherence to which the story has been so much injured.

Perhaps the point in which the difference between the author and the writers in vogue at present is most curiously shown is in the way sensational incidents are dealt with. For they are not avoided; on the contrary, the author always resorts to a suicide to get rid of a troublesome character. Readers of *The Initials* will remember the death of Count Raimund. In this book, Mina, having had an intrigue with Sigmund, is engaged to be married to his father, and being compelled to meet the former by midnight on the bank of a lake, drowns herself when he expresses his determination to expose her. This is all narrated in the most matter-of-fact way; and the son, after doing his best to save the woman he once loved, calmly remarks that he cannot help her having jumped into the water, and that his best plan will be to keep his share in the misfortune to himself. What would not such a scene be in the hands of Miss Braddon? On the other hand, passion has more influence over people than our author sometimes allows. When a young man is in love with a pretty young woman, who is actually his wife, but from whom he has been separated hitherto by constant misunderstandings; and when he gets so far towards a reconciliation as to tell her that the only thing which prevents him from declaring his passion is a vow he has made that the next overtures must come from her; and when she replies that the first proposal must come from him, but that to save his vow he may make it a command,—nothing will induce us to believe that he would persist in his foolish pride any longer. Frank, the young man in question, is preëminently flesh and blood—and flesh and blood would have kissed her on the spot. On the whole, this book will hardly add to the author's reputation; but it is a pleasant tale nevertheless, and a great boon to novel-readers who have no taste for the spasmodic.

IV. *A History of England during the Reign of George the Third.* By William Massey, M.P. Vol. IV., 1793-1802. London: Parker, Son, and Bourn, 1863.

It is scarcely matter for surprise, from one point of view, that Mr. Massey has determined to bring his book to a premature conclusion; for the end of the reign of George the Third is a singularly bad terminus. If, as the title would seem to indicate, the central idea of the author was to show how the personal character of George the Third affected the history of this country, his labours would naturally conclude with the commencement of the Regency. But such a subject is better suited, perhaps, for an essay than a historical narrative, for it would leave England in the very thick of the greatest conflict in which she was ever engaged. If, on the other hand, the literal promise of his title were fulfilled, he would equally conclude at a point of time which affords no adequate historical resting-place. The natural plan would have been to undertake the narration of affairs either from the king's accession, or from the conclusion of the American war (the point at which Lord Stanhope stops), down to the peace of 1815. The revolutionary war, though not concluded till George the Third had ceased to exercise royal power, was commenced by the nation under the influence of the modes of thought and the feelings of which he was preëminently the representative, far more so than the great minister who is commonly held responsible for it; and thus such a plan would have enabled Mr. Massey to work out the leading idea which we have ventured to attribute to him, and at the same time to give us a careful review of an important section of English history. The peace of Amiens, with which his work now ends, is merely the conclusion of the first act of the war, and in no sense fulfils the promise of his title-page. This is the more to be regretted, because we are convinced that if the history of England is to be written at all, it must be written piecemeal, each writer choosing some well-marked portion of time. No very long continuance of his labours would have enabled Mr. Massey to complete such a design; as it is, he has given us only the fragment of a fragment.

It is idle to attempt to ascertain, and indeed the public have no concern with, his motives for this resolution. It may well be, however, that he may have been much influenced by the increasing difficulties of his task. Whatever shortcomings criticism may detect in his treatment of domestic events, it cannot be denied that he possesses some qualities which peculiarly fit him for the discharge of that part of his undertaking. He has, for instance, great moderation of temper, and very considerable constitutional learning; but in dealing with military events he may not improbably have found himself engaged in an uncongenial employment. His limits scarcely allowed him to give more than an outline, and an outline of military operations written by a civilian can hardly be otherwise than uninteresting. In Mr. Massey's hands the outline must be pronounced singularly dull. His narrative is clear indeed, but it is diffuse and spiritless. If there is a battle in modern history more dramatic in its incidents than another, it is Marengo. The Austrian victory, where defeat was ruin; the opportune arrival and heroic death of Desaix; the decisive charge of Kellerman; the strangely sudden change of fortune; and the veteran Melas receiving the news of his utter overthrow as he was writing the despatch which was to announce his triumph,—are all circumstances which impress the most sluggish imagination. If any curious person wishes to know how dreary and uneventful that 14th of June may be made to appear, let him turn to page 499 of this volume, and satisfy his soul. And Mr. Massey might very fairly have contented himself with a mere allusion to it. Its incidents are perfectly well known to every person of ordinary reading; and though the terms of the subsequent treaty of Campo Formio had considerable influence on the policy of this country, the details of Bonaparte's Italian campaign might well have been dispensed with. It was, however, impossible to escape the necessity of narrating those operations, in which our own forces were actually engaged; and had Mr. Massey prolonged his history he would have been involved in a period in which the war becomes of predominant importance and interest. If he felt that this was a period of which he was scarcely suited to be the historian, there is, we think, in this volume enough to show that he has formed a just estimate of his own powers.

But perhaps the most curious part of this volume is the tone in which the author writes of the actors in the French Revolution. He seems to have studied the literature of the period until he has imbibed its feelings, and writes in a sort of strain with which it is difficult to find fault, and which is nevertheless a little unfair as well as a little absurd. For instance, all persons "concerned in the murder of the king of France," including, therefore, such men as the Girondists and Carnot, are termed "blood-thirsty miscreants" (p. 14). The French armies are "led or *driven on*" by their generals; and the generals are "desperate men, conscious of inexpiable crimes, and animated by a mingled fear and hatred of their adversaries" (p. 25): as Bernadotte, for instance, and Moreau. With a phraseology pompous enough for Burke, and which intervenes strangely amid the tame sentences of Mr. Massey, Philippe Egalité is branded as a "recreant prince and gentleman" (p. 31). After this it is not surprising to read that "Bonaparte was a genuine child of the Revolution. No fear of God or man influenced his actions. No feeling of humanity, no sense of honour, ever checked the career of his ambition or restrained him from any word or deed which his interest or the exigency of the moment seemed to require. His proceedings in Egypt were a tissue of cruelty, blasphemy, and lying" (p. 459). And the old story of the murder of the sick at Jaffa is raked up again, and represented in the colours in which it was painted at a time when Englishmen feared and hated Bonaparte, as perhaps they never feared and hated man. As a matter of fact, the proposal referred only to incurables, whom it was necessary to abandon to the mercy of the Turks, and was not entertained by the medical officers; and whatever proof it may afford of the unscrupulousness of Bonaparte, the character of that great bad man was his own, was borrowed from no revolution, and would have been the same in the golden age or the millennium. Of course all men agree that, if the deeds of the actors in the French Revolution are to be considered by themselves, from the point of view of a judge trying criminals, they are among the worst by which human nature has ever been stained. But that is not the point of view of the historian. He may and ought to take into consideration the provocation which the French people had received, the ignorance in which the populace was steeped, the frenzied fear by which they were driven. After all, the cruelty and infidelity of the Revolution was less than the cruelty and infidelity which had for years distinguished the nobles and priests of France. The French people was like a faithful dog flogged by a savage master into flying at his throat. Its excesses were only proportionate to its previous patience, and its guilt must to a great extent be borne by those who had brutalised it by oppression. The historian is bound to modify his judgments by reference to that law, rightly, indeed, repudiated by the legislator, but nevertheless not of man's devising, nor capable of being altered by him,—that law which enacts that the sins of the fathers must be visited on the children.

The best part of Mr. Massey's book is, however, that which treats of domestic affairs, and their bearing on our constitutional progress. Here he is on ground with which he is more familiar, and the narrative of the trials of Hardy, Horne Tooke, and Thelwall, is even spirited. His general view of the state-prosecutions of the period is the same as that which has been successively taken by Lord Campbell and Mr. May, but has the advantage of treating them historically, from which Mr. May was precluded by his plan of dividing the events of the period of which he treated, by subjects, and not according to the order of their occurrence. There is however proof in this volume that the author shares to some extent the reactionary spirit of the present day, not only in the opinions which he expresses as to the French revolution, but even with reference to the internal policy of Pitt. Take, for instance, the prosecution of Mr. Reeves, the author of the *History of English Law*. The Government was compelled by the clamours of the Opposition to prosecute him, although a Tory, for writing a violent tract, in which he said that Parliament was a branch which could be lopped off the monarchy without endangering the constitution. He was properly acquitted; for merely speculative opinions ought to be free: but it was certainly of importance to show at that evil hour that the Government did not intend actually to proscribe liberty. Neither was Mr. Reeves quite so insignificant a person as Mr. Massey makes him. His *History of the English Law* may or may not be "a mere compilation," but it remains to this day the only book on the subject to which the student can be referred. And it is not altogether unimportant to observe that Sheridan, so far from proposing that Reeves should be prosecuted, distinctly opposed it, although he did demand his dismissal from the public service, that he should be summoned to the bar and reprimanded, and his book burned by the hangman. The prosecution was the choice of the Government, who did not care to be involved in a question of privilege. We could wish, moreover, that plainer language had been used as to the financial extravagance of the period. Pitt's expedients —such as the suspension of cash-payments—were not always unexceptionable; and the enormous sums wasted on expeditions which, even if successful, would have effected nothing towards bringing the war to an end, form the bulk of that extravagant debt under which the nation still groans. The most completely satisfactory part of the work is the chapter on Ireland. And whatever may be thought of the means by which the Union was effected, it is at least satisfactory to reflect that it has put a stop to the barbarities which either faction in that unhappy country was wont to inflict upon the other. The rebellion of 1798 probably owed its origin in no slight degree to the acts of 1795, by which Pitt, in pursuance of his policy of repression, silenced the political societies. Up to that time they had courted publicity; thenceforth they became secret associations. The United Irishmen, deserted by the more timid or more moderate of their number, began to scheme for a

French invasion instead of the rights of man. Coercion thus led to its natural conclusion—rebellion. The Croppies were cruel, as was to be expected from the degraded condition to which they had been reduced; but they were not licentious. The Protestant militia added rape to robbery, while Lord Cornwallis reported to the secretary of state that "murder appeared to be their favourite pastime." The use of torture was freely resorted to. Confessions were extorted by "tearing the scalp off the head with pitched caps, penetrating the soles of the feet with pointed stakes, cutting with swords, and flogging to the peril of life." The Irish Parliament eagerly covered these atrocities by an act of indemnity; and even in the British Parliament, after the Union, Beresford, an Irish member, and Lord Clare, the Irish chancellor, ventured to defend them. The worst of these ruffians, Fitzgerald, the high-sheriff of Tipperary, was actually rewarded with a baronetcy. Whatever other injuries the act of Union may have inflicted on Ireland, it at least gave the death-blow to the system of government which had produced such results as these.

V. *The History of the Jews, from the Earliest Period down to Modern Times.* By H. H. Milman, D.D., Dean of St. Paul's. 3 vols. Third edition, thoroughly revised and extended. London: Murray, 1863.

In comparing this new edition of Dean Milman's work, revised and enlarged as it now is, with its earliest appearance more than thirty years ago, we are made to feel most strikingly how wide is the interval in the progress of human thought which separates them, and how many questions then first budding into the possibilities of future speculation, have since that time expanded into positive and well-defined conditions of biblical inquiry, which no competent scholar with any regard to his own reputation can venture henceforth to evade. To Dean Milman belongs the merit—and no slight one we regard it—of having first introduced to the general public of this country, a rational and at the same time a religious view of the history of the Jews,—and of enabling the mass of readers to form a conception of the marvellous fortunes and the still more marvellous literature of that extraordinary people, not through the distorting glasses of theological systems, but in the clear, natural light of common sense, and with the unforced sympathies of the common heart of man. For the first time in our literature he made the history of the Bible readable, by making it human. Others have subsequently followed in the same direction, but he broke up the ground and led the way. To undertake such a work for English readers in the earlier part of the present century, not only a learning then rare, but a yet rarer moral courage, was required; and these are claims on the respect and gratitude of the friends of religious truth, which richer harvests reaped by later hands from the same fields can never supersede. It is no discredit to the most exact and thoughtful writer, that after the lapse of many years, marked as the last three decades have been by unparalleled activity in every branch of critical and historical research,—on a subject running out into many collateral inquiries, and involving not a few very complicated problems, he should find that he had advanced some positions which can no longer be maintained with the same undoubting confidence; that with the accession of fresh and indisputable facts, the old solution of difficulties was no longer available; and that points which he once supposed definitively settled, had to be reconstructed and set in a new light. To acknowledge such deficiencies, and to endeavour to supply them with the candour and moderation which signalise the corrections and additions to the volumes now before us, is no small praise.

The extension of the present edition consists partly in the interpolation of numerous passages in the text, but still more in a large body of notes, confirming and sometimes qualifying the statements in the text, and not unfrequently affording the reader materials for coming to a conclusion at variance with that of the author himself. His reading, indeed, is immense. Of every thing which the scholarship of France, Germany, and even Italy has contributed during the last quarter of a century to the manifold subjects of his work, he seems to have industriously made himself master. The additions and corrections are not in the same proportion to the original text in all parts of the work. We speak from a comparison of the present with the earlier edition. The notes, if not the most abundant, are certainly the most important, and furnish the largest amount of corrective and illustrative matter, in the opening part of the history, to which recent controversy has naturally attracted a more than ordinary attention. The most copious additions to the narrative occur in the later books, which have been greatly expanded, and contain a very interesting account, not readily accessible to the English reader from other sources, of the state of Judaism in medieval and modern times. In this part of the work we would notice with special commendation the characters of Maimonides, Spinoza, and Mendelssohn. They are discriminating and just, and written in a spirit of genial appreciation. Throughout, the recent researches of Jost, Geiger, Depping, and Herzfeld, have been diligently used and turned to good account. The author's studies, it is evident, have never been intermitted; he has not reposed under the laurels of his early fame. We might rather say, he has been almost too anxious to read every thing that had the remotest affinity with his subject. As a consequence, he has hardly left himself time to digest his multifarious materials, and to reduce the infinite variety of ideas which the open candour of his mind so readily admits, into order and harmony. Sometimes he merely notices a book and its contents, without further comment, leaving it to the reader to infer what bearing it may have on the views maintained in the narrative. On the whole, there is a want of keeping between the text and the notes. Notwithstanding the effort to reconcile them, they still bear the trace of belonging to different stages in the history of the author's mind—they still belong, so to speak, to the opposite ends of the long interval which divides his last from his first edition. Furnished with so much new matter, which has had a marked effect upon himself, we cannot but regret, as well for his own reputation as for the instruction of the public, that Dean Milman did not recast his history, and produce, like Jost, an entirely new work. On a theme of such importance, there is, to our apprehension, something slovenly in reprinting an old text here and there interpolated, with a running margin of qualifying commentary which ought to have been incorporated into a new one, and which, if it does not itself directly contradict the text, supplies the reader with the means of seriously questioning its statements. The work has the appearance of having been somewhat hastily brought out. Its publication was, perhaps, accelerated by the Colenso controversy, to which the author alludes in an excellent spirit at the conclusion of his preface. Of course we do not mean that the materials of this new edition had been suddenly got together. They are, doubtless, the accumulation of years, and their very richness makes us the more regret that sufficient time should not have been given to develop them into greater completeness and self-consistency. When Dean Milman takes pains, he can write excellently well. There are passages in his works of remarkable graphic power. But in the present volumes, especially in his long notes, partly we presume from want of time and partly from the pressure of his redundant matter, his style is more than ordinarily loose and careless, at times scarcely grammatical; and in the citation of Greek and German authorities we have observed frequent errors of the press, which should not have been allowed to disfigure the pages of so accomplished a scholar.

On the much-debated question of the origin and authorship of the Pentateuch, Dean Milman adheres to the view which he maintained in his first edition, namely; that in its substance, with some recent interpolations, it belongs to the Mosaic age, and is an authentic embodiment of the primitive Mosaic legislation. He lays stress on the fact, that all recent discoveries render it next to certain, that the Hebrews must have been acquainted with the use of alphabetic characters at the time of the Exodus; that many of the laws still furnish evidence in their peculiar phraseology, of their origination in the desert; and that if the Law (*Torah*), as it was subsequently called, did not proceed from Moses, no period can be assigned between the Exodus and the extinction of the monarchy, when such a collection could have been put forth under his name without the imposition being discovered, and the authority claimed under it repudiated. These are the old arguments, and to this day they satisfy many minds. But there are considerations of great weight on the other side, which the author has had the candour not to withhold from the reader in his notes.

Every one who dispassionately considers this subject, must be struck with the remarkable failure of all allusion to Moses and the Law in the earlier literature and history of the Hebrews, after we quit Joshua. The name of Moses does not once occur in any of the older prophets; and we believe not more than three times in the whole compass of the books of Kings. In Judges and Samuel it is wholly wanting. Dean Milman himself has called attention to this singular fact (i. 134, note). The condition of the people corresponds to the silence of their records. As far as any inference can be drawn from the books of Judges, Samuel, and even Kings, the elaborate system of sacerdotal ordinances contained in the Pentateuch, and issued complete, it is usually supposed, by Moses, under the direct authority of Jehovah,—seems to have existed without any perceptible effect on the popular mind and character for many centuries, and not to have made any approach to a realisation till after the return from exile. Between that time and the age of Moses a long interval elapsed, during which the Mosaic legislation, *as we now have it*, might as well never have existed for any visible trace which it has left behind it. It is difficult to conceive, why such a prospective scheme should have been promulgated so many centuries before it was wanted, before it was even practicable. Such a proceeding is not in harmony with the usual order of God's providence. This is a fact patent on the surface of the Old Testament history, which yields evidence appreciable by every one; not at all dependent on the critical faculty of discriminating the age and authorship of ancient documents, or on those subtle deductions from the niceties of a particular language, which lie beyond the reach of a vast majority of even studious men. Our author has evidently felt the difficulty involved in this fact, and meets it in his own way, though he does not, we think, either carry the difficulty to its full extent, or effectually reply to it. "I have a strong opinion," he says (i. 135, note), "that at the time of the Exodus the Israelites, at least their leaders, were in a higher state of civilisation in many respects than at any period of their history before the Captivity, excepting, perhaps, during the later reign of David and that of Solomon."

Every thing seems to show, that the old, what we may call the classical, literature of the Hebrews in its three main branches—the legal, the prophetic, and the devotional—was collected, arranged, digested, and, to use a modern phrase, reëdited, on the reconstitution of the national life after the return from Babylon. The nature and extent of the revision to which their old writings were then subjected, to adapt them to a new state of things, our strong Protestant prejudices have hindered us from even yet adequately appreciating. Perhaps the nearest parallel case in the history of literature was the reëditing of the old Greek poets by the critics of Alexandria. Certainly some of the early fathers use a language on this subject, which would shock our modern orthodoxy as much as the heresies of Bishop Colenso; and that is saying a great deal. Irenæus, in a well-known passage cited by Dean Milman (i. 134, note), does not hesitate to speak of the dispersion and corruption of the Scriptures (*διαφθαρεισῶν τῶν γραφῶν*) during the Captivity, and of the restoration of the Law of Moses (*ἀποκαταστῆσαι*) by Ezra, who was inspired for the purpose; and Jerome, repeating his statement, calls Ezra "instauratorem Pentateuchi." It must be remembered that the question under discussion is the Pentateuch in its present form and compass, with Joshua as an appendix.

We have some difficulty in determining what Dean Milman's own views are. He makes concessions in his notes which furnish data for going beyond the conclusions apparently affirmed in his text. He thinks the argument from language overdone, and charges the critical school with having fallen into the same fallacy as the upholders of a verbal inspiration—that of assuming the soundness and reliability of the text on which they ground their reasonings. But we may surely ask, what other ground have they to reason from at all? If our actual text is so uncertain, that we can draw no inference from it as to age or authorship, we must give up all criticism, and with it all history. Ignorance of the history of a text, admission even of extensive corruption, does not disqualify us for discerning those traces of mental individuality which are too deeply stamped on all genuine writings ever to be effaced, except by intentional and systematic depravation; and this in the present case no one ventures to impute. We can feel what belongs to Homer—the peculiar genius of his diction, his rhythmus, and his thought—though we cannot trace the history of his text with much distinctness beyond the Alexandrine age, and cannot tell what changes and interpolations his lays may have undergone since they were first sung by wandering minstrels. It seems to us a strange mode of rescuing the history of the Bible, to discredit to such an extent the language in which it has been transmitted to us. The Dean's supposition of the "gradual and insensible modernisation"—to use his own words—of the text of the Old Testament, to adapt it to later times, offers quite as much violence to all received notions on the subject, and leaves us at last quite as much in doubt as to what is or what is not authentically Mosaic, as any of the hypotheses of the critical school, to which he is so strongly opposed. The following observations, which we extract from a long note (i. 134), seem to us as bold as any thing advanced by Davidson or Colenso, without being at all more satisfactory:

"I must confess that so many objections that have been raised, and on which great stress has been laid, against the historical value of the Hebrew writings, vanish away, in my point of view, as palpable interpretations, glosses which have crept into the text, errors in numbers. Even in linguistic difficulties so much may have grown out of gradual and insensible modernisations, the accommodation to the prevailing vernacular usage of the people, that the argument from language—however unimpeachable to a great extent—is not a guide quite so sure and infallible as it is sometimes assumed to be. And what if there be ground for the reconstruction or redintegration of all the sacred books by Ezra, as seems to have been the belief of many, if not most, of the early fathers? They attest that Ezra was specially inspired for this function; but, setting aside the question of his divine inspiration, if the sacred books really were recomposed (this is hardly too strong a word) by Ezra, or in the time of Ezra, supposing the most scrupulous fidelity as to legal and religious provisions, what extensive modifications may have been made as to the smaller historic facts (some for the sake of perspicuity, some to harmonise discrepancies), above all in the language, which would in many places inevitably and insensibly take a varying cast!"

In speaking of the enormous numbers that characterise the narrative of the Exodus, the author remarks in a note (i. 189): "If we might suppose that a cipher has been added in the total sum, and throughout the several particulars, or if we might include men, women, and children under the 600,000, the history would gain, in my opinion, both in clearness and consistency." But the only plea for such wholesale alteration would be the assumption of the strict historical veracity of the original statement, which is the very matter in dispute. Every history may be brought more within the limits of credibility by thus pruning it at will. The excess in numbers here is uniform, pervading, and self-consistent. Besides, there is every reason to believe that the numbers were from the first expressed in words, which afford less opportunity for corruption. The citation of parallel instances of numerical exaggeration from other Oriental works explains the fact, but does not redeem the history.

Assuming the probability of changes so constant and extensive, as are here supposed, to adapt the document to the "vernacular usage" of the time, what guarantee have we left that they would not extend to the "legal and religious provisions," which are quite gratuitously excepted in the foregoing extracts? If we admit any growth in the national character and institutions, such as the extant history distinctly attests, these are precisely the points in which some change might be most naturally expected to occur. Indeed, unless we suppose the Mosaic Law to have been throughout a mere abstract ideal, with no practical influence on the people, we are reduced, apart from the admission of some progressive change, to this dilemma: either the laws enacted by Moses for the use of nomades, must have been wholly unavailable in the time of Ezra; or else laws suited to the new state of things which followed the exile, must have been unsuited to the need and capacity of a warlike horde, fighting its way to a new settlement through the wilderness. In the face of evidence which he has so candidly collected in his notes, we are surprised that Dean Milman should still leave unqualified the broad statement of his earlier edition,—that there can be no doubt "that the statute-book of Moses, with all his particular enactments, still exists, and that it recites them in the same order, if it may be called order, in which they were promulgated."

This question is often so put, as if it lay between the recognition of the whole existing Pentateuch as the work of Moses, and the entire repudiation of him as in any sense the primitive legislator of the Hebrews. Such a statement may serve the purpose of extreme partisans, who desire to enlist the religious prejudices of the uninstructed on their side; but those who only seek truth, will perceive that there is an intermediate view which best meets and reconciles the several conditions of the case. We presume that none but the most unreasonable sceptics venture to call in question the historical existence of Moses, or attempt to reduce him to a simple myth. His name is too deeply impressed on the subsisting laws of the Jewish people, and too closely interwoven with their oldest traditions, to permit us to entertain so extravagant a supposition. On the other hand, there is every probability that much has been ascribed to him, which is not his, and that his name by its commanding attraction has gathered to it, and put under its high sanction, many usages and ordinances which had come into existence with the increasing demands of the national life, and brought with them no distinct evidence of a particular occasion or a certain author. His personal history is so interwrought with the marvellous, which few even of the most cautious critics now accept as historical, that it seems impossible to doubt that much of it must have come to us through the mythic and legendary medium of oral tradition. Granting, then, the existence of a Mosaic nucleus of legislation in the Pentateuch, which gave its first impulse to the national existence, and even determined to a large extent by its powerful precedent the form of subsequent enactments, we are still compelled to suppose, by the undeniable results of critical analysis, by the existence of laws substantially the same in different forms of enunciation, by the traces of distinct groups of laws which must have preceded the present Pentateuchic collection, and by other phenomena of a similar kind—that around this primitive nucleus new enactments continually accumulated as the political and sacerdotal elements of the commonwealth developed themselves, which still carried with them the venerable name of Moses. Such extension of a name beyond the limits of its own proper sphere is not without example. David has imparted his to the whole Psalter, though only a small portion of its contents was actually written by him. The Proverbs are ascribed to Solomon, though the book itself speaks of various authorship. In our own country, how many institutions, that date from the Anglo-Saxon period, has the popular reverence gratuitously associated with the name of Alfred! This view, it must be admitted, is at variance with the general belief, and even with the impression, which the Pentateuch and Joshua (reduced to the form in which we now have them, at a later age) are calculated to produce. Instead of conceiving Moses to have announced the Law in its whole extent, and to have revealed the religion on which it is based, in its full perfection, all at once, with reference to a distant state of things, centuries before it did or could exist—it compels us to believe, that the Mosaic legislation, and the Jehovism associated with it, commenced with a few rudimental principles, involving the seed of a progressive self-development, which slowly and gradually, through their inherent strength and vitality, quickened by ceaseless prophetic action, forced their way into wider acknowledgment against a dense mass of grossness and ferocity, and even to the close of the monarchy had to sustain a doubtful contest with formidable hostile agencies.

This view is certainly most in accordance with the evidence of the history from Judges onwards, and with two facts that are prominently brought out by the learned and enlightened author of the present work. First, it is quite clear (Dean Milman every where acknowledges it) that, beside the polytheistic idolatries of the surrounding nations which threatened the purity of the national belief,—there were two forms of Jehovistic worship prevalent in Palestine,—one lower and symbolical, perhaps even idolatrous, of which the seats were the old high places where Samuel had once ministered; the other pure and spiritual, represented by Isaiah and the prophets, of which Jerusalem was the centre;—and that between these two forms there arose a deadly antagonism, which increased in bitterness in the last days of the kingdom, and was hardly exceeded by that which existed between Jehovism itself and the Baal worship of Ahab. This lower Jehovistic worship is usually regarded as a defection from the primitive Mosaic standard, occasioned more particularly by the separation of the kingdoms and the political necessities of the first king of Israel. We seem to encounter fewer difficulties by viewing it as the perpetuation of an earlier and ruder faith, from which the Jehovism of Jerusalem, cherished by a higher civilisation and developed by the prophets, was effectually disengaging itself; while it still subsisted in vigour in the northern and remoter districts, and had one of its principal seats at Bethel, which Jeroboam selected as a new sacerdotal centre for his kingdom.—The other fact is the change which appears to have come over the religious tendencies of the Jews, under the influence of the people among whom they were for a time transplanted. On their return from exile they were strict and even bigoted monotheists, and had worked off apparently all those idolatrous proclivities which had so deeply infected them to the very termination of the monarchy. "It is by no means improbable," says Dean Milman, "that at this period the Persians were pure Theists;" "and this probability," he adds in a note, "has been much increased by the cuneiform inscriptions, those especially of which the interpretation appears to me the most trustworthy,—the translations from the first or Zend column of Behistun." We cannot indeed suppose that the words of Isaiah, Micah, and Jeremiah were without deep effect in the concluding period of the kingdom of Judah; but their ministry had to maintain a sharp struggle to the last. The sorrow and humiliation of exile proved the truth of what they had uttered; and in that sad season their countrymen became acquainted with a great and powerful nation, the conquerors of the world, who repudiated all idolatry, and worshiped through their grand dualistic symbolism one Sovereign Intelligence. Such an example was not lost upon them. It perfected their spiritual training, and infused into it, through the doctrine of individual immortality, new elements of motive and hope. When their Law was reconstituted and put forth afresh on their return to their native country, it completed the work of preceding influences, and impressed on the national mind a fixed and enduring type, which all the wanderings and persecutions of ensuing centuries have been unable to efface. Such a type, had the Law previously existed in equal force, carrying with it as it did a divine sanction, and assisted, as was believed, by miraculous interposition,—it is surprising it should never have exhibited, during all the centuries that elapsed between the Exodus and the Exile, even a proximate tendency to produce.

For ourselves, we feel so sure that the solemn warnings, the grand suggestive exhortations, and the sublime anticipations of the prophets contain a truth, which carries its own evidence along with it, and could only come from God,—a truth which found its destined issue and fulfilment in the Gospel of our collective humanity,—that, in a religious sense, we are quite indifferent as to the solution of these critical questions. Our interest in them is purely intellectual,—to ascertain, if possible, what result is yielded by accessible evidence, and what view best meets the acknowledged difficulties of the case. Whatever that view and that result may be, religion, we are perfectly certain, will remain uninjured. We think it will even be an advantage to religion, that the theology of the Bible should be delivered, by the unavoidable effect of these inquiries, from too servile a dependence on the assumed history of the Bible. With all that the venerable author of the present work has so well said on this subject, we find ourselves in perfect harmony; and we heartily wish his own enlightened and catholic spirit were more widely diffused through the church of which he has long been so distinguished an ornament. We cannot do better than close this article in his own beautiful words (Preface, p. xxii.):

"For the perpetuity of religion, of the true religion,—that of Christ, —I have no misgivings. So long as there are women and sorrow in this mortal world, so long there will be the religion of the emotions, the religion of the affections. Sorrow will have consolation, which it can only find in the Gospel. So long as there is the sense of goodness, the sense of the misery and degradation of evil, there will be the religion of what we may call the moral necessities of our nature, the yearning for rescue from sin, for reconciliation with an All-holy God. So long as the spiritual wants of our higher being require an authoritative answer; so long as the human mind cannot but conceive its imaginative, discursive, creative, inventive thought to be something more than a mere faculty or innate or acquired power of 'the material body;' so long as there are aspirations towards immortality; so long as man has a conscious soul, and feels that soul to be his real self, his imperishable self,—so long there will be the religion of reason. As it was the moral and religious superiority of Christianity,—in other words, the love of God, diffused by Christ, 'by God in Christ,'—which mainly subdued and won the world, so that same power will retain it in willing and perpetual subjection. The strength of Christianity will rest not, in the excited imagination, but in the heart, the conscience, the understanding of man."

VI. *The Plain of Troy described, &c.* By Charles Maclaren, F.R.S.E. Edinburgh: Black, 1863.

Mr. Maclaren published in 1822 a *Dissertation on the Topography of the Plain of Troy.* Since that period so much light has been thrown upon the geography of Homer, especially by the publication of Dr. Forchammer's Memoir in 1842, and the Admiralty map in 1844, that Mr. Maclaren, having himself visited the Troad in 1847, has been induced to re-write his essay with considerable additions. Some of these, more particularly the reproduction of the Admiralty map, are important.

Never have the merits of a good map been more strikingly illustrated than in the case of the Troad. Kauffer's map was published somewhere about 1800: it is far from a scientific performance, and yet from Clarke's copy of Kauffer, engraved in 1803, have been derived almost all the maps of the Troad down to a very recent period. We cannot be surprised, therefore, that the Admiralty survey was an epoch in the history of Homeric topography. It did much to establish the geographical reality of Homer; but above all it confirmed the substantial accuracy of Strabo.

Sinking minor details, it is surprising how well Strabo has described the Trojan plain. If we take the Admiralty map, and fix our attention upon its more salient features, we get unmistakably the three ridges of the ancient geographer. These are the Rhœtean or Northern, the Chiblak or Central, and the Udjek or Southern ridge. Starting from Ida, and running in the direction of the Hellespont, very nearly parallel to each other, but with a perceptible inclination of the two outer ridges towards the inner, these perfectly unpretending hills enclose two valleys, each with its river-course. Between the Rhœtean and Chiblak ridge we have the Dombrek, between the Chiblak and Udjek the Menderé. It is upon the slopes of these hills and in the recesses of these valleys that all students of Homer, with few exceptions, have agreed to search for the site of *wind-swept* Troy. The field of investigation is thus narrowed to an area some ten miles by seven; and within these limits three principal points have been selected: the Novum Ilium of Strabo at Hissarlik, a village just upon the Western end of the Central ridge; Strabo's Ancient Ilium, near the Eastern extremity of the same ridge; and the village of Bunarbashi, on the Menderé, in the fork between the Central and the Southern ridge. Mr. Maclaren defends the claims of the first. The second, in some one or other of its modifications, has been adopted by several eminent geographers, particularly by Major Rennell. The third has perhaps found more friends than any other claimant, and was first suggested by M. Lechevalier in 1785.

Mr. Maclaren does not principally rely upon authorities. If he did, we do not think he would be badly off; for with the exception of Strabo, or rather Demetrius of Skepsis, from whom Strabo derived his information, the uniform testimony of antiquity is with him; and as to modern writers we can heartily enter into the honest pride with which he refers to the favourable opinion of Mr. Grote. But authorities are by no means Mr. Maclaren's sheet-anchor. His reliance is much more on facts and figures, in handling which he is evidently a veteran. His method is simple enough. He endeavours to establish two propositions: first, that *the Novum Ilium of Strabo is the modern Hissarlik*; secondly, that *Ilium Novum was really the Ilium Vetus of Homer*.

The identity of Ilium Novum with Hissarlik was first discovered by Dr. Clarke; but for the final settlement of this question we are indebted to the Admiralty map, and the indefatigable rule and compass of Mr. Maclaren. Not that Mr. Maclaren is without his difficulties. Strabo's figures look obstinate at first, but no figures are invincible.

Strabo places Ilium Novum 20 stadia from Sigeum, and 12 from Rhœteum. Now, if lines starting from these points be produced until they meet towards Hissarlik, the one will measure 33, the other 22 stadia. At this crisis Mr. Maclaren calls in Scylax. Scylax wrote about 400 years before Strabo; he gives 25 stadia between Ilium and the Hellespont, and this is actually the distance, as shown on the Admiralty map, between the bottom of the hill at Hissarlik and a point about midway between the mouth of the Menderé and that of the Dombrek. But is Strabo wrong? It does not follow for an instant. Mr. Maclaren propounds a theory which bids fair to be the true one, and which certainly reconciles the apparent discrepancy. It is briefly this. Scylax describes Troy before, Strabo after, its enlargement under the Romans. This enlargement would naturally be towards the coast, and thus the distance would become less. But, however this may be, the first proposition is proved to satiety, and we must accept Hissarlik as the Ilium Novum of Strabo.

But was this Ilium Novum the Ilium of Homer? Strabo says not. Here Mr. Maclaren divides his argument. First, there is the question of magnitude: is the hill of Hissarlik large enough to have been the site of Homer's Troy? Secondly, there is the question of distance from the shore and relation to the rivers: does the Iliad suppose an interval of some 6 or 8 miles between Troy and the Greek camp; or would the conditions of the poem be better satisfied by a distance of some 3 or 3½ miles? Again, is the Simois the prominent river in the battle-scenes, or is it not rather the Scamander? The area of the hill at Hissarlik is about half a square English mile; the area of that portion which Mr. Maclaren would identify with the *Pergamus* is about 11 English acres. Now we know that Tyre, with its 45,000 inhabitants, covered only about one-sixth part of a square mile; that East London has a population of 290 to the acre; and, as regards the *Pergamus*, that the acropolis of Argos, and also that of Athens, present areas of not more than eight acres. We do not see, then, how Mr. Maclaren can be blamed for inferring that the question of size is not against the claims of Hissarlik to be considered the site of ancient "wide-streeted" Troy.

The question of distance is a question to be determined by the Iliad itself; and here we think that Mr. Maclaren has it all his own way. Whether we read the details of the first, the second, or the third battle, it seems impossible to resist the conviction that the poet had in his mind a comparatively brief interval between the city and the camp of the Greeks. In fact, the evidence on this point has always seemed to us perfectly irresistible; and we think that Mr. Maclaren might fairly have been excused if he had treated it less fully than he has done. Now Hissarlik is 3½ miles, Strabo's Ilium Vetus 6 miles, and Bunarbashi 9 miles, from the Dardanelles. Strabo felt this difficulty, and therefore proposed to abridge the space between his Ilium Vetus and the Hellespont by supposing the shore to have been advanced seaward by the detritus of the Scamander.

This theory has been adopted to a certain extent by Major Rennell;

and of course it has been eagerly grasped at by Major Leake and other patrons of M. Lechevalier, whose maps exhibit a deep bay at the mouth of the Dombrek. Mr. Maclaren has convincingly shown that there is no river in the Troad which could produce such a change in the shore-line; and even Major Rennell admits that "to attribute the addition supposed [by the Lechevalier school], amounting to three feet per annum on the low shore of the Rhœtean bay, to a river like the Menderé, which is only occasionally full enough to make any deposits, is to ascribe to it an effective power of deposition proportionally greater than the Ganges possesses, with all its floods, with its perpetual great stream, and its never-ceasing load of sediment." The testimony of Scylax has a material bearing on this point; and, as his 25 stadia are something very like 25 stadia still, it seems evident that no considerable projection of the shore can have taken place between his time and ours.

The relation of the city to the rivers brings Mr. Maclaren into still sharper collision with M. Lechevalier. M. Lechevalier explored the Troad in 1785-1786, and read the results of his investigations before the Royal Society of Edinburgh in 1791. Lechevalier was neither an engineer nor a geographer, but simply a volatile Frenchman, with all the reckless positivism and pseudo-sentimentalism of his race. He surveyed with a graphometer, and made blunders innumerable, and yet his theories have found a host of supporters. They cannot, however, stand before the Admiralty map, and the fierce onslaught of Mr. Maclaren. Never was there a more hapless stream than the Kirk Jos. From being exalted to the high dignity of the Homeric Scamander, it has been degraded by Mr. Maclaren successively into a brook, a rivulet, a drain, and a quagmire. That the Scamander is the Menderé we think there can be no doubt whatever: a glance at the map shows this at once. Unless we give up Homer's geography as desperate, the Scamander must certainly have been the largest river of the Troad. It must have flowed in such a direction that the Greeks in marching against the city would cross it, and it only, and cross it once, not twice. These are the conditions; and no river fulfils them but the Menderé, nor fulfils them with reference to any site but that of Ilium Novum, or Ilium Vetus, both on the Chiblak ridge. In the face of any thing like an accurate map, the Kirk Jos must be given up. It is neither the Scamander nor the Simois, but in all probability a canal of comparatively recent construction.

The next question is, where are we to find the Simois? Mr. Maclaren determines it to be the Dombrek. But there are difficulties connected with this hypothesis. The Scamander and the Simois, as late as the time of Pliny, became one river before entering the sea. Ptolemy separates their embouchures, and they are separate now. It is true the Kalifatli Asmak, which is after all little more than a muddy ditch, communicates both with the Menderé and the Dombrek, and thus forms a kind of junction. But on the whole Mr. Maclaren is not quite so satisfactory upon this point as upon some others. Indeed, if our topographer can be supposed capable of any thing like special pleading, we venture to think that he has yielded to that weakness here.

The fact is, that the appetite for identification is always in great danger of becoming morbid; the broad, general features of resemblance come at last to lose their piquancy; and the very gravest of archæological mouths may at times be observed to water for a titbit of special discovery. Mr. Maclaren is no exception to this rule.

There is yet one great difficulty which stands between Mr. Maclaren and the goal of triumphant identification. This is the present course of the Scamander. Running close under Sigeum, it leaves a space on its western bank utterly inadequate for the position of the Greek camp. This is a difficulty which besets all theories as to the site of Troy; and Mr. Maclaren has been quite as successful as any of his predecessors in attaining that prime necessity of Homeric realists, a more easterly channel for the lower Scamander. Here again the Admiralty map is used with effect. From the peculiar projection towards the north-east of the line of three-fathom soundings, Mr. Maclaren infers a deposit which suggests two successive channels: one, and that probably the older, at En Tepe Asmak, or the mouth of the Dombrek; the other at a lagoon rather more to the west. We need hardly say that either of these channels, but especially the former, would leave a very considerable space on its west bank for the Naustathmos.

Mr. Maclaren has done good service to all students of Homer: he has written a book which promises to be *the* book on the subject of which it treats. But we really never saw such Greek quotations. Mr. Maclaren has published a table of *errata*. Can he possibly be aware of the portents which still disfigure almost every page? In the earlier part of the book we have copious extracts from Dr. Clarke's Latin translation: it might perhaps have been as well if this *pis aller* had been adhered to throughout. We have one other complaint to make. Possibly we may be pardoned if we venture to submit that the tone of some passages in this work is slightly in excess of that vigorous warmth which is only just admissible in questions of archæology. There is a quasi-Bentleian ferocity in one or two of the assaults upon poor M. Lechevalier which might well have been spared. Nor do we think that Mr. Maclaren will be angry with us if we suggest that it has long ceased to be the habit of accomplished authors, even though they be sprung from the *perfervidum genus*, to call each other hard names.

VII. *The Polish Captivity.* By Sutherland Edwards. W. H. Allen and Co.

Any body who has lived much on the Continent must be aware that in every European country there exists a pro-English party of more or less importance. As a rule, the influence of English opinion on the masses of a Continental nation is very small compared with that of France. To what cause this fact is due, whether to our language, our insular position, or our peculiar state policy, is a question too wide for us to enter on. The fact, however, is, that the party which studies English literature, and copies English manners, and admires English institutions, is rarely, if ever, the national one. They represent a sect, often a very influential and respectable sect, but they do not represent the country; and therefore their opinions as to the prospects and condition of their own land are seldom reliable. On the other hand, an Englishman is remarkably apt to make acquaintance with this pro-English party, and adopt their views and sentiments as being those of the country he is visiting. Unless we are mistaken, Mr. Sutherland Edwards has fallen a victim to this common mistake. Apparently, during his sojourn in Poland, he became intimate with the small section in that country who represent the Anglo-loving community, and has been indoctrinated by them with their peculiar views. Unfortunately, in this instance, the error was a serious one. By this time the notion that England is likely to interfere actively in behalf of the popular cause on the Continent is pretty well exploded. The party therefore in Poland who favour the English in preference to the French alliance are virtually advocates of moral intervention in preference to physical. Now as the most enthusiastic of Poles scarcely believe it possible that Poland can overthrow the dominion of Russia without the aid of foreign arms, this preference is tantamount to an acquiescence in the supremacy of Russia. In other words, the pro-English Poles consider that the best chance for their country lies in coming to terms with the Czar, not in attempting to dissolve the partnership by force. This opinion may possibly be a wise and just one, but it is not the national opinion of Poland; and the views based upon it are likely to mislead the readers of *The Polish Captivity*.

What renders this bias of Mr. Edwards the more unfortunate is, that the peculiar tenets of his Anglo-Polish informants happened to tally exactly with his personal prejudices. We never met with a writer who had a greater number of partisan animosities. It is hard to say whether he dislikes the French or the Germans, the Manchester party or the European democrats, more cordially. Mr. Carlyle is an antipathetic—in Italian phrase—to him, as Mr. Cobden and Frederick the Great and the first Napoleon are the objects of his indiscriminate abuse. As far as we can understand the author's views, he would sooner see Poland amalgamated with Russia than emancipated by the aid of French armies; and indeed the brightest prospect he can look forward to for that unhappy country is, that the Czar should recover her lost provinces from Austria and Prussia, and incorporate the whole into a Russian dependency. Throughout the book, amidst much generous and—what is more—much genuine sympathy for the Poles, there runs a strong undercurrent of pro-Russian sentiment. The moral of the work might be conveyed in the proverb, which the author remarks could be applied appropriately to the relations between Russia and Poland, "Nec sine, nec cum te vivere possum." It is clear that, in despite of his conservative prejudices, he believes the inexorable logic of facts to have decided the fate of Poland. She is henceforth bound to Russia, and the only thing she can do is to make the best of an indissoluble union. There is a story told of King Victor Emmanuel in whose moral Mr. Edwards would heartily coincide. At the outbreak of the Polish troubles, somebody spoke to his majesty on the subject. The king twisted his moustache, and remarked, "If I were Czar of Russia, I would end this difficulty at once: all I should say to the Poles would be, 'Soyons amis, annexons la Prusse.'" Of all their persecutors, the Poles, in our author's opinion, dislike the Russians the least, and would gladly combine with them in an attack on Austria and Prussia. Mr. Edwards, therefore, is disposed to look leniently on the errors of the Marquis Wielopolski and other pro-Russian Poles, and to believe that their policy was in itself the wisest for their country. We are by no means clear that these views are mistaken ones, but we dispute the accuracy of receiving them as the popular opinions of educated Poles.

Disagreeing, as we do, with Mr. Edwards' political sentiments, we yet wish to render full justice to his literary merits. In the first place *The Polish Captivity* is a very readable and pleasant book; and in the second place it gives us a great amount of information we could not easily obtain elsewhere. As a mere work of art it would be more perfect if the latter half of the second volume were omitted. The lengthy disquisition on the first faltering steps of constitutional life in Russia is the least interesting portion of the book, and bears only indirectly on the question of Poland. We could perhaps wish, too, that Mr. Edwards had given us more of description and less of political discussion; not, indeed, that the latter is not worth reading, but that the former is so very light and easy. As a specimen of the author's descriptive powers, let us quote the following:

"Even in the thoroughly Polish city of Cracow, where there is no prohibition against the national dress, it is a rare thing to see a complete and authentic Polish suit. I remember one old Pole there, however, who, but for the reality of his look, the calm dignity of his manner, and the intimate relations evidently existing between him and his clothes, might have been taken for a Mazurka-dancing Pole out of some Polish ballet, produced with unusual magnificence, and with scrupulous accuracy in the costume department. He was old enough to have seen the constitution of the 3d of May adopted, supposing that his father had carried him to the Assembly, as Suchorzewski did his son, that he might swear a theatrical oath to slay him on the spot if the wise measure which abolished the *veto*, and made the crown hereditary, became law. The first time I saw this ancient Pole, I found myself looking involuntarily to see whether he still wore the sabre which was formerly the distinguishing sign of a Polish gentleman. No, he had abandoned that; but he kept to the silken semi-oriental robe, and to the close-fitting tunic worn beneath, and the silver ornamented girdle, and the long black boots of soft shiny leather; and on great days (such, for instance, as the anniversary of the Union of Poland with Lithuania) actually appeared in a species of hussar cap, and made a point, according to the ancient custom, of wearing in his dress the colours of his coat-of-arms."

It is a pity that an author who can write so well as this should tarnish his pages with frequent, and invariably unsuccessful, attempts at fine writing. Here, for example, is an indignant apostrophe, though to whom it is addressed we are unable to discover. We presume it is meant for Prussia, and that for 'Prussia' in the first sentence you should read 'Russia.' This, however, is only a conjectural emendation.

"'Tu l'as voulu, Georges Dandin!' You tied yourself to Prussia without thinking how much younger, stronger, more powerful, more enterprising, and even more unscrupulous, she is than you. The Poles may yet rise against you; your long, thin country may again be broken in pieces, as it was in 1806, and as it remained until 1813; when finding that your French master was running from the Russians, you turned upon him and magnanimously kicked him!

"But, whatever happens to Prussia, it will still have Mr. Carlyle for its historian, only it must not lose Posen till the *Life of Frederick II.* is quite finished: for if a nation does not prosper, it does not deserve to prosper. The historian will justify the ways of Providence towards Prussia up to the moment of going to press. It must not, then, before the last volume is completed, fall back to the position it occupied fifty years ago."

These blemishes, however, are incidental, and hardly affect the intrinsic value of the work. The two points which Mr. Edwards throws the greatest light upon are, to our mind, the state of the Poles in the non-Russian provinces, and the relations of the peasantry to the nobles. On these points he writes from observation, not from theory, and therefore his researches possess an especial importance. If his facts are true, they completely dispel the popular English notion that Austria and Prussia have succeeded in reconciling the Poles, more or less, to their governments. On the contrary, according to our author's views, though the political position of the Poles is more favourable in Posen and Gallicia than in Russia, their social and personal comfort is greater in the latter. "In spite of most reforms, in spite of liberty of the press, as great almost as in Prussia, and perfect liberty of speech in the Gallician diet, there is still, on the whole, far less political liberty in Gallicia than in Posen, though of course far more than in the Kingdom where there is indeed none whatever. On the other hand, of that kind of freedom, scarcely appreciable by those who have never felt the want of it, which consists in being able to speak, learn, teach, and transact all kinds of business in the national language, and without the interposition of foreigners, there is less in Austrian Poland than in that portion of Russian Poland called the 'Kingdom,' where every one speaks Polish, where Polish money circulates, and accounts are kept in the old Polish currency; where such phantoms of journals as appear are all printed in Polish; where Polish is the language of the public offices, churches, and schools; and where until quite lately (when, in consequence of the Poles refusing to attend it, it was closed) there was a national Polish theatre, at which Polish pieces were played by Polish actors. This is just the kind of freedom which is denied to the Poles by the government of Prussia, and which, in spite of copious promises, has only been partially granted by Austria. In short, a Pole is surrounded by more of what is called 'Polonism' in the kingdom than in Gallicia or Posen; but he finds in Posen the greatest amount of political liberty. In Austria, he has a little of both, but not very much of either."

This statement, if correct, will account for the vitality of Poland, and is therefore promising for the hopes of its future regeneration. On the other hand, Mr. Edwards' narrative of the feelings prevalent amongst the peasants towards the nobles is a gloomy one for the friends of Poland. Entertaining as he does a strong prejudice in favour of the old aristocratic Polish government, he strives hard to prove that the peasants have no real cause to entertain ill-will towards their former masters. He dwells enthusiastically on the liberal provisions with regard to the serfs contained in the constitution of 1791. He declares, possibly with reason, that the Polish nobles have long been anxious to emancipate their serfs, but were continually prevented by their rulers from carrying out their wishes; and he affirms that the permanence of serfdom would have been far less long-lived, had it not been for the partition of Poland. All this may be true, but it does not affect facts. The truth seems to be, that the serfs were miserably ill-treated under the old Polish governments, and that since their country has been enslaved their condition has been marvellously improved. In consequence they regard the government as their friend, and the nobles as their enemy. The conclusion may be wrong, but it is not unnatural. Supposing the result of the American civil war should be to free the blacks, it is certain that the Negroes will always regard the Federal government as their protector, however logically you may prove to them that the planters, if left to themselves, would have liberated them with equal or greater rapidity. The condition of the Polish serf appears to have been little, if any thing, better than that of a field-hand in the cotton-states; and the Poles are reaping now the curse which sooner or later falls on all slave-owners. It is hard that the Polish nobles should be ruled by foreigners at the present day, because their grandfathers were tyrants; but it is the law of the world that children do suffer for the sins of their parents. The Polish peasantry are very likely brutal, ignorant, and selfish; but still we cannot exaggerate the importance of Mr. Edwards' admission, that practically the emancipated serfs would regard the restoration of an independent Poland as a national calamity. We do not say, for one moment, that this state of things justifies the enslavement of Poland; but it accounts for the fact that the country has been enslaved, and causes us not to be over-sanguine of its ultimate liberation.

BOOKS OF THE QUARTER SUITABLE FOR READING-SOCIETIES.

The History of England during the Reign of George III. By William Massey, M.P. Parker and Bourn.

[Reviewed in the Short Notices.]

The Life of Lacordaire. By the Count de Montalembert. Bentley.

[Interesting in itself, and for the light it throws on French Ultramontanism.]

Six Months in the Federal States. By Edward Dicey. Macmillan.

[Reviewed in the Short Notices.]

The Naturalist on the River Amazon. By H. W. Bates. Murray.

A Memoir of Charles James Blomfield, Bishop of London. By his Son, A. Blomfield, M.A. Murray.

Fish Hatching and the Artificial Culture of Fish. By F. Buckland. Tinsley Brothers.

The Life of Sir Howard Douglas, G.C.B., &c. By S. W. Fullom. Murray.

The Heroes of the Sahara, and the Manners of the Desert. Translated by J. Hutton. Allen and Co.

Travels on Horseback in Mantchu Tartary. By G. Fleming. Hurst and Blackett.

John Leifchild, D.D., his Public Ministry, Private Usefulness, and Personal Characteristics. By J. R. Leifchild. Jackson, Walford, and Co.

[Badly written, but interesting as the life of an eminent Nonconformist.]

The Court of Peter the Great. By an Austrian Secretary of Legation: translated by Count Mac Donnell. Bradbury and Evans.

Narrative of a Secret Mission to the Danish Islands. By the Rev. J. Robertson. Longman.

Essays on the Pursuits of Women. By Frances Power Cobbe. Emily Faithfull.

Heat considered as a Mode of Motion. By J. Tyndall, F.R.S. Longman.

[Popularly written.]

Memoirs of Miles Byrne, Chef de Bataillon, &c. Paris, Bossange.

The Roman Poets of the Republic. By Professor Sellar. Edmonston and Douglas.

A Yachting Cruise in the Baltic. By S. R. Graves. Longman.

Pictures of German Life in the Eighteenth and Nineteenth Centuries. Second Series. By Gustav Freytag. Translated by Mrs. Malcolm. Chapman and Hall.

Lectures on the History of England. By William Longman. Vol. I. Longmans.

War Pictures from the South. By Colonel P. Estvan. Routledge and Co.

A Painter's Camp in the Highlands. By P. G. Hamerton. Macmillan.

A Visit to Russia. By Henry Moor, Esq. Chapman and Hall.

History of Christian Missions during the Middle Ages. By G. F. Maclear. Macmillan.

Austen Elliot. By H. Kingsley. Macmillan.

[Full of hearty vigorous writing and animal spirits; but not as well put together as the author's earlier works.]

Lost and Saved. By the Hon. Mrs. Norton. Hurst and Blackett.

[Pervaded by a most unpleasant tone on moral subjects.]

The Water-Babies. By the Rev. C. Kingsley. Macmillan.

Deep Waters. By Miss A. Drury. Chapman and Hall.

Giulio Malatesta. By T. A. Trollope. Chapman and Hall.

Arrows in the Dark. By the Author of "Said and Done." Smith, Elder, and Co.

A First Friendship. Parker and Bourn.

Chesterford. By the Author of "A Bad Beginning." Smith, Elder, and Co.

THE NATIONAL REVIEW.

OCTOBER 1863.

Art. I.—THE CRITICISM OF THE OLD TESTAMENT.

An Introduction to the Old Testament, Critical, Historical, and Theological. By Samuel Davidson, D.D. of the University of Halle, and LL.D. 3 vols. Williams and Norgate, 1863.

In the primitive text-books on the canon of Scripture there was a respectable custom that under the heads of inspiration, genuineness, and authenticity, should be arranged all that could be plausibly made out with regard to the canonical authority of each book. The proofs were collected with care, and set forth in unadorned simplicity. The Rev. Hartwell Horne devotes a page and a half to the genuineness and authenticity of Daniel, observing that with regard to that book there is every possible evidence, both external and internal; the former embracing "the general testimony of the whole Jewish church and nation," and the latter the convincing fact that the "language, style, and manner of writing are all perfectly agreeable to that age." It is true that the proofs of other books are somewhat meagre in comparison. The Song of Solomon, for example, rests upon the argument that, as the canon of the Hebrew Scripture was settled by Ezra, who "wrote, and we may believe acted, by the inspiration of the Most High," the Song, which was placed by him in the same volume with the Law and the Prophets, must have been a sacred book. As regards Ecclesiastes, again, "there can be no doubt of its title to admission; Solomon was eminently distinguished by the illumination of the Divine Spirit, and had even twice witnessed the Divine presence." The learned author naïvely adds—we are quoting the edition of 1828—that "the tendency of the book is excellent, when rightly understood; and Solomon speaks in it with great clearness of the revealed truths of a future life and of a future judgment."

Now we have no more wish to exclude the Song of Solomon from a collection of Hebrew literature than any other well-meaning love-song. The little idyll in question is pastoral, and perhaps pretty; not rigidly decorous throughout, according to our modern ideas, but ardent, and—to speak seriously—distinctly virtuous in its tendency. The Established Church does not introduce it into its services, and is content with the modest remark, which, if it were only at all true, would be certainly applicable,—that of this, in common with the rest, there was never any doubt in the Church. The other books, too, which we have just mentioned, we are most happy to receive, though perhaps in a different sense from the author of the celebrated "Introduction." But it is difficult to help wondering whether its writer really believed that there was nothing more to be said on the subject than the few words which he devotes to it in each of these cases. The Canticles, for example, are never quoted by our Lord or his Apostles, by Josephus or Philo. Daniel contains Greek words. There is hardly an educated man at the present time who will not feel that we have advanced somewhat beyond such criticism as that above quoted. It so happens that one of the books in question is of antiquity now almost undisputed, and that the other is, according to the opinion of nearly every critic, a production of the age of the Maccabees. But, whether by the diligence of English or Germans, orthodox or heretics, the present knowledge of the Old Testament has advanced many steps beyond that of forty years ago.

The study of the Jewish records is one for which many men have no time, and still more have no taste. But the results of that study there are few who do not wish to understand, and there are even some who are willing to accept. The minds of Englishmen have been lately aroused to the fact that there is something yet to be learnt beyond the truth that all Hebrew writers were infallible. The students of the Old Testament have been so loud in their assertion of novel ideas, so persistent in their refusal of cherished beliefs, that it has become evident to an ordinary observer that, whatever the new views are, they are not the results of mere caprice. At the same time, the knowledge of Scripture in English society has been as yet deplorably small, and all but the simplest arguments are beyond the understanding of the public. It needs some matter-of-fact numerical calculation, or some broad and picturesque view of a difficulty, to enable a layman to recognise the facts which critics themselves have learnt on their first entrance upon scriptural study. The words 'Biblical criticism,' 'canon,' 'recension,' 'authenticity,' are to ordinary eyes invested in one general fog. Something, they feel, is going on in the background, which is at all events interesting, and which the bishops consider shocking. Reason is a very good thing in its way; why has rationalism such an awful and malignant sound? Religious liberty has been a watchword of Englishmen for two centuries; it cannot be stinted now. But why, it is generally felt, cannot the critics say distinctly what there is to be said, instead of imploring the laity to grant them the religious liberty of talking to one another in a tongue not understanded of the multitude?

Nothing can account for the popularity of the late books of theological inquiry in England, but the distinct understanding that they are the mouth-piece of a large and increasing school. It was commonly declared by the antagonists of Bishop Colenso's first volume on the Pentateuch, that if it had appeared in Germany, that land of theological learning, it would have created no sensation at all. If the statement be even partially true,—for the greatest critics of the Continent have spoken of the book with considerable praise,—the simple reason is, that the main ideas which it contained were in themselves no novelty to the Germans. The intellectual conservatism of England was about half a century, roughly speaking, behind its neighbour. And true as this is in regard to the results of inquiry, it is still more true in respect of the way in which the questions themselves are looked at. Here, it is well understood, when a theological professor sits down to write a book, that he has some cause to advocate. There, it is charitably supposed that he wishes to elucidate the subject. Here, a clergyman is considered as competent to deal with a disputed topic, if he is a good man and keeps his Sunday-schools in order. There, it is believed to be necessary to have examined the controversy with care. A German student will inform an inquirer at once which branch of theology it is to which he has chiefly devoted himself, and will hesitate to dogmatise upon others. An English bishop will publish a statement that he has been credibly informed that one particular interpretation of a text is right, and that he is confident that a complete refutation of a given heresy will be found in the work of a friend of his own. Except among the educated laity, who preserve an emphatic silence, the criticism of the Scriptures is treated in England with prejudice, violence, and haste; and prejudice, violence, and haste alike exclude the golden virtue of candour.

The secret of German success in criticism is to be found in the system of division of labour. Every one of the great names that are mentioned in connexion with theological progress can be classified and set down in his own peculiar niche in history. The study of the Old Testament has been the work in reality of but a few men. All the philosophy of Germany, a century or a century and a half ago, was concentrated on the New; and it was long before real progress was made in the investigation of the Jewish Scriptures. The first great name is that of Michaelis, the thorough German, the man of hard solid learning, whose researches into the details of Mosaism are far from obsolete now. Rosenmüller trod somewhat in the same steps, and Herder added the element of a more modern literary zeal; to listen to him, said

J. Paul Richter, was like beholding the red dawn amid the moonlight. It was not till popular attention had been roused almost painfully towards the subject of criticism by the publication by Lessing of the Wolfenbüttel fragments, that Eichhorn appeared on the stage. He was the model of a critic—serious, acute, calm. His "rationalism"—we use the word in the technical sense—has indeed died out, but much of his spirit and much of his work remains. Röhr, the German Stanley, with Bertholdt and Vater, are the next names that meet us; the tone of criticism then experienced some change. The influence of Schleiermacher in Germany was such that his disciples introduced even into the study of the Old Testament, upon which he himself had not entered, something of his earnestness and depth; and, strange as it may appear, one of the results of the change was the happy divorce of criticism from dogma. The old master had exalted the individual religious life above the formularies of belief; and some of his successors adopted from him the religious spirit, and left the questions of orthodoxy to fight their own battle, while they devoted themselves to historical study. De Wette is the most eminent example of the school of which we are speaking; he died not very long ago, after years of patient labour, animated by a keen critical sagacity, and recommended by a blameless life. The later Tübingen school must be mentioned with him, though their chief work has been on the New Testament, and though in many of their number the polemical spirit of the partisan destroys the earnestness of the critic. De Wette has been followed (we are speaking of Old-Testament criticism only) by Tuch, Maurer, Winer the lexicographer of the Bible, Knobel of Basle, Hitzig, whose study of the Prophets has been invaluable, Hupfeld, Lücke, and the accomplished Bunsen, whose skill it was to pursue doctrinal theology as a theologian, ecclesiastical theories as a politician, and Scriptural studies as a critic, and to know how to keep them apart. The rising Dutch school of criticism must be added to the German list; Leyden is beginning to be a university of high theological reputation, and there are few contemporary names which stand higher in the critical world than that of Kuenen. Last of all, as isolated from the rest, far above them in mastery of Oriental language and ideas, acute, obstinate, apparently almost reckless in a conjecture, but indestructible in an argument, of keen sensibility, poetic temperament, profound piety, relentless in self-assertion, quick in apprehension, untiring in patience, stands Ewald of Göttingen, foremost of German critics.

We sometimes hear on platforms, and find echoes even in episcopal letters, of an orthodox reaction in Germany. The destructive school has died out, it is said, under the efforts of Hengstenberg, Neander, and Tholuck. It would be equally true to assert that English heterodoxy is disappearing through the zeal of Mr. Hartwell Horne, Dean Milman, and Mr. Maurice. The only "orthodox" names of any note in the particular branch of which we are now speaking are Delitzsch, Keil, and possibly Hävernick; and the first of these, the only writer of real power among them, is by no means rigorously conservative. The truth is, there are two distinct movements to which the term "orthodox reaction" has been applied. The first was by no means a reactionary movement. It was the religious tendency in criticism, which showed itself in the disciples of Schleiermacher; the emotional and subjective element of thought brought forward in opposition to the Hegelian method, which first created religious doctrine on an *à priori* basis, separated it, till the era of Strauss, from critical and historical study, and then systematised it as a body of objective divinity. This is the school which in one direction produced De Wette, and in the other Neander; from which, in fact, all the best German criticism has proceeded. But the later Berlin school, the true "orthodox reaction," is a very different thing. It is a semi-political móvement, strongly conservative, supported by the court-party, ultra-Lutheran, ecclesiastical, and even sacramental in its tendency. It silences criticism by church authority, as it wishes to silence political liberalism; and it has as yet produced no great names, unless perhaps that of Kurtz, in the world of letters. Some of our own religious journals which echo the cry of a German orthodox reaction would be somewhat surprised if they were told that they were cheering on the banner of the *Kreuz Zeitung* to victory.

Meanwhile a school of critical inquiry is rising in France. Strange to say, it began among the mysticism and excitement of a revival movement, and its German authors were such men as Schleiermacher and Tholuck, and not such as Tuch and De Wette. Its importance will not shrink in English eyes from the fact that its prominent leaders have been men of strong religious feeling. The Coleridge of France, if such an expression may be used, was Vinet, the celebrated divine of Lausanne. He had all Coleridge's determination, his strong subjectivity, his wonderful power of influencing others. Like him, he was a metaphysician among theologians; "conscience in harmony with revelation" was the one staple of his teaching. It was in virtúe of his persistent assertion of individual liberty that he gained the almost patriarchal position which he so long held, and through which his name is now almost a household word among French Protestants. Gradually the seed of liberty which Vinet sowed grew up and began to yield fruit. On the one hand, a Pressensé now bears the flag of an orthodoxy which is not narrow-minded, and such men as Astié, Arnaud, and Secretan are no unworthy followers. On the other, criticism and scholarship have their representatives in Schérer, whose faithfulness to his principles cost him his professorship fourteen years ago; and Réville, the pastor of Rotterdam, whose articles in the *Revue des Deux Mondes* always seem to combine French elegance with German thoroughness. Reuss the historian is with him, and Colani the eloquent preacher of Strasbourg, and the younger Coquerel, and Nicolas the essayist; Renan can hardly be counted among the list. It is only a rising school, and has done but little as yet; and it is not without its faults. One sees a disposition to conquer all theology in one essay, an impatient eagerness for generalisation, which will sober down in time. *Le voilà, le chameau,* is too much the motto even of theology in France. It appears perhaps more than any where else in the spirit of true French eclecticism, which insures completeness of theory at the cost of elaborateness of proof. The references are constantly not verified; and, indeed, it is not always that there are any references to verify. But these are matters of detail. The French school, it cannot be doubted, will soon have made itself a name; and it has now the merit of being the only school of known theologians which does not habitually condescend to invective. One of its leaders declared in England not long ago, that the recriminations of English polemics were to him perfectly surprising, in contrast with the mutual forbearance with which such topics are usually treated by his countrymen.

As a deliberate attempt to found an English school of criticism the *Essays and Reviews* might have gained some credit if they had been content to tell the world only what it knew before. It had been found impossible to establish a *Studien und Kritiken*, an unsectarian journal of sacred criticism, in England with any prospect of a wide circulation. The authors of the new volume wished simply to make scriptural inquiries popular; and if they had but adopted a conciliatory tone, or had dressed heresy in orthodox language, they might have escaped the storm. Nothing is more clear from the recent controversies than that it is possible to advance liberal views in such a way that they shall seem perfectly commonplace. And there is, it is evident, in the public mind an instinct against meddling with science. The *Dictionary of the Bible* escaped adverse criticism not because it was so well-meaning, but because it was so big. It was clearly not advisable to adopt a "platform" of confessed ignorance by taking up arms against some fifty of the leading Biblicists of the country. The divergence would have been made more painfully evident between the religion of the people and the religion of the men of science.

The fact is, that a destructive criticism is not enough. Englishmen must have some belief, and it is necessary to show them that when the trust in Biblical infallibility is removed, there is something worth believing still. But it was necessary first to destroy. It will be no easy task even now to clear away the one great obstruction to criticism which age after age has heaped up. We are persuaded that the majority of critics have no idea of the extent to which the belief in an infallible record has spread, or the extent of time during which it has prevailed. It has been often said, and it has been said even in courts of law, that the belief of which we are speaking is a new one, unknown to the Reformers, and *à fortiori* unknown to the ages before them. After some study, we are convinced of the contrary. In spite of the looseness which prevailed in the usage of religious terms, it is certain that the schoolmen as a body considered that the Scriptures cannot err. Aquinas, Nicolaus de Lyrâ, and many others, though they do not state the doctrine in words, convey it implicitly in their writings. We are speaking, it will be observed, of infallibility, and not of inspiration; the one is a tangible property, capable of proof and disproof, and has been denied in later times by Baxter, Horsley, Tillotson, Paley, Whately, Thirlwall, and Heber; the other is an attribute which may vary in degree, which may be ascribed in some sense to ordinary men, which has even in its higher sense, that of a plenary and "special" inspiration of God, been applied by a canonising Pope to Thomas Aquinas himself. But once the Reformation movement began, Bibliolatry declined. "That Spirit," writes Erasmus, "who guided the minds of the apostles, allowed them to be ignorant of some things." It is needless to quote the views of Luther and other Reformers; it is evident that the struggle in favour of liberty, which overthrew the authority of the Church, also partially overthrew the superhuman authority of the Bible. That it has again revived, both in England and abroad, is to be attributed to the one vice of indolence, the fruitful parent of superstition. A very little study would have shown that holy men might sometimes be mistaken, as Ezekiel when he prophesied the utter destruction of Tyre. A week's candid searching of the Scriptures might bring any reader within reach of a hundred self-contradictions which render perfect accuracy chimerical, and it needed but a superficial knowledge to assure him that no one writer in the Bible, on any single occasion, lays claim to infallibility at all. And yet this strange belief grew up alike under the fostering care of the Church, and in the unfettered freedom of Nonconformity, and men, not contented with surrendering their lives to spiritual authority, performed as well the voluntary sacrifice of their intellects.

It is curious to remark how easily, when the work of destruction is done, that of reconstruction commences. Since his first volume Dr. Colenso has practically changed his position.

Whether as a preface to a larger plan or not, he occupied himself at first entirely with disproof of the details of Exodus; in a few months he appeared again as the framer of a new theory of its composition. Valuable as his positive arguments are, it may be questioned whether he was not more useful in his negative. The public attention was aroused by a clear statement of certain incoherencies and impossibilities: there is some fear that, amid the hazardous and doubtful proofs of a special theory, the interest may slumber again. The minute analysis of the Psalms, for example, is a work which has not been attempted in England before; but it is one thing to lay before fifty thousand readers the plain fact that every critic knows, and another to ask their assent to minutiæ upon the import of which the critical world is divided. As a matter of fact, the argument for a Samuelic authorship of one of the original documents does not appear to us sufficiently cogent, however much we may admire the tact and learning which recommend it; and the main theory of the third volume, in like manner, seems probable, but not irresistible. Would it not have been better, for the present at all events, to have pursued the original line of demolition, even at the sacrifice of a reputation for thorough scholarship, and at the cost of the hostility which is sure to fasten most on the negative side of an argument? In his forthcoming volume of Genesis, it is to be presumed that Dr. Colenso will again revert to the simple and popular method which he can pursue with such skill. If our recommendation could have any weight, we should urge him first of all to devote his labour to the not inglorious task of convincing the public of a wide-spread error: when this is once thoroughly done, when once the character of the historic details is made plain to every one who will take the trouble to read and examine, let him then enter on the higher paths of criticism. Let him then bring his countrymen to understand that there may be some interest in the study of books which possess no supernatural protection from human frailty, and some profit to be derived from the history of a race whose writers and poets have something in common, even in their errors, with the writers and poets of our own.

At the head of this article is placed the name of a work which has lately appeared on the Old Testament. It is an expansion of a previous work by the same author, and it is the most complete which has yet been produced in this country. As a compendium of the opinions which have been held on the several books of the canon, and as an impartial judgment upon them, it will probably be for some years the most satisfactory within the reach of Englishmen. As far as we have been able to form an opinion, the merits of the book are very high, and especially in the purely literary part of the subject: the questions of date, language, and authorship, are examined with great care and research, and the conclusions are clearly stated. The author devotes the greater part of the first volume to an elaborate examination of the Pentateuch. He himself places the date of the Elohist writer in the reign of Saul, and the Jehovist in that of Uzziah; and maintains the existence of a "junior Elohist" at about the time of Elisha. The composition of Deuteronomy, and the final editing of the five books, he places, with most critics, somewhere in the reign of Manasseh. The historical books are well treated as regards their sources and their relation to one another, though it might have been as well to dismiss the explanations of disputed passages in a book of the kind. The Psalms, again, require a more careful handling than the nature of Dr. Davidson's work could permit him; nor will the student be thoroughly satisfied with his treatises on the poetical books. But the examination of the prophets is excellently conducted, and but for the perplexities which render it impossible to place perfect reliance on the results of any criticism of the prophets, however sagacious, it might almost serve for a commentary to the general reader. It is hardly necessary to say that the author does not for a moment seek to disguise his obligation to the German scholars who have preceded him.

We have spoken in sincere commendation of the matter of the great part of Dr. Davidson's work. It is difficult to yield the same unqualified admiration to its style. In the first place, considering that the author is himself a convert to the views which he now professes, it might have been well if some of the conclusions at which he arrives were stated with a little more reserve. "Neither of these hypotheses is correct;" "to say that the . . . is to assert what is false,"—such are some of the formulæ in which questions are disposed of. Very frequently the reasons are given for the judgment, and no doubt they are often very good ones; but the reader expects, in such a work as Dr. Davidson's, a little more of the student, and not quite so much of the prophet. Another fault which we have to find is to be referred to the circumstances of the author. A great part of Dr. Davidson's life has been spent in the midst of controversy, not to say persecution; and his book bears witness to the fact. There is a polemical tone running through it which constantly offends the ear. One is glad sometimes, in pursuing theological inquiries, to be able to dismiss from the mind the conviction that one's opponents must be very wicked men; and if the book before us does not always exactly state as much as this, it too frequently hints that they are very foolish ones. The author seems as if, with all his learning and ability, he could never quite remove from his mind the idea that he is fighting for a professorship. And if in any writer some calmness of argument to be looked for, it is surely in one who but twenty years ago published, with a great deal of emphasis, opinions exactly the opposite of the present. We have in our hands a volume called Davidson's *Sacred Hermeneutics*, published in 1843. At p. 37 we read thus: "The next office of reason, with regard to the Bible, is to acquiesce in its statements." A little further on: "The Bible is infallible, because its Author is so." The writer who now speaks of the "narrow notions of noisy religionists" is the same who inveighed before against the "bold and blasphemous assertions of Strauss;" the antagonist of an orthodoxy which "heartily blackens the characters of men who dare to differ from its dogmas" is the same who had no hesitation, twenty years back, in calling Rationalism "the offspring of the Evil One."

In the midst of theological controversy, the most candid minds may well become bewildered. There are two questions which are often asked, and are asked most naturally, by men who expect in such topics as these the same distinctness which they find in political or social contests. On the one hand, they ask, "Where will all this stop?" and on the other, "What are the things that the critics have actually found out?"

To the first of these questions the only suitable reply is a refusal to answer it at all. Let us examine for an instant what the question means. It assumes that there exists a body of religious facts in which most men find satisfaction and comfort, from which learned writers are in the habit of taking away first one and then another; and it expresses a fear that the progress of learning will end in abolishing the heap altogether, and leaving nothing worth calling a religion in the world. Men come with their interpretations, their mythical theories, their rationalism—

> "Geology—ethnology—what not—
> Greek endings with the little passing bell
> That signifies some faith's about to die"—

and cut away at belief till it almost seems to be toppling over on their heads. How many more strokes will there be? Is it really going to fall in ruins? Such is the sentiment which asks where criticism will end. Let those who adopt it consider seriously this dilemma. Religion is in the main either a bad or a good thing. If it is a bad thing, the sooner a remorseless logic sweeps it away the better for the world. If it is not, it will not be destroyed by reasoning; and the more pains that are spent on it, the more thorough the inquiries which bear upon it, the greater will be the general gain. Criticism will not stop any where. The critics of the present day are for the most part candid and religious men; and therefore they will not teach falsehood wilfully. In free discussion none but the most learned will obtain a long success; and therefore the general results of criticism are likely to be true. Those who fear for the issue must take their choice between one of two alternatives: either they wish one set of views to prevail, whether true or not; or they wish the truth to prevail, and do not believe that free inquiry will conduce to it.

But, after all, the world has a right to know whether there are fixed laws of criticism or not; whether the conclusions to which they are called upon to yield assent are simply at the mercy of Teutonic caprice; whether, when we say that we will follow criticism to its furthest lengths, we mean that it is really going to conduct us to an absolute negation. A clever writer lately remarked that the theological belief of the great mass of his personal friends consisted simply of self-gratulatory confidence that they did not themselves "go as far" as some one else did. Now, restricting ourselves to the present subject, —the criticism of the Old Testament,—we may remark that no student of theology has yet definitely proved that Abraham lived in the reign of Queen Elizabeth, or that the book of Kings is a compilation by Lord Macaulay. So far from such research being wild and vague, it is conducted as severely and rigorously, and perhaps with as great a sense of responsibility, as any investigation of literature or science. Divines who talk of the random guesses of critics are evidently unaware of the nature of their inquiries. The date of the Pentateuch is determined by minute and systematic argument; where conjecture has to be employed, as with regard, for example, to the authorship of some parts of Isaiah or of the book of Job, it is only employed because of the insufficiency of the existing evidence. Suppose that we meet with the case of a legislator ordaining the rest of a seventh day to men who had no work to do on the other six, and enjoining a periodical rest from cultivation to a nation which had not a yard of ground to cultivate, what are we to say? That the ordinances were prospective, and therefore useless to his hearers, or that they were the legacy of past tradition, or that the injunctions were put into his mouth by the uncritical piety of subsequent ages? Must the choice be made at random, or must it not? In this particular case we should be inclined to choose sometimes one hypothesis, and sometimes another. But if there appears to be a vagueness in the result of such inquiries, theological science would be deeply grateful to any coming reformer who could suggest a means of rendering the determination of such problems any thing else than hazardous.

But what have the critics actually found out? To those who want a full answer, we might reply by recommending to their notice such books as that which heads these pages. But what if we were to ask them in return, What do they know without the critics? What is the Bible, why do they reverence it, and how do they know that this is the Bible which is in their hands? It may be convenient to some readers that we should set down in a condensed form a few of the simplest facts ascertained about the Bible, even at the risk of stating what is well known to others.

For several generations after Christ there was no such thing as a Bible, in the modern sense of the word. There was no one authorised book, bound between covers, and common to all Christians. There were a number of separate gospels and epistles, many of which were accounted sacred by all churches, and some by a few only. At a later period the churches were nearly all agreed in accepting some and rejecting others, though the only Christian authority for the books of the Bible as one body of sacred writing is, in the Catholic Church the Council of Trent, and in the Protestant the authority of the Queen and of the fourth Article; and, as is well known, the Catholic Church receives many more books as scriptural than the Protestant. But one thing is quite certain with regard to the claim of some books to form part of the Bible, that that claim can never be fully made out. It is on the whole most probable that the second epistle which bears St. Peter's name was not written by that apostle; on the other hand, some epistles unknown to most Protestants, such as the "Shepherd" of Hermas, were received among some of the earliest collections of the New Testament. But, to confine our attention for the present to the Old, it may be taken for granted that the books which the Palestinian Jews of our Lord's time held sacred were the same as those which we have at present. They did not hold them all in the same value; Esther, for example, they highly prized, while they spoke slightingly of Daniel and Ecclesiastes. But the Jews of other countries, Egypt for instance, placed others among them; the author of the epistle of St. Jude quotes the book of Enoch in the same way as St. Paul quotes Isaiah; and so difficult was it to find out which books were Biblical and which were not, that a bishop of Sardis, a century and a half after our Lord's death, made a journey to the East on purpose to find out the genuine writings, and came back with a list in which Ezra and Esdras are specified, and Nehemiah, unless included in them, is not. But to return. The Jews of Palestine read these books in their synagogues, and our Lord himself, by reading and quoting them, implied his assent to the general respect in which they were held, and pointed emphatically to the passages in them in which the prophets had directed the eyes of the nation, not to the present, but to the future. So far back we can trace the history of the Bible—and even farther, to the time when a Greek translation was made, less than 180 B.C., in Egypt. Beyond this the whole is a total blank. Nothing whatever is known of the composition of the books of

Scripture beyond the statements of the Talmud (which contain absurdities), and a vague tradition, which may possibly have some foundation in fact, that Ezra had something to do with the arrangement of the sacred books. The date and authorship of each writing must be found out by internal evidence alone.

Few of the books of the Old Testament are single and connected compositions, created by one person at one time. It is probable that the greater number of them, not including the prophetical books, owe their origin to two great periods of literary activity, the one about or a little after the time of Solomon, the other towards the close of the monarchy of Judah. The two periods are very different in character, and their productions have hardly any thing in common; but whatever history is to be referred to either of them is modified, rather in form than in substance, by the prevailing characteristics of the age. No Jewish writer seems ever to have composed a consecutive and original history. He adopted other documents, arranged and sometimes modified them, added existing traditions and episodes from the materials to which he had access, and so produced rather an edition of older works than a new one of his own. We shall now endeavour to exhibit in a tabular form the conclusions which have been most generally adopted by critics as to the dates of the literary history of the Jews; only, of course, as indicating the sort of results to which criticism at present approximates, without binding ourselves to precise details. One or two books, of quite uncertain date, are omitted.

CONTEMPORARY HISTORY.	LITERATURE.
	Fragments of early history, the sources of Genesis.
	Primitive annals, *e.g.*
Period of	Book of the wars of the Lord.
Judges.	Book of Jasher, or the Upright.
	JUDGES,
Saul.	[a compilation; some materials evidently ancient].
	Elohistic document of Pentateuch.
	[Mention of kings—not of divided kingdom or centralised worship.]
	Book of Samuel the Seer.
	Book of Nathan, &c.
Solomon.	*Literary activity—foreign intercourse—perhaps* (Renan) *foreign school of literature.*
	JOB—PROVERBS (part)—SONG OF SOLOMON—RUTH (?)
Earlier	*Jehovistic* document of Pentateuch.
Monarchy.	[Mention of Assyria, and of centralised worship.]
	Book of Shemaiah the prophet.
	Book of Iddo the seer, &c.
	SAMUEL,
	[a compilation; slight contradictions].
	Book of Jehu, and Chronicles kept throughout.

CONTEMPORARY HISTORY.	LITERATURE.
	Rise of prophetic literature.
	HOSEA—JOEL—AMOS.
Captivity of Israel.	ISAIAH (the great part of chaps. i.–xxxix.).
	NAHUM—MICAH.
Later Monarchy.	ZEPHANIAH—HABAKKUK—OBADIAH (?).
	Author of Zechariah ix.–xiv.
	Revival of letters—discovery of "the Book of the Law."
	DEUTERONOMY, and completion of PENTATEUCH, and (?) JOSHUA.
	The Words of the Seers that spake to Manasseh.
	JEREMIAH.
Captivity of Judah.	EZEKIEL.
	BOOK OF KINGS.
	LAMENTATIONS—Author of Isaiah, last twenty-seven chapters.
Return from Captivity.	*Supremacy of sacerdotalism.*
	HAGGAI—ZECHARIAH (i.–viii.)—MALACHI.
	EZRA—NEHEMIAH.
	PSALMS (completed)—ECCLESIASTES (?).
Later still.	CHRONICLES.
	ESTHER (?).
	[speaks of Persian monarchy as of something past].
Maccabæan age.	DANIEL,
	[separate from prophets in Jewish canon; never alluded to in O.T.; obscure in history; prosaic style; late language; minute and hence unprophetical predictions; Greek words].

We have endeavoured to state what are the prevalent views in the critical world on the composition of the books of the Old Testament. With the exception of the prophetical books, the author of every one of them is unknown, and though conjectures may be made on the subject, our knowledge can never reach beyond conjecture. But it is important to remember that to produce a literary compilation in the days of which we are speaking was by no means the same thing as in our own. The very slowness of the process of writing may have carried the composition of a single work over a long period of time. When the book was made, how many were to read it, and how was it to become generally known? A startling prophecy, especially if it were short, might easily be copied and circulated, or it might be publicly read. But the annals of the nation were no doubt preserved in the safe custody of priests, away from the eyes of the vulgar; and the people themselves can have had for the most part but an irregular tradition to depend upon. When the critic comes to examine the tone and character of the historic books, and their relation to the history of the nation, he is startled at once by a crowd of difficulties which hardly present themselves at all to the ordinary reader. Inconsistencies in the subject-matter of the history are of course intelligible to those who assume no standard of perfection at the outset; but anomalies in the character and spirit of the writings are much more difficult to deal with. How, for example, are we to account for the fact that while so many of the Old-Testament writings are imbued with a strict sacerdotal and legal spirit, the story gives evidence of other forms of worship simultaneously existing for centuries unchecked and even encouraged? How is it that, while the temple-worship had confessedly a political as well as a religious object, the literature of the Jews is by no means consistently hostile to the northern tribes? How is it that the prophets are found at one moment disparaging priestly ceremonies, and at another upholding them? If, in attempting an answer to inquiries such as these, we devote some space to a somewhat careful consideration of the religious influences which would be likely to act upon the literature of the Jews, it is because it appears to us that the subject of which we shall attempt a sketch has not received as much attention as it deserves from the hands of English writers.

When Moses brought out the tribes of Israel from Egypt, he had a work before him such as no chieftain since his times has ever had. The race over which he ruled was one without, as far as we can see, any one element of the heroic character. They were without enthusiasm, and he had to supply it; they were without endurance, and he had to train them to it; they were a nomad race, and he had to fit them for a settled life; their ignorance of the practical arts was such, that the mere artificers of their holy shrines obtained at once a character for divine inspiration. That Moses himself was the author of the numerous details of the Levitical legislation, we cannot admit; but that he inspired this degraded people with the germs of certain splendid ideas, and even paved the way for their development by some definite institutions, there is no valid reason for questioning. Some part of the genuine Mosaic legislation undoubtedly came from Egypt: we trace the ark, the Urim and Thummim, and many minor customs, in the extant Egyptian records. But he had the adaptive talent which could give to most of these a new and significant value. Did the Jews practise circumcision as a popular custom, he sanctioned it as an observance of the Lord's own people. Did they kill the victims for their food with peculiar rites, he made every slaughter a sacrifice to the Almighty. It is not, however, in such observances as these that we must look for the true genius of the Mosaic legislation. "I spake not unto your fathers," says a later poet, "nor commanded them in the day that I brought them out of the land of Egypt, concerning burnt-offerings or sacrifices;

but this thing commanded I them, saying, Obey my voice, and I will be your God, and ye shall be my people." There were two ideas chiefly which seem to have sprung from the desert-chief, and which may be traced in the history of the people, gradually and slowly penetrating their rudeness, struggling with their waywardness, making their way against prejudice, custom, and example. One we may call the principle of the theocracy, the other, in imitation of a late French writer,* the principle of Jehovism.

The two, though allied, are sufficiently distinguishable. The theocratic idea of Mosaism was different from that of the numberless superstitions of antiquity. It depended on no ceremonial array: the priests were no heralds of the divine will, no interpreters of the decrees of Heaven. On the contrary, the priesthood was for some part of Jewish history clearly antagonistic to the true theocratic principle. The idea was far simpler; it was that the Lord was the King of Israel. Wherever the half-abandoned idea is recalled in a later age, it is always in this sense; Israel was not only the sanctuary of God, but still more emphatically his dominion. That which we have ventured to call the principle of Jehovism demands for its explanation a reference to a subject which is now recognised as a part of Jewish history. The earlier title of God was Elohim; the later word Jehovah. The first is a plural word, the 'God' of our version, either implying power and dignity, or suggesting a primitive stage of polytheism; the second, translated in English Bibles 'the LORD,' in French 'l'Eternel,' represents eternity. Two different ideas attached among the earlier Hebrews to these two words. Elohim was the name by which the patriarchs knew the Deity; it was the name originally belonging to the race, and perhaps common to other tribes as well; it is also used of heroes and kings, and even employed as a kind of superlative in ordinary language. Moses first introduced, if we may trust the narrative of Exodus, the word Jehovah among the people. The word was adopted, though with a slowness which has induced Bishop Colenso with some critics to refer its introduction to a much later date, as the name of the theocratic, the national, the covenant God. It has sometimes been supposed that the title was brought from Egypt. Without denying what is incapable of disproof, we can only say that of such a derivation there is not a single trace to be found. Nor is the hypothesis necessary. In its etymology the word is easily referable to a Hebrew root, though, as is now generally known, the present pronunciation is not that which the word originally

* Nicolas, *Etudes critiques sur la Bible*, p. 111. We are disposed to believe with M. Nicolas in the Mosaic origin of these ideas. But any statement as to personal teaching of Moses himself must, after all, be very far from certain.

had. But, independently of its origin, it is indispensable to an understanding of Hebrew history to form a distinct estimate of the difference of the titles. Elohim is most often the God whose "fear" is wisdom; Jehovah is the Lord in whom men can put their "trust." Elohim is exalted far above all knowledge; upon Jehovah Moses could look, and not die. The object of Moses was to announce to the people that Jehovah was the Elohim of Abraham, Isaac, and Jacob.

The central feature of this new conception was that of unity; Jehovah not only allowed no divided service, but required even a refinement of spiritual worship for which the Jews were not prepared. We shall have occasion to observe that the national worship of Elohim was in the main an idolatrous one; that of Jehovah loudly and constantly repudiated every material symbol. We have, then, these two ideas as the cardinal principles of Mosaism: Jehovah who is the king of his people, and Jehovah whose worship must be spiritual. Let us now inquire how far these principles penetrated the people. The evidence—or rather the absence of it—is extraordinary. So far from being generally accepted, the Mosaic ideas seem to have hardly made themselves felt at all for the first five hundred years. With other principles deeply rooted in their nature, the Hebrews were incapable, generation after generation, of seizing and embracing the teaching of the desert. A higher faith was put before them, but the national practice was unchanged. "Was it to *me* that ye offered sacrifices and offerings in the wilderness forty years, O house of Israel?" Moloch and Chiun on the one side, and the calf of Aaron on the other, tell a very different story. Nor is there any reason to accuse the nation of any excessive stubbornness, any obstinate conservatism. It has been well remarked that the very reverse is the character presented by its history. The ease with which it passed from a nomad to an agricultural life, and in later times to the pursuits of commerce; the versatility with which it could appropriate to itself the manners and habits, now of the nations of Canaan, now of the Syrian races, afterwards of the Persian conquerors, then Greek science at Alexandria, then Arab philosophy in Spain,—all this is a sufficient disproof of the charge. It is rather to the intellectual culture of the nation and its physical position that the apparent obstinacy must be attributed. How could a people cling to a single theocratic rule, which found itself at once hopelessly broken up for centuries into the original tribe-organisation, which was, after all, so congenial to its character? How was it possible for a nation to apprehend firmly the nature of a spiritual Jehovah, in whose language it is impossible to express without circumlocution a single abstract term? The result is not surprising. Once the land was occupied, the invading tribes forgot nationality and covenant alike; instead of conquering the territory, they preferred to amalgamate with its races. Occasionally it might happen that some prophet would appear to speak in the name of Jehovah and recall the high mission of the race; but tradition was too powerful and the social disorganisation too complete. For five—we had almost said for ten—centuries, the Jewish state is founded on principles which present no trace of Mosaic legislation; the relations of the people, the practices of religious worship, are exactly those which it had been the object of that legislation to discountenance.

Henceforth, then, we are to witness the spectacle of a higher creed combating with a lower one, and by slow degrees winning its way to power. The chief field of battle was the question of divine worship. There is every reason to suppose that the worship of Elohim was not necessarily, and not generally, free from material symbolism. When we say that the national religion of the Jews from the time of Joshua to that of David, or even longer, was idolatrous, we do not imply that a worship of heathen deities was practised. There was no polytheism, except when the rites of Moloch and Baal were introduced from abroad; and "false gods" and "strange gods" are in the Scriptures every where equivalent expressions. But an idolatrous monotheism there certainly was. The idea of Elohim is clearly one which admits of symbolic representation: "Let us have Elohim, who may walk before us," is the cry of the rebellious people. When even Christianity can, in the eyes of some of its disciples, appear to sanction the use of material images of the Deity, it is hardly to be wondered at that a semi-barbarous people should think they worshipped the Creator in worshipping the calf which symbolised him. There is no ground to suppose that Aaron conceived his conduct in setting up the calf as other than pious: "These be thy Elohim, O Israel!" The men of Judah did no harm, as they thought, in prostrating themselves before the brazen serpent; the ephod which Gideon consecrated was meant, like Laban's teraphim, for an idolatrous, and yet for a sincere and well-meaning, worship; Micah set up his images—his priest being, as the book of Judges declares, a grandson of Moses himself—and thought that "the Lord would do him good." The cherubim which guarded the ark were representatives of the divine presence; the winged bulls of Nineveh were not more idolatrous than they. Nor was it only in the recognised centres of religious service that these practices prevailed. Wherever there was a "high place," there, we may believe, the altar and the symbols stood. "To cast down high places and cut down images" is the recognised form of words in the later writings for the abolition of the ancient worship. In Josiah's time the priests of the high places are spoken of; and within the space of half-a-dozen verses they are called the "idolatrous priests." And what seems the strongest argument of all to prove the thoroughly national character of the worship is this. The sources from which the book of Judges was compiled are allowed by the severest criticism to be of a high authority and value; and in these records, when allusions to this idolatry are made, they are made without surprise or reproof.

Where, it may be asked, was all this time the priesthood, with its array of national ceremonies, its solemn festivals, its hegemony of the Israelitish people? Those who read without prejudice the earlier records of the nation can have no difficulty in answering the question. This "Established Church" did not exist. Whatever details of religious observance are rightly attributed to Moses were, as far as regards their influence in the land, utterly dormant. Priests there were; but they were the priests of the "high places," the ministers of the unreformed faith, the servants of Elohim. Micah consecrated one of his sons to be priest of his teraphim, and afterwards he placed a chance Levite in his stead. The men of Kirjath-jearim sanctified the son of one of their inhabitants as priest. In the time of David the same men were priests and generals, and military leaders offered sacrifices when they pleased. There was no doubt a centre of religious worship, which may possibly have retained the true Jehovist principles; but there is nothing to lead us to conclude that it had any weight with the nation. The genuine Mosaic ideas—the unity of a spiritual Lord, the suzerainty of Jehovah over his people—were maintained by the prophets alone. The place which a Protestant preacher might hold in a nation of Catholics, the prophets held in Israel. The multitude would cling, piously enough, to ceremonies and symbols; the few would uphold principles and abstractions. They never named the name of Moses; the law they preached was not the later Deuteronomic law, but the law of which the book of Psalms speaks; not the law that cleanses the hands, but the law which converteth the heart. They did not tell of Sinai, or of a written code, for they knew none; the appeals which a Christian will make to the Gospel, a Mussulman to the Koran, a Hindoo to the Vedas, have no counterpart in the prophets of Israel; they knew simply the guiding ideas which had been bequeathed to them by one whose title in Scripture is that of prophet, in the days when a theocracy could really be said to exist.

The establishment of royalty was the severest blow that the principle of the theocracy could receive. It was a practical dissolution of the holy covenant. Samuel struggled hard against it, and failed; then, when it was hopeless to resist, he attempted to make the best of the altered circumstances, and modify the kingdom to his will. He himself would anoint the monarch to be the divine vice-regent upon earth; Saul should reign, and he himself would rule; Saul should lead the hosts to battle, and he would give the signal for attack. The attempt was a failure; it was but one of the series of disappointments which the prophetic order was ever doomed to experience. "I gave thee a king in my anger," was the sad reflection of a successor of Samuel many centuries after. With David there was more hope. His accession—or, if we were to call it by a harsher name, his usurpation—had been the resource of the old prophet when the hopes fixed on Saul had failed. David had visited in his exile the schools of the prophets, and had shared his misfortunes with more than one of their number. Indeed there is every reason to think that upon his personal character the influence of the prophets was very great. Gad and Nathan were among his constant advisers; the language of the fiftieth Psalm is in the very tone of Isaiah or Amos. The fact which the Bishop of Natal has pointed out, that Elohism is the uniform character of his earliest Psalms, and Jehovism of his later, is very significant, though we do not draw from it the same inferences as Dr. Colenso. It seems to us rather to indicate the increasing hold which the ideas connected with the name of Jehovah had upon the mind of the same king who in his earlier days kept idols in his very household.* At the same time the political effect of the prophets was but small. David centralised, indeed, the ceremonial worship to some extent at Jerusalem, but it was no doubt with a political, and not with a religious object that the step was taken; and great as was the authority which the king bestowed upon the high-priest, he created and deposed him at his pleasure. The chief sanctuary might be at Jerusalem, but there was a rival altar at Gibeon—another, it would seem, at Enrogel; and when Absalom wished to pay a vow at Hebron, the request was granted immediately. And it is strange to observe how, though it was by Nathan's own advice that Solomon was named as the successor of the aged monarch, it is distinctly recorded that, in the very beginning of Solomon's reign, the "high places" were numerous and popular.

It is most important, in order to understand the historical books which bear upon the Jewish monarchy, to form a clear conception of the relations of prophets and priests. We have seen enough to enable us to understand how the existence of a national Elohistic worship explains the absence of a strongly

* 1 Sam. xix. 13. With reference to the latter part of the paragraph, it is worth remarking that Dr. Colenso is in error in stating (§ 637) that the idea of a centralised worship at Jerusalem does not occur at all in the earlier books of the Pentateuch. It is to be found in Miriam's song, Ex. xv. 17.

sacerdotal element in the Elohistic record of the Exodus. On coming to the narratives of later times, we are struck by a similar difference in the tone of the two parallel histories. While the Book of Kings, bearing as it does every mark of candour in its composition, has but little in it that tends to the glorification of the Levitical priesthood, the Chronicles, on the contrary, are imbued with a priestly spirit throughout. Everywhere the priests have the post of honour; everywhere their influence is magnified, and their errors extenuated. One fact is suggestive of the explanation of this divergence. While the Chronicles, composed at a time when the priests were the absolute rulers of the nation, stand by themselves at the end of the Hebrew canon, the Books of Kings are grouped with the prophetical writings. Not that they were composed by prophets; they were no doubt compiled from records existing at Jerusalem. But they were the work of men who had no exaggerated or traditional sympathy with the priests. During the greater portion of the monarchical history the prophetical spirit was distinctly the rival of the sacerdotal spirit. The prophet was not one of a separate family; he was not confined to one place; he was not a slave of ceremonies. He preached in the streets and markets, taught the unimportance of religious rites, proclaimed against kings and priests alike the ties that bound the people to their Lord. Whether it was a Baal-worship or a worship of "high places," a vice of the court or a corruption of the temple, the denouncing voice of the prophets was heard. They adopted no arts or sciences, they joined in no commercial enterprise, they gave themselves to no secular literature; their intellectual activity was one long struggle in the service of Jehovah. There is, as far as we know, but one prophet, Hosea, who seems in any passage directly to point to idols as a desirable appendage of religious worship; and it must be noticed that Hosea is the only prophet who appears to have belonged to the northern kingdom, and that he speaks of the teraphim not as laudable in themselves, but simply as a customary part of ceremonial observance. In a similar way the complaint that "they have digged down *thine altars*" is put into the mouth of a northern prophet in the story embodied in the book of Kings, without any hesitation arising in the writer's mind on the score that such altars were heretical: for we may remark, that for Dr. Pusey's statement that the northern prophets were in the habit of acting as priests there is no foundation whatever in the sacred records. It is true, again, that Joel never alludes in terms of dispraise to idolatrous observances, though he has many opportunities of doing so; but Joel, though his utterances are couched in a prophetic tone, has a priestly spirit running through the whole of them, and indeed was possibly a priest himself. It is impossible, therefore, to agree with Professor Newman in regarding the prophets as having at one time seen nothing amiss in the symbolic representations of their time: the 45th Psalm in the original Hebrew speaks of polygamy without reproof, and yet no one would think of inferring from one single instance of the kind a general sanction of the custom. Still less can we think with him that the Levitical priesthood formed in any sense or at any time the cradle of the prophetical order. On the contrary, the temple-worship at Jerusalem was never Jehovistic, in the full sense of the word, till the days of the later monarchy. It is remarkable that the Elohistic Psalms seem in almost every case to be those most adapted for public religious service; and we doubt whether there is any evidence that the priesthood before the days of Hezekiah ever regarded with any thing but perfect complacence the existing orthodox idolatry. Would it have been possible that Phœnician architects should be employed in the building of the temple, if it had been designed with a theocratic and spiritual object? or is it possible that, if this were the case, the prayer of dedication, even if composed at a later date, should have been composed with hardly a word of reference either to the author of Mosaism or to any of its leading ideas? "The high places were not taken away"—such is the constant burden of the subsequent records. The priest Urijah was facile enough in altering the temple furniture to the model of a heathen shrine. Hangings for the idols of an impure worship were fabricated within the very limits of the sacred enclosure.* When Athaliah introduced the rites of Baal into Jerusalem, she never cared to intermeddle with the tolerant priesthood. The fact is, that the priests who ministered in the temple now were the descendants of the same men who had served the images before. There is no reason to suppose that the Levites—or priests, for the words seem to have been at one time merely synonymous—were at first a separate family. In the earliest passage in which they are mentioned, they are described as "scattered in Israel." Micah's Levite was a Levite of Judah, Samuel was at once a Levite and an Ephraimite, and the Aaronite warriors who came to David at Hebron have no Levitical characteristic. David's sons were priests as much as the sons of Eli were. It may perhaps be the case, as Kalisch suggests, that the substitution of the Levites for the firstborn may have reference to the gradual process by which the sacerdotal duties, naturally performed in a semi-barbarous time by the head of the house, transferred themselves gradually to a distinct order of men; at any rate, it was not long before the profession became a caste, and the word "Levite," which implies a "union,"

* 2 Kings xvi. 10; xxiii. 7.

became truly representative of their history. It was then between this hereditary priesthood and the prophets, the Protestant preachers of the Jews, that a settled warfare arose. Isaiah denounces a curse on priest as well as people; Micah proclaims that they teach for hire; even the later Jeremiah declares them false to their office. "Like people, like priest," is the burden of many a mournful prophetic song.

It was indeed with a singularly light regret for the sanctuary at Jerusalem that one of the prophets suggested the idea of a secession of the northern tribes. Here he doubtless hoped the experiment of a theocratic royalty might be tried again, perhaps with better success. A young officer of public works, under the guidance of the prophet Ahijah, raised the standard of revolt, and the prophets at Jerusalem defended him from the attack of Rehoboam. It was useless. The first act of the new king was to revive the image-worship at two of its ancient shrines, and the phantom-like appearance in the story of the denouncing "man of God" indicates the failure of the prophetic hopes. In Judah the prospect was as bad. On every high hill and under every green tree the ancient worship went on; and even the hideous rites of Moloch began now to be customary at Jerusalem. The champions of Jehovah did not yet abandon their political efforts: it seems as though it was necessary for them to learn by experience, what their counterparts in modern times too often forget, that it is not by state intrigue or the struggles of well-meaning faction that the kingdom of God must be established upon earth. "Art thou he that troublest Israel?" might have been in many cases a far from unsuitable address. And now the worst was at hand. Ahab took the Sidonian princess to wife, and with her came Baal and Ashtoreth.* It must have been only by degrees that their worship was established, as the daughter of Ahab and Jezebel is called by a Jehovistic name; but the king built Baal a temple, and 400 idolatrous worshippers dined at the table of the queen. The crisis of the nation was indeed come; the stories of Elijah and Elisha seem hardly too marvellous for the times. The defenders of Jehovism nerved themselves for one more attempt. A prophet —true to his political schemes—inspired Jehu with the design of overthrowing the idolatrous house, and Samaria was bathed in blood. But the false worship reappeared, and in the history of the northern tribes it was never abolished again. Ephraim was joined to idols; human victims fed the accursed flames; "the statutes of the house of Omri were kept." One pictu-

* Ashtaroth is the Hebrew plural of Ashtoreth, as Baalim of Baal. M. Nicolas, to whose work we are much indebted, speaks of the "culte des bocages." The Asherah (so often translated 'grove' in the E. V.) may perhaps have no connexion with Ashtoreth; but it certainly has none with groves of trees.

resque incident will be sufficient to show the state of the national religion in later Israel. There stands among the gray stony hills which separate Ephraim from Judah, close to the central high-road, but desolate in its scenery as the old sanctuaries of Cornish rites, the royal shrine of Bethel. Century after century has seen king and people bow down, while the priests of the ancient worship burn the solemn meat-offerings before the idols. There are winter and summer palaces, "great houses and houses of ivory," magnificent among the wildness of the hills. Not a morning but sees the offering of a victim; not a worshipper but brings his tithe to the priest. On a day of solemn assembly there will be drinking of wine and anointing with oil, and sacrifice of lambs and of calves, and chanting to the sound of the viol. Amid this rich array a herdsman prophet from the south stands, among the royal court and by the splendid sanctuary, and denounces it in burning words. We can picture to ourselves the consternation of the priestly throng at the uncouth figure in their midst; we may fancy the smile passing over their faces at the contemptuous words in which the high-priest himself dismisses the unwelcome intruder. "O thou seer"—thou 'antiquated visioner,' we might almost render the word—"go, flee away into the land of Judah, and there eat bread, and prophesy there; but prophesy not any more at Bethel."

In Judah, however, the books of Kings and of Isaiah point to brighter prospects for Jehovism. Thanks to the priest Jehoiada, the Baal-worship was soon destroyed, and only briefly appeared again in the reigns of Manasseh and Amon. From this time the sacerdotal element in the councils of the southern kingdom rapidly increases. The temple itself is repaired; and we now hear for the first time of a Sabbath, and of a written book of the Law. But as yet there was no idea of abolishing the popular religious customs; the priesthood made no more attempt than the monarchy to put down the high places in the land. It was a work reserved for Hezekiah, a king on whose reign the subsequent annalists dwell with an enthusiasm that knows no bounds. Never before him or after him was there such a king in Israel. At a feast which now appears for the first time in the history of the monarchy—the Passover—came a great concourse of Jehovists from all quarters of Palestine. With a resolutely iconoclastic spirit, which reminds us of the Puritan bands of modern times, these reformers spread through the land, and destroyed and shattered the idols. The violence of this religious revolution was overpowering; it must have had some such effect as the revocation of the Edict of Nantes upon the Protestant villages of France. Many of the dispossessed ministers must have been reduced to the state in which we find them in Deuteronomy (xvi. 14, &c.)—poor and needy, and coupled with the fatherless and widows; a juxtaposition which has not hitherto, as far as we are aware, been explained. Not that the influence of the prophets upon Hezekiah was solely political; a purer and more devotional spirit seems henceforth to animate their zeal. We read of prayer almost for the first time in the story; and the cordial alliance between Isaiah and the king seems to have been uninterrupted. But it is not to be supposed that the reforms of the reign were accomplished without discontent; religious reform is too often in the world's history but another name for religious persecution. The herald of Sennacherib knew well where the weak point of Hezekiah's popularity was, when he reminded the people of the altars and high places which the king had taken away.

But they were taken away irretrievably. It was a time of change and of progress, and old institutions once abolished were not to be revived again. Foreign relations were now beginning to be more extended, and foreign politics more complicated. It is true, that no people in history has ever found itself more incapable of grappling with political questions than the Jewish; but the course of events was forcing the nation onwards. The men who had denounced the mere census of the population with the judgment of Heaven, now saw Jewish merchantmen crowding the harbours of Elath, and luxury, the companion of commerce, invading the Jewish homes; from Damascus a king will even go so far as to borrow the pattern of an altar. Above all, with commerce came literature. There was room for literary leisure at Jerusalem; the writings of the time begin now to drop the poetic form, and a cultivated prose is attempted. The legendary element ceases; we find new combinations of language, new forms of thought; one writer will imitate and borrow from another; a school or college appears in the capital of the kingdom. Unfortunately we have but little accurate knowledge of the extent to which literature, or even the art of writing, was diffused among the people; if we had more, it might perhaps be possible to found some safe conjecture upon that mysterious subject, the "finding of the Book of the Law"—a story at the true interpretation of which it seems impossible to arrive with certainty. But at any rate there was now a "revival of letters" in Israel; a change was working itself out, comparable only to that which followed the introduction of Greek culture at Rome, or classical literature in England. There arose a school of philosophising Mosaism, if we may use the term; and historical records henceforth assume a different and a more thoughtful phase. "Books of the Kings" are framed, in which the actions of each sovereign are looked at according to the standard of the law. Legal forms are thrown back into the earliest history of the race; Moses is now considered as the author of the minute details of ceremony, much in the same way as Napoleon is now regarded as the author of all the statutes in France. The Pentateuch is completed by the edition of Deuteronomy; a book of which Ewald's remark, whether true or not, is at all events suggestive, that it bears the same relation to the earlier books of the Old Testament that St. John's Gospel bears to the New,—that of a philosophic and thoughtful view of the subjects which had hitherto been looked at only from their historic and objective side. And amid all this the internal change is brought about which would be almost inexplicable without the commentary which the history of the time affords—the *rapprochement* of prophets and priests. The reign of Josiah sees Jehovism at last triumphant; were there no other proof of the fact, its growing inclination to formalism would be sufficient to stamp it as the prevailing faith. And now, from the seat in which Isaiah and Amos had thundered against the claims of ceremony and sacrifice, an Ezekiel mourns the indifference to clean and unclean, and the neglect of the Sabbath-day; and a Jeremiah, even though struck and imprisoned by a priest, still speaks of the temple as one persuaded that there alone was the place where men ought to pray. His thirty-third chapter seems almost to echo with the cry of "church and king." It is now the star-worshippers who chiefly give pain to the reformed faith, and whom more than one prophet, and the author of Deuteronomy, attack. There are still some (Deut. xxxiii. 11) who "hate" and "rise against" the growing priesthood; but there is no evidence that the party is a large one. The old forms of idolatry have vanished; unless they hide themselves behind the doors or in the wine-fats. "Our heart is not turned back," it might now be said, for the first time in all the history, "neither our steps gone out of Thy way." The strong doom pronounced against rebellious cities in Deuteronomy seems to us to imply not, as Bishop Colenso infers, that idolatry was now prevalent, but rather that it was no longer so; in civilised times draconic punishments are seldom proposed for common and frequent offences; and it is certain that there was a great part of Jeremiah's ministry in which the worship of false gods was far from popular with the nation. The *rapprochement* of which we spoke had but little from without to interrupt it; in Josiah's ceremony prophets and priests mingle harmoniously together. Too often both alike were untrue to their calling; oftentimes the prophet was but a dreamer of dreams after all. Yet, whether they prophesy truly or falsely, the priests now "bear rule by their means;" and the author of the Lamentations, on calling to mind the causes which have brought his country to ruin, declares that the evil came upon

Jerusalem alike "for the sins of her prophets, and for the iniquity of her priests."

And so the principles of Moses were victorious, at the very moment when the people of Moses perished. Was it in vain? Did the champions of the "old covenant" waste their efforts upon a shadow? Did the race which "lived for an idea" do nothing towards bringing it to a result? Some, perhaps, will call to mind the words of the most prophet-like of the Christian apostles, how the seed is not quickened except it die. There are those to whom the idea of the theocracy has become a living reality, for it means the kingdom of Christ. There are still more to whom the spiritual adoration of one Lord is more than a habit of the intellect, even though a Virgin, a Church, or a Bible may seem to usurp the honour of the Deity upon their tongues. We may be glad indeed that the Jewish nation did not live to exhibit more fully the fatal influence of success. Already, in the 33d chapter of Ezekiel, may be seen a picture of the religious world of his day, which gives the reader but little trust in its power for good, and of the displays of rival prophets which remind us too forcibly of the worst type of the "popular preachers" of our time. The remnant of the Jews returned from the captivity accurate observers of a modified Mosaic code. The Samaritans are repulsed when they wish to help in the work of restoration, in the spirit which a high churchman might now display towards the efforts of a Calvinist sectarian. A few noble Messianic ideas gleam dimly through the fog of barren orthodoxy. The prophets are thoroughly Levitical;* it is now

* We had intended to enter at greater length upon the question of the veracity of the Book of Chronicles; but the subject is already too large. The case stands thus. It is admitted by those who do not hold to a theory of Biblical perfection, that the Books of Chronicles are not to be depended upon when any question of temple-worship or sacerdotalism is at issue. They are so deeply imbued with a Levitical colouring, and so downright in their maintenance of later Levitical ideas, that it may be safely said, not only that they give an erroneous view of many subjects, but that they have altered the history purposely towards such views. Are we, then, to say, as is so often said, that the Chronicler is dishonest and reckless? Is there a *mala fides* in his assertions? Admitting that the opposite view may be religiously and devoutly held, we are yet inclined to the belief that the Chronicler used his materials as he thought right, altering them to suit his own views, with the conviction that the things could not possibly have been otherwise than as he states. It was not a time for severe criticism in matters of fact; and the author of the book, as Dr. Davidson has shown, is credible in matters not connected with the worship of Jerusalem. Dr. Davidson's chapters on Chronicles are some of the best in his book. We may remark, as a specimen of the ignorance which prevailed among the later Jews with regard to their own religious history, that the author of Tobit confuses together the monotheistic symbolism of earlier times with the foreign rites of Baal, and speaks of sacrifices offered to Baal the calf, τῇ Βαὰλ τῇ δαμάλει. It is much the same comparison as that of which Lord Byron was guilty, when he declared, as a result of the destruction of Sennacherib's host, that

"The widows of Asshur are loud in their wail,
And the idols are broke in the temples of Baal."

Sennacherib's army had probably never seen an altar of Baal in their lives.

the priests that should keep knowledge, and to them that the people should seek; Zechariah seems even to doubt whether the coming Saviour of the race is not to be found in the high-priest Joshua. Perhaps the most striking picture of the hopes of the time, half-looking to priests for help, half-rising above the priesthood, is that where Malachi speaks of the Messiah as one whose first work it shall be to purify the sons of Levi.

We have seen that the history of the Jews, as far as its bearing upon their literature is concerned, is essentially a history of religious ideas. As such, it will never be successfully treated by any one who is unable in some degree to appreciate such ideas himself. But, on the other hand, persons of the most fervent piety may read these writings, and arrive at a totally false estimate of the story they contain. Any method short of that by which a rigorous scrutiny is exercised upon every statement, must be as imperfect as it would be in treating the history of Rome or England. Professor Stanley has lately published some lectures on the history of the Jewish Church, of which, though with every respect for the writer, critics have nevertheless the right to make some complaint. After calmly reviewing the present position of sacred literature in this country, Professor Stanley seems to have determined upon a distinct line of action. It is that which he himself is fond of attributing to his prophets —the position of a mediator between old and new, a harmoniser and reconciler of different modes of thought. He will present criticism to the world in as favourable a guise as possible; he will shock no prejudices; he will even court good-will by a reticence on doubtful points. We do not say that he does not do good—every learned and sincere man must. But we do say, that it is hardly fair upon those who do not profess to take every historical statement of the Bible for granted, that he should attempt to veil under courtly forms of language the fact that he does not do so himself. It is as though a history of the Jews meant a history of facts, while a history of the Jewish Church meant a series of photographs from Palestine, taken in a pious spirit. Mr. Kingsley, whom we quote as a preacher and not as a critic, takes something of the same ground in his recently published Sermons on the Pentateuch. Good plain people, he says, are moved with no critical misgivings: "when they read the story of the exodus, their hearts answer: *This* is right. This is the God whom we need. This is what ought to have happened. This is true; for it must be true. Let comfortable people who know no sorrow, trouble their brains as to whether 60 or 600,000 fighting men came out of Egypt with Moses." Mr. Kingsley speaks in the preface to his book of his happiness n having enjoyed a Cambridge education, which could teach him how to treat Old-Testament criticism aright. We wonder whether it was at Cambridge that he learnt that an individual judgment on the moral fitness of a narrative is an adequate intellectual criterion of its truth. We wonder whether it was at the university, or since leaving it, that he first began to think it consistent with charity to speak of critics who differ from him as "comfortable"—dead, that is, to religious feeling. The first of these errors is a manifest fallacy: the second is a grievous wrong. Both Mr. Kingsley and Dr. Stanley seem to us to begin at the wrong end of their subject. Both seem to urge upon their readers that the moral of the story is what chiefly deserves attention. It may be so; but how can we tell what the moral of a story is, if we do not know what the facts are? Mr. Kingsley writes, that the Jews heard the sound of a trumpet exceeding strong, and a voice "most divine and yet most human." What does it mean? How can a sound be divine and human at the same time? Did the Israelites hear with their outward ears the vibrations caused by a current of air passing through a metallic tube, or did they not? Some writers seem to think that there are portions of religious history too solemn to be related according to the common forms of narrative. It will soon, in all probability, be affirmed that religion is too complex a subject to be treated by the ordinary rules of grammar.

Professor Stanley's history has nevertheless received a high encomium in the last few months from one writer whose name ought to carry weight. In eulogising the semi-orthodox professor, and attacking the out-spoken bishop, Mr. Matthew Arnold asserts a distinction between edification and instruction, the former being for the unenlightened many, the latter for the enlightened few; and he declares that every book ought to aim at one of these two objects exclusively. Without minutely considering how far each of the two writers above mentioned purposely set themselves to either task, our objections to the theory may be very briefly stated. In the first place, it allows no means by which the enlightenment can penetrate to the masses, and assumes that upon theological questions the few must always think differently from the many. Yet, from a historical point of view, it is remarkable that the work which has been most famous in this century in connection with religious inquiry, the *Leben Jesu*, was intended mainly for the critics, and not for the multitude. In the second place, the theory involves, as far as we can see, the obligation upon the learned edifier of being deliberately and wilfully uncandid. And finally, we utterly deny that a writer is bound in every case to put before himself any such alternative as that stated, or indeed any one set purpose at all. Let there be free trade in thought, as there is a free market in buying and selling. Such limitations as these are the old-fashioned props of error. If any one had objected on the appearance of M'Culloch's *Commercial Dictionary* that it was a bad book, because it neither enriched the British farmer, nor promoted civil liberty among the populations of the European continent, the argument would seem to be precisely as fair a criticism of the Dictionary as that which Mr. Arnold brings against the Bishop of Natal.

It is strange that, in a country of freedom, it should be so difficult to say these things aloud. The virtue that we want is that of courage, and the places where it is chiefly wanted are the places where it ought to flourish most. The time when the mind is most plastic, most active, most splendidly versatile, is the time that a young man spends at college; and here, if any where, it might be expected that the air would be congenial to free study. We believe that it needs a considerable knowledge of the English Universities fully to appreciate the intellectual cowardice which characterises the older portion of their members. The exceptions are notorious; and it is in such a case as this that, in the true meaning of the phrase, the exceptions prove the rule. It would not be so well known who were the advocates of freedom, if the disposition to acquiesce in prejudice were not so widely predominant.* A young man at the university begins to think that the Flood was not historical, or that the maledictions of David are not couched in a very forgiving spirit. One set of advisers speaks to him in tones of severity; like the Brahmin who crushed the microscope which first revealed to him the living insects in his vegetable food, they urge him to turn from such thoughts at once, and believe by an effort of the will. Should he be man enough to resist this counsel, there are others who will advise him in friendly tones to fly to action as a remedy for doubt; a better frame of mind will come, if he will but do his duty and shut his eyes. It is a suggestion which implicitly assumes the monstrous hypothesis, that the best way of arriving at truth is by deliberately abstaining from the search for it. Adolphe Monod was so advised, and Arnold; and they followed the advice—with more or less effect. Perhaps the inquirers may yield to their incessant temptations, and maintain and subscribe and swear whatever college and university and church set before them. There are many who do so, and who never recover their freedom again. Ecclesiastical authority closes upon them—an authority incompatible with independent thought. Soon the questioner begins

* While we write, attempts are being made at each of the Universities to set on foot a plan for a critical commentary on the Old Testament. Notwithstanding that they will both be undertaken in a somewhat conservative spirit, we wish the schemes every success.

to care less for the old questions, theory is swallowed up in action; he is happy, he wishes nothing further; the world is not the better for the intellect God gave him to use. Contentment, the great vice of middle age, settles gradually upon him—a vice all the more fatal from its being so often called a virtue.

Any one who embraces, on the other hand, the task of candidly working out for himself the religious problems before him will find it a harder task, even if it be a higher one. It is a task to which our country now emphatically summons men who are not afraid to think. At the commencement of one of his essays, Renan speaks of a painter who would never attempt except upon his knees the head of a Virgin or her Son. Some such intense reverence for the issues before him a theological critic may well feel; to pause and adore seems but the fitting preface to the study. But it is not a pause of fear, or a reverence which unmans the intellect. The object of the inquiry is not an impious one, and free-thinking is, in the simple meaning of the term, the highest gift of humanity. The true critic is one who will deem the most perfect humility to lie in the abandonment of prejudice, and the highest faith in the conviction that truth will win. He will have intellectual labour while others are at rest, and perplexities where others cannot feel them. His aims and hopes will not be understood; his candour will seem presumption, and his courage ill-will to what is holy. Persecution may not attack him, but social suspicion will. He will work as one whose reward is not before his eyes, and who, in giving up the secure assumptions which bring peace to others, has not sacrificed to God that which cost him nothing. Again and again he will be called to surrender a fancied discovery, a treasured paradox, a literary revenge, a polemical retort. He will often pause on the brink of a theory, and summon all his self-restraint to aid him in the refusal to tread hastily on a tempting path. He will not believe, with the Dean of Carlisle, in the "ever-deteriorating tendency of the unaided human intellect;" he will rather trust that good endeavours lead in the end to good results. And as he began his task for the sake of truth, and not for the sake of reputation, he will regard his conclusions as not his own, but given and offered to truth, and will support them no further for the sake of sustaining a thesis than he would maintain them for the sake of preserving a creed. Thus, with whatever lowliness of spirit and loftiness of determination he can, he will brave the terrors of public opinion, and the more imposing terrors that lurk in the weakness of the human soul; and will not doubt that in destroying a religious error, or making known a discovery of critical study, he is doing something, however small it be, to assist and educate his race.

Art. II.—DISTORTIONS OF THE ENGLISH STAGE: "MACBETH."

The Works of William Shakespeare. Edited by William George Clark, M.A., Fellow and Tutor of Trinity College, and Public Orator in the University of Cambridge; and John Glover, M.A., Librarian of Trinity College, Cambridge. Cambridge: Macmillan and Co., 1863.

Art is art because it is not nature, is the motto of the Idealisti; Art is but the imitation of nature, say the Naturalisti. The truth lies between the two. Art is neither nature alone, nor can it do without nature. No imitation, however accurate, for imitation's sake makes a good work of art in any other than a mechanical sense. And every work of art in which the objects represented are inaccurately or imperfectly imitated is in so far deficient. But art works by suggestion as well as by imitation. Whatever is untrue to the imagination fails to produce its proper effect, however true it be to the fact. The most absolute realism will not answer the higher demand of the imagination for ideal truth. Art is not simply the reproduction of nature, but nature as modified and coloured by the spirit of the artist. It is a crystallisation out of nature of all elements and facts related by affinity to the idea intended to be embodied. These solely it should eliminate and draw to itself, leaving the rest as unessential. A literal adherence to all the accidents of nature is not only not necessary in art, but may even be fatal. The enumeration of all the leaves in a tree does not reproduce a tree to the imagination, while a whole landscape may be compressed into a single verse.

Between the ideal and the natural school there is a perpetual struggle. Under the purely ideal treatment art becomes vague and insipid; under the purely natural treatment it becomes literal and prosaic. The pre-Raphaelists, in protesting against weak sentimentalism and vague generalisation, and demanding an honest study of nature, have fallen into the error of exaggerating the importance of minute detail, and, by insisting too strongly on literal truth, have sometimes lost sight of that ideal truth which is of higher worth. But their work was needed, and it has been bravely done. They have roused the age out of that dull conventionalism in which it had fallen asleep. They have stimulated thought, revivified sentiment, and reasserted with word and deed the necessity of nature as a true basis of art.

As in the arts of painting and sculpture, so in the drama and on the stage a strong reaction is taking place against the stilted conventionalism and elaborate artifice of the last generation. Such plays as the *Nina Sforza* of Mr. Troughton, the *Legend of Florence* of Mr. Leigh Hunt, and the *Blot on the Scutcheon* and *Colombe's Birthday* by Mr. Browning, are vigorous protests against the feeble pretensions and artificial tragedies of the previous century. The poems and plays of Mr. Browning breathe a new life; and if as yet they have only found "fit audience though few," they are stimulating the best thought of this age, and slowly infusing a new life and spirit into it.

But the traditions of the stage are very strong in England, and are not easily to be rooted out. The English public has become accustomed to certain traditional and conventional modes of acting, which interfere with the freedom of the actor, and cramp his genius within artificial forms. There is almost no attempt on the English stage to represent life as it really is. Tradition and convention stand in the stead of nature. From the moment an actor puts his foot on the stage he is taught to mouth and declaim. He studies rather to make telling points than to give a consistent whole to the character he represents. His utterance and action are false and "stagey." In quiet scenes he is pompous and stilted; in tragic scenes ranting and violent. He never forgets his audience, but, standing before the footlights, constantly addresses himself to them as if they were personages in the play. Habit at last becomes a second nature; his taste becomes corrupted, and he ceases to strive to be simple and natural. There is, in a word, no defect against which Hamlet warns the actor which is not a characteristic feature of English acting. It never "holds up the mirror to nature," but is always "overdone," without "temperance," full of "mouthing," "strutting," "bellowing," and "noise." It "tears a passion to rags, to very rags, to split the ears of the groundlings." And "there be players whom I have heard play, and heard others praise, and that highly, not to speak it profanely, that, having neither the accent of Christians, nor the gait of Christian, pagan, nor man, have so strutted and bellowed, that I have thought some of Nature's journeymen had made men, and not made them well, they imitated humanity so abominably;" and this needs to be reformed altogether.

These words of Shakespeare show that even in his time the inflated, pompous, and artificial style still in vogue on the English stage was a national characteristic. We have scarcely improved, since old traditions cling and hold the stage in mortmain. Reform moves slowly every where in England; but the two institutions which oppose to it the most obstinate resistance are the church and the theatre. In both of these tradition stands for nearly as much as revelation. Each adheres to its old forms, as if they contained its true essence; each believes that those forms once broken, the whole spirit would be lost; just as if they were phials which contained a precious liquid, and must be therefore preserved at all costs. The idea that the liquid can be quite as well, and perhaps better, kept in different pihals has never occurred to them. They will die for the phial.

Still it is plain that a strong reaction against this bigoted admiration of traditional and conventional forms is now perceptible. The facilities of travel and intercourse with other nations have engendered new notions and modified old ones. It is impossible to compare the French and Italian stage with the English, and not perceive the vast inferiority of the latter. In the one we see nature, simplicity, and life; in the other the galvanism of artificial convention. It cannot be denied that the recent acting of Hamlet by Fechter was to the English mind a daring and doubtful innovation. It was something so utterly different in spirit and style from that to which we have been accustomed that it created a sensation; and while it found many ardent admirers, it found quite as many vehement opposers. The public ranged themselves in two parties; the one insisting that the traditional and artificial school, as represented by Garrick, the elder Kean, and Cooke, was the only safe guide for the tragic actor; and the other, arguing that as the true function of the stage was to hold up the mirror to nature, acting should be as much like life and as little like acting as possible. The former, at the head of which were the friends of Mr. Charles Kean, made a public demonstration in his behalf, and scouted these new-fangled French notions of acting. Was it to be supposed that any school of acting could be superior to that created and established in England by the genius of such actors as Garrick, the elder Kean, and Cooke? Should foreigners presume to teach us how to interpret and represent plays which had been the study of the English people for centuries? To this it was opposed that, however mortifying to us, it was a fact that the Germans had led the way to a profounder and more metaphysical study of Shakespeare, and had taught us in many ways how to understand his plays, and that therefore there was no reason why foreigners might not teach us how to act them. The very fact that their eyes were not blinded, nor their tongues tied by traditional conventions, enabled them to study Shakespeare with more freedom and directness. There was no deep rut of ancient usage out of which they were forced to wrench themselves. And, besides, it was affirmed, and with truth, that the English stage is the jeer of the world, and needs thorough reform.

We have indeed made little progress in reforming the stage.

Mr. Charles Kean has devoted his talents to improving the wardrobe and scenery, and has so far done good service; but in the essential matter of acting we are nearly where we were in the past century. While the background and dresses are reformed, and the bag-wig in which Garrick played Hamlet is thrown aside, we have carefully preserved all the old points, all the stage-tricks, and all the stilted intonations of the artificial school; and the consequence is, that the sole reality is in that which is the least essential. The attention is thus withdrawn from the actor to the scenery, and we have a spectacle instead of a tragedy. The background is real, but the actor is conventional; the blanket has usurped the prominent place, and Shakespeare retired behind it. The bursts of genius with which Garrick startled the house, and made the audience forget his bag-wig, are wanting, but all his tricks are preserved; the corpse is still there, but the spirit he put into it is gone.

In comedy there is as little resemblance to real life as in tragedy; humour and wit are travestied by buffoonery and grimace. Instead of pictures of life as it is, we have grotesque daubs and caricatures, so exaggerated and farcical in their character as to "make the judicious grieve." The actor and the audience react upon each other. The audience are generally uneducated, and for the most part agree with Partridge in his comment on *Hamlet*: "Give me the king for my money," says he. The actors must bow to this low taste,

> "For they who live to please must please to live."

But tradition has worse sins to answer for. It has not only ruined our national acting, but in some cases has overshadowed the drama itself, and perverted the meaning of some of the greatest plays of Shakespeare. Hamlet is not Hamlet on the English stage; he is the tall imposing figure of John Kemble, dark, melodramatic, and dressed in black velvet. Strive as we will, we cannot imagine him as the light-haired Dane, easy and dreamy of temperament, "fat and scant of breath," essentially metaphysical, hating physical action, and wanting energy to put his thoughts into deeds. The whole spirit of the acted Hamlet is southern, that of the real Hamlet is purely northern. We have indeed broken through an old tradition, according to which, incredible as it may seem, Shylock used to be acted as a comic character, though we are still far from a real understanding of his character. But of all the plays of Shakespeare none is so grossly misunderstood as *Macbeth*. Nor is this misapprehension confined to the stage; it prevails even among those who have zealously studied and admired Shakespeare. As John Kemble stands for Hamlet in our imaginations, so does Mrs. Siddons for

Lady Macbeth. She has completely transformed this wonderful creation of Shakespeare's, distorted its true features, and so stamped upon it her own individuality, that when we think of one we have the figure of the other in our minds. The Lady Macbeth of Mrs. Siddons is the only Lady Macbeth we know and believe in. She is the imperious, wicked, cruel wife of Macbeth, urging on her weak and kind-hearted husband to abominable crimes solely to gratify her own ambitious and evil nature. She is without heart, tenderness, or remorse. Devilish in character, violent in purpose, she is the soul of the whole play; the plotter and instigator of all its horrors; a fiend-like creature, who, having a complete mastery over Macbeth, works him to madness by her taunts, and relentlessly drives him on against his will to the commission of his terrible crimes. We hate her as we pity Macbeth. He is weak of purpose, amiable of disposition, "full of the milk of human kindness," an unwilling instrument of all her evil designs, who, wanting force of will and strength of character, yields reluctantly to her infernal temptations.

Nothing could more clearly prove the great genius of Mrs. Siddons than that she has been able so to stamp upon the public mind this amazing misconception, that, despite all the careful study which of late years has been given to Shakespeare, this notion of the character of Lady Macbeth and Macbeth should still prevail. Yet so deeply is it rooted, and so universal, that whoever attempts to eradicate it will find his task most difficult. But, believing it to be an utter distortion of the characters as Shakespeare drew them, and so at variance with the interior thought, conduct, and development of the play as not only entirely to obscure its real meaning, but to obliterate all its finest and most delicate features, we venture to enter upon this difficult task.

Macbeth and his wife, so far from being the characters above described, are their direct opposites. He is the villain, who never can satiate himself with crimes. She, having committed one crime, dies of remorse. She is essentially a woman—acts suddenly and violently, and then breaks down, and wastes her life and thoughts in bitter repentance. He is, on the contrary, essentially a man—who resolves slowly and with calculation, but once determined and entered upon a course of action, obstinately pursues it to the end, haunted by no remorse for his crimes, and agitated by no regrets and doubts, so long as his wicked plans do not miscarry. The spring of his nature is ambition;* and in working out his ends he is cruel, pitiless, and

* "I have no spur
To prick the sides of my intent, but only
Vaulting ambition."

bloody. He is without a single good trait of character; and from the beginning to the end of the play, at every step, he develops deeper abysses of cruelty and inhumanity in his nature. When first presented to us, we, in common with Lady Macbeth, are completely unaware of his real baseness. He is a thorough hypocrite, and deceives us as he deceived her. We see that he has a grasping ambition, but we believe that he is amiable and weak of purpose, for so Lady Macbeth tells us; but as the play goes on, his character develops itself, and at last we find that he has neither heart nor tenderness for any body or any thing; that his will is unconquerable; that he is utterly without moral sense, is hopelessly selfish, and wickedly cruel. All he loves is power. His ambition is insatiable. It grows by what it feeds on. The more he has, the more he desires, and he is ready to commit every kind of horror for the sake of attaining his object. He is restrained by no scruples of honour, by no claims of friendship, by no sensitiveness of conscience. He murders his sovereign, from whom he has just received large gifts and honours in his own house; and then instantly compasses the death of his nearest friend and guest, Banquo. Not content with this, he then seeks the life of Macduff; and, enraged because he has fled, savagely and in cold blood puts the whole of his family to the sword. There is a steady growth of evil in his character from the beginning to the end, or rather a steady development of his evil nature.

Malcolm and Macduff, who at first were his friends and companions, afterwards, when they had learned to "know" him, call him "treacherous" and "devilish." So far from agreeing in the character given of him by Lady Macbeth, they say,

> "*Macd.* Not in the legions
> Of horrid hell can come a devil more damned
> In evil to top Macbeth.
> *Malcolm.* I grant him bloody,
> Luxurious, avaricious, false, deceitful,
> Sudden, malicious, smacking of every sin
> That has a name."

Yet even they admit that

> "This tyrant, whose sole name blisters our tongues,
> Was once thought honest."

As he had deceived the world, so he deceived his wife. His bloody and treacherous nature was at first as unknown to her as to his friends. As they thought him "honest," she thought him amiable and infirm of purpose, greatly ambitious, and one who would "wrongly win," but yet kindly of nature. Fiery temptations had not as yet brought out the secret writing of his character. It was with Macbeth as it was with Nero: their real natures did not exhibit themselves at first; but when once they began to develop, their growth was rapid and terrible. And in each of them there was a vein of madness. Essentially a hypocrite, and secretive by nature, Macbeth had passed for only a brave and stern soldier when he first makes his appearance. Yet even in his fierce Norwegian fight we see a violent and bloody spirit. In the very beginning of the play one of his soldiers describes him, in his encounter with Macdonald, as one who,

> "Disdaining fortune, with his brandished steel,
> Which smoked with bloody execution,
> Like Valour's minion,
> Carved out his passage till he faced the slave;
> And ne'er shook hands nor bade farewell to him
> Till he unseam'd him from the nape to the chaps,
> And fixed his head upon the battlements."

This is rather a grim picture, and scarcely corresponds to the character usually assigned to Macbeth. Here is not only no infirmity of purpose, but a stern unwavering resolution, carving its way through all difficulties and against all opposition. Thus far, however, all his deeds had been loyal and for a lawful purpose. Still within his heart burnt, as he himself says, "black and deep desires," and only circumstances and opportunities were needed to show that he could be as fierce and bloody in crime as he had shown himself in doing a soldier's duty. They were already urging him in the very first scene; but, secretive of nature, he kept them out of sight.

> "Stars, hide your fires;
> Let not light see my black and deep desires;
> The eye wink at the hand. Yet let that be,
> Which the eye fears, when it is done, to see."

Thus he cries to himself as he speeds to his wife The "murder," which was but an hour before "fantastical," has now become a fixed resolve.

A nature like this, secretive, false, deceitful, and wicked, which had thus far satisfied itself in a legitimate way, and having no temptation in his own house, had never shown its real shape there, would naturally not have been understood by his wife. Glimpses she might have of what he was—but not a thorough understanding of him. Blinded by her personal attachment to him, and herself essentially his opposite in character, as we shall see, she would naturally have misinterpreted him. The secretive nature is always a puzzle to the frank nature. Accustomed to go straight to her object, whether good or bad, she was completely deceived by his hypocritical and sentimental pretences, and supposed his nature to be "full of the milk of human kindness." But time also opened her eyes, though, perhaps, never even to the last did she fully comprehend him. "What thou wouldst highly, that wouldst thou holily," she would never have said after the murder of the king. But however this may be, that her view of his character is false is proved by the whole play. When did he ever show an iota of kindness? what crime did his conscience or the desire to act "holily" ever prevent his committing? When did he ever exhibit any want of bloody determination—infirm of purpose? He was like a tiger in his purposes and in his deeds. The murder of Duncan did not satisfy him. The next morning he in cold blood kills the two chamberlains to gratify his wanton cruelty. It was impossible that they should testify against him—they had been drugged, and he could have had no fear of them. Then immediately he plots the murder of Banquo and Fleance, and all the while hypocritically conceals his foul purposes even from his wife; and because Macduff "failed his presence at the tyrant's feast," he determines also to murder him. Foiled of this, he then cruelly and hideously puts to the sword his wife and little children. In all these murders, after the king's, Lady Macbeth not only takes no part, but he keeps her in ignorance of them. She drive him to the commission of his crimes? She does not know of them till they are done. They are plotted and determined upon in secret by Macbeth alone, and carried into execution with a bloody directness and suddenness. 'Tis he is "bloody, false, deceitful, sudden,"—essentially a hypocrite, false in his pretences, secret in his plotting, loud in his showy talk, but sudden and bloody in his crimes and in his malice.

Thus far, however, we have seen but one side of Macbeth. The other side was its opposite. Bold, ambitious, and treacherous, he was also equally imaginative and superstitious. In action he feared no man. Brave as he was cruel, and ready to meet any thing in the flesh, he was equally visionary of head, a victim of superstitious fears, and a mere coward before the unreal fancies evoked by his imagination. He has the Scottish second-sight, and visions and phantoms shake his soul. Show him twenty armed men who seek his life, he encounters them with a fierce joy. Show him a white sheet on a pole, and tell him it is a ghost, and he trembles abjectly. He conjures up for himself phantoms that "unfix his hair and make his seated heart knock at his ribs;" he is distracted with "horrible imaginings." His excited imagination always plays him false and fills him with momentary and superstitious fears; but these fears never ultimately control his action. They are fumes of the head, and being purely visionary, they are also temporary.

They come in moments of excitement, obscure for a time his judgment, and influence his ideas; but having regard solely to things unreal, they vanish with the necessity of action.

These superstitious fears have nothing to do with conscience or morals. He has no morals; there is no indication of a moral sense in any single word of the whole play. The only passage which faintly indicates a sense of right and wrong is when he urges to himself, as reasons why he should not kill Duncan, that the king is not only his kinsman, his king, and his guest, but that he has borne his faculties so meekly, that his virtues would plead like angels trumpet-tongued against the deep damnation of his taking-off. This, however, is mere talk, and has only reference to the indignation which his murder will excite, not to any sorrow he has for the crime. His sole doubt is lest he may not succeed; for, as he says,

> "If the assassination
> Could trammel up the consequence, and catch,
> With his surcease, success; that but this blow
> Might be the be-all and the end-all here,
> But here, upon this bank and shoal of time,—
> We'd jump the life to come."

The idea of being restrained from committing this murder by any religious or moral scruples is very far from his thought. Right or wrong, good or bad, have nothing to do with the question; and as for the "life to come," that is mere folly.

But while his moral sense is dead, his imagination is nervously alive. It engenders visions that terrify him: after the murder is done, he thinks he hears phantom-voices crying, "Sleep no more, Glamis has murdered sleep; and therefore Cawdor shall sleep no more, Macbeth shall sleep no more;" and these voices so work upon his superstitious fears that he is afraid for the moment to return to the chamber, and carry the daggers back and smear the grooms with blood. He is, as Lady Macbeth says, "brainsickly," and "fears a painted devil." This is superstition, not remorse—a momentary imaginative fear, not a permanent feeling. In a few minutes he has changed his dress, and calmly makes speeches as if nothing had occurred,—nay, this cold-blooded hypocrite is ready within the hour to commit two new and wanton murders on the chamberlains, and boastfully to refer them to his loyal spirit and loving heart, inflamed by horror at the hideous murder of the king, which he has himself committed.

The same superstitious fear attacks him when he hears that Birnam Wood is moving to Dunsinane Hill; but it does not prevent this creature, so "full of the milk of human kindness," from striking the messenger, calling him "liar and slave," and threatening,

> "If thou speak'st false,
> Upon the next tree thou shalt hang alive
> Till famine cling thee."

So too when Macduff tells him that he was "not of woman born," awed for a moment by his superstitious fears, he cries,

> "Accursed be that tongue that tells me so,
> For it hath cow'd my better part of man!
> . . . I'll not fight with thee."

At times, under the influence of an over-excitable imagination acting upon a nature thoroughly superstitious, his intellect wavers, and he is subject to sudden aberrations of mind resembling insanity. They are, however, evanescent, and in a moment he recovers his poise, descending through a poetical phase into his real and settled character of cruelty and wickedness. In the dagger-scene, where he is alone, these three phases are perfectly marked. The visionary dagger "proceeding from the heat-oppressed brain" soon vanishes, then follows the poetic mania, and then the stern resolution of murder. In the banquet-scene, when the ghost of Banquo rises, the poetic interval is less marked, for he is under the restraint of the company and under the influence of his wife; but scarce has the company gone when his real character returns. He is again forming new resolutions of blood. His mind reverts to Macduff, whose life he threatens. He is bent "to know by the worst means the worst;" "strange things I have in head, which will to hand."

This aberration of mind Macbeth has in common with Lear, Hamlet, and Othello. But in Macbeth alone does it take a superstitious shape. The trance of Othello is but a momentary condition, in which his goaded imagination, acting upon an irritated sense of honour, love, and jealousy, obliterates for an instant the real world. Hamlet's madness is but the "sore distraction" of a mind essentially dreamy and metaphysical on which the burden of a great action is put, which he can neither refuse nor accept, and while thus struggling with himself he rejects all ideas of love as futile and impertinent. The very notion of love maddens him while he has his dreadful problem to solve. Lear, again, is "heart-struck." His madness comes from wounded pride and affection. The ingratitude and cruelty of his daughters shake his mind, and to his excited spirit the very elements become his "pernicious daughters:" "I never gave you kingdoms, called you children." In all except Macbeth, the nature thus driven to madness is noble in itself, moral in its character, and warm in its affections. The aberrations of

Macbeth are superstitious, and have nothing to do with the morals or the affections.

Macbeth's imagination is, however, a ruling characteristic of his nature. His brain is always active; and when it does not evoke phantoms, it indulges in fanciful and poetic images. He is a poet, and turns every thing into poetry. His utterance is generally excited and high-flown, rarely simple and real, and almost never expresses his true feelings and thoughts. His heart remains cold while his head is on fire. On all occasions his first impulse is to poetise a little; and having done this, he goes about his work without regard to what he has said. His sayings are one thing; his doings are quite another. Shakespeare makes him rant intentionally, as if to show that in such a character the imagination can and does work entirely independently of real feelings and passions. There is no serious character in all Shakespeare's plays who constantly rants and swells in his speech like Macbeth; and this is plainly to show the complete unreality of all his imaginative bursts. In this he differs from every other person in this play. Yet when he is really in earnest, and has some plain business in hand, he can be direct enough in his speech, as throughout the second interview with the weird sisters, and in the scene with the two murderers whom he sends to kill Banquo and Fleance;* or when, enraged at the escape of Fleance, he forgets to be a hypocrite, and his real nature clearly expresses itself in direct words, full of savage resolve. But on all other occasions, when he is not in earnest and intends to deceive, or when his brain is excited, he indulges in sentimental speeches, violent figures of speech, extravagant personifications, and artificial tropes and conceits. Even in the phantom-voices he imagines crying to him over Duncan's body, he cannot help this peculiarity. He curiously hunts out conceits to express sleep. He "murders sleep, the innocent sleep; sleep, that knits up the ravell'd sleeve of care, the death of each day's life, sore labour's bath, balm of hurt minds, great nature's second course, chief nourisher in life's feast." No wonder that Lady Macbeth, amazed, cries out, "What do you mean?" But he cannot help going on like a mad poet. His language is full of alliteration, fanciful juxtaposition of words, assonance, and jingle. At times, so strong is this habit, he makes poems to himself, and for the moment half believes in them. Only compare, in this connexion, the natural simple pathos of the scene where Macduff hears of the barbarous murder of his wife and children with the language of Macbeth when the death of Lady Macbeth is announced to him. Macduff "pulls his hat upon his brows," and gives vent to his agony in the simplest and most direct words. Here the feeling is deep and sincere:

"All my pretty ones?
Did you say, all?—O, hell-kite!—All?
What, all my pretty chickens, and their dam,
At one fell swoop?
Mal. Dispute it like a man.
Macd. I shall do so;
But I must also feel it like a man:
I cannot but remember such things were,
And were most precious to me.—Did heaven look on,
And would not take their part? Sinful Macduff,
They were all struck for thee! Naught that I am,
Not for their own demerits, but for mine,
Fell slaughter on their souls:—Heaven rest them now!
. . . .
O, I could play the woman with my eyes."

But when Macbeth is told of the death of his wife, he makes a little poem, full of alliterations and conceits. It is an answer to the question, What is life like? what can we say about it now?

"To-morrow, and to-morrow, and to-morrow,
Creeps in this petty pace from day to day,
To the last syllable of recorded time;
And all our yesterdays have lighted fools
The way to dusty death. Out, out, brief candle!
Life's but a walking shadow; a poor player,
That struts and frets his hour upon the stage,
And then is heard no more: it is a tale
Told by an idiot, full of sound and fury,
Signifying nothing.

Enter Messenger.

Thou comest to use thy tongue; thy story quickly."

Has this any relation to true feeling? Do men of any feeling, whose hearts are touched, fall to improvising poems like this, filled with fanciful images, when great sorrows come upon them? This speech is full of "sound and fury, signifying nothing." There is no accent from the heart in it. It is elaborate, poetic, cold-blooded. "Life is a candle," "a poor player," "a walking shadow," "a tale told by an idiot." We have his customary alliterations: "petty pace," "dusty death," "day to day;" his love of repeating the same word, "to-morrow, and to-morrow, and to-morrow," just as we have "If 'twere done when 'tis done, then 'twere well 'twere done quickly;" and his "Sleep no more, Macbeth doth murder sleep; sleep, that knits up," &c.; "Sleep no more, Glamis hath murdered sleep, and therefore Cawdor shall sleep no more, Macbeth shall sleep no more." He cannot forget himself enough to cease to be ingenious in his phrases. As a poem this speech is striking; as an expression of feeling it is perfectly empty. At the end of it he has quite forgotten the death of his wife; he is only employed in piling up figure after figure to personify life. What renders the unreality of this still more striking is the sudden change which comes over him upon the entrance of the messenger. In an instant he stops short in his poem, and his tone becomes at once decided and harsh; his wife's death has passed utterly out of his mind. When the messenger tells him that Birnam Wood was beginning to move, with a sudden burst of rage he turns upon him, strikes him, calls him liar and slave, and threatens to "hang him alive till famine cling him," if his report prove to be incorrect. This is the real Macbeth. From this time forward he never alludes to Lady Macbeth; but, in a strange condition of superstitious fear and soldierly courage, he calls his men to arms, and goes out crying,

> "Blow wind! come wrack!
> At least we'll die with harness on our back."

And this throughout is the character of Macbeth's utterances. He is not like Tartuffe, a religious hypocrite; he is a poetical and sentimental hypocrite. His phrases and figures of speech have no root in his real life; they are only veneered upon them. "His words fly up, his thoughts remain below." When he is poetical he is never in earnest. Sometimes his speeches are merely oratorical, and made from habit and for effect; sometimes they are hypocritical, and used to conceal his real intentions; and sometimes they are the expressions of an inflamed and diseased imagination stimulated by superstition. But they are generally bombastic and swelling in tone, and are so intended to be. His habit of making speeches and inventing curious conceits is so strong, that he even "unpacks his heart with words" when alone, so as to leave himself free and direct to act. Thus, in one of his famous soliloquies, mark the unreal quality of all the pretended feeling, the mixture of immorality, bombast, and hypocrisy, the assonances and alliterations, the plays upon words, the extravagant figures, all showing the excitability of the brain and not of the heart:

> "If *'twere done*, when 'tis *done*, then *'twere*
> Well *'twere done* quickly. If the assassination
> *C*ould trammel up the *c*onsequence, and *c*atch,
> With his *surcease, success;* if but this blow
> Could *be* the *be-all* and the *end-all here*,
> But *here*, upon this bank and shoal of time,—
> We'd jump the life to come."

Then, after some questionings about killing his guest, his kinsman, his king, which would seem honest, but for what comes after and for the utter reckless immorality which has gone before these words, his imagination excites itself, and runs into a wild and extravagant figure which means nothing. Duncan's virtues, he says,

"Will plead like angels *trumpet-tongued* against
The *deep damnation* of his *taking-off*."

No sooner did he begin to swell and alliterate again than he goes wild:

"And pity, like *naked newborn babe*,
Striding the blast, or heaven's cherubim, hors'd
Upon the sightless couriers of the air,
Shall blow the horrid deed in every eye,
That tears shall drown the wind."

This is pure rant, and intended to be so. It is the product of an unrestrained imagination which exhausts itself in the utterance. But it neither comes from the heart nor acts upon the heart.

Again, in the soliloquy of the air-drawn dagger, the superstitious visionary Macbeth, who always projects his fancies into figures and phantoms, after addressing this

"false creation
Proceeding from the heat-oppressed brain,"

falls at once into poetic declamation about the night, and indulges himself in strange images and personifications. A man about to commit a murder who invents these conceits must be a poetical villain:

"Now witchcraft celebrates
Pale Hecate's offering: and wither'd murder,
Alarum'd by his sentinel, the wolf,
Whose howl's his watch, thus with a stealthy pace,
With Tarquin's ravishing strides, towards his design
Moves like a ghost."

Can any thing be more extraordinary and elaborate than this pressing of one conceit upon another? Wither'd murder has a sentinel, the wolf, who howls his watch, and who with stealthy pace strides with Tarquin's ravishing strides like a ghost! Shakespeare makes no other character systematically talk like this.

But the fumes of the brain pass, and leave the stern determined man of action:

"Whiles I threat, he lives;
Words to the heat of deeds too cold breath gives.
I go, and it is done; the bell invites me.
Hear it not, Duncan; for it is a knell
That summons thee to heaven, or to hell."

We have no such rant as this in Lady Macbeth. In the scenes of the murder, she does not befool herself with visions and poetry. She is practical, and her attention is solely given to the real facts about her. Contrast the simple language in which she speaks, while waiting for Macbeth, with his previous rhodomontade. Agitated, in great emotion, listening for sounds, doubting whether some mischance may not have befallen to prevent the murder,—she speaks in short broken sentences; but she does not liken her husband to Tarquin, and say now is the time when "witchcraft celebrates pale Hecate's offering," nor employ this interval in making a poem full of conceits.

He goes in to the king, and commits the murder; no scruples of any kind prevent him. But when that is secure, he has a superstitious fit, and imagines phantom-voices, that talk as no phantoms ever did before. Still he is a coward in the presence of phantoms, and will not go back. The deed has been done, and ghosts alarm him.

But, as has been before observed, all this raving as usual passes by at once. In a half-hour he is cold and calm as ever. The phantom-voices did not reach his conscience and awakened no remorse. They were the children of superstition and imagination, and they vanish with cockcrow and daylight, leaving no trace behind in his memory. They have not altered his mood nor his plans.

We now come to a consideration of Lady Macbeth's character. At all points she was his opposite, or rather his complement. Where he was strong, she was weak; where he was weak, she was strong. He was poetical and visionary of nature; she was plain and practical. He was indirect, false, secretive; she, on the contrary, was vehement and impulsive. Between what she willed and what she did was a straight line. She was troubled by none of his superstitious fears or visions. Her imagination was feeble and inactive, her character was energetic; she saw only the object immediately before her, and she went to it with rapidity and directness of purpose. She was skilful in management and ready in contrivance, as women are apt to be; while Macbeth was wanting in both these qualities, as men generally are. For herself she seems to have had no ambition, and not personally to have coveted the position of queen. Her ambition is but the reflection of Macbeth's, and her great crime was wrought in furtherance of his suggestions and promptings. Mistaking entirely his character at first, proud of his success for his sake, and rightly reading him so far as to see that his ambition, which was insatiable, grasped at the throne, she lent herself to the murder of Duncan, in the belief that the throne once obtained, Macbeth's ambition would be satisfied. Her moral sense was inactive, and not sufficient to lead her to oppose his project. It was not, as we shall see, utterly wanting in her, as in Macbeth. She seems to have been warmly attached to Macbeth, and always, after the murder is committed, she endeavours to soothe and tranquillise him with gentle and affectionate words. But she could not understand his superstitious hesitations when once resolved on action. His poetry and his imaginative flights, as well as his visions, were to her incomprehensible, and she made the natural mistake of supposing him to be infirm of purpose. Her mind was one of management and detail. The determination and suggestion of the murder is his; the management and detail of it is hers. This is a master-stroke of Shakespeare's, by which he at once distinguishes the masculine from the feminine nature. Man is quick to propose and suggest a plan in its general scope; woman is always his superior in adjusting the details by which it may be carried into execution. Her nature was not wicked in itself. It was susceptible of deep feeling and remorse. But her moral sense was sluggish, while her impulses were sudden and vehement; and, as such women generally are, she was irritably impatient of the postponement of any project already decided upon. She had a strong will, and gave expression to it in an exaggerated way:

> "I have given suck, and know
> How tender 'tis to love the babe that milks me:
> I would, while it was smiling in my face,
> Have pluck'd my nipple from its boneless gums,
> And dash'd the brains out, had I so sworn as you
> Have done to this."

This is but a vehement, passionate, and exaggerated way of saying that if she had sworn to herself to do *any thing*, however shocking, as deliberately and determinedly as Macbeth had to commit this murder, she would do it in spite of consequences, and not like him be "afeard to be the same in thine own act and valour as thou art in desire." She does not mean, nor did Shakespeare mean, that so hideous an act would be possible either for her to plan or to commit; but to prove her contempt of that condition of mind when "I dare not waits upon I would," she seizes upon the most horrible and repulsive act that she can imagine, and declares energetically that, shocking as that is, she would not hesitate to do even that, "had *she so sworn*" to do it as Macbeth had. Yet this wild and violent figure of speech is generally taken as the key of her whole character. It is nothing of the sort; for the very line preceding it proves that she had a tenderness of nature under all her energy, and a power of love as well as of will:

> "I have given suck, and know
> How tender 'tis to love the babe that milks me."

Well, despite that tenderness and love, which you, Macbeth, know I have, I would have done what is so contrary to all my nature, had I so sworn as you.—Throughout this scene her sole object is to urge, as vehemently as she can, upon Macbeth the folly of dallying and hesitating to carry out a project which he alone had conceived, suggested, and determined, merely for fear of consequences, and lest it should do him injury in the eyes of the world. He never feels nor suggests any moral objection; he does not pretend to feel it. His sole fear is lest he may not succeed; he only doubts whether it would not be better to postpone the execution of his project until a more fitting time. His decisions are less rapid than hers. She must at once act on the first strength of her resolve. She is impetuous, and would spring upon her prey at once. He, knowing that his fell purpose will only strengthen with meditation, and doubting whether the time has come to secure his object, proposes to postpone its execution. But there is no time for this. There are but a few hours in which all must be accomplished, and he is not ready with the detail. But to this proposal of postponement she says "No." She knows that he never will rest till it is accomplished. Neither time nor place adhered when you "broke this enterprise to me," she says; and now, when both "have made themselves," execute your design, and let no longer "I dare not wait upon I would." To this he feebly opposes, "If we should fail," failure being the only thing that troubles him. She then suggests the plan in detail by which the murder can be effected; and he cries out, in a burst of admiration and delight,

> "Bring forth men-children only,
> For thy undaunted mettle should compose
> Nothing but males."

Still, when the time approaches, Lady Macbeth needs all her courage, and she stimulates it with wine, lest it should break down:

> "That which hath made them drunk hath made me bold."

She preserves her courage, however, to the end, never loses her self-possession, and takes care that the plan is carried out fully in all its details. But once accomplished, she utterly breaks down. She has over-calculated her strength; she was not utterly wicked, and her remorses are terrible. From this time forward we have no such scenes between her and her husband; he performs all his other murders alone, without her knowledge or connivance.

And here the main feature of this play must be kept in mind. Lady Macbeth dies of remorse for this her crime; she cannot forget it; it haunts her in her sleep; the damned spot cannot be washed from her conscience or her hand. What a fearful cry of remorse and agony is that of hers in her dream!

> "Here's the smell of the blood still. All the perfumes of Arabia will not sweeten this *little* hand! Oh! oh! oh!"

There is no poetising here, no sentimental and figurative personifications; it is the cry of a wounded heart and conscience. It is written too in prose, not in verse. It is real, and not fantastic like the rant and poetry of Macbeth. That terrible night remains with her, and haunts her, and tears her like a demon, and at last she dies of it.

How is it with Macbeth? does the memory of that night torture him? Never for a moment. He plots new murders. He has tasted blood, and cannot live without it. On, on, he goes, deeper and deeper into blood; till he is slain, and never to the last one cry of conscience.

Yet it is thought that Lady Macbeth urged on this amiable man, so infirm of purpose, so filled with the milk of human kindness, and was the main-spring of his crimes. Suffice it to say, in answer to this view, that after Duncan is killed he keeps her in complete ignorance of all he does, and his murders are thenceforward more terrible and pitiless, and with no faint shadow of excuse or apology. This cold-hearted villain stops at nothing; even her death does not awaken a throb in his heart. Is it not preposterous to suppose that the so-called fiend of the play, she who instigates and drives an unwilling victim to crime, should die of remorse for that crime; while the amiable victim, far from sharing any such feeling, only plunges deeper into crime when she does not instigate him, and develops at every step an increasing brutality and savageness of nature?

No; it is not the tall, dark, commanding, and imperious figure of Mrs. Siddons, with threatening brow and inflated nostrils, that represents Lady Macbeth; she is not at all of that character or features. She is of rather a delicate organisation, of medium height, her hair inclining to red, her temperament nervous and sanguine, with a florid complexion, and "little hands." So was Lucrezia Borgia; and so was Lady Macbeth. She was personally fair and attractive. Can any one imagine Macbeth calling the dark, towering, imperious woman like Mrs. Siddons his "dearest love," "dear wife," or his "dearest chuck"?

But it is commonly thought that the murder of Duncan was suggested and planned by Lady Macbeth, and he was urged into it against his will and contrary to his nature. Such a view is utterly in contradiction of the play itself. The suggestion is entirely Macbeth's, and he has resolved upon it before he sees her. The witches are a projection of his own desires and superstitions. They meet him at the commencement of the play, prophesying, in response to his own desires, that he is thane of Cawdor, and "shall be king hereafter;" but they respond also to his fears, by adding that Banquo's "children shall be kings." Those are the very points upon which all his thoughts hinge—his ambition to be king, his fears lest the throne shall pass from his family. Hence his hate of Banquo and Fleance. From this time forward he thinks of nothing else. As he rides across the heath, he is self-involved, abstracted, silent, sullen, revolving in his mind how to compass his designs, which are nothing less than the murder of the king. He does not dream that the prophecies of the weird women will accomplish themselves without his assistance, for they are projections of his own thoughts. He instantly receives news that he is made thane of Cawdor, and scarcely gives a thought to this honour, scarcely expresses his satisfaction; when the news is announced he says,

> "Glamis, and thane of Cawdor:
> *The greatest is behind.*—Thanks for your pains."

And then immediately his mind reverts to the promise that Banquo's children shall be kings:

> "Do you not hope your children shall be kings,
> When those that gave the thane of Cawdor to me
> Promised no less to thee?"

Then he falls again into gloomy silence, and talks to himself inwardly. What does he say and think? He resolves to murder the king:

> "This supernatural soliciting
> Cannot be ill; cannot be good. If ill,
> Why hath it given me earnest of success,
> Commencing in a truth? I am thane of Cawdor:
> If good, why do I yield to that suggestion
> Whose horrid image doth unfix my hair,
> And make my seated heart knock at my ribs,
> Against the use of nature? Present fears
> Are less than horrible imaginings;
> My thought, whose *murder* yet is but fantastical,
> Shakes so my single state of man, that function
> Is smothered in surmise; and nothing is
> But what is not."

Yes, already he dreams of murder. He sees not his way clear; he will trust to chance; but he dreams of murder. And full of these thoughts, he rushes to his wife to fill her mind with his project, to consult her as to how it can be carried into execution; for he cannot plan in detail; and though the thought crosses him, that

> "If chance will have me king, why chance may crown me,
> Without my stir."

Yet this is but a hope; for in the next scene he has determined to take the matter into his own hands and trust nothing to chance. As soon as he hears that Malcolm is made prince of Cumberland and heir to the throne, he determines absolutely to kill the king:

> "The prince of Cumberland!—That is a step
> On which I must fall down, or else o'er-leap,
> For in my way it lies. Stars, hide your fires;
> Let not light see my black and deep desires:
> The eye wink at the hand. Yet let that be,
> Which the eye fears, when it is done, to see."

He has already written to Lady Macbeth; and his letter has but one thought and one theme,—the promise that he shall be king. Much as she "fears his nature," she knows thoroughly his desires, and has faint glimpses of his real character; she knows that he *means* to be king, and sees that he would "wrongly win;" that his ambition is great, and that his mind is filled solely with one idea. But she fears that he is "too full of the milk of human kindness to catch the nearest way;" and when she hears that Duncan is coming to the castle, and that Macbeth is hurrying to see her before the king's arrival, she doubts no longer his plan. For a moment she is aghast. "Thou'rt mad to say it," she says to the messenger who announces the king's approach; for she sees that he comes to his death:

> "The raven himself is hoarse
> That croaks the fatal entrance of Duncan
> Under my battlements."

He has been lured here by Macbeth to compass his destruction; and in a moment Macbeth will be with her. Then, summoning up all her courage at once, she resolves to aid him in his ambitious and murderous design. She calls upon "the spirits that tend on mortal thought" to "unsex her," to alter her nature, to make her cruel and remorseless, to let nothing intervene to shake her purpose; for she is not quite sure of herself. She knows what "compunctious visitings of nature" are, and she strengthens herself against them. She is not naturally cruel; and she cries out to the "spirits" to "stop up the access and passage to remorse" now open in her nature, to change her "milk for gall," and to cover her with "the dunnest smoke of hell," so that her

> "keen knife *see* not the wound it makes,
> Nor heaven peep through the blanket of the dark,
> To cry, Hold, hold."

In this tremendous apostrophe, in which she goads herself on to crime, the woman's nature is plainly seen. Macbeth never prays to have his nature altered, to have any "passages of remorse" closed up; never fears "compunctious visitings of nature," nor desires darkness to hide his knife, so that he may not *see* the wound he makes. But she knows she is a woman, and that she needs to be "unsexed," and feels that she is doing violence to her own nature; still her will is strong, and she cries down her misgivings, and resolves to aid Macbeth in his design.

Macbeth meets her in this mood. There is no salutation or greeting on his part; he has but one idea,—Duncan is coming, and is to be murdered. His first words are:

> "My dearest love,
> Duncan comes here to-night."

To which she asks, "And when goes hence?" "To-morrow," he answers, and pauses; and adds, "as he purposes." But in the look and in the pause Lady Macbeth has read his whole soul and intent. There is murder in that look; and she cries:

> "O, never
> Shall sun that morrow see!
> Your face, my thane, is as a book, where men
> May read strange matters."

There is no explanation between them. He has conveyed all his intention by a look and a gesture, as she herself distinctly says. He has ridden headlong, as fast as horse could carry him, away from the king full of this one idea; and the king has vainly "coursed him at his heels," having "the purpose," as he himself says, "to be his purveyor." And his thoughts have spoken in his looks so unmistakably, that they are perfectly understood. If there be any doubt by whom the murder was suggested, it is made perfectly clear by what Lady Macbeth subsequently says to him in the next scene in which they are presented. When he begins to doubt whether the murder had not better be postponed, she says:

> "What beast was it, then,
> That made you break this enterprise to me?"

It was not of my plotting, but of your own: "Nor time nor place did then adhere, and yet you would make both;" you desired it and still desire it, but are afraid of consequences. These words of hers would indeed seem to indicate that he had urged the crime upon her against her will at a previous interview not reported in the play, or perhaps by a letter; for she says distinctly, that when he broke the enterprise to her,

> "Nor *time*, nor *place*,
> Did then adhere, and yet *you would make both*:
> They have made themselves."

It would, therefore, plainly seem that Macbeth had broken this enterprise to her, and urged it on her, even before the king had determined to come to his castle, and that he intended to "make time and place." This would account for her opening speech completely, and for the fact that he does not make any explanation to her of his intentions other than by his look and intonation when they first meet; for certainly there is nothing in the play about the "time and place" of the murder except as herein indicated. It would also explain the surprise of Lady Macbeth when she hears her husband is coming, and the king after him: "Thou'rt mad to say it," she says; and "the raven himself is hoarse that croaks the fatal entrance of Duncan under my battlements." The time and place had made themselves, then; and on hearing this it is that she suddenly changes from calm to vehement emotion, and makes that wonderful apostrophe to the spirits to "unsex her." She sees that all has been resolved, and that she has need of her utmost resolution.

There is no warrant of any kind that she, in the simple words, "And when goes hence," meant more than she said. It was the most natural question that she could possibly ask. Granting that she intended equally with him to commit the murder, what is more natural than that she should wish to know how long the king was to stay, so as to know how soon it was necessary to carry out the plan of murder, and what time there was in which to make all the arrangements? Not only Macbeth pauses after saying "To-morrow" (so, at least, is the punctuation in all editions), before adding "as he purposes," but Lady Macbeth, in her answer, says that she sees in his face that he intends that "never shall sun that morrow see." Yet, in the recitation of these parts on the stage, and as generally read, the meaning is given to Lady Macbeth's simple words; and Macbeth is made perfectly innocently to answer without showing in his look any "strange matter." But the king is coming close on his heels; there is no time to arrange details; and Macbeth goes away to receive him, saying, "We will speak further."

The characters, as exhibited in the next scenes, have been already sufficiently discussed. He, with his superstitions, his visions, his poetry, and his hesitations; she, with the stern determination of a woman who has "screwed her courage to the sticking point," is agitated by no visions; but who, feeling the necessity of immediate action, occupies herself in the arrangements of details, and thus dulls her conscience.

After all the excitements which have agitated Macbeth—after his soliloquy, in which he says, "there is no spur to prick the sides of his intent but only vaulting ambition;" but if he were sure of "success," he'd "jump the life to come"—there comes a moment when he either has or pretends to have a hesitation about "proceeding further in this business." He does not hesitate for conscience-sake, but because, being ambitious, he now would like to wear the golden opinions he has won, "in their newest gloss," and not "cast them aside so soon," before he has had the satisfaction of being wondered at and admired a little longer. Praise and high position he had gained, and his vanity was gratified. Before committing a hideous murder he naturally would pause. But he never pretends that this feeling comes from any moral sense. His mind had been too long strained with one thought; and, as in all men of excitable brain, there was a moment of reaction. He cannot see his way clear. He fears the effect of his crime. He does not see how it can be done so that he may avoid suspicion, and attain the object beyond the murder, and for which he commits it, without running too great risks, and thus exposing himself to the vengeance of the king's friends. He fears that his "bloody instructions may return to plague the inventor"—not hereafter, but "*here*." But what most troubles him is, that he cannot see the practical way, cannot arrange the details so as to secure a chance of avoiding suspicion. Here his wife comes to his aid. She has thought out a plan and arranged the details. She opposes sternly his proposal to abandon his design, for she knows that his hesitation is only for a moment, and that nothing less than to be king can ever satisfy him. Better, then, do the deed at once. His only opposition after this is, "If we should fail?" But as soon as he sees the feasibility of her plan, all his scruples are gone; he is more than convinced, he is delighted, and enters upon it with a joy which he does not pretend to conceal.

During all these scenes, up to the murder of Duncan, Lady Macbeth is labouring under an excitement of mind which sustains her in carrying out the design of her husband. The time is purposely made very short—only a few hours between the arrival of Duncan and his death—so that she may not break down. All is hurry and movement, and arrangement of detail. There is no time for reaction. The very necessity for immediate action acts as an irritant on the nerves, and strains all her thoughts and feelings to an unnatural pitch. Still, when the murder is on the point of being done, she keeps up her courage by drink; for the strain is almost too great. In this excited state her inflamed will has got completely the command of her; and to have it all over, and not caring about the dreadful design longer, she says, that had Duncan "not resembled my father as he slept, I had done it." But though she can talk of dashing out the brains of her babe while it was smiling in her face, she was not, even in this excitement, able to strike Duncan, because she thought he looked like her father. Her woman's hand would have failed her had she attempted it. But all her powers are bound up in this one design. She has come to a violent determination, and this she will carry out, come what may. She thrusts aside all compunction of conscience, and makes such a noise by action in her brain, that its still small voice cannot be heard.

Macbeth, on the contrary, is of a colder and more brutal nature. His determination is sullen, and it lies like an immovable rock, on which the flames of his imagination burn like momentary fires of straw, and over which his superstitious visions pass like clouds or fogs, and then clear away, leaving the rock unchanged. Just before he commits the murder, Banquo comes in and tells him that the king

> "hath been in unusual pleasure, and
> Sent forth great largess to your offices:
> This diamond he greets your wife withal,
> By the name of most kind hostess; and shut up
> In measureless content."

But this does not touch Macbeth, nor induce a moment's hesitation. Banquo then speaks of the three weird sisters, and says, "To you they have show'd some truth;" and Macbeth answers falsely:

> "I think not of them;
> Yet, when we can entreat an hour to serve,
> Would spend it in some words upon that business,
> If you would grant the time."

Thus, cold and collected, he bids him "Good repose," sends off the servant, and waits for the bell to ring, which is the sign that all is ready for him to murder Duncan. In this interval we have his three characteristic features brought out one after the other: the cloudy vision of the air-drawn dagger; then the straw-fire of his poetry about Hecate and withered murder's sentinel the wolf, and "Tarquin's ravishing strides;" and, as these clear off, the stern sullen resolution underneath—"Whiles I threat he lives;" "I go, and it is done."

When the murder is done, they are equally distinct in character; she energetic and practical, he visionary and superstitious; and so they part.

Thus far, be it observed, Lady Macbeth has supposed her husband to be merely "infirm of purpose;" but the next scene is to open her eyes to a glimpse of his real character.

Macbeth has become perfectly calm and cold again in a few minutes, and makes his appearance immediately after the knocking. He is completely master of himself, offers to conduct Macduff to the king, and when Macduff says he knows "it will be a joyful trouble" to him, answers like a proverb, calmly, "The labour we delight in physics pain." The king is then found dead, and the noise brings Lady Macbeth from her room. What a difference is now visible in the way in which she and he speak and act! When Banquo says, "Our royal master's murdered," she cries out, "Woe! alas! what, in our house?" and says not a word more. Macbeth, however, who is only afraid of shadows, but who, with the daylight, has no fear of looking at dead bodies, or adding one or two more with his sword, goes to the room of Duncan, and then reappears, without the faintest shadow of feeling, and makes a little hypocritical poem on the event:

> "Had I but died an hour before this chance,
> I had liv'd a blessed time; for, from this instant,
> There's nothing serious in mortality:
> All is but toys: renown and grace is dead;
> The wine of life is drawn, and the mere lees
> Is left this vault to brag of.
> What is amiss?" (says Donalbain).

And Macbeth cries, "You are, and do not know it. The spring, the head, the fountain of your blood is stopped; the very source of it is stopped."

This is Macbeth's rant and fustian. He has no feeling, and, as usual, he makes the pretence of poetry serve him. The head, the spring, the fountain, the source is stopped, is stopped.

And this stuff he recites coolly, although he has but a moment before wantonly killed the two grooms; nay, he does not mention it until afterwards, on their being spoken of by Lenox, when this hypocritical villain cries:

> "Oh, yet I do repent me of my fury,
> That I did kill them.
> *Macd.* Wherefore did you so?
> *Macb.* Who can be wise, amaz'd, temperate, and furious,
> Loyal and neutral, in a moment? No man:
> The expedition of my violent love
> Outran the pauser reason.—Here lay Duncan,
> His *silver* skin lac'd with his *golden* blood;
> And his gash'd stabs look'd like a breach in nature,
> For ruin's wasteful entrance: there the murderers,
> Steep'd in the colours of their trade, their daggers
> Unmannerly breech'd with gore: who could refrain,
> That had a heart to love, and in that heart
> Courage to make his love known?"

During this amazing speech, in which he poetises so elaborately, and with such curious artifice coldly paints the picture of the man and friend he had just murdered, Lady Macbeth had been looking and listening in silence. Suddenly, for the first time, she sees what her husband really is; she sees that he has neither heart nor conscience; for no man possessing either could have acted or talked as he has since the murder of Duncan. So far from having any feeling of shame or remorse, he, without provocation, wantonly, and with no sufficient object, has added two other murders to it; and, with a cold-blooded artificial hypocrisy, he paints in his stilted way the scene of Duncan's death, and has command of himself enough to seek out elaborate and high-flown phrases. But Lady Macbeth, whose courage, stimulated by excitement, had carried her through the murder, now suddenly breaks down. This new revelation of her husband's character, and the ghastly picture which he summons up before her of the scene of the murder, are too much for her. She swoons, loses all consciousness, and is carried out. In her violent excitement, while there was something practical to busy her mind and her body with, she could carry back the daggers and smear the grooms with blood; but she could not bear the vivid remembrance of it when there was nothing to do, and when the excitement was over: as women will go through extreme dangers, stand at the surgeon's table during terrible operations, be great and strong in a great crisis, and then suddenly faint and fall when the work is over, unable to bear the remembrance of what they have gone through.

This swooning of Lady Macbeth is the crisis of her nature. From this time forward she is no more what she has appeared; we hear no more urging of Macbeth to strengthen his throne by other crimes; no more taunts by her that he is infirm of purpose; no more allusions to his amiable weaknesses of character. She has begun to know him and to fear him. She only endeavours to tranquillise him and content him with what he has got. But still she does not know him; for his nature, before hidden, like secret writing, comes out little by little before the fire of his heated ambition and superstitious fears.

At this swooning-point the two characters of Lady Macbeth and her husband cross each other. She has thus far only made the running for Macbeth, and he now takes up the race and passes her; she not only does not follow, but withdraws. Henceforth he rushes to his goal alone; alone he arranges the death of Banquo and Fleance.

When next they meet she is no longer the same person we have known; she feels the gnawing tooth of remorse; she is calmed and cowed by what she has done:

> "Nought's had, all's spent,
> When our desire is got without content:
> 'Tis safer to be that which we destroy,
> Than, by destruction, dwell in doubtful joy."

And as Macbeth enters she endeavours to tranquillise his mind. She has his confidence no longer; he avoids her, and keeps alone after the murder of the king. She, not yet aware of the abysses of his nature, and little imagining that he has been plotting the murder of Banquo, supposes that the secret of his perturbations, of the solitude he now seeks, and of his avoidance of her, is the remorse that he begins to feel, and says as he enters:

> "How now, my lord? why do you keep alone,
> Of sorriest fancies your companions making?
> Using those thoughts which should indeed have died
> With them they think on. Things without remedy
> Should be without regard: what's done is done."

His answer shows it is no remorse which is haunting him; his sorry fancies are new plots of murder:

> "We have scotch'd the snake, not kill'd it;"

and we are still "in danger of her former tooth."

> "But let
> The frame of things disjoint, both the worlds suffer,
> Ere we will eat our meals in *fear*, and sleep
> In the affliction of these terrible dreams,
> That shake us nightly: better be with the dead,
> Whom we, to gain our place, have sent to peace,
> Than on the torture of the mind to lie
> In restless ecstasy. Duncan is in his grave;
> After life's fitful fever, he sleeps well;
> Treason has done his worst: nor steel, nor poison,
> Malice domestic, foreign levy, nothing,
> Can touch him further!"

Here is one of those cases where he uses his poetry as a cloak to his real thoughts. Yet despite his hypocrisy, which takes in his wife, his real meaning is clear. He would rather die than go on in this fear: rather be like Duncan, whom they have at all events "sent to peace," and whom nothing can "touch further," than on "this torture of the mind to lie in restless ecstasy." What is this "fear"? what is this "torture of the mind"? Is it, as Lady Macbeth supposes, from remorse? Oh, no! he tells us himself what it is; it is solely because Banquo and Fleance are alive:

> "O, full of scorpions is my mind, dear wife!
> Thou know'st that Banquo and his Fleance lives."

This it is that tortures him, and this only.

> "But in them nature's copy's not eterne,"

says she; meaning, as she has throughout this scene, solely to console him and draw his thoughts away. They may die; a thousand accidents may happen to them; you may outlive them; don't torture yourself with vain fears. "*There's* comfort yet," he cries, "they are assailable;" and now, after his old fashion, he breaks into poetry:

"Then be thou *jocund:* ere the bat hath flown
His cloister'd flight; ere, to black Hecate's summons,
The shard-borne beetle, with his drowsy hums,
Hath rung night's yawning peal, there shall be done
A deed of dreadful note."

"What's to be done?" she cries; for having completely misunderstood him through all the previous part of this interview, she completely fails to see what he now means. But he has no longer confidence in her; he knows she would not uphold him in this new crime; and so, with caressing words, and probably with some caressing act, he answers her:

"Be innocent of the knowledge, dearest chuck,
Till thou applaud the deed."

How could she suspect his real meaning? This murdering hypocrite had just told her that Banquo was coming to the feast that night, and bade her be jovial, and said to her,

"Let your remembrances apply to Banquo,
Present him eminence both with eye and tongue."

And this he proposes to her after having just left the murderers whom he has hired to waylay and kill Banquo, and entertaining no real doubt in his mind that Banquo will never reach the supper—certainly never reach it unless his plot miscarries. Well might she "marvel at his words." What follows is full of poetry and wickedness; but it is plain that he was a mystery to her now, a riddle which she could not read.

The banquet-scene now comes, and Macbeth, believing that he has secured the death of Banquo and Fleance, is happy, until the murderers come in and tell him that Fleance has escaped. This upsets him:

"Then comes *my fit* again: I had else been perfect:
Whole as the marble, founded as the rock;
As broad, and general, as the casing air:
Now I am cabin'd, cribbed, confin'd, bound in
To saucy doubts and fears."

So he poetises his condition, for superstitious fears always inflame his imagination; but he cannot regain his composure; his "fit" is on him, as "it hath been from his youth." He conjures up the phantom of Banquo to threaten him and his throne, and this ghost shakes him with superstitious terror. Lady Macbeth, to whom it is invisible, rouses herself at this; and not only not comprehending these starts and flaws of fear, but having a contempt for him, endeavours to recall him to himself by sharp words; but it is useless, his fit will not leave him, and the company is dismissed in confusion. When they have gone, Lady Macbeth's spirit and courage, which were momentary, have fled. She does not taunt him, but soothes him. He, as soon as he recovers himself, begins with Macduff, whom he also means to murder:

> "Strange things I have in head, that will to hand,
> Which must be acted, ere they may be scann'd."

To this she only says, not imagining his meaning,

> "You lack the season of all natures, sleep."

Henceforward Lady Macbeth disappears; we hear nothing of her save in the terrible sleep-walking scene; she is dying of remorse. But Macbeth goes to the weird sisters, to learn whether "Banquo's issue shall ever reign in this kingdom." They answer, "Seek not to know:" and he cries out, "I *will* be satisfied; deny me this, and our eternal curse fall on you." And when they show him the issue of Banquo, kings, he is enraged beyond control, and curses them. Henceforth for him no hesitations, no delays. He speaks directly enough now. From this moment,

> "The firstlings of my heart shall be
> The firstlings of my hand. And even now
> To crown my thoughts with acts, be it thought and done:
> The castle of Macduff I will surprise;
> Seize upon Fife; give to the edge o' the sword
> His wife, his babes, and all unfortunate souls
> That trace his line. No boasting like a fool;
> This deed I'll do before this purpose cool:
> But no more *sights!*"

And no more *sights* he has; but he is still haunted by fears. And when "the English power is near, led on by Malcolm, his uncle Siward, and the good Macduff," burning for revenge, Macbeth's spirit falters. He rushes into violent rages and then subsides into vague fears, and then endeavours to strengthen his heart by recalling the mysterious promises of the weird sisters that he shall not fall by the hand of any man of woman born, or before Birnam wood come to Dunsinane; but, do all he can, "he cannot buckle his distempered cause within the belt of rule," though he declares,

> "The mind I sway by and the heart I bear
> Shall never sagg with doubt, nor shake with fear."

Still he does fear; and in one of his dispirited moods, after blazing out at the messenger who tells him of the approach of Birnam wood,

> "The devil damn the black, thou cream-fac'd loon!
> Where got'st thou that goose look?"

He says, finding that there are ten thousand men coming to attack him, and his followers are not stanch:

> "This push
> Will cheer me ever, or disseat me now.
> I have lived long enough: my way of life
> Is fallen into the sear, the yellow leaf:
> And that which should accompany old age,
> As honour, love, obedience, troops of friends,
> I must not look to have; but, in their stead,
> Curses, not loud, but deep, mouth-honour, breath,
> Which the poor heart would fain deny."

But in a moment he is himself again, and cries:

> "I'll fight till from my bones the flesh be hack'd.—
> Give me my armour."

In this mood the illness and death of the queen is nothing to him: he fights bravely to the end; though, superstitious to the last, "his better part of man" is cowed by the knowledge that Macduff "was from his mother's womb untimely ripped," and so not of woman born.

And so, by the sword of Macduff, perishes the worst villain, save Iago, that Shakespeare ever drew.

We have called the witches the projections of Macbeth's evil thoughts, and suggested that they were only objective representations of his inward being. To this it may be objected that they were seen also by Banquo. But this may well be; for Banquo also seems to have had evil intentions, which are vaguely hinted at in the play. He constantly harps on the idea that his children are to be kings. Approaching the castle of Inverness at night, before the murder of the king, he says:

> "Hold, take my sword. . . . .
> A heavy summons lies like lead upon me,
> And yet I would not sleep:—Merciful powers!
> Restrain in me the cursed thoughts that nature
> Gives way to in repose!—Give me my sword."

Meeting then Macbeth, he gives him the diamond sent by the king to Lady Macbeth; and after speaking of Duncan's "measureless content," he says:

> "I dreamt last night of the weird sisters:
> To you they have shown some truth."

At which Macbeth proposes an interview, to

> "Spend it in some words upon *that* business."

To which he readily consents.

The "cursed thoughts," then, are connected with his dreams about the weird sisters.

At his next appearance the same thoughts agitate him in Macbeth's palace at Fores. His first words are—in soliloquy—

"Thou hast it now, king, Cawdor, Glamis, all,
As the weird women promised; and, I fear,
Thou playd'st most foully for't: yet it was said
It should not stand in thy posterity;
But that myself should be the root and father
Of many kings. If there come truth from them
(As upon thee, Macbeth, their speeches shine),
Why, by the verities on thee made good,
May they not be my oracles as well,
And set me up in hope? But, hush; no more."

When it is recollected that, after this scene on the heath with the soldiers, these are nearly all the words we have from Banquo, it seems to be pretty clearly indicated that his thoughts at least were not perfectly honest and what they should have been.

The weird sisters are but outward personifications of the evil thoughts conceived and fermenting in the brains of Banquo and Macbeth; both high in station, both generals in the king's army, both friends, and both nourishing evil wishes. They are visible only to these two friends; and though they are represented as having an outer existence independent of them, they are, metaphysically speaking, but embodiments of the hidden thoughts and desires of Banquo and Macbeth: as such they are a new and terrible creation, differing from the vulgar flesh-and-blood witches of Middleton. They look not like the inhabitants of the earth; they vanish into thin air; wild, vague, mysterious, they come and go, like devilish thoughts that tempt us, and take shape before us, as if they had come from the other world. The devils that haunt us and tempt us come out of ourselves, like the weird sisters of Macbeth.

Art. III.—HEALTH OF THE BRITISH ARMY AT HOME AND ABROAD.

Report of Commissioners on the Sanitary Condition of the Army. Parliamentary Proceedings. 1858.

Report of Commissioners on the Sanitary State of the Army in India. Parliamentary Proceedings. 1863.

Army Sanitary Administration, and its Reform under the late Lord Herbert. By Florence Nightingale. 1862.

Sanitary Condition of the Army. By the Right Hon. Sidney Herbert. 1859.

Hansard's Parliamentary Debates. Vol. clxv., pp. 966 et seq. 1862.

Mortality of the British Army. Illustrated by Diagrams and Tables. Prepared by Miss Nightingale.

To a people whose civil rights are secure, whose political liberties have been long established and are now beyond the reach of imaginable danger, whose Government provides them peace and order, and among whom the administration of justice is prompt, efficient, and beyond suspicion, it would seem that scarcely any subject of public importance remains which concerns them more closely, or ought to interest them more vividly, than the condition of the army which defends their homes and is recruited from their ranks. It is the guardian of their national security; it is intrusted with the vindication of their national honour; their power and grandeur, the extension of their empire, the maintenance of their influence in the councils of the world, the protection of their citizens in distant lands, depend in the last resort upon its efficiency; they are taxed for its support, and taxed to such an extent that every man of property, and almost every consumer of ordinary commodities, actually feels the burden. Of an Englishman's annual contributions to the *active* expenditure of the State, about three-fifths go to the military and naval forces of the country. All classes are concerned: the army is recruited from the lower class; it is paid, clothed, and fed by the middle class; and it is officered from the higher class.

Again: if there be any section of the community whom we are bound by every motive to care for with the greatest vigilance, on whose condition the best forethought, the keenest science, the most conscientious moral consideration, should be ceaselessly and anxiously brought to bear, it is the army. And this for three special reasons. The soldier is a peculiarly valuable, a peculiarly costly, and a peculiarly helpless animal. If he be not courageous, stubborn, admirably disciplined, and thoroughly effective, he may be the cause of much turbulence and mischief at home, and our dearest and highest national concerns will suffer—nay, even our national position and security may be endangered. Of all our creations he is, when perfect, that in which the best result is produced out of the poorest materials. Most recruits are drawn from the class of whom all communities are ashamed and afraid. The finished first-rate British soldiers, into whom such recruits are often formed, are citizens of whom any community might be proud. The process is a costly one, so costly and so troublesome that the article, when produced, ought to be hoarded almost like a gem. A thoroughly trained and disciplined soldier, any thing like a veteran, takes many years to create, and costs about 100*l.* every year. He is worth all that and more when obtained and perfected; but if he dies or is squandered, the raw recruit who is to replace him is comparatively of the scantiest value. Then, again, of all classes there is none whose individuality is so completely merged and taken from him as the soldier. Every thing is ordered for him, every thing is done for him; he is allowed no will of his own; the place in which he is to sleep, the food he is to eat, the clothes he is to wear, the mode in which he is to employ every moment of time, are all regulated for him by absolute decree; he may not murmur, he may not remonstrate, he may not give an opinion, he is never taken into council; he is at the total and despotic disposal of another; he is literally and almost dreadfully at the mercy of the ignorance, caprice, injustice, temper, or want of consideration of his immediate superior. We need scarcely point out what a terrible weight of responsibility this absorbed and dictated existence imposes on those superiors, and how heavy is the sin of those who from selfishness, or thoughtlessness, or avoidable errors, or obstinate ignorance and wilfulness, or bad passions, or any other defect, either neglect their duties or abuse their powers. Those who have fellow-creatures so utterly and helplessly dependent upon them ought of all men to be most unselfish, most vigilant, most scrupulously considerate and just.

But this is not all. The life of the British soldier is an unnatural one,—actually to a sad extent, necessarily perhaps to a great extent. At the age of the most imperious passions he is precluded from marrying save in rare exceptions; at the age of temptation he is thrown where temptations are rife, and where there is little or nothing to counteract them, among hundreds of others as weak, as ill-educated, and as tempted as himself; at a most impressible period of life he is removed from domestic influences, and submitted to barrack influences; at the age of activity and mobility of mind he is subjected to a daily routine rife with the most dreary and killing *ennui*,—divided between tedious formalities and absolute inaction. Probably nothing could go far to counteract the evil effects of this unnatural life except war and work; but war comes seldom, and work our military authorities appear resolutely, and, as we believe, insanely and wickedly, to oppose.

"It must be remembered that an army is a body to which the state stands in peculiar relations. It is the instrument by which the state protects itself, and for this purpose of protecting the community the army—and the same remark applies to the navy—is placed in circumstances of life which are totally different from those of the rest of the community, and are quite exceptional and abnormal. There can be no doubt that the natural life of man is domestic; as a rule, every grown-up man in town and country has his wife and children about him. The army is cut off from this domestic state, and put into a wholly artificial form of life. We mould our instrument exactly according to our own uses, without reference to the wants within the instrument itself, the natural individual requirements of those whom we use as our instrument. There can be no doubt that we *must* have a standing army, and that an army cannot be a community living in a domestic manner. But this being the case, the state is certainly under peculiar obligations to these men, whom it thus uses as one great corporate tool. It places these men, entirely for its own convenience, in circumstances of the greatest peril to themselves—peril moral and physical. These men, who are no better than the rest of the community, and a certain proportion of them very wild and impulsive fellows, must either exert such a command over their passions as belongs to philosophers—we might almost say anchorites—or they fall into vice, and, with vice, into terrible disease. That is the alternative which the state puts before them. The alternative is undoubtedly a hard one, a very hard one; and the power which imposes it upon them is under an obligation, as a matter of common benevolence, to see that it does not work more mischievously than can be helped; that it does not produce a greater amount of disaster than by reasonable expedients it can be restricted to. The state has brought these men together, has placed them in this abnormal and eccentric condition, has made them its own instrument for one great purpose. Having made the life of these men, then, thus irregular and exceptional, and exposed them to peculiar danger, the state is especially bound to look after their health, to counteract the bad causes at work as much as it can, and to reduce the source of disease to the smallest possible dimensions. We can hardly think of immense physical evil, and of physical evil brought on to a large extent by our own arrangements, made in subservience to the necessities of the community, but still our own arrangements, without feeling that we are bound to take all the precautions possible to modify this evil. Society at large must look after itself, its temptations are of its own raising, and it has no right to expect the state to look after it; but here is an exceptional body, a creature of state necessity. It has peculiar claims on the state. If remedial hospitals, then, devoted to the reception of an unfortunate class, can largely modify this danger and diminish the root of disease in the army and navy, there can be no serious objection to the state supporting such institutions in the quarters where they are wanted."

Well: all subjects have their innings in England sooner or later. Sooner or later Englishmen always awake to their duties and responsibilities. And some years ago they did awake—some of them at least, and the late Sidney Herbert among the first—to a sense of the condition of the soldier, to a perception of how much they owed him, and how little they had paid. A searching inquiry was instituted into the matter, especially in reference to his health and comfort, and the result was sufficiently startling. Since then the matter has not slept, and the Blue Books just issued on the "Sanitary State of the Indian Army" are the last consequence of the public attention which was aroused some years ago. Before examining these, however, we wish to recall to the recollection of our readers the facts in reference to the mortality of the English army at home which came to light in 1859, and the practical effect which has followed those disclosures. The various publications we have placed at the head of this article give us ample materials for a very definite picture of the state of affairs; which is appalling enough.

The idea which naturally occurs to the uninformed mind, when the mortality of the army is mentioned, is that soldiers die because they are killed; that they are slain in battle or die of their wounds; and that it is their *métier*, a natural concomitant of their profession, thus to end their days. Nothing can be further from the truth. It has been stated by the sanitary reformers, with Mr. Chadwick at their head, that during all our Napoleonic wars, which lasted on and off for twenty years, we only lost 19,000 men upon the field; and the statement, startling as it is, was authenticated by reference to official documents, and, so far as we are aware, has never been contradicted. Sidney Herbert reminds us that of 405,000 French troops that crossed the Niemen to invade Russia in 1812, only

55,000 re-crossed it five months afterwards; and that of the balance of 350,000 lost, only 54,000 fell of killed and wounded at Borodino, and not more, it is believed, than 46,000 in minor actions. Miss Nightingale shows in carefully constructed tables that in the Crimean war, which lasted two and a quarter years, and included one of the most disastrous sieges and three of the hardest battles we have ever fought, the aggregate annual mortality among our troops reached 22·78 per cent—only 3 per cent of which came under the denomination of violent deaths. Lastly, it appears from the Report of the Royal Commission just published, that even our bloodiest wars in India seldom raised the average mortality more than from 70 to 84 per 1000, or in former days from 90 to 117. "Out of 9467 men dying among regiments in India prior to the mutiny, or sent out in 1857-58, only 586 were killed in action or died of wounds"—scarcely more than 6 per cent. Our soldiers die of disease, and of preventible disease; and they die—or at least used to die—at a fearful rate—far faster than any other class of their countrymen. Yet they ought to be peculiarly healthy. They are all picked men, and are subjected to a rigorous medical examination before they are borne upon the rolls; they have the best medical attendance gratis; and they are clothed, lodged, and fed at the cost of the nation, and with no sparing of expense, as our annual estimates testify. The following comparison, which we extract from Sidney Herbert's paper, gives the main facts:

Annual Deaths per 1000 of Men at the Soldiers' Ages.

London fire-brigade	7·0
Metropolitan police	7·6
Navy on home stations	8·8
City police	8·9
Healthy districts of England	7·7
Agricultural labourers	8·0
All England	9·2
Twenty-five large towns	12·0
Household cavalry	11·0
Dragoon-guards	13·3
Infantry of the line	18·7
Foot-guards	20·4

The mean rate of mortality of the entire army was 17·5 per 1000. Thus the British troops—a body of men out of whom all diseased and ill-organised subjects have been carefully eliminated to begin with, and who enjoy the special supervision of the state—die twice as fast as average Englishmen, and more than twice as fast as policemen and other selected bodies; while the Foot-Guards, the finest and most carefully chosen of all our troops, die faster than any other, and nearly three times as fast as the corps commanded by Sir Richard Mayne, which lives in the same city and performs nearly the same duties.

The causes of this excess of mortality were easily discoverable, and were clearly pointed out, and the existence and tolerated continuance of them were in the highest degree discreditable to the authorities. We have no intention of doing more than simply enumerate them. It was shown that the food of the soldiers, though ample in quantity and not defective in kind, was so unvaried as to become almost unsanitary, through monotonous insipidity; their daily life was so dreadfully idle and irksome as to affect materially the vital energies; they had few duties, little amusement, and no work; and, as a natural result, intemperance and debauchery were their habitual resources, and the number always in hospital from syphilitic affections was enormous. But the *teterrima causa* was the condition of the hospitals and barracks, and mainly the bad construction and defective ventilation of the latter. The degree to which the most ordinary and best-established principles of *hygiène* had been perpetually neglected in these buildings, when once made public, appeared utterly incredible.

The late Lord Herbert perceived the full importance of the subject, and devoted his whole energies, both in and out of office, to the rectification of the evils which had been brought to light: and among all his assistants in this great work none were more efficient or more indefatigable than Florence Nightingale. It is scarcely too much to say that the life of the one and the health of the other have been sacrificed in the soldier's cause. The success which has attended their exertions has been signal and most encouraging. By simply following out the plainest rules of health, by carrying common sense and common science into the daily routine and daily *entourage* of the soldier's life — though regular and full work, the most efficient of all sanitary influences, is still withheld through the irrational prejudices prevalent in high quarters—they have succeeded in reducing the mortality of the troops at home *below* that which obtains in ordinary civil occupations, instead of being, as formerly, more than double. The annual deaths per 1000 among the infantry of the line *was* 18, it *is* now 8½; the rate among the English male population between fifteen and forty-five years of age is 9¾. Sir G. C. Lewis, in moving the army estimates in March 1862, gave the following most encouraging contrast between the present and the past. More attention has been paid to cleanliness and ventilation in barracks; marriage has been less discouraged; hospital and medical attendance has been improved; clothing and diet have been amended; and recreations of various sorts have been provided; and the result has been as follows:

Annual Deaths per 1000 *among Troops serving at Home.*

	1830-36.	1859-60.
Household cavalry	14	6
Cavalry of the line	15	7
Royal artillery	15	6
Foot-guards	21	9
Infantry of the line	18	9

Annual Deaths per 1000 *Soldiers in the Colonies.*

	1837-56.	1859-60.
Gibraltar	13	9
Malta	18	14
Ionian Islands	16	10
Bermuda	35	11
Canada	17	10
Jamaica	60	17
Ceylon	39	27

In a word, before the Crimean war we *murdered* our troops at home, by mismanagement and neglect, to the number of more than 2000 annually. The deaths in fifteen years, 1839-1853, were 58,139; they ought only to have been, and would now be, 16,211. In those years, therefore, official ignorance, incapacity, and carelessness *slew* 41,928 trained soldiers, and kept at least an equal number constantly in hospital; costing the country a sum probably not less in that period than 5,000,000*l.* sterling.

What has been done in Great Britain and in the Colonies may be done, on an equivalent scale, in India also; and reform is even more needed there than here, for that country will henceforth be, in all likelihood, our chief military field, and the great drain upon our recruiting powers. From 70,000 to 80,000 men we shall require always to maintain there, and at times even more. The lives of our soldiers, therefore, in India are peculiarly valuable, and hitherto seem to have been peculiarly disregarded. The commission issued by Lord Stanley in 1859 has not reported one hour too soon; but it has reported well, and in great detail. It has laid before the public a series of facts which will arouse the most painful interest, and it has concluded its labours with a number of practical recommendations, which the circumstances it has brought to light naturally suggest and irresistibly enforce.

It was to be expected that nearly all the causes of military sickness and mortality which prevail at home would prevail in India in an aggravated form. The climate is dangerous in itself, and neither official vigilance nor official skill and knowledge are likely to be increased by distance from home. Of course, therefore, the mortality in regiments stationed in the East was sure to be much greater than at home, for India is dangerous even to civilians; but *how* much greater the public could scarcely have anticipated. The deaths in the British army at home were 17 per 1000; those in the British troops serving in India for forty years averaged 69 per 1000; of which, according to Sir A. Tulloch, about 10 per 1000 were attributable to our wars. That is to say, the mortality was four times greater than among soldiers in England, and eight times greater than among ordinary Englishmen at the soldier's period of life. But this is not the whole extent of the mischief; for it appears that out of an aggregate force of 73,000, nearly one-twelfth, or 5880 men, are always in hospital, which is about six regiments out of *seventy*. Now, as the commissioners show conclusively that both the sickness and the mortality might be reduced to the rate which prevails among civilians in India, it follows that the excess of sickness is equal to a loss of 3800 men, and the excess of annual deaths is equal to 3500 men; that the two together amount to the strength of more than *seven* entire regiments, and that the cost thus incurred to the public is not short of 800,000*l.* per annum.

The Commissioners first explain their grounds for assuming why the rate of mortality might be vastly reduced, and then enumerate the causes which make it now so high. It is excessive, it is gratuitous, it is clearly not attributable to unavoidable influences of climate, because it varies enormously at different stations in India, among different ranks, and in different occupations. Thus, "the station at Trichinopoly is within the tropics, in Southern India, and is reckoned one of the hottest to which troops are exposed. The mean temperature is 82°." Yet the rate of mortality per 1000 was 44 for 19 years, 31 for 11 years, and only 20 for the last 4 years (1850-1853) of which we have returns. "Crossing the Ghauts, we come to Cannanmore, low on the Malabar coast, where the rain-fall is 140 inches, and the temperature still tropical; the mean rate was 21 per 1000 for 10 years." At Bangalore it was 20; at Belgaum, where it used to be 28, and even 41, it has fallen to 19; at Kirkee it ranged from 6 to 19; and at Poonah from 11 to 26. Now compare these figures with those recorded of the various stations on the Ganges, by the unhealthy delta of which river all the Bengal regiments enter India, and in which they contract diseases which they carry with them to other districts. At Fort-William the mortality was 102 per 1000 during 10 years, and for longer periods has seldom ranged below 60 or 70. At Dumdum it was 77; at Chinsurah 54 and 70; at Dinapore 78; at Cawnpore from 66 to 91; at Meerut from 32 to 44. The Calcutta stations are naturally the worst. "The 29th regiment of foot arrived in India on July 29, 1842, and was stationed at Chinsurah, where it lost 106 men before April 1843. Proceeding to Ghazeepore, it lost 158 men one year, and 260 the next." It then went into a bloody campaign, and lost 190 more in action. It remained in India 17 years, losing 1091 men in that time, of whom one half died in the first three years.

The health of the officers is far better than that of the rank and file. Yet they are not originally more carefully selected or endowed with better constitutions; and they are subject to the same severe heat, and to perhaps even greater exposure, and certainly to more anxiety. While the soldiers die at the rate of 69 per 1000, the officers only die at the rate of 38 per 1000; and even this proportion varies greatly in the several presidencies, and in the two divisions of the army. Thus, among the military officers of the Company, the annual mortality was 31 for Bengal, 39 for Bombay, and 45 for Madras. Among the officers of the Royal army, it was 34 in Bengal, 33 in Bombay, and 36 in Madras. The case of the civil servants of the Company is still more instructive. They are as a rule pretty hard-worked men; they have often to sit whole days together in crowded courts; they are dispersed over all districts, and generally in the same stations and towns as the military men with whose sanitary condition theirs is brought into comparison, and of course the climate is just as trying and insalubrious to civilians as to soldiers. Yet their death-rate has only averaged, for a long series of years, 20 per 1000; or, to give it more in detail, it ranges from 20 to 41 according to age, in the Bengal presidency; from 24 to 26 in Bombay; and from 14 to 18 in Madras. The Commissioners therefore conclude, and we think with perfect justice, that "the experience of the civil service, of the military officers, and their wives and children, of the English troops in many stations, and of the native troops, proves that in the present state of India the mortality of the British troops there can be reduced to the rate of 20 in 1000. Any excess beyond this is due, not to the climate, but to other causes."

What are these causes? There seems to be little doubt and little difference of opinion on this branch of the subject, either among the experienced witnesses or the judicial Commissioners.

The bad influences to which the excessive military mortality in India is to be attributed are very obvious, very powerful, all greatly mitigable, and nearly all removable with time, care, sense, and science.

1. In the first place, it is found that very young soldiers suffer most and die fastest in the climate of Hindoostan, and that the longer a man stays there, the more severely does the climate tell upon him. Nearly all observers agree on this point, which may be considered to be established beyond dispute. Every year the soldier becomes less and less able to resist the enervating combination of heat and moisture. He becomes enfeebled by it, not inured to it. The Commissioners, therefore, recommend that in future no recruits shall be sent out under the age of 21 years, that they shall complete their drill at home, and, in order that they may arrive in good health, that they shall be shipped so as to reach India in November, and that no spirits, but only malt-liquor, shall be served out to them during the voyage. It is also thought desirable that, as a rule, service in India should not be prolonged beyond ten years.

2. The locality and the construction of the barracks in which the troops are placed are unanimously pronounced to be the most fatal influences to which they are exposed. It appears that most of the military stations were not *selected* at all, in any intelligible meaning of the word, but were retained and made permanent simply because they chanced to be the spots on which the troops were first landed or located, or where temporary accommodation was most easily found. Others were chosen for purely strategic or political reasons, without the slightest reference to sanitary considerations, and without any consultation with the medical authorities, and have since been kept up, as those in the West Indies were for so long a period, in spite of every warning, and from pure stupid and wilful inertia. It happens, therefore, as might be anticipated, that a great proportion of these stations "are situated in low, damp, unhealthy positions, deficient in means of natural drainage, or on river-banks, close to unwholesome native cities or towns." A more careful selection of the locality for our barracks is therefore the first point to be attended to. "Hill stations" are strongly urged by Sir Ronald Martin; and no doubt, as a rule, these have been found more healthy, *cæteris paribus*, than those on the plains, though by no means invariably so; but political and military authorities both agree that, in order to hold the country and govern it effectually, not more than one-third of our whole force could be stationed in the hilly districts, properly so called. This, however, would of itself be a vast resource, by reason of the frequent reliefs of enfeebled or invalided regiments which it

would render possible. Independently, however, of such stations, an immense change might be effected by removing the troops who must continue to be stationed in the plains to *the highest ground in the vicinity* of their duties and their dangers, instead of (as is often the case now) placing them in the lowest and the worst. It appears that such moderate elevations are to be found scattered over even the flattest parts of India, and a very few thousand, or even hundred, feet are sufficient to rise out of the malaria of the plains, as well as to afford facilities for thorough drainage and sewerage, and other sanitary arrangements. Many of the most pestiferous stations might probably be abandoned at once.

At the same time the Commissioners declare that it is not easy to pronounce what stations are necessarily and inherently insalubrious, since nearly all are surrounded by removable and gratuitous sources of disease. The description given of the beastly and wretched condition of the generality of the stations, and the ground immediately around them, is actually sickening and most disgraceful. The filth from both camps and towns is allowed to soak into the soil, and thus to poison both the air and the water for acres and for miles around;—and this in a moist climate and under a tropical sun! Indian cities are proverbially nasty, British camps in India appear not to be much better; the two together would seem to be carefully contrived hot-beds of pestilence. The following is the summary given in the Report:

"The towns and bazaars in the vicinity of lines are in the worst possible sanitary state, undrained, unpaved, badly cleansed, often teeming with offensive and dangerous nuisances; with tanks, pools, and badly-made surface-gutters, containing filth and foul water; the area overcrowded with houses put up without order or regularity; the external ventilation obstructed, and the houses overcrowded with people; no public latrines, and every square plot of ground covered with filth in consequence; no water-supply, except what is obtained from bad shallow wells and unwholesome or doubtful tanks. These towns and bazaars are the earliest seats of epidemics, especially of cholera, before their ravages extended to the European troops in the vicinity.

None of the stations have any subsoil drainage; and there are no other means of removing the rain-fall except surface gutters. The ground about the lines is often broken up in pits and hollows filled with stagnant water, or it is traversed by unwholesome ravines or nullahs. In certain states of the weather and wind, nuisance is experienced in the lines from these causes, and from the foul state of neighbouring native dwellings. Many of the older stations are irregularly built; and the buildings are so arranged as to interfere with each other's ventilation."

In all these respects the hill stations are often as bad as those on the plains. The Simla stations, as well as some of those in the Neilgherries, are disgraceful. At Simla, which should be the sanatorium of India, "the 'conservancy' is described as having been as bad as could be; the ravines full of dead animals and the ordure of many thousand natives. There are no public conveniences. The water supply was scanty, and liable to pollution. The effluvia from the ravines was as strong as on going into a sewer." . . . . "At Mount Aboo (in the Simla group) the barracks are erected in a malarious gully; at Nynee Tâl, 7600 feet above the sea, the huts have been built in a narrow defile, where the earth is damp, and a perfect marsh during rains, and where the huts are exposed to violent gusts of wind. The bazaars are filthy and overcrowded. There are neither drains nor latrines, and the stench is at times overpowering, causing nuisance in the barracks." Generally speaking, the hospitals are about as ill-situated and ill-drained as the barracks. Was there ever such a sinful state of things?

3. The barracks in which the troops in India reside are stated to be, almost without exception, constructed in either simple ignorance or in open neglect of the most recognised and rudimentary principles of *hygiène*. "Raising the floors (says the Report), with free passage of air underneath, is necessary not only to avoid malaria, but to avoid damp, in flat or low-lying districts, where there are small natural facilities for drainage. The stational returns show that the barracks throughout India have been constructed without reference to this primary condition of health. While it is a native habit to sleep only on upper floors, in order to avoid malaria, the European soldier, who is a much more susceptible subject, has all along slept at or near the level of the ground. The usual mode of constructing barrack-floors has been to raise a plinth a foot or two in height, *to fill up the space with earth* or some other material, and to lay the floor upon it. . . . . Major-General Goodwyn states that he knows of only one instance (at Calcutta) in which the barracks are raised above the ground; and that he considers the absence of arcaded basements as a great fault; they should be raised at least twelve feet from the ground."

Having provided for the barracks being damp and malarious, the next care of our military authorities appears to have been to provide for their being ill-ventilated. Now bad ventilation—the necessity for breathing insufficient or vitiated air—is noxious and enfeebling in any country: in a climate like that of India it is simple poison. It is found impossible to secure a flow of pure air into the rooms, especially during the night, if the rooms are above a certain size and contain above a certain number of men. "The healthiest of all sleeping-rooms are those which, like the huts of the native troops, contain only one or two people, because they are so easily ventilated. Whenever the number of inmates exceeds 20 or 30 per room, it is practically far more difficult to ensure fresh air, and beyond that number it soon becomes impossible. Sad experience has proved that long rooms, like passages, with 100 or more persons sleeping in them, may become highly dangerous during epidemics, and absolutely pestilential if occupied by sick." Yet nearly every barrack in India, even the most recent and those built on the most admired models, has been constructed in open defiance of this warning. Among the smallest rooms are those at Mean Meer, a new station, and these are 48 feet long by 24 wide; at Secunderabad they range from 124 to 274 feet long; at Allahabad they are 335 feet long; at Trichinopoly 1000 feet; at Fort St. George, Madras, there is one 2124 feet long. In rooms like these the only choice is found to lie between breathing a thoroughly impure air, or lying in a thorough draught—either alternative about equally fatal. Then, again, the natives, we have seen, seldom sleep more than two or three in a room; at home the barrack-rooms rarely hold more than ten, fifteen, or twenty men; but at Secunderabad they hold 104; at Allahabad 100; at the Dalhousie barracks, at Fort William (the newest of all), 306 men; at Fort St. George 400 and 600.

4. After this, we shall not be surprised to learn that the supply of water—which next to air is most essential to life and health—is in the Indian barracks almost invariably inadequate in quantity and bad in quality. The water in India is seldom very good or very abundant; when not obtained from the rivers, it is collected in tanks, or drawn from shallow wells, twenty or thirty feet deep. To many of our stations it is conveyed by bullocks, and often in skins. It is usually full of impurities and organic matter, to a degree which scandalises even men accustomed to our London element. The water from shallow wells is in most countries impure—in India particularly so. The nasty habits of the natives aggravate the evil both in well and tank water. The obvious remedy is to sink wells of sufficient depth, and to filter all suspicious water before use;—and these precautions the Commissioners urge should be insisted on in future. Better cooking and more careful clothing are also recommended as likely to be attended with the happiest results.

5. We now come to the moral causes of the excessive sickness and mortality of the troops in India—intemperance, debauchery, and ennui. We will take the last first, as one of the chief inducements to the others. No one who reads the following passage can wonder that the British soldier in India is both drunken and licentious:

"There is no period of military service in which the soldier is thrown more upon his own resources, and has fewer opportunities of employing them advantageously, than during his service in India. He rises at gun-fire, attends his parade or drill, over soon after sun-rise. He then returns to his barrack, and during the hot season he is not allowed to leave it till late in the afternoon. At one o'clock he consumes a large amount of both animal food and vegetables, porter (perhaps a quart), and spirits. He has few or no means of occupying himself rationally. He lies on his bed and perhaps sleeps most of the day. He has his evening parade or drill, and his turn of guard-duty once in every five, seven, or ten days. Even at home this kind of regimen would be far from conducive to health. In India, both physically and morally, it helps to destroy health in men in the prime of life, with abundance of nervous power to dispose of.

The whole of this unwholesome proceeding is considered necessary for preserving the soldier; but it is not considered necessary to subject the officer to the same ordeal. He goes about, and even goes shooting, not only without detriment, but with great advantage to health, for the officers are much more healthy than the men.

The men's amusements, such as they are, are always connected more or less with drink; and they are every where most deficient in amount. The men suffer much from ennui. For all practical purposes, they are entirely idle, and they complain of what they feel every where, 'the weary idleness' of their lives, and that so little has been done in the way of giving them occupation.

The want of exercise, and a coincident high rate of sickness and mortality, falls most heavily on the infantry. The cavalry regiments and artillery, who have, one way or other, much more physical exertion to undergo, are much more healthy."

Now soldiers are rarely reading men, and though libraries and reading-rooms ought, no doubt, to be provided for them, and to a certain limited extent have been, yet we cannot say that we anticipate any vast improvement from the acquisition of this sort of recreation. Nor will the artificial contrivance of theatres do much. Gardens they might have, and do have occasionally; and the slight practical difficulties in the way might easily be overcome. But two things might and ought to be provided, and between them would do much to remedy the evil complained of—the insupportable irksomeness of life. The soldiers ought to be allowed and encouraged, and even made to work, and they ought to be subjected to gymnastic training. The value of this last resource can scarcely be overestimated. It would render the soldier a far more valuable man professionally. Indeed, without it he is and must remain professionally very imperfect. The French understand this well; and their picked troops go through almost the training of athletes and acrobats. Gymnastics, too, would harmonise with the soldier's tastes and habits. Both the evidence and the Report are very clear and strong upon this head. Such discipline would be popular as well as salutary, and would supply the exercise so much needed. All the best officers agree that there need not be, and should not be, any strict confinement to barracks; even shooting should be encouraged—indeed, any activity and any amusement that is innocent. Wherever this system has been tried, as Colonel Greathed shows, it has been attended with the best results. It is clear, too, that work should be both encouraged and rewarded. There can be no reason why the soldier should not employ those long hours during which he is now absolutely idle and useless in labouring for himself and his regiment, in working at some trade, in producing articles wanted by the troops,—such as cabinet-making, shoe-making, iron-work, &c. We quite agree, moreover, with those witnesses and Commissioners who would extend this permission still further, and employ the men, wherever practicable, in out-door work—in building, carpentering, road-making, &c. If they were paid for it, they would like it; and they would become instantaneously incomparably more moral, more contented, and more sober. This is no mere theory: the trial has already been made in some districts, and has succeeded admirably. Every barrack in the Punjab has a workshop attached to it.

Intemperance would diminish enormously and rapidly with the introduction of employment and recreation. At present the soldier in India is driven to drink by the insupportable irksomeness of his idle hours, and encouraged to drink by the canteen system, as it is called, under which spirits are provided for the soldier, and brought close within his reach, on the plea that if the authorities did not supply him with good liquor, he would buy worse stuff from the natives. The Commissioners, while admitting the difficulty of the case, are of opinion—in which they are supported by much testimony—that if, instead of spirits, malt-liquor, acidulated drinks, and light wines, were provided in ample quantities at the cantonments, the consumption of ardent spirits would be much reduced, and that, whatever the original cost, the diminution of sickness among the men would render the measure one of wise and certain economy.

6. The next point is a matter difficult to deal with, both in life and on paper. A very large proportion of the disabling sickness which prevails in the Indian army arises from debauchery. Nearly one-fourth of the men in hospital are there for syphilitic affections. Altogether, one-third of the entire force is said to suffer from this class of disease, viz.—345 per 1000 in Bengal; 314 in Bombay; and 249 in Madras. Not only are the soldiers thus temporarily rendered useless, but they are often permanently invalided by this wretched malady,

and may trace their premature death by other diseases to the enfeebling of their constitution by this one. Now, as long as the great majority of the army consists of young and unmarried men (and we suppose it must always consist of such), no one appears to believe that the licentious habits from which these disorders spring can be effectually cured. But all military witnesses and authorities agree that much might be done to mitigate the evil. In the first place, a greater number of the men might be allowed to marry, and to have their wives accompany them. It is purely a question of trouble and expense; or rather of trouble only, for every one bears testimony to the fact, that the married soldiers are by far the steadiest and most healthy; and the extra cost, therefore, would be more than counterbalanced by the increased efficiency and the diminished sickness of the force. At present the number of married soldiers who have a claim to accommodation in the barracks for their wives at home is six per cent. In India the proportion has been augmented to twelve per cent. The best authorities advise a still further enlargement of the limit up to 25 per cent, and the provision of better quarters for the women. Considerable reduction in the severity of the scourge might also be secured by the establishment of lock hospitals under strict and cogent regulations. But, as General Jacob declared, moral forces alone are of much value, and these must act both slowly and, for the most part, indirectly. Occupation, instruction, and recreation, brought within the soldier's reach, urged upon him, and made agreeable to him, would do more than any thing else to reduce the force of those temptations to illicit indulgence which now entail such deplorable results. Licentiousness and intemperance would be brought within much narrower limits than at present, if the men could employ their time pleasantly and profitably without being driven by the *tedium vitæ* to the brothel and the canteen.

To sum up the whole: three or four points are made perfectly clear by the Report of the Commissioners, and by the other authentic documents to which we have referred. *First,* That the excessive mortality and sickness which has hitherto prevailed in the Indian Army taxes our recruiting power to a dangerous extent, and may make it a very difficult matter to maintain there a sufficient force for the security of our dominion. *Secondly,* That this excessive mortality might, with absolute certainty, and with no insuperable difficulties, be removed in India, as it has been among the British troops serving at home and at other foreign stations. *Thirdly,* That *it would pay* splendidly to introduce the needed sanitary reforms. And, *fourthly,* That the simplest dictates of common sense, common justice, and common morality, demand that we should set about the incumbent and very feasible work without an hour's delay. The guilt of manslaughter on a portentous scale will lie at the door of all who can be fairly chargeable with either neglect, opposition, or avoidable procrastination.

Art. IV.—MR. FREEMAN'S HISTORY OF FEDERAL GOVERNMENT.

History of Federal Government. By Edward A. Freeman, M.A., late Fellow of Trinity College, Oxford. Vol. I. General Introduction; History of the Greek Federations. Macmillan & Co.

To the reader of a work on a subject of great and permanent interest there is something very unsatisfactory in the impression that it has owed its origin to the excitement of events passing at or immediately before the time when it was written. And it must be confessed that a title-page which begins with "History of Federal Government," and ends with the date 1863, is not unlikely to convey this impression. It is, therefore, with no common pleasure that we notice the disclaimer which Mr. Freeman has placed in the opening sentences of his Preface:

"I trust that no one will think that the present work owes its origin to the excitement of the War of Secession in America. It is the first instalment of a scheme formed long ago, and it represents the thought and reading of more than ten years. All that late events in America have done has been to increase my interest in a subject which had already long occupied my thoughts, and, in some degree, to determine me to write at once what might otherwise have been postponed for some time longer" (p. ix.).

Nor is it possible to read Mr. Freeman's volume carefully without feeling that in this statement he has done himself no more than justice, and that what he has written is the product of substantial learning and independent research. Thus in the discussion of the characteristics of federal government, which precedes the more strictly historical part of the book, the opinions which he expresses are formed on much broader grounds, and deserve a much larger measure of our respect, than the hasty diatribes, either in favour of federalism or against it, with which newspapers and pamphlets have made us only too familiar. And if in the course of the history itself allusions to modern politics are occasionally unduly frequent, it is much rather of references to French imperialism than to American federalism that we have to complain.

The present volume is apparently the first of a series of four, devoted respectively to the histories of the four greatest federal commonwealths which the world has yet seen: the Achaian League, the Confederation of the Swiss Cantons, the Seven United Provinces of the Netherlands, and the United States of America. Mr. Freeman tells us that his object is "to exhibit the actual working of federal government in ages and countries widely removed from each other;" and he proposes, while considering in detail only the preëminent four which we have mentioned, to complete his treatment of the subject by giving some account of the minor federations, of which history presents so many examples to us. Thus with the Achaian League he couples notices, first, of the imperfect federal unions, or attempts at federal union, which existed in Greece in the pre-Macedonian times; secondly, of the numerous federations of the Macedonians in the federal period (as it may fairly be called) of Greek history; and lastly, of one outside the limits of Greece proper, the Lycian League, the independence of which dates from the fall of the kingdom of Macedon, and lasted to the reign of the Emperor Claudius. Similarly, with the Swiss Confederation he proposes to join the Hanseatic and other German leagues of the middle ages; and with the great American union the hitherto unsuccessful federal unions which have been formed in imitation of it in various parts of Spanish America. The only federations omitted from this list are those of ancient Italy, of which, however, the nature and institutions are, as Mr. Freeman may justly plead, too obscure to be treated historically.

We are not disposed to underrate the interest attaching to the theory of federalism. But it may well be doubted whether that interest is sufficient to give unity to a work comprising four such different subjects as the history of federal Greece, of Switzerland, of the Netherlands, and of the United States. To us this seems a weak point in Mr. Freeman's extensive plan. The single point of resemblance, the federal form of government, is not in itself of such overwhelming importance, and cannot so far counterbalance the innumerable diversities in the national life of these great republics, as to make it easy for us to look upon them simply as manifestations of one and the same political phenomenon. All that interests us most in each of them is peculiar to it; to make their histories into one, by means of the principle of federalism, seems arbitrary and unnatural. Nor is it only this want of unity of which we complain; for, after all, the want of sufficient connexion between the four volumes of a work is a very tolerable evil. We could well be content to receive from Mr. Freeman four separate histories each complete in itself, and we should willingly allow him to bind them together, if he pleases, by a slender thread of federal ideas. But it is, as we conceive, in the execution of the separate parts of his design that he is placed at a very serious disadvantage by the nature of the object which he proposes to himself. Such, at least, is certainly the case in the volume before us. A history of the Achaian League, written to illustrate federal principles, is not the history of that league which English readers will care to have. The period during which the league existed is one well worthy the pains of the writer and reader of history; and one, though only one, of its claims to attention is that in it, for the first time, we meet with an important and successful development of federal institutions. It may even be admitted that more of direct political instruction is to be obtained by regarding it from this point of view than from any other. But while few will care to open a history of Greece during the Macedonian period, in order to study in it the uncertain outlines of imperfectly known federal institutions; a comparatively numerous class will be attracted by the melancholy interest with which we must ever regard the closing scenes of Hellenic independence. Again, the minor confederations of ancient Greece, those of Phocis, Acarnania, Epirus, and Bœotia, are of interest and importance to the scholar who wishes to have the whole history of Greece before him; but surely they yield no lessons to the student of federal polity, who can derive but little edification from the scanty and imperfect accounts we possess of their constitutions. To scholars we can confidently recommend the pages which Mr. Freeman has devoted to the Amphiktyonic council, and to the place of Bœotia in Greek history; but we can hardly imagine that any searcher for political instruction will find that his conception of the actual working of federal institutions is rendered any clearer by them. When we have been told that the fate of Bœotia is a warning against the danger of allowing an over-powerful capital in a federal state, and that the Lycian League was the only federation of ancient times which adopted the simple plan of giving to cities of unequal size unequal numbers of votes in the national assembly, we believe that we have learnt the only lessons on federal politics which are to found in a considerable, and far from uninteresting, part of Mr. Freeman's work. Nor can we but expect that in other parts of his great task, Mr. Freeman will find himself equally embarrassed by having to write from a federal point of view of important events in which federalism plays but an accidental part. One exception, indeed, we must make to this remark. The United States of America, owing to their isolated position on that continent, have experienced but few external embarrassments, while, in consequence of the political and social diversities originally existing among them, aggravated by their rapid and unequal development, they have never been free from abundant sources of internal disturbance. Thus a history of federal government in the United States will tell us all that we most care to know concerning them, and, indeed, will come very near to a complete history of the nation. But a history of federal government in the Netherlands, if it be strictly confined within the limits which the title prescribes, will certainly miss all that most interests us in a people whose place in the world's history cannot be said to depend on the peculiarity of their internal polity. The heroic struggles of the Dutch against Spain and France for existence, and against ourselves for maritime dominion; the religious and literary activity of the days when they printed for all Europe; the growth of their commerce and colonial empire,—these are things which have but a remote connexion with federal government, and which even singly, and much more taken together, surpass in interest and importance all the political knowledge we are likely to derive from the most luminous exposition of the details of the Dutch constitution.

"As a historian of federalism" (writes Mr. Freeman, in words which seem to us to imply a consciousness of the difficulty in the task before him), "I look to every thing mainly as illustrating or not illustrating the progress of federal ideas. I dwell upon events, or I hurry over them, not according to their intrinsic importance, but according to their importance for my particular purpose. I have disposed in a line or two of battles which were of high moment in the history of the world, and I have dwelt at length on obscure debates and embassies, when their details happened to throw light on the Achaian constitution, or on the mode of proceeding in the Achaian assembly. It so happens that much of the information most valuable for my purpose comes in the form of details of this kind, which a general historian would, naturally and properly, cut very short" (p. x.).

It is a consequence of the intention which is here so frankly avowed, that Mr. Freeman is occasionally led to rely too much on the knowledge of his readers, or, at least, on their spirit of research. Every educated Englishman can read a constitutional history of England with pleasure and with profit, because he is sufficiently acquainted with the general history of his country, which is the framework of its constitutional history. But a constitutional history of the Achaian League, unless it be accompanied by and intermingled with a general history of the period, can only be approached by the readers of Polybius and Plutarch, or at least by those who are willing to take the pains to prepare themselves for it by a preliminary reference to Bishop Thirlwall's eighth volume. We cannot but regret that Mr. Freeman should have moulded his work in a form calculated to diminish so seriously the number of his readers. The extent to which the histories of Bishop Thirlwall, Mr. Grote, and Mr. Merivale are read by persons who are not scholars by profession, shows that there is nothing in classical history, even when treated with the profoundest research and the greatest fulness of detail, which is repulsive to the educated feeling of our days; and it is a pity that Mr. Freeman should have missed the opportunity of doing for the federal period of Greece what Mr. Grote has done for its earlier and greater days. Fortunately, however, as we think, for his readers, he has not found it possible to adhere quite rigorously to the principle laid down in his preface; and the spirit and animation of the considerable amount of direct narrative which he has given us (it occupies nearly one-half of the volume), only make us regret the more the lacunæ which here and there he somewhat arbitrarily leaves in it.* We venture to hope that in Mr. Freeman's second volume he will find it still less practicable, than in his first, to be simply the historian of Federalism. We believe we are right in asserting that the history of Switzerland (excepting a few brilliant passages here and there) is a sealed book in England; and as we do not know of any English work to which Mr. Freeman can refer his readers for information on the affairs of Switzerland, as he does to Bishop Thirlwall on those of Peloponnesus, we trust that he will be tempted to write a history of Switzerland for us himself.

Mr. Freeman's introductory discussion of the characteristics of a federal government is conceived throughout in the spirit of a historian, and not of a jurist. His definition of a perfect federal government comes to this, that it is one in which each member of the federation is sovereign in all internal matters, and the federation is sovereign in all external matters. For the purposes of history we believe that this definition, if rightly understood, will be found sufficient. But the use which is made in it of the term "sovereign" is open to some objections. It raises the very difficult question, "what is the sovereign power in a federal state?" a question which, for the right understanding

* For example, Mr. Freeman purposely omits to give us any account of the brilliant adventures by which Aratus liberates Sicyon and Corinth. It is a little hard upon the reader, unless he happens to be in a library, to be told that "the Greek of Plutarch, the German of Droysen, and the English of Thirlwall are enough." Besides, the omission is important, as bearing on the character of Aratus for skill and courage; for Mr. Freeman gives us the details of his failures, and thus an impression unduly adverse to him is created.

of the history of some federations, it is quite unnecessary to raise, and which in the case of very many it is quite impossible to answer. And unfortunately the answer which the definition suggests is untenable. It recognises a plurality of sovereignties—that of the federal government, and those of the component states—within the federation; and this consequence of his definition Mr. Freeman explicitly admits. "The sovereignty is in fact divided; the government of the federation and the government of the state have a coördinate authority, each equally claiming allegiance within its own range" (p. 15). The coexistence of coördinate authorities under a common superior is a matter of every-day occurrence, and presents no speculative or practical difficulty; but it hardly needs the irrefutable logic of Mr. Austin to convince us that the coexistence of two independent sovereignties in the same state implies a contradiction in terms.* A state, on entering a federation, either retains its sovereignty or relinquishes it; for sovereignty is a thing which cannot really be divided,—it cannot be half relinquished and half retained. If the states of a union retain their separate sovereignties, they do not form a composite state, or a true federal union, at all, but are simply a confederation (intended to be permanent) of independent states; in a true federal union the sovereignty resides not in the individual states, but in the aggregate of the states. But it is difficult to apply this abstract doctrine (which has the high authority of Mr. Austin) to the federations we meet with in history. It would probably reduce the number of true federal unions to a very few; and it would certainly compel us to class either with mere confederations or with consolidated states, states the whole political history of which has the closest analogy to that of states certainly federal. It is also specially inapplicable to ancient times, not only because our knowledge of the constitution of ancient federal states is too imperfect to admit of our applying it, but also because it would seem that the importance of the question of sovereignty in a federal union had not (in ancient times) as yet made itself practically felt; although, as we see from the Politics of Aristotle, the nature and attributes of sovereignty had been, by him at least, carefully considered.

A set of Greek independent communities, in forming themselves into a league, had, we may be quite sure, a clear conception of the motives which induced them to take this step; but they are very likely to have had no clear conception of its legal effect on their position as sovereign states. The league was intended to be permanent; it was also intended that the common government should have the sole management of foreign

* Austin's *Province of Jurisprudence determined*, cap. vi.

relations, and that it should not interfere with the domestic affairs of individual states. That these points should be secured by the constitution of the league was the important object. Probably none of the states intended to relinquish its sovereignty; but probably also no one thought of inquiring whether that sovereignty had or had not been relinquished. Nor was the inquiry likely to be of practical importance until a time came when a state seceded, or when it was proposed to introduce an amendment into the constitution. And we may add, that in ancient times even an act of secession would not go very far to raise the question of sovereignty; for whether a seceding state were sovereign or not, the league would equally make war upon it,—in the one case for a breach of treaty, in the other for rebellion; a distinction which, in the state of international law in those days, may well have seemed evanescent. On the other hand, we have unfortunately no record of any amendment to the constitution of the Achaian league, with which we are so much better acquainted than with any other Greek federation. The result on the whole probably was, that, conscious of subjection to a double government, the people divided their allegiance in very uncertain proportions between the two. If circumstances fostered a tendency to union, the sovereignty of the individual state may have come to be wholly forgotten, and that of the league to be admitted as supreme; if disintegrating influences prevailed, the state governments were always there, ready to resume the authority they had delegated to the federal government. In the particular case of the Achaian league, it would appear that the consciousness of imminent peril from powerful neighbours occasioned, on the part of the majority of the Achaian people, a gradual transference of their allegiance from their respective states to the league; a transference which no doubt was greatly facilitated by the circumstance, that in Greek democratic communities the sovereignty always resided in a general assembly of all the citizens, and that the legislature of the league was such an assembly. We cannot imagine that before the Cleomenic war Aratus could have attempted, in carrying out a course of federal policy, to partition a loyal state of the league. Yet this Philopœmen, a generation later, did at Megalopolis. If this measure was carried out without the consent of Megalopolis (and any other supposition seems inconceivable), it must have been done by the sole authority of the general assembly of the Achaian states; from which we may safely infer that at the time in question that assembly regarded itself, and was regarded by the people, as sovereign in the states as well as in the league. But it is not in the leagues of the ancient world alone that we find the allegiance of the people wavering between the state and the federation. Of this we have ample evidence in the Sonderbund war of Switzerland, and in the American war of secession. Probably at this moment the idea which a citizen of New York, or even of Berne, forms of the government under which he lives, is in most cases adequately represented by Mr. Freeman's phrase, however illogical we may think it,—a divided sovereignty. And it is precisely because the interpretation which the popular feeling of a nation puts upon its constitution is at least as important in its history as the more accurate interpretation of it which would be given by a jurist, that we accept Mr. Freeman's definition, with all the vagueness which he has intentionally left in it, as more really applicable to the facts of history than the precise and carefully-reasoned statement of Mr. Austin. Nevertheless, it is not uninteresting to observe how the progress of political experience has forced more and more clearly on federal statesmen the conviction that a federation cannot "serve two masters," and that it is requisite, for the preservation of its institutions, to define clearly the political body or bodies in which the sovereignty is vested. The fifth article of the constitution of the United States of America* gives the ultimate power of altering the constitution to a majority of not less than three-fourths of the states; and it cannot be doubted that the effect of this article is to substitute for the sovereignty of the separate states the sovereignty of the aggregate of them. Similarly, in the constitution of Switzerland now in force, the power of altering the constitution, and with that power the sovereignty of the Swiss Confederation, is given to a majority of the cantons and a majority of the Swiss people.† Thus, in the United States the sovereignty resides in a body which is wholly distinct, not only from the legislatures of the individual states, but also from the federal legislature; whereas the Demos at Athens, and the Queen, Lords, and Commons in England, combine the ordinary functions of a legislature with the exercise of sovereign power. Hence the necessity in the United States for a supreme federal court,—an institution which has no parallel either in Athens or in England. It is necessary in the United States to prevent the legislature from usurping the sovereign power, or, which is the same thing, from making laws which change or violate the constitution. And this necessary check

* "The Congress, whenever two-thirds of both houses shall deem it necessary, shall propose amendments to this constitution; or, on the application of the legislatures of two-thirds of the several states, shall call a convention for proposing amendments: which amendments in either case shall be valid, to all intents and purposes, as parts of this constitution, *when ratified by the legislatures of three-fourths of the several states, or by convention in three-fourths thereof.*"

† This is the effect of arts. 111-114 of the Swiss Constitution of 1848.

is provided by the institution of a court, which may be said to represent the sovereignty of the nation, so far as it can be represented by a judicial tribunal, and which has the right to pronounce acts of the federal legislature or of the state legislatures illegal, and to direct the inferior tribunals to disregard them. By this memorable institution the constitution of the United States is differenced not only from non-federal states, but also from the less perfectly organised federations of ancient times. It is at least certain that we find no trace of any such institution in the Achaian League; nor, indeed, can there have been any room for it there, if we suppose the sovereignty of the league to have resided in the general assembly, which formed the federal legislature. We wish to direct attention to this circumstance, because Mr. Freeman (who, in his comparison of the Achaian constitution with that of the United States, chiefly fixes his attention on administrative arrangements) has omitted to take notice of it.

It has been proposed to divide federations into two classes: those in which the federal government acts on the people only indirectly and through the state governments, and those in which it acts directly and independently of the state governments. Theoretically the distinction is of little importance, because the authority of the federal government may be greater under a constitution of the first than under one of the second kind; and also because it is possible that neither of the two principles may be adopted to the exclusion of the other. For example, the taxes may be federal, and the military force may be raised by requisitions from the federal government to the state governments. It is therefore certainly erroneous to confuse this distinction with that other and more important distinction between a composite state and a confederacy of states. Nevertheless the practical experience of the American confederation of 1778, which preceded the Union of 1787, clearly showed that it was impossible, at least under the circumstances of that country, to make the federal government a reality to the people, so long as its action upon them was only exerted through the state governments. We may therefore, on the whole, agree with Mr. Freeman's judgment, though it is a little vaguely expressed, that "the real difference between the two classes is, that the one is a good, the other a bad, way of compassing the same objects" (p. 12). To show how really ignorant we are of the constitution of the Achaian League, and of the other leagues of ancient Greece, we may observe that it is impossible from the evidence before us to decide to which of the two classes they belonged. We know indeed that the Achaian League had a federal revenue, but we do not know whether this revenue was raised by federal tax-collectors or by requisition to the different towns. Perhaps, however, we have the less reason to be surprised at our want of information on this head, when we remember how imperfect our knowledge is of the fiscal arrangements of the ancient world. We know that the league had a federal army; but the vague phrases of Polybius* do not enable us to conjecture in what manner this force (so far as it consisted of a militia, and not of mercenaries) was levied upon the different municipalities. We should have been glad to have known something of the courts of judicature in the Achaian League, but on this subject our authorities are silent. We certainly hear nothing of federal courts, any more than of a supreme federal court. Polybius indeed tells us† that the union of the Peloponnesians was so complete, that they had the same laws, the same weights, measures, and currency, the same magistrates, senators, and judges. But we believe that in this passage Polybius is speaking not of the Achaian League in the days of its independence, but of the Roman times, when, after the nominal restoration of the constitution, the union was probably more perfect than it had ever been before.‡ It is hardly conceivable that, while the feeling of city independence was in vigour, Corinth or Megalopolis would have admitted a federal jurisdiction within its domain. The strength of the tradition in Greece in favour of "autonomy" would rather lead us to imagine that the Achaian League adopted the less perfect form of federal administration, in which the action of the federal government is only indirect. But it is probable that this imperfection, if it is to be considered as such, tended to impair the federal unity much less than was found to be the case in the American confederation of 1778. In a territory so small as that of the Achaian League, the federal government came much nearer to every man's home; and besides, the league was almost always at war, and we know that in military

* Lib. v. 91.

† Lib. ii. 37,—Freeman, p. 259; and compare Polyb. ii. 62 and iv. 32.

‡ The league, however, had a federal coinage during the period of its independence. The coins were struck by the cities, but were all of one type; the copper coins, for example, having on one side a full-length Zeus Homagyrius holding a Victory, with the name of a magistrate generally at full, and on the other side a Demeter Panachaia seated, with the names of the Achaians and of the coining city, thus—ΑΧΑΙΩΝ ΚΟΡΙΝΘΙΩΝ. The magistrates whose names appear are municipal and not federal officers, so that numismatic evidence does not help us to complete the list of the generals of the league. But it supplies many names to the list of cities: thus we learn from coins the names of six of the townships separated from Megalopolis by Philopœmen, and united as independent cities with the league. We learn also from coins inscribed ΑΧΑΙΩΝ ΠΑΓΑΙΩΝ, ΑΧΑΙΩΝ ΕΛΙΦΑΣΙΩΝ, that Pagæ and Eliphasia had similarly been separated from Megara and Mantinea respectively. In all, there are about forty cities of the league, of which federal coins are extant. (See the truly excellent Essay on Greek Federal Coinage, which Mr. Leicester Warren has written for the express purpose of illustrating Mr. Freeman's work.)

affairs the authority of the general of the league was supreme. There is a remarkable passage in the *Federalist*, which Mr. Freeman has taken for the motto of his volume: "Could the interior structure and regular operation of the Achaian League be ascertained, it is probable that more light might be thrown by it on the science of federal government than by any of the like experiments with which we are acquainted." We feel that so long as we are obliged to give purely conjectural answers to questions such as we have been here considering, the *desideratum* of the *Federalist* remains a *desideratum* still, and that we must not entertain exaggerated expectations of the political lessons to be learned from institutions which have to be completed by guess.

But, after all, the most important question that can be asked with regard to any form of government is, whether it is calculated to promote the well-being of its subjects; and Mr. Freeman has done well in addressing himself principally to this question, though perhaps we have a right to complain that he has a little neglected in its favour some legal and constitutional points. His theory is, that federalism is a compromise between the systems of large and small states; an effort to secure, so far as possible, the advantages and avoid the disadvantages of both; and the pages in which these advantages and disadvantages are enumerated are among the most interesting in the volume. The comparison evidently reduces itself to one between the political system of Greece in its best days, and that with which we are familiar in modern Europe. Such a comparison has of course often been attempted before, but we do not know where we can find it drawn out with so much completeness, or with greater impartiality and care. It is perhaps the favourite bias of Mr. Freeman's taste to compare continually remote parts of history with one another; and what he is so fond of doing he naturally does extremely well. His account of the Greek conception of "an autonomous city community" is well worth reading, even after the lavish illustration which the subject has received from Mr. Grote. Some points in the working of the constitution natural to an independent town community are placed by him in a clearer light than even by that great historian.

That the great advantage of the Athenian constitution was the high intellectual and political education which its operation conferred on all Athenian citizens has often been pointed out; and the words of De Tocqueville, quoted by Mr. Freeman (p. 40), —"C'est en participant à la législation que l'Américain apprend à connaître les lois, c'est en gouvernant qu'il s'instruit des formes du gouvernement,"—are applicable with tenfold force to the Athenian. But it is a somewhat hazardous step to compare the political education which an Athenian might derive from attendance at the meetings of the assembly with that which a member of the House of Commons receives by virtue of his parliamentary position. Nevertheless, Mr. Freeman succeeds, we think, in showing that, in one respect at least, the former had the advantage of the latter. The existence of a ministry in modern representative constitutions, coupled with the system of government by party, practically takes the responsibility of deciding on almost all very important questions out of the hands of individual members of the legislature. Many most important acts of the administration are never submitted to the House of Commons beforehand; the House has only the power of approving and disapproving after the fact; and the effect of a vote of disapproval is probably simply to remove ministers from office, and not to obtain a reversal of what has been already done. Thus it comes that the cases in which a member of Parliament has to express a really independent opinion are not usually questions of the highest national importance. He has to decide whether he will keep a ministry in office; and this decision he practically makes once for all when he decides on the party to which he will belong. Widely different from this was the position of the Athenian in the Pnyx. He sat there not to approve or disapprove of the policy of officers of state, but to give them directions as to the policy they were to pursue. The Demos had of course the power of electing its officers, and held them responsible for their conduct in office; but it did not trust its interests to their discretion in the same way in which those of a modern state are intrusted to its cabinet of ministers. It discharged itself many of the functions of a government as well as of a parliament. It listened to its officers, but it also listened to, and often preferred, the plans proposed by private citizens, without its being thought in the least necessary for its officers to resign, and indeed without its being implied that they had forfeited the confidence of the nation. One striking instance of this is presented by the case of Nicias, who, after opposing the Sicilian expedition to the uttermost, was sent himself to command it; and sent too with every mark of popular confidence. Such an occurrence would be impossible in our days, whose political morality will allow a soldier, but not a statesman, to carry out measures of which he disapproves. But it is clear that the Athenian's position required a greater and more frequent exercise of his private judgment; he had to judge for himself of important questions, perhaps affecting the highest interests of the state, each on its own merits; while, no less than the English member of Parliament, he had the advantage of hearing all that could be said on either side by great orators and statesmen.

Mr. Freeman, however, does not forget the dark side of the picture. It may fairly be questioned whether a town community is more liable to internal revolutions than a larger state; and whether its revolutions are, in proportion to its size, more sanguinary than those which are enacted on a larger scale. Except in this one respect of scale, there is not much to choose between the Corcyræan revolution described by Thucydides, and the scenes of the Reign of Terror. But there can be no doubt that a system of independent town communities is more liable to foreign war than a system of larger states; and that in a system of the former kind war produces an incalculably greater amount of misery in proportion to the number of the belligerent populations. The tendency of a system of large states, as the experience of modern Europe shows, is to confine the worst evils of war within limits increasingly narrow. There has been a tendency in recent times to strain to the utmost every point of public law affording protection to non-combatants. And this has been done not so much, we may fear, from an increasing reverence for principles of right, as from a conviction that such a course is in the long run for the interest of all; and in large states the calculations of interest are powerful enough to make themselves heard, in some measure, above the passions which produce war and are produced by it. On the other hand, the public law of a system of small states is less open to humanising influences. Struggles between neighbouring city communities are for life or death, not for dominion —the injuries received and inflicted on either side are such as are felt by the whole people—and the passions roused far surpass in intensity the national hatreds of which we have any experience in the present day. In Greece, the rights of noncombatants had absolutely no existence, under a public law which at least tolerated the killing of the adult male inhabitants of a conquered town in cold blood, and the selling of the women and children into slavery. It is of course difficult to estimate how much of the great improvement which has taken place in this respect is due to the influence of Christianity, and how much to that diminution of the bitterness of the passions of war which is consequent on the substitution of large states for single cities. But we cannot doubt that Mr. Freeman is right in attributing much importance to the latter cause.

Between these two political systems federal government occupies a middle place. It proposes, so far as possible, to combine the local and municipal independence, which a small state or a town community guards so jealously, with the external and massive strength which is characteristic of a large state. Of course this combination is, rigorously speaking, impossible. The individual state on entering the federation relinquishes its sovereignty, or promises not to exercise it; and the resulting federation is weak as compared with a consolidated state, though strong as compared with the isolated units which it has absorbed into itself. But, in truth, federations are formed, not upon any calculation of a balance of advantages or disadvantages, but from the strongest of all possible motives—the instinct of self-preservation. A federation is the natural, and even the only, resource of small states threatened by the proximity of larger ones. The leagues of the federal period of Greece owed their origin to the fact that the independent city communities had come in contact with large states, and that they must either unite or perish. Consolidation was impossible, as well as repulsive to the old feeling of the nation; they could do nothing but form a league. This, no doubt, is the explanation of the fact, that federalism became as characteristic of Greece during the Macedonian period as town autonomy had previously been. In like manner, the origin of the Swiss and Dutch leagues is attributable simply to the fear of their Austrian and Spanish enemies. The American colonies, after the War of Independence, must have felt that a union of some kind was essential to their preservation. There is something almost unmeaning in a discussion of the strength or weakness of the principle of federalism. It may be weakness as compared with consolidation, but it is strength compared with total disunion; and, above all, it is the only possible course by which a system of smaller nations can maintain their independence in the presence of more powerful enemies—a condition of things which has over and over again occurred in the world's history.

Mr. Freeman complains more than once that the federal period of Greek history is neglected in England. If this complaint refers to English scholars, so few works on ancient history are published in England, that it is very hard to say whether any one part of it has been more neglected than another. We are not a learned nation, nor is this generation a learned generation. And yet, what with Bishop Thirlwall and Mr. Freeman, we think as much has now been done for the federal period as can be expected from the not very numerous body of English scholars. But if the meaning of the complaint is, that the history of federal Greece forms no part of English classical education, the fact is undeniable—Polybius is not read in English schools and universities. But we are not prepared to concede that a change in this respect is desirable. If Polybius is to be read, at least let it be the Punic wars, and not the affairs of Greece, that we may be sure of having a great subject, even if we have not a great author. The truth is, that there is an immeasurable inferiority in the later as compared with the earlier Greece. The causes of this inferiority may be obscure, but the fact itself is certain. All that has made Greece the admiration of the world and the teacher of the world ceases, with a surprising suddenness, within a generation or two at most from the beginning of the Macedonian ascendency. On this point it is impossible not to sympathise with Mr. Grote as against Mr. Freeman. It is not a question of Greek democracy against Greek federalism, but of national greatness against national mediocrity. We find the same sudden falling-off in art, in poetry, in eloquence, in philosophy. The last name of commanding greatness in the long catalogue of Greek sculptors is Lysippus, and Lysippus is not Phidias or Praxiteles. "The list of mighty poets is made up" when the names of Theocritus and of the masters of the new comedy have been added to the roll. After Demosthenes and his contemporaries there is not a single orator who can be named beside them. After the founders of the Stoic school (and the speculation of the Stoic school is feeble compared with Plato or Aristotle), philosophy dwindles more and more. It is singular that science, which had begun latest, survived longest. The old man who defended Syracuse against Marcellus, and who perished at its capture, was probably the last of the many Greeks whose lives have marked an epoch in the intellectual development of mankind. The history of Greece is no longer the history of a people unrivalled among the nations of the world for its fertility of men of genius; it is the history of a people which is resplendent only with the light reflected on it from its past. The Greece which created human civilisation is gone; we have instead a race of men able indeed to preserve and to appreciate, but unable to increase the intellectual wealth transmitted to them by their forefathers. Outside of Peloponnesus there is not during the whole federal period a single general or statesman whose name is worth preserving from oblivion. Inside the Isthmus there is not quite the same blank: we have the Spartan kings Agis and Cleomenes, and the Achaian generals Aratus and Philopœmen,—all four deserving to be placed where Plutarch has placed them, by the side of their great countrymen in former generations. Many incidents which we find in Polybius and Plutarch show that, if the genius of the people was gone, the old "greatness of heart" was still to be found here and there among them. No one can read the story of the death of Agis, or of Cleomenes and the Spartan exiles who accompanied him to Egypt, without feeling that the true Spartan spirit had revived in them, rendered perhaps less rugged, but not less devoted, by the softening influences of an increased civilisation. Nor are the simple words with which Philopœmen takes the cup of poison unworthy of the last of the Greeks, or of the pupil of a school of philosophy which had learnt from Socrates how to die. But, notwithstanding individual instances of true nobleness, it is clear that the spirit of the people, as a whole, had sunk deplorably. And it is in this, even more than in the want of great men, that the inferiority of federal Greece manifests itself. The Achaians, it is true, never sank to the depths of degradation into which Athens had now fallen. But the spirit by which they were animated at the best of times was never comparable to that of the great Athenian days. They seem to have cared much for good government, but much less for that perfect independence from their powerful neighbours without which national greatness was an impossibility. Above all, they do not seem to have felt the duty and necessity of fighting for themselves; or that freedom is, and can be, nothing if men are not willing to defend it with their own hands and at the risk of their own lives. They paid mercenaries in an enormous disproportion to their citizen forces. We hear, on one occasion, that the troops voted for the year were 10,000 mercenaries and 3300 citizens. They were only too ready to get a king to fight for them, even when they had to pay and support his army. Doubtless Aratus was a bad teacher for them; but the Athenian people in their best days would never have learned the evil lesson. One useful political quality the Achaians did possess—that of keeping a great leader when they had found him; and for this they receive and deserve the approbation both of Polybius and of Plutarch. But this quality did not depend on the simple appreciation of greatness; there was a kind of docility in it which is not a national merit of a very high order. It led them to obey the call of Philopœmen, when, a generation too late, he tried to rouse the martial spirit of his countrymen. But it also led them to cleave to Aratus through a course of policy which was fatal to their independence; and at last it led them, at the bidding of men like Critolaus and Diæus, to rush headlong into a war with Rome. Of all historical speculations, the most worthless are those on what might have been; but, without risking any such conjectures, it is at least certain that, in an age when it was universally felt that union and vigour alone could preserve the independence of Greece, the Greek nation displayed but imperfect tendencies to union, and but little vigour. And what vigour they did display was against themselves, and not against their enemies; not a single exploit of Philopœmen was directed against the external enemies of Greece. The growth of a Panhellenic spirit is clearly visible all the time; the misfortune is, that it grew too slowly, and that, with the Macedonian and the

Roman at their gates, the Achaian League and Sparta could not keep from an internecine war.

The comparison between the "Greece of Thucydides" and the "Greece of Polybius" naturally suggests to Mr. Freeman a comparison between Thucydides and Polybius themselves.

"Thucydides never went out of the immediate Greek world; but for his fortunate exile, he might never have gone out of the dominions of Athens; his reading was necessarily small; he spoke only one language; he knew only one form of political and civilised life. But an inborn genius, an intuitive wisdom, a life spent amid the full youth and freshness of the first of nations, set him at once above all who have come after him in ages of greater experience. Polybius, on the other hand, is like a writer of our own times; with far less of inborn genius, he possessed a mass of acquired knowledge of which Thucydides would never have dreamed. He had, like a modern historian, read many books and seen many lands; one language at least besides his own must have been perfectly familiar to him; he had conversed with men of various nations, living in various states of society and under various forms of government. He had himself personally a wider political existence than fell to the lot of any historian before or after him. The son of a statesman of Megalopolis, he could remember Achaia a powerful federation, Macedonia a powerful monarchy, Carthage still free, Syria still threatening; he lived to see them all subject provinces or trembling allies of the great municipality of Rome. In his youth he bore to the grave the ashes of Philopoimên, a Grecian hero slain in purely Grecian warfare; he lived to secure some little fragments of Grecian freedom as contemptuous alms from the Roman conqueror. A man must have lived through a millennium in any other portion of the world's history to have gained with his own eyes and his own ears such a mass of varied political knowledge as the historian of the decline and fall of ancient Greece acquired within the limits of an ordinary life" (p. 226).

For our part, we should be disposed to put the contrast briefly thus: Thucydides is a great historian, a great thinker, and a great writer. Polybius is a good historian, a feeble thinker, and an indifferent writer. There is, therefore, much in Mr. Freeman's estimate of him with which we cannot agree. To recommend an ancient historian to the notice of modern readers because he had read many books and seen many lands, and because he was perfectly familiar with one language at least beside his own, is to suggest a comparison between ancient and modern historians which is not likely to turn out to the advantage of the former. But it is undeniable that Polybius lived in an age of great events, that he was an eye-witness of some of them, and that he had had himself experience of the transaction of affairs —advantages of which we should, perhaps, have thought more highly, if there were not something offensively self-sufficient in his consciousness of them, and in his criticisms on less fortunate historians. His one transcendent merit is, that he is careful to ascertain the truth, and to tell it when he has ascertained it; he is not only a great authority when we have others beside him, but he is also of incalculable value to us as our only authority for the history of many important events. His style is free from rhetorical affectation, but it is often cumbrous and unpleasant. He is perfectly destitute of imagination, yet his use of language is certainly not remarkable for precision. His reflections are commonplace, and withal pedantically expressed, even when they are just; and they are not always just. Perhaps, of all writers of a reputation comparable to his, he is the one to whom the words "inborn genius" are the least applicable. There is also something in the tone of his history not altogether creditable to him. That he should regard with complacency the condition of his country under the Romans; that he should look upon it as the crowning result of the lives and labours of Aratus, Philopœmen, and Lycortas, argues indeed that "utter absence of all merely sentimental patriotism" for which Mr. Freeman elsewhere gives him credit. Plutarch tells us that when an orator in the Achaian assembly was insisting on the necessity of a policy of subserviency to Rome, Philopœmen interrupted him with the exclamation, "Man, why do you hasten to look upon the fate of Greece?" The youth who carried the ashes of Philopœmen to his tomb lived to look upon the fate of Greece, and thought it the best thing that could have happened.* Again, it is certain that in his history of Achaian affairs he is not exempt from partiality. If his account were the only one that had reached us, we should never have recognised the noble patriotism of Cleomenes, and we should never have suspected the grave faults in the public character of Aratus. The policy of the latter in the Cleomenic war placed the Achaian League at the mercy of the Macedonian kings, yet it is represented by Polybius as a masterpiece of diplomatic skill, without the slightest inti-

* This feeling of Polybius would be inexplicable, if we did not bear in mind that the result of the Achaian war with Rome, though fatal to the city of Corinth, and though leading to the temporary dissolution of the league, did not in a technical sense deprive the Greek communities of their freedom. "If we look to the formal sovereignty of the free communities, it must be granted that the position of Greece was not altered in point of constitutional law by the events of the year 146 B.C. It was a difference *de facto* rather than *de jure*, when, instead of the Achaian League, the individual communities of Achaia now appeared by the side of Rome as tributary protected states." Mommsen's *History of Rome*, book iv. cap. 1, note.—[Engl. Trans.] We must remember also that Polybius was the legislator of the Achaian cities, and that he naturally looked with favour on the work of his own hands. Of the catastrophe itself, as opposed to the restoration which followed it, he speaks in terms which imply perhaps too keen a perception of the demerits of his countrymen, but which, on the whole, do him no dishonour. See the Vatican Excerpts, lib. xxxviii.

mation that it was even misdirected. The wide discrepancy, with respect to that policy, between the judgment of Polybius on the one hand, and of Plutarch and nearly all modern historians on the other, cannot be explained by the Achaian or Megalopolitan patriotism of Polybius; it is simply a result of that imperfect perception of moral greatness, or, indeed, of any moral element in human affairs, which is conspicuous in his history. The passage in which he justifies the infliction of death by torture on the Argive Aristomachus, is perhaps a fair example of the worst faults of which he is capable. It is evidently prompted by a desire to criticise the historian Phylarchus; it is historically disingenuous, inasmuch as the fact is half admitted and half denied, and inasmuch as the charge against Aristomachus, which is alleged in justification of his punishment, is, as Mr. Freeman has shown, of very questionable truth; while the vindication of torture at all is unworthy of Greek humanity, and reminds us that Polybius was a Romanised Achaian, and accustomed to the barbarity of Roman punishments. In striking contrast to all this, it is impossible not to admire the impartiality of his attitude with regard to the Roman power, the establishment of which in the world is the subject of his history. It is to him simply a great fact, the causes of which he does his best to analyse. "In all great matters," says Mommsen, "he has no interest for one state or against another, for this man or against that." This is true, if we remember that with Mommsen, Achaian matters, and others standing on the same level, are not great matters.

If Mr. Freeman overvalues Polybius, he makes up for it by undervaluing Livy. Thus he tells us that "there are several narratives in Livy which are translated from Polybius to the best of Livy's small ability." He is "tempted to believe that Livy had never heard of either Aratus till he came to the events of B.C. 208." The temptation to which Mr. Freeman has in this instance succumbed we do not quite understand; but we must admit that Livy blunders when, speaking of the year B.C. 195, he tells us, that Sparta had been subject to tyrants *per aliquot ætates;* the truth being that Sparta at that time had been subject to tyrants for about thirty years. Other charges of Mr. Freeman's against Livy do not seem so clearly made out. It is surely unfair to infer from the words "Eleorum accensi odio quod à cæteris Achæis dissentirent," that Livy had an "idea that Elis was a state which had seceded from the Achaian League," and to ask, "What can he have found and misunderstood in his Polybius?" Elis had never as yet belonged to the Achaian League, and therefore the expression "*cæteris*

Achæis" is strictly speaking incorrect; but we submit Livy's obvious meaning is the truth, that Elis sympathised with the enemies of the Achaian League. We deprecate altogether the fashion of decrying Livy which has set in since the time of Niebuhr, though we do not hold Niebuhr responsible for it. There are few historians indeed whose character for accuracy would stand the microscopic scrutiny which it is occasionally in our power to bring to bear on Livy. We would remind Mr. Freeman that he himself has made it very probable that his favourite Polybius has confounded the Argive Aristomachus, whom we have already mentioned, with one of his predecessors, and that he has thus attributed to the Aristomachus who was put to death by torture a crime which he never committed. Yet this error in a Peloponnesian historian would imply far greater carelessness than Livy's incidental confusion of the great Cleomenes with one of his successors.

We have already had occasion to observe how imperfect our knowledge is of the constitution of the Achaian League. Like the constitutions of the United States and of the Swiss Confederation, it must have been formally enacted and accepted by the cities of the league at some definite period of its history. Unfortunately for us, this original treaty of union has not been preserved, and we have to infer its provisions from incidental notices in Polybius, Livy, Plutarch, and Pausanias. One source of difficulty in the attempt to put these notices together is, that they relate to very different periods of Achaian history; and it is possible that the constitution may have undergone modifications more or less important. Another is, that Polybius (himself an Achaian statesman, and perfectly familiar with every detail of the constitution) is not very careful in his use of words;* and when we find that Polybius is occasionally confusing, we cannot expect less from those who used him as an authority. The supreme power of the league resided in an assembly, in which every citizen of the age of thirty years, of

* Mr. Freeman tells us that Polybius speaks of the assembly as *Ἀχαιοί, ἔθνος, σύνοδος, πλῆθος, οἱ πολλοί, ἐκκλησία, ὄχλος, ἀγορά*. Of these, *Ἀχαιοί, ἔθνος, πλῆθος, οἱ πολλοί, ὄχλος*, are evidently not constitutional names. But whether the assembly was properly called *σύνοδος ἐκκλησία* or *ἀγορά* we cannot make out. Yet it is inconceivable that it should not have had some proper constitutional name; and if so, a really careful writer would have let us know it. The word oftenest used by Polybius is *σύνοδος*; but perhaps the chances are in favour of *ἀγορά*. An extraordinary meeting is called *σύγκλητος* by Polybius, which may or may not have been its formal name. *Τὸ κοινὸν τῶν Ἀχαιῶν* is not the formal title of the Achaian assembly, but of the Achaian state. Again, such an expression as *οἱ τῆς γερουσίας* (Polyb. xxxviii. 5) must mean either the body which is elsewhere called *βουλή*, or the council of officers of state elsewhere called *ἄρχοντες* or *ἀρχαί*. In either case the plurality of names for the same political body is probably attributable to a not very culpable carelessness in Polybius's way of writing.

any city of the league, had a vote. The limitation of age appears requisite to explain an obscure passage in Polybius, to which we shall presently refer. As the constitution of the cities of the league was in all cases more or less democratic, the assembly was itself in theory a democratic body. But the provisions of the constitution and the circumstances of the country rendered the assembly at once less powerful and less democratic than it was theoretically. The Athenian "ecclesia" met every ten days in the Pnyx. The Achaian assembly met regularly only twice a year, in spring and autumn; and as its extraordinary sessions were limited by law to three days, we may presume that its ordinary meetings were similarly limited to a certain number of days. Thus, it can never have attempted to exercise those administrative functions which the Athenian assembly took upon itself, but must have entrusted the whole executive power to the annually elected officers of the league, who thus became a government in the constitutional sense of that term. These officers were a general, an under-general, a general of cavalry, a secretary, and ten demiurgi.* The general was the president of the league; his office was civil as well as military; he was the keeper of the common seal of the league; and we find the curiously modern phrases "to lay down the seal," "to receive the seal," used as equivalent for resigning and entering on the office. On the other hand, the functions of the under-general and general of cavalry seem to have been purely military. Those of the secretary are probably sufficiently characterised by the title of the office. The demiurgi appear, from one or two narratives in Polybius, to have formed a kind of cabinet council for the general, though it does not appear how far his power in time of peace was limited by theirs. It would seem that the important power of summoning extraordinary meetings of the assembly was vested, not in the general alone, but in the general and demiurgi.† The demiurgi, not the general, presided in the assembly, and put questions to the vote. They could refuse to put an illegal question to the assembly at all. We may infer, from the whole tenor of the history,

* An "admiral of the Achaians" is mentioned, Polyb. v. 94. But as it does not appear that the Achaians maintained a fleet, although we hear afterwards of royal presents of ships accepted by them, these words are probably to be understood with reference to the six ships mentioned in cap. 91. In the difficult passage in cap. 94, *αὐτὸς μὲν ἧκε πρὸς τὴν τῶν Ἀχαιῶν σύνοδον, τοὺς δὲ μισθοφόρους συνέστησε Λύκῳ τῷ Φαραιεῖ, διὰ τὸ τοῦτον ὑποστράτηγον εἶναι τότε τῆς συντελείας τῆς πατρικῆς* (quoted by Mr. Freeman at p. 281), it is surely simplest to interpret the words *τῆς συντελείας τῆς πατρικῆς* of the national contingent (see cap. 91), as opposed to the mercenary forces. If this interpretation be correct, it would imply that the under-general was ordinarily commander of the national forces, and that, as the name of the office implies, he was the natural person to take the chief command in the absence of the general.

† Polyb. xxiii. 10.

that the general was supreme in time of war, and that his cabinet council had then no power to control him. But what the ordinary powers of the government were, we have no means of ascertaining with precision; only it is clear that an assembly, whose session lasted but a few days, must have left a large discretion to its officers. The assembly voted the supplies of men and money for the year; it gave audience to ambassadors, and declared peace or war; it elected its officers, and no doubt called them to account when their year of office was over; but beyond this it can have interfered very little. In these circumstances Mr. Freeman justly discerns a nearer approximation to what we term constitutional government than is elsewhere to be found in ancient history.

If the meetings of the assembly had really been attended by the whole adult population, they would have been of ungovernable size, and unfit for the despatch of business. But, except on very rare and stirring occasions, it is not to be supposed that any such concourse took place. In its later days the league included the whole of Peloponnesus, and even at the beginning of the Cleomenic war it included Megara and the north-eastern half of the peninsula. The citizens of the town in which the assembly was held might be present *en masse*, but only a fractional part of the citizens of any other state could attend; only those, in fact, who had time and money to spare. The assembly thus acquired, as Mr. Freeman clearly shows, an aristocratic and conservative tendency; though the danger of an oligarchical development of this tendency was obviated by the certainty that the democracies which were left at home could come at any time they pleased, and outvote their *quasi*-aristocratic representatives. The attendance at the meetings of the assembly was often very thin: it would even seem that sometimes none but members of the senate or council (a body which we have not yet mentioned) were present. A proposal to send an auxiliary force to the Ptolemies is thrown out because it could not lawfully be considered in an ordinary assembly; some time after an extraordinary assembly is held; and there come together to it, so Polybius tells us, not only the council, but also all the citizens of thirty years of age.* The inference is obvious: that meetings commonly were not so well attended. Under these circumstances, it was natural that considerable precautions should be taken to prevent a surprise of the majority by a minority. We have just seen that there were some matters which could

* The word which we have ventured to translate an "ordinary meeting" is *ἀγορά*. It is very improbable that it means a market-place, as Tittmann supposes. It will be remembered that *ἡ πρώτη ἀγορά* is elsewhere used for the spring meeting.

not be taken into consideration at an ordinary meeting; and we know from Livy that it was unlawful to submit to an extraordinary meeting a resolution foreign to the matters which it was convened to consider.

The vote of the assembly appears to have been taken by cities, and the vote of each city to have been given by the majority of its citizens present. This is nowhere distinctly stated; but it is not in itself improbable, and is perhaps implied by the passages cited from Livy. To take the vote of the majority of those present by heads would have been more conformable to the practice of Greek democracies; but when the assembly met at Corinth or Megalopolis it would have been swamped by Corinthian or Megalopolitan citizens. The vote by cities must have had the effect of giving something of a representative character to the assembly; for though the voters who attended from each city did not attend as delegates from the city, yet we may be quite sure that if an important question arose on which opinion in a particular city was divided, the majority in the city took care that its vote in the assembly was not given in favour of the minority. An obvious disadvantage of the vote by cities was, that it placed great states, like Argos or Corinth on a par with little townships whose names are almost unknown to history. This inequality might easily have been compensated by allowing, as was done in the Lycian League, a plurality of votes to the larger cities; but if this had been the case, we can hardly imagine that Polybius, where he extols the generosity of the Achaians to those whom they admitted into their league, would have omitted to mention this signal instance of it. It may well surprise even those who remember an unreformed parliament that such a state of things could have been tolerated by the larger cities. Yet we cannot show historically that any evil consequences came of it; a fact which we can only attribute to the spirit of fairness and moderation (unexampled in the ancient world) which characterised the Achaian people. And when we find that in the later times of the league Philopœmen and Lycortas pursued a policy of dismemberment with regard to such states as Megalopolis, Sparta, and Messene, we believe that this was done much more to break the power of those states than to swamp the original Achaian cities by increasing the total number of votes; especially as every such increase put unpartitioned states, like Corinth and Argos, in a worse position than they were in before.

The functions of the senate or council cannot, we think, be divined from the casual expressions of Polybius. Such, indeed, is the vagueness of his phraseology, that the passage which we have already quoted is probably the only one which clearly proves its existence as a separate body. In other places it seems to be confused with the general assembly. Mr. Freeman infers its functions from those of the bodies similarly named in other Greek states, and supposes "that the government brought their proposals before it to be discussed, and perhaps amended, by this smaller body before they were submitted to the final decision of the assembly." His statement, that it consisted of 120 members, is, if we are not mistaken, without any foundation in the passage to which he refers in proof of it. King Eumenes offers a present of 120 talents to the Achaian League, which they are to invest, using the interest to pay the councillors for their attendance at the public meetings of the assembly. The offer, much to the honour of the Achaians, was declined, with a very emphatic intimation that they were not grateful for it; but the interesting debate which Polybius records does not inform us either of the number or of the duties of the council. It is not even quite certain, though it is very probable, that the councillors were unpaid; for the proposal of Eumenes may have gone to relieve the league from a burden, and not to introduce an entirely new practice into the constitution. Whether the high Achaian offices were paid or unpaid must also be left undecided, and we think that Mr. Freeman has over-estimated the evidence on this point. But that they were not remuneratively paid we may be sure, not only because we find them uniformly in the hands of men of wealth and position, but also from a particular case in which it is mentioned, that Archon, a general of the league, had incurred such heavy expenses in his year of office, that he was unwilling to support an application of King Attalus, for fear it should be thought that he wished to indemnify himself by accepting a royal present; a thing which, as we learn from the debate on the offer of Eumenes, was forbidden by law not only to officers of the league, but also to private citizens. So long as office could only be held at a pecuniary loss, it is not surprising that the administration of the league remained constantly in the hands of the upper classes, and that we hear of nothing resembling the demagogy of the earlier periods of Greek history. It is also remarkable, and greatly to the credit of the Achaian people, that we hear nothing of bribery being employed at elections, though in the worst days of the league we find federal officials, even federal generals, taking bribes. The instance of a corrupt election, which Mr. Freeman mentions, is not really one. Polybius does not say that Callicrates had used bribery to carry his election, which is attributed to other causes, but that he had himself been bribed, probably by the Spartan and Messenian exiles, whose restitution, on entering upon his office, he immediately effects.

With regard to the precise relation of the federal authority to the individual cities, we are again left to draw our inference from the incidents of the history itself. It would seem that the act by which a new city entered the league took the form of a treaty with the league—a treaty recorded in the usual Greek manner, upon a monumental pillar. These pillars are frequently alluded to in the course of the history. Unfortunately, not one of the inscriptions on them has been preserved to our time. One thing, however, is perfectly clear, that the management of foreign affairs was vested absolutely in the federal government, and that each city on entering the league simply ceased to exist as an independent state in the presence of foreign nations. One of the most striking proofs that this was the rule is presented by an exception to it. The city of Megalopolis, in the Cleomenic war, sends an embassy to Antigonus Doson to ask for his help. But it asks and obtains the leave of the federal assembly before it takes this step. And the reply of Antigonus is, that he will send the assistance requested, "if the Achaians give their consent." Later, however, when Rome was preparing the way for the dissolution of the Achaian League, we hear of frequent embassies from discontented states (as Lacedæmon and Messene) to Rome. But this, it cannot be doubted, was a violation of the federal constitution, as it also was of the treaty with Rome, in which, according to Pausanias,* it was expressly provided that ambassadors should be received at Rome only from the federal government, and not from the individual states. In earlier times, we hear of cities belonging to the league sending ambassadors to represent them at the assembly (see the cases of Mantinea and Megalopolis, in Mr. Freeman's work, pp. 448-466). In this (though it is contrary to the usage of the United States of America) there is clearly nothing contrary to the principle of a federal union: nor do we quite understand the surprise at it which Mr. Freeman expresses. Since the Mantinean or Megalopolitan citizens who attended a meeting of the assembly, attended only as private citizens, and not as accredited representatives of their city, it is clear that, in order to address the assembly in the name of the city, special commissioners were necessary. This necessity is not felt in America, where the states are represented in Congress, not only as populations, in the House of Representatives, but as states, in the Senate. In Switzerland, however, although the cantons are represented precisely as the states in America, it is,

* Paus. vii. 9, 12.

nevertheless, in addition provided that a canton shall have the right of communicating directly, by correspondence, with either house of the legislature.

We should gladly, if our limits had permitted, have followed Mr. Freeman's course through the events of the Achaian history, as well as through the somewhat dry details of the Achaian constitution. We can only refer to one or two points. Few histories are so biographical as that of the Achaian League. The lives of Aratus and Philopœmen exhaust between them nearly the whole story. To these names the filial piety of Polybius has induced him to add that of his own father Lycortas, who, after the death of Philopœmen, endeavoured steadily to carry out his policy of temperate resistance to Roman aggression. Mr. Freeman, we are sure, would wish to complete the list with Markos, the first general of the Achaians, and Lydiadas, the tyrant of Megalopolis, who voluntarily laid down his tyranny, and united the "great city" to the league. On Aratus Mr. Freeman is severe, perhaps even hardly just. The picture that he gives us of his military character is certainly over-coloured. "No man," we are told, "risked his life more freely in a surprise, in an ambuscade, in a night assault;" but "this man, so fearless in one sort of warfare, was in the open field as timid as a woman or a slave. . . . . History puts the fact itself beyond a doubt: Aratus in the open field was a coward." Human nature presents many strange contradictions; but the contradiction here described seems to us to pass the bounds of credibility. The fact, which history puts beyond a doubt, is, that Aratus lost almost every battle that he fought, and never fought a battle when he could help it. What he was afraid to risk was the Achaian army, and with it the Achaian commonwealth; his own life he probably held as cheap by day as by night. And something might be said in his defence. The Achaian troops were not to be depended on; they had confidence neither in their leaders nor in one another. It is true that, under Philopœmen's training, they showed that they could become good soldiers; but Aratus did not possess Philopœmen's military genius. In one instance, at least, the military demerits of Aratus are exaggerated by Mr. Freeman. At the battle of Ladocea he is accused of halting his heavy-armed troops on the brink of a trench, and refusing to allow them to cross it. In this he was probably wrong, though Plutarch says he was inferior in numbers to Cleomenes. But, at any rate, it is fair to observe that the obstacle which, in Mr. Freeman's English is a trench, in the Greek of Plutarch is a deep ravine. Lydiadas, perhaps with more courage than judgment, called to the cavalry to follow him, and charged the enemy. Still Aratus did not stir. In the broken ground Lydiadas was overpowered and killed. The popular judgment of the Achaians was probably the truth; it was, that Aratus had not supported Lydiadas as he ought to have done, and that through his fault Lydiadas had perished.

Lydiadas is a great favourite with Mr. Freeman; he places him "among the first of men." It is disappointing, after his ardent panegyric, to turn to Polybius, or even to Plutarch; we are made to feel how scanty the materials are for so much enthusiasm. Something of greatness there must have been about this man, or he could not have divided with Aratus the affections of the Achaian people. We feel that Cleomenes did well when he wrapped the body of the fallen hero in a kingly robe and sent it crowned to Megalopolis. We wish to believe all that Mr. Freeman has found to say about him; but the utmost that we can bring ourselves to credit is, that it may be true. We read in Plutarch that Lydiadas, when he was yet a youth, made himself tyrant of Megalopolis. On this text we have the following comment:

"In his youth he seized the tyranny of his native city; but he seized it with no ignoble or unworthy aim. We know not the date or the circumstances of his rise to sovereign power, but there is at least nothing to mark him as one of those tyrants who were the destroyers of freedom. He is not painted to us as a midnight conspirator, plotting rebellion against a state of things which made him only one free citizen among many. Still less is he painted as the chief magistrate of a free state, bound by the most solemn oaths to be faithful to its freedom, and then turning the limited powers with which his country had intrusted him to overthrow the liberties of which he was the chosen guardian. We do not read that he rose to power by driving a lawful senate from their hall by the spears of mercenaries, or by an indiscriminate massacre of this fellow-citizens in the streets of the Great City. We do not read that he reigned by crushing every noble feeling, and by flattering every baser passion, of his subjects; we are not told that every man of worth or talent shrank from his service, and left him only hirelings and flatterers as the agents of his will. There is no evidence that the dungeons of Megalopolis or the cities of free Greece were filled with men whose genius or whose virtue was found inconsistent with his rule. We do not hear that his foreign policy was one of faithless aggression; that he gave out that tyranny should be peace, and then filled Peloponnêsos with needless wars. It is not told us that he seized on city after city, prefacing every act of plunder with solemn protestations that nothing was further from his thoughts. Still less do we find that he ever played the basest part to which tyranny itself can sink; that he stretched forth his hand to give a hypocritical aid to struggling freedom, and then drew back, that he might glut his eyes with the sight of a land wasted by anarchy and brigandage, to which a word from him would at any moment put an end. No; Lydiadas was" &c.

For Mr. Freeman's sake, no less than for that of his readers, we enter our protest against this mode of writing history. We have no partiality for Louis Napoleon, nor have we any wish to spare him a single invective, so long as invective does not intrude into history. But we instinctively feel that invectives against him, which might suit the columns of the *Saturday Review*, are out of place in a history of the Achaian League. To tell us what Louis Napoleon has done, under pretence of telling us what Lydiadas did not do, neither helps us to understand Achaian history, nor really does any honour to Lydiadas. Unfortunately the passage we have cited is not the only instance of the fault—so grave, and yet so easy to avoid—of carrying the passions and the language of a journalist into history. It is a real blemish in Mr. Freeman's book; it is a serious drawback to the pleasure with which we read his comparisons of the ancient and modern world, and it gives an ephemeral character to a work the interest of which is not, and ought not to be, ephemeral.

ART. V.—POLAND AS IT IS.

[It may be right to say that we give in the following Article the exact words of a most intelligent eye-witness of the Polish Revolution. The policy of this country with regard to Poland is discussed in Article IX.]

La Pologne Contemporaine. Par Charles de Mazade. Paris: Michel Lévy.

Recueil des principaux Traités. Par Martens. Vols. VIII. and X.

THE saying of the Emperor Nicholas, "there is no Poland except among the *émigrés*," may now take place with the similar aphorism of Metternich, that Italy was only a geographical expression. At the very moment when the work of the Holy Alliance seemed to be complete, the accident of a political dinner among a few third-rate politicians in Paris shook it to the ground. The first Italian War, and the reappearance of a Napoleon in France, led up so naturally to Sebastopol and Solferino, that the new order might almost seem to have been inherited. The instinctive hatred which the Tory and Legitimist party every where have felt for the Crimean War, and their unreasoning previsions of evil, have been fully justified by the results on the absolutist system. We are making a new world every where in Europe; or rather, perhaps, we are stripping off the lath-and-plaster with which certain kingly architects defaced the natural work of time nearly fifty years ago. There has been much bloodshed in the operation, and not a little blundering and intrigue. But the final results at present attained have been Italian liberty, serf-emancipation in Russia, a constitution in Austria, and a great expansion of material progress in France and England. Perhaps fifteen years could hardly have been expected to do more.

With the first beginnings of troubles, all eyes were turned upon Russian Poland. To the surprise of all, it remained quiet. There was insurrection in Posen and a war in Hungary, in which Poles did gallant service; but they seemed still to be the true countrymen of Sobieski, doing battle for every banner except their own. The Crimean War came and passed with no armed uprising against the Russian yoke in Warsaw. The campaign of Solferino had almost produced an insurrection in Hungary; but Poland was still apathetic, or at least peaceful. Suddenly, in 1861, the news came, not of insurrection, but of massacre. Europe heard with consternation of an unarmed crowd shot down in a public square without warning, and, as it seemed, with no better motive than the caprice of a subaltern of police. Presently, however, it appeared that a struggle of a kind never yet known had commenced throughout the Polish provinces of Russia. On the one hand, the Russians were striving to provoke a revolt, in order, as Wielopolski once expressed it, that they might bring the abscess to a head. On the other hand, the Poles had resolved to offer themselves to death on every possible occasion, in the belief that the spirit of martyrdom would at length be too strong for despotism itself. The parallel steadily kept in view, and unflinchingly acted up to, was that of the early Christians under the Empire. "The crown of thorns," said a manifesto, "has been our emblem for a century: . . . it means patience in grief, self-sacrifice, deliverance, and pardon." The crown of thorns is never long waited for. Not two months after the first massacre a second crowd assembled near the castle, refused to disperse, and received fifteen volleys with the solidity of veterans. Only prayers and hymns answered the roll of musketry. It might seem that this enthusiasm would be as short-lived as all violent emotions commonly are. But months passed; and the Poles were still readier to offer themselves to death than the Russians to slay. The whole country wore the garb and the aspect of a funeral. Such depth of national sentiment, the growth of long misery, confounded observers in happier distant countries, and was at first mistaken for a mere masquerade. The *Saturday Review*, which is professedly incapable of understanding that there is a noble side to humanity, accused the Poles of acting like petulant children. That fatal contempt for weakness, which clings to Englishmen, added to the general misconception of the drama whose first scenes had been already acted, and the demonstrations were disregarded precisely because the actors were unarmed. At last the fatality of great crimes hurried the Russian Government into a new step. It was resolved to draw the new conscription entirely from the towns, with the double view of sparing the peasantry and of thinning the educated class, who are the eternal enemies of misgovernment. The deed seemed to be done, when some unlucky official conceived the idea of insulting the victims. Europe was told in a telegram that the conscription had been carried out in perfect tranquillity. The jest was one of questionable good taste even for an *employé* of the school of Nicholas, and its results were disastrous. A majority of one in the secret government decided that war at any hazards was preferable to extinction without a sign; and the conscripts not already in custody were instructed to take to the forests, and defend themselves as they could, unarmed in mid-winter, against a disciplined army. "And now," a Polish gentleman lately said to us, "Europe believes that we are alive because we are fighting. Is it not horrible that all our sufferings, all our struggles after constitutional reform, were actually unheeded till we appealed to arms,—the last argument of the barbarian?"

Without wishing to defend English apathy on the Polish question, we are constrained to admit that it is not quite inexcusable. The Poles have been too apt to rest their cause primarily on the injustice of the two partitions of Poland, and to date all their demands for redress from 1772. We believe this to be a mistake in principle. The spoilers of Poland were certainly not sovereigns of high character, and they carried out their designs with a mixture of low intrigue, hypocrisy, and brutal violence, which made the injustice additionally revolting. Perhaps the only extenuating circumstance was, that they did not invoke a blessing upon their plunder, like the Congress of Vienna a little later, in the name of the Holy and Indivisible Trinity. But their victim deserved its fate. Since the rescue of Vienna by Sobieski, Poland had governed itself worse than any nation is permitted to do and live. It had the most disorderly form of government, the most intolerant Church, and the most degraded peasantry in Europe. Its one redeeming virtue was the courage of its people, and, thanks to its nobles, it had no army. It was a perpetual occasion of war on the confines of countries that might wish to be at peace. To have saved such a nation from its natural fate, foreseen for more than a century, and to have propped up its decrepitude by European guarantees, would have been policy eminently worthy of the cabinet that now keeps the Turks in Constantinople. But it was not the statesmanship of Chatham or his contemporaries in England, any more than of Choiseul in France. Sensible men regretted that another bulwark against the Muscovite had been broken down, and that even such a shadow of freedom as the Polish constitution had been was replaced by very actual tyrannies. But it would have been the extreme of political quixotism for England to declare war against Russia and Prussia, its old and late allies, in behalf of a people who scarcely protested by words, and in no wise protested by acts, against the usurpation. At the time of the second partition we were in no condition to interfere, if we had wished it; the war with France absorbed every energy.

The real second life of Poland dates from the second partition. Short-lived as the struggle for liberty was, it had a few glorious memories. A body of insurgents in Warsaw, never stronger than 1500, by the admissions of the Russian general opposed to them, drove out a garrison of more than 10,000 disciplined troops from the town. Kosciusko invented the terrible Polish scythemen,—imitated, perhaps, from the old flailmen of Ziska, who are still the only known instances of peasants that have been able to cope with regular troops. Crushed by overwhelming forces, and by the ferocious energy of Suvarof, the insurrection now became an emigration, and traversed Europe under the banners of Napoleon. But Napoleon in his heart regarded Polish nationality as a chimera, useful only as a phrase in bulletins and a stalking-horse in diplomacy. He consented at the treaty of Tilsit to dismember the country for the benefit of the man he most hated and despised, the King of Prussia; he declared Lithuania Russian; and in reconstituting a sort of shadowy Poland in the grand duchy of Warsaw he made it the appanage of a petty German prince, the King of Saxony. Nevertheless, under all discouragements, the Polish name made itself so well respected, that the conquerors of Vienna, who punished Saxony and Denmark for adherence to the fortunes of the fallen chief, were well disposed to reconstitute Poland. The time was eminently favourable for reconstruction, and Austria and Prussia would have made sacrifices to keep a few hundred miles of neutral ground between themselves and their Muscovite ally. To Russia alone Poland was too important to be given up. It was the richest province of the empire, the point of contact with the West, the advance-post upon Europe, and it symbolised Russia's retribution on an old foe. In face of the colossal Russian force occupying the country, and bound as they were by recent obligations to the Czar, the allies did not care to enter upon a war for the sake of reconstituting a fallen nationality. But they made it the very first article in the treaty of Vienna, that "the Poles, the respective subjects of Russia, Austria, and Prussia, shall obtain a representation and national institutions;" and, in the peculiar phraseology, "the duchy of Warsaw" "shall be united irrevocably by its constitution" "to the empire of Russia," they implied, as Lord Russell has well observed in his despatch of August 11, that the constitution was the consideration for which Poland was surrendered. Europe wished to mitigate as much as possible the sacrifices it was obliged to ratify.

But the allies did even more than this. By the 14th article they decreed that the regulations for free trade and free use of rivers, canals, and ports throughout the whole extent of ancient Poland,—that is to say, the Poland of 1772,—which Russia, Austria, and Prussia had agreed to by private treaties, should become of international force, and be maintained inviolably. The intention obviously was to minimise the evils of the partition, and preserve a shadow as it were of the old Poland, which might some day, under favourable chances, become a reality. If therefore the persistence of the Poles in claiming Lithuania and parts of Little Russia is to be treated as irrational, it must be remembered that the chimera has been sanctioned by the public law of Europe, and agreed to by the spoilers. In the same spirit, no doubt, article 6 decreed the independence of the free town of Cracow under the protection of Russia, Austria, and Prussia. The royal town was left inviolate, as a sort of symbol of the unimpaired right of the nation to exist. Its seizure in 1846 by its protectors was a flagrant violation of the compact; and Prince Metternich's explanation, that the treaty only gave a hypothetical right of inquiry and remonstrance, was enough to sap the foundations of all international good faith. In saying this, however, we are not caring to waste regret upon the fallen fortunes of Cracow. Its position fitted it for nothing but to be an emporium of smuggling, of secret presses, and of conspiracies; and it fully availed itself of its position. A free town of Cracow between three enslaved provinces was an anomaly; and more tolerant men than Metternich and Nicholas I. might have been tempted to suppress it. Still in 1815 its establishment was one of several articles that all tended to the same end,—the ultimate restoration of the old Poland,—every one of which has been violated.

Up to a certain point, then, the efforts of the Polish patriots, if not altogether successful, had not been useless. Poland was once more a name in Europe, and a name for which those who bore it need not blush. The next fifteen years were the Lehr-Jahre of the people born again. If the constitution given them by Alexander had been loyally carried out, the Poles would have been mad indeed to try the chances of war for the mere phantom of nationality. That memorable instrument must, as Lord Russell has observed, "when once promulgated, be taken to be the constitution meant by the framers of the treaty," and as such, we may add, cannot be revoked arbitrarily. It guaranteed freedom of the press, freedom from arrest before conviction, and the secure possession of property, confining the government to natives, and making the ministers responsible to the bicameral parliament. The functions of the Czar as king were virtually confined to proposing laws, nominating life-judges and life-senators, and commanding a native army within the country. The whole reads like Utopia or England. The system at first worked so well that opposition was scarcely known in the Chambers; and Alexander declared his intentions of extending representative institutions to Russia. Population and wealth increased as it were by miracle. But the beginnings of evil were soon evident. We do not wish to hold the Poles blameless. These were times of revolution every where, of Carbonari, and Turn-vereine, and Luddites. There were men in Poland for whom every thing was insufficient short of national independence. In England such dissentients would have been allowed to talk till they were dumb, or the public tired out. The Russian Government at once established a censorship of the press (1819). Opposition transferred itself to the parliament, and the parliament was no longer summoned, or when it met, once in ten years, was packed. Readers of De Custine, who may perhaps be trusted when he reports conversations, will remember how he admires the remark of Nicholas, that all representative monarchy was "the government of falsehood, fraud, corruption." It was so in Poland, because the Czar, who never recovered the panic of Pestal's conspiracy, degraded it by intrigues and violence; but after all said he could never fashion it to his pleasure. The case for Poland, however, is best summed up in the manifesto which the Polish Committee issued in 1831 (Jan. 10): "The union of the crown of an autocrat and of a constitutional king is one of those political anomalies which cannot long exist. Every body foresaw that the kingdom would become the germ of liberal institutions for Russia, or succumb under the iron hand of its despotism. The question was soon decided. Public instruction was corrupted . . . The people were shut out from all means of obtaining instruction. An entire palatinate was deprived of its representatives in the council. The Chamber lost the power of voting the budget. Monopolies were created calculated to dry up the resources of national wealth . . . Calumny and espionage had penetrated even into the privacy of families. . . . Personal freedom, which had been solemnly guaranteed, was violated; the prisons were crowded; courts-martial were appointed to decide in civil causes, and imposed infamous punishments on citizens whose only crime was that of having attempted to save from corruption the spirit and character of the nation."

Nevertheless, whatever its excuses may have been, the insurrection of 1831 had the worst of all faults,—it was a political blunder. The revolution in Paris had by this time died out, with no better issue than that of replacing M. Sotenville by Jérome Paturot,—the most foolish of sovereigns by the most undignified. Never man was less disposed to risk his family fortunes for any abstract principle of good, or more inclined to pay his debts of honour with frothy phrases, than was Louis Philippe. He had studied the English constitution with no other result than to believe that corruption was the main-spring of representative government. He cheated in statesmanship from a simple feeling that life was a sharper's game, and that it was due to himself to have the winning hand. In one respect, however, he was beyond his country and his time. The principle of non-intervention, which he first put forward as a European programme, was so little appreciated in 1831 that it only provoked contempt and incredulity. Men persisted in believing that the strong nation ought to protect the weak, and that the interests of Belgium and Poland were those of free countries every where. For a moment it seemed as if the little province of Luxembourg would be the apple of discord between West and East, Russia and the German Empire maintaining the principles of the Holy Alliance against France, and perhaps England. We know now that Louis Philippe would have blustered up to the last moment, and truckled at the last; but it was not so understood then, and the Czar prepared for a campaign on the Rhine. The whole forces of the empire were actually in march to the frontier when the insurrection in Warsaw broke out. Well might Marshal Diebitsch say to the Polish deputies that their movement at least had not the merit of being *à propos*. But if the blunder was a great, it was also a splendid one. Never men fought with more reckless heroism than the Poles of that generation. At Grochow less than 50,000 men repelled the main Russian army of 180,000, under Diebitsch. On one occasion 500 Polish gentlemen, in court-dress and armed with small swords, threw themselves in mere wantonness of battle on a detachment of the Russian guards, and were cut to pieces to a man, not unavenged. The population of Warsaw by the time order was restored in it had sunk from 140,000 to 75,000. Had Prussia been neutral, or Poland itself more firmly united, the issue might still have been different; for the Russian army was almost disorganised by the loss of officers, who have always been disproportionately few in its ranks. As it was, fortune remained on the side of great battalions.

The wrongs of the present generation of Poles may be said to date from the surrender of Warsaw. Nicholas told the deputies, in language strangely characteristic of the man, that he would destroy Warsaw at the first symptom of an outbreak; and that it was a real happiness to belong to Russia. A single incident of the punishment dealt out to the conquered will illustrate the absolutist conception of happiness. The mother of Prince Roman Sanguszko addressed a petition to the Czar, imploring mercy for her son, who had been condemned to Siberia. The Czar wrote at the bottom of the petition, "He shall go on foot." The leader of the convoy in which the prince actually went, with a sort of grim poetry, led a riderless horse, to the saddle of which a huge knout was attached, and from time to time pointing to it, with the words "The Czar's instrument," forced the prisoners to make genuflexions before it, as to a cross. Even in Siberia the exiles found that there were distinctions in misery, and that Poles and Russians were on a very different footing. Generally all depended on the character of the governor of the district, from whose caprice no appeal was possible. An exile who spent seventeen years in the country assured the author that six of his companions had been punished with six thousand blows a-piece. Horrible to state, one of them survived the infliction for years with a broken spine. Nevertheless the Emperor was so well satisfied with the expedient of transportation, that he actually issued an order to transfer five thousand families, by force if necessary, to the crown lands on the frontier of the Caucasus, the latter position being of course exposed to all the horrors of a border war. In the kingdom itself all independence was destroyed. The government recoiled indeed before a total change of the laws, and the Code Napoléon still subsists accordingly. But the troops were incorporated in the Russian army, where there is no distinction of nationality in the regiments, but all are arranged by height. Russian officials were introduced; the Chambers dissolved; the Catholic religion persecuted; the university and upper schools abolished or put under control;

and an attempt was even made to force the Russian costume upon the peasantry. But the most effectual engine of despotism undoubtedly was the conscription. Throughout the reign of Nicholas it was maintained at the rate of fifteen in the thousand, ten in the thousand being the highest proportion which statists regard as consistent with steady increase. In fact the population of the country districts remained almost stationary throughout the reign. The present insurrection would scarcely have been possible if the Treaty of Paris had not stipulated that the Russian army should be reduced within limits which practically made it impossible to draught soldiers during the last six years. That breathing-time has given the country a new generation of combatants.

Englishmen are not inclined to extenuate the vices of such government as this. But there is a tendency to look back on the stormy past of Poland,—an almost unbroken history, for two centuries before the partition, of wars, or civil feuds, or internal anarchy,—and to ask if such a people, however chivalrous and richly endowed, can ever be capable of self-government. There are races which seem fitted only for peculiar phases of civilisation, and which die out by some natural process when the appointed term has expired. The Pole, like the Hungarian and the Spaniard, was eminently a warrior; his very tribe-name, Lech, means "soldier." He bivouacked in the broad plains which the Vistula and the Bug water, and held his own manfully, without mountain fastnesses or fortified towns, against all comers. Once, indeed, the Tartar swept over him; but the wave of conquest broke as it passed on, and ebbed back again. Placed between the heathen Prussian, the barbarous Muscovite, and the fanatical Turk, Poland was for ages the border-garrison of Latin civilisation. But for more than three centuries a change has been coming upon the world; and the tradesman is supplanting the feudal soldier, buying him out of his estates, multiplying in terrible disproportion around him, and at last beating him in the field by dint of endurance and drill. The Pole did not move with a moving earth. His country, admirable for corn and timber, was comparatively unfitted for commerce, and had never been studded with towns instinct with municipal life. In the absence of a middle class the peasantry will always be unduly depressed; and in the old Polish provinces there was a difference of race between them and their nobility sufficient to widen the gulf between high and low. They were not lower than the Irish peasantry of the last century; perhaps not than the Continental peasantry generally, whom the Hohenzollerns kidnapped or an Elector of Hesse sold; but there was less chance that they would ever be elevated. Meanwhile the Pole was the Frenchman of Eastern Europe,—gay-hearted, prodigal, thoughtless, dividing his time between the faro-table and his seraglio. But whereas the French nobility—held in check by the towns, decimated by civil war, and controlled by able sovereigns—had surrendered the essentials of power and clung only to the most meaningless and vexatious privileges, the Polish nobles had seized the opportunity of the dying out of the Jagellons to establish their own power on the ruins of the throne. In 1572 the crown for the first time was thrown open to the world by the fatal advice of a Zamoiski, and the right of election extended to the lesser nobility; that is, from 200 or 300 magnates to 100,000 gentlemen. From that hour the ruin of Poland was sealed. Under competent kingship it might have done almost any thing in the sixteenth century, at the period of Russia's greatest weakness and of the Thirty Years' War. But with its kings mere titular presidents it lost provinces even under the ablest: under Sigismund III., who burned Moscow, and under John Sobieski, who saved Vienna.

Admitting all this, and without seeking to extenuate the excesses of a rampant liberty, we can hardly regard it as the very worst form of political error. The Polish nobles were perhaps not more factious than the Swedish; the difference was that the former were placed between great powers, whose interest it was to maintain disorder. From the time of Sobieski to the first partition, the country had three sovereigns; the first an Elector of Saxony, nominated by Austria and maintained by Russia; the second his son, nominated by Russia and Austria; and the third an old lover of Catherine II., nominated by a Muscovite army. Great political virtue in all classes of the nation might still have saved the country, or retarded its fall; but the eighteenth century was not the epoch of great political virtues in Europe generally. The Poles fell, as we have said, unjustly, but not undeservedly. The question really is, whether they are to be condemned to all time for having committed a gross political blunder in the sixteenth century, which they clung to as a privilege in the seventeenth, and which they were not allowed to reform in the eighteenth. For the influence of the Saxon court and Russian arms were steadily employed to maintain the Polish constitution in its most obnoxious form. In 1773 the partitioning powers declared, as fundamental laws which they would not allow to be disputed, that the crown should be elective for ever, and that no son or grandson should succeed his father until after an interval of two reigns; and further, that the republican form of government should be maintained. In 1788-1791 the Polish

Diet, notwithstanding, declared the throne hereditary, gave political rights to the middle classes and peasants, and reformed other flagrant abuses of the old system. The reforms were made the excuse of the second partition.

There is a common idea in England that nations are born free, and without special natural endowment cannot be made fit for constitutional government. It is the fashion to assume, accordingly, that the past failures of the Poles are decisive against them; that having enjoyed and lost liberty, they are clearly unfit for it. We venture to think that this view is at least overstrained. Even, taking our own country, it may fairly be asked whether an observer in 1689, recalling the history of the past fifty years,—the misgovernment of Charles I., the rebellion, Cromwell's military government, the servility of all classes under Charles II., and the open defiance of law by his Catholic brother,—might not have pronounced representative institutions an utter failure in England, and only possible in states like Holland or Sweden. But there are even better instances at hand. Down to 1815 Norway was a Danish province, with absolutely no rights; since then it has had the freest government in Europe. Spain failed for forty years, and has yet succeeded within the last ten in making her constitution work. Italy seemed to want almost every element of the system; the people were of the Latin race, unused to self-government, with the aristocracy abased, and the peasantry uneducated; yet the Italian Chambers are not sensibly below the English standard The fact is, Europe generally has become familiarised with the parliamentary system, and the errors of the first French experimentalists have been fruitful of good to their successors. But, besides this, there is a sensible difference between generations of the same people. The pictures of Vandyke and Reynolds tell their own tale. The Polish gentleman would be more or less than human, if the events of the last century, the struggles and sufferings of at least three generations, had not left their impress on the national character. A French traveller in the seventeenth century remarked a general carelessness about religion; the *Times* correspondent now speaks of a morbidly religious sentiment. The people was the most outspoken of all; it is now one vast conspiracy under a secret government. Two generations have grown up under the Code Napoléon. But, above all, the position of classes is changed. There is now a large middle class of native tradesmen and artisans; it is, in fact, the only part of the population that tends steadily to increase. The peasants were serfs; they are now not only free, but copyhold proprietors, the only question unadjusted being that of compensation to their landlords.

Railroads and steamers are binding the different provinces together. A national literature of singular fertility and depth has grown up. It is, of course, impossible to say beforehand that even these advantages would enable the Poles to govern themselves well; but we may fairly regard them as elements of hope, if a new trial were given. That trial, be it remembered, has never been vouchsafed since the Treaty of Vienna, except for a few years under Alexander; and the success then was considerable. Even the secret government may be fairly cited as proof of the people's capacity. In spite of its immense difficulties, it commands the entire confidence of the nation, and beats the Russian police on their own ground. We are constantly told, in "inspired" newspapers, of disunion among the leaders. Differences of opinion there no doubt are and must be, but there are no signs as yet of disunion, or even of such opposition as Fox and his followers maintained throughout our greatest national struggle. Even the class jealousies which have existed in Poland, as every where, and which the Russian government has steadily fostered, appear to melt away before partnership in danger.

Assuming, however, that the Poles have been misgoverned, and that they are capable of self-government, the question still remains whether they were justified in insurrection. We are most of us apt to think that it is better to endure certain grievances than to redress them at the risk of extinction. Could not the Poles have developed the institutions actually conceded to them by a certain exercise of political tact and long-suffering? And, if so, is Europe to bear the penalty of the impatience that preferred appealing to arms? A glance at the relations of Poland with Russia, and at the history of the last seven years, will answer this question. Poland and Russia represent two opposite civilisations. The central idea of Russian government, from time immemorial, has been the Czar-father, the paternal despot; of the Polish, the independence of a large governing class. Distinctions of rank in Russia are bureaucratic, and the pride of family is a modern exotic; in Poland, the feeling of race has often bordered on insanity. Leave a Russian village to itself, and its peasants organise a communistic system; in a Polish settlement the divisions of land are broadly marked and jealously guarded. Traditions and immobility are the principles of the Russian Church, and of its most powerful sectaries; it has no political ambition, except so far as its patriarch and priests are the instruments of the Czar. In Poland, the adopted land of Socinus, Catholicism has constantly represented, as it does even now, the divorce of church and state, and has thus been a principle of spiritual liberty. Lastly,

Polish civilisation has been Latin from the earliest times, and that of Russia has been Byzantine. Each nation, therefore, represents opposite principles of life. The experiment of Russian civilisation is one to which every thinking man must heartily wish success, not only for the sixty millions whose happiness is involved in it, but because the very novelty of the conditions under which it has been developed, promises to throw new light on the whole history of man. But the possession of Poland rather hinders than assists the working out of the problem. It produces the worst antagonism of all, the bitterness of the conqueror towards the conquered; and Russia, having reached a point where contact with the West has become necessary, is in danger of isolating herself from the sympathies and influences of all Europe. Political liberty and freedom of thought will be for ever proscribed in St. Petersburg, if they are put down at Warsaw.

We dwell upon this antagonism of character between the two nations because we believe it explains in great measure why they have never been able to assimilate. The idea at St. Petersburg has been that a propaganda of Panslavism would finally remove all difficulties. There have been moments when it had some chance of success. In 1846, when Austria encouraged the Jacquerie of the Gallician peasants against their landlords, Wielopolski called upon all his countrymen to sink their nationality in the Russian, that they might be revenged on their German enemies, and a deputation waited upon the Czar offering to put Gallicia into his hands; receiving the characteristic answer, that if he wished for the province he would conquer it, but would never take it as the gift of revolted subjects. At the accession of Alexander II., when milder measures were promulgated, the exiles released, and a certain liberty allowed, the comparison of Russia to Austria, not yet chastened by Solferino, was more than ever favourable to the former. Men hoped every thing from a young prince. But Alexander II., himself a partisan of new ideas, was under the influence of men of the old order. Poland, to the generation of Russians that has grown up under Nicholas, is a conquered province that must be absorbed. These men know nothing, think nothing, of the Treaty of Vienna, and of international obligations. They imagine that the war of 1831 has annulled all; as if a revolt provoked by misgovernment could cancel Russia's obligations to France, England, and Germany. Alexander II., reluctantly, it is said, but resolutely, made himself the mouthpiece of the old Muscovite party. Addressing a people who had thronged to do honour to him, he told them: "I mean the order established by my father to be maintained.

Therefore, gentlemen, and before all, no dreams, no illusions. The happiness of Poland depends on its entire fusion with the other peoples of my empire. What my father has done, therefore, was well done, and I will maintain it. My reign shall be the continuation of his. . . Have you understood me? I love better to reward than to punish; but know, and take it as my word, gentlemen, that if need be, I shall know how to repress and to punish, and it shall be seen that I will punish severely." This speech, to say the least, was ungracious and unkingly from a sovereign to the subjects whom he saw for the first time. But words, after all, are words. It remains to be seen by what acts that declaration was commented on and explained.

The leading man among Poles for the last thirty years, and therefore a fair type of the national aspirations and character, on one side at least, has been the Count André Zamoiski. He belongs to a family which is professedly *Anglomane*, and several of whose members have been educated in England, while some of them are said to speak English better than their native tongue. Certainly no man could better represent than Count André the English horror of war, or our belief in material progress and in all gradual processes of constitutional growth. In Count Cavour, also a student of English institutions, the acquired culture was only subservient to a passionate Machiavellic Italian temperament, that would have wrapped Europe in flames at any moment to save a single province of Italy. But to Count André Zamoiski's temperament peace was necessary, as the condition of self-culture and self-government. His great works have been industrial enterprises: stud-stables, a line of steamers on the Vistula, a society for lending money on mortgage, and the famous Agricultural Society for improving the staple of Polish industry. In England such a man, however respected and respectable, would have no great political influence. In Poland he was regarded by his countrymen as the leader of the patriotic party, and by the Russians as a conspirator; the more dangerous because acting with steady legality. In fact, the Agricultural Society served first as a small bond of union between Polish gentlemen in distant counties, then as an excuse for meetings in which social questions, such as serf-emancipation, were discussed privately, within the limits of the existing laws. That a portion of its members would have liked to go further, and give the society a distinctly political character, is no doubt true; but their president never permitted this deviation from their statutes. At last, after the massacre of February, Prince Gortschakoff, trembling for the safety of the town, invited Count André to provide for public security. The result was, that during a week of unparalleled ferment, with a crowd of 100,000 spectators invited to assist in the funeral of the victims, perfect order was maintained. The success was a fatal one. "All the town obeys you," said Prince Gortschakoff, indignantly. "Things cannot remain in this state; I do not fear you; I have troops now." Five weeks later the Agricultural Society was dissolved. Its dissolution occasioned the second massacre, the crime of the victims being that they petitioned for its reëstablishment. Then power passed definitely into the hands of the Marquis Wielopolski; and in August 1862 Count André, having committed the crime of encouraging some hundred gentlemen to sign a petition to the Czar for national institutions and official union with the old provinces of Poland, was insulted by the Grand Duke, sent to St. Petersburg, and dismissed into honourable exile.

Those who care to follow out at length the complications of 1861-1862 must seek them in the excellent *résumé* of M. de Mazade, from which we have drawn freely. It is perhaps a misfortune that the book is made up of articles which have not been recast, so that the whole has a rather fragmentary character; but this fault of composition is abundantly redeemed by the author's thorough knowledge of his subject, and by his candour and breadth of view. Our own object is simply to point out, that ever since April 1861 Alexander II. has been carrying out his programme to govern Poland as his father did, and that the second tyranny has been even worse than the first. Except that the commissioners of roads are now to be elected by districts instead of by provinces, a change of very doubtful value, no single organic reform has been promulgated. On the other hand, schools have been shut up by hundreds, industrial enterprise has been discouraged, the clergy have been threatened, leading nobles and authors imprisoned or transported as a precautionary measure; and finally, a conscription organised with the express object of forcing the men most averse to service into the ranks. Since the revolt provoked by these measures, the government has set no limits to its severity. Twenty-three thousand men have been imprisoned as a precautionary measure. Hundreds are sent every week to Siberia. Torture and flogging are now among the means employed to extract confessions. The country is filled with spies. In Lithuania the infamous Mouravieff has offered rewards of from three to five roubles (from nine shillings to fifteen shillings) for the head of every insurgent. He has levied a fluctuating property-tax of at least 10 per cent, or two years' income; and the goods of those who cannot at once discharge this monstrous imposition are put up to public auction at nominal prices. We have before us the list of 397 persons whose estates, down to the 4th of July last, he had sequestered. He causes every village in which insurgents have been harboured to be burned down. For these and other such atrocities he enjoys the unbounded admiration of his countrymen, demoralised by the war, and has received the order of St. Andrew and a letter of thanks from his sovereign. Unhappily he has imitators among the Russian generals; and Annenkoff in Podolia, Kieff, and Volhynia, is said to be not inferior. But even when the Russian generals are humane, well-meaning men, they cannot control the troops under them, embittered by a guerrilla war and constantly drunk. Burning alive, burying alive, flogging, are among the horrors of the present campaign that relieve the ordinary incidents of violation and massacre. At first the Russian organs attempted to represent the revolt as excited by the emigrants, and exclusively carried on by the upper classes. Both statements have been emphatically disproved. Not only are the emigrants not in the national government, but the services of such a man as Mieroslawski have been steadily declined, for fear his reputation as a red republican should excite distrust in Europe. As regards the different classes of the nation, the list of official victims alone proves that all are represented, about half hitherto having been peasants, farmers, or artisans, though of course the higher heads are the first struck. But the strongest testimony has been that of the Russian general Boggawout, who excuses the disorders of his troops on the ground that the peasants burn the villages at their approach, and fly into the woods to join the insurgents. We will just add, that in two corps we ourselves saw in Poland above a third were peasants, and only a small proportion educated men. But the lower classes in towns, especially Warsaw, have no doubt furnished the chief number of combatants.

Is compromise possible? The Czar has in fact answered that question by rejecting all mediation, accepting solemnly the responsibility of his acts, and refusing to treat the insurgents as belligerents. After seven months' struggle, with from 20,000 to 30,000 men in the field against him and baffling his best troops, Alexander II. allows no exchange of prisoners, and shoots or even hangs as traitors the unhappy gentlemen who have formerly served against their will in the Russian army. Sierakofsky, who was dragged from the bed on which he lay wounded to the gallows, had made himself honourably famous through the length and breadth of the empire by procuring the abolition of corporal punishment in the army. To ask the Poles to lay down their arms after the bitterness of such a struggle, in blind reliance on the mercy of a prince who permits these atrocities, would surely be to expect too much of human nature. Would any sane man like to pledge himself that the Czar-father would not respond to their confidence by sending them Mouravieff? But if Alexander II. were not the weak man he is,—*qui a des velléités mais qui n'a pas de volonté*, —and who is swayed by every impulse of popular animosity or rancour, a capitulation of the weak, considered as revolted subjects, to the strong, being a foreign despot, is hardly a measure to be taken while there are yet a hundred men with arms in their hands. What the Czar really counts on is the coming winter. His troops have been repeatedly beaten, and barely keep the field in spite of numbers and superior equipment. His treasury is bankrupt, and heavy arrears of pension and pay are even now said to be due. But he believes that four months' frost will save Russia again, as in the campaign against Napoleon. Having amused and baffled the Western powers by a half-evasive, half-insolent diplomacy, he now looks forward in confidence to extirpating their *protégé* during the winter. The weak will have learned a new lesson on the value of moral sympathies.

It is not for us or for any one to predict the future. Considering the national jealousy of France, the dislike to commence a war of which the issue cannot be foreseen, and the weakness of the present ministry, who dare not have a decisive policy for good or evil, the chances are certainly considerable that England will remain at peace during the next six months, and that Austria will follow her example. We need not discuss the possibilities which are still talked of in Vienna of an Austrian army of occupation taking possession of Poland up to the gates of Warsaw. But there is more than one step short of war which would seriously derange the Russian combinations. The recall of the English, French, and Austrian ambassadors, in imitation of what was done in Naples in 1859, would be something more than a mere moral remonstrance. It would shake the prestige of the war-party; it would necessitate fresh armaments on the Baltic, and ruinous expenses throughout the empire. Another and even simpler step would be to acknowledge the Poles as a belligerent power. The *Presse* of Vienna—the Austrian *Times*—has already declared in favour of this step, and it is generally believed that Franz Joseph and his ministers only wait the signal from St. James's, and the assurance that they will not move alone. There are several precedents for this measure. In the conference held at London in July 1826, between the cabinets of London, Paris, and St. Petersburg, it was postulated "that an intervention is justifiable not only when the safety and essential interests of a state are affected by the internal events taking place in a neighbouring state, but also when the rights of humanity are violated by the excesses of a cruel and barbarous government." The Porte refusing to grant an amnesty, the three powers at once recognised the belligerent rights of the Greeks. Similarly the belligerent rights of Belgium were recognised; and in this case England was not eventually drawn into any war with Holland. The insurrection of the Spanish colonies was recognised by England, the United States, and Sweden. We recognised the belligerent rights of the Southern Secessionists without even sufficient delay to show that they could hold their own against the government of Washington. Here then appears to be a distinct principle, that it is in the option of any power to recognise insurgents of any kind, and at any time during the struggle, as belligerents.

What, it may be said, would be gained by this? The immediate and immense gain would be the winter. During those very months when the Russians expect to draw their enemy, as in a net, the Polish combatants would emigrate into Austria, leaving perhaps a few of the best-seasoned bands to harass the enemy. The insurrection would become something impalpable and yet terribly near. It would buy its munitions of war at a fourth of their present price, and would recruit soldiers from every country in Europe. The men who are now imprisoned on suspicion by the Austrian police, and sent back over the frontier, would be allowed to traverse Gallicia at will, so long as they did not do it in regular companies. It is not too much to say that the whole labour of subjugation would have to be recommenced. Yet in one particular at least the war would have a tendency to be less bloody. It would be difficult for the Czar's government to persist in treating as brigands men whom the rest of Europe recognised as regular belligerents. We might fairly hope to hear of flags of truce between the two combatants and of mercy to the wounded.

It rests with Russia to prevent this recognition, and to reconcile herself with civilised Europe. She is still in a position, if she will only use it, to yield with dignity. The reconstruction of Congress Poland with a native parliament, under a Russian grand duke, and with international guarantees for the honest carrying out of the amnesty that has been so often talked about, would be nothing more than the Court of Peterhof is already pledged to by the Treaty of Vienna, and yet would suffice to satisfy public opinion. France and England have nothing to gain by the continuance of an internecine struggle, which occupies their diplomacy, produces constant fluctuations in the money-market, and keeps cabinets and press in a wearisome state of tension. The fee-simple of Poland would not pay us for the disquietude of a year's European war. That the Poles would dislike such an accommodation as we have suggested is more than probable; but there is just sufficient equity about it to make it certain that they would forfeit the sympathies on which they now rely if they refused to entertain it. Besides, their faith in cabinets must by this time have undergone several disenchantments. As the scheme is in fact that which the Russian organs steadily represent as already contemplated, the only humiliation for the Emperor would be in admitting European intervention in the case of a province which he only holds in trust for Europe. The revolt of 1831 no more transferred Poland to the Russian empire than the revolt of 1848 in the Ionian Islands changed them from a trust into a dependency of the British empire. Sooner or later the Czar's government will discover that it is not wise to disregard public opinion and European treaties; and it may have occasion to learn before many months are over that there are other means of punishing bad faith than by drawing the sword.

Art. VI.—THE ROYAL SUPREMACY, AND THE HISTORY OF ITS INTRODUCTION.

State Papers of Henry VIII., published by Royal Commission. Correspondence of Cromwell in the State-Paper Office.

The anxiety of the episcopal bench to get rid of Bishop Colenso by some legitimate means brings us once more face to face with the Act of Supremacy and its authors. Hitherto, churchmen have upheld that statute with as much vehemence and tenacity as if the existence of the Church itself depended upon it. The greatest of English theologians, from the days of Hooker, have flourished it in the face of their enemies as a weapon of proof not less effective against Romanism than Dissent. To the old thick-and-thin supporter of "Church and State," the royal supremacy seemed a tower of strength. He was not ashamed to be told that he belonged to a church which owed its superiority solely to its political advantages. He would not have flinched from the assertion, that the Reformation was a political movement; that the state church was under greater obligations to the king than the bishops. He rather gloried in the fact. He saw in this alliance a pledge that the powers of the state should be employed in securing for the church a supremacy above all other religious societies. However they might fluctuate and decay, he was perfectly secure. It was the business of the state, not his, to see that the church sustained no damage; to prevent any attack upon its outworks, and put down the promulgators of schism from within. It was a comfortable doctrine; it saved a world of thought, of labour, and of reading; better than all, it saved him from the necessity of forming a judgment on the difficult problems sometimes thrown in his way. It is pleasant to have others to think and provide for you; it is especially pleasant when thought and labour bring with them no other reward than "laborious days," and the imputation of singularity.

There did, indeed, happen times when the church ran off the accustomed rails, and this state-support became oppressive. The yoke, which bore equally on the necks of both animals in the straight furrow, fell in rougher ground with disproportioned weight on the shoulders of the smaller beast. It was hard for the nonjuring clergy in the reign of William III. to stand up and hold their own against the whole bench of bishops; still more hard when the whole weight and influence of the crown were thrown into the scale of the stronger. Then the clergy began, if not to disavow the royal supremacy, at least to question its true and legitimate limits. The same authority which seemed unfavourable to dissent when it pleaded for liberty of conscience, was equally unfavourable to the exercise of the same liberty on the part of the clergy. Their strength was to sit still. The moment they attempted to stir a hand's-breadth beyond the established formularies of the church, the moment they attempted to walk alone, without recognising the support of the state,—that moment they received unmistakable warnings of their helplessness. The Church of England claims in its Articles the right of every individual church "to decree rites or ceremonies" as it shall think needful; and the state indorses that claim. It claims authority to determine what is right or wrong in "controversies of faith;" and the state, with equal complaisance, sanctions that authority. It denounces the man who is cut off from the unity of the church as "a heathen and a publican;" and the state has not a word to say against so wholesome and so charitable a doctrine. But the moment the church attempts to put these abstractions into practice, the state steps in with its Act of Supremacy; and woe to the unhappy churchmen, singly or collectively, who, deluded by these fair promises, should venture to act upon them. With authority to decree rites and ceremonies, rites and ceremonies have remained precisely as they were more than three centuries ago. The whole nation has been torn with controversies of faith, almost without intermission, from the Reformation to the present hour; but the church has never ventured to interpose an authoritative voice in these matters. And as for denouncing a dissenter as "a heathen and a publican," we take it that a jury of twelve enlightened citizens would very soon show the denouncers how far such advice was allowable. In fact, the state-support is very much like Sancho Panza's state-physician in his island of Barataria. "He had hardly put one bit into his mouth, before the physician touched the dish with his wand, and then it was taken away by a page in an instant. Immediately another with meat was clapped in the place; but Sancho no sooner offered to taste it, than the doctor with the wand conjured it away as fast as the first." Any actual exercise of authority on the part of the church is neutralised by the state, whether it relates to doctrine or to ceremonies; and therefore, like Sancho Panza, compelled to solace his hunger, in the absence of more savoury and substantial dishes, "with a hunch of bread and some four pounds of raisins," the action of the church rises no higher than to a crusade against pew-rents or the recommendation of thanksgiving for a plentiful harvest.

Sooner or later the whole subject will provoke, as it has long since demanded, grave consideration. Not that, in the present distracted state of religious parties, we are anxious to see those restrictions removed from the independent action of the church, which would be inevitably turned to mischief, and end in its total ruin. But, as we have stated, we are brought face to face with the practical difficulties of the question by the case of Bishop Colenso. As the law now stands, the church can pronounce no judgment on the Bishop of Natal. It has no jurisdiction over him or any other bishop, heretical or orthodox. He may write and preach as much Hoadleyism or neologianism, or any other *ism*, as he pleases. The church is absolutely powerless. Long before the Reformation the right of punishing a bishop had been vested solely in the pope. The Act of Supremacy transferred this, with other ecclesiastical privileges, to the crown; and we might live to witness the anomaly of a bishop, ordained to drive away false doctrine, maintaining it in his own person, without any power in the church to restrain or to punish it. In fact, the time cannot be long distant when a much greater amount of freedom of opinion will be claimed both by bishops and clergy. In the rapid advance of art and science, it is impossible that theology alone can remain stagnant. It is equally impossible for the clergy of the Church of England, brought up at the universities, accustomed to the broader and profounder views which a philology unknown to the sixteenth century has opened to mankind, to remain satisfied with the theological axioms of the Reformers, often based on a total misapprehension of the original language of the New Testament, and always more or less crippled by those narrow habits of thought in which they had been trained. Of the Fathers of the Reformation, as they are called, to whom we are indebted for the Articles and Homilies of the Church of England, who is there that would now be quoted as an authority in any great question of ecclesiastical history, of philology, of philosophy, or even of theology? It is impossible to turn over a single page of their writings and not be struck with the total absence of power and originality. Even in the most learned, such as Cranmer, the learning consists mainly in scraps and commonplaces from the Latin Fathers, or miserable translations of the Greek, valued solely for their apparent efficacy in the pending controversy against Catholic opponents, but indicating the smallest possible familiarity with the true spirit of antiquity. It is impossible that the clergy can be long content to walk in the theological gyves of the sixteenth century. And unwilling as the Church of England may be, and, in its present relations with the state, unable to grapple satisfactorily with the question, the time is not far distant when it must be prepared to reconsider its past decisions on many theological difficulties, and claim for itself and its adherents a greater liberty of expression and of action.

Of the history of that Act, which has produced such important consequences, and modified the whole existence of the Church of England, we should have been glad had Mr. Froude furnished us with a little more explicit information in his history of Henry VIII. To us it is far more interesting, and in itself infinitely more important, than Anne Boleyn's robes or the feuds of the Geraldines. Whose genius was it that upset the traditions of fifteen centuries, and devised an organisation without parallel in ancient or in modern times? Who first conceived the bold idea—not of a parity of power between the spiritual and temporal jurisdictions, not Warburton's figment of an *imperium in imperio*, not modern Anglicanism, watching to steal a feather out of the tail of the imperial eagle, —but a transfer of the whole authority of the church from a spiritual to a temporal ruler? Who was it that, with one stroke of the pen, to use the phrase of Bishop Andrews, "transubstantiated Henry VIII. into the pope," and converted the church from an independent rival to a ready and submissive dependent on the state? With all the papers and documents before him needful for the satisfaction of such an inquiry, we should have been glad if Mr. Froude had availed himself of his precious opportunities; if he had told us by what steps the authors of such a policy arrived at this result,—how they emancipated themselves from the long prejudices of ages,—how they ventured, not only in the teeth of Roman Catholic tradition, but of that new ecclesiastical liberty then awakening in the breasts of Continental reformers, to set up an ecclesiastical headship which was neither old nor new, foreign nor Anglican, Catholic nor Puritan. Whose ingenious brain conceived, who shaped into practical form, this alliance between church and state, wherein both should seem to be equal, but one in reality was extinguished? Was it the natural consequence of English constitutional tendencies? Was it the inevitable result of English Protestantism? Did it find acceptance with the mass of the people from its own intrinsic excellence, or was it forced upon them as a state necessity by the subtle ingenuity of Cromwell, or the iron resolution of Henry VIII.? Every man who cares to read the history of those times feels at once that this is *the* question, this is the keystone of the Reformation; all other topics dwindle into insignificance beside it. This is the real point at issue between the advocates of the old and the new system; this, and not purgatory, not pilgrimages, not transubstantiation; not what Mr. Froude seems ever and anon to suppose, the different degrees of loyalty and morality in Romanist and Protestant. There were men as loyal and pure-hearted as More whose consciences would not suffer them to acknowledge that Henry VIII. was "Head of the Church;" there were men as vulgar and worldly as Bonner, leaders of rebellion, like the Bigots, the Husseys, and the Constables, who were ready to die themselves, or at least put others to death, in defence of the king's supremacy. The coronations of kings and queens, the pomp of Cardinal Pole's ceremonials, even the death of the unhappy monks of the Charterhouse, sink into nothing in comparison with this. They were but temporary; they scarcely stirred the hearts of men familiarised with such spectacles, and too much occupied with their own griefs and perplexities to spare much sympathy for others. This, on the other hand, has spread its broad shadow across the range of centuries. It has fallen like a thing of evil on Puritans and Romanists alike. If it brought More and Fisher to the scaffold in the reign of Henry, it wrung the hearts and wasted the life-blood of Cartwright and the Puritans in the reign of Elizabeth. If it hung like a sword over the head of the Tudor bishops, and prevented all relapse to Rome, it equally drove out from the pale of the national church every conscientious nonconformist, who was a zealous Protestant in every thing with the exception of this one article. It kept the church obedient to the sovereign and to the first principles of the Reformation, but it effectually prevented all organic expansion, whatever the circumstances of the times.

We do not hope to throw much light upon these topics; a full elucidation of them must be left to the historian of the Reformation. The acts which transferred to the king the supreme headship of the church made it treason in any one to dispute or to doubt it in writing or conversation. Further than this, and with a stretch of arbitrary power unknown even in the darkest times, it was not necessary to prove any overt offence against the statute; it was enough to involve a man in the penalties of high treason if, when examined by oath *ex officio*, his answers were not deemed satisfactory by his judges. Such powers concentrated in the hands of one man, or one set of men, could hardly escape abuse even in the most peaceful and regular times. But the great minister of Henry VIII. whose genius conceived these measures, and whose ability directed them, was, as Mr. Froude tells us, beyond the passions and temptations of ordinary statesmen. The severities occasioned by them might be bitter, but they were in his estimation necessary and salutary. He entertains a charitable hope that these powers were not abused, and that those who passed these measures were not "betraying English liberties in a spirit of careless complacency." He finds a necessity for these proceedings and excuse in the insecurity of the times; and as Romanists had been persecutors in the days of their ignorance, he reconciles himself with a sigh to the righteousness of this retaliation: "the even hand of justice was but commending the chalice to the lips of those who had made others drink it to the dregs. They only were like to fall under the Treason Act who for centuries had fed the rack and the stake with sufferers for opinion."* In the present condition of historical literature we are not so unreasonable as to expect that no materials should escape the notice of the historian, which can throw light on his inquiries. A few years only have elapsed since the judicious liberality of the Master of the Rolls has thrown open to the student the true sources of English history, and many years must still elapse before those sources can be fully explored. But when Mr. Froude wrote his history there were materials within his reach which we think he ought to have consulted; materials of which ample use had been made by Sir Henry Ellis—we mean Cromwell's own correspondence, formerly in the State-Paper Office, now at the Record Office. The authenticity of these letters cannot be disputed. They furnish the most complete insight into the life and history of this wonderful man.

* History of England, ii. 330.

"Cromwell," says Mr. Froude,* "the malleus monachorum, was of good English family, belonging to the Cromwells of Lincolnshire. One of these, probably a younger brother, moved up to London, and conducted an iron-foundry, or other business of that description, at Putney. He married a lady of respectable connexions, of whom we know only that she was sister of the wife of a gentleman in Derbyshire, but whose name does not appear. The old Cromwell dying early, the widow was remarried to a cloth-merchant named Williams; and the child of the first husband, who made himself so great a name in English story, met with the reputed fortune of a stepson, and became a vagabond in the wide world. The chart of his course wholly fails us. One day in later life he shook by the hand an old bell-ringer at Sion House, before a crowd of courtiers, and told them that 'this man's father had given him many a dinner in his necessities.' And a strange random account is given by Foxe of his having joined a party in an expedition to Rome, to obtain a renewal from the pope of certain immunities and indulgences for the town of Boston; a story which derives some kind of credibility from its connexion with Lincolnshire, but is full of incoherence and unlikelihood. At length we catch for a moment an accurate sight of him. In the autumn of 1515 a ragged stripling appeared at the door of Frescobaldi's banking-house in Florence, begging for help. Frescobaldi had an establishment in London, with a large connexion there; and seeing an English face, and seemingly an honest one, he asked the boy who and what he was. 'I am, sir,' quoth he, 'of England, and my name is Thomas Cromwell; my father is a poor man, and by occupation a cloth-shearer; I am strayed from my country, and am now come into Italy with the camp of Frenchmen that were overthrown at Garigliano, where I was page to a footman, carrying after him his pike and burganet.' Something in the boy's manner attracted the banker's interest; he took him into his house, and after keeping him there as long as he desired to stay, he gave him a horse and sixteen ducats to help him home to England. If this story is true, the future minister must have had a rough training; and in the midst of it this noticeable fact further shows itself, that he knew by heart Erasmus's translation of the New Testament. After his return from Florence, he found employment in the household of the Marchioness of Dorset in some uncongenial capacity; and at length found his way into the general asylum of ability in want of employment, the service of Wolsey. Here he made rapid progress. Wolsey soon discovered the nature of the man with whom he was dealing, and in 1525 employed him in the most important work of visiting and breaking up the small monasteries."

Circumstantial as this narrative seems to be, there is hardly a statement in it correct, with the exception of the last. We cannot disprove every assertion made by Mr. Froude, because we cannot always discover when he speaks from authority.

* History of England, ii. 108.

Having assumed that the minister of Henry VIII. belonged to the Cromwells of Lincolnshire, Mr. Froude assumes the probability of Foxe's story, borrowed from Bandello. And though he doubts in his notes, as reasonably he might, how Cromwell could, according to Foxe, be at the storming of Rome with the Duke of Bourbon in May 1527, when he was employed in Wolsey's household in England, Mr. Froude is inclined to prefer the more dramatic but unsubstantial narrative of the martyrologist to the drier but indisputable testimony furnished by official documents. We are sorry to dissipate such a pleasant illusion. But the whole account is little else than a mistake. If the story told by Camden and Broke, and repeated by Fuller, be true, it is certain that Cromwell did not belong to the Cromwells of Lincolnshire. "Formerly there flourished," says Fuller, "a notable family of the Cromwells at Tattershall in Lincolnshire, especially since Sir Ralph Cromwell married the youngest sister and co-heir of William, the last Lord Deincourt. Now there wanted not some flattering heralds (excellent chemists in pedigrees, to extract any thing from any thing) who would have entitled this Lord Cromwell (minister of Henry VIII.) to the arms of that ancient family. His answer unto them was, 'that he would not wear another man's coat for fear the right owner thereof should pluck it off over his ears,' and preferred rather to take a new coat." Mr. Froude describes his widowed mother as marrying again to a cloth-merchant named Williams, "and the child of the first husband, who made himself so great a name in English story, met with the reputed fortune of a stepson, and became a vagabond in the wide world." But this part of the story he fails to authenticate. Cromwell had a sister married to a man of obscure parentage, named Williams or Williamson, who died about 1533, leaving a daughter, whom the minister was anxious to place under the care of some noble lady, and induct her into the manners of fashionable society. It is possible that the mother may have been a widow and married a man of the same name as her daughter's husband, but not very probable. At all events, until better authority be forthcoming the statement must stand for what it is worth.

The facts known of Cromwell's life, so far as they can be drawn from the indisputable data furnished by his own correspondence, are briefly these. The first notice that occurs of him is that of a merchant trading in 1512, at the mart of Middleburgh, to all appearance a member even at this early period of the Society of Adventurers who had dealings with the Low Countries. Sir Henry Ellis has published a letter addressed to him, at a later date, from Antwerp, in which the writer wishes to engage Cromwell in a speculation for buying cheese; and the whole style of the letter shows that the future minister was perfectly well versed in such operations. In 1520 and the following years he was practising in London as a scrivener and attorney, combining with his other occupations that of a cloth-dyer. He was then living in Fenchurch Street. On wandering scraps of dirty papers, and dry-as-dust heaps in the Record Office, quite beneath the notice of the hero-worship of history, we stumble upon queer bits of information relating to his early career. Here is the back of a bill for cloth-dressing and facings mixed up with items paid in the course of his business at the law-courts; here the draft of a petition in Chancery, or a list of his creditors, hopeful and desperate. As early as the year 1521 he was flourishing in business and lending money. In 1525 Lord George Grey is his debtor for 30*l*., and Lord Harry Percy, Ann Boleyn's unfortunate suitor, for 40*l*. in 1527. Here again is a letter sent to him by one T. Tressell, dated from Worcester, 20th October 1522: "Mr. Cromwell, I commend me unto you, and I trust that ye have dressed my cloth long ere this time. I pray you to send me word what ye paid for dyeing of my cloth. But, sir, I do suppose unkindness in you that you do not send unto me my pouch of velvet, &c. Commend me to Mr. Wodall and Anthony Bonvysy." This reference to Antonio Bonvyx, a wealthy Italian merchant to whom Sir Thomas More addressed his last letter from the Tower, is worth observation. He continued a constant correspondence with Cromwell long after his greatness. And possibly it was this connexion with Bonvyx which gave occasion to the rumour that Cromwell had been an agent to the Italian merchants in Lombard Street.* Mr. Froude refers with scorn to the conversation narrated by Cardinal Pole between himself and Cromwell in the house of Cardinal Wolsey. Pole states that in the excitement caused by the divorce, and the differences of opinion existing among the king's councillors, Cromwell took occasion to sift Pole's sentiments, then just returned from Italy. At that time it must be remembered that Wolsey was moving heaven and earth to accomplish the divorce, nervously conscious that all chance of retaining Henry's favour depended on his success. It is piteous to read his earnest appeals to the pope, and witness the excitement which dragged the omnipotent minister out of his bed before daybreak. All other business was forgotten in the one absorbing topic. If successful, he might still hope to retire and spend his declining years in the service of God, and in watch-

* "He was a merchant's clerk," says Pole, "and kept his accounts; and I know the merchant well, a Venetian, in whose employment he was." This merchant was undoubtedly Bonvyx.

ing over the welfare of his growing colleges; if unsuccessful, no past services could protect him from the resentment of an implacable master. In this state of things Cromwell and Pole met. "I told him," says Pole, evidently alluding to the cardinal, and those who shared his sentiments, "that it was the duty of a councillor to consider above all things the honour and interests of his sovereign; I enlarged on these subjects as they are enforced by the law of nature and the writings of pious and learned men." Cromwell replied, that he did not deny that what I had urged were popular topics in the schools, and were received with great applause when uttered from the pulpit; but, he said, in the secret councils of princes such arguments were insipid; whoever attempted to urge them at the council-table must change his tone, or bring his counsels and himself into discredit; and he added that such principles rarely agreed with the tempers of sovereigns, and were entirely out of fashion at court. It was a wisdom, he said, not to be gained from the schools; and they who come fresh from college to the councils of princes often make shipwreck against these rocks from want of this experience." In the end he advised Pole to give up his studies, and read Machiavelli.*

If this story be a mere invention of Pole's, it displays an insight into character and a power of imagination not usually found in his writings. The sentiments expressed in it are too much in accordance with the times, and the great change then rapidly approaching, to be altogether imaginary. Nothing could mark off in stronger relief the statesman of the old and the new era. It is precisely the feeling which would reign in the heart of the new man, who owed his advancement solely to his knowledge of the world, and despised the less practical wisdom of the schools. Nor, does it need much insight into Cromwell's character to perceive that there lurked in his mind this sort of contempt for learning; as a factor to Antonio Bonvyx he had made himself master of Italian, probably the only language with which he was familiarly acquainted besides his own. We find him recommending the study of it to Bonner and lending

* After giving in his text the story of Cromwell's appearing in 1515 at the door of Frescobaldi's banking-house in Florence, Mr. Froude adds, "this noticeable fact further shows itself that he (Cromwell) knew by heart Erasmus's translation of the New Testament." The fact is more noticeable than Mr. Froude seems to be aware of, and adds one more marvel to Cromwell's marvellous career; for by Mr. Froude's account he must have learned Erasmus's translation of the New Testament by heart a year before it was published. But, unconscious of his blunder, Mr. Froude continues: "A fact (this reading the translation of Erasmus) which qualifies Reginald Pole's accusation of Machiavellism against Cromwell. He says Cromwell told him to read Machiavelli. If he did, there is no occasion to be surprised. Men may read and learn from books which they do not wholly admire." A platitude no one would dispute.

him "The Triumphes of Petrarche in the Italian Tongue."* But it was to his knowledge of men and his experience of the world that he owed his advancement. These were the qualifications which placed him at once above all his clerical rivals in the court of the cardinal. Though his person was plain and ungainly even to ugliness, the flexibility and fascination of his manners were universally admitted. His contemporaries could attribute it to nothing less than magic. And there is still preserved at the Record Office the confession of a simpleton charged with resorting to necromancy for the purpose of obtaining a magical ring such as that by which Cromwell had risen so rapidly in favour. Traces of these qualities are to be found in the following letter, which we insert entire, not only as disproving the absurd stories of Foxe, which Mr. Froude is too fond of reproducing with little embellishments of his own, but also because we believe it is the earliest letter now preserved in Cromwell's handwriting. It has other claims to attention. It gives an account of the parliament held in 1523, where Cromwell sat as a burgess. That parliament was remarkable as the scene in which Sir Thomas More, then for the first time chosen speaker, is said to have hit upon this singular device of outwitting the cardinal and preserving the privileges of the Commons: "It fortuned at that parliament," says Roper, "a very great subsidy to be demanded, which the cardinal fearing would not pass the Commons' House, determined for the furtherance thereof to be there present himself. Before whose coming, after long debating there, whether it were better with a few of his lords, as the most opinion of the house was, or with his whole train royally, to receive him there amongst them:—'Masters,' quoth Sir Thomas More, 'for as much as my lord cardinal lately, ye wot well, laid to our charge the lightness of our tongues for things uttered out of this house, it shall not in my mind be amiss to receive him with all his pomp; with his maces, his pillars, his pole-axes, his crosses, his hat, and the great seal too; to the intent that if he find the like fault with us hereafter, we may be the bolder from ourselves to lay the blame on those that his grace bringeth hither with him."

But here is Cromwell's own account of the matter, addressed to "his especial and entirely beloved friend John Creke," then residing at "Bylbowe in Biscaye."

"Maister Creke, as herteleye as I can I commende me, and in the

* We doubt if he understood Latin beyond what was necessary for his legal business. The letters addressed by him in that language to persons in official employment might be written by the regular clerks. But if he did, this would be an additional presumption against his shoeless and neglected condition. Very few boys in his rank of life would be taught Latin at that time.

same wise thanke yow [for your] gentill and lovyng lettres to me at sundrye tymys sent; and wher as I accordinglye have not in lyke wise remembrid and rescribid, it hath bene for that I have not hade any thing to wryt of to your advancement; whom I assure yow yf it were in my lytyll power I coulde be well contentyd to preferre as ferre as any one mann lyvyng; but at this present I being at sum layser, entending to remembre and also remunerate the olde acquaintaunces and to renew our not forgoten sundrye communycacions, supposing ye desyre to know the news curraunt in thes partyes, for it is said that news refresshith the spy[rit] of lyffe; wherfor ye shall understonde that by long tyme I amongist other have indured a parlyament, which contenewid by the space of 17 hole wekes, wher we communyd of warre, pease, stryffe, contencyon, debatte, murmure, grudge, riches, poverte, penwrye, trowth, falshode, justyce, equyte, discayte, opprescyon, magnanymyte, actyvyte, force, attempraunce, treason, murder, felonye, consyli[s], and also how a commune welth myght be edeffyed and a[lso] contenewid within our realme. Howbeyt, in conclusyon, we have do[ne] as our predecessors have bene wont to doo, that ys to say, as well as we myght, and lefte wher we begann. Ye shall also understond the Duke of Suthffolke, furnysshyd with a gret armye, goyth over in all goodlye hast; [whit]her I know not: when I know I shall advertyse yow. Whe have in our parlyament graunytd unto the Kinges highnes a right large subsydye, the lyke wherof was never grauntyd in this realme. All your frendes to my knowlage be in good helth, and specially thay that ye wott of; ye know what I meane: I thinke it best to wryt in parables be caus[e] I am in dowt. Maister Vawhan fareth well, and so doth Maister Munkcaste[r]. Maister Woodall is merye withowt a wyffe and commendyth hym to yow; and so ys also Nycholas Longmede, which hath payd William Wilfforde. And thus as well f[are] ye as I woolde do my self. At London, the 17th daye of August by your frende to all his possible power,

THOMAS CRUMWELL."

Of his other belongings at this period it is not easy to speak with precision. But there is not a tittle of evidence to justify belief that he was an erratic and shoeless adventurer. In fact, all evidence points to an opposite conclusion. He was a steady thriving merchant, married and settled in life, at the very time when he is supposed to be wandering in Italy, dependent on the charity of the Frescobaldi. So fall all Mr. Froude's anecdotes—of the bell-ringer at Sion whom he shook by the hand, and told the crowd of courtiers that "this man's father had given him many a dinner in his necessities;" of the manner, still more romantic, in which he repaid Frescobaldi, who afterwards came to poverty—a story dressed up with great dramatic effect by Foxe.

To speak of his family. Of his wife frequent notice occurs in his correspondence; and the "tattered stripling" must have been married at the time he is described as appearing before

Frescobaldi. He had a son named Gregory, a dull boy,* not very well educated, who had already been under several masters, when he was placed at Cambridge, under a tutor named Chekyngs. This could not have been later than 1528 or 1529, when Cromwell was in Wolsey's service. Supposing Gregory was the eldest child, and was between thirteen and fourteen at the time he was sent to the University, we must assign his birth to the year 1515, or at the latest 1516; a date much too early for Foxe's story. We find Mr. Chekyng dunning the future great man, then a wealthy merchant, for the shabby sum of 6*l.*, and the repayment of thirty shillings, which he had been out of pocket for Gregory's commons; and, to add to the shabbiness of the whole affair, Cromwell, who had innumerable bags of ducats to relieve the imaginary poverty of Frescobaldi, pays the poor schoolmaster only a part of his bill, under the plea that Gregory had not "got on well with his learning."

How Cromwell was taken into Wolsey's service we have only conjecture to help us. But we cannot be far wrong in supposing that he owed this advancement to his knowledge of business, and his skill as a lawyer. From early times he had been employed in this capacity. The numerous drafts of leases and agreements in his handwriting, now at the Record Office, add probability to this conjecture. He was not admitted to any part in Wolsey's political negotiations. The cardinal was at this time busy in suppressing the smaller monasteries, and conferring their houses and estates upon the two colleges he was then erecting at Ipswich and Oxford. The transfer of the property, the settlements with the tenants, the adjustment of different claims fenced in by canon and by common law, was a work of great intricacy,—far more than the cardinal had anticipated. The suppression of the smaller religious houses roused up a host of powerful enemies, not only among the abbots and bishops, but among the most influential nobility, whose progenitors had been the founders of these houses, and who still claimed a sort of right over them by virtue of these foundations. It wanted but this one act of aggression—for aggression it was then considered—to fill up the measure of Wolsey's unpopularity, and provoke the vengeance of those who were already bent upon his destruction. Stories were industriously circulated of unhappy monks who had been turned out of their ancient homes and sent adrift upon the world to starve. The nobility and the bishops regarded the act as an unjustifiable aggression on their property, to be followed by others not less alarming. Had he succeeded in effecting the divorce, it is possible that Wolsey might have outlived this storm; de-

* He was "almost a fool," says Hills, a stern Puritan, writing to Bullinger.

feat boded irretrievable ruin. Still this mighty man kept on his way, and concentrated all his energies for this last effort. Shorn of his strength, hated by Charles, deceived by Rome, betrayed by Suffolk (of all betrayals the most ignominious and disgraceful), detested by Anne Boleyn, and coldly supported by the king, he was not to fall an inglorious victim. His despatches, always bold, vigorous, and comprehensive, are at this time infused with the energy and rhetoric of despair. It was his last appeal; the die was cast; the world was against him. Men looked tamely on his dying struggle with a sort of curiosity, not unmixed with awe and even satisfaction. No wonder the effort was too great; and the over-strained nerves of the expiring minister gave in their reaction no other proof of what he had been except tears and imbecility. But under these overwhelming cares he had little thought or time to spare for the adjustment of leases and the settlement of rents. It was a relief to find an able man, not unambitious to please, to whom he could delegate the business. His concern for his colleges survived all other considerations. They were the last thought of his dying moments; and if any of his old affections still survived from the wear and pressure of political life, they survived to fix themselves with exclusive energy on that one object which, to Wolsey's apprehension, seemed the sole relic of his herculean labours and better aspirations. His greatness had passed away never to return; the purposes to which he had devoted his life had been shipwrecked; his colleges still survived to embalm his memory, and pray for their founder. With this anxiety strong upon him even in the heaviest moments of his life, it is not surprising that Cromwell should have attained a high place in his favour; still less that he, then a burgess in parliament and accustomed to parliamentary business, should have been selected by the cardinal to watch the bill of attainder preferred against his master, which Mr. Froude rightly characterises as "violent, vindictive, and malevolent." It was much too violent and vindictive to have any chance of passing the House. In fact, his enemies—even the Duke of Norfolk, the most formidable—had already begun to relent. Satisfied with humbling the cardinal and removing him from the court, they had no wish to proceed to extremities. Mr. Froude is rapt in admiration at Cromwell's chivalrous and disinterested conduct on this occasion, and speaks of the gallant service rendered by him in serving Wolsey. We have no wish to detract from the merits of that service; but what other line of conduct could he have pursued with decency, and what disgrace or peril did he incur by its espousal? It might have been inferred from Mr. Froude's language that

Cromwell stood alone in this respect, but others were equally forward, and certainly quite as disinterested, in their intercessions. "Master Russell told me," says Chapuys, an authority to whom Mr. Froude will readily defer, "that, on account of a few words in favour of the cardinal which he had repeated (*porté*) to the king, *the Lady* (Anne Boleyn) had held him in great displeasure, and refused to speak to him for a whole month; and that a week ago the Duke of Norfolk told Russell how much the *said Lady*, his niece, was irritated with him, and also against the Duke, because he had not done his worst against the cardinal." We have the same authority for the assurance that, the irritation of the moment once over, the king's favour was rapidly returning. "A gentleman told me," says Chapuys, writing on the 27th of November, "that a short time ago, the king was complaining to his council of something that had not been done according to his wish, and exclaimed in great wrath, that the cardinal was a very superior man in managing business to any of them. And he repeated this twice. Since then the duke, *the Lady*, and her father have not ceased from their machinations against the cardinal, *the Lady* especially, who does not cease to bewail her lost time and her blemished reputation, threatening the king that she will leave him. They say that the king has had trouble enough to quiet her; and that he prayed her most earnestly, *with tears in his eyes*, not to talk of leaving him; but nothing would satisfy her without a promise that the cardinal should be arrested." That the king therefore should not be sorry to see that justice done to the cardinal he had not the firmness to do himself, was natural enough. Mr. Froude says, with an air of solemnity, commenting on this part of Cromwell's history, "I cannot call him ambitious; an ambitious man would scarcely have pursued so refined a policy, or have calculated on the admiration which he gained by adhering to a fallen minister." Mr. Froude seems to us simply to misapprehend the real position of parties. Such magnanimity has been as frequently exhibited in the nineteenth as it was by Cromwell in the sixteenth century. It was a struggle for preëminence between two factions: that of the nobles, headed by Norfolk, backed up by Charles, and supported by Anne Boleyn; and that of the cardinal,—a head without followers. Till the day of Wolsey's death, it was almost universally expected that he would be restored to favour; and the paroxysms of fright into which his enemies were thrown the moment the king exhibited any signs of relenting only show how well those apprehensions were founded.* What could Cromwell expect by throwing him-

* James Clyffe, a priest, writes to Bonner, Wolsey's chaplain: "My Lord of

self into the arms of Wolsey's opponents? He had no favour to anticipate from that quarter. He would have been looked upon as a deserter; and he had other inducements of a personal nature we cannot now stop to insist upon. He chose the more graceful and more generous path—that of supporting the cause of his old master; but in serving him he served himself.

From Wolsey's, Cromwell passed into the king's service, but how soon and by what steps we have no evidence to tell. We find him in the Michaelmas term of 1531 addressed as the king's trusty councillor, if the date be correct, and appointed to confer with the king's learned "counsaell," much on the same business as he had been employed on by Wolsey. The candidates at this time for royal favour were the Duke of Norfolk, who had been mainly instrumental in Wolsey's downfall, and Stephen Gardiner, secretary of state, and bishop of Winchester. Probably both looked upon the new pretender with infinite disdain; one as a mere upstart, the other as his former inferior in Wolsey's household. Norfolk had the reputation of being hard and imperious; his treatment of Wolsey had not heightened his popularity; to Henry he was never acceptable, though he did every thing in his power to secure the king's good graces. But besides the influence of his rank, his services, and his riches, he had the support of Anne Boleyn, of her father and brother, and, such as it was, of the Duke of Suffolk. Gardiner, wily, ingenious, and supple, had recommended himself to the king by his zeal and ability in conducting the negotiations for the divorce. The confidence reposed in him by the king was unbounded; and his great experience as a diplomatist, picked up under Wolsey, gave him signal advantages. Had he combined his forces with Norfolk, the two together might have succeeded in excluding Cromwell from power. But why should they? Who would ever have dreamed of such an advancement? Had it not been the boast of the king to surround himself with scholars? to have about his court the best educated ambassadors and ministers in Europe? No one up to this time had ever been preferred to any post of importance who did not seem to possess some claim to it from the eminence of his attainments, or who did not command it by the eminence of his birth. The whole administration of the reign

Wiltshire is in the French King's court. Mr. Leye is come home; it is thought he hath not brought such news as have been longed (longyt) for. In divers pleas where my Lord Card. grace is communed of, and among lords of the council specially, they fear that they shall of necessity be compelled to ask for my Lord Card. grace again. God continue their minds in that behalf. The King's grace and the Queen as this day lie at Hampton Court, and my Lady Anne. 29 May [1530]."

had been managed by scholars and nobility. Here was a new man who could lay claim to neither distinction. He had been unknown when he made his appearance at court, except for his damaged reputation and his faithful adherence to a disgraced minister. He had no friends, and apparently he looked to none. He does not seem to have paid extraordinary court to Anne Boleyn, or any of her numerous relatives and hangers-on, who now monopolised the king. Perhaps he did not expect favours from one whose resentment was sharp, if not lasting, and who would not forget that he had been the confidant of the man she hated above all others. Possibly Mr. Froude may set down this indifference to the sense of virtue, and to a conviction in Cromwell's mind of the queen's immorality. We attribute it to lower motives; for we cannot, after due examination, accept his estimate of the character of this minister. To Mr. Froude we must apply the language he has used in examining and condemning the conduct of Queen Anne: "If Protestant legends are admitted as of authority, the Catholic legends must enter with them, and we shall only deepen the confusion. The subject is one on which rhetoric and rumour are alike unprofitable. We must confine ourselves to accounts written at the time by persons to whom, not the outline of the facts only was known, but the circumstances which surrounded them."* We accept these conditions with pleasure, and only regret that Mr. Froude himself should so often have departed from them.

Certain it is, then, that the new candidate for power regarded Anne Boleyn with indifference, if not with positive dislike. He is even accused by Alexander Ales,† the Scotch reformer, then resident in London, with having poisoned the king's ear against her. But whatever may be thought of this charge, this very isolation of Cromwell turned to his advantage. He had but one anxiety—to please the king; and in this he was eminently successful. Whilst his two grand and learned rivals were despatched on foreign missions, he, much too humble and obscure for such splendid employments, remained at home in close attendance on the king. He might have found a dangerous rival in Sir Thomas More; and a few years before no one bid so fair as More to engross the favour of Henry. The smiles for which other men grovelled in the dust, and bartered their faith and their principles, fell unsolicited on More. On no man's neck did the king hang with greater familiarity; in no man's conversation and society did he take so much delight. If he attempted to be familiar with Wolsey, there was something in the very character and sur-

* ii. 462. † In a letter addressed by him to Queen Elizabeth, Sept. 1, 1559.

roundings of the cardinal, something perhaps in the supremacy of his intellect, which forbade ease and raised up a shadow between them. If the king was willing for a time to forget his crown and his dignity, Wolsey never forgot, in the proudest achievements of diplomacy, that he was the king's "most humble chaplain and bedesman." But More, witty, charming, easy, and refined, would not bate an iota of his principles; he had turned a deaf ear to the blandishments of courts to employ himself in writing against heretics. His opinions on the divorce were too well known; and he hastened to get away from the uncongenial atmosphere of a palace. So the whole field was left to Cromwell; and he was not a man to let his opportunities lie idle. In the autumn of 1532 he attended the king to the interview with Francis at Calais; in 1533 he was master of the jewel-house and recorder of Bristol; in 1534 he was secretary of state, chancellor of the exchequer, and master of the rolls; in 1535 and the next year visitor of all monasteries, vicar-general, or king's vicegerent in all ecclesiastical matters, and lord privy-seal. Within these few years he had engrossed in his own hands powers such as no subject and no sovereign in this country had ever possessed before or will ever possess again. As secretary of state he had the ear of the king exclusively; he opened despatches of ambassadors and dictated their instructions; he issued commissions; filled up appointments; disciplined and dictated to the House of Commons. As visitor of monasteries he appointed abbots and priors, disposed of monastic pensions, corrodies, and leases; interfered with discipline, punished offenders. As vicegerent in ecclesiastical matters he presided in person or by deputy over Convocation, taking precedence of the Archbishop of Canterbury; he summoned, dissolved, managed it at his sole will and fiat. To him archbishops and bishops rose up and bowed down as to the great golden image which Nebuchadnezzar, the king, had set up. He disposed of livings, he granted church-leases, he regulated the punishment and promotions of ecclesiastics from the highest to the lowest. Great and unconstitutional as were these powers, wielded at the will of one individual, without the check of public opinion or the control of an independent House of Commons, they were infinitely increased by the Acts of Supremacy and High Treason. By these acts any man's house could be ransacked without notice at any moment, his papers and books seized and sent to London, and himself committed to prison and the rack,* on the

* Notice of the use of the rack is found more than once in this minister's papers and correspondence. Few were able to resist such an argument in support of the king's supremacy.

most frivolous accusation. If at any time, in the carelessness of conversation or the heat of discussion, he had dropped an incautious or angry word which could be construed as expressing a doubt of the king's marriage, or the spiritual nature of the king's supremacy; if he possessed a book or paper, however secret, in which these topics were discussed; if he had by carelessness failed to obliterate the name of the pope or Thomas à Becket from every Ms. which he possessed; if he expressed commiseration for Queen Katherine, or questioned the virtues and good qualities of Queen Anne,—he fell under the penalties of high treason; and if he did not forfeit his life, he was committed to prison, there to remain for an indefinite period, until Cromwell sent down an order for his release or execution. Nor was it necessary that the unhappy culprit should know the offence precisely with which he was charged, or be confronted with his accuser. Malice, ignorance, even a blunder, were active causes in bringing many to gaol.

But Mr. Froude will tell us these powers were seldom abused; at least, he has so much confidence in the goodness of Cromwell as to assure us, if any mistakes were made or any undue severity shown, they fell only on those who had monopolised for centuries religious persecution. We cannot accept such an assurance. We do not see how it would excuse the arbitrary proceedings of the times, if we did. We do not believe that the punishment fell only on men who, themselves or their forefathers, had been actively engaged in persecution; or that these considerations weighed with those who administered the laws. Far from it. Men like Bonner and Gardiner escaped, not because they abhorred persecution, but because, if they had scruples of conscience they swallowed them, and took the oath; More and Fisher, and men of tender and scrupulous consciences,—and there were thousands such,—whose objections to the king's supremacy did not, as Mr. Froude terms it, consist merely in sarcasm, but in a real difficulty,—these men, we say, were executed, not because they or their fathers had been persecutors for centuries, but simply because they refused to forswear themselves. A very superficial acquaintance with the correspondence of the times will show how bitterly these laws were carried into execution;—how every parish bailiff, headborough, justice of the peace, and knight of the shire, was forward to recommend himself to the great man and his favour, and his multitudinous means of preferment, by hunting down unhappy subjects. The more numerous the victims, the more unquestionable the loyalty of the persecutor, the better his chances of promotion. Even the officious zeal of modern policemen has to be kept in check by magisterial caution and restraint; what was it, then, when the whole kingdom was converted into spies, informers, and sharp executors of the law, stimulated to their task by the hopes of gain or distinction at court? The correspondence of Cromwell is filled with cases of this kind. Here is one instance of administering justice, for which Sir Roger Townshend doubtless expected the thanks of the minister:

"Please it your good Lordship to be advertized that there was a poor woman of Wellys beside Walsyngham that imagined a false tale of a miracle to be done by the image of Our Lady that was at Walsyngham, sith the same was brought from thence to London; and upon the trial thereof by my examination from one person to another to the number of 6 persons, at last it came to her that she was the reporter thereof and to be the very author of the same, *as far forth as my conscience and perceiving could lead me.* I committed her therefore to the ward of the constables of Walsyngham. The next day after, being market day there, I caused her to be set in stocks in the morning; and about 9 of the clock, when the said market was fullest of people, with a paper set about her head written with these words upon the same, *A reporter of false tales,* [she] was set in a cart and so carried about the market stede and other streets in the town, staying in divers places where most people assembled, young people and boys of the town casting snowballs at her; this done and executed, was brought to the stocks again and there set till the market was ended. This was her penance, for I knew no law otherwise to punish her but by discretion; trusting it shall be a warning to other light persons in such wise to order themself. Howbeit, I cannot perceive but the said image is not yet out of some of their heads. I thought it convenient to advertize your Lordship of the truth of this matter, lest the report thereof coming in to many men's mouths might be made otherwise than the truth was: therefore I have sent to your Lordship by Robert Touneshend the said examination. Thus I beseech Almighty Jesu evermore to have your good Lordship in his best preservation. Written, the 20th of January."

In another, written about the same time, from Sir Thomas Blount, we find eight poor men and two women hanged for offences against the Act of Supremacy; and a poor tailor, Miles Denison of Kidderminster, for expressing his indignation at the proceedings, was committed to prison: "Your lordship shall be advertised that Dr. Taylor, chaplain unto my Lord Bishop of Worcester (Latymer), was one which preached on Saturday, 27th July last past, at the place of execution, where eight men and two women suffered death. And his sermon did set forth the king's authority of supremacy, and persuaded the prisoners to take their death charitably, and to take the same death for the satisfaction to the world only, and Christ for the satisfaction of their sins; by reason of which sermon the prisoners so did, and gave thanks to the king and his officers for their just execution and death." The offence of the tailor consisted merely in passing a very unceremonious remark on the preacher: "This is a foolish knave-priest, come to preach of the new learning, the which I set not by." A pewterer of Hereford was committed to gaol by the mayor for saying, "I trust to see Queen Katherine's banner spread again, and she shall be queen of England in her old place, by the grace of God." These are but a few of the numerous instances of the way in which the statutes were enforced against the laity. Those against the clergy are more numerous, but equally disproportioned to the offence. One priest is committed to prison for saying that he thought the king could not be supreme head of the church, "for he could not give a man that thing that he should have when he came into the world, nor when he went out of it," *i. e.* the sacraments;—a remark which at least indicates, what no careful student of these times will deny, a persuasion in the minds even of the educated that the king did claim by his supremacy precisely the same spiritual powers which had been exercised by the pope. On another occasion, a schoolmaster was sent to gaol for having a Bible in his possession of which three or four lines in the preface relating to the supremacy were cancelled and blotted out, though he denied it was his doing. Two friars are subjected to the same penalty for saying that they would not for a year or two buy new habits for "by that time, perchance, there will be another change." A Cambridge undergraduate is imprisoned for saying, what nowadays few would deny: "If the pope would have consented that the king might have married Anne Boleyn, he would have been pope still, and been called holy father." Two active magistrates write to Cromwell to inform him, that they had committed to ward a curate who had confessed that his conscience would not serve him to speak against the papal supremacy, "because he heard that the Bishop of Rochester and the fathers of Sion had suffered death for it. But he confessed to us that he prayed every Sunday in the pulpit, where he was curate, for our sovereign lord King Henry VIII., supreme head of the Church of England, and for Queen Anne his wife, and the Lady Elizabeth princess their daughter." He professed his sorrow for his omission, and offered to comply; but notwithstanding he was sent to prison. Richard Thompson, a clerk, is committed to the King's Bench, for praying for the bishop of Rome "at the compulsion of his parishioners, whom he durst not contrary at that time." In some cases the statute assumes a more aggravated form: Clerk, the bishop of Bath and Wells, and whose sympathies leaned to the old religion, informs Cromwell that he had imprisoned a priest for not having preached to his parish "against the bishop of Rome's usurped authority." Another had been committed to gaol, there to continue until Cromwell's pleasure be known, for omitting to erase the popes' names from his own private books. One minister, apparently a puritan, is brought up before the justices for exclaiming in his pulpit, "the king is naught, the bishops and abbots are naught, and himself was naught too." Another for tripping on a similar occasion: "that the holy bishop Urban, sometime *pope* of Rome, and then he advised himself and said, holy Urban *bishop* of Rome, had granted pardon," &c. Sir Anthony Brown is examined by the council solely for expressing a wish, "that God would give the Lady Mary grace to submit herself to the king;" and this was interpreted "as bold talking of the king's succession." In fact, the whole land swarmed with informations. Malice or ignorance might convert into high treason the most innocent or the most careless expressions; and men found themselves hopelessly immured in the walls of a prison, and their goods confiscated, for crimes they had never committed, solely because they had no friend at court to recommend their case to the consideration of the minister.

It is difficult to see in many of these instances, and they might be easily increased, on what fair principles of construction such offences could be legitimately interpreted as offences against the statute; and it may be urged that Cromwell must not be made accountable for the blunders and misapplied zeal of country justices and incompetent magistrates. But no one who has studied the phraseology of the act can doubt that it was thus loosely worded in order to allow of its widest possible application. It was a net intended to catch the weak equally with the subtle; an instrument which threw into the hands of an arbitrary minister indefinable powers of oppressing his enemies. This is a harsh judgment we admit. But even those who take a more favourable view must acknowledge that, though these instances of the perversion of the law were brought immediately to the notice of Cromwell, and are found in his correspondence, no attempt was ever made by him to correct the evil, or moderate the intemperate zeal of his informers. In fact, the reverse is true. He grew more arbitrary; he endeavoured to surround himself and his exorbitant authority with a sanction that should make it high treason to dispute his acts, or breathe a censure on his character. Far as the crime of treason had been extended by his legislation, he sought to extend it yet farther. There is a draft of an act among his papers in his own hand, in which, among other offences to be punished as high treason, we find that of leaving the realm without a license; living in the dominions of a foreign prince; annoying the king, his ambassadors or servants; causing them to disclose the king's secrets;—offences even more vague than those included in the Act of Supremacy. And therefore these arbitrary extensions of the act, already too vague and comprehensive in its penalties, are not to be attributed to the subtle interpretation of the crown-lawyers, as Mr. Froude would have his readers believe, but were part of the original intention of its framer;* and Cromwell is the first, and we believe the only minister, who placed himself on a level with the sovereign, by bringing offences and words against himself under the statute of high treason. Magistrates were taught to make no distinction. Was it likely they would? Expressions against Cromwell were visited with the same penalties as words against the king, his crown, his marriage, his supremacy. We find the justices of Ludlow acting upon this understanding. They write to Cromwell to say that they have apprehended a priest for speaking words against him, sealed his house and taken an inventory of his goods, delivered his plate and property to certain persons for the use of the king. They had searched his house and examined his papers, to find if there was "any untruth" to our lord the king, but had found nothing. From a bag belonging to the priest, containing 76*l.* 16*s.*, they had taken 20*l.* to pay their own expenses; 10*l.* for engrossing the inventory, and 10*l.* for the messenger appointed to carry this information to Cromwell!

We could easily fill the whole of our space with instances of such arbitrary proceedings, but we must press on. They show a systematic attempt to force the consciences of men, to punish them for their religious convictions, and strain the law to the utmost for this purpose. Mr. Froude will excuse it as a state necessity; he will draw a subtle distinction between punishments inflicted for offences against the state and punishments merely for religion; he will contend that these were civil, not religious crimes, and were only punished as dangerous to the safety of the state. We, on the other hand, contend that no such distinction existed at the time in the mind either of sovereign or of people; that the king, as spiritual head of the church, assumed to himself the right of punishing such offences, not as contrary to the laws of the state, but as contrary to what he was pleased to determine was the law of God,—offences as much against his spiritual as against his temporal power. He never stopped to consider how far this or that creed might be excused or condemned,

* ii. 329.

and its assertors brought to the scaffold as rebels or as heretics. That was a distinction first set up by the subtle statesmen of the reign of Elizabeth, when persecution for religion was growing unpopular. It had no place in the mind of Henry. The passing of the Six Articles, and the punishment of those who transgressed them; the persecution of Tyndal, and the death of Frith and Barnes,—all show this. When he transferred to himself the supremacy of the church, he transferred with it all those powers which the church had ever exercised for the punishment of heresy or disobedience to its authority. If the pope was the bishop of bishops, so was he; if the pope could of himself determine controversies of faith, so did he. If the doctrine of purgatory, or the sacrament of penance, or the worship of saints, were or were not to constitute part of the creed and the teaching of the Church of England depended upon the king alone. It is true that he did not administer the sacraments and ordain priests and bishops, but if any man had questioned his power to do so, he would have incurred the penalty of high treason. "A bishop," says Cranmer, "may make a priest by the Scripture, and so may princes and governors, and by the authority of God committed to them." In common with other reformers, Cranmer looked to all spiritual functions as absolutely dependent on the will of the king, as temporal commissions, like those of any other magistrate; and consequently, when Edward VI. came to the crown, he made an offer of resigning his bishopric as if it had been extinguished by the death of the sovereign. And precisely as the power of the pope was supposed to over-ride that of the ordinary, so were the clergy taught to believe that obedience to their diocesans was superseded by the Act of Supremacy. Thus Adam Becansaw, one of Cromwell's visitors, writes to him that it was considered that no priest "was obedient to any ordinary immediately, but only unto the king's highness, as unto the supreme head, *which is one of our chief articles of visitation.*" If these facts indicate the utmost confusion in the minds of men of real religious convictions like Cranmer, to what dangerous purposes might they be applied by a minister like Cromwell, who, as Mr. Froude seems to admit,* had no clear religious principles! They were used by

* Mr. Froude says of Cromwell: "His Protestant tendencies were unknown as yet (1530) perhaps even to his own conscience; nor to the last could he arrive at any certain speculative convictions. He was drawn towards the Protestants as he rose into power by the integrity of his nature, which compelled him to trust only those who were honest like himself." What Mr. Froude means by "speculative convictions" must be left to others to explain. Does he mean to say that while Cromwell passed for a Protestant, and allowed his partisans to believe that he was the great champion of the reformed doctrines, he was in fact opposed to them? Are we to assume that though Cromwell was a Catholic,

him as political engines; they were employed to damage and crush his political rivals; they were made the instruments of his hate, the furtherance of his worldly interests;—not exclusively, we allow, but still they were misused to these purposes. And just as he never scrupled at the means he employed, however unconstitutional, to carry his measures in the House of Commons, so he never scrupled to make use of the spiritual power when by so doing he could obtain his purposes more speedily and more securely. If he packed the House of Commons with his own creatures, would he be more scrupulous in packing a jury? If he interfered with the functions of the bishops, was he likely to be more reserved in interfering with the freedom of elections? These are not hypothetical cases. We find him writing to the king in 1539:* "For your grace's parliament I have appointed your majesty's servant Mr. Morison to be one of them; no doubt he shall be ready to answer and take up such as would crack (boast) or face with literature of learning, or by indirected ways, if any such shall be, as I think there shall be few or none; forasmuch as I and other your dedicate councillors be about to bring all things so to pass that your majesty had never more tractable parliament." What those means were of making parliaments "tractable" we need be at no loss to divine, but they were such as had never before entered the head of the most arbitrary sovereign. It was not merely undue influence at elec-

yet, on finding that all Protestants were honest men, and all Catholics dishonest, he was drawn to the former by the integrity of his nature, and persecuted the latter in spite of his religious convictions? That is precisely what Foxe might have said in his honest, blunt, and immovable bigotry. Meanwhile there is this difficulty. Supposing that so shrewd an observer as Cromwell could have passed his life among the merchants and aldermen of London without paying any attention to the great controversy of the times, it is certain he had been in correspondence with the favourers of the new doctrines (among others, with Miles Coverdale) some years before 1530. In the first draft of his will, dated June 1529, he leaves 20*s.* to every one of the five orders of friars within the City of London to pray for his soul: and he enjoins his executors to engage a priest "to sing for my soul three years next after my death, and to give him for the same 20*l.*" The will was corrected by himself throughout some years after, to make the alterations required by the death of his two daughters, and by other circumstances. The bequests are in general increased one-third throughout, and in some instances doubled. Added to the fact of these alterations having been made in a later hand, we must infer that they were inserted some years after the original draft, unless this augmentation of his wealth was gained by indirect means. Suppose the period to be five or six years, this would bring the date of them to 1534-5, after the passing of the Act of Supremacy and the death of More and Fisher. Yet in its amended form, not only are these two bequests for his soul retained, but in the latter the term is enlarged from three years to seven, and the money from 20*l.* to 46*l.* 13*s.* 4*d.* To us the inference seems to be incontrovertible, viz. that while Cromwell, like his master, was a political Protestant, he adhered in his religious belief to the ancient faith. If there was one tenet to which the Protestants of that period were most opposed, it was that of prayers for the dead.

* State-Papers, i. 603.

tions, it was not bribery, it was not intimidation; it was even more. On the 20th May the corporation of Canterbury write to Cromwell, then chief secretary, to say that they have complied with the king's command certified to them in Cromwell's letter, and according to the king's pleasure have chosen as their burgesses in parliament Rob. Darkenall and John Bryges, notwithstanding that on the 12th of May the sheriff had returned two other burgesses as already duly elected,—John Starky and Christopher Levyns,—whose election was thus disregarded and set aside by this unconstitutional interference. We could produce instances scarcely less flagrant of his tampering with juries and escheators in relation to crown property, but we must forbear. We have already put the patience of our readers to a severe test, and are therefore almost ashamed to beg their attention to the following paper addressed by Cromwell to Cranmer. It shall stand in its colours of good and evil without any comment, for we know of no document which sets forth in so true a light the real feelings of the nation at the time on the principles by which its rulers, civil and ecclesiastical, were actuated. We will only premise that it was written just after the marriage of Henry VIII. and Anne Boleyn,—that marriage which Mr. Froude insists was earnestly demanded by the people, out of deference to whose wishes the king was driven into measures often otherwise inexecusable. It is endorsed

"*Reasons to clear the Clergy for condescending to the King's second Marriage, and for abolishing the Pope's Supremacy.*

There be (I think) in this realm that be not in their minds full pleased and contented that our Sovereign hath married as he hath done, some bearing their favour to the Lady Katharine Princess Dowager, some to the Lady Mary, some because the Pope's authority was not therein; and for this they lay the blame alonelie on some of the prelates. And albeit that the prelates have none otherwise done in this matter but as it became them, and according to the very law of God, yet many of the inconstant commons be not therewith satisfied. And though they forbear to speak at large for fear of punishment, yet they mutter together secretly; which muttering and secret grudge within this realm, I think, doth not a little enbolde the king's adversaries without the realm. And forsomuch as this muttering and grudge is not against our most gracious Sovereign Lord the King, for every man seeth that he is the most gentillest prince, and of the most gentillest nature, and the most upright that ever reigned among men, but only against some of the prelates, and specially against the Archbishop of Canterbury; therefore I would deem it right expedient, that he should show himself to have done nothing (as he hath not in very deed) but according to the law of God. And although the suspicion and muttering be both false and untrue, and of the people unreasonably conceived against him, yet must he endeavour himself to pluck it out of their heads, and that by loving manner. And also if the Pope be excluded out of this realm, the Archbishop must be chief of all the clergy here, the which will not lightly be accepted in the people's hearts, because it hath of so long time continued otherwise, except that the people perceive themself (by reason of the said alteration) to be in better case than they were before. Wherefore I think it were very necessary for those considerations that the said Archbishop should make out a book, not over long, to declare that it that he hath done is not only according to the law of God, but also for the great wealth and quietness of all this realm; and this book would be from him written to all the clergy of this realm. And in the said book let him exhort in charitable wise all the said clergy, and specially such as be in great authority and advanced to dignity in the church, as Bishops, Abbots, Priors, Deans, Provosts and such other, that they at length now call to their remembrance that they be not called unto those rooms and dignities for their own sakes but for the people—not for their own ease, rest, and quiet, but for the quiet, rest, and ease of the people—not for their own winning and lucre, but to make the people rich and plentiful—not to the intent to eschew labour and travail, but by their labour and travail to ease the people of their burthens—not to reign in abundance of all delights and pleasures and the people in misery, but by their temperance and sober living to help the people at the least to plenty of suffisaunce—and finally, not to be served worshipfully, but for Christ's sake (like as he did) to serve other; for woe to us (let him say) if we do not thus! and let him thunder out here and there the vehement exclamations of the prophets and specially of Jeremie against spiritual pastors; and let him persuade the said clergy to avoid clean all pomp, all pride, all vain glory, and specially all manner of covetousness, that hath been occasion of so many evils in the Church of Christ. Let them avoid all ambition, all delicate fare, and to be ready with heart and mind to depart and dispose among the people of this realm lands, goods, money, and whatsoever other thing they now possess superfluously, and that they never hereafter seek for the riches or lordship of this world, nor show themselves desirous of any honour in this world, but diligently to seek for the kingdom of heaven, and there to make their treasury, and clene cast away all care of this world. And let him say:—Most dear brethren in Christ, let it never be seen in us that we seek for any ease or for any pleasure in this world, but only to joy in the cross of Christ and in the health and salvation of the people, both in body and soul; for this is our charge, and for this we shall give a straight accompt. If you, most dear brethren, will gladly go with me this way at my loving exhortation, ye shall greatly merit for your obedience; but in case ye will not, I will compel you by the law of God thus to do, and then ye shall lose your merit of obedience. Thus our Lord Jesus Christ send us grace, both you and I, to accomplish this mine intent to the wealth of all the people both in body and soul. Amen.

I am very sure if he would set out a little book after this tenour, though he could never bring his purpose about, yet should he by this mean greatly content the people's minds and make them think that they be happy thus to be rid of the Pope's oppression, and that the Archbishop is a perfect and a good Bishop, and that he intendeth truly according to the Word of God, and that he never did any thing for his prince's pleasure so much to win him promotion as he did for the truth's sake, seeing he pretendeth to stamp under foot all pleasure, all ease, all delight of this world, and utterly give himself to travail and pain in this world: for my mind is and ever hath been that the King's highness should not be seen to be most busy to defend his most righteous cause himself, but let the Clergy specially do it, and namely, the Archbishops. But if there be any so stubborn that he will not believe the truth, then the King's highness to punish him according to the laws in that case provided. For I wote well if it come to the hearing of the Pope and the Emperor that the whole clergy of England is fully bent to defend our Sovereign Lord the King's cause to the very death, they will not meddle much further."*

There are other points in the inquiry on which we should gladly have entered had our space permitted us; inquiries for a satisfactory solution of which we have searched Mr. Froude's pages in vain. The hero of his story is Henry VIII., and yet he seems to attribute the conception and execution of the most eventful and characteristic measures of the reign to the genius of Cromwell. We are told by Mr. Froude "that Cromwell struck the line on which the forces of nature were truly moving—the resultant, not of the victory of either of the extreme parties, but of the joint action of their opposing forces. To him belonged the rare privilege of genius, to see what other men could not see." And yet in a page or two after, it is the Tudor spirit that wakes; it is the king that speaks. We should be glad to know which was the wheel, and which the index; which the substance, and which the reflection. Did Henry set his seal to measures suggested to him by his minister, or did his minister merely carry out the ideas of his master? Mr. Froude will point out to us letters and sign-manuals; he will call our attention to passages in which *he* feels "the noble spirit" of the monarch breathing in every line. We confess we cannot be satisfied with these evidences; and we fancy—though it may only be fancy—that we trace in the laboriously corrected drafts of the secretary indications of those qualities which Mr. Froude regards as the exclusive attributes of the sovereign. It may be that the secretary was writing to dictation; it may be that he was no more than the hand upon the dial-plate.

* With a view of making the clergy more dependent on the crown, he proposed to confiscate the episcopal revenues, and make the bishops pensioners on the state. Each one of them, with the exception of the archbishop, was to receive 1000 marks a year. Had he lived longer, the bishops would have followed the abbots and priors.

But this is the point we desire to see cleared up. If Henry was indolent and disinclined to business, if he was engrossed in his amorous passion for Anne Boleyn, if Mr. Froude's favourite metaphor of his "waking up" is to be construed literally,—then it might happen that his able and obsequious servant would not willingly obtrude on his master's slumbers. He might be satisfied with a general conception of his master's wishes; he might shape out his policy after his own fashion, satisfied that the king should affix his signature, or that he himself should apply the signet to acts bearing the king's authority, and running in the royal name, but of which the king himself had very little cognisance. If this seems a hazardous supposition, it must be remembered that it was his theory that the king should not be too much seen in his own causes. And even if it were not so in all measures, it is probable that the king would confine himself mainly to questions of foreign politics, and leave domestic reforms to his vicar-general and vicegerent. To Henry it was of much greater moment what the emperor thought of his doings, or how he should draw Francis I. into following his own example of renouncing the pope, than to punish discontented subjects for calling Queen Anne "a churl's daughter," or setting curates in the pillory for haggling over his title of supremacy. At all events, the doubt is as old as the days of Cromwell. "They that rule about the king," said people, "make him great banquets and give him sweet wines, and make him drunk; and then they bring him bills and he putteth his sign to them, whereby they do what they wish, and no man may correct them." "That Cromwell," exclaimed one John Hampson, in a street-brawl at Oxford—"that traitor hath destroyed many a man; an I were as nigh him as I am to you, I would thrust my dagger into the heart of him." Whether these prejudices were well founded or not, there can be no doubt that they existed; and, in fact, Mr. Froude admits that Cromwell was the most unpopular man of his time, without a friend in either party; but then he falls back on the poetical commonplace, that he was friendless from the excess of his integrity.

On that point we must conclude, and then leave our readers to judge for themselves. We have shown before with what unexampled rapidity this minister rose from the utmost obscurity within six years to the highest honours of the state—how, in less than three years, he saw all his rivals at his feet, whatever their rank, their abilities, or their advantages;—he, a man in trade, not distinguished by learning, not trained to politics, a subordinate in Wolsey's household. If he owed this rapid promotion solely to his virtue, then should Mr. Froude comfort himself that virtue is sometimes highly rewarded. But there are questions which will immediately occur to men of ordinary sense, and to which they will demand a satisfactory answer before they consent to surrender their convictions to the most bland and graceful of historians. When Cromwell entered Wolsey's service, he was a thriving merchant, but no more; when he entered the king's service, on the death of the cardinal, he had given up business. To live at court, and that so splendid and extravagant as the court of Henry VIII., required a fortune; the mere presents that every minister must distribute—the New Year's gift alone—would have swallowed up a moderate income. His official emoluments as secretary of state were of the scantiest kind; yet we find him early launching out into great expenses. Within a few years he has five establishments,—one at Austin Friars, another at Hackney, another at Stepney, another at Mortlake, another at Canonbury, besides his official residence at the Rolls. At Austin Friars, Hackney, and Stepney, he was carrying on extensive repairs and buildings all at the same time, and employing upon each of them from fifty to seventy workmen at 6*d.* a day. Not long after he was erecting a mansion at Ewhurst, of which his steward reports that it was "the goodliest and the mightiest he had ever seen." He kept from three to four stewards, he had a staff of clerks, servants, hunters, hawks, and all the expensive *impedimenta* of a noble establishment. In July 1537 the expense of his household, not to mention wages, was 101*l.* 13*s.*; in August, 98*l.* 9*s.* 6½*d.*; in September, 240*l.** Next year, in the same month, it had increased to 300*l.*, not including 133*l.* 6*s.* 8*d.* for provisioning Lewes priory, which had then come into his hands. On the 19th November 1537 he paid 2000*l.* for a diamond and a ruby. In June 1538 he purchased Sir George Somerset's house at Kew; in November following, the manor of Brampton for 1000*l.* In January the next year he bought the demesnes of the priory of Folkestone; next month the manor of Holden for 3450*l.* The same year he lent Gastwick 2000*l.*, the year before, 2253*l.*, for the king's use. Besides these outlays he lost money at dice and cards, in sums varying from 20*s.* to 20*l.* Nor were his outgoings as a courtier inconsiderable. On the birth of Prince Edward he gave the messenger 6*l.* 13*s* 4*d.*; to the ladies attending on the prince, 20*l.*; and 3*l.* 10*s.* to the poor of St. James. To the king he presented a gold cup, and an "outlandish beast" with a velvet collar; to the poor queen herself his new-year's gift in 1537 was a cup of gold and

* These sums must be multiplied by ten to bring them near to modern computation.

22*l.* 10*s.* With these exceptions, his liberality was most conspicuous to the Princess Mary. In 1537 he sent her 24*l.* as a new-year's gift, then 11*l.* 5*s.*, and immediately after 6*l.*; and next month, as her "fallantyne" (valentine), 15*l.* In November of the same year he paid Wriothesley 38*l.* 6*s.* 8*d.* "to make my Lady Mary a new-year's gift," and in December "a salt of gold and 10 sovereigns." Her only acknowledgment of this bounty was "a dish of quinces," for which the minister rewarded the bearer with 5*s.* Whether she remained inexorable, or money grew scarce, her next new-year's gifts were only 11*l.* 5*s.* Besides these he was fond of masques. In the January of 1539 he exhibited a masque before the court which cost him 30*l.* 7*s.* 6*d.*,—the stuff, 13*l.* 17*s.* 11*d.*, the copper-plates and disguises, 9*l.* 2*s.* 1*d.*; and among the curious items is one of 21*s.* 2*d.* "paid for the trimming of Divine Providence when she played before the king." To Woodhall, the schoolmaster of Eton, he gave 5*l.* for playing before him at Christmas; and to Bole, afterwards bishop of Ossory, and his fellows, on a similar occasion, 30*s.*; to Grafton, the furnisher, 10*l.* for masks. His installation as Knight of the Garter, in 1537, cost 25*l.*; his gown, 6*l.* 13*s.* 4*d.*, his collar and George, 7*l.* 6*s.**

When churchmen were ministers, the scanty emoluments of office were supplemented by bishoprics; but Cromwell could enjoy no such advantages. Henry was not unkind to his virtues, and he had numerous grants from the crown; but such grants brought in little ready money, certainly none adequate for such heavy expenses. Then, how were these expenses defrayed? A glance at his correspondence explains. In Wolsey's service he had learned to take douceurs,—we should call them bribes,—to obtain the cardinal's favours for suitors. When he became chief minister to Henry VIII., he continued the practice; and his letters furnish ample evidence of the extent to which this practice was carried. His appointments as visitor and as vicar-general gave him ample opportunities of enriching himself by indirect means; and the numerous applications made to him afford ample indications—even if we had not his private accounts to produce—that his virtue was not impregnable. Sir Ant. Cope writes to him to say that seven convicts had escaped from the Bishop of Lincoln's prison in Banbury; and this will be a good opportunity to extort from the bishop

* There are other curious items for which we cannot afford space; *e. g.* such as "two ribbands for his George, 8*d.*, and a lace for his spectacles, 4*d.*; two stools to set his legs on, 1*s.*, and 20*d.* for a pewter pot to wash a running sore with which he was troubled," like his master. He was by no means conspicuous for charity. His alms in 1537 were 8*d.* to a poor woman in March; 8*d.* to two poor men in July; 1*s.* to three poor women, and 2*d.* at Christmas. Next year he was more liberal, but chiefly to the poor of Putney.

the fee-farm of the hundred of Banbury, which he holds of the king, and bestow it on one of Cromwell's friends; and he ends with offering Cromwell 200*l.* to obtain it for him. Sir Simon Harcourt writes to him to procure him from the king a little house of Canons in Staffordshire: "His grace shall have 100*l.*, and your mastership, if it be brought to pass, 100*l.* for your pain, and 20*l.* fee so long as you live." But if it be dissolved, and Cromwell can obtain the grant of its farm for the petitioner, he will give him 100 marks. Thos. Candell offers him, when privy seal, 10*l.* to obtain the king's patent and seal for a friar's house and lands. Lady Mary Capell offers him 20*l.* to buy a hobby, if he will get the arrears of her annuity paid up. Sir Piers Eggecombe desires a grant of the suppressed priory of Totness. He offers the king 800 marks for it, and Cromwell a present of 100*l.* to procure the king's favour. He obtains his request, and then asks for two manors in Devonshire. A wretched constable employed by him as a visitor of the religious houses begs him to stay the conclusion of a bargain between one Broke and the abbot of Bardsley. "Hear me speak or you conclude with him: it shall be in the way of 200 marks." Archbishops and bishops, noblemen and widows, purchased his smiles with eager hands. The black-mail which he levied under the name of new-year's gifts, fees, and annuities, was enormous: 40*l.* a year from Cranmer, 20*l.* a year from the other bishops, and 10*l.* a year besides in the shape of a new year's gift; sums of 2*l.*, 5*l.*, 10*l.*, and 20*l.* from most of the abbeys and priories in England; 40*l.* from the Earl of Wiltshire, 20*l.* from Queen Jane Seymour, the same from the unhappy Countess of Salisbury; 20*l.* from Dr. Lee, the same from Dr. Leighton, and 10*l.* from Dr. Landon, his visitors of the monasteries. The entries in his steward's book reveal the same tale: 6*l.* 13*s.* 4*d.* in a little white purse; "in a pair of gloves," 13*l.* 6*s.* 8*d.*; "in a handkercher," 66*l.* 13*s.* 4*d.*; "in a black velvet purse," 20*l.*; and 10*l.* "with a purse of silver and gilt." "A purse of crimson satin," containing 66*l.* 13*s.* 4*d.*; in "another crimson satin purse," 20*l.*; 20*l.* "in a white paper;" 20*l.* "in a glove under the cushion in the gallery window;" "under a cushion in the middle window in the gallery," 10*l.* "Under the cushion in the gallery window, in a purse of white leather," 100*l.*; "the same day 50*l.* in a purse of red leather;" "in a purse of white leather," 10*l.*;—all lying close together in those eventful months, when nobles and peasantry were dissipating and plundering the abbey lands.

We might enlarge these instances almost to any amount. The poor monks at Canterbury, who paid him an annuity for his protection, had a summer's residence at Bekesborne, the envy of the neighbourhood. The king was desirous to have it, and offered the prior any lands of equivalent value in exchange. In great trepidation he laid his griefs before the minister; the monks could not consent to part with it on any terms, it was their only place of recreation, nothing could be an equivalent for its loss. The powerful intercession of the minister saved it from the clutches of the crown, and the monks were profuse in their gratitude: but in his very next letter he demanded and obtained a lease of it for himself. Pensions and annuities from abbots and priors trembling for existence; presents of money from grasping squires and nobles eager to clutch at the prey and forestall each other; hampers of game, fish, and poultry; eggs, cheeses, and venison pasties from less wealthy suitors, all anxious to bespeak the favour of this man, more powerful than the king himself, poured in at his gates. The venison sent him fed his servants and saved his butcher's bills, as his thrifty steward informs him;—if it got a little damaged by the journey, it was baked in a pie, and that was food for the man which was no food for his master. For though he rose to the highest offices in the state, and his income was enormous, the business-like habits and frugality of the merchant still reigned in his heart and his household. No wonder whilst the minister grew wealthy the crown grew poor. It was thought a great thing that Cardinal Wolsey, once in his magnificent administration, with foreign wars and continual loans to Maximilian, to Charles, and after his captivity to Francis I., should have once demanded a subsidy from the House of Commons; now, in a period of profound peace, with parliamentary subsidies, the enormous fines paid by the clergy to escape the premunire, with annatys and first-fruits, which had hitherto rolled a stream of gold to Rome, all turned into the exchequer, the king "woke up," after six years, to find himself on the eve of a rebellion, with no funds to meet it, unless he melted his plate and sold his jewels.

These details are not taken from Protestant or from Popish legends, so much deprecated by Mr. Froude; they are not the blind suggestions of malice and envy; they are derived from an authority which Mr. Froude himself will not dispute—Cromwell's own correspondence. We do not contend that they present the whole account of the matter, and that Cromwell's character is to be judged by these facts alone, to the exclusion of others: that would be to fall into the fault we condemn. But whether they bear out Mr. Froude's views, and whether an impartial historian ought to have ignored them, our readers can decide for themselves.

Art. VII.—MR. BROWNING'S POEMS.

The Poetical Works of Robert Browning. Three volumes. Third Edition. Chapman and Hall.

Mr. Browning, though commanding a wider intellectual sweep of view than almost any artist of our day, is yet a poet not of European, nor even of national celebrity, but rather the favourite of an intellectual sect; and this, not from any sectarian tendency in his poetry,—nothing could be more catholic, —but from the almost complete absence of that atmosphere of fascination about his verse, that melody of mind and speech, which is the main attraction of poetry to ordinary men, and but for which, mere imaginative power, however great, would scarcely arrest their attention at all. Coleridge once defined poetry—very badly we conceive—as "that species of composition which is opposed to works of science, by proposing for its *immediate* object pleasure, not truth; and from all other species (having *this* object in common with it) it is discriminated by proposing to itself such delight from the *whole* as is compatible with a distinct gratification from each component *part*." Now Coleridge certainly did not *intend* to exclude Mr. Browning's works by anticipation from all claim to the title of poems; if he had lived to read Mr. Browning, Coleridge's profound, rich, and catholic imagination would scarcely have failed to appreciate fully the power and insight of the younger poet; but no definition of a poem could have been contrived more ingeniously calculated to exclude Mr. Browning's works from that class of composition. Most of Mr. Browning's poems might be described precisely 'as proposing for their *immediate* object truth, not pleasure, and as aiming at such a satisfaction from the whole as is by no means compatible with any very distinct gratification from each component part.' In other words, Mr. Browning's poems, though, when clearly apprehended, they seldom fail to give that higher kind of imaginative satisfaction which is one of the most enviable intellectual states,—give scarcely any immediate sensitive pleasure. There is none of the thrill through the brain, of the vibrating melodious sweetness, of the tranquillising touch and atmosphere of loveliness which we usually associate with the highest powers of poetical expression. And then, as to the relation of the whole to the part, which is Coleridge's second test of a poem, Mr. Browning's poems are not so organised that the parts have any gratification for you at all, till you catch a view of his whole. Coleridge says, that "the reader should be carried forward, not merely or chiefly by the mechanical impulse of curiosity, or by a restless desire to arrive at the solution, but by the pleasurable activity of the mind, excited by the attractions of the journey itself. Like the motion of a serpent, which the Egyptians made the emblem of intellectual power, or like the path of sound through the air, at every step he pauses and half recedes, and from the retrogressive movement collects the force which again carries him onward." Nothing could be farther from describing the movement of Mr. Browning's poems. Instead of fascinating you with his harmony of movement, and gradually insinuating the drift and spirit of the poem into your imagination, Mr. Browning rushes upon you with a sort of intellectual *douche*, half stuns you with the abruptness of the start, repeats the application in a multitude of swift various shocks from unexpected points of the compass, and leaves you at last giddy and wondering where you are, but with a vague sense that, were you but properly prepared beforehand, and warned as to its laws of approach, you might discern a unity and power in this intellectual water-spout, though its first descent only drenched and bewildered your imagination. Take the following short poem for example, one of really marvellous force, indeed of true genius, but which we purposely decline to present to our readers with any further introduction than Mr. Browning has himself accorded us; in order to illustrate this characteristic of his, that the whole must be fairly grasped before any of the "component parts" are intelligible,—the component parts, indeed, being little more than diminutive wholes, too diminutive in scale to be clearly legible until you have seen the whole, whence you go back to the component parts again with a key to their meaning that at last gradually deciphers them:

"*Soliloquy of the Spanish Cloister.*

"Gr-r-r—there go, my heart's abhorrence!
Water your damned flower-pots, do!
If hate killed men, Brother Lawrence,
God's blood, would not mine kill you!
What? your myrtle-bush wants trimming?
Oh, that rose has prior claims—
Needs its leaden vase filled brimming?
Hell dry you up with its flames!

At the meal we sit together:
Salve tibi! I must hear
Wise talk of the kind of weather,
Sort of season, time of year:
*Not a plenteous cork-crop: scarcely
Dare we hope oak-galls, I doubt:
What's the Latin name for 'parsley'?*
What's the Greek name for Swine's Snout?

Whew! We'll have our platter burnished,
Laid with care on our own shelf!
With a fire-new spoon we're furnished,
And a goblet for ourself.
Rinsed like something sacrificial
Ere 'tis fit to touch our chaps—
Marked with L. for our initial!
(He-he! There his lily snaps!)

Saint, forsooth! While brown Dolores
Squats outside the Convent bank,
With Sanchicha, telling stories,
Steeping tresses in the tank,
Blue-black, lustrous, thick like horsehairs,
Can't I see his dead eye glow,
Bright as 'twere a Barbary corsair's?
(That is, if he'd let it show!)

When he finishes refection,
Knife and fork he never lays
Cross-wise, to my recollection,
As do I, in Jesu's praise.
I, the Trinity illustrate,
Drinking watered orange-pulp—
In three sips the Arian frustrate;
While he drains his at one gulp!

Oh, those melons! If he's able
We're to have a feast so nice!
One goes to the Abbot's table,
All of us get each a slice.
How go on your flowers? None double?
Not one fruit-sort can you spy?
Strange!—And I, too, at such trouble,
Keep them close-nipped on the sly!

There's a great text in Galatians,
Once you trip on it entails
Twenty-nine distinct damnations,
One sure, if another fails:
If I trip him just a-dying,
Sure of Heaven as sure as can be,
Spin him round and send him flying
Off to Hell, a Manichee?

Or, my scrofulous French novel
On grey paper with blunt type!
Simply glance at it, you grovel
Hand and foot in Belial's gripe:
If I double down its pages
At the woeful sixteenth print,
When he gathers his greengages,
Ope a sieve and slip it in't?

Or, there's Satan!—one might venture
Pledge one's soul to him, yet leave
Such a flaw in the indenture
As he'd miss till, past retrieve,

Blasted lay that rose-acacia
  We're so proud of! *Hy, Zy, Hine* . . .
'St, there's Vespers! *Plena gratiâ*
  Ave, Virgo! Gr-r-r—you swine!"

When we have caught the idea that Mr. Browning is painting the jealous disgust and tricky spite felt by a passionate, sensual, self-indulging, superstitious monk for the pale, blameless, vegetating, contented sort of saint who takes kindly to gardening, and "talks crops" at the monastery table, we see how living and strongly conceived the picture is: but the wording, though vigorous, and one verse at least (that concerning Sanchicha) highly picturesque, is neither melodious nor even very lucid for its purpose; and the parts, as we said, are diminished images of the whole, and hence enigmatic till the whole has been two or three times read. Yet we take it that the versification, and the verbal *efficiency* generally, in this little poem is a good deal above the average power of expression of the pieces called "lyrical," chiefly because it is lyrical only in name, and does not attempt to be in form much more than it really is in essence, a dramatic fragment.

Mr. Browning's deficiency in the power of sensuous expression, and in the art of giving an *independent* interest and attractiveness to the component parts of his poems, as distinguished from the whole, is of course most strikingly seen in the deficiencies of his metre and rhyme, which are the natural gauge of poetic expressiveness and harmony of poetic structure. A metre that does not fit the movement of the thought gives the painful sense of a man rattling in a case of armour quite too large for him; and rhyme that is only rhyme, and that does not bring with the regular beat of the language something of new power to the sense, annoys with a sense of something artificial, ingenuity at best, which interferes with the imaginative effect instead of heightening it. Mr. Browning is never happy in his lyrical metres, and his rhymes have the careless wilful effect of being cast off at random in order to conform to a barren and tyrannic custom. His versification is almost always best where it is nearest to prose, where, as in the dramas, the metre is blank verse without rhyme. Elsewhere there is no elasticity in the rhythm; and rarely indeed, when he tries rhyme, does he use it to effect its legitimate function,—the delicate and definitive *clasping* of thought to thought. Except in "The Lost Leader," "Bringing the Good News from Ghent to Aix," and one or two other ballads of the same kind, which have a stately gallop in their movement that corresponds well to the movement of the thought, there is not a metre or a rhyme in the poems that strikes you by its felicity, and but few, except some of the blank metres, that do not painfully drag or jar. And this deficiency in the *verse* is only the reflection of the deficiencies of the style generally; whenever, at least, it attempts to be lyrical.

Mr. Browning has himself suggested to us, not perhaps with any conception of the full scope of his remark, the reason why many of his so-called lyrics are unsatisfactory in form; and if we follow the clue his suggestion gives, we shall probably find that it accounts for much both of his great power and great uncouthness. He says in a note to the first of the "Lyrics," "Such poems as the majority in this volume might also come properly enough, I suppose, under the head of 'Dramatic Pieces;' being, though often Lyric in expression, always Dramatic in principle, and so many utterances of so many imaginary persons, not mine." This is most true, except that we should very seldom indeed allow these pieces to be truly "lyric in expression." They try to be indeed, but fail. They make an effort to take the lyric form; but having another essence, they wriggle about uncomfortably in their artificial attitude, and show, by the rasping and the friction of the style that they have somehow got embodied in a wholly unsuitable poetic organism. The truth is, we think, that Mr. Browning combines in his own person the *half* of a great dramatist with a large capacity for pure intellectual thought, but has none of that liability to flashes of emotion tingeing his whole creative power which generates lyric poetry. His mind seldom or never seems to fall under the dominion of a single sentiment or passion, without which poetry cannot properly be lyric. He can *throw* himself into such a mood as a dramatist, but that has an altogether different effect. A dramatic picture of emotion has not the same spontaneity, the same ease, the same singleness of effect; for almost always (usually even in soliloquies) it has direct relation to the minds and actions of others. Mr. Browning is a dramatic thinker,—always thinking within the imaginative fetters of dialogue, even when not throwing his thoughts into that external form; always speaking and writing for a resisting medium of thought or feeling foreign to that which he is expressing at the moment. You feel that he invariably contemplates some other phase of character, against which his thought has to justify itself, or into the heart of which it has to force an entrance. A genuine lyric is not written under the sense of external limits, and with direct reference to the presence of some other form of thought or character. Dramatic thought must always be a *compressed* form of imaginative power; it must be distinctly outlined, and fit piece into piece. Lyrical poetry is "a law unto itself," defined by its own nature, but without defined end or purpose, falling into shapes due only to the inward harmony of the mind in which it originates, and essentially free from the control of any immediate foreign influence. It is obvious that far more variety and flexibility of metre is needed for the lyric than for the drama. Dramatic verse must be open to all sorts of moods alike; must be the common ground on which they meet; and consequently takes a very general form, which will suit alike the most different humours and admit the sharpest collisions. But a lyric is complete in itself, and should justify itself by the perfect individual organisation of its versification.

Why, then, it may well be asked, does a mind so essentially dramatic ever feel tempted to adopt the lyric form? The answer we believe to be, because Mr. Browning is only *half* a dramatist,—his dramatic powers being controlled entirely by intellectual interests, and never hurrying on his imagination deep into the play of those practical forces which constitute the life of a great drama. He does not enter into character as a prelude to the excitement of a conflict, but at most only indicates the conflict to illustrate the character. He conceives men in their relation to each other, and in mental collision with each other; but, after all, he does not care which way the battle goes, except so far as it is involved in his intellectual conception. There is no *narrative* force in him at all. He never enters into the story, and even in his dramas evades a plot as far as he possibly can. The consequence is, that he is constantly tempted to throw his dramatic conceptions into a form which rids him altogether of the necessity for affecting a plot. It is intellectual dramatic sketches to which his genius leads him, not drama; intellectual portraits of dramatic *states of mind*, never of dramatic scenes and *dénouements*. And in order to disguise more effectually the fragmentary character of these pieces torn from their dramatic connexion, they are too often forced into an artificial mould of lyrical shape. Yet, as they are really bits of dialogue addressed to a visionary but half-indicated auditor, the lyrical metres and rhymes are too often the most awkward of artificial accomplishments, which, instead of setting them to a soft melody, produce the same kind of effect as paving-stones placed at regular short intervals in the track of a carriage. Of course the periodic jolt marks a kind of time, and to nerves of bendleather might serve to measure the flow of the thought; but it is the measure of artificial obstacles methodically upsetting the thought at fixed intervals, not of its natural ebb and flow. A very short extract will show what we mean; we take it from a poem of fine conception, called "The Grammarian's Funeral;" the idea of which is to bring out the strong implicit faith in an eternal career which there should be in any man who devotes this life wholly to the preliminary toil of mastering the rudiments of language:

> "Was it not great? Did not he throw on God
> (He loves the burthen)
> God's task to make the heavenly period
> Perfect the earthen?
> Did not he magnify the mind, show clear
> Just what it all meant?
> He would not discount life, as fools do here,
> Paid by instalment!
> He ventured neck-or-nothing—heaven's success
> Found, or earth's failure:
> 'Wilt thou trust death, or not?' He answered, 'Yes!
> Hence with life's pale lure!'
>
> * * * *
>
> So, with the throttling hands of death at strife,
> Ground he at grammar;
> Still, through the rattle, parts of speech were rife:
> While he could stammer
> He settled ὅτι's business—let it be!
> Properly based οὖν—
> Gave us the doctrine of the enclitic δε
> Dead from the waist down."

Now that is a very dramatic defence of a grammarian's life; and if the substance of it had fallen naturally into a grammarian's own mouth, instead of being forced out of shape into a kind of hoarse triumphal recitative—chant we cannot call it—over his grave, it might have made a fine dramatic fragment. But as it is, this is in form not meant to be dramatic, but a sort of rhapsody of praise. While the *thought* throughout suggests simply an imaginative effort in the poet's mind to explain and defend the narrow range of a grammarian's studies, the form of the expression tries to pour out a flood of lyrical enthusiasm over him which the writer does not feel, and the striving after which, therefore, comes out in the quick awkward limp of the lame metre.

Nothing is easier than to multiply instances of the same kind of blunder in Mr. Browning's so-called lyrics. As a rule, wherever we have a peculiarly jarring metre and jingling rhymes, there Mr. Browning is attempting to disguise sharp dramatic sketches in the flowing forms of lyrical melody,—to disguise a speech in a song, to throw over the tight-fitting costume of dialogue the easy undress of spontaneous feeling,—in short, to give the effect of "wandering at its own sweet will" to a stream of thought or emotion which is strongly and pointedly directed on a specific object. Here, for instance, is a young lady complaining of her lover for ceasing to care for her, because she had allowed him to see too fully her love for him. She makes a fair speech, but a wretched monody, or whatever else this species of confession ought to be called; and the attempt to put it into a lyrical form results in a funny compromise between a firm step and the beat of wings, which reminds one most perhaps of a duck's waddle:

"Never any more
    While I live,
Need I hope to see his face
    As before.
Once his love grown chill,
    Mine may strive—
Bitterly we re-embrace,
    Single still.

Was it something said,
    Something done,
Vexed him? was it touch of hand,
    Turn of head?
Strange! that very way
    Love begun:
I as little understand
    Love's decay.

When I sewed or drew,
    I recall
How he looked as if I sung,
    —Sweetly too.
If I spoke a word,
    First of all
Up his cheek the colour sprung,
    Then he heard.

Sitting by my side,
    At my feet,
So he breathed the air I breathed,
    Satisfied!
I, too, at love's brim
    Touched the sweet:
I would die if death bequeathed
    Sweet to him.

'Speak, I love thee best!'
    He exclaimed.
'Let thy love my own foretell,'
    I confessed:
'Clasp my heart on thine
    Now unblamed,
Since upon thy soul as well
    Hangeth mine!'

Was it wrong to own,
    Being truth?
Why should all the giving prove
    His alone?

I had wealth and ease,
Beauty, youth—
Since my lover gave me love,
I gave these," &c.

This marked genius of Mr. Browning for sketching character *in position*, as we may say—that is, in its most characteristic attitude towards the rest of the world—is probably the secret not only of his lyrical failures, but of his generally defective powers of poetical expression; for it implies an intellectual basis for his dramatic power, and suggests that Mr. Browning is rather a highly-intellectual actor, throwing himself into a new part, and feeling its characteristic points, as a good rider just feels his horse's mouth with the bit,—or, to use a better image, perhaps, that he throws out all his nervous perception into the defining outline and moral profile of his part, as a blind man will finger the contour of a face that is dear to him, to secure his image of the characteristic lines,—rather than that he works, like Shakespeare or Goethe, by intense sympathy from within, leaving the final outline to crystallise as it may, according to the internal law and nature of the life thus germinating in his imagination. And no doubt the basis of Mr. Browning's whole genius is keenly intellectual,—not meditatively intellectual, but, on the contrary, observingly, definingly, speculatively intellectual,—of which we may see one great proof in the far superior character of his masculine than of his feminine sketches, of his "men" than of his "women." Educated *men's* characters are naturally *in position*, and most vigorous masculine characters of any kind have a defined bearing on the rest of the world, a characteristic attitude, a personal latitude and longitude on the map of human affairs, which an intellectual eye can seize and mark out at once. But it is not so usually with women's characters. They are not best expressed by attitude and outline, but by essence and indefinite tone. As an odour expresses and characterises a flower even better than its shape and colour, as the note of a bird is in some sense a more personal expression of it than its form and feathers; so there is something of vital essence in a great poet's delineations of women which is far more expressive than any outline or colour. When Shakespeare makes Cleopatra say, over the body of Antony,

"And there is nothing left remarkable
Beneath the visiting moon,"

he somehow contrives to embody in a sentence the concentrated essence of the imperial and voluptuous queen. When Goethe makes Klärchen, in *Egmont*, sing,

"Freudvoll und leidvoll,
Gedankenvoll seyn,

Langen und bangen
In schwebender Pein,
Himmelhoch jauchzend
Zum Tode betrübt,
Glücklich allein
Ist die Seele die liebt,"—

he has given you the whole character in an aroma of brief but surpassing sweetness. There is no trace of this power in Mr. Browning. He throws his feminine characters into as strongly-defined attitudes as his masculine, and the consequence is, that they are not nearly so effective; and also that, half-conscious of this intellectualising mould of his mind, he attempts them very much less often. He has drawn women, indeed, of a certain grandeur of outline,—as, for instance, the guilty Ottima, in "Pippa passes," who stimulates her lover to the murder of her husband, and then asks him to crown her his queen, his "spirit's arbitress, magnificent in sin;" but the picture is painfully inflamed, and though it impresses one as true, it is because, under such exceptional circumstances, the pronounced attitude which Mr. Browning loves to draw is to be found even more sharply defined in the passionate woman, fearful that the guilt may alienate love, than in the most masculine of men.

Otti. "Well, then, I love you better now than ever,
And best (look at me while I speak to you)—
Best for the crime; nor do I grieve, in truth,
This mask, this simulated ignorance,
This affectation of simplicity,
Falls off our crime; this naked crime of ours
May not, now, be looked over: look it down, then!
Great? let it be great; but the joys it brought,
Pay they or no its price? Come: they or it!
Speak not! The Past, would you give up the Past
Such as it is, pleasure and crime together?
Give up that noon I owned my love for you?
The garden's silence! even the single bee
Persisting in his toil, suddenly stopt;
And where he hid you only could surmise
By some campanula's chalice set a-swing:
Who stammered—'Yes, I love you?'"

But this too is essentially an intellectual picture; a passionate attitude, with its swollen veins and starting muscles, delineated powerfully by an intellectual mind. And of the only other feminine pictures that strike us at all,—those, namely, in the fine piece called "In a Balcony,"—it may be equally said that they are not perhaps overdrawn, but drawn on the stretch, and not in the way in which women most naturally express themselves. In general, all Mr. Browning's power is expended on masculine characters in intellectually defined relations to the rest of the world.

And, again, this defective, because too intellectual, basis of Mr. Browning's powers of expression betrays itself most clearly in his choice of language. In that strange freak of creative self-will, *Sordello*, which probably no man or woman except the author ever yet understood,—we do not at all doubt that he understands his own drift clearly enough,—there are one or two flashes of intelligible thought which give us some insight into Mr. Browning's own troubles. Sordello is an ambitious poet of the ancient Troubadour type and times, divided with himself whether he should try to influence the world directly or only through his song. And it is the psychological history of this conflict which Mr. Browning apparently wishes to describe. One of Sordello's first difficulties, during his poetic period, in getting at mankind, is, language. He is oppressed apparently (like our Lake poets of the end of the last century) by the unreal character of the poetic phraseology, and he leaves off imagining for a season, to see if he can make something more effective of the medium through which his imaginations must be presented to the world:

> " He left imagining, to try the stuff
> That held the imaged thing, and—let it writhe
> Never so fiercely—scarce allowed a tithe
> To reach the light,—his Language."

Certainly Sordello was quite right in supposing that this was the great obstacle to fame, if we have any measure of his powers of expression in this poem; for a more completely opaque medium than the wording either of his own thoughts or of the author's thoughts about him, Talleyrand himself would have failed to invent. However, it is something that he so keenly felt the obscurity, while the attempt to remedy it, and the reason of the failure, are instructive:

> "How he sought
> The cause, conceived a cure, and slow re-wrought
> That Language,—welding words into the crude
> Mass from the new speech round him, till a rude
> Armour was hammered out, in time to be
> Approved beyond the Roman panoply
> Melted to make it,—boots not. This obtained
> With some ado, no obstacle remained
> To using it; accordingly he took
> An action with its actors, quite forsook
> Himself to live in each, returned anon
> With the result—a creature, and, by one
> And one, proceeded leisurely to equip
> Its limbs in harness of his workmanship.
> 'Accomplished! Listen, Mantuans!' Fond essay!
> Piece after piece that armour broke away,
> Because perceptions whole, like that he sought

To clothe, reject so pure a work of thought
As language: thought may take perception's place,
But hardly co-exist in any case,
Being its mere presentment—of the whole
By parts, the simultaneous and the sole
By the successive and the many."

Whether this expresses Sordello's process of poetical construction or not, we strongly suspect that it expresses Mr. Browning's. To cast his language, like bronze armour, in moulds of its own; to conceive and imagine in a separate intellectual world far removed from this verbal armour of the imagination, and then bring "the result, a creature," to have the armour of language "leisurely" fitted on to it; and finally to find that armour break away,

"Because perceptions whole, like that he sought
To clothe, *reject so pure a work of thought*
As language,"—

seems to us a very graphic, though not very poetical—in one small respect only erroneous—account of Mr. Browning's own struggles with the difficulties of poetic expression. We say, in one respect erroneous, because it is only to intellects like Mr. Browning's that language *is* "so pure a work of thought;" and to them only because they see mainly the intellectual side of language, and look at its defined meanings so much more than its often far more vital undefined associations. Instead of language being too pure a work of thought to clothe Mr. Browning's perceptions adequately, we suspect that it would be nearer the truth to say that his perceptions are too much overruled and concentrated by thought to admit of the most poetical use of language.

This may seem obscure; but we can explain what we mean about Mr. Browning's style, and we think justify it, in a few words. Every one must have noticed that the style introduced by Mr. Carlyle is far from poetical, and yet in the highest degree picturesque, while also open to the charge of being not a little obscure. It is a style the essence of which consists in driving your perceptions into the service of your intellect, and talking a sort of hieroglyphic, every picturesque symbol in which expresses a thought. Thus, to open Mr. Carlyle at random: "To such length can transcendental moonshine, cast by some morbidly radiating Coleridge into the chaos of a fermenting life, act magically there, and produce divulsions and convulsions and diseased developments. So dark and abstruse, without lamp or authentic finger-post, is the course of pious genius towards the eternal kingdoms grown." Here we have the rather ordinary thought that the 'high philosophy of a genius like Coleridge's is able to cast a charm over minds in difficulty and doubt, and persuade them this way and that, when they have no really safe guide to look to,'—illuminated, like the old missals, by a little series of images, in which vision is made the instrument for sharply accentuating thought. Hence it is a style crowded with stress, and makes the same kind of fatiguing impression on the mind which a handwriting sloped the wrong way makes on the eye, —an impression of strain and effort. It is therefore apt to be obscure, and certain not to be poetical, for one and the same reason,—namely, that over-emphasis is both exhausting and unnatural; and while an exhausted attention is necessarily enveloped by a mist of obscurity, emphasis too crowded for nature misses the under-tones and the neutral tints which are absolutely essential to the harmony of poetry. Now we do not mean to say that Mr. Browning's style is the illuminated style of Mr. Carlyle. He is too much of a poet for such disproportion of the picturesque, such fatiguing gold-and-crimson. But it is true that *his* style also is fatiguing and destitute of lower tints and under-tones, and that when he is pictorial, as he very often is, he crowds and accentuates the striking points, so as to miss the harmony of poetry. It gives one the impression of a vigilant intellect noting all the principal features of the scene acutely, and concentrating his perceptive faculties so completely in the gaze of attention as to miss those numberless under-growths of half-dreamy observation which constitute so great a charm of poetic insight. Mr. Browning's style is too keen, too restless, too startling,—his soul is too much in his eyes, his mind too devoid of that *lazy* receptiveness which fills-in and softens and warms the effect of the whole,—for a really high poetic style. Compare, for instance, his purely descriptive talent, which is highly picturesque, but not poetical, with Tennyson. Thus Mr. Browning describes a lunar rainbow:

"For lo, what think you? suddenly
The rain and the wind ceased, and the sky
Received at once the full fruition
Of the moon's consummate apparition.
The black cloud-barricade was riven,
Ruined beneath her feet, and driven
Deep in the West; while, bare and breathless,
North and South and East lay ready
For a glorious Thing, that, dauntless, deathless,
Sprang across them, and stood steady.
'Twas a moon-rainbow, vast and perfect,
From heaven to heaven extending, perfect
As the mother-moon's self, full in face.
It rose, distinctly at the base
With its seven proper colours chorded,

Which still, in the rising, were compressed,
Until at last they coalesced,
And supreme the spectral creature lorded
In a triumph of whitest white,—
Above which intervened the night.
But above night too, like only the next,
The second of a wondrous sequence,
Reaching in rare and rarer frequence,
Till the heaven of heavens were circumflext,
Another rainbow rose, a mightier,
Fainter, flushier, and flightier,—
Rapture dying along its verge!
Oh, whose foot shall I see emerge,
WHOSE, from the straining topmost dark,
On to the keystone of that arc?"

This is powerful, keen-eyed, piercing,—too much of all these for the full harmony of poetry. The style is to the poetic like the secondary rainbow to the primary, "fainter, flushier, and flightier:" "fainter," because the colours are washed on with a thin hasty hand; "flushier," because they come and go with a certain flush of attentive perception that subsides back into pure thought; and "flightier," from the palpitating breathless air of the whole metre. The sense of rest which a still lunar rainbow after a storm should produce on the heart is entirely absent. Tennyson also is one of the greatest of poetic painters; but how much of the still undergrowth of perception, or rather reception, which does not, nay cannot, come if you watch for it which steals into the brooding mind when the attention is relaxed and the mind's eye half shut, is there in every fragment of his descriptions! Take a fragment from *In Memoriam*, for instance:

"Doors, where my heart was used to beat
So quickly, not as one that weeps
I come once more; the city sleeps
I smell the meadow in the street.

I hear a chirp of birds; I see
Betwixt the black fronts long withdrawn
A light-blue lane of early morn,
And think of early days and thee."

That is poetry in which the brooding, silent, receptive mind drinks-in much that the restless eye and ear could never catch; that *absorbs* the silence as well as the sound, the middle tints as well as the flashes of light and colour. And the want of this power in Mr. Browning seems to us to show that for him language is not in reality "too pure a work of thought" to contain his perceptions, but that his perceptions are too pure a work of thought, too full of vigilant intellectual activity, to give him the full command of the associative charms and latent riches of language. His imagination is impatient; it never *broods*.

And hence, too, all the obscurity of style there is in Mr. Browning; and in some of his works it is predominant. It is mere abruptness and hurry, the rapid sketchy accumulation of too many points of emphasis tumbling one upon the other in a bewildering crowd. In the dramas, where Mr. Browning's dramatic genius corresponds to the *form* of his thought, and in the confessedly dramatic fragments called "Men and Women," where there is no effort to be lyrical, nothing can be more lucid and simple than his style, so soon as you have once found your true latitude and caught the spirit of the situation. The only really unintelligible poem is *Sordello*, and that, not because there is any great mysticism, as far as we can see, in the substance of what he wishes to say, but because it is elliptical, laconic, crowded with hints, and pronouns which may belong to half a dozen distinct nouns; because it is a mere *tangle* of thought. It reads like a *corrupt* edition of an old poem, in which the very language has got into hopeless confusion. Mr. Browning has attempted to guide the guesses of his readers by a running head-line to the pages, directing their attention to his real drift: but, after all, this can do but little, and we suspect that, if it be true, as his dedication appears to indicate, that there is really one mortal who to his own satisfaction has understood him, it would be found on cross-examination of that one, that (like Hegel's sole philosophical confidant) even he has *mis*understood him. A specimen of the sort of obscurity we mean is the following. Sordello, at Palma's advice,—Palma is his lady-love, and (we believe) the daughter of Ecelin, one of the tyrants of Treviso, and sister of the second Ecelino, called "the enemy of mankind,"—decides to enter with her upon a political career, instead of the musing, solitary life of a troubadour. Palma has just left him, after exhorting him to aid her, and he has been debating with himself the comparative value of the dreamy poetic life and the practical. The poet goes on:

"Thus
I bring Sordello to the rapturous
Exclaim at the crowd's cry, because one round
Of life was quite accomplished; and he found
Not only that a soul, whate'er its might,
Is insufficient to its own delight,
Both in corporeal organs and in skill
By means of such to body forth its Will—
And, after, insufficient to apprise
Men of that Will, oblige them recognise
The Hid by the Revealed—but that, the last
Nor lightest of the struggles overpast,

His Will, bade abdicate, which would not void
The throne, might sit there, suffer be enjoyed
Mankind, a varied and divine array
Incapable of homage, the first way,
Nor fit to render incidentally
Tribute connived at, taken by the by,
In joys. If thus with warrant to rescind
The ignominious exile of mankind—
Whose proper service, ascertained intact,
As yet (to be by him themselves made act,
Not watch Sordello acting each of them)
Was to secure—if the true diadem
Seemed imminent while our Sordello drank
The wisdom of that golden Palma,—thank
Verona's Lady in her Citadel
Founded by Gaulish Brennus, legends tell:
And truly when she left him, the sun reared
A head like the first clamberer's that peered
A-top the Capitol, his face on flame
With triumph, triumphing till Manlius came."

Now, whoever can construe this, we confess ourselves altogether unable to do so. What, for instance, the parenthetic

"to be by him themselves made act,
Not watch Sordello acting each of them,"

means, we have not the most distant notion. Mr. Browning might as well have said, "to be by him her himself herself themselves made act," &c., for any vestige of meaning we attach to this curious mob of pronouns and verbs treading on each other's heels. The style is faulty from no mysticism, but sheer clumsiness. And this is the case in large portions all through. It gives the impression of breathless hurry, not even caring to be articulate, so long as the style should jot down to the writer's mind what he meant to say. Mr. Browning should publish an annotated edition, with a note on every ellipsis, obscure pronoun, and abrupt turn of the subject,—in which case the notes would be three times as long as the poem. There are fine sentences in it, but, for the most part, reading it is like walking in the catacombs with a light falling vividly here and there on the emblems of a great life and a greater death.

But we have devoted enough, perhaps more than enough, space to the discussion of Mr. Browning's poetic deficiencies. They mark distinctly the limits of his imaginative power, which is nevertheless very high. In range of thought he certainly surpasses *all* his poetic contemporaries, and in vividness of conception he is second to none but Mr. Tennyson, though far his inferior. Altogether he must certainly rank second of our living poets; though Mr. Arnold, and perhaps even others, may greatly surpass him in the gift of harmoniously expressing what they have once conceived. To a considerable extent he has lost merited popularity by belonging neither to this country nor to this time. Saturated with foreign, and especially with Italian, culture, possessed by the human genius, though keenly alive to the frauds and falsehood of Roman Catholicism, and occupying himself with both forms of character and modes of thought that seem more native to the Middle Ages than to modern England,—Mr. Browning's poems have naturally failed to take quite their true level in English literature. Still, the place he does take is undoubtedly a very high one, and is likely to rise steadily the more thoroughly he is studied. We shall be satisfied if we can diminish in any degree the obstacles to a true appreciation of his genius.

We have said that Mr. Browning's chief power lies in the intellectual side of drama,—the dramatic delineation of characters, especially of masculine characters, in their characteristic relation to the world, but that his interest in the dramatic "situation" is purely intellectual, and fails therefore to impart any vigorous movement or practical excitement to the plot. We must add, that there is one cardinal interest which so greatly overpowers all others in Mr. Browning's creations that it forms more or less the staple interest of all his best poems, and not only explains his wonderful artistic grasp of the genius of the Catholic Church, but gives an additional reason why the living centre of his imaginative power is almost always in a *man's* mind, and never in a woman's heart. This central imaginative interest of Mr. Browning's arises from his intimate and keen apprehension that human knowledge and worldly wisdom are faint shadows, often just blending with the actual substance, of divine knowledge and spiritual wisdom; and that the desire for the latter is often temporarily assuaged by the possession or the vision of the former. Mr. Browning has the keenest sympathy with the passion for knowledge, at least for the knowledge of living minds, of man, and God; and has, too, an intuitive sense of how easily the one takes the place of the other, and how subtly they mingle in all the more artful and politic forms of character. It is evident how much a long residence in the country of Machiavelli and Cavour, and a close study of the ecclesiastical wisdom, craft, and subtlety produced by the system of the confessional, must intensify his interest in this border-land between the supernatural and the worldly wisdom. The command of motives which is given by a constant study of the secrets of the heart, either for saintly and mystical or for worldly and selfish reasons, is necessarily of the same order of practical importance; and none knows better than Mr. Browning how strangely they interweave. By far the greatest intellectual fascination of his poems consists in his marvellous mastery of the infinitely various compounds between the religious and the worldly wisdom, and the passionate respect and yearning that both alike, in their higher degrees, whether pure or blended, inspire in the simpler minds over which they cast their influence. Every one of the greater poems includes in some shape—very seldom indeed involving a repetition, for his power of dramatic variation of this theme is endless—a study of some striking conflict or some still more striking combination between the craft of the visible world and the craft of the invisible, and of the many threads of connexion between the two.

Mr. Browning's earliest poem, "Paracelsus," which bears all the marks of youth, is nothing but a study of the craving for a knowledge of the absolute principle of life on the mind of a medieval aspirant who might have hoped eventually to attain such knowledge. The poem is one of the least successful, partly because it is scarcely more than in name dramatic, and wants the local colour, and the intimate knowledge of the ambitious heart and intellect, which his later poems abundantly show. Paracelsus aspires at first only to absolute *knowledge;* when, after long wanderings, his heart is beginning to fail him, he meets a true poet, who in like manner has aspired passionately to love, and has failed even more bitterly than Paracelsus in attaining the fulfilment of his desire. From him Paracelsus learns that true life consists in seeking to blend love for man with knowledge (however incomplete) of the laws of man's life; and accordingly begins to devote himself to teaching (at Basle) what little he knows. Then comes the temptation to affect more knowledge than he has, in order to gain a fit audience for what he has, and the consequent dabbling in pretended magic. The only powerful part of the poem consists in the delineation of the strange mixture of self-scorn and self-belief, —the compunction for affecting false powers, and the lingering faith in a transcendental method of mastering the secret of life,—the conviction that God disapproves his pious frauds to gain influence with the world, and that He approves the effort to teach and serve the world, which seems to necessitate them. This struggle, no doubt, is finely delineated. The bitter hope that even in *cheating* the world for its good he is doing better than in mere solitary study without any attempt to serve it; at all events, that thus, if not doing "most good," he is yet effecting "least harm;" the almost cynical remonstrance with God for not showing him his way clearer—are all powerfully drawn:

> "You little fancy what rude shocks apprise us
> We sin: *God's intimations rather fail*
> *In clearness than in energy:* 'twere well
> Did they but indicate the course to take,
> Like that to be forsaken."

That is a very fine expression of the half-angry, half-mournful disappointment of a proud and shadowy mind; and all this portion of "Paracelsus," where he is openly and furiously at war with himself for the false assumption of secret lore by which he renders his teaching popular, and with God for not either giving him knowledge enough to do without falsehood, or else at least relieving him from the heavy obligation to teach others with the imperfect knowledge he has, is strikingly brought out. But, on the whole, "Paracelsus" appears to us vague and unimpressive in execution, though not perhaps in the design.

Mr. Browning's favourite, and perhaps highest, exercise of art, however, is shown in the various delineations of the worldly force of ecclesiastical dignities struggling with, or flavouring, the Catholic faith. Of this he has given us many and very remarkable dramatic pictures, ranging from the childish, full-fed, superstitious, sensual-creeded "bishop, who orders his tomb at St. Praxed's church," to the shifty, unscrupulous, gallant old papal Nuncio, who, standing boldly at bay, and gaining time by lie upon lie, makes so many skilful though useless bids to gain over the wavering Druses for his church, in the piece called "The Return of the Druses." And these are but two out of many of the same genus, though different species. We scarcely know whether the St.-Praxed's bishop's flushed *physical* appetite for the splendid Roman Catholic rites, or the keen laughing twinkle that glitters in the eyes of the aged Legates and Nuncios, when they deal with captious children of the church, is the more powerfully painted. No painting can be more striking than the pleading of the dying bishop with his own natural sons to fulfil their pledge to him in giving him a tomb of jasper handsomer than that of his rival Gandolf, who died before him, with an inscription of purer Latinity:

> "Nay, boys, ye love me—all of jasper, then!
> 'Tis jasper ye stand pledged to, lest I grieve
> My bath must needs be left behind, alas!
> One block, pure green as a pistachio-nut,
> There's plenty jasper somewhere in the world—
> And have I not Saint Praxed's ear to pray
> Horses for ye, and brown Greek manuscripts,
> And mistresses with great smooth marbly limbs?
> —That's if ye carve my epitaph aright,
> Choice Latin, picked phrase, Tully's every word,
> No gaudy ware like Gandolf's second line—

> Tully, my masters? Ulpian serves his need!
> And then how I shall lie through centuries,
> And hear the blessed mutter of the mass,
> And see God made and eaten all day long,
> And feel the steady candle-flame, and taste
> Good strong thick stupefying incense-smoke!"

The piece is full of passionate superstition, equally voluptuous and equally dramatic; but the shades of thought in it are perhaps less delicate and difficult to draw than in some other of Mr. Browning's ecclesiastical sketches. Perhaps the most striking contrast to it, showing, in its way, equal art and insight, is the wonderful picture of the Göttingen Professor and his Christmas-eve discourse, on the mythical character of Christianity, in "Christmas-Eve and Easter-Day." There you have the thin intellectual ghost, or hardly distinguishable shadow, of Christian faith, in the place of the high-fed physical form of it we have just seen; and each is painted with such strict dramatic truth, that we scarcely know whether we are most fascinated by the picture of the faith which steams with the "burnt-offerings of rams and the fat of fed beasts," or of the faded and pallid rationalism that seems just disappearing into the inane:

> "That sallow, virgin-minded, studious
> Martyr to mild enthusiasm,
> As he uttered a kind of cough preludious,
> That woke my sympathetic spasm
> (Beside some spitting that made me sorry)
> And stood surveying his auditory
> With a wan pure look well nigh celestial,—
> Those blue eyes had survived so much."

No theological student in a German university can miss the type; and the lines which follow might certainly have been painted from personal experience:

> "He pushed back higher his spectacles,
> Let the eyes stream out like lamps from cells,
> And giving his head of hair—a hake
> Of undressed tow for colour and quality—
> One rapid and impatient shake,
>
> * * * *
>
> The Professor's grave voice, sweet though hoarse,
> Broke into his Christmas-Eve's discourse."

This discourse, no less than the portrait, is a striking pendant to the delirious address of the bishop of St. Praxed to his sons, as it explains,

> "How the ineptitude of the time,
> And the penman's prejudice, expanding
> Fact into fable, fit for the clime,

Had by slow and sure degrees translated it
Into this myth, this Individuum,—
Which, when reason had strained and abated it
Of foreign matter, gave for residuum
A Man !—a right true man, however,
Whose work was worthy a man's endeavour."

And Mr. Browning's subtle and striking criticism on his Göttingen Professor's mythological lecture, though apparently needless for the portrait, really adds its most dramatic touch, when he concludes it by saying to his lecturer,

"Go on, you shall no more move my gravity
Than, when I see boys ride a-cockhorse,
I find it in my heart to embarrass them
By hinting that their stick's a mock horse,
And they really carry what they say carries them."

The whole picture of the exhausted intellectual receiver in the Professor's mind, of his constant effort to remove husks till the grain was gone, of his cough, which,

"like a drouthy piston,
Tried to dislodge the husk that grew to him,"—

is completed by this hint, that if you could get at the centre of his mind, his weary and wan and joyless air would be explained by the constant spiritual labour of actually carrying "what he says carries him."

A poem quite as impressive from its strange mixture of physical and voluptuous passions (richly set in an artistic nature), with an implicit faith in all the legends of the Church, is the sketch of the Florentine monk and artist Fra Lippo Lippi. His promise to himself of how he will atone for his irregularities of life, and paint the fashion of his pardon, is one of the most powerful conceptions in all Mr. Browning's poems:

"I shall paint
God in the midst, Madonna and her babe,
Ringed by a bowery, flowery angel-brood,
Lilies and vestments and white faces, sweet
As puff on puff of grated orris-root,
When ladies crowd to church at midsummer.
And then in the front, of course a saint or two—
Saint John, because he saves the Florentines;
Saint Ambrose, who puts down in black and white
The convent's friends and gives them a long day."

Into this saintly crowd, secured at their devotions, the artist is to introduce himself in his old serge gown, coming "as one by a dark stair into a great light," "mazed, motionless, and moonstruck," and looking anxiously for escape:

"Then steps a sweet angelic slip of a thing
Forward, puts out a soft palm—'Not so fast!'
—Addresses the celestial presence, 'nay—
He made you and devised you, after all,
Though he's none of you! Could Saint John there, draw—
His camel-hair make up a painting-brush?
We come to brother Lippo for all that,
Iste perfecit opus!' So, all smile—
I shuffle sideways with my blushing face
Under the cover of a hundred wings
Thrown like a spread of kirtles when you're gay
And play hot cockles, all the doors being shut,
Till, wholly unexpected, in there pops
The hothead husband!"

This, of course, though a wholly different picture, is closely akin to the St.-Praxed bishop in intellectual conception; showing the same strong mixture of eager fleshly naturalism beneath the robe of superstitious awe; but it is the infinitely varied transformations under which Mr. Browning can present the same elements, which prove how great an intellectual dramatist he is.

The intermediate place between the bishop of St. Praxed and the Göttingen Professor, but embodying also some of the shrewd political instinct which Mr. Browning so subtly and thoroughly penetrates, is "Bishop Blougram," who gives us a rather too extended apology for continuing to hold his place in the Catholic hierarchy, though admitting that a large part of its creed is either doubtful or false to him. Nothing can exceed the tortuous dramatic sophistry of this admirable special-pleading; but for the subject of a work of art it is a bad one, presenting too few points of living interest, and lying wholly in the leaden-coloured region where moral fallacies have their roots. Of course there is as real drama in this subtle struggle between the claims of the world and the claims of sincerity, as in any other region of human life; but to interest men in it as a work of art there should at least be more condensation in form, and some fate hanging on the issue of the struggle. As it is, the great force of the picture is lost for the world in general. It ought to interest deeply clergymen in a false position, who are striving to draw consolation from Mr. Jowett's theory of casuistry; but few else will recognise the marvellous minuteness and fidelity of this Denner-like painting of every wrinkle on the ecclesiastical conscience, and every pucker in its understanding.

The most wonderful picture of the ecclesiastical politician and diplomatist is certainly the pontifical legate Ogniben, in "A Soul's Tragedy," who trots into a papal town to suppress a popular revolution, alone on muleback, humming "*Cur fre-*

muere gentes?" and saying, as he laughs gently to himself, "I have known three-and-twenty leaders of revolts." The acute knowledge of human motives, and still acuter manipulation of them, which this not unkindly old man shows; the courage, and the real spiritual power over man which the confessional has given him, at the expense of course of uprightness; the Socratic address with which he draws out the selfish ambition in the new leader of revolt, and lures him with it into renouncing the popular cause, and finally disposes of him in words curiously mingling a genuine kind of piety, not unascetic, and ecclesiastical craft, concluding with, "I have known *four*-and-twenty leaders of revolts,"—constitutes one of the most subtle and striking pictures in modern drama. The pity is that all the subsidiary characters—even Chiappino, the leader of revolt, himself, who is not ill-conceived—are as usual so far inferior to this figure, that the drama is a poor one, though the dramatic sketch is inimitable. Nor is it only the intersecting line between worldly and spiritual wisdom that Mr. Browning has traced so finely. The jealous hatred of the bishop of St. Praxed for his rival Gandolf, and the first extract we made for another purpose from his poems, called the "Soliloquy of the Spanish Cloister," both show how finely he can conceive the union of earthly passions with monastic and ritual ideas. The same power is shown, with much more of poetic form and expression, in the short piece called "A Heretic's Tragedy," though here the picture is of the blending of inquisitorial cruelty with the passionate bigotry of faith. The triumphant joy of vindicating the Infinite Justice in the torture applied to the recusant heretic, the pitiless gaiety which the natural cruelty of savage natures engrafts on this directly the belief that the suffering is *deserved* absolves them from the duty of sympathy, the fine shading-off of the consciousness of wreaking divine retribution into human brutality,—is a work of rare art. It is a pity that Mr. Browning has not chosen a great inquisitor for the theme of one of his longer plays.

Perhaps, however, the most original of all Mr. Browning's many poems on this class of subjects is the "Epistle containing the strange Medical Experience of Karshish, the Arab Physician;" which is an attempt to bring such medical science, or rather empirical skill, as might have existed in the time of Christ into direct contact with the "case" of the risen Lazarus, whom the Arab physician encounters in Bethany at the time when the siege of Jerusalem by Titus has just begun. Karshish, questioning himself and his friends as to the asserted resurrection, reports his opinion on it to his master in a letter vibrating helplessly between a guess that it was really a cure of unusually prolonged epilepsy which had left mania behind, and a proudly-resisted inclination to believe that there was something divine in the matter, as Lazarus himself asserted. The artist's skill, however, is shown, as usual, in delineating the influence of the two opposite sorts of thirst for knowledge in this dignified Arabian leech,—the pride of human science and craft, which makes him eager to penetrate the secret of a new and remarkable cure, and the yearning for divine knowledge, which thrills him with a humiliating sense of awe and hope at the very words he affects to despise from the ignorant peasant. The letter is highly dramatic, beginning with stealthy Oriental subtlety, far from his mark (for he is evidently bewildered and ashamed at the impression made upon him by the story of Lazarus), explaining, after compliments, a few new recipes; describing his temporary abode at Bethany, which lies, he says, from Jerusalem

> "scarce the distance thence
> A man with plague-sores at the third degree
> Runs till he drops down dead;"

chronicling his new pathological experiences—"a viscid choler is observable in tertians," "scalp disease confounds me, crossing so with leprosy," and so forth; until at length he comes, with many apologies, on his "case of mania subinduced by epilepsy:"

> "The man,—it is one Lazarus a Jew,
> Sanguine, proportioned, fifty years of age,
> The body's habit wholly laudable,
> As much indeed beyond the common health
> As he were made and put aside to show."

And then gradually the physician allows it to be seen how much thought he has spent on his diagnosis of the mania, how its very simplicity subdues and bewilders his wisdom. The effect, he says, on the mind of the patient is as if some new and vast world had been opened out to him, making this world worthless, which he is yet forbidden to leave. The patient has no measure of the true proportions of things; the armaments assembled round Jerusalem are trivial to him, while he is lost in wonder that others do not see the value of the most trivial facts with his "opened eyes." "Wonder and doubt come wrongly into play, preposterously at cross purposes." Unbroken in cheerfulness if his child be ill or dying, a word or gesture from the child that he disapproves will startle him into an agony of fear. In short, the patient clings to "a narrow and dark thread of life, which runs across an orb of glory" into which he may not enter, though it gives its law to his spirit. His notions of right and wrong, instead of being adapted to the narrow conditions of this thread of life and its continuance, are always taking into account a whole universe of invisible and apparently imaginary facts:

> "So is the man perplext with impulses
> Sudden to start off crosswise, not straight on,
> Proclaiming what is Right and Wrong across
> And not along, this black thread through the blaze—
> 'It should be' balked by 'here it cannot be.'
> And oft the man's soul springs into his face,
> As if he saw again and heard again
> His sage that bade him rise, and he did rise!"

In this antique and patient enumeration of the mental symptoms of the patient, the most startling and impressive is reserved, with a sort of scientific shame, to the last, and only then oozes out involuntarily with the half apology, that, "in writing to a leech, 'tis well to keep back nothing of a case."

> "This man so cured regards the curer then
> As—God forgive me—who but God himself,
> Creator and Sustainer of the world,
> That came and dwelt in flesh on it awhile!
> —'Sayeth that such an One was born and lived,
> Taught, healed the sick, broke bread at his own house,
> Then died, with Lazarus by, for aught I know,
> And yet was . . . . what I said nor choose repeat,
> And must have so avouched himself in fact,
> In hearing of this very Lazarus,
> Who saith—but why all this of what he saith?
> Why write of trivial matters, things of price
> Calling at every moment for remark?
> I noticed on the margin of a pool
> Blue-flowering borage, the Aleppo sort
> Aboundeth very nitrous. It is strange."

But the subject fascinates him, in spite of his scientific scorn for it. He goes back to relate the mode of his encounter with Lazarus; and finally there is wrung as it were from him, reluctant as he is to mention the mere ravings of a madman which have no pathological bearing on the case:

> "The very God! Think, Abib; dost thou think?
> So the All-great were the All-loving too—
> So, through the thunder comes a human voice,
> Saying, 'O heart I made, a heart beats here!
> Face, my hands fashioned, see it in Myself.
> Thou hast no power nor mayst conceive of Mine,
> But love I gave thee, with Myself to love,
> And thou must love Me who have died for thee!'
> The madman saith He said so: it is strange!"

Certainly no more original poetic conception has been worked out in our time than this,—brief as the poem is,—and very dramatically is it sustained, the dignity and satisfied wisdom of the physician giving way at times beneath the glory of the poor Syrian's dream and the strange consistency and simplicity of his demeanour,—but returning again with full elastic force wherever he can regain his complete assurance of the impossibility of the story, and the wholly unprofessional character of the explanation. It is only here and there that Mr. Browning has drawn worldly skill or wisdom half-worshipping, with dazzled eyes, a simplicity above it. Generally in his poetry, as in the world, the prevalent type of sagacity freely makes use of an established faith, but is not willing to recognise it when it is new and disturbing. But this Oriental physician, who has evidently given up his life to study all diseases and remedies with open eyes, is one of the exceptions. When a light shines upon him, if he cannot gaze at it, it is his nature not to ignore it. Mr. Browning finds a deeper humility in science, with all its pride, than in the shifty talent of worldly knowledge.

The true pendant to this picture of the stately Arab physician, bewildering himself with the faith and simplicity of the Syrian peasant, is the striking drama of *Luria*, which, like all Mr. Browning's best dramas, is a drama of but one focus of intellectual interest. The idea of it is, the extraordinary spell cast upon the powerful and magnanimous mind of a less intellectual race by the elaborate statecraft and unfathomable political subtlety of a race of born schemers and politicians. Luria is what Othello should have been,—not a negro, but a Moor, commanding the Florentine army during the war with Pisa in the fifteenth century. His courage and genius have all but won the game for Florence when the scene opens, but the suspicious jealousy of the Florentines has already undermined his authority, and is prepared to spring the mine the moment that Luria's services have answered their purpose and are no more required. This he discovers before he completes his work by the final defeat of Pisa; and the interest of the piece lies in the struggle which ensues in his own mind between the faithless republic's claim on his imagination, if not on his honour and devotion, and the wrath of retributive justice. The spell on his imagination is very finely portrayed. It is the calm depth and universality of Florentine political intrigue which takes hold of his simple mind as the cold craft of Ulysses took hold of ancient Greece, by embodying the divine subtlety of infinite calculation. Florence appeared to wield with a mighty ease the whole motive force which lies spread like a living nerve beneath the quiet surface of every human society,—and so to have almost a divine right to the use of Luria's mere physical courage and strategic skill, even though it were thankless and treacherous in return. Before the discovery of the treachery, when a Florentine remarks that Luria, in place of a Moorish captain, desires to be one of them, he replies:

"Oh no!
Not one of you, and so escape the thrill
Of coming into you, of changing thus,—
Feeling a soul grow on me that restricts
The boundless unrest of the savage heart!"

And even after Luria is aware of the treachery meditated to him, there remains a chord in his mind which answers to the cold proud claim of the wily Florentine who lays it down that the republic has a right to break hearts and ruin heads, however liberally, in her own service:

"And when the fresh heart breaks,
The new brain proves a martyr, what of them?
Where is the matter of one moth the more
Singed in the candle, at a summer's end?
But Florence is no simple John or James
To have his toy, his fancy, his conceit,
That he's the one excepted man by fate,
And, when fate shows him he's mistaken there,
Die with all good men's praise, and yield his place
To Paul and George intent to try their chance!
Florence exists because these pass away;
She's a contrivance to supply a type
Of Man, which men's deficiencies refuse;
She binds so many, that she grows out of them—
Stands steady o'er their numbers, though they change
And pass away—there's always what upholds,
Always enough to fashion the great show.
As, see, yon hanging city, in the sun,
Of shapely cloud substantially the same!
A thousand vapours rise and sink again,
Are interfused, and live their life and die,—
Yet ever hangs the steady show i' the air
Under the sun's straight influence: that is well!
That is worth heaven to hold, and God to bless!
And so is Florence,—the unseen sun above,
Which draws and holds suspended all of us,—
Binds transient mists and vapours into one,
Differing from each and better than they all.
And shall she dare to stake this permanence
On any one man's faith? Man's heart is weak,
And its temptations many: let her prove
Each servant to the very uttermost
Before she grant him her reward, I say!"

This mighty shadow of an omniscient cunning, this earthly edition of the celestial craft of secret government by unattainable knowledge, produces on Luria's far higher nature much the same kind of irresistible impression which, in the reverse direction, the simplicity and fidelity of a peasant's faith had made on the accomplished physician. In the one case faith penetrates worldly knowledge with a sense of its own deficiencies; in the other, wide and worldly knowledge penetrates a generous and sensitive nature with a still profounder sense of its own deficiencies. All knowledge, Mr. Browning thinks,—even the mean diplomatic cunning,—has in it a sort of shadow, however faint, of divine fulness, which gives an excuse if not a justification for its magic spell over human nature. If not really a hem of the divine garment of omniscience, it is at least so striking a forgery that the idolatry may be almost noble. In Luria's nature certainly it is infinitely noble, and is mingled with every thing short of Christian virtue. The picture is worthy of Mr. Browning's genius, and constitutes the essence of quite his finest drama.

We must conclude with a few words in review of Mr. Browning's genius. Its most striking characteristic is the great vigour of his intellectual and spiritual imagination, and of his carnal imagination (if we may be permitted a technical Scripture phrase to express the imagination of *all* the passions and perceptions), and the almost complete absence of the intermediate psychical or sentimental imagination, which is with most poets the principal spring of all their poetry, and perhaps the only spring of lyrical poetry. We do not know a poem of Mr. Browning's which can be said to express a *mood*, as Shelley expresses so vividly moods of passionate yearning, Wordsworth of meditative rapture, Tennyson of infinite regret. Mr. Browning has no moods. His mind seems to leap at once from its centre to its surface without passing through the middle states which lie between the spirit and the senses. Hence we may see from another side why Mr. Browning's women are so imperfect, for their truest life is usually in this middle region, which seems totally absent from his poems. The nearest approach to a sentiment which he has drawn is, on the one side a passion, which he has drawn repeatedly and powerfully,—on the other a spiritual affection, "the devotion the heart lifts above and the heavens reject not," such as he has so finely painted in that love of David for Jonathan, which comes flowing in in great waves, like a spring-tide, till it pours on into his love for God; and this he has drawn as scarcely any other man could draw it. But both these are essentially different from what is properly denoted by sentiment, which is apt to lean upon the occasional, lives on memory and association, tinges every thing around it with a secondary glow of its own, and has neither the immediate physical origin of a passion, nor that absolute independence both of circumstance and instinct, which characterises what is here called a spiritual affection. It is, as we have said, in sentiment that the tempering moods are rooted which give rise to so much of our highest poetry, and touch with a sort of illuminating magic so much more which would otherwise have no intrinsic charm. Gray's *Elegy*, for instance, is popular solely for the tender melancholy that hangs around it, and almost constitutes it an incarnation of evening regret. Now, of those sentiments which *tune* the imagination Mr. Browning's poems seem destitute, and the consequence is that he is apt to plunge us from cold spiritual or intellectual power into the fever of passion, and back again from this fever into the cold. But we suspect that his dramatic intellect has *gained* through this hiatus in his imagination. Sentiment, *because* it is lyrical, because it tempts the mind into dwelling on its own moods, is a great hindrance to that strategic activity of the intellect which enables it to pass easily from one intellectual and moral centre to another. A great dramatist is in some sense a great intellectual and spiritual ventriloquist, and nothing should, one would think, more interfere with the ease of spiritual ventriloquism than the clinging personal sentiments, which never leave the creative mind really free and solitary. For it must require a habit not merely of physical, but, if we may so speak, of spiritual solitude, to migrate rapidly in this way from your own actual centre in the world of intellect and feeling to a totally different centre, where you not only try to speak an alien language, but to think unaccustomed thoughts and feel unaccustomed passions. Mr. Browning says very finely in one of his dramas,

> "When is man strong until he feels alone?
> It was some lonely strength at first, be sure,
> Created organs such as those you seek
> By which to give its varied purpose shape,—
> And, naming the selected ministrants,
> Took sword and shield and sceptre—each a man!"

This seems to us to describe a dramatic poet's work not much less powerfully than it describes the royally creative thought of the divine administration. Mr. Browning's intellectual and spiritual strength has apparently been much braced in this cold solitude. And it has been perhaps easier to him, from the absence of that refracting atmosphere of personal sentiment, which, even when we *are* alone, creates a kind of twilight of customary influences, and environs us with crowds of associations which are apt to fritter away the creative powers of the mind, and to diminish its power to issue those sharply-defined imaginative decrees which may be said to originate *proprio motu*, as the papal language of absolute free-will aptly expresses it. To a dramatic intellect (unless the imagination be of the very highest spontaneous fertility) the power of completely controlling the thoughts and images, of saying to one "go," and to another "come," must be of the first moment. No poet of modern days gives us more distinctly this sense of an imagination which acts *proprio motu* than Mr. Browning. It is one reason why his poems have a cold air; for that resisting medium of restraint,—the atmosphere which surrounds the dramatic intellect,—though it may hamper the practice of intellectual migration, will, if it does *not* prevent it, lend a warmth and natural ground-colour of harmonising feeling to the new creations which will blend them into a more perfect work of art. Mr. Browning's mind appears somehow to travel *in vacuo*, and therefore with greater rapidity than almost any part of his genius; but he carries no vestige of his former self about with him, which necessitates, therefore, a perfectly new plunge for the reader into quite a new world in every new poem. But hence also the bracing effect which his masculine and rugged poetry has on the intellect. Poetry is apt to be enervating, producing the effect of intellectual luxury; or if, like Wordsworth's, it is as cool and bright as morning dew, it carries us away from the world to mountain solitudes and transcendental dreams. Mr. Browning's—while it strings your intellect to the utmost, as all really dramatic poetry must, and has none of the luxuriance of fancy and wealth of sentiment which relaxes the fibre of the mind—keeps you still in a living world,—not generally the modern world, very seldom indeed the world of modern England, but still in contact with keen, quick, vigorous life, that, as well as engaging the imagination, really enlarges the range of one's intellectual and social, sometimes almost of one's political, experience. Mr. Browning cannot, indeed, paint action; but of the intellectual approaches to action he is a great master. And in spite of more grating deficiencies in the power of expression than any eminent English poet perhaps ever laboured under, these poems cannot fail to win for him slowly a substantial and an enduring fame.

Art. VIII.—THE EFFECTS OF THE GOLD DISCOVERIES.

A Serious Fall in the Value of Gold ascertained, and its Social Effects set forth, with two Diagrams. By W. Stanley Jevons, M.A., formerly of the Sydney Royal Mint. London: Stanford.

The meeting of the British Association has once more recalled public attention to the effect of the gold discoveries, and the discussion opened in section F has been continued in the columns of the *Times*. We cannot say that we think much light has been thrown on the complicated question of monetary depreciation by the recent contributions to the controversy; nor do we think that the exhibitions of economic dialectics which it has called forth, if these are to be taken as an indication of the present state of economic knowledge in the country, afford us much reason for self-congratulation upon this head. Far from political economy being, as we have been accustomed to regard it, an established science, resting on solid foundations of fact and reasoning, with recognised principles applicable to the solution of practical questions, its most elementary doctrines seem still to be open to dispute: each speculator excogitates a theory for the nonce, apparently in entire ignorance that his sudden inspirations conflict directly with principles which have been wrought out by the labours of a series of able thinkers, and verified by a long course of experience. One writer, for example, in the recent discussion (and he merely gave distinct expression to what appeared to be the latent thought of many more) denies point-blank that an increase in the precious metals has any tendency to lower their value: it did not do so in the sixteenth century; it will not and cannot do so now. "The new gold and silver have been so much new capital added to the wealth of the world; they have acted as a stimulus to industry, and caused the production of commodities equal in value to themselves. The world is, in fact, richer than it was fifteen years ago by the whole amount, not only of the precious metals, but by all the property they represent." "I can discover nothing in this," he naïvely adds, "contravening the acknowledged principles of political economy." Another writer qualifies this position: he admits that increased supply may lower value, but gold, he informs us, distributes itself, not according to the principles expounded by Ricardo, but after the analogy of water:* it runs first to the lower levels, and does not touch

* The writer referred to thus explains his meaning: "England is in the very centre of the mouth of a very wide and very long estuary, and as the water rises it extends over a constantly increasing area in length and width; but the quan-

the table-lands till these have been filled. England is now table-land, and hence no effect on its monetary system need be apprehended, at least until India, China, and all the lower currency levels have been raised to its height. A third tells us that we should compare the new supplies, not with the existing stock of the precious metals, but with currency in general—including with gold and silver every form of paper and credit medium. Mr. E. Ashworth, who, as a practical man, seems to consider himself dispensed from assigning reasons, thinks the question sufficiently disposed of by declaring his belief, that, "however large might be the annual production of gold, *it would all be absorbed;*" an opinion which strikes us as eminently safe, but the bearing of which on the question of depreciation is not by any means obvious, unless, indeed, there are persons who contend that depreciation can only be accomplished by leaving the new gold to accumulate at the pit's mouth. Even Mr. Fawcett does not appear to have seized the principles of his subject with any firm grasp. A year ago he denied the existence of any sensible depreciation of gold, founding himself upon the fact that the gold-price of silver had not sensibly risen; now he admits depreciation to the extent of from ten to fifteen per cent, although the price of silver—his own criterion—remains precisely where it was. Finally, the *Times* sums up the whole controversy by declaring that the one thing evident in the discussion is, that political economy is at fault. "Gold ought, according to the laws of science, to have been depreciated long ago; but every writer in succession has been compelled to acknowledge that this result, at least in the proportions which science requires, has not occurred."

In this chaos of opinion among those who take part in economic discussions, it will not be out of place to advert briefly to some of the elementary principles applicable to the matter in hand. In the first place, then, in opposition to the ingenious theory as to the "stimulating" effect of gold on industry and the "absorbent" influence of wealth on gold, we must contend that gold is no exception to the universal rule, that whatever facilitates production promotes cheapness, and that less will be given for objects in proportion as they are obtained with less trouble. The authors of the theory in question have not favoured us with their notion of the manner in which the alleged stimulus to industry operates and the supposed absorption is effected. We are told, indeed, that "the new gold and silver

tity of tidal water sufficient to raise the channel at dead low water a foot would not be the thousandth, or perhaps millionth, part of what would be required for a foot rise over the whole estuary at the top of a spring-tide." *Times*, 12th September 1863.

have been so much new 'capital' added to the wealth of the world;" but if by this it be meant that the productive power of industry is increased in a direct ratio with each additional ounce of gold added to the world's stock, we must simply deny that gold possesses the attribute which is here assigned to it. We deny that gold and silver can exert any effect on the increase of wealth till they are exchanged for commodities suitable for productive operations; and it has yet to be explained how the stock of such commodities is increased *pari passu* with the stock of gold and silver. When the obvious *reductio ad absurdum* has not restrained such speculations, it is perhaps idle to meet them by serious argument. We say the obvious *reductio ad absurdum;* for if the doctrine be good for any thing, it would prove that under no circumstances could gold fall in value. The theory applies to every conceivable augmentation of the precious metals. The stimulus is represented as in proportion to the supply. However great, therefore, the increase, in the same degree would be the stimulus—in the same degree the amount of wealth produced, and in proportion to the wealth would be the absorption. Gold might, according to this doctrine, be as abundant as copper, as common as sand, and yet as valuable as ever: a given quantity would still command as much of all other things as before. When such a consequence is boldly faced, it is perhaps idle to appeal to reason. Still we will suggest this one consideration: How is the extension of productive industry which the theory assumes to be carried out? In the last resort it is only possible through a more extended employment of labour. But when once all the hands in a community are employed, the effect of further competition for labour can only be to raise wages; and, wages once being generally raised, profits can only be maintained either by a corresponding rise of prices, or by increased productiveness of industry, prices not undergoing a corresponding decrease; either of which implies a depreciation of money. When, therefore, the influence of the new money has once reached wages,—a point which has long ago been attained in this country,—it is evident that there will be no motive to continue production to the length which, by acting on supply, would bring prices to their former level: a depreciation of money must therefore at this stage of the movement be permanently established.

We hold, then, by the old doctrine, that an increased supply of money does tend to lower its value; and, further, we maintain that, not only does the value of money decline from an increase of supply, but that, other things being the same, the decline proceeds in inverse proportion to the amount of augmentation. We shall now endeavour to show that gold, so far forth as it is money, has, under the recent addition to its stock, in fact submitted to this law.

In attempting to deal with this subject in the brief space at our disposal, we do not of course aim at more than tracing its main features; and even as to these we make no pretence to minute accuracy in details; we must take round numbers and aggregate results, and confront them with general principles. We accept, then, as substantially correct the statement that the amount of gold produced since the gold discoveries is not less than 300,000,000*l.* sterling, and that the bulk of this has been already added to the monetary systems—including under this expression hoards as well as current money—of the world. Let us consider what, according to theory, ought to be the effect of this immense addition on the value of the metal concerned.

And first, with what principal sum are we to compare the new money? At first blush one would say, with the stock of gold already in existence. A brief consideration, however, will show that the mass of money on which the new supplies of gold are acting is not simply the gold already in existence, but the aggregate stock of gold and silver combined.

When two commodities happen to be largely available for common purposes, and admit therefore of extensive mutual substitution, no change can take place in the value of one without affecting, in a greater or less degree, that of the other. A familiar illustration of this principle is supplied by the different cereals. An unusually large wheat-crop will throw down the price of oats as well as of wheat, by causing wheat to be employed in many uses in which oats is employed in ordinary times; the effect of the excess in one grain is distributed over both, and shows itself in a fall in the value of both. Another example of the same kind is furnished by cotton and flax; but the most striking of all is afforded by the precious metals. Gold and silver are largely employed for common purposes: they are both extensively used in ornamental manufactures; they both serve for currency; they are both hoarded; in some countries they are both legal tender. It is impossible, therefore, that a sensible fall should occur in the value of either without the other sharing the decline. Accordingly, from the commencement of commercial history down to the present time, the relative value of gold and silver has experienced very little change, as compared at least with that which has occurred in other commodities. During the Middle Ages they generally exchanged in the proportions of 12½ to 1. After the discovery of America a large increase took place in the supply of both metals, but far the most in silver. It has been estimated that, for nearly half a century after the opening of the Potosi mines, the annual supply of silver was, in quantity sixty times, in value about five times, greater than that of gold; yet, notwithstanding this immense excess, continued over so long a period, the value of the more abundant metal was not lowered in its relation to that of the other by more than 20 per cent. This is the more striking, as general prices are considered to have risen from 300 to 400 per cent during the same time. Since the Californian and Australian discoveries an analogous phenomenon has occurred. But the mutuality of the two metals is now, owing to the wider range of commerce, combined with the closer connexion existing between all parts of its domain, even better established than in the sixteenth and seventeenth centuries; and the consequence has been a still greater steadiness in their relative value. About two years after the first supplies from the new sources began to arrive, the gold-price of silver rose about 2 or 3 per cent; this was sufficient to furnish a motive for substituting the falling metal for the other over an extensive field; and the result has been that, notwithstanding the large excess in the supply of gold which has since occurred, the gold-price of silver has scarcely risen above the point which it then reached. The circumstance which has most conspicuously facilitated this interchange has been the existence of a double standard in the currency of France. Up to 1852 France had constantly imported silver for the purpose of her currency; in that year, however, the tide turned. Silver then began to be exported and gold imported. In 1857, the date of M. Chevalier's first publication upon this subject, 45,000,000*l*. of silver had left France, and 100,000,000*l*. of gold had been received. Since that time the interchange has continued, but, in consequence of the gradual exhaustion of silver in the French currency, on a constantly-decreasing scale.* We should expect that the substitution of gold for silver must, so far as France is concerned, have by this time nearly, if not quite, run its course. But, though it is not improbable that the closing of the French market may lead to a further depreciation of gold in its relation to silver, there is,

* The silver drawn from the French currency was in the very early stages of the movement purchased chiefly by Holland, which had in the year 1850 adopted a law demonetising gold, and constituting silver the sole legal tender. Latterly, however, the great bulk of the French silver has come to England. Now during the years from 1853 to 1858 the imports of silver to England from France ranged between 4,000,000*l*. and 10,000,000*l*. sterling annually. In 1858 there was a sudden diminution, almost cessation, of the drain; but it recommenced in 1859, and reached in that year the amount of 6,000,000*l*.: since then, however, it has again declined, and for the last three years the average importation has been little more than 3,000,000*l*. sterling.

in our opinion (and on this point we venture to differ from M. Chevalier), no reason to suppose that this depreciation will take place in any marked degree. Though a double standard of value undoubtedly facilitates the mutual substitution of the metals in currency, it is not an indispensable condition towards this end. Gold, for most purposes of circulation, answers quite as well as silver; in the case of the larger transactions much better. In our own currency, for example, every one must be conscious of the large increase in the number of half-sovereigns in circulation during recent years. For the purpose of hoarding, gold is even better adapted than silver, and it is probable is already taking the place of the latter metal in many countries where hoarding prevails; at least we think we see indications of this in the recent returns of precious metals sent to the East. For example, in 1857, out of a total of 17,601,428*l.* exported, only 305,996*l.* was gold, or less than 2 per cent; while in 1862, out of 12,629,830*l.* exported, 1,919,621*l.* was gold, or 15 per cent. This increase, too, has been gradual; the proportion for the two middle years—1859 and '60—being on an average 7 per cent.* These are signs that gold is already forcing its way into the monetary systems of the East; and there is only need, we have little doubt, of a slight further advance in the gold-price of silver to accelerate powerfully this process. On the whole, then, although the increased supplies of gold have unquestionably told with greater effect on gold than on silver, still the disturbance which they have effected as between the two metals cannot be regarded as considerable; in the main the action of the new money has been distributed over the combined mass; it is therefore with this, and not merely with the existing stock of gold, that it must be compared.

In adopting this principle, however, with reference to the preëxisting stock, we must adopt it also with reference to the annual supplies. To the 300,000,000*l.*, therefore, of new gold which have been produced since 1850, we are bound to add the amount of new silver which has been brought into use during the same time. This is a very considerable sum; for it has happened that while these large accessions have been received to our stock of gold, the production of silver, chiefly in consequence of the discovery of new mines of quicksilver, and in some degree owing to improved processes, has also largely in-

* The following are the returns for the period 1857-62, as given in the statistical abstract:

Precious Metals sent to the East viâ Egypt.

	1857.	1858.	1859.	1860.	1861.	1862.
Total of gold and silver =	£17,601,428	5,220,136	16,616,531	9,426,122	8,036,334	12,629,830
Gold	305,996	131,286	613,264	1,301,886	796,495	1,919,621

creased. The annual production for some years previous to 1848 was estimated at 8½ millions sterling; the new facilities for its production came into operation about the year 1853, and in 1856 the annual supply, according to Mr. Newmarch's estimate, had risen to 12,000,000*l.* sterling. For the purpose of a general comparison, we shall probably be sufficiently close to the mark if we set down the annual supply of silver from 1850 to the present time at an average of 11,000,000*l.* This would give at the end of 1862 a total addition of 132,000,000*l.** to the preëxisting stock; but the loss from wear and tear in silver is considerably greater than in gold. Making allowance for this, we shall therefore set down the new addition at 120,000,000*l.* sterling. We have thus altogether an aggregate addition of 420,000,000*l.* of precious metals to the stock already at the time of the gold discoveries in existence in the world. That stock, according to Mr. Newmarch, was in 1848 somewhat under 2000 millions sterling. Assuming, then, Mr. Newmarch's estimates to be correct, and supposing all the other conditions of the case to have remained substantially as they were in 1850, we should have reason to expect, as the result of the recent augmentations, an average depreciation of the monetary medium to the extent of about 21 per cent; or, if we choose to state the case separately for each of the metals, a depreciation of about 22 per cent in gold and 20 per cent in silver.

Of course the other conditions of the problem have not remained as they were; on the contrary, the trade of the world has during this period undergone a very remarkable development, principally owing to the growth of free trade principles, but in some degree in consequence of the impulse given to emigration by the gold discoveries,—an impulse which has resulted in the addition of two new and thriving members to the society of industrial nations. A large increase has thus undoubtedly taken place in the aggregate wealth of the world since the epoch of the

* A writer in the *Times* (Mr. Crawfurd) sets the addition of silver down at 300,000,000*l.* On what grounds does the reader suppose? Simply because silver (so he alleges) has maintained its value in relation to gold, while gold has been increased by this amount. "No appreciable difference in the relative value of silver and gold has taken place [the difference which was sufficient to transform nearly the whole French currency not being "appreciable" by this financier's mind], *it follows* that silver equal in value to the new gold must have been produced; so that the actual amount of the precious metals which has been added to the old stock is 600,000,000*l.*" Here is faith in abstract reasoning with a vengeance! In direct defiance of notorious facts, silver is concluded to have increased as fast as gold in virtue of a principle! and what principle? The existence of a constant relation between value and quantity. To make the argument complete in all its parts, it is only necessary to add that this astounding inference is made in a letter, the whole purpose of which is to show that an increase in the quantity of gold has *no* tendency to lower its value.

gold discoveries. The population of the world has increased, and probably on an average each individual is richer. There are, therefore, more commodities to be exchanged; and to effect the more numerous exchanges on the same terms as before, a larger circulating medium would be required. Taking into account, therefore, merely those elements of the problem which we have already stated, though we should expect a fall in the value of money (for of course we do not suppose that the increase in general wealth has been at all commensurate with the increase in the monetary medium), yet we should not expect a fall in proportion to the augmentation of the supply. But there is another and very important element still to be taken account of—the element of credit. An extended use of credit as a medium of circulation is (subject to certain qualifications which it is not necessary to advert to here) entirely tantamount, as regards its effects on price, to an increase of money.* So far as it is used, it renders unnecessary a corresponding amount of coin; and therefore, if the employment of credit media only keeps pace with the extension of business, prices may be maintained in the midst of a growing commerce without the necessity of any addition whatever to the precious metals. Now that the use of credit has received an immense extension during the last fifteen years is a fact obvious to the most cursory observation. It is not merely in the larger transactions of the wholesale trade that this extension has taken place—in these it has been very considerable; but the remarkable feature in the recent history of credit is its growing use in ordinary retail business. Thousands of transactions are now settled every day by means of cheques where ten or fifteen years ago gold or notes would as a matter of course have been employed. To what lengths this movement has been carried during the period since the gold discoveries can of course only be matter for conjecture; nothing like certainty on such a point can be attained. In the absence, however, of accurate knowledge, both as to the increase of credit throughout the world and as to the increase of wealth, it will be convenient, and we do not think we shall be guilty of substantial error, if we set off roundly these two items as balancing each other. On this assumption, that the recent extensions of

* Yet it does not follow from this, as has been contended by a writer in the *Times*, that the new gold should be set against the whole credit and coin circulation together. When an addition of coin is received permanently into a circulation which, like that of England, is composed largely of credit, the augmentation of currency which follows will not be in the ratio of the new addition to the whole circulation, but in that of the new addition to the metallic stock only; for the proportion of credit to coin will still be maintained. The new coin, or a part of it, will itself be made the basis of a superstructure of credit; and the augmentation of the whole will correspond with the augmentation of the metallic portion.

credit will about neutralise, as regards the value of the circulating medium, the recent extensions of trade, the increased supplies of the precious metals would then tell upon the value of money in proportion as they have augmented its amount; and we are inclined to believe that this is substantially* what has happened.

The assertion is indeed constantly made, that no rise in general prices has yet occurred; but this assertion, when examined, will, we apprehend, be found to rest on no better foundation than the "impressions" of those who make it. Now it must be plainly stated, once for all, that such "impressions," even though backed by a few selected examples, are, in a controversy of this kind, absolutely without value. It is by no means likely that a rise in general prices,—such a rise as the circumstances of the present case give us warrant for expecting,—would be apparent to ordinary observers. The action of an increased supply of money in raising prices must of necessity be exceedingly gradual. Besides this, money is not the only cause which affects prices. Simultaneously with the increase of money, a great variety of other agencies,—the seasons, wars, the state of credit, changes in fashion—each, probably, with reference to particular commodities, and for a short time, more powerful than the new gold,—have been acting upon prices. These have greatly complicated the phenomenon, and thus in a great degree concealed the effect of the constant cause. Not only so, but the effects of the new money, even where they are perceived, are liable to be misinterpreted. Writers, for example, who adopt the view to which we adverted in the opening of these remarks, that gold can never fall in value, when they find on examination that prices have in fact extensively risen, imagine that they may evade the inference involved in this fact by saying that the rise is due to changes in demand and supply.† Such a remark simply shows that those who make it have yet to learn the rudiments of their subject. *Of course* it is due to changes in demand and supply—there is no other means by which prices can be altered; and if the new gold did

* We say substantially, as we cannot here enter into several influences of a minor kind, whose joint effect would be in some degree to neutralise the action of the increased supply of the precious metals, and thus render the actual depreciation less than the proportions of the new additions to the stock would lead us to expect. The most important of these minor influences will be found pointed out in an article in the *Edinburgh Review* for July 1860, pp. 14, 15.

† "According to my view," says Mr. John Crawfurd, in a letter to the *Times*, "there is not an article of Mr. Jevons last list the rise and fall in which may not be satisfactorily accounted for on the usual principle of demand and supply;" and, we imagine, according to Mr. Jevons view also. Mr. Crawfurd adds: "There has been a rise in the price of ordinary corns of nine per cent, but this small increase simply shows that supply has not kept pace with demand."

not act on demand and supply, it could have no effect upon prices. An increase in general demand is in fact *the specific means* through which an augmentation in the supply of money depresses its own value; for an increase in the supply of money is only another name for an increase in the demand for commodities. For these reasons no opinion as to general movements in price is deserving of the slightest consideration which is not based upon a wide induction of facts carefully sifted and systematically arranged. Fortunately for the purposes of this discussion, an inquiry conducted in this manner has recently been made by a competent statistician. Mr. Jevons, of the Sydney Royal Mint, has lately published a pamphlet, in which he states the results of a very extended inquiry into prices. We shall now describe briefly his method of procedure, and the conclusions at which he has arrived.

Mr. Jevons has comprised in his investigation altogether 118 commodities. These he divides into two classes, one consisting of 39 "chief," the other of 79 "minor" commodities. The "chief" commodities include such articles as the metals, the principal raw materials, agricultural produce, butcher's meat and provisions, tea and sugar; the "minor" commodities, the less important varieties of several of the "chief" kinds, together with others, as coffee, seeds, rice, fruits, wines, spices, &c. Of both, tables of prices are constructed, reaching from 1845 to the present time. As a general rule, Mr. Jevons has not attempted to eliminate special causes of disturbance: he has acted on the principle, that where the induction is sufficiently extended, these may be trusted to neutralise each other. He has, however, departed in two instances from this rule—in his returns of hemp and flax during the Russian, and in those of cotton during the present American, war. The actual prices of hemp, flax, and cotton are not given during these periods; but in their stead he has, in the case of the hemp and flax, interpolated numbers in a geometrical series between the prices of 1852 and 1856; while in the case of cotton he has substituted for the actual prices of 1861 and 1862 those of 1860, as being obviously unaffected by the present cotton "famine." Thus his only deviations from a strict record of the phenomena are cases in which he has substituted averages for exceptionally high prices. In no case has he applied this principle to prices which were exceptionally low. As his standard he takes an average of the period 1845–50; a period which, in allusion to the periodical fluctuations which prices are observed to undergo, he describes as one of "mean level of the commercial tide." With this he compares prices during the years 1860–62, a period not of "mean level," but of "commercial low water." The result is as follows: in the class of "chief" commodities a rise has occurred in five cases out of six; in the minor, in two cases out of three: in the former to the extent, on an average, of 16 per cent; in the latter to that of about 6½ per cent. Combining these results, Mr. Jevons arrives at the conclusion that general prices stand at present 10½ per cent higher than during the period of 1845-50. But the present being a period of "commercial low-water," while that with which the present is compared was one of "mean level," Mr. Jevons, allowing for the difference in the *natural* elevation of the two periods, is of opinion that 15 per cent would more correctly describe the actual depreciation of gold.

Such is the result of the latest systematic investigation into the subject of prices. We have no hesitation in saying that it is not only not at variance with "the laws of science," but that, soundly interpreted, it affords to these laws a very remarkable corroboration.

We say soundly interpreted, because we are not prepared to accept Mr. Jevons's interpretation of his tables in all respects as economically sound. He shows an advance in prices to the extent of 10½ per cent, or, making allowance for the exceptionally depressed condition of the market, of nearly 15 per cent; and he says that this indicates a proportional depreciation of gold. In our opinion it indicates a more than proportional depreciation. For it must be remembered that the values of other commodities have not been constant while this change has been taking place in gold. As a general rule, in advancing communities, the tendency is towards a fall in price in the mass of commodities—the natural consequence of progress in the industrial arts. Mr. Jevons has observed, that from 1820 down to the time of the gold discoveries this feature is very noticeable. In ordinary times, indeed, the tendency is principally operative in the products of manufacture; improvements in the modes of raising raw produce being for the most part not more than sufficient to counteract the causes inherent in the limited fertility of the soil, which are constantly pushing up the value of such produce. But in the period since the gold discoveries the progress of invention and enterprise has not been less marked in agriculture than in manufactures. The repeal of the corn-laws has acted on the value of food, scarcely less by the spur which foreign competition has applied to domestic agriculture than by opening up new sources of supply. Thorough draining, artificial manures, rotation of crops, the thrashing-machine, the reaping-machine, if not the inventions and discoveries of this period, have at least during it, for the first time, come extensively into use. Contemporaneously, too, improvement has been active in pastoral farming. It is impossible but that such causes should have had a powerful effect in cheapening every description of raw produce—an effect which, had nothing occurred in the interval to derange our monetary standard, would have shown itself in a corresponding depression of prices. The mere fact, therefore, of general prices maintaining their ground during the last fifteen years (supposing nothing more than this could be shown) would, fairly considered, be a very conclusive proof that depreciation of our monetary medium had set in. What amount of decline would be indicated by the mere maintenance of the former range of price is one of those points in our case which must of necessity be left to conjecture. There is no reason, however, that we should ignore facts* because we are unable to measure them. We hold, therefore, that the sound economic inference from the facts which Mr. Jevons has presented is not that which he has drawn. The mere maintenance of the former range of prices would show a fall—a substantial fall—in the value of money; an advance beyond that range to the extent of 15 per cent argues, therefore, an amount of depreciation still greater than in proportion to the advance. We do not think we are overstating the case in setting down the actual depreciation of gold at 20 per cent.

Such is the result to which a careful examination of the facts of the movement up to the present time leads us. Absolute coincidence between fact and theory in such an investigation is of course not to be looked for. The utmost that can be expected is a general agreement in the main aspects of the case with those which theory foreshadows; and this, we think we have shown, has, in the present instance, been, even in a remarkable degree, realised. Before, however, leaving Mr. Jevons's pamphlet, we wish to point to one result brought out by his inquiry, as it bears upon a theory referred to in the opening of these remarks, which has been started by a correspondent in the *Times*, and has since been endorsed by that journal in its leading columns. The doctrine is thus expounded by the *Times:* "To give an idea of the argument, let us compare the influx of gold to the irruption of water. The water would flow over the area opened to it, but before settling on the surface it would fill up the hollows, and it would be only when these were filled that the general depth of the flood would be calculable. In the sixteenth century England was a hollow,

* We do not mean to charge Mr. Jevons with ignoring the fact to which we here call attention; indeed, he has very distinctly pointed out that "it is not the simple change of price which is due to the gold, but *the difference of the change* between the two second periods [1844-50 and 1851-62] from the change between the two first periods [1833-43]" (p. 70). We think, however, that his language is calculated to conceal the fact which he here states.

with but a little water at the bottom, and the golden flood rushed into it accordingly. At the present time England is a high table-land, and many a hollow must be filled before we shall find much experience of the flood. Prices will rise no doubt, but it is elsewhere, and to our level, that they will rise."

If this be sound doctrine, then Ricardo's most notable achievement in political economy—his theory of foreign trade—is merely an extravagant blunder; and Mill, in adopting and developing Ricardo's view, has only blundered more egregiously. "Gold and silver," says Ricardo, "are, by the competition of commerce, distributed in such proportions among the different countries of the world as to accommodate themselves to the natural traffic which would take place if no such metals existed, and the trade between countries were purely a trade of barter;" a principle which, as he proceeds to show, leads to much and permanent diversity in local prices among different countries. The *Times* and its correspondent were probably quite unaware that they were propounding a heresy. But there is no need that we should enter on the ground of principle; it will suffice for our purpose to appeal to facts. "The groups," says Mr. Jevons, commenting on the evidence of his tables, "which have risen in the highest degree [are] . . . hides, tallow, leather, wines, butcher's meat, and oils, . . . articles of which the demand increases rapidly with the wealth and population of the country, while the supply is naturally limited: they comprise the principal animal materials. On the other hand, all the groups which have fallen in price [and we add, from an inspection of his tables, almost all those in which the advance in price has not been considerable] are of vegetable origin and chiefly of foreign growth:" for example, sugar, tea, foreign spirits, spices, rice, sago, seeds, jute; these have all either fallen in price or but slightly risen. Facts thus exactly reverse what we may venture to call the hydrostatical theory of monetary distribution. Commodities—the products of England and of the more advanced commercial countries—which the theory tells us are not to rise at all, at least not till a late stage of the movement, are precisely those in which the rise has been greatest, while those in which we are told to look for an extraordinary advance obstinately refuse to move, or, if they move, move but slowly, and as often in the wrong as in the right direction. The whole theory was probably suggested by the exceptional activity presented by certain localities in India which have lately been brought under special influences.

So far as to the effects in the past. In estimating the probabilities of the future, speculation has here also followed divergent courses. Those who, in one form or another, adopt what we may call "the absorption theory" hold consistently enough that under no circumstances is depreciation of any moment to be anticipated; on the other hand, those who think that gold is not exempt from the common lot of commodities, which dooms them to fall in value as they become abundant, while admitting that little effect has been produced hitherto, yet—as if to compensate for the meagre programme of the present—seem to foreshadow, though dimly, something like a catastrophe impending.* For ourselves, while we agree with these that gold is undergoing depreciation, we differ from them both as to what has been already accomplished and as to what remains to be done. We think there is a disposition to exaggerate the latter as much as to underrate the former.

The question of future depreciation divides itself into two branches; one, as to the extent to which the fall may ultimately be carried; the other as to the rapidity with which it is likely to proceed. The solution of the former question turns in the last resort on the fertility of the fields of supply, or, more correctly, on this, combined with the efficiency of industry in working them. On these two variables depends the cost of gold, and the cost of gold must in the end regulate its value. The question of ultimate depreciation can therefore only be solved by estimating future probabilities upon these two points. On this ground we cannot now enter. We shall content ourselves with saying that, taking the assumption that the present fertility of the principal mines now worked is maintained,—maintained, we mean, till all the gold required at the present cost is produced,—and that no more productive mines are discovered, we do not think that a greater depreciation need be apprehended than, at the utmost, to the extent of from 40 to 50 per cent on the value as it stood before 1848. This at first hearing sounds formidable, and no doubt, supposing it realised, will involve serious consequences. Still, as we hold that a depreciation of nearly half this amount has already occurred, and as we see that the sensible effect of this is so slight that its existence is still disputed, we do not expect, even on the contingency of a depreciation to the extent we have stated, that the result would be by any means overwhelming. The progress of the industrial arts would, as it has hitherto done, steadily neutralise and conceal the decline: the effect would be complicated with the action of many independent influences; and we have no doubt

* "From that moment" [the time when the substitution of gold for silver in the French currency is complete], says M. Chevalier, "the fall in gold will be rapid. In a word, if, down to the present time, the immense production of which Australia and California have been the theatre has not produced a greater fall in gold, it is France which is the cause." Cobden's *Chevalier*, p. 62.

there would to the end be people to deny that any depreciation had in reality occurred, even as there are people now who make the same denial regarding the great monetary revolutions of the past.

But the practical consequences of depreciation will depend in no slight degree on the second of the two points to which we have adverted—the rapidity with which it proceeds. With reference to this, the consideration which at first strikes one is, that every addition made to the precious metals, by augmenting the aggregate stock, increases its stability; and that, on the other hand, as the depreciation goes forward the inducement to produce will diminish, and therefore the supply may be expected to fall off. These considerations unquestionably point to a steady retardation of the pace of depreciation as the movement proceeds. On the other hand, the present condition of the world's trade threatens a contingency which may, we think, very seriously modify the normal course of monetary events, and may even convert what has hitherto been a gentle descent into a rather sudden leap. We refer to the possible cessation of the Eastern drain. This topic has been adverted to more than once in the course of the recent discussion; but we do not think that either its true connexion with the gold movement, or the conditions on which the contingency in question depends, has been very clearly apprehended by any of those who have touched upon this point.

The Eastern drain has been spoken of as if it were a phenomenon apart from the gold discoveries—an independent counteracting cause. Doubtless the Eastern drain is due in some degree to causes not connected with the new gold. For example, the failure of hemp during the Russian war, of silk in consequence of the disease in silk-worms, of cotton at present—each of these occurrences has sent us to the East to supplement our supply of the commodities thus diminished. The ordinary course of trade has thus been deranged, and every derangement in trade necessitates for a time—until prices in the exchanging countries have adapted themselves to the new conditions—an increased use of the precious metals. So far as the Eastern drain is traceable to occurrences of this kind, it may not improperly be regarded as a counteracting agency to the course of depreciation; though it would be more instructive, as well as more philosophical, to assign as the principle of counteraction the commercial disturbances themselves, since these came into play in other quarters than the East. But the influence of such occurrences in determining the drain has, we believe, been but slight. The most cursory inspection of the returns will show, what indeed might have been guessed without their aid, that the augmented proportions of the Eastern drain (for it will be remembered that the phenomenon itself is coeval with the history of commerce) are principally referrible to the gold discoveries themselves. Thus during the five years ending 1852 (at which time the new gold had begun to pour into Europe) the average annual exportation did not exceed 1,100,000*l.* sterling; in the five following years ending 1857 it almost reached 9,000,000*l.* sterling; and in the five years since that time it has risen to more than 10,000,000*l.* The relation of these facts to the occurrences in California and Australia can scarcely be missed; and the least consideration will reveal its true nature. The new gold has come in the first instance to the markets of Great Britain and the United States, and has acted on prices and salaries in those countries. People here and in America have found themselves in possession of larger monetary incomes, their expenditure has increased, and that expenditure has been turned largely upon commodities produced in Oriental countries. The result has been an immense increase in our imports from those countries* —an increase, however, which has not been balanced by any corresponding exportation; and this for two reasons, first, because the principal demand of the gold countries being for English and American productions, the bulk of the new gold has, in the first instance, come to our and the American markets; and secondly, because, owing to the inelastic nature of the currencies of Oriental countries, and the habits of hoarding which prevail, a given amount of the precious metals does not produce the same effect on general prices and wages there as with us. The Eastern drain in its present proportions is thus mainly the direct result of the gold discoveries: it represents the main channel through which the new money diffuses itself in the world. The question, therefore, of the continuance or cessation of this drain is mainly but another form of the question as to whether the gold supplies will continue or cease. If they continue, and the commercial condition of the East remains substantially as at present, it is scarcely a prediction to say that the phenomena which we now witness will continue. Salaries and prices here will advance upon salaries and prices

* Mr. Newmarch, writing in 1857, thus sums up the principal causes acting on the drain up to that time: "As the general result of the whole of these circumstances, we may correctly describe the efflux of silver to the East during the six years 1851-56 as occasioned fundamentally by the increased demand for the tea and silk of China excited in England and the United States, principally in consequence of the enlarged employment and expenditure in those countries arising out of the gold discoveries. . . . . . On the one side, England has received from China and India the products for which there has been an active European and American demand; and, on the other side, England has collected and forwarded to the East the amounts of gold and silver required to adjust the general account of each year." *History of Prices*, vol. vi. pp. 718-19.

there, as they have hitherto done; there will be an overflow, and this overflow will discharge itself in an Eastern drain.

But will the present industrial condition of the East remain substantially as it now is, pending the monetary development consequent on the gold discoveries? Mr. Jevons's tables show us that prices in the East have as yet responded but feebly to the action of the new money, copious as has been the tide that has been turned on them. We believe that this has been owing to the causes which we have just indicated—the inelastic character of the Oriental currencies, combined with the habits of hoarding, and, we may add, with the passion for ornamentation, which prevail in the East. But a note circulation (somewhat homœopathic in character, it is true) has lately been introduced into India: bills have long been in use there; cheques and other forms of credit will, it is probable, gradually win their way. In proportion as these media come into use, a given quantity of coin will support a higher range of prices. The habit of hoarding and the taste for ornaments are persistent propensities; but it will be strange if they do not, sooner or later, give way in the presence of English commercial civilisation. Supposing that on any extended scale the practice of investment takes the place of hoarding, the result will be the same as if so much new money were added to the world's stock. That which was before inert will at once begin to act upon the markets, and prices will feel the effect as if a new mine were opened in India. Nor is it in India only that these results are possible. As our commerce with China extends, it is probable that China also will feel the influence of our commercial ideas; and China is a magazine of the precious metals. These are topics which, in connexion with the problem started at Newcastle, appear to us be of the last importance. Supposing that, under the action of the influences we have described, general prices should rapidly advance in the East, this would, on the one hand, check European demand for Eastern commodities, and on the other stimulate Eastern demand for the commodities of Europe: the balance would be rapidly reduced, perhaps disappear; and this grand vent for the precious metals would be closed. Such a contingency could not fail to accelerate powerfully the depreciation of money; and it seems to us to be by no means an improbable one. Indeed, supposing we maintain ourselves in India, the assimilation of Oriental commercial habits to those of Europe can only be a question of time: time, however, is an important element in the present problem.

It will be seen that the conclusion to which we have come exactly reverses that contended for by some of those who have taken part in the recent discussion. According to them, the progress of English ideas in the East is to open up new channels for currency, which are to "absorb" the new supplies of gold, and thus prevent depreciation. If our view be sound, the effect of this progress will be to dam the old, not to open new, channels—possibly (for it is impossible to say what may be the effect of extensively setting free the hoarded money of the East) to turn back the tide of metallic wealth to its sources.

On the whole, we perceive two influences acting in opposite directions on the course of depreciation: the one proceeding from the constantly increasing dimensions of the total mass of the precious metals, and tending to retard the decline; the other, arising from the progress of English commercial civilisation in the East, tending to accelerate it. From one point of view, in so far as it multiplies real wealth, the latter cause will no doubt create an increased necessity for currency, and thus operate in the same direction as the former; but no multiplication of real wealth which is at all probable can be expected to keep pace with the expansion of currency which *may* occur, supposing both paper credit and the hoarded money of the East combine their resources in the Oriental circulation. The commercial development of the East, therefore, we regard as the grand influence on the side of acceleration, as the increasing mass of the metals forms the most potent drag on the descent. Hitherto they have perhaps about neutralised each other; which of the two causes will prevail, as the movement proceeds, is a question which we do not here attempt to solve, but remit to the consideration of those whose larger acquaintance with the present state and prospects of Oriental society renders them better fitted for the task.

Art. IX.—FOREIGN POLICY OF THE ENGLISH GOVERNMENT AND THE ENGLISH NATION.

Correspondence relating to the Affairs of China, Japan, Mexico, and Brazil. Parliamentary Papers, 1862-3.

Correspondence with Mr. Seward relating to the Commerce of the Bahamas. Parliamentary Paper, 1863.

Hansard's Debates. Sessions 1862-3.

The British people and the British government are not always at one in their notions of foreign policy. Both are swayed to a great extent by the national interests, real or supposed; both are often compelled to bow to what it is now the fashion to call "the inexorable logic of facts;" both occasionally "drift" at the mercy of currents which they did not calculate on, and cannot stem. But in the main the one is guided by its traditions, and the other by its instincts;—and of the two, the instinctive policy is usually the soundest, the wisest, and the most generous. The people think much of what is *characteristic*, of what is just, of what is beneficent, noble, and disinterested. The government consider largely what they did in their youth, and what their predecessors did in the old time before them, of diplomatic usage, of the obligations of international etiquette, of the completion of inchoate plans, of adherence to established precedent, of fidelity to old engagements and entanglements, of consistency with rash, unwarrantable, and even conflicting professions and promises inherited from a foolish and discrepant past. Sometimes the government acts before the people have had time to think or speak, and then we find ourselves committed to a line of conduct which we cannot heartily support or long endure. Sometimes the people get wind of what is going on, and make themselves heard before it is too late; and then ministers are forced into language and proceedings which somewhat astonish themselves, and utterly bewilder their diplomatic interlocutors. At one period the party whose watchwords are "Economy" and "Non-intervention" get the public ear; at another period, the votaries of "National honour" and the "Due influence of Great Britain" are in the ascendant; and our policy is swayed in one direction or the other according to the oscillations of the parliamentary and popular pendulum, greatly to the perplexity of the observers who watch us, and the nations that have to deal with us. On the whole, however, the several parties act as wholesome checks upon each other. The people preserve the government from any gross iniquities, and the government keep the people out of any very flagrant follies. The peace party prevent the meddlers from being too mischievously busy; and the upholders of the national dignity and position prevent their antagonists from driving us into any thing desperately mean. The statesmen who are in bondage to the traditions of the Foreign Office, who think much of precedent and little of principle, are a salutary counterpoise to their younger and more unfettered rivals who dream only of material interests and "common sense."

Our foreign minister generally has his hands full. England, by her greatness and the extent of her dominions, is in contact with all the world, and usually in collision or in discussion with half of it. England, by her history, is mixed up in nearly every international question, and has entangling engagements or unsettled controversies with nearly every state in Europe, Asia, or America. She has always some "difficulty" on hand, either with one of the great powers of the Continent, or with some maritime rival, or with some semi-civilised Oriental potentate, or with some wholly savage tribe. Earl Russell is ever "at it," as the formidable list of Foreign-Office blue-books annually laid before Parliament, and now lying in an appalling pile upon our table, testifies. Either he is negotiating with France, or remonstrating with Russia, or pleading for Poland, or arguing with the United States, or bullying Brazil, or assisting China, or sitting on Japan. This "quadrumanous activity," as Burke calls it, may well task the powers of the strongest head, and put a severe strain on the serenest temper; and nothing can enable any minister to steer his way through it with credit and success, or without much stumbling and many blunders, except the guidance of some fixed principle, some magnetic pole, some distinct aim and purpose, well-defined and grasped with the tenacity due at once to a conviction and to an affection. Unfortunately this settled principle and clear goal are precisely what both minister and people lack. The nation loves influence, loves dominion, loves justice, worships good faith, hates oppression, sympathises with those who are struggling for liberty and civil rights; but it also loves peace, loves money, hates trouble, and is too sensible at bottom to care to do other people's work for them, or to attempt work which no power on earth could do at all.

In the various grave questions of foreign policy that have troubled us during the last two years, England has, on the whole, come off with very considerable credit. In one or two cases perhaps our course has been such as we cannot look upon with any satisfaction, but then it has been where *no* course would have been satisfactory. In at least two other matters the minister has committed great errors both of judgment and of temper, but the country has not sustained or encouraged him in either case. In the most knotty and important of all, both the government and the people have behaved with singular dignity, justice, and forbearance; and, without having made a single false step, have incurred a degree of enmity and vituperation which only the most persistent series of false steps could have righteously deserved.

Earl Russell has been severely assailed for having permitted and encouraged Mr. Lay and Captain Sherrard Osborn to take service under the Chinese government; the one as Inspector-General of Customs, the other as a sort of naval chief, at present at the head of a special force, but destined ultimately in all likelihood to become virtually First Lord of the Admiralty to the Celestial Empire. There is no doubt that the proceeding is a most important one, and is pregnant with future consequences both far-reaching and momentous, and as such perhaps should not have been ventured upon without previous parliamentary discussion and sanction. Some years ago, viz. in 1854, the Chinese government, conscious of the incurable rascality of its own functionaries, and anxious to improve and protect its revenues, applied to Mr. Rutherford Alcock, then our consul at Shanghai, to nominate a British inspector of customs duties at that port, to see that they were fairly levied and properly brought to account. In 1855 Mr. Lay succeeded Mr. Wade in this post, and soon produced a remarkable and most welcome result. The revenue paid into the Chinese exchequer was speedily quadrupled; and the Regent was so delighted that, as soon as he had satisfied himself of Mr. Lay's incorruptible honour as well as vigorous ability, he appointed him by direct commission to the control of the Customs department at all the open ports, *i. e.* in fact for the whole empire. Mr. Lay has now a large staff of clever and well-paid officials, partly English and partly American, under him, holds a distinct and independent post in the Chinese administration, and bids fair to become virtually the finance minister of the empire, either nominally or through the influence which his acknowledged superiority in mental and moral qualities will enable him to exercise. The success of this first attempt at the employment and naturalisation of foreign agency answered so well, that Prince Kung applied for English private assistance in putting down smuggling, and creating an efficient navy that should be able to deal both with contrabandists, pirates, and Taeping rebels; and Captain Sherrard Osborn was authorised by the British government to undertake the task, and become a sort of Chinese admiral and surveyor of the navy—to provide a marine for the Celestial Empire and to command it. By two orders in council, dated respectively August 1862 and January 1863, not only are the enterprises of Mr. Lay and Captain Osborn formally sanctioned, but those gentlemen are authorised to equip vessels and enlist men (even officers of our army and navy) for the service of the Chinese government.

The measure is a bold one; and much may be said and has been said both for and against it. On the one side it is urged that this is not only undertaking an important portion of the administration of a distant and semi-barbarous empire, but involves actually taking part in a civil war, and may involve participation in the future foreign wars of China; that it is commencing in China the course we have run in India, with the probability, amounting almost to certainty, that it will end here, as it has ended there, in our becoming virtually, if not actually, the rulers and managers of that vast empire;—since year by year English energy, knowledge, and honesty, will assuredly make their way in all posts, distance all native competitors, absorb all administrative functions; and when the inevitable consequence comes of native jealousy, native recalcitration, native injustice, and cruelty exercised on British subjects, the *civis romanus* doctrine is sure to come up; English sympathy will be vehemently awakened on behalf of deserving, beneficent, and ill-treated Englishmen; government interference will be insisted on; and what was originally but the enterprise of *individuals* will be adopted and carried out by *the nation* in its collective and corporate capacity. On the other hand, Earl Russell and his friends replied with considerable effect—all the more effect because they were addressing an audience of Britons—that the reconstitution of Chinese finances, the purification of Chinese administration, the suppression of piracy and smuggling in Chinese seas, were eminently good works, and that it was not the habit of Englishmen to refuse participation in such works; that it was directly for our interest that they should be carried out, and that they could not, we well knew, be carried out by native agency; that we had by our previous wars (not always scrupulously just ones) done so much to weaken the Celestial Empire, that we were in a manner bound now to do what we could to strengthen it; and that only by thus aiding and consolidating it could we enable it to carry out its treaty engagements with us, and to afford efficient protection to the vast amount of British property invested there, and the numerous British subjects whom we had encouraged to visit or to settle there. It was declared moreover—but this was mere special pleading—that the Englishmen who had taken service with the Chinese government were now their servants and not ours, and must undergo the conditions and accept the risks incidental to such service, with the usual Oriental probabilities of treachery, fickleness, ingratitude, and cruelty.

Both the antagonistic pleas are irrefutable. To our minds the fault of our government in this matter lies not so much in what they have done,—for we do not see that they could or ought to have acted otherwise,—as in having done it with no avowed principle, on no settled system, and with no clear prevision or acceptance of the sure results. But this is the very fault of which we have complained already as pervading all our foreign policy and indeed all our national action; and it is one which the country shares in equal measure with its government. We may be quite certain that the nation would not tolerate any needless or arbitrary impediments being thrown in the way of the free and useful enterprise of its citizens; that it will insist upon efficient protection being afforded them in whatever part of the world legitimate trade or legitimate occupation may have led them; and that the permission to Englishmen to engage themselves in the civil and naval and military administration of China is probably the best and cheapest way of securing this protection. *Individually* it is not to be expected that we should look far to ulterior issues, either in the way of deprecation or welcome; but our statesmen and our government ought to do this. And, therefore, though we do not think that Earl Russell and Lord Palmerston should have withheld the royal sanction to such unquestionably beneficent and valuable undertakings as Mr. Lay's and Captain Osborn's, yet we do think that they were bound to have given this sanction with a full purview and a clear comprehension of the inevitable consequences, and with a distinct resolution how to deal with those consequences when they arise. For our part, we in no way deprecate the ulterior issues we foresee; we do somewhat dread their coming upon us as surprises, and finding us without any decided plan or principle of action. We are sure that we cannot avoid being concerned more and more deeply, year by year, in the administration of Oriental countries; nay more, we do not think that we ought to aim at this avoidance; but this at least will not be disputed, that we should know clearly whither we are going and what we shall do when we get there; that wherever we sail to, we should *steer* and not *drift;* that we should not, like fools or children, habitually suffer and enforce the cause, and then whine over or denounce or stand amazed at the result,—habitually order the expenditure and then grumble at the bill. *We* believe we have a "manifest destiny" in the eastern world; we do not shrink from it; we are not ashamed of either the qualities or the propensities which force it upon us;—if in a spirit of timidity, or humility, or self-denial, we determine to renounce it, let us renounce it avowedly, consistently, and on principle, and let us be sure that in the hour of temptation we shall adhere to our renunciation. But if we pursue it, let us pursue it manfully, systematically, righteously as far as human weakness will allow, and with an open-eyed acceptance of all its issues. This "manifest destiny" we see accomplished in India, in progress in China, incipient, but in its main features unmistakable, in Japan. In India the particulars of our progress were varied by the fact that there our mercantile *encroachments* (we do not use the word in a bad sense) were conducted by a powerful and chartered company, and were therefore at once better regulated and more irresistible. But every where commercial enterprise is the first and political ascendency the last step in the uniform and inevitable process. Our merchants see tempting openings for interchange and profit in a foreign land. They go thither, they establish themselves, they grow rich; they develop wealth in those who deal with them. Their energy, their talents, their integrity,—so far beyond those of the native population, and, we may add without vanity, usually so far beyond those of other foreign visitants,—naturally win for them a position, undefined indeed, but not the less substantially influential on that account. Some rulers and some parties favour them more than others, and become therefore insensibly their allies, offer them special privileges, and bargain for assistance in return. They thus gradually become involved in native disputes and native strife. Their services are repaid with territory; a factory becomes a settlement, and a settlement becomes a national possession. They make bargains with native princes. These bargains at times assume something of the magnitude and dignity of treaties. Occasionally these treaty-bargains are infracted by the natives, who have not always the same sense of fidelity to obligations that we have. In such cases the merchants or the company demand redress, and, if need be, enforce it; sometimes they ask the assistance of their government to compel reparation. Redress involves both indemnity for past and security against future wrong. These are often most readily given in the shape of added territory and augmented privileges. Thus little by little, with or without design, by the mere natural ascendency of superior capacity, by the mere inevitable operation of natural causes, we—either our merchants themselves, or the official representatives of our government to which the merchants have appealed for justice and protection—become native powers in various Eastern countries; and as soon as they have attained this position, their innate superiority to other native powers insures first preponderance, then ascendency, and finally, perhaps, absorption.

Now, as an historical fact, no one can deny that this process has usually been attended with much arrogance, and often with much wrong, on our part. But it need not be so. From the first establishment of European, and especially of British, merchants at the ports of an Asiatic country, all the rest follows sooner or later as a matter of course, and almost of necessity. We cannot avoid making agreements. Agreements, once made, must be enforced. Wrongs inflicted, outrages sustained, must be atoned for and punished, or the safety of British subjects and peaceful traders in distant parts of the world is at an end. Often redress can only be obtained by taking the law into our own hands, by British fleets and British soldiers. These fleets and soldiers in the end require harbours and *pieds-à-terre,* where they can refit, repose, and perhaps entrench themselves. If wrongs and quarrels become frequent, it is found so costly and troublesome to send expeditions *pro hâc vice* to the extremities of the earth, that we prefer taking possession of, or purchasing or obtaining by treaty, some island or promontory where our perpetual presence may overawe wrong-doers, and may thus save us the pain of punishing injuries by preventing them. We seize Chusan; we exchange it for Hong-Kong. We have then a military and naval settlement in the Chinese empire, and a British fleet permanently in the Chinese seas. Presently the Chinese are in difficulties. Pirates swarm in the Chinese waters, and prey upon native and foreign commerce indiscriminately. English men-of-war can deal with these far more efficiently than Chinese imperial junks. The Chinese authorities therefore beg us to sweep away these sea-ruffians; and we are willing enough to do so, for the sake of our trade as well as theirs. Again, rebellion breaks out: the power or the very existence of the government is threatened. On its power depends obviously its means of keeping its engagements with us. We have therefore a direct interest in sustaining it, more especially when its assailants are more unfriendly and barbarous than itself. Then, to complete our involvement, some imperial city like Shanghai, full of European property and swarming with European residents, is menaced or assailed, and is certain to be sacked unless all British indwellers and visitors, mercantile, civil, naval, and military, at once join in its defence. Of course only pedantry would order us to fold our hands and wait for reinforcements from Pekin. The defence is organised; the Taepings are driven off; and we have become embroiled in the civil strife. Finally, the celestial government has now had ample experience of the superiority of British soldiers, and even British adventurers, to its own best troops, and of British administrators to its own picked officials:—it therefore entreats individual Britons to collect its customs and organise its brigades, naval and military. They are nothing loth; and the British government, when appealed to, sees no reason why it should withhold its sanction and encouragement. Such is the regular course of affairs; such is the normal development of our "manifest destiny." We do not see how we can avoid carrying it out in the far East, nor why we should; but it lies with us to decide whether we will carry it out clumsily or skilfully, empirically or systematically, in such a way as to bring about the maximum of benefit to our clients and ourselves, or in such a way as to do the least possible good to them at the greatest possible cost and discredit to ourselves.

No mock modesty shall ever make us disguise our conviction, that there are few Eastern races to whom British influence with all its drawbacks, and even British rule with all its blunders, are not, or might not be made, an almost incalculable gain. We have, no doubt, in our Oriental career been sometimes violent, often wilful, often stupid, often strangely and perversely blind. But nothing will persuade us that to the semi-civilised races of the East in general the governing ability and the conscientious sense of duty which characterise most Englishmen, as compared with the corresponding qualifications of their own chiefs, must not prove an incalculable blessing. Can any man doubt that Borneo under Rajah Brooke would not be a vast improvement on Borneo under the Dyaks? or that Chinese finance under Mr. Lay, and Chinese naval warfare and police under Sherrard Osborn, will not offer an *immeasurably* favourable contrast to the same departments under Governor Yeh, or any Chinese mandarin ever yet born?

Nor can we picture to ourselves a grander or nobler field for English energy and talent. To remodel, to purify, to develop the resources of a magnificent empire like that of China,—imposing from its magnitude, but corrupt and rotten to its very core; to introduce honesty and purity and skill where now there is nothing but incapacity and peculation; to render taxation light and commerce fair; to avert famine and infanticide; to elicit order where there is now only confusion, and regular and organised law where there is now only an alternation of frightful license and still more frightful severity of repression; —these are surely tasks worthy of the ablest and most enterprising of our citizens. Equally clear is it that to suppress piracy and murder, to inaugurate law and justice, education and trade among a people like the bloody Dyaks of Borneo, to substitute peaceful and civilising occupations for sanguinary wars and perpetual devastation over an island as extensive as a continent, are functions which might employ a virtuous and ambitious man for his whole life, and enable him to lie down in joy when the time comes to give an account of his stewardship. We believe these superb and beneficent careers are now open to our countrymen almost without stint, if we can only a little systematise and regulate our proceedings; and that all these blessings might be conferred upon the races in question, under a sound and settled line of policy, without committing the British nation nearly so much as its authorised and unauthorised citizens are now committing it every day, and without entailing upon it the expenditure of one extra shilling; nay more, without doing one act of greediness or wrong, or being chargeable with one violent or questionable deed.

The principle to be laid down appears to us evident and simple. All action should be the action of individuals: the government as government, the nation as nation, should abstain from all participation as completely and as long as possible. As a rule, Englishmen succeed and manage well; as a rule, the English government usually blunders and often fails. The reason is plain enough:—individuals undertake enterprises and enter on careers because their hearts are in the cause, or because they feel some special aptitude or calling for the work;—when the government acts, on the contrary, *it looks out for agents*, and partly from the inveterate habits, and partly from the incurable necessities of a parliamentary system, it selects and nominates these agents, not for their pecular fitness for the place, but from altogether domestic and irrelevant considerations. These men blunder and fail, and the nation has to rectify the failures, to endorse the blunders, to bear the discredit and the cost of both. But if individuals like Sir James Brooke, Mr. Lay, Sherrard Osborn, and others that might be named, choose to go out on their own account, and place their organising and governing capacity at the service of an Oriental people, either as recognised *employés* of its government or as private adventurers, keeping within the legitimate bounds of morality and justice, we would allow them to do so without let or hindrance;—establishing at the same time the strict rule that, while affording them every moral sustainment and encouragement, so long as their enterprises and functions are useful and worthy, our government entirely declines to interfere for their protection against the laws of the country in which they may settle, or the decrees and proceedings of the government under which they may have taken service. If Sir James Brooke had been murdered by the Dyaks, there would have been no call on the

English authorities to demand punishment or indemnity. If the Chinese government should have reason to believe Mr. Lay to be guilty of peculation, or Captain Osborn to be corrupt or treacherous, and should, in the exercise of its despotic authority, order their decapitation, we *ought not* to interfere with the course of justice, or what the Emperor of China deems to be such. Nor, we apprehend, should we interfere, had not the case been complicated by the sort of governmental or national participation in their enterprises which the Order in Council we have before noticed would seem to indicate or imply.

Such appears to us the clear principle which should guide and control English intervention in the administrative affairs of Asiatic countries. Government *quà* government—Great Britain *quà* Great Britain—should in no wise participate, direct, or be mixed up with it. The real difficulty will lie in persuading the nation to act up to this rule in all instances. For, *first*, Englishmen have an invariable disposition to lay all their acquisitions, whether of influence or territory, at the feet of their country. When Brooke has made himself the supreme ruler of Sarawak, instead of glorifying himself with the notion of independent sovereignty, he immediately wishes to become instead the mere governor of a British settlement. When Lay and Osborn have rehabilitated the navy and finances of China, they will think only how far and how best their high position may be made conducive to English interests and English reputation. England is thus constantly tempted by her loyal and patriotic sons. And *secondly*, if any act of flagrant cruelty or injustice were to be perpetrated by the Oriental government against the English officials who had served it, if they were brutally punished though clearly innocent, or treacherously and in breach of promise dismissed or made away with by jealous or ungrateful potentates or ministers, then it would be by no means easy for our rulers to resist the clamour that would arise, both among the people and in Parliament, for vengeance against a power which had "treated Englishmen ill." Still, if English unofficial ability is to be made largely available for Oriental administration, some strict rule of the sort we have indicated must be adopted and adhered to.

We confess to a strong wish that our "manifest destiny" had not led us to Japan. We are by no means certain that strict principles of morality and justice warrant us in being there. And we are quite certain that our position there will entail upon us, almost of necessity, many proceedings which morality and justice can never sanction. At the same time, it would be idle to blame our merchants for what they have done, inasmuch as they merely followed their ordinary mercantile instincts, which in the main are innocent and sound; and it is not easy to blame our government for what *they* have done, inasmuch as we do not clearly see how they could have abstained from all action, or at what point of the proceedings which have brought about the present menacing and painful situation they could have acted otherwise than they have done. There have, perhaps, been some errors, but there has been much more of irresistible fatality.

The Japanese are not only a peculiar people, but a people whose peculiarities are the very opposite of ours. They are singularly clever, ingenious, and persevering, courageous, fierce, and indifferent to life. Their system of government, moreover, is so singular and complicated, that it is doubtful whether even now we rightly understand its mechanism or its functions. One of the chief peculiarities of this people, and one of the most settled maxims of its rulers, consists in a rooted dread and detestation of foreigners, a great dislike to their appearance on the islands, a disinclination to have any dealings with them, and a determination to get rid of them by any of the various methods familiar to Asiatics,—by overreaching and intimidation, if possible; by open and pertinacious violence, if necessary. These sentiments of the Japanese were always well known to us; and being thus known, it would seem to have been the part of wisdom and of kindness to have left that people in their resolute isolation, and to have abstained from forcing our unwelcome presence upon them. Beyond curiosity and vague speculative hopes, there was no very strong motive for our intrusion; for Japan could supply us with no commodities which we could not procure from China in still greater abundance; and so exclusive, so ingenious, and so manufacturing a race was not likely to furnish a very brisk market for our productions.

Unhappily, however, the restless enterprise of British commerce, and the jealousy and ambition, and perhaps the duty, of British diplomatists, combined to override these prudential considerations. We were the chief commercial people in those Eastern seas. The Russians and Americans had both made treaty arrangements of some sort with Japan, and permitted their merchants to go thither and trade. Our mercantile adventurers, naturally enough, did not choose to be shut out from this new market and possible El Dorado, and they urged both their own interests and considerations of political prestige as reasons why England, as well as her rivals, should make a treaty and obtain a footing. They *would* go thither, whether our government liked it or not; and if our government stood aloof, they would simply hold an inferior and disadvantageous and unprotected position,—a state of things which neither English pride, nor English sense of fair dealing, nor, perhaps, English interests in that quarter of the globe, could tolerate. Accordingly Lord Elgin was instructed to open political and mercantile relations with Japan, and, if possible, to conclude a treaty, which should include the authorised residence of a British minister in the principal island, with, of course, the usual immunities and assurances of safeguard enjoyed by all embassies in all civilised countries, and with some further ones which we are in the habit of exacting from semi-barbarous and Oriental states,—such as the exemption of our citizens from Japanese law and Japanese tribunals, and their control by our representative as a substitute. Lord Elgin succeeded in effecting such a treaty, and the ratification of such engagements by the Japanese authorities; who, like all Asiatics, succumbed readily to pressure accompanied with a display or an impression of superior power, but were fully determined to evade the fulfilment of these unwelcome engagements as soon as the fear and the pressure were removed. The usual results followed. Offence was given, recklessly but unintentionally, by some European visitors; the people were annoyed by the increased price of the necessaries of life; the government grew anxious about the export of bullion; and the latent hostility of the ruling classes, and, we believe, of the majority of the population also, soon showed itself. The mission was more than once treacherously attacked by ferocious ruffians acting under superior command, or stimulated by spontaneous fanaticism; some of its members were severely mutilated and narrowly escaped with life, and several of its servants were slain; similar outrages have from time to time been repeated on the persons of British subjects and other Europeans; and there was, and continues to be, every indication of a fixed determination on the part of the people and their feudal chiefs to render our position in Japan unpleasant and untenable, by every means within the reach of a fierce, unscrupulous, and crafty race. Of course we demand redress, apology, and the punishment of the offenders. Of course we are met with delays, shuffling, expressions of regret, confessions of powerlessness, and the like; to which we reply by fresh remonstrances, distinct menaces of retaliation, and after which we feel a strong conviction that, ultimately, we shall have to take the law into our own hands, and to avenge ourselves. Earl Russell intimated in one of his despatches to Col. Neale that he was prepared for this contingency; for he writes that "it would be better the Tycoon's palace should be destroyed, than that our rightful position by treaty should be weakened or impaired."

Unfortunately, however, our case is complicated by two circumstances. There can be no doubt that *primâ facie*, and in strict law interpreted according to European usage, we seem to have a rightful position in Japan by treaty; and it is certain that, being there peacefully and by consent, we cannot submit to ruffianly outrage, nor permit ourselves to be driven away by violence, whether authorised or spontaneous. But, in the first place, it is by no means certain that the authorities with whom we made the treaty—in virtue of which we established ourselves in Japan, and which was the *fons et origo* of all subsequent calamities and offences—had any legal right or power to make such a treaty, or were in fact the true and supreme government of the state. It is now known that the ruler with whom Lord Elgin fancied he was negotiating, and by whom the Japanese negotiators were assumed to be, and probably had been, delegated, had been dead some days before the treaty was concluded; and it is surmised that he was assassinated in consequence of his consent to treat. It seems certain also, from information subsequently gathered, and most of which is contained in Sir R. Alcock's book or despatches, that this dead Tycoon—even if he had been alive—would have had no authority to abrogate or violate any of the fundamental laws of the empire; and it is positively stated that the exclusion of foreigners from Japan (as well as the right and duty of every native to slay and exterminate such foreigners) *is* a fundamental law of the empire, and one of its most sacred and dogmatic laws. There is little doubt, finally, that the Japanese polity is not only a monarchy, and a *double* and limited monarchy, but a feudal aristocracy; that the Daimios, or great semi-independent princes, have a sort of concurrent jurisdiction with the sovereign, and have nearly as much right and power to say what shall and what shall not be done as the Tycoon or the Mikado; and that these Daimios are rootedly and fiercely averse to foreign residents and foreign commerce. It is not improbable, therefore, that this treaty—concluded by Lord Elgin with a dead Tycoon of limited authority, and in reliance on which we were a few months ago on the point of going to war—may have little more real or legal validity in Japan than would belong to a treaty negotiated in England with the late Lord Mayor of London and the Archbishop of Canterbury or the Viceroy of Ireland.

In the second place, it is admitted on all hands that the Tycoon, who is the head of the temporal government of Japan, is rather friendly to us, has acted on the whole very fairly by us, and is well disposed both to protect and afford us redress so far as his power extends. But his position is full of difficulties. He is ill looked upon among his fellow-countrymen on account of his friendly or conciliatory inclinations towards us.

His power, too, is very limited,—limited by law, still more limited most probably in fact,—as is usual in semi-barbarous and feudal countries such as Japan. Combined, the great Daimios are more than a match for him; singly even, some of them might set him at defiance. *They* commit the outrages; *he* deplores them, but is really, we apprehend, unable to prevent or to punish them. Yet it is from him, as the nominal ruler, that we have to demand reparation; he whom we have to coerce and menace with our vengeance. Earl Russell freely admits all this; he even draws a practical inference therefrom, inasmuch as he desires our admiral to take measures *directly* against the Prince of Satsuma, a great Daimio and an enemy of the Tycoon, by whose followers the worst outrages upon us are believed to have been committed, and whose estates, luckily for us, lie near the seacoast. Earl Russell also foreshadows a theoretical conclusion to which his mind has been led by the position of affairs: "For my own part (he writes), I shall be very glad to see the authority of the Tycoon maintained, and the authority of the Daimios diminished." It is not at all clear what is the actual situation at this moment in Japan: by the last accounts it seemed that pecuniary indemnity had been conceded, but not the punishment of the offenders; it was understood that a sort of struggle, which might probably end in civil war, was going on in reference to us and our quarrel between the Tycoon and the feudal princes, aided, perhaps, by the Mikado or spiritual emperor; and that into this conflict, as it originated about us, we might very probably be dragged. For if the Tycoon gets into trouble by adhering to us, honour seems to demand that we should assist him; and as he is our chief friend and protector in Japan, the instincts of self-defence point in the same direction. But however the present dispute may terminate, others are certain to arise not so easy of adjustment. We shall be injured and insulted, and shall demand redress; if refused or delayed, we shall enforce it. To prevent future repetitions of the injury, we shall insist on fresh securities, on a territorial *locus standi*, or some efficient control over a weak or unfriendly administration. These things, with a semi-civilised state like Japan, means, as our Oriental experience must satisfy us, a continued course of gradual though reluctant encroachment on native rule, and probably an ultimate assumption of supremacy. Now all this is greatly to be deplored, but we fear cannot now be prevented, nor perhaps could at any time have been averted by any action or inaction which the English people would have tolerated. Practically, all that our government can now do is to give full powers to our minister in Japan to control and punish all British subjects who offend against Japanese laws, or wilfully irritate Japanese prejudices; and having done this, to be at once as firm and as conciliatory as possible when any causes of dispute arise.

The affairs of Mexico, and our intervention therein, next demand attention. Mexico is naturally one of the finest and richest countries in the world. Though situated within the tropics, it combines within its range every variety of climate, for it has every degree of elevation. Near the coast it is unhealthy; in the interior it is salubrious enough. Its soil is good, and can grow any thing from sugar down to apples. Its silver mines are the most extensive and productive in existence. Its resources in every way are vast, and under a good government, and inhabited by a decent people, it would be prosperous and progressive in a high degree. Unfortunately its inhabitants are a mongrel and unsatisfactory race,—partly pure Indians, partly mixed blood, partly effete Spaniards; and its government is probably the worst known—worse even than that of Greece. In fact, for a long series of years Mexico has been a prey to the most absolute anarchy. The central government has been seized by one military adventurer after another—nearly all rascals, and all alike unable to enforce their authority, and unable or unwilling to maintain order, to protect property, to punish crime, or to observe engagements. The condition of the country and the offences and atrocities of its rulers are delineated in the despatches of Sir C. Wyke, our resident minister there, in language which is very unusual in diplomatic correspondence. Here is an extract or two:

"It will be very difficult, if not impossible, to give your lordship a correct idea of the present state of affairs in this unfortunate country, so utterly incomprehensible is the conduct of the government which at present presides over its destinies. The religious feelings of a fanatic population have been shocked by the destruction of churches and convents all over the country, and disbanded monks and friars wandering among the people fan the flame of discontent. . . . In the mean time the congress, instead of enabling the government to put down the frightful disorder which reigns throughout the length and breadth of the land, is occupied in disputing about vain theories of so-called government on ultra-liberal principles; whilst the respectable part of the population is delivered up defenceless to the attacks of robbers and assassins, who swarm on the high roads and in the streets of the capital. The constitutional government is unable to maintain its authority in the various states of the federation, which are becoming *de facto* perfectly independent. . . . Patriotism, in the common acceptation of the term, appears to be unknown, and not one man of any note is to be found in the ranks of either party. Contending factions struggle for the possession of power only to gratify either their cupidity or their revenge; and in the mean time the country sinks lower and lower, while its population becomes brutalised and degraded to an extent frightful to contemplate. Such is the actual state of affairs in Mexico, and your lordship will perceive therefrom that there is little chance of justice or redress from such people except by the employment of force to exact that which both persuasion and menaces have hitherto failed to obtain. . . . .

Since this day month, when I had the honour to write to your lordship describing the state of affairs here, matters have been going on from bad to worse; and every day's experience only more clearly proves the imbecility and bad faith of a government now generally detested, and against which various conspiracies are on foot. . . . .

A more disgraceful state of things than that now existing here it is impossible to conceive in any country pretending to call itself civilised. The civil war now raging, and the weakness of the government, have encouraged the Indian population to rise against the whites at a place about twenty miles from hence, where they have committed dreadful atrocities, thus adding a new element of discord and misery to those already existing. This movement, if not at once checked, may lead to terrible results, as the immense majority of the inhabitants of this republic belong to the Indian race, which is quite strong enough utterly to exterminate the degenerate and vitiated descendants of the old Spanish conquerors. All the respectable classes look forward to foreign intervention as the means of saving them from ruin, and preventing the dissolution of the confederation, as well as a general rising of the Indians against the white population. . . . . I see no hope of improvement, except it comes from a foreign intervention, which may render possible the formation of a respectable and rational government composed of the leading men of the moderate party, who, however, are at present devoid of moral courage, and afraid to move without some material aid from abroad."

But, independent of all this, there had been a long series of wrongs and outrages against foreigners generally, and Englishmen in particular, to be atoned for and punished. Successive Mexican administrations had broken numberless engagements, pecuniary and otherwise, entered into with our countrymen and our government. Debts long overdue remained unpaid. Funds specially set apart by solemn convention to meet special loans or obligations, had been audaciously confiscated. The British legation had been forcibly robbed of a large sum of money by Mexican officials. Another sum of British gold had been seized *in transitu.* For none of these shameful spoliations had any redress been rendered, and against a daily repetition of such no security was, or could be, obtained. But this was not the worst. British travellers and British residents had been repeatedly murdered under circumstances of great atrocity; the lives of foreigners generally were threatened; several of these assassinations had been committed by the soldiery; and in other cases neither justice nor the punishment of the offenders could be obtained by the utmost efforts of our minister. In fact, it was by no means certain that the Mexican rulers, who succeeded one another so fast, and hated each other so much, would have prevented these atrocities if they could; and it was quite certain that they could not, even if they would. The French and Spaniards had similar, though less flagrant, wrongs to avenge.

There was, therefore, every reason to justify, and even to call for, armed intervention on the part of ourselves and our allies to exact redress for the past, and some sort of security for the future. If there ever was a case in which foreign interposition was imperatively needed, was dictated by every generous as well as by every selfish motive, was certain to do much good, and could not possibly make matters worse, this was such a case. It was clear, too, that though we might pay ourselves for the debts righteously due by seizing Mexican property and assuming the direction of Mexican customs dues, yet that we could not protect British subjects from Mexican outrage by any such means. It was clear that it was worse than useless to make any agreement with any Mexican administration, since none would have power to carry out their engagements, and we should have no power to force them. It was clear, therefore, that only by the establishment of a strong, stable, and decent government in that country, could we hope to gain the objects of our armed interference. France saw this plainly, and continued to see it. We appeared to see it plainly also at first, but Foreign-Office vision soon became confused and misty.

A joint expedition was arranged between England, France, and Spain for the attainment of their common aims. Joint expeditions are always objectionable; but perhaps joint action in this case was unavoidable. A convention was agreed upon between the three European Powers, of which the purpose was "to demand from the Mexican republic more efficacious protection for the property and persons of their subjects, as well as a fulfilment of the obligations contracted towards their Majesties;" and an expedition, naval and military, was sent to enforce this demand, "the commanders of which were to seize and occupy the several fortresses and military positions on the Mexican coast, and were authorised moreover to execute such other operations as may be considered, *on the spot*, most suitable to effect the object specified in the preamble of the convention, *and specifically to insure the security of foreign residents.*" The contracting parties engaged, further, "not to seek for themselves, in the employment of the coercive measures contemplated by the present convention, any acquisition of territory or any special advantage, and not to exercise in the internal affairs of Mexico any influence of a nature to prejudice the right of the Mexican nation to choose and constitute freely the form of its government."

Now, bating a certain indefiniteness in this last clause, the convention was rational and business-like. As soon, however, as it began to be carried out, a difference of opinion arose between the contracting parties,—in which, as it seems to us, we were clearly wrong, and the French were clearly right. France, however, made the great mistake of taking Almonte with them, under the impression that a strong party of moderates in Mexico would rally round him. They thus appeared to embrace his views, and to intend to urge his claims. It soon transpired, however, that Almonte was deservedly unpopular, and would do harm to the cause. After a while, therefore, he was quietly suppressed. England, however, or rather Lord Russell (for the English press almost unanimously blamed his proceedings), made the far greater error, and adhered to it, of losing sight, at the very first practical step taken, both of the real object of the enterprise, and of the special clause by which the allied commanders on the spot were to determine the best measures for carrying out that object. The representatives of the three powers agreed at Vera Cruz upon a brief proclamation to the Mexican people, stating that they had a higher and more beneficent object than the mere enforcement of pecuniary claims or the exaction of satisfaction for past outrages, and came to hold out a friendly hand, and to aid the nation in putting down anarchy and restoring order. Nothing could well be more sensible and moderate. But Lord Russell,—a very *doctrinaire* in all that relates to the right of every people, even the most barbarous, to absolute freedom of choice as to its polity,—disapproved the proclamation in the strongest terms, declaring that we had not undertaken the regeneration of Mexico, but that our objects were limited to the exaction of redress and the protection of British subjects and British property. The rejoinder of France was unanswerable. It was to the effect "that the proclamation condemned by Lord Russell was the production of the authorised allied commanders 'on the spot;' that they had all agreed upon it; that it was in strict conformity with the terms of the convention; that only by the establishment of a decent and strong government in Mexico could protection either to life or property be secured; and that such government could not be established without foreign aid." In a word, that if the expedition was not prepared to help decent Mexicans to elect and maintain an honest and capable administration, it had better never have left Europe. This seemed self-evident;

but jealousy and mistrust had arisen between the allies—for which it cannot be denied that French antecedents had given some colourable pretext, perhaps more; so Lord Russell withdrew the English forces, and Spain followed his example.

Louis Napoleon was greatly annoyed, and even irritated, by this withdrawal, and we think with considerable reason. It threw upon the French the whole weight and the whole responsibility of an undertaking which might turn out ill, and which was not popular in France; and he argued with much cogency, that to set on foot an expedition for a particular purpose, and then at the very beginning to shrink from the only means by which that purpose could, by any possibility, be effected, was not a very rational proceeding. We hold him to have been quite right: probably diplomatic pedantry and slavery to watchwords never led England to stultify herself more completely and more uselessly. But for the discreditable features of this transaction, however, we should incline to rejoice in it. We have no wish to run in double harness with France, if we can help it. We believe, too, that France does work of this sort better and more efficiently than we should. She is more direct, more dogmatic, and less scrupulous. She has, too, ideas and projects of her own, which ours would mar, and with which they could rarely harmonise.

The rest of the history is well known. Louis Napoleon persevered. At one time the enterprise seemed jeopardised; for the resistance of Juarez was more obstinate than had been expected, and the French army suffered severely from the climate. At last, however, Mexico was taken, the country to a certain extent subdued, an assembly of notables summoned, who declared for an empire, and offered the crown to the Austrian archduke Maximilian. The task of conquest and pacification is not yet completed, but we have full confidence that it will be ere long; and if Louis Napoleon shall really have succeeded in establishing a strong and stable rule in that miserable country, he will have done a meritorious deed, and will deserve well of Europe and humanity. We, at least, shall never grudge him either the glory or the influence he may derive from the transaction. He showed logic where we showed only inconsistency, confusion of sentiment, and feebleness of will. He showed resolution and good sense where our Foreign Office displayed only red-tapism and a slavery to words.

In the case of Poland, the views and feelings of the British nation appear to have been natural and sound, and its silence, under the circumstances, to have been judicious. Not knowing exactly what to think, nor seeing clearly what to do, nor being able to satisfy themselves that any thing effectual could be done, our people, though far from indifferent or unsympathising, have abstained both from speech and action. A few small meetings have been held indeed, a few unimpassioned addresses have been delivered, and a certain amount of discussion has taken place in the public papers; but no one who remembers the manifestations of popular sentiment when the destinies of Hungary and Italy were at stake, can fail to appreciate the meaning of our comparative apathy in reference to the Polish insurrection. Unfortunately the Foreign Office could not follow the national example. Its position, perhaps correctly, appears to its present chief to impose upon it the obligation of expressing an opinion and offering advice on all political occurrences. Earl Russell does not appear to have seen more distinctly than Englishmen in general what ought to be desired, what could be said, or what might be done, in this singularly perplexing conjuncture; but he could not well, like Englishmen in general, fold his arms and look on in silent pain and grief. Moreover, France was urging him to some decided steps; so, under the joint pressure of Louis Napoleon, circumstances, and perhaps his own cacoëthes, he took up his pen and descended into the arena. Once there, he acted of course according to his kind. Being a Whig and a *doctrinaire*, he recommended parliamentary institutions and a national representation as the panacea for Polish as for all other evils. Being a colleague of Lord Palmerston's, and minister for foreign affairs, he followed the traditions of Downing Street, and took his stand on the treaties of 1815. He wrote a despatch indorsing and repeating the errors committed by Lord Castlereagh forty-eight years ago; and because that singularly blundering statesman had arranged an unworkable compromise then, Earl Russell insisted on the enforcement of that unworkable compromise now.

The difficulties of the case lay here; and unquestionably they are grave enough. In all serious disputes between the Czar of Russia and his Polish subjects of the Grand Duchy of Warsaw, the principles and etiquette of international law give us a sort of claim to interfere; because we were arranging and guaranteeing parties to those European treaties which made those Poles subject to Russia, and because the non-fulfilment of the conditions of those treaties is alleged to be the cause of the actual Polish insurrection. In consequence of our participation in those treaties Russia is bound to listen to us when we remonstrate against her alleged violations of them, and we are bound to listen to the Poles when they appeal to us to enforce the terms which we sanctioned. Thus much is clear. Another point is clear also. There can be no doubt that Poland has not possessed—at all events since 1831—that national representation, or that constitutional freedom, which were supposed to have been secured for her by the treaty of Vienna. There can be no doubt that the misgovernment of Poland by her Russian masters has been systematic and extreme; that it has, especially of late, been directed to the object of fusion, *i.e.* of trampling out the elements and the fostering causes of distinct national life; that the oppression inflicted during peace, and the cruelties inflicted since war broke out, have been revolting to civilisation and disgraceful to the Russian government and soldiery. There can be no doubt, in a word, that the Poles have suffered enough both of barbarity and of wrong to warrant them most amply in their endeavours to throw off the Russian yoke, if they saw any reasonable prospect of success.

So far is clear. Every thing beyond this is dark and disputable. It appears certain that the terms which the Western Powers stipulated for on behalf of the kingdom of Poland implied a political arrangement which was simply absurd and impossible, which is now repudiated as such both by the oppressors and the oppressed, and which, as soon as it is stated in plain language, is repudiated by common sense. It appears almost equally certain that no other political arrangement can be suggested which is at once feasible, desirable, and just. The problem admits of no diplomatic solution, and it is not worth a war to solve it.

The intention of the more liberal of the statesmen who negotiated treaties of Vienna was, no doubt, to erect the Grand Duchy of Warsaw—*i. e.* that portion of Poland which remained Poland after the three partitions—into a constitutional kingdom under the dynastic supremacy of the Czar of Russia. It was felt that the Poles had suffered great wrongs, and deserved some indemnity for the past and some security for the future. It was felt that Alexander had rendered such vast services in the rescue of Europe from Napoleon's grasp that he merited every concession that could decently be made to him. Personally he was inclined to be mild and just, and had coquetted with liberalism. He was not indisposed to meet our wishes, and to see if he could govern Poland constitutionally. But he was not willing to have his hands tied. It was arranged, therefore, that Poland should have a sort of quasi-independence—which was to be and not to be at the same time—which was to be asserted and denied in consecutive sentences of the same parchment instrument. Thus it was agreed that she should have *bonâ fide* representative institutions; but, lest this should bind Alexander to something too definite, these institutions were to be "réglées d'après la mode d'existence politique que chacun des gouvernements auxquels ils appartiennent *jugera utile et convenable de leur accorder.*" It was impossible to bind autocracy with a slighter or a silkier chain. Poland was to be a constitutional country, governed by Poles, legislated for by a parliament really representing the several classes of the community; but the system on which this representation should be organised was to be determined by the absolute will of the ruler; and this country was to be governed constitutionally by an autocrat who was perfectly absolute in every other portion of his dominions. He was to be an unfettered despot on one side of the frontier, and a limited monarch surrounded by a haughty aristocracy on the other. He was to govern on one bank of a river and to reign only on the other. And the empire, one small section of which was to have this anomalous favour shown it was an agglomeration of conquests from races more free and civilised than itself. And the section thus distinguished was inhabited by a turbulent and warlike people, who hated their new rulers with a fierce, a national, and a well-motived animosity, both as ancient oppressors, as repeated spoliators, as aliens in race, and as fanatically hostile in religion. Russia was to govern Poland mildly, justly, by the agency of Polish statesmen, through the medium and according to the enactments of a Polish parliament chosen by the Polish people. In a word, the Poles hated the Russians and burned to free themselves from the detested foreign yoke; yet the Russians were to govern these same Poles *with their own consent*, through their own instrumentality, in accordance with fair and free representative institutions. This was the polity which the Congress of Vienna thought fit to inaugurate; which Alexander really fancied he could manage for a time; which the harder and shrewder Nicholas took advantage of a rebellion to sweep away as too absurd for further trial or discussion; yet which Earl Russell has again urged on the Czar as what he once promised to England and France, and what he is bound therefore, on the demand of England and France, to set up once more.

Our foreign minister sees all the incongruities involved in such a polity; but, strange to say, he fails to draw the conclusion that so incongruous a polity is and must ever be a mere dream. His arguments, when defending his diplomatic intervention and his refusal of armed intervention in July last in the House of Lords, are so amazing that if we had not the words before us in black and white, we should fear we were misrepresenting, instead of merely condensing, him. "No man," he declared, "expects that the Poles will ever lose the hope of establishing their independence. Lord Castlereagh did not expect it. *I do not. I hope and believe this spirit in the Polish people will never die.* Feeling all this,—and feeling at the same time that it is impossible for us to propose any terms which do not assume that *the Russian government is to prevail in Poland,*—I have urged that Russia shall establish a genuine national representation in that country, shall appoint Poles to all the great posts of administration, shall maintain the Polish language and religion. And I cannot see why Russia should not accede to all these proposals. Russia must of course continue to rule over and govern Poland. That is the basis of the whole arrangement. But why should she not govern it *according to the wishes and the nature of the people of the country?*"

Such was really and without exaggeration Earl Russell's pleading. *First,* the Poles wish, and always will wish, and our foreign secretary trusts they always may wish, for national independence. *Secondly,* God forbid, however, that we should further that desire, for Russia must continue to govern Poland, and Earl Russell can entertain no proposal which even hints at any other arrangement. But, *thirdly,* Earl Russell cannot, for the life of him, conceive why Russia (which wants to govern and must govern Poland) should not at once concede self-government to Poland (which desires, and naturally and rightly desires, to govern herself)! And, *finally,* if Earl Russell shall succeed in persuading despotic and sovereign Russia to restore to aristocratic and vassal Poland a government which "shall preserve not only in the homes of Poland, but in her municipal councils and national assemblies, that spirit of the Polish people which he (Earl Russell) believes will never die, and hopes will never die,"—then he (the said Earl) "will have achieved a feat of diplomacy of which he need not be ashamed."

It is well for the foreign minister, and well for England, that Russia met our remonstrance and demands with a refusal instead of with acceptance. For, as Lord Derby in a very few words showed, Russia by acceding to our demands might have entangled us in an inescapable logical and moral obligation to aid her in her future wars against Poland, or in this one if too obstinately prolonged. "It is a question," he said, "whether this country may not be dragged into a war, *not for Poland, but against Poland.* For, if we impose certain conditions on Russia, if we find those conditions impracticable, and if Russia, having acceded to those conditions, shall find that the arms thus placed in the hands of the Poles are used for the destruction of Russian power (as we know they would be), then Russia will have the right to say, 'You compelled me to make these promises, and you compel me to adhere to them. I have adhered to them, and am now suffering in consequence.' In such a case we should be bound to throw into the hands of Russia the whole of our moral influence, the whole of our moral support."

Fortunately for us, Russia has distinctly declined to concede self-government to the Poles, or to consent to the establishment of an obviously impossible and self-contradictory polity. Happily also, the Poles with equal distinctness have refused to listen to a compromise so hollow and so condemned by the experience of the past and the clear common sense of the case. Both belligerents have declared that no half-scheme will work or shall be attempted. Russia insists on complete subjection. Poland insists on complete independence. If Russia is to gain her end, she must do her work herself. If Poland's demand is just or for the good of Europe, Europe must help her to obtain it. Now is it desirable or expedient that an independent kingdom of Poland should be established? We cannot tell. It is not easy to answer confidently in the negative. It is still more difficult to answer confidently in the affirmative. It is very sad to see horrible cruelties committed. It is very sad to see an ancient and courageous nobility trodden out. It may be that a free and constitutional kingdom established in the heart of north-eastern Europe might be a germ of good that would fructify in time. It might be a barrier to Russian despotism, if Russia again ever became formidable to Western Europe. But, on the other hand, we remember what Poland was when formerly independent; and we know that it was not then a blessing,—either as an enlightener or a peace-maker. We know that its aristocracy, though brave and patriotic, was about the most oppressive, the most ignorant, and the most turbulent in the world; and that unless it were to be very different from what it used to be, and to act on very different principles, its reëstablishment would be not only a questionable good, but an unquestionable wrong. It *might* come purified and changed out of the fire of adversity; but also it might *not*.

Then, again, if set up, could it be kept up? In the *Kingdom of Poland*—the only portion of old Poland which European statesmen appear even to dream of nationalising and acknowledging as independent—there are only 3,800,000 Poles. In all parts there are only 6,800,000 Poles. Could a nation with either the larger or the smaller number maintain its independence, surrounded as it is by three vast and powerful empires, with every one of which it would be in a state of chronic controversy? Is it not certain that on England and France would devolve the permanent task of supporting the monarchy they had set up? And how when England and France were no longer at one? Do we see any such certain good, any such undeniable duty, any such righteous aim, as to induce us to bind such a fearful burden on our shoulders? But the Poles have distinctly avowed that they would not be satisfied with the independence merely of the Grand Duchy of Warsaw, of "Congress" Poland, as it is sometimes termed. They declare that all the provinces formerly wrested from them shall be restored,—in other words, that the portions of their former territory now incorporated into the Russian, Austrian, and Prussian monarchies respectively shall be restored and reannexed. And there can be little doubt that even if no demand of this sort had been put forward, the *kingdom* of Poland could scarcely be established in full national independence without arousing in the minds of the Poles who reside in the outlying provinces, reft away in previous partitions, a restless longing to be reincorporated with their former compatriots,—a longing that would give rise to constant rebellions, and to incessant hostilities between Poland and her powerful neighbours. Now it is abundantly obvious that no such claims could be enforced against Russia, Prussia, and Austria, except at the cost of an obstinate and general war,—a war, moreover, which might not terminate to the advantage of the claimants or their allies. But there is yet another consideration behind. The seizure and separation of the provinces in question was unquestionably at the time of its commission a great act of wrong and spoliation. But it by no means follows that their restoration to Poland now would be an act of right and justice. On the contrary, it is certain that such a proceeding would be rather the commission of a fresh injustice than the rectification of an old one. In all the provinces in question the Poles, once the sole or the main inhabitants, are now a minority of the population;—and to hand them over to Poland, therefore, would be to place them under foreign domination, *i. e.* to do the very thing which the Poles themselves complain of. Thus: the population of the Duchy of Posen, now belonging to Prussia, is 1,494,000, of whom only 780,000 are Poles. In Gallicia, out of 3,100,000, only 1,100,000 are Poles. In the incorporated *ci-devant* Polish provinces of Russia, the entire population is about 10,000,000 of whom 5,950,000 are Russians of the Greek church, 1,400,000 are Jews, and only 2,600,000 are Poles and Catholics.

In spite, therefore, of all our sympathy, which is both sincere and deep, for the sufferings of the Poles and their aspirations after recovered or preserved nationality; in spite of our detestation, which is general and vivid, at the barbarisms and brutalities of Russia, it is impossible not to feel the cogency of the practical conclusions to which the English people have been driven. It is clear that to demand from Russia that she shall grant real self-government to a part of her dominions, which yet she is really to govern and retain,—that she shall rule a people who detest her as they wish to be ruled, and through their own instrumentality and consent, is to demand a contradiction and an absurdity. It is clear that to give independence to a small country with less than four millions of national citizens, surrounded by hostile and mighty neighbours and foes, would be to give her what she could not maintain. It is clear that to nationalise and liberate the four millions of Poles who reside within the kingdom, without restoring and reannexing to them the other three millions who dwell in outlying provinces, would be only to create a perpetual blister and a running sore in the heart of Eastern Europe. It is clear that these outlying provinces could only be reannexed at the cost of a desperate, sanguinary, general, and doubtful war. It is quite clear that such a war would be a great evil. It is not at all clear that such a re-creation of old Poland would be a great good. It is clear, therefore, in conclusion, that the silence of the English nation in the matter has been wise and right; and equally clear that the conduct of our Foreign Office in demanding the fulfilment of absurd and impossible arrangements, and announcing at the same time that there was not the faintest intention of *enforcing* this demand, was neither dignified nor judicious. It was a case, we fully admit, in which it was peculiarly difficult either to do nothing or to do right. But we need not have done at once so little and so ill.

When we turn our eyes from Europe to America, we are charmed to find a case in which the British people have been quite in unison with the British government, and in which no fault can justly be found with the conduct of either. The civil war which broke out more than two years ago between the two divisions of the great republic of the West offered a conjuncture in which there was every facility both for the nation and for ministers to go astray. The questions of right, of wisdom, of propriety, involved were numerous and very complicated. Both our sentiments and our interests were deeply and immediately concerned. We felt almost as vividly in the matter as if it had been an English question, and as if the struggle had taken place at home. Many of us had strong prepossessions and even affections in favour of one side or the other. Some of us detested and condemned both sides impartially. Vehement convictions and passions on the Slavery question inclined numbers among us to favour the North. Personal and national interests as to the supply of cotton, as well as logical regard for political liberty, disposed others to wish success and emancipation to the South. Nine-tenths of Englishmen found it impossible not in their hearts to rejoice at the dissolution of a Union which was fast becoming too powerful either for the tranquillity of others or for its own good. The upper classes generally felt relieved by the *écroulement* of a violent and aggressive democracy, from which England had much to fear. The working-classes to a considerable extent mourned over the failure of republican institutions, from whose example and success they had hoped so much. Our merchants were severe sufferers by the interruption to their trade; and two millions of our most industrious and skilful population were menaced with the loss of their daily bread, and have actually had to endure much privation and to live on charity for two years. Scarcely any war could have interested us so keenly or affected us so much.

We need not go through the details of the struggle. The determination both of this nation and this government was taken at the outset. It was resolved to be absolutely impartial and to be very patient; to allow the established principles of international law to be carried out to their fullest extent, at whatever inconvenience and injury to ourselves; and to be as forbearing and considerate as possible whenever either belligerent, in haste or ignorance, in anger or under pressure, overstepped the recognised limits of respect or justice. In accordance with this resolution, we acknowledged both parties as belligerents, not only because we were bound by usage to do so, but because we could not have done otherwise in justice to either party or to our own commerce. In accordance with this resolution we resisted every temptation to go further, and to secure a supply of American cotton by breaking the blockade or acknowledging the South. We permitted without complaint the repeated seizures of our merchant-ships, when these were engaged in furnishing munitions of war or other articles to either combatant, and only remonstrated where belligerent rights were carried beyond all bounds of right, or were exercised with undue insolence and harshness. We have borne much which it is thought by many we should not have borne, and which other countries wonder at our bearing, because we feel that every allowance is to be made for men engaged in a struggle for political existence, and with all their passions wound up to the highest pitch. The Nassau correspondence supplies proof enough of the extent to which American audacity and British forbearance have been carried. Once only have we spoken and acted with peremptory indignation—viz. in the case of the *Trent,* when envoys were forcibly taken from the deck of a British packet-ship proceeding from one neutral port to another, and when the case was so clear that all Europe cried shame upon the Federals for the outrage. On this occasion we acted in the most friendly way possible. We demanded immediate restitution of the captured envoys, and the disavowal of the offending officer; and we accompanied this demand by proceedings which showed the United States that we were peremptory and in earnest, and thus made it necessary and comparatively easy for them to make atonement before they had got committed to a wrong course by protracted controversy. Of late we have gone perhaps too far in soothing their susceptibilities and meeting their exacting claims. We have, at the instance of the government at Washington, ventured to seize a ship of war said to be designed for the Confederates,—and it is believed that we have given direction to detain two others:—it now appears that in acting thus our government has not only gone to the very verge of the law, but has probably outstepped it, and will have to pay heavy damages in consequence. On the whole, our conduct as a nation has been almost admirable. With every need for cotton, we have adopted no questionable steps to obtain it. With every wish for a dissolution of the Union, we have not aided it by any single partial proceeding. Under every provocation we have kept our temper. Under every inducement to action we have been absolutely passive,—and have induced others to be passive also. It is owing to discouragements from our government that France has not long since recognised the Confederacy, and broken the blockade, and consummated the disruption of the republic. Yet we meet with nothing but misrepresentation, enmity, and vituperation from those whom we have thus served in obedience to law and principle, and in defiance of our own interests and predilections. We do not expect that the United States will ever do us justice, but history most certainly will.

Art. X.—THE LATE SIR G. C. LEWIS.

A Dialogue on the Best Form of Government. By the Right Hon. Sir G. C. Lewis, Bart. M.P. London, 1863.

Few more curious sights were, not long since, to be seen in London than that of Sir G. Lewis at the War Office. What is now a melancholy recollection was, when we used to see it, an odd mixture of amusing anomalies. The accidental and bit-by-bit way in which all minor business is managed in England has drifted our public offices into scattered, strange, and miscellaneous places. It has drifted the war minister into the large drawing-room of an old mansion, which is splendid enough to receive fashionable people, and large enough to receive a hundred people. In this great and gorgeous apartment sat, a few months since, a homely scholar in spectacles, whose face bore traces of sedentary labour, and whose figure was bent into the student-stoop. Such a plain man looked odd enough in such a splendid place. But it was much more odd to think that that man in that place supremely regulated the War Department of England. The place should have been a pacific drawing-room, and the man was a pacific student. He looked like a conveyancer over deeds, like a scholar among treatises, like a jurist making a code; he looked like the last man to preside over martial pomp and military expeditions.

So *unique* a man as Sir George Lewis has, in truth, rarely been lost to this country. Most men, most politicians even especially fall easily into some ready-made classification, belong to one of the recognised groups of ordinary character. Political life has gone on so long that we have ascertained the principal species of statesmen, and have a fixed name ready for each. But Sir George Lewis, as all who knew him in the least well will testify, did not belong exactly to any received type. People were puzzled how to classify a man who wrote on the Astronomy of the Ancients, the Fables of Babrius, and Roman History *before* there was history, and who was yet able to fill three difficult cabinet offices in quick succession. He wrote what most cabinet ministers would think it too much and too hard to read. No German professor, from the smoke and study of many silent years, has ever put forth books more bristling with recondite references, more exact in every technicality of scholarship, more rich in matured reflection, than Sir George Lewis found time, mind, and scholarlike curiosity, to write in the very thick of eager English life. And yet he was never very busy, or never seemed so. In the extremity of the *Trent* difficulty, when, as he was inclined to think, a war with America was impending, when a war minister might be pardoned for having no time for general reflection, Sir George Lewis found time, at three o'clock on a busy parliamentary day, to discuss with the writer of these lines, for some twenty minutes, the comparative certainty, or rather *un*certainty, of the physical and moral sciences. It was difficult to know what to make of such a man.

The difficulty was the greater because he made no pretence to be a marvel of versatile ability. When Lord Brougham was chancellor, he was always doing—his enemies said for display, his friends said from a certain overflow of miscellaneous activity—many out-of-the-way matters. According to one legend, he even wrote a treatise on hydrostatics for the Society of Useful Knowledge which was so full of blunders that it could not be published. Many statesmen have had the vanity of variety. But if ever there was a plain man, an unpretending man, a man who in matters of business affected to be *par negotiis neque supra*, that man was Sir George Lewis. The objection to him was that he was too prosaic, too anxiously safe, too suspicious of every thing showy. It was not possible for an enemy or for an opponent—for he had no enemies—to hint that Sir George Lewis's miscellaneous books were written from a love of display. They were written from a bent of nature—from the born love of dry truth.

To those, however, who had an opportunity of accurately observing Sir G. Lewis there was no difficulty in making him out. He was so simple and natural that he explained himself. His principal qualities were all of a plain and homely species, and though it may not be possible to give a likeness of them, yet a brief description may easily give an idea and an approximation.

The specialty of his mind was a strong simplicity. He took a plain, obvious view of every subject which came before him. Ingenuities, refinements, and specious fallacies might be suggested around him in any number or in any variety, but his mind was complication-proof. He went steadily through each new ambiguity, each new distinction, as it presented itself. He said, in unadorned but apt English, "The facts are these and these; the new theory concerning them is so and so: it accounts for facts Nos. 1, 2, and 3, but fails to account for facts Nos. 4, 5, and 6." Of course he was not uniformly right. We shall show that there were some kinds of facts, and some sorts of events, which he was by mental constitution not able wholly to appreciate. But his view of every subject, though it might not be adequate, though it might be limited, was always lucid. His mind was like a registering machine with a patent index. It took in all the data, specified, enumerated them, and then indicated with unmistakable precision what their sum-total of effect precisely was. The index might be wrong, though it pretty generally was right; but nobody could ever mistake for a moment what it meant and where it was.

Few men ever kept apart, in civil matters, so well what, in medical matters, would be called the diagnosis and the prescription. Most men mix, even to themselves, their view of what is with their suggestion of what should be. You could not have made Sir G. Lewis mix the two. His mind on such points was almost a tedious formality. He would say, "The facts proved are so and so; from these there are the following probable inferences. If you wish to alter the present circumstances and to produce others, you must do so and so." When a man came to him with a plan, he asked, "What is your object?" Until he got a plain answer to that, and a proof that the object was good, he never looked at the plan. All this in theory may seem very obvious and very trite. Nothing is so easy as to be sensible on paper. The only true theory of transacting business is a simple matter which has been known for hundreds of years. Any part of that theory in print looks stupid, and not worth saying. Yet in real life, especially in political life, how few great actors are there! In politics the issues to be determined are for the most part plain and simple; but they are exciting, are embedded in rhetoric, and overlaid with irrelevant matter. A certain strong simplicity sweeps all these outside matters away. Talking to Sir G. Lewis on a pending political matter was like reading a chapter of Aristotle's Politics; you might think the view incomplete, but there were the same pregnant strength and matter-of-fact simplicity.

One great advantage of this sort of mind Sir George Lewis noted in an article in the *Edinburgh Review*, which, though when published anonymous, may now be quoted as his: "When Demosthenes was asked what was the first and second and third qualification of an orator, he answered, 'Delivery;' in like manner, if we were asked what is the first and second and third qualification of an English statesman, we would answer, 'Intelligibility.' As in oratory the most eloquent words and the wisest counsels will avail but little if they are not impressed by voice and manner upon the minds of an audience; so integrity and public spirit will fail to command confidence, if the course adopted is intricate or inextricable." Sir G. Lewis could not have described his own sort of mind better if he had been trying to do so; he *could* not be intricate or perplexed. On those rare occasions in politics when it is useful to be ambiguous he failed. When he was Home Secretary he could not diffuse that useful mist over delicate difficulties which was now and then desirable, and in which Sir G. Grey has succeeded. An unbroken fluency in indefinite half-truths was simply impossible to Sir George Lewis. He could not be said to fail in it, for he did not attempt it. His mind was unsuited to ambiguity, whether artful or natural. But on those all but universal occasions when only a plain intelligible statement of an important proposition was required his solid vigour was appropriate. He could never have appealed to the people by the felicitous attraction of his words, but he had an even surer source of popularity in the certain intelligibility of his plans.

The last words of his last book show the sort of grave moderation with which he regarded politics, as wise as any of which he ever made use. They are the judgment in which the reflective man of the world sums up the arguments of the advocates of different forms of government.

"Each one of you, in to-day's discussion, has been able to show specious, perhaps strong, grounds in favour of his opinion.

Monarchicus can say with truth that the testimony of experience is in his favour; that the vast majority of nations, now and at all former periods of time, have been governed by monarchs; and that a plural or republican government is an intricate machine, difficult to work, and constantly tending to relapse into monarchy. Aristocraticus can argue that aristocracy is the government of intelligence and virtue; and that it is a just medium between the two extremes of monarchy and democracy; while Democraticus can dwell upon the splendid vision of a community bound together by the ties of fraternity, liberty, and equality, exempt from hereditary privilege, giving all things to merit, and presided over by a government in which all the national interests are faithfully represented. But even if I were to decide in favour of one of these forms, and against the two others, I should not find myself nearer the solution of the practical problem. A nation does not change the form of its government with the same facility that a man changes his coat. A nation in general only changes the form of its government by means of a violent revolution. This is not a moment when reason is in the ascendant, and when the claims of force can be safely disregarded. The party which is uppermost in the revolution dictates the form of government, and pays little attention to abstract theories, unless it be those which coincide with its own views. The past history of a nation, its present interests, its present passions and antipathies, the advice of favourite leaders, the intervention of foreign governments, all exercise a powerful influence at such a crisis in determining the national decision. Such is the rude process by which one form of government is actually converted into another; very unlike the gentle and rational method which is assumed by the constructors of Utopias. Besides, the political preferences of a people are in general determined by habit and mental association; and though the newly introduced constitution may be intrinsically better than its predecessor, yet the people may dislike it, and refuse it the benefit of a fair trial. It may therefore fail, not from its own defectiveness, but through the ill-will and reluctance of those by whom it is worked.

"There are some rare cases in which a nation has profited by a revolution. Such was the English revolution of 1688, in which the form of the government underwent no alteration, and the person of the king was alone changed. It was the very minimum of a revolution; it was remarkable for the absence of those accompaniments which make a revolution perilous, and which subsequently drew upon it a vindictive reactionary movement. The late Italian revolution has likewise been successful; by it the Italian people have gained a better government, and have improved their political condition. It was brought about by foreign intervention; but its success has been mainly owing to the moderation of the leaders in whom the people had the wisdom to confide, and who have steadily refrained from all revolutionary excesses.

"The history of forcible attempts to improve governments is not, however, cheering. Looking back upon the course of revolutionary movements, and upon the character of their consequences, the practical conclusion which I draw is, that it is the part of wisdom and prudence to acquiesce in any form of government which is tolerably well administered, and affords tolerable security to person and property. I would not, indeed, yield to apathetic despair, or acquiesce in the persuasion that a merely tolerable government is incapable of improvement. I would form an individual model, suited to the character, disposition, wants, and circumstances of the country, and I would make all exertions, whether by action or by writing, within the limits of the existing law, for ameliorating its existing condition, and bringing it nearer to the model selected for imitation; but I should consider the problem of the best form of government as purely ideal, and as unconnected with practice; and should abstain from taking a ticket in the lottery of revolution, unless there was a well-founded expectation that it would come out a prize."

This sober simplicity is not to the taste of many people. Many wish to find in politics a sort of excitement. They wish that public affairs should be managed in a rather theatrical way, in order that they themselves may have the pleasure of reading a stimulating series of brilliant events. People who went to Sir George Lewis for excitement were very likely to be disappointed. He was sure to knock the gloss off things. "People," he would observe, "who know how things are managed, know that the oftener cabinets meet the better. Ignorant persons fancy that when cabinets meet often there is something wrong; but that is a mistake. It is in the long vacation and in the country that some ministers do something brilliant and extraordinary that is much objected to. When ministers get together, they can agree on something plain and satisfactory." He always talked of the cabinet as if it were a homely sort of committee.

At bottom, perhaps, he did not much object to be thought a little commonplace. "In *my* opinion," he said (and perhaps there is no harm in adding that it was in reference to the Suez canal), "in nine cases out of ten cure is better than prevention. If it be ever necessary to hold Egypt, then fight for Egypt. By looking forward to all possible evils, we waste the strength that had best be concentrated in curing the *one* evil which happens." Those who wish that the foreign affairs of England should be managed according to a far-seeing and elaborate policy will not like such voluntary shortsightedness; but the English people themselves rather like to have the national course fixed by evident, palpable, and temporary circumstances.

Some people thought Sir George Lewis obstinate, and in one sense he was so. No one was a better colleague; no one, after full discussion, was readier to take a share in the responsibility for measures of which he did not entirely approve the whole. But though he gave up his proposals, he did not alter his opinion. It may be said of him that he could not alter it. Most men's conclusions are framed upon fluctuating considerations, some of which are very indistinctly present to their minds, and most of which it would puzzle them to state shortly. Sir George Lewis knew exactly what were the facts upon which he grounded his opinion, and what his inference from those facts. Unless you gave him new facts, he could not help drawing the same inference. This was one of the comforts of dealing with him. You always knew exactly where you would find his mind. Unless the data had altered, you might be sure his inference from the data would be unchanged.

It may be added that his inference was almost sure to be exactly sound. His *data* might be limited. As we shall show, there were some kinds of facts which, from a limitation of nature, he did not thoroughly appreciate. When such facts were in question, his conclusion was likely enough to be wrong; for he was arguing rightly on incomplete premisses. But no one could gainsay the correctness of his inference from what he did see. He was the soundest judge of probability we have ever known. The facts being admitted to be so and so, what will be the consequence of those facts? Upon this question few judgments, if any, in England were better than that of Sir George Lewis.

It is this judgment of probability which makes the man of business. The data of life are accessible; their inference uncertain: a sound judgment on these data is the secret of success to him who possesses it, and the reason why others trust him. It is this that men call a *sound* understanding; it is this that Napoleon had in mind when he said that a man should be *carré à la base*.

To this straightforward simplicity of understanding Sir G. Lewis added the most complete education perhaps of any man of his time. He did not believe in what has been called *specialty;* at least he confined it to the lower grades of practical life and literary labour. He has observed: "The permanent officers of a department are the depositories of the official traditions, they are generally referred to by the political head of the office for information upon questions of official practice; and knowledge of this sort acquired in one department would be useless in another. If, for example, the chief clerk of the criminal department of the Home Office were to be transferred to the Foreign Office or to the Admiralty, the special experience which he has acquired in the Home Office, and which is in daily and hourly requisition for the assistance of the Home Secretary, would be utterly valueless to the Foreign Secretary or to the First Lord of the Admiralty. . . . . The same person may be successively at the head of the Home Office, the Foreign Office, the Colonial Office, and the Admiralty; he may be successively President of the Board of Trade and Chancellor of the Exchequer; but to transfer an experienced clerk from one office to another would in general be like transferring a skilful naval officer to the army, or appointing a military engineer officer to command a ship of war. A similar distinction may be observed in other branches of practical life; thus, an architect may direct the execution of different classes of buildings; he may give plans for palaces, churches, courts of justice, bridges, private dwellings; but the subordinate workmen whom he employs retain their separate functions unchanged—a carpenter does not become a mason, a painter or glazier does not become an ironmonger or plasterer."

He sincerely believed (and perhaps acted to excess on the belief) that a well-educated man was competent to undertake any office and to write on any subject. He would have acknowledged the truth of the saying, that the end of education was to make a good *learner*. He was at the day of his death perhaps the best learner in England; there was no sort of definite information, whether relating to public business or to books, which he did not know how to acquire and where to find. Some public men may know where to find as much political information; some scholars may know where to find as much learned information; but what other man knows so precisely the best sources of both kinds of knowledge?

He had a nearly perfect mastery over the keys of knowledge. He derived from Eton and Oxford a perfect knowledge of the classical languages, and he extended it to the day of his death. An article published in *Notes and Queries* within a week or two of that time showed that he had read Mr. Freeman's history,—a rather formidable work, which we elsewhere review, relating to the Ætolian and other Greek leagues, which was only then just published, and which is as much as many busy men read in ten years. Many English statesmen have been good classical scholars, and it is happily not difficult for those who have once well learned the languages of antiquity to retain a familiarity with its masterpieces. The very business of life, indeed, adds to these masterpieces an additional charm, for it reveals touches of discerning thought, and traits of eternal human knowledge, which the writers learned from experience, and which no one can appreciate without it. Mr. Pitt, Mr. Canning, Lord Grenville, the Marquis Wellesley, and many others of our conspicuous statesmen, have had this sort of scholarship. The knowledge of the Classics was to them an intellectual luxury. But Sir George Lewis had a far more laborious scholarship than this. He had read and knew, not only the classical writers themselves, but also terrific German treatises, in many volumes and upon the worst paper, *about* the Classics, which no intellectual voluptuary would touch or look at.

In addition to his Eton and Oxford scholarship, Sir George Lewis was excellently acquainted with modern languages, and had a fair knowledge of mathematics. But a mere enumeration of this sort does not in the least give a notion of the sort of knowledge he had—a phrase, not of the purest English, alone expresses it: it was a knowledge which "turned up" every where. Hardly a subject could be started on which he could not throw an unexpected light, and to which he could not add some new fact. The sort of way in which this happened is aptly enough illustrated by Lord Stanhope's *Miscellanies*, published last year: "Mr. Windham," writes Lord Stanhope, "in his speech of December 9, 1803, observes of the Martello towers that they were so called from a place of that name in Corsica; and I have quoted that sentence from him in my *Life of Pitt*.

"Since my own publication, however, there has been suggested to me, by a very high authority upon all such subjects, a derivation far more probable than Mr. Windham's, and certainly, as I conceive, the right one. S.

"*Right Hon. Sir George C. Lewis to Earl Stanhope.*

[Extract.] "April 2, 1862.

"The origin of Martello towers I believe to have been that when piracy was common in the Mediterranean, and pirates like the Danes made plundering descents upon the coasts, the Italians built towers near the sea in order to keep watch and give warning if a pirate ship was seen to approach the land. This warning was given by striking on a bell with a hammer; and hence these towers were called *Torri da Martello*.

"*The same to the same.*

"May 7, 1862.

"I think that I have discovered, with the assistance of a

friend, the origin of Windham's statement respecting Martello towers. An attack was made on the tower of Mortella, in Corsica, by the British forces both by sea and land, in February 1794. The tower was taken after an obstinate defence, but the two attacking ships were beaten off. This circumstance is likely to have given rise to the confusion between Martello towers generally and this tower of Mortella."

And Lord Stanhope adds some additional facts showing that the derivation suggested by Sir George C. Lewis was correct. Again, in p. 40, Lord Stanhope gives an extract from a letter of Sir George Lewis:

"Lord Grenville told my father that Pitt had formed a plan for abolishing all Customs Duties, and that he would have carried it into effect, if the war of the French Revolution had not broken out, which defeated all his financial and commercial schemes. Lord Grenville said that the amount of the public expenditure at that time rendered such a plan quite feasible."

These are two instances casually occurring in one little volume. But any one who knew Sir George Lewis would know that these sort of miscellaneous odd facts were accumulated in his memory, to what seemed an infinite number, and were at once brought out when they could be useful in illustrating any thing.

As a writer this great knowledge, especially when connected with the strong love of bare truth which led him to acquire that knowledge, was not advantageous to him. He gave a mistaken credit to his readers; he fancied they loved fact and truth as much as he did. "Woe to the writer," goes a wise saying, "that exhausts his subject; his readers are exhausted first." Sir George Lewis always exhausted his subject if he could, and you could not have persuaded him not to do so. In proposing the dowry of the Princess Royal he amused the House of Commons by an elaborate reference, not only to the dowry of George III.'s daughters, who seemed quite far enough back for an impatient audience that wanted its dinner, but also to a perfectly forgotten Princess Royal who was George III.'s aunt. Most of his books are too full of citations and explanations; and to the last he would have been more read and more influential if he had thought often of Sidney Smith's precept, "Now, remember Noah, and be *quick*."

But though a tendency to overlay a subject with superfluous erudition was one of Sir George Lewis's defects, the possession of that available erudition was one of his greatest powers. In the present day the usefulness of a public man is largely measured by the number of subjects which he can get up—Sir George Lewis could get up any subject. There was no probable topic on which he could not form, from the very best sources, with ease and pleasure, a clear, determinate, and exact opinion. His memory helped him. It has been compared to Macaulay's —not that it was equal to such marvellous displays, but that it contained as much, or nearly as much, miscellaneous knowledge. And there was this peculiarity in it. Macaulay's memory, like Niebuhr's, undoubtedly confounded not unfrequently inference and fact: it exaggerated; it gave, not what was in the book, but what a vivid imagination inferred from the book. Sir George Lewis had none of this defect: his memory was a dry memory, just as his mind was a dry light; if he said a thing was at page 10, you might be sure it was at page 10. Somebody called him a "sagacious dictionary," and there was felicity in the expression.

Apart from this massive simplicity of understanding, and this immense accumulation of exact knowledge, there was nothing *very* remarkable in Sir George Lewis. It would be the greatest injustice to his memory, and be the very last thing which he would have desired, to mar the picturesque outlines of his character by concealing its limitations. He had, as we explained, some great qualities in an extraordinary measure, but in other respects he was no more than an ordinary man, and in some he was even less than one.

There was a want of brisk enthusiasm about him both in appearance and in reality. He looked like a scholar, a thinker, and a man of business; he did not look like—he was not—a buoyant ruler or a popular orator. He was quite conscious of this himself, and would sometimes allude to it. The late Mr. Wilson—a very vivacious and active man—who was Secretary of the Treasury when Sir G. Lewis was Chancellor of the Exchequer, used to relate, that when he once was urging something rather strongly, Sir George answered: "No; I can't do it. The fact is, Wilson, you are an animal, and I am a vegetable." Taken literally, this would have been a satire on himself, but it indicated his main defect. He had always, or nearly always, sufficient judgment for a great statesman, but he had not always sufficient impulse.

He was *puzzled* about the passions of mankind; he had so little passion himself that it seemed to him an unknown force which might take men to a distance which it was impossible to foresee, and in a direction that could not be calculated. "When," we have heard him say, "you know a man will act for his own interest, you know how to deal with him; but if he is likely to be guided by feeling, it is impossible to predict his course." Such extreme calmness of mind is not favourable to a statesman; it is good to be without vices, but it is not good to be without temptations. It would always have been a difficulty to Sir G. Lewis that he did not share the impetuous part of human nature whether for good or evil. He was ever liable to impute to a settled design and intellectual self-interest what was in fact owing to an impulse of philanthropy or a gust of mere passion. He was apt to be thought cynical in opinion, though goodnatured in manner and action,—and in some sense he was so. He took too external a view of human nature, and ascribed to consistent selfishness what was really produced by mixed motives and a close combination of good and evil.

He was so defective in the more conspicuous sorts of imagination, that he was often thought to have no imagination. But this was an error. He could conceive well the working of a polity, the operation of a scheme, the details of a plan. His criticism on the working, say of the American constitution, would show great power of conceiving distant causes, and of predicting and analysing strange effects. He had the business imagination. But he had no other. He could not imagine great passions, or overwhelming desires, or involved character; he knew that there were such things, but he had no image of them in his mind and no picture. He was like a man on the edge of a volcano, who dreaded an eruption, but had no vision of the flames. He was thus apt to be out of sympathy with, and even to be impatient of, some elements in ordinary men's judgment. He was a little too critical of public opinion, too critical, that is, for a parliamentary statesman, for one who should try to sympathise with the master whom he must obey. Sir G. Lewis hated exaggeration as much as he could hate any thing,—and popular opinion is always exaggerated. "There is," said Sir Stafford Northcote, "no quality for which Sir George Lewis is more remarkable than for a quiet courage, which emboldens him to give utterance from time to time, and sometimes without any apparent necessity for his doing so, to propositions of the most alarmingly unpopular nature." And such courage is admirable. In this day it is much to have a statesman who, on any occasion and for any object, will withstand public opinion. But such opposition should be reserved for great occasions, and too much must not be expected from the mass of men. A vague tendency and loose approximation to what is right is all we can hope of miscellaneous popular opinion; and it is not wise in a statesman to criticise too nicely, or to attempt to give to the rough practical judgment of men a fine accuracy which it can never in fact possess. Sir G. Lewis was the antithesis of a demagogue; he could not take a test without a qualification; he was sure to distrust, and apt to despise, a popular dogma.

A slight survey—and we have only space or powers for a very slight one—will show that these qualities were as conspicuous in Sir G. Lewis's writings as in his political career. Indeed, if there ever was a man whose mind was always and every where one and the same, Sir George was that man. He had not really a versatile mind, though his pursuits were varied. He was far too modest and wise to aim at what was impossible to him, and nature had given him sharp limitations. It was said by the *Times* of Lord Brougham, "that he might have been any *one* of ten first-rate kinds of men, but that he had tried to be *all* ten, and had failed." Sir G. Lewis had none of this flexibility, and none of this vanity. He never tried to be a great poet or a great orator, or to be any thing else but what nature made him—a shrewd and solid thinker. He had a great faculty of research, but his matter is every where of the same sort. It is the same imperturbable homely sense upon finance in his Budgets, upon the Egyptology of Baron Bunsen in his Ancient Astronomy.

Sir G. Lewis's principal writings may be divided into two classes, the historical and the speculative; and it is hardly too much to say that the whole of the historical are developments in many forms of one central idea. He always devotes himself to the refutation of an hypothesis: some previous writer has elaborated a theory which, Sir G. Lewis maintains, rests on no basis of evidence, and which he wishes to dispel. Some one has seen a *mirage*, and related it as a fact; Sir G. Lewis wishes to dispel the mirage.

His earliest work of this sort was the *Origin and Formation of the Romance Language*. M. Raynouard, a distinguished French scholar, had expounded a very curious and remarkable theory as to the breaking-up of the Latin language. It is certain that good Latin was once spoken at Rome; it is certain that the Romans conquered the rest of Italy, France, and Spain; it is certain that in each of these countries a modern language, analogous to the Latin, and derived from the Latin, is now spoken. How, then, did the Latin break up? how, then, were the new languages formed? M. Raynouard maintained that they were formed by means of an unintermediate language. He held that the Romance language, which was purely spoken in the times of the Troubadours, and which is still corruptly spoken in Provence, was a language once used in the same form all over Europe; that it was the same tongue in France, in Portugal, in Italy, and in Spain; and that as a person who spoke Latin would have been universally intelligible at one time, so a person who spoke Romance would have been universally understood at a subsequent time. This idea of a single diffused

Middle-Age language Sir G. Lewis undertakes to dispel; he thinks it a dream and a theory. He says that the Latin broke up under different circumstances, with different velocities, and in different modifications, in the different states of Europe. There was a certain general resemblance, he holds, in the changes which were in progress, whether in Italy or Spain, France or Portugal, because those changes in all these countries were produced by the same causes. The invasion of the barbarians, the fall of the Roman empire, and the somewhat mysterious movement which tends to break up the old rhetorical and synthetic languages, and replace them by analytic and conversational languages, were common causes, operating alike in all countries where Latin had been spoken. But though the change in all the languages was in the same general direction, it was not at the same rate, nor was it identical in details. There has, according to Sir G. Lewis, never been a single vernacular language spoken through Europe since Latin was so spoken. The theory of Raynouard is, according to Sir G. Lewis's characteristic language, an "unsupported and imaginary hypothesis."

This essay on the Romance language was republished by Sir George within a few months of his death, and is worth reading as an illustration of his mode of thought and argument. The burden of proof is upon Raynouard. He says there was a common language at a certain date; where, then, is that language? what were its parts of speech, its verbs, its pronouns, and its substantives? Let us look at them in the different countries of Europe at the time in question, and prove that the language was uniform by the identity of its forms. Accordingly Sir G. Lewis goes through the earliest known forms of the Italian, Spanish, Provençal, and French languages, and he shows that at the earliest stage they were *not* identical. He characteristically says, "The importance and interest of the philological problem which is treated in the following pages are much increased by the fact that it lies entirely within the historical period; and that not only the original and the derivative languages, but also the circumstances attending the transition, are known by authentic evidence and by an unbroken tradition. It is therefore a problem which admits of solution by demonstrative arguments, and without recourse to a series of hypotheses and conjectures, weakening as the chain lengthens." Sir G. Lewis revels, we may almost say, in the plentifulness of the evidence. He has lists of the "tenses and inflexions of Romance nouns," "new Romance nouns formed by affixes," of the degrees of comparison, pronouns, and numerals, in the Romance language, with endless similar information. He elaborately compares the earliest stages of the Italian, Spanish, and French languages with the earliest form of the Provençal; and he shows clearly and fully, what was probable enough in itself, that the earliest forms of these languages differ; that they have pursued a different history; that the Provençal is only one of the derived languages, with a history of its own; that there never was any one derived language generally diffused through Europe; that as soon as the use of Latin ended, distinctions of speech began. A very close political observer, who did not himself easily relinquish any thing, once described Sir G. Lewis as the most pertinacious man he had ever known: "He returns," it was added, "to the charge again and again, and he hardly ever fails." This was said by one who seldom read any thing, who had read very little of Sir G. Lewis's writing, who assuredly had never opened the treatise on the Romance languages. But if he had studied the treatise, he could not have described it better. Sir George returns again and again, with verbs and pronouns, to the charge, and he hardly ever fails. A student who continued to believe Raynouard's theory must be impervious to argument and detail-proof.

The largest of all Sir G. Lewis's writings, and his acutest, strikes with the same tactics at a nobler game upon a larger field. The reception of Niebuhr's *History of Rome* is one of the most curious of recent literary phenomena. Though he really is a bold theorist on Roman history, though his narrative is by admission constructed by the imagination, he has obtained something like the credit due to an almost contemporary authority—to a person who had some special information. He believed he had acquired, by long study and brooding, a special faculty, a peculiar divination. He tells us, "All my faculties were directed to a single object for sixteen months, without any intermission except now and then for a few days. My sight grew dim in its passionate efforts to pierce into the obscurity of the subject, and unless I was to send forth an incomplete work, which sooner or later would have had to be wholly remodelled, I was compelled to wait for what Time might gradually bring forth. Nor has he been niggardly, but, though slowly, has granted me one discovery after another." "The true account, it must be owned, is not always the most probable. But when an inquirer, after gazing for years with ever renewed undeviating steadfastness, sees the history of mistaken, misrepresented, and forgotten events rise out of mists and darkness, and assume substance and shape, as the scarcely visible aerial form of the nymph in the Sclavonic tale takes the body of an earthly maiden beneath the yearning gaze of love,—when by unwearied and conscientious examination he is continually gaining a clearer insight into the connexion of all its parts, and discerns that immediate expression of reality which emanates from life,—he has a right to demand that others, who merely throw their looks by the way on the region where he lives and has taken up his home, should not deny the correctness of his views, because they perceive nothing of the kind. The learned naturalist, who has never left his native town, will not recognise the animal's track, by which the hunter is guided: and if any one, on going into Benvenuto's prison, when his eyes had for months been accustomed to see the objects around him, had asserted that Benvenuto like himself could not distinguish any thing in the darkness, he would surely have been somewhat presumptuous." It is beautiful to see the heavy care and sluggish diligence with which Sir G. Lewis reckons all this poetry back into mere prose.

"The history of Niebuhr," he tells us, "has thus opened more questions than it has closed, and it has set in motion a large body of combatants, whose mutual variances are not at present likely to be settled by deference to a common authority, or by the recognition of any common principle.

"The main cause of the great multiplicity and wide divergence of opinions, which characterise the recent researches into early Roman history, is the defective method, which not only Niebuhr and his followers, but most of his opponents, have adopted. Instead of employing those tests of credibility which are consistently applied to modern history, they attempt to guide their judgment by the indications of internal evidence, and assume that the truth can be discovered by an occult faculty of historical divination. Hence, the task which they have undertaken resembles an inquiry into the internal structure of the earth, or into the question, whether the stars are inhabited. It is an attempt to solve a problem, for the solution of which no sufficient data exist.

"The consequence is, that ingenuity and labour can produce nothing but hypotheses and conjectures, which may be supported by analogies, and may sometimes appear specious and attractive, but can never rest on the solid foundation of proof. There will, therefore, be a series of such conjectural histories; each successive writer will reject all or some of the guesses of his predecessors, and will propose some new hypotheses of his own. But the treatment of early Roman history, though it will be constantly moving, will not advance; it will not be stationary, but neither will it be progressive; it will be unfixed and changeable, but without receiving any improvement; and it will perpetually revolve in the same hopeless circle. Like the search after the philosopher's stone, or the elixir of life, it will be constantly varying its aspect, under the treatment of different professors of the futile science; but truth and certainty, the aim of all rational employment of the intellect, will always be equally distant. Each new system of the early Roman constitution will be only (to use Paley's words) one guess among many; whereas he alone discovers who proves. There is indeed no doubt that long habit, combined with a happy talent, may enable a person to discern the truth where it is invisible to ordinary minds, possessing no peculiar advantages. This may be observed, not only in historical researches, but in every other department of knowledge. In order, however, that the truth so perceived should recommend itself to the convictions of others, it is a necessary condition that it should admit of proof which they can understand. Newton might have perceived, by a rapid and intuitive sagacity, the connexion between the fall of an apple and the attraction of the earth to the sun; but unless he could have demonstrated that connexion by arguments which were intelligible and satisfactory to the scientific world, his discovery would have been useless, except as a mere suggestion. In like manner, we may rejoice that the ingenuity and learning of Niebuhr should have enabled him to advance many novel hypotheses and conjectures respecting events in the early history, and respecting the form of the early constitution, of Rome. But unless he can support those hypotheses by sufficient evidence, they are not entitled to our belief. It is not enough for a historian to claim the possession of a retrospective second-sight, which is denied to the rest of the world; of a mysterious doctrine, revealed only to the initiated. Unless he can prove as well as guess; unless he can produce evidence of the fact, after he has intuitively perceived its existence, his historical system cannot be received. The oases of truth which he discerns amidst the trackless expanses of fiction and legend, may be real; but until their existence can be verified by positive testimony, we have no certainty that these 'green spots in memory's waste' may not be mere mirage and optical delusion. It is an excellence in a historian of antiquity, who has sufficient data to proceed upon, that he should form a vivid conception of the events described; that he should live, as it were, among the persons whose acts he recounts; and that he should carry his reader back into the bygone times in which his drama is placed. On the other hand, it is a fault in the modern writers who first narrated Roman history that they should have related the events as if they had never happened. But when there is a want of solid evidence, we do not render the history true by treating the events as if they were real."

Almost the whole of Sir G. Lewis's two volumes are an expansion and development of this passage. He turns Niebuhr's revelations into fancies, and his divinations into mere guesses. Since Sir G. Lewis's work on Roman history, no English scholar at least has ventured to defend Niebuhr's essentially arbitrary treatment of legendary history. An historian, it is now agreed, cannot accept one legend because it suits a preconceived hypothesis, and reject another because it is inconsistent with that hypothesis. He must take both or must reject both. We may not, and perhaps have not, attained to a complete and accepted theory of the value of traditional evidence; there are many points on that subject which require much more delicate handling than they have received. But no one will ever revive Niebuhr's notion of an occult tact. A long acquaintance and a familiar meditation upon any sort of *truth* does indeed give an instinctive sense with respect to that truth. A constant habit of comparing accurate truth with legendary versions of the same truth would really give a student a verified knowledge, and even a quick instinctive idea what sort of inventions popular tradition is prone to. But Niebuhr had studied legends as to times of which there are only legends; he had not compared truth with fiction, but fiction with fiction. He had not acquired a test of truth by a contact with truth; but his hot brain had brooded so long on a favourite subject that he mistook its own fancies for realities. Sir G. Lewis did not mistake them.

It is sometimes said that Sir G. Lewis would accept no fact of which there was not contemporary evidence, and that he set no value whatever upon any tradition in any case. But this is a mischievous exaggeration. Sir G. Lewis was not the most exacting of historical critics. He considered Polybius as too strict and sceptical. Polybius thought that an historian without books, and with only oral information, could not be sure of events more than twenty years before his own birth. Sir G. Lewis held that a sort of memory of leading events, accurate in substance though probably inaccurate in detail, might be preserved by tradition for about a hundred years, and that special events from special circumstances might be remembered longer; but that in such cases it was only the general outline which could be faintly traced, and only events of interest that would be preserved. After about a hundred years—after the period about which a man could hear from his grandfather—he thought, for the most part, there was no reliable knowledge.

Sir G. Lewis's Ancient Astronomy might seem a deviation from his general studies. Astronomy is a physical science, and Sir George, though well enough acquainted with such sciences, did not profess to have made them a special study. He was often enough heard to say, half in jest but still with a certain meaning, "That on matters of practical interest the physical sciences were less certain than the moral: as long as you are dealing with abstractions, with perfectly elastic beams and a world without fiction, physical science is quite certain; but as soon as you introduce the actual conditions of life, and talk of the real world in which we live, most physical sciences become as uncertain as any moral science. Take, for example, physic. If you will question your medical man, you will find that, if he cures you, it will not be by the goodness of his *arguments*. A great deal of what is set down upon that subject in grave treatises appears to me to be inconsistent rubbish. And my experience at the War Office shows me that scientific evidence may be accumulated in almost any quantity for any given invention and against any given invention." A man who talked in this spirit was scarcely likely to devote many hours out of the scanty leisure of English public life to the history of physical science. Nor was Sir G. Lewis attracted to the subject by its abstract scientific interest. He is at great pains to explain that he makes no pretension to such abstract mathematical knowledge as was possessed by Delambre and others, his predecessors, and that astronomy is conversant with obvious realities which have always excited human curiosity. In truth, he encountered ancient astronomy in his investigations of ancient history. He found many pretensions to ancient scientific knowledge which it was much in his way to scrutinise and disbelieve; he was in all his inquiries compelled to deal with ancient chronology, which is not to be understood except with reference to the astronomical notions of those who framed it. Such questions as, Was there a Roman year of ten months? met him at every step. He was thus led to write a clear, compendious, and popular account of the rise of astronomical science in ancient Greece. It is not exhaustive, as most of his treatises are exhaustive; it is not, like his other treatises, supported by an available accumulation of all appropriate knowledge, for he was in some places cramped by the deficiency of his mathematics. It is not, therefore, one of the works on which his fame as a great scholar will hereafter rest. But it is a very clear, sensible, and interesting account of the interesting subject to which it relates.

But bound up with the history of Ancient Astronomy, and having but a very slender relation to it, are three essays: one on the Early History and Chronology of the Egyptians; another on the Early History and Chronology of the Assyrians; and a third on the Navigation of the Phœnicians. Here Sir G. Lewis is all himself, dealing with the subjects which he liked best, and dealing with them as he liked best. Any body who wishes to know the sort of mind he had may read—and it is not unamusing reading—his criticism on the Egyptian history of Baron Bunsen. At the risk of tediousness we will condense a little of it:

"The principal manipulator," says Sir G. Lewis, "of the ancient Egyptian chronology is Baron Bunsen, who, in his recent work on Egypt, has avowedly applied the method of Niebuhr to Egyptian antiquity. Now the method with which Niebuhr treated the early history of Rome was to reject the historical narrative handed down by ancient, and generally received by modern writers; and to substitute for it a new narrative reconstructed on an arbitrary hypothetical basis of his own. Every thing that is original and peculiar in Niebuhr's historical method, and in its results, is indeed unsound. But it possessed advantages, when employed in the transmutation of Roman antiquity, which are wanting to it when applied to Egyptian antiquity. The early Roman history, whatever may be its authenticity, presents at least a full and continuous narrative, most parts of which are related in discordant versions by different classical writers. As none of these versions rests on an ascertained foundation, or can be traced to coeval attestation, great facility is afforded for ingenious conjecture, for bold and startling combinations, for hypothetical reconstruction by means of specious analogies, and for the display of imposing paradox and dazzling erudition. But the so-called history of ancient Egypt consists of little more than chronology. It is, for the most part, merely a string of royal names. Now this is a most unattractive field for the hypothetical historian: he is condemned to make bricks without straw. Instead of demolishing and rebuilding constitutions, instead of creating new states of society out of obscure fragments of lost writers, he is reduced to a mere arithmetical process. Accordingly, the operations of Bunsen and other modern critics upon the ancient history of Egypt rather resemble the manipulation of the balance-sheet of an insolvent company by a dexterous accountant (who, by transfers of capital to income, by the suppression or transposition of items, and by the alteration of bad into good debts, can convert a deficiency into a surplus), than the conjectures of a speculative historian, who undertakes to transmute legend into history.

"Egyptology has a historical method of its own. It recognises none of the ordinary rules of evidence; the extent of its demands upon our credulity is almost unbounded. Even the writers on ancient Italian ethnology are modest and tame in their hypotheses, compared with the Egyptologists. Under their potent logic all identity disappears; every thing is subject to become any thing but itself. Successive dynasties become contemporary dynasties; one king becomes another king, or several other kings, or a fraction of another king; one name becomes another name; one number becomes another number; one place becomes another place.

"In order to support and illustrate these remarks, it would be necessary to analyse Bunsen's reconstruction of the scheme of Egyptian chronology. Such an analysis would be inconsistent with the main object of the present work; but a few examples will serve to characterise his method.

"Sesostris is the great name of Egyptian antiquity. Even the builders of the pyramids and of the labyrinth sink into insignificance by the side of this mighty conqueror. Nevertheless, his historical identity is not proof against the dissolving and recompounding processes of the Egyptological method. Bunsen distributes him into portions, and identifies each portion with a different king. Sesostris, as we have already stated, stands in Manetho's list as third king of the twelfth dynasty, at 3320 B.C., and a notice is appended to his name clearly identifying him with the Sesostris of Herodotus. Bunsen first takes a portion of him, and identifies it with Tosorthrus (written Sesorthus by Eusebius), the second king of the third dynasty, whose date is 5119 B.C., being a difference in the dates of 1799 years—about the same interval as between Augustus Cæsar and Napoleon; he then takes another portion, and identifies it with Sesonchosis, a king of the twelfth dynasty; a third portion of Sesostris is finally assigned to himself. It seems that these three fragments make up the entire Sesostris; who, in this plural unity, belongs to the Ancient Empire; but it is added that the Greeks confounded him with Ramesses, or Ramses, of the New Empire, a king of the nineteenth dynasty, whose date is 1255 B.C.; who, again, was confounded with his father, Sethos; which name again was transmuted into Sethosis and Sesosis.

"Lepsius agrees with Bunsen that Sesostris in the Manethonian list, who stands in the twelfth dynasty, at 3320 B.C., is not Sesostris; but, instead of elevating him to the third dynasty, brings him down to the nineteenth dynasty, and identifies him with Sethos, 1326 B.C.; chiefly on account of a statement of Manetho, preserved by Josephus, that Sethos first subjugated Cyprus and Phœnicia, and afterwards Assyria and Media, with other countries further to the east. Lepsius, moreover, holds that Ramses, the son of Sethos, was, like his father, a great conqueror, but that the Greeks confounded both father and son under the name of Sesostris.

"We therefore see that the two leading Egyptologists, Bunsen and Lepsius, differing in other respects, agree in thinking that Sesostris is not Sesostris. The notice appended to his name in Manetho, which identifies him with the Sesostris of Herodotus, Diodorus, and other Greek writers, is regarded by Lepsius as spurious. But here their agreement stops. One assigns Sesostris to what is called the Old, the other to what is called the New Empire, separating his respective dates by an interval of 3793 years. What should we think, if a new school of writers on the history of France, entitling themselves Francologists, were to arise, in which one of the leading critics were to deny that Louis XIV. lived in the seventeeth century, and were to identify him with Hercules, or Romulus, or Cyrus, or Alexander the Great, or Cæsar, or Charlemagne; while another leading critic of the same school, agreeing in the rejection of the received hypothesis as to his being the successor of Louis XIII., were to identify him with Napoleon I. and Louis Napoleon?"

It is well known that all these conjectures on early Egyptian history are supported by the recent discovery of the true meaning of the long-unintelligible hieroglyphic inscriptions. But Sir George Lewis does not believe they have discovered their meaning. He states the problem certainly with formidable force. It is something like this: "Here you have inscriptions composed in a lost *language*, and written down in a *character* which is also lost. Is it to be believed that the imagination of man can first guess rightly the system of written symbols, and then guess the meaning too? It is the old story; you have to interpret the dream without knowing what it is. Even supposing that you have found out, as you think, one set of written symbols, and made a language in these symbols which you can read, who will assure us that some other person will not find another set of symbols with another set of meanings in a new imaginary language?" "The question," says Sir George Lewis, "as to the possibility of interpreting a language whose tradition has been lost, is further confused by a deceptive analogy derived from the process of deciphering. A cipher is a contrivance for disguising the alphabetical writing of a known language by a conventional change of characters. The explanation of this conventional change is called the *Key*. If a document written in cipher falls into the possession of a stranger ignorant of the Key, and if he can conjecture with tolerable certainty the language in which it is written, he can proceed to apply to it the rules for deciphering, which are founded upon the comparative frequency of certain letters and certain words in the given language. This process, if the document be tolerably long, is almost infallible. It is difficult to devise a cipher, sufficiently simple for frequent use, which cannot be deciphered by a skilful and experienced decipherer. But this operation supposes the language to be understood; it is a merely alphabetical process;

it does not determine the meaning of a single word; it merely strips the disguise off a word, and reproduces it in its ordinary orthography. No process similar to deciphering can afford the smallest assistance towards discovering the signification of an unknown word, written in known alphabetical characters. The united ingenuity of the most skilful decipherers in Europe could not throw any light upon an Etruscan or Lycian inscription, or interpret a single sentence of the Eugubine Tables. In like manner, assuming an Egyptian hieroglyphical text to be correctly read into alphabetical characters, no process of deciphering could detect the meaning of the several words."

It is possible, for example, that Champollion may have discovered by comparison on some proper names some phonetic characters, and it is also possible that the ancient Egyptian may have had some analogy with the modern Coptic,—the same sort of analogy, perhaps, which Italian bears to Latin. But it is very difficult to be satisfied that any great knowledge could be derived from the spelling of a few letters, and the guessing of a few words as expressed in these letters. "Where," says Sir George Lewis, "the tradition of a language is lost, but its affinity with a known language is ascertained or presumed, the attempts to restore the significations of words proceed upon the hypothesis that the etymology of the word can be determined by its resemblance, more or less close, to a word in the known language, and that the etymology of the word is a certain guide to its meaning. But although there is a close affinity between etymology and meaning, yet etymology alone cannot be taken as a sure index to meaning. When the signification of a word is ascertained, it is often difficult to determine the etymology. The Lexilogus of Buttmann, the Romance Dictionary of Diez —in fact, any good etymological vocabulary—will furnish ample evidence of this truth. But when the process is inverted, and it is proposed to determine the signification of the words of an entire language from etymological guesses, unassisted by any other knowledge, the process is necessarily uncertain and inconclusive, and can be satisfactory only to a person who has already made up his mind to accept *some* system of interpretation.

"Thus in Italian the word *troja* signifies a sow. Diez refers the origin of this word to the old Latin expression *porcus Trojanus*, which meant a pig stuffed with other animals and served for the table; the name being an allusion to the Trojan horse. He conceives that this phrase first became *porco di troja*, and afterwards *troja* simply, with the signification of a pregnant sow. Assuming this etymology to be true, what possible ingenuity could have enabled any body to invert the process, and to discover the meaning by the etymology, if the meaning were unknown?"

The alphabet of Baron Bunsen is very complicated. He has four classes and an extra, or later class. He has 1000 characters altogether:

Ideographics	620
Determinatives	164
Phonetics	130
Mixed	55
Later alphabet	100
	1069

And he can read a very large number of words; but we are not surprised to hear that "the system of reading the hieroglyphic characters, as expounded by the Egyptologists, is flexible and arbitrary. It involves the hypothesis of homophones; that is to say, of a plurality of signs for the same sound. It likewise involves a mixture of ideographic and phonetic symbols."

Altogether, though Sir George Lewis may not be right in his bold assertion that *no* early Egyptian history is possible, he is clearly successful in proving that Baron Bunsen's history is untrue. As he expelled the conjectures of Niebuhr from Roman history, so he has expelled the conjectures of Niebuhr's great pupil from Egyptian history. Nobody who reads Sir George Lewis can doubt that Bunsen, for the most part, indulges in conjecture as to the language, as to the written character, and as to the history of ancient Egypt. *His* theories in future will not be accepted as facts. A better feat of iconoclasm has seldom been performed.

These historical works might well have exhausted the leisure of a man almost always occupied in civil business. But Sir George Lewis wrote another long series of books on philosophical politics also. We have not left ourselves much space to speak of them at great length, and we do not think that they need be spoken of at such great length as his historical works. We think that they represent less perfectly the best parts of his mind, and that they bear more marks of his deficiencies.

The earliest and among the most curious is an essay on the *Use and Abuse of certain Political Terms*, published in 1832. It is curiously characteristic of Sir G. Lewis that, at a time when England was convulsed by the almost revolutionary struggle of the Reform Bill, when all Europe still gazed with wonder at the prosperous effect of the most happy of French revolutions, Sir G. Lewis should have sat down, to write not on the facts of political revolution, but on the *words* of political science. After he became a practical statesman he became more alive to political passions and less occupied with political terms; but to the last he was too apt to wonder at great conflicts, and to be pleased with verbal inquiries. In 1833 he was under the mastery of a remarkable teacher. The late Mr. Austin had little fame in his lifetime, and was so discouraged by neglect that he could not nerve himself to complete great works, of which he had finished what most men would consider the difficult part, and had only to add that which most people would think the easy part. He in this point resembled Coleridge. That great thinker has left no work which embodies his philosophy, and yet his philosophy has permeated his generation. Mr. Austin seized hold, some thirty years ago, of several strong minds, and by the help of these great minds he greatly influenced his time. You will find thoughts distinctly traceable to him far away among people who never heard of him. His few lectures and his years of conversation were a peculiar source of nice expression and accurate thought for more than half a century; a little bit of just though almost pedantic thought cropped suddenly up in our crude and hasty English life. Thirty years ago Mr. Austin, at the London University, explained what may be called the necessary part of political science, and illustrated it by the best of all illustrations—Roman law. He analysed not a particular government, but what is common to all governments; not one law, but what is common to all laws; not political communities in their features of diversity, but political communities in their features of necessary resemblance. He gave politics not an interesting aspect, but a new aspect; for, by giving men a steady view of what political communities *must* be, he stopped in the bud many questions as to what they ought to be, or ought not to be. As a gymnastic of the intellect, and as a purifier, Mr. Austin's philosophy is to this day admirable,—even in its imperfect remains; a young man who will study it will find that he has gained something which he wanted, but something which he did not *know* that he wanted; he has clarified a part of his mind which he did not know needed clarifying. Sir G. Lewis was deeply penetrated by this abstract teaching; to the last day of his life, in the unphilosophical atmosphere of the War Office, he would use the phrases of, and would like allusions to, this philosophy. One source of his power as a political thinker was, that he had, under Mr. Austin's guidance, studied political questions as it were in their skeleton. Once a jurist, always a jurist. The vast and easy command of the whole sources of juridical literature which Sir G. Lewis showed in his essay *On Foreign Jurisdiction, and the Extradition of Criminals*, and elsewhere, is largely due to his early studies. Yet it may be doubted whether Mr. Austin's influence was entirely favourable to him. A certain school of thinkers magnify the effects of human language. Calm and simple-minded students, when they see the hasty world of human beings using inaccurate and vague words, are apt to ascribe all their errors to those words, and to believe that, if you could put human language right, you would set the world in order. There is no greater mistake. Men are mainly deceived by their passions and their interests; they care but little for abstract truth, and rush forward to small, petty, but concrete, objects. They catch hastily at any sort of word that justifies what they wish to do, and if it sounds well care little for fallacies and ambiguities. The language is inaccurate no doubt, but it is a symptom only of a mental disease. You cannot calm the passions of men by defining their words. Mr. Austin's school was apt to forget this. The early treatise of Sir G. C. Lewis on the *Use and Abuse of Political Terms*, and some of his later too, are not exempt from this defect, though his strong sense and really practical turn of mind always kept it in check. A person wishing to watch his intellectual history, should look carefully at this book; it is a series of exercises in Mr. Austin's class-room.

A more serious defect mars the popularity of Sir G. Lewis's writings, and we think Mr. Austin is partly to blame for that too. Mr. Austin was always talking of the "formidable community of fools;" he had no popularity; little wish for popularity; little respect for popular judgment. This is a great error. The world is often wiser than any philosopher. "There is some one," said a great man of the world, "wiser than Voltaire, and wiser than Napoleon, *c'est tout le monde.*" Popular judgment on popular matters is crude and vague, but it is right. And it is even more certain that a great writer on morals and politics ought not to adopt a mode of writing which excludes him from popularity. Mr. Austin's mere style did this for him. He wrote on the principle that people would be sure to comprehend what was completely expressed, but could never be trusted to supply an *hiatus* in what was incompletely expressed. His writings accordingly read like a legal document; every possible case is provided for, every ambiguity is guarded against, and—hardly any one can read them. The ordinary human mind cannot bear that method of expressing every thing; it is more puzzled by such elaborate precision than by any thing else. Sir G. Lewis did not err in mere language, but he erred in treatment. Mr. Austin expands all thoughts, new and old, at just the same length; and he taught Sir G. Lewis to do so also. In the present state of the moral sciences, this is absurd. Much of them is very well, though a little vaguely, understood by the world at large. It is often of great consequence to reduce them to a principle; it is often of great importance to add new truths, and to give a new edge to old truth. But it is not advisable to begin with a principle and to work steadily through all its possible applications at the *same* length. If you do, the reader will say, "How this man *does* prose! why, I knew that;" and he did know it. Some of the applications of a principle are new, and should be treated at length; some are of pressing importance, and should be treated at length too; but all the consequences should not be worked out like a sum. An atmosphere of commonplace hangs over long moral didactics, and an equal expansion of what the world knows and what it does not know will not be read by the world.

Sir G. Lewis did his fame serious harm by neglecting this maxim. He wrote, for example, *An Essay on the Influence of Authority in Matters of Opinion*, which was described by a hasty thinker as a book to prove that when "you wanted to know any thing, you asked some one who knew something about it." The essay certainly abounds in acute remarks and interesting illustrations, and if these remarks and these illustrations had been printed separately, it would have been a good book. But the systematic treatment has been fatal to it. The different kinds and cases of authority are so systematically enumerated, that the reader yawns and forgets.

The case is even worse with his great treatise *On the Methods of Observation and Reasoning in Politics*, in two large volumes. Scarcely any one has read these volumes, and those who have are sure that their bulk was a mistake. They are written upon the principle that "two and two make four" is as much unknown to the mass of men as the integral calculus. Easy things are explained exactly with the same care as difficult things, and in consequence very few people read the explanations. There are many admirable parts and essays in the book. It contains an account and criticism of "political induction" as described by Mr. Mill, and an account and criticism of jurisprudence as described and understood by Mr. Austin. Both these discussions are very good, and the speculations of the two thinkers are well spliced together; but they are overlaid with long explanations of what requires no explanation, and discussions of what need never have been discussed. Charles Fox used to say of a very dull but able speaker, "I always listen to that man, and then speak his speech over again." A dishonest writer might well do so with Sir G. Lewis's writings. There are many thoughts, and a million facts in them, which the world would be glad to hear, though it cannot extract them from the rest. A writer of this sort naturally did not look for profit from his laborious writings; few men have done more gratuitous work. He was disposed to agree with Mr. Mill, that the notion of "thinkers giving out doctrines for bread was a mistake," and even to hold that speculators should *pay* for the opportunity of placing their opinions before the world.

We own that we much regret this misconception of the conditions of modern writing, now that Sir G. Lewis's career has been cut short in the midst. When he had life before him, it seemed less important that he should throw away fame; but now that all is over we wish he had desired popularity more, for he would have been remembered better. He really had considerable powers of pointed writing. The little treatise at the head of this Article shows that when he did not aim at completeness he could write easily that which would be easily read. He had not, indeed, the powers of a great literary artist; it was not in his way to look at style as an alluring art; he wanted to express his opinion, and cared for nothing else. He had no literary vanity; and without the vanity that loves applause few indeed cultivate the tact that gains applause. "If you can do without the world," says the cynic, "the world can do without you;" and it is as true to say that few, if any, gain literary fame who do not long and hunger after it.

As a sort of compensation, Sir G. Lewis rose more rapidly as a parliamentary statesman than any of his contemporaries. He was in the first rank of the Liberal party, yet he entered parliament five years after Mr. Cardwell, fifteen years after Mr. Gladstone, nineteen years after Sir C. Wood, and forty years after Lord Palmerston. It is curious at first sight that he should have done so. He was not an attractive speaker, he wanted animal spirits, and detested an approach to any thing theatrical. He had very considerable command of exact language, but he had no impulse to use it. If it was his duty to speak, he spoke; but he did not want to speak when it was not his duty. Silence was no pain, and oratory no pleasure to him. If mere speaking were the main qualification for an influence in Parliament,—if, as is often said, parliamentary government be a synonym for the government of talkers and *avocats*,—Sir G. Lewis would have had no influence, would never have been a parliamentary ruler. Yet we once heard a close and good observer say: "George Lewis's influence in the House is something wonderful; whatever he proposes has an excellent chance of being carried. He excites no opposition, and he commands great respect, and generally he carries his plan." The House of Commons, according to the saying, is wiser than any one in it. There is an elective affinity for solid sense in a practical assembly of educated Englishmen which always operates, and which rarely errs. Sir G. Lewis's influence was great not only on his own side of the House, but on the other. He had, indeed, probably more real weight with moderate Conservatives than with extreme Liberals. Enterprise neither seemed to be nor was his forte, and bold men thought him rather tame. His influence was like that of Lord Palmerston: he was liked by the moderate members, whether Whigs or Tories, who think just alike, whatever they call themselves; and who are likely nowadays to rule the country, whatever name the party in power may chance to bear. He was a safe man, a fair man, and an unselfish man. He had a faculty of "patient labour," which, as he himself remarked, "*was as sure* to be appreciated when Englishmen meet together to transact business, as wit or eloquence;" and therefore it was that he had great influence in the House of Commons; therefore it was that he rose rapidly.

He filled three cabinet offices; the first was that of Chancellor of the Exchequer, and this was the one which he liked best, and for which he conceived himself best qualified. He had no easy time, however, during his actual tenure of the office. He had to find money for the Crimean war, the heaviest draft on the resources of the exchequer since Waterloo; he had to break the "fundamental law of the currency," as he called it, Peel's Act, in the unexpected panic of 1857. He gave universal satisfaction as finance minister, and especial satisfaction in the City. He was clear, considerate, and it was at once felt that argument would move him if good argument could be found. He had to borrow much money, and he so managed as to be able to borrow it without undue charge to the state, and with that immediate success which sustains the credit of the state, and secures a *prestige* in the money-market. It is scarcely possible to speak of him as finance minister without alluding to his differences with Mr. Gladstone in the cabinet and out of it. Yet it is not possible to discuss the subject accurately. Mr. Gladstone's views of the budget of 1860, we all know; but Sir G. Lewis's views have never been set forth at length, and it is not wise to base an argument on scraps of oral conversations. It may be as well, however, to point out that, in addition to their intrinsic and considerable differences of temperament and character, they approached finance from two different and even opposite points of view. Mr. Gladstone is the successor, the legitimate inheritor of the policy of Sir R. Peel. He made his reputation as a financier and as a statesman by the budget of 1853, in which the prominent object is to remove old taxes, that cramp and harass industry. He regards the public purse as donative, out of which trade may be augmented and industry developed. Sir R. Peel used the public purse in that manner, and Mr. Gladstone has done so also. Sir G. Lewis was led, perhaps from temperament, and certainly from circumstances, to take a stricter and simpler view of finance. He came into office on a sudden, during a great war, and he had to find the resources for that war. He had to consider, not how taxation could be adjusted so as to help trade, but how the exchequer could be filled to pay soldiers. On all financial matters he looked solely at the balance of the account, Will there be a deficit, or will there not be? Forms of account, and all minor matters, were in his mind of very small importance; he looked to the simple question, How much will there be in the till at the end of the year? With two such different prepossessions as these, it is no wonder that men so intrinsically different as Sir G. Lewis and Mr. Gladstone did not very well agree upon finance; it is rather a wonder that they could act together at all. There is no use, over Sir G. Lewis's grave, in reviving financial controversies; every body will now admit that while he was in office and responsible he was a sound and sure Chancellor of the Exchequer.

In the panic of 1857, we have heard, he was even amusing. His perfect impassivity and collectedness contrasted much with the excitement of eager men; and in a panic most men are eager. A deputation of Scotch bankers attended at the Treasury to ask Sir George to induce the Bank of England to make advances to them in certain possible cases. Sir George said, "Ah, gentlemen, if I were to interfere with the discretion of the Bank, there would be a run upon me much greater than any which there has ever been upon you." He was a man who probably *could* not lose his head.

At the Home Office he had the opportunity of displaying great judicial faculties. The Home Office is the high court of appeal in cases of criminal justice. When any one is to be hung, it is almost always argued before the Home Secretary that he should not be hung. If Sir George Lewis had practised at the bar, for which he studied, he would have been a bad advocate; his mind was not futile in ambiguous fallacies, and was incapable of artificial belief; and a great pleader should excel in these. One of the greatest judges of our generation, when at the bar, could only state the point once, and when the court did not understand him, could only mutter, "What fools they are! awful fools, infernal fools!" Sir George Lewis would not have indulged in these epithets, but he would have been nearly as little able to invent ingenious suggestions and out-of-the-way arguments. He probably would have said, "I have explained the matter. If the court *will* not comprehend it, *I* cannot make them." But no man was fitter for a judge than himself. He would never have shirked labour,—which is not unknown even among judges,—and his lucid exposition of substantial reasons would have been consulted by students for years. At the Home

Office he could not display all these qualities, but he was able to display some of them.

At the War Office he shone far less. It did not suit his previous pursuits; and no other man with such pursuits would have taken it, or, indeed, would have been asked to take it. He pushed in this case too far the notion that an able and educated man can master any subject, and is fit for any office. The constitutional habit in England of making a civilian supreme over military matters, though we believe a most wise habit, has its objections, and may easily look absurd. It *did* look rather absurd when the most pacific of the pacific, the most erudite of the erudite, Sir George Lewis, was placed at the head of the War Department. In great matters, it cannot be denied, he did well. When the capture of the *Trent* made a war with the Federal States a pressing probability, the arrangements were admitted to be admirable. Much of the credit must belong in such a case to military and other subordinates,—all the details must be managed by them; but the superior minister must have his credit too. He brought to a *focus* all which was done; he summed-up the whole; he could say distinctly why every thing which was done was done, and why every thing left undone was left undone. He would have been ready with a plain intelligible reason on all these matters in Parliament and elsewhere. And this was not an easy matter for a civilian after a few months of office. But on minor matters Sir George Lewis was not so good at the War Department as at the Exchequer or the Home Office. He had been apprenticed to the Home Office as Under-Secretary, and to the Exchequer as Financial Secretary to the Treasury; but he had never been apprenticed to the War Office. On matters of detail he was obliged to rely on others. He held, and justly, that a parliamentary chief of temporary, perhaps *very* temporary, tenure of office should be very cautious not to interfere too much with the minor business of his department. He should govern, but he should govern through others. But the due application of this maxim requires that the chief minister should know, as it were by intuition and instinct, which points are important and which are not important. And no civilian introduced at once to a new department like that of War can at once tell this. He *must* be in the hands of others. In the House of Commons, too, Sir G. C. Lewis could never answer questions of detail on war matters in an offhand manner. He had to say, "I will inquire, and inform the honourable member." At the Home Office he could have answered at once and of himself. It was an act of self-denial in him to go to the War Office. He felt himself out of place there, and was sure that his administration of military matters could not add to his reputation. But he was told it was for the interest of the Government that he should accept the office, and he accepted it. Perhaps he was wrong. The reputation of a first-rate public man is a great public power, and he should be careful not to diminish it. The weight of the greatest men is diminished by their being seen to do daily that which they do not do particularly well. A cold and cynical wisdom particularly disapproves of most men's *best* actions. Few men were less exposed to the censure of such wisdom than Sir G. C. Lewis; but his acceptance of the War Office was a sacrifice of himself to the public, which injured him more than it advantaged the public,—which it would be better not to have made.

The usefulness of men like Sir George Lewis is not to be measured by their usefulness in mere office. It is in the cabinet that they are of *most* use. Sir George Lewis was made to discuss business with other men. "If," we have heard one who did much business with him say,—"if there is any fault in what you say, he will find it out." In council, in the practical discussions of pending questions, a simple masculine intellect like that of Sir G. C. Lewis finds its greatest pleasure and its best use. He was *made* to be a cabinet minister.

The briefest notice of Sir George Lewis should not omit to mention one of the most agreeable, and not one of his least rare, peculiarities—his good-natured use of great knowledge. It would have been easy for a man with such a memory as his, and such studious habits as his, to become most unpopular by cutting-up the casual blunders of others. On the contrary, he was a most popular man; for he used his knowledge with a view to amend the ignorance of others, and not with a view to expose it. His conversation was superior either to his speeches or his writings. It had—what is perhaps rarer among parliamentary statesmen than among most people—the flavour of exact thought. It is hardly possible for men to pass their lives in oratorical efforts without losing some part of the taste for close-fitting words. Well-sounding words which are not specially apt, which are not very precise, are as good or better for a popular assembly. Sir George Lewis's words in political conversation were as good as words could be; they might have gone to the press at once. We have compared it to hearing a chapter in Aristotle's Politics, and perhaps that may give an idea that it was dull. But pointed thought on great matters is a very pleasant thing to hear, though, after many ages and changes, it is sometimes a hard thing to read. The conversation of the Dialogue at the head of this Article has been admired, but it is very inferior to the conversation of the writer. There was a delicate flavour of satire lurking in the precise thought which could not be written down, and which is now gone and irrecoverable.

"When," says Lord Brougham, commenting on the death of a statesman once celebrated and now forgotten,—"when a subject presented itself so large and shapeless, and dry and thorny, that few men's fortitude could face, and no one's patience could grapple with it; or an emergency occurred demanding on the sudden access to stores of learning, the collection of many long years, but arranged so as to be made available at the shortest notice,—*then* it was men asked where Lawrence was." And now, not only when information is wanted, but when counsel is needed,—when parties are confused,—when few public men are trusted,—when wisdom, always rare, is rarer even than usual,—many may ask, in no long time, "Where is Lewis now?"

Art. XI.—M. RENAN'S LIFE OF JESUS.

Vie de Jésus. Par Ernest Renan, Membre de l'Institut. Paris: Michel Lévy Frères, 1863.

Every attempt to re-write the "Life of Jesus" implies an opinion that the four Evangelists have not been finally successful in their task. Had there been only one gospel, the grand figure which it presents might for ages have left a satisfying image on the mind. But when the simplicity of the impression is broken, when the outline appears in parts double or treble, and the movements separate on different lines, when tones of incompatible colouring are laid on, the eye instinctively endeavours to clear the confusion; first, by suspecting itself, and correcting its own point of view; and, failing this, by criticising the representations themselves, and discharging the touches least true to nature. As early therefore as the second century, Tatian's Diatessaron redisposed the four gospels into one, and began the long and not very harmonious procession of "Harmonies." Their method consists simply in a mechanical rearrangement of parts, a cutting-up of four threads into convenient lengths, to re-tie them in an order which omits nothing but the duplicates. The task may be achieved with more or less skill: the pieces may be too long or too short: the joints may be neat or clumsy: the geographical windings may be excessive: the time-measure may be open to dispute. But you are to criticise nothing except the manipulation: you are to assume that the material is all right, and, like a dissected map, admits of being put together as a whole, when the rule of combination has been found. The result is not encouraging. So primary a point as the duration of Christ's ministry,—the size of the framework within which the detail is to be distributed,—remains undetermined. Not to mention the startling assertion of Irenæus that it extended to the Saviour's fiftieth year at least,—we have bipaschal, tripaschal, quadripaschal systems, each giving to the sacred life different sequences, different proportions, a different *mise-en-scène*; and all involving jerks of incident and contortions of character which would be deemed unbearable in any other biography. The very repute of infallibility which would seem to secure reverential treatment for the gospels really exposes them to unparalleled violence; for it benumbs in the reader all historical tact, excuses him from applying the delicate measures of humanity, and sets him in a sphere beyond nature, where, all things being possible, nothing is arbitrary. In any but sacred history, the outrages on probability sanctioned by every Harmonist would be deemed intolerable. Because, for instance, one Evangelist* puts the "cleansing of the Temple" at the commencement of the Saviour's ministry, the others† at its close, Dr. Carpenter assigns it to *both*:‡ and, for a similar reason, he makes Jesus *twice*§ utter his lament over Jerusalem, in the same words; as if it were a passage got up for delivery now in Galilee, then at the Temple! The last meal before the crucifixion has, in each type of narrative, its symbolic incident;—in John, the washing of the feet; in the rest, the institution of the Supper: the Harmonist introduces first one, and then the other.‖ The risen Christ who, in one account, appoints to meet his disciples exclusively in Galilee,¶ and, in another, restricts his interviews to the neighbourhood of Jerusalem,** does not object, on the pages of a Harmony, to appear in both localities. A mosaic work thus pieced together from several distinct memoirs mars the design and chafes away the peculiarities of each; it dissects living unities to death, that it may use the *disjecta membra* in framing an artificial one. It puts out of sight the significant phenomena, of language and idea, which mark the place, the school, the era, whence each record comes; and creates in the mind an interest against the main source of light with regard to the beginnings of our religion. For if ever a clear image is reproduced of those sacred days, it will be gained, not by assimilating, but by differencing the early Christian memorials. The "Horæ Paulinæ" of an age of "Evidences" may find the "coincidences,"—of an age of History will interpret the deviations,—of Acts and Epistles:

* John ii. 13. † Matt. xxi. 12; Mark xi. 15; Luke xix. 45.

‡ Apostolical Harmony, pp. 27. 206.

§ Ibid. pp. 189. 221; Luke xiii. 34; Matt. xxiii. 37.

‖ Ibid. pp. 237. 244; John xiii. 1; Matt. xxv. 26; Mark xiv. 22; Luke xxii. 19.

¶ Matt. xxviii. 7. 10. 16. ** Luke xxiv. 13. 36. 49.

and the critic who shall explain the contrasts between the fourth gospel and the rest will in no slight degree clear the mist which hangs around the person of Christ. The Monotessaron conception which represents the first rude attempt at a "Life of Jesus" has long been the chief obstacle to any approximate success.

The modern demand for a clear "Life of Jesus" has however a much deeper source than any discrepancies of the Evangelists: it would remain, were there no gospel but one. It is quite impossible for the present age to accept the simple Jewish record as an adequate account of the divinest agency in history, or to replace its central figure in just the light with which Galilean thought invested it. Christianity has turned out other than its first votaries expected;—an unspeakably greater, purer, more enduring power than their final little "kingdom of heaven;" not alarming the world with magical and revolutionary surprise, sudden as the pangs of travail, but born into it, like some child of rarer beauty and higher conscience in a home, and growing silently into the affections of kindred natures. The look therefore which it had to a prospective eye cannot satisfy our wants in retrospect: we require causes for other effects than were then in sight: we can dispense with causes provided for effects that never came. Even those who do not absolutely recoil from the miraculous element in the narrative must feel that it often assumes its form from untenable and obsolete beliefs, and needs to be either dropped as legendary, or corrected into intelligible history. To us, the demons vociferate in vain their superhuman recognition of the Christ; the healing virtue that oozes from the hem of a garment is not persuasively divine; and the payment of a tax by catching a fish with a shekel in his mouth is hardly credible. Nor can the traces escape us, even within the limits of the same gospel, of incompatible ideas impressed upon the record by different hands at different times: as when Jesus, for instance, at one time forbids his missionaries to address themselves to Samaritans or Gentiles (ἐθνῶν),* assuring them that, ere they have gone the round of the cities of Israel, the last Advent would have come; and at another commands them to go and teach all nations (πάντα τὰ ἔθνη).† For these reasons we cannot but feel that, could we be transported to the evangelic time and place, we should see and tell the story differently; that in the extant narrative there is present much which is not due to the personality of Jesus; and that in the residue which *is*, some elements belong simply to his inheritance of national thought, and only within and beyond these are the sacred characteristics reached of his divine originality. To conduct us to this final essence of our religion, to show us how it

* Matt. x. 5, 6. 23.

† Matt. xxviii. 19.

acted and suffered amid historical conditions, and comported itself in its influence on the succeeding period of the world, is the aim of M. Renan's work. The brilliant and impressive volume now published is to be followed by a second on the Apostolic age; a third will exhibit the state of Christianity under the Antonines; and a fourth terminate the history with the settlement by Constantine. The latter half of this great enterprise enters upon firm historical ground: but in the earlier half the sources are so scanty and their authority so obscure, that it needs a refined and exhaustive ingenuity of combination to frame a connected narrative, and a rare power of psychological divination to construe and complete the interrupted lines of thought and character. The genius of M. Renan, eminently subtle and apprehensive, works congenially in such a field, and often opens to us delicate lights which at once reveal and beautify. Notwithstanding his large erudition, we are more disposed to trust his constructive imagination than his critical judgments. This book, conceived in the spirit of a devout philosophy, and executed with poetic tenderness and reverence, is nearly perfect as a work of art: and so far as it fails to recover the historic figure of Christ and the true drama of his life, the defect is due, we think, to no weakness of sympathy or fancy, but to imperfect discrimination in estimating his authorities, and too vague a theory of the relation between the Divine and the Human.

A pupil, we believe, of Ewald, M. Renan has not always, in his History of the Semitic Languages, accepted the authority of the master: but in his present work, especially in the fundamental place it assigns to the fourth gospel, he is true to the school from which he springs. From that gospel he adopts, as authentic, the general program of the life of Christ; interweaving from Matthew chiefly the *discourses*, which he regards as the basis of the first gospel, and identifies with the Hebrew λόγια mentioned by Papias; and from Mark chiefly the recitals of *incident*, supposed by the same witness to contain the recollections of Peter.* In its groundwork therefore, notwithstanding its free dealing with details, our author's volume is essentially a *Harmony*, incorporating into one system the materials of the Johannine and the synoptical gospels; and assigning the primary place to the later composition, the secondary to the earlier. He allows that weighty

* This distinction between Matthew's gospel as containing *discourses*, and Mark's as containing *incidents*, is not borne out by the terms in which Papias speaks of them, ap. Euseb. *Hist. Eccles.* iii. 39. The term λόγια cannot be restricted to *spoken words*, but is certainly used of narrative as well: and Mark's production is expressly said to have contained τὰ ὑπὸ τοῦ Χριστοῦ λεχθέντα as well as πραχθέντα. On Schleiermacher's attempt (*Theol. Stud. und Krit.*, 1832, p. 735 seqq.) to limit the word λόγια to discourses, see Bleek's *Einleitung in das N. T.*, p. 93, and Baur's *Krit. Untersuchungen über die kanon. Evangelien*, p. 580.

doubts attach to the authorship of the fourth gospel,—doubts not yet resolved; but on the whole inclines to an hypothesis of this kind: The Apostle John, whose exclusively Judaic expectations were embodied, about A.D. 68, in the Book of Revelations, gave up this order of Messianic ideas after the destruction of Jerusalem in A.D. 70; and, removing into Asia Minor, insensibly imbibed the speculative and Gnostic modes of thought prevailing there, till they tinctured and transformed all his memories, and changed for him the Galilean Son of Man into an Incarnation of Divine Truth. Thus converted from a theocratic zealot into a metaphysical mystic, he is not satisfied with the current evangelical memoirs: he finds inaccuracies in them: they do not assign to himself his due place among the personal disciples, and make relatively too much of Peter: and to correct these faults, he dictates to those about him a recital of things better known to him than to others. This recital, circulating in the immediate school of John, was the source of those traditions which Papias was fond of collecting from personal associates of the Apostles; which especially Presbyter John and Aristion orally brought him from the circle of the beloved disciple, without telling him that they had been committed to writing.* This view of the origin of the fourth gospel places its *narrative* in the first rank of historic value: but its *discourses* are dismissed by our author as free compositions, deserving of no credit as reports, and in themselves little else than "pretentious heavy, ill-written tirades" (p. xxx.), which could never have proceeded from the same lips with the Sermon on the Mount. It is difficult to reconcile M. Renan's thorough-going repudiation of the Johannine discourses,—which constitute the very essence of the book,—with his dependence upon the Johannine narrative. At times,† he throws the responsibility of the discourses on the secondary compilers and editors of the gospel,—"the school of John." But again,‡ as if conscious of the indivisible unity of the book, he accounts for the peculiar colouring of the speeches by the psychological revolution in the Apostle himself; who, on looking back, saw every thing through his own medium; and to whom the recollections of the past came altered by the intellectual atmosphere around. But surely, the same refracting medium which so changed the *voices*, must no less change the *images*,

* Introduction, pp. xxiv.-xxxvi. The silence of Papias (declared by Irenæus to have been a hearer of John) as to any Gospel of John drives M. Renan to this strange assumption, that his informants kept its existence a secret. It does not appear, from the citation in Eusebius (*Hist. Eccl.* iii. 39) that Aristion and Presbyter John were personally known to Papias.

† Introd. p. xxxvi. "Les discours aux moins ne sont pas du fils de Zebédée."

‡ Ibid. p. xxxi. "En prêtant ces nouvelles idées à Jesus, il ne fit que suivre un penchant bien naturel."

of distant years: things and thoughts, action and speech, must suffer in common by any subjective process which melts away the sharp lines and degrades the pure tints of truth. Critically, it seems to us impossible to give the incidents to a first hand and the discourses to a second: and psychologically, no less impossible to save or sacrifice the one without the other.

We regret our author's half-and-half verdict on this *quæstio vexata,* because it impairs the firmness of his hand and clearness of his eye as he proceeds to fill his canvas. For one who would recover the real portraiture of Jesus, the first condition is, to choose between the two types of Evangelist: the Johannine Christ is not the synoptical Christ: and to blend the two is to take away all outline from the personality, and all natural sequence from the drama in which it acts. The contrast between them is far from being confined to the discourses, and seems to us much deeper than M. Renan allows. A gospel in which Jesus never meets a demoniac, and never utters a parable,—is neither baptised nor tempted,—partakes of no last Passover, and institutes no Lord's supper,—announces no coming of the "kingdom of heaven," no fall of Jerusalem, no return of Messiah to judgment,—speaks of himself as the "Son of God," and as carrying a preëxistent glory in disguise,—and finally is crucified in coincidence with the slaying of the paschal lamb,—belongs to quite a different world from its predecessors, and could never proceed from the same little group of personal disciples whose memorials we meet in the other evangelists. Least of all can we assign it to the son of Zebedee, whom, in the Apocalypse, we know as the Chiliast and Judaist, and find excluding Paul from the number of Apostles,* denouncing his principles,† expecting the return of Nero to the world,‡ and then the Messianic judgment. To suppose this "son of thunder" subdued and attenuated into the theosophic evangelist is to do violence not only to nature, but to history: for, as it happens, we are able to follow him into Asia Minor, and to see that he was still steadfast to Judaic usage and tradition,—and *that* upon the very point on which emphatically the fourth gospel contradicts them. In the second century, it is well known, the Christians of the West and of the East observed a different rule for the celebration of Easter.§ The Latins, constant to the sacred day of the *week,* merely singled out a particular Sunday at the vernal equinox to celebrate, with exceptional intensity, the same resurrection of which every Sunday was a memorial: and, having determined this πάσχα ἀναστά-

* Rev. xxi. 12-14. Comp. ii. 2.

† Rev. ii. 14.

‡ Rev. xvii. 9-11.

§ Irenæus and Polycrates; epp. ad Victor. ap. Euseb. *Hist. Eccles.* v. 24.

σιμον, they appointed, as a prelude to it on the previous Friday, a remembrance of the crucifixion; a *πάσχα σταυρώσιμον*: and the fast of that season continued unbroken through the week. They thus took no notice except of distinctively Christian facts, marking the two grand incidents in the crisis of redemption,—the life laid down, the life resumed. The Asiatics, on the other hand, adhering to the Old-Testament rule for the Passover, consecrated a given day of the lunar *month* (the 14th Nisan), and celebrated their eucharistic supper simultaneously with the Jews' paschal meal, whatever might be the day of the week on which this breaking of their fast might fall: and it does not appear that they appended any special commemoration of the resurrection, the weekly remembrance of it being regarded as adequate. In defence of their practice, repeatedly objected to from Rome, the bishops of Asia Minor,—Polycarp of Smyrna A.D. 160 (*Ἰωάννου ἀκουστής*), Melito of Sardes A.D. 170, Polycrates of Ephesus A.D. 190,—advanced two cogent pleas;—that they did but follow the authoritative example of their Lord, "who had himself kept the passover with his disciples on the 14th Nisan, and then suffered on the great day of unleavened bread,"* and that they had received their usage direct from the Apostle John, who, like other of the apostles, had always observed it among them, and established a custom respected by all their venerated men.† We have thus the Apostle's name used as a tower of strength in support of the very tradition,—of the last supper as a paschal meal,—which the fourth gospel excludes: and the Jewish Christian usage founded on that tradition has its citadel in his special school, its upholders in his associates and followers, its authority in his personal example; and, on the other hand, its conclusive refutation in the history attributed to him. May we not reasonably prefer the historical evidence of his continued Jewish identity to the fictitious hypothesis of a psychological metamorphosis turning the millennarian Boanerges into the mystic form of the "beloved disciple"?

The external theatre of the ministry of Jesus, and its whole order and duration, are no less affected than its internal character, by our historical estimate of the fourth gospel. Exceptional in this as in every thing else, it makes Judæa, not only his native country,‡ but the main scene of his labours, places

* Apollinaris: Fragm. ap. Chronicon Paschale, p. 14. ed. Bonn.

† Iren. ap. Euseb. H. E. v. 24, 16 and 2·7.

‡ M. Renan indeed (p. 20) appeals, in proof of the birth at Nazareth, to passages in this gospel, viz. i. 45. vii. 41, to which may be added xix. 19. But in these passages Jesus is assigned to Nazareth only by others, speaking from common repute: and in vii. 27. 41 the very gist of the Evangelist's purpose is to let "the Jews" exhibit their *ignorant* confidence in regard to the nativity of Christ, and by an act of judicial blindness reject him on the *false* ground of a Galilean

him in Jerusalem for five festivals, including three passovers, and thus nearly trebles the chronology of the synoptics, and renders him familiar from the outset with that wonderful society of priests and canonists into which the other evangelists bring him only to die. All these peculiarities hang together and belong essentially to the idea and plan of the work. "The Jews" collectively (the writer placing himself outside of them) are to be exhibited as incorrigibly hostile and insensible to the impersonated Divine Word,—as the dark medium amid which that veiled glory, escaping nevertheless in words of insight and works of power,—shone in vain: and it is only in the centre of the nation, not in its rural outskirts, that this divine controversy can be tried in the person of its proper representatives, and the necessity be shown of seeking "other sheep, not of this fold." But the more the evangelist's scheme is consistent within itself, the less is it susceptible of disruption into fragments for amalgamation with the far different plan,—not ideal but historical,—of the synoptics. To treat either narrative as consciously composed of unconnected parts, and needing to be supplemented by the other, sacrifices the true genius of both. M. Renan indeed (p. 205) reproduces the argument, so often urged in favour of the Johannine frame-work of place and time, that even in the other evangelists Jesus alludes to sojourns at Jerusalem which they do not describe; when he exclaims,—"*How often* would I have gathered thy children together,—as a hen doth gather her brood under her wings;—and ye would not!" (Matt. xxiii. 37.) But the more closely this passage is studied, the more evident does it become that these repeated appeals to Jerusalem refer, not to the personal visits of Jesus at the festivals, but to the whole series of Divine opportunities given to the city throughout its history. They go back avowedly into anterior ages:—"Lo, I send unto you prophets and sages and scribes; and some of them ye will kill and crucify." They go forward to incidents in the siege under Titus (Joseph. Bell. Jud. iv. 5):—"That upon you may come all the righteous blood shed upon the earth, from the blood of righteous Abel to the blood of Zacharias son of Barachias, whom ye slew between the temple and the altar" (Matt. xxiii. 34, 35). Be the cause what it may, Jesus is here made to speak, not in his historical individuality, but as impersonating the entire Providence of the

birth. The rule that "a prophet hath no honour in his own country," Jesus himself gives (iv. 44) as his reason for going *away from Judæa* (iv. 3), and *resorting to Galilee*, where he was well received (iv. 45: comp. vii. 1). By the synoptics this same rule is applied (also through the lips of Jesus himself) to explain the unbelief of the people of *Nazareth*, and the consequent turning of Jesus to other Galilean places. This inverse citation of the rule proves that the πατρὶς was held to be Judæa in the one case, Nazareth in the other.

the Jewish nation through its vicissitudes: and no inference therefore can be drawn from these words with respect to his attendance at the festivals of the metropolis. That Jesus himself should slip insensibly from speaking in his own person to speaking in that of God is at variance with all analogy; and betrays, even more than the anachronism with regard to the son of Barachias, the hand of a later evangelist throwing back upon the sacred year what was present to the eye and thought of a new generation.*

In estimating the relative value of the primitive Christian records, we are left mainly to internal indications: and no conclusions fairly deduced from the phenomena of the gospels themselves can be materially affected by the scanty and doubtful testimony of ecclesiastical witnesses. Even if we had direct citations of the fourth gospel by name in the very earliest of the Christian fathers, Papias, Polycarp, and Justin, they would carry us no further back than the middle of the second century; leaving us at a distance still of two generations from any probable apostolic authorship, and of nearly four from the events related. In an age prolific of supposititious writings, and a society quite uncritical, this interval is ample for the diffusion of a book amid a halo of unauthentic tradition; as may be seen from instances both within and without the canon of the New Testament,—the Epistle to the Hebrews, that of Barnabas, and some of the Clementine writings. But we have no such citations: and M. Renan is not justified in saying, "no one doubts that the fourth gospel existed and *was attributed to John* about the year 150:" or even in adding, of the first epistle, "it is recognised as John's by Polycarp, Papias, and Irenæus" (xxv. xxvi.). The "texts of Justin" to which he appeals in support of the first assertion certainly are closely related to words in the gospel, though not accurately representing them: but John is not mentioned as the authority for them; and the only time when his name occurs in Justin, he appears as author, not of

* In Luke (xi. 49) the words, "I will send unto you prophets," &c. are introduced as a *quotation* from the "Wisdom of God:"—"Wherefore *the Wisdom of God said*," &c. This "Wisdom of God," it has been suggested, was probably a lost Christian production of the first age, in which the Divine Wisdom was represented as addressing warnings and appeals, in the tone of the old prophets, to the Jewish people. If the work was produced under the excitement of the Jewish war, it might well contain the allusion to the murder of Zacharias. Luke, by avowedly citing, clearly exhibits the change of person which in Matthew remains confused, and, but for the parallel passage, could only be conjectured. The quotation extends, according to Strauss, to the lament over Jerusalem, which, in Matthew, immediately follows, though Luke less naturally transposes it to another connexion (xiii. 34), and represents it as spoken already in Galilee, before the approach to Jerusalem. In this way it is not *Jesus*, but the *Wisdom of God*, that exclaims, "*How often*," &c. See an Essay by D. F. Strauss in Hilgenfeld's Zeitschrift für wissensch. Theologie, 1863, p. 84.

the Gospel, but of the Apocalypse. So of the Epistle: in the same anonymous way Polycarp's letter to the Philadelphians includes one of its short sentences: and of Papias Eusebius simply says that he "used testimonies from it." Of Irenæus alone, and his contemporaries, in the latter part of the second century, does our author's remark hold good. The external evidence, in short, is so little definite as to be compatible with any conclusion suggested by comparative criticism of internal historical features.

How far the voice of M. Renan in favour of this justly venerated book will be acceptable to conservative theologians we do not know. On the one hand, it has the weight belonging to a judicial voice, removed beyond suspicion of interest or affection. On the other hand, it is pronounced with such qualifications as to take away almost as much as it gives. When the Gospel is discharged of all its miracles and all its discourses, the residuary shreds scarcely retain any characteristic value. And not even these are left intact, as honest remnants of reality. The suspicion is raised against the Apostle of deliberate falsehood in stating that he was present at the crucifixion, and that the mother of Jesus was then consigned to him as a sacred trust; —of falsehood prompted by the wish to make himself important:

"His disciples had fled. John, however, declares that he was present, and remained throughout standing at the foot of the cross. With better assurance we may state that the faithful women of Galilee, who had followed Jesus to Jerusalem and attended on him, still did not desert him. Mary wife of Cleopas, Mary Magdalen, Johanna wife of Chuza, Salome, and others, kept some way off, with eyes fixed upon him. Were we bound to accept John's statement, we should add that Mary too, the mother of Jesus, was at the foot of the cross; and Jesus, seeing his beloved disciple and his mother together, said to the one, 'Behold thy mother,' and to the other, 'Behold thy son.' But it is inconceivable that the synoptic evangelists, who mention the other women, should have omitted her whose presence made so striking a feature. Nor perhaps is such a trait of personal tenderness in Jesus itself accordant with his extreme loftiness of character at the moment when, singly absorbed in his work, he ceased to be but for humanity."

To this passage is appended the following note:

"Here, in my view, is one of the traits revealing the personality of John, and his desire to give himself some importance. It appears to have been a fact that, after the death of Jesus, John received and in a manner adopted the mother of his master (xix. 27). The great consideration enjoyed by Mary in the rising church induced him doubtless to pretend that Jesus, as whose favourite disciple he gave himself out, had in his dying moments commended to him what he held most dear. The presence about him of this precious deposit secured him a sort of precedence of the other apostles, and gave a high authority to his doctrine" (pp. 421-423).

On these terms the apostolic authorship guarantees us nothing historical; if the pen claimed as original is liable, at the seduction of vanity, to become mendacious. Where is the advantage of securing an eye-witness if, when you have him, he does not tell you the truth? What ground of confidence can there be in an apostle who would tamper with the most sacred affections, and abuse his power of pathetic imagination, in the service of a boastful lie; who could look upon the self-sacrifice of Calvary with self-glorifying gaze; and either live in the house with Mary the life of mutual dissimulation, or, if she were gone, make a dishonest investment in her repute? Must we not say, that what our author's critical conservatism attempts to keep, his moral scepticism here throws away?

In the treatment of literary and historical questions, we look with distrust on all pretensions to divination; whether it be rationalistic, reducing every thing to the "common and unclean;" or devout, exalting every thing into an intangible holiness. Refined and delicate indications, combined by the hand of a master-critic, may often no doubt lead to momentous conclusions which are not easily justified to untrained apprehensions: but under the mask of these rare cases it is easy for gratuitous conjecture and arbitrary assumption to obtain unmerited respect. As M. Renan can see the veins and feel the pulses of fiction beneath the surface, so can more evangelical critics discover the apostolic author by the mysterious sympathies of piety, and verify the narrative by its own self-light. The secrets of the past, the problems of history, are not amenable to this clairvoyance: and whoever appeals to it applies a subjective test to objective facts; which is to invert the Divine order of things, and set up himself and his wishes as the measure of God's transactions. No doubt it is a tender reverence, which clings to each long-consecrated scripture: but the piety which dominates evidence, and must have it so, is less noble than the piety which submits to it and lives with it as it is. When, in discussing such a question as the origin of the fourth gospel, a theologian becomes pathetic about "robbing the Christian of his treasure," and drops into commonplaces about "destructive criticism," we see at once, beneath that saintly perturbation, the inner heart of unbelief, the absence of repose upon realities, the secret purpose to remain within some nimbus of coloured dreams. Cleared vision can "rob" us of nothing, except as daylight "robs" the night of ghosts. "Criticism" can "destroy" nothing but illusions; the disappearance of which either restores the substituted truth, or at least leaves its place duly "swept and garnished" for its return. Criticism can "construct" nothing but hypotheses; which are not divine facts, but mere human representations, and at best can only fill the chasms of knowledge with ideal shadows of probability. The reproach of "negative," the boast of "positive" theology, are alike intrusions, under disguise, of personal desires on the very field consecrated to self-sacrifice. Nothing is "positive" or "negative" except in relation to *our pre-conceptions*, according as they are affirmed or contradicted: and to use such words as tests of merit and expressions of what "we need," is tacitly to stipulate with the nature of things to let our dreams alone. This is the very idol-worship and pride of intellect: and we have yet to learn our first lesson in the religion of thought till we feel that it is not ours to choose where the light shall fall or how much of it there shall be; still less to play tricks with it, and fling its images hither and thither with the mirrors and lenses of our own desires; but to watch it as the dawn, and let it steal in where it will, and show the solid forms of things, though it turn the dark hollow into a nest of beauty, and melt our visionary mountains into clouds.

In the absence of all historical sources (for the stories, in Matthew and Luke, of the nativity and infancy, are plainly legendary), there can be no proper "Life of Jesus" beyond the brief period of his Ministry. That he was born in Nazareth about three years before our ill-computed era, that his parents' names were Joseph and Mary, that he had brothers (James and Joses, Simon and Judas) and sisters, and that his father was a carpenter, is all that we really know.* Scanty, however, as the

* That is, if we limit ourselves to the synoptics. M. Renan adds (p. 24) that Mary had a sister, *whose name was also Mary*; whose two *sons* bore the same names as are, perhaps erroneously, given to their cousins *James* and *Joses*, and, under the title of "*brothers of the Lord*," became "bishops of Jerusalem," the *real* brothers remaining unbelievers; and whose *husband* went by two unconnected names, Alphæus (*Halphai*) and Cleophas (Κλεόπατρος). This tissue of confusion, whose "enormous difficulty" no hypothesis relieves, comes entirely of "harmonising." Keep the fourth gospel apart, and the threads of relation remain clear. (1.) As to the *two sisters* with the *same name*: John alone mentions the *sisterhood* (xix. 25); the synoptics alone identify *the names* (Matt. xiii. 55. xxvii. 56; Luke i. 27. xxiv. 10): for it is remarkable that the fourth evangelist never gives the name of "the mother of Jesus," and doubtless thought of it as something other than *Mary*, which he applies to her sister (ii. 3. 5. 12; vi. 42). With him the two women had different names: with the synoptics, they were not sisters: and so the incompatible phenomena never meet. (2.) As to the *namesake brothers* in the two families: John, who makes them cousins, never gives their names: the synoptics, who give the names (Matt. xiii. 55. xxvii. 56; Mark xv. 40; Luke xxiv. 10), do not make them cousins. (3.) As to *the two names* for *the same man*: it is only in the fourth gospel (xix. 25) that he is called *Cleophas*: it is only in the synoptics (Matt. x. 3; Mark iii. 18; Luke vi. 15; Acts i. 13) that he is called *Alphæus*. The person named Cleopas in Luke xxiv. 18, the evangelist cannot have identified with the father, whom he always calls Alphæus, of the Apostle James mentioned just before (xxiv. 10). In these

personal data are, and impossible therefore as any proper biography is of the youthful Jesus, much may be said of the conditions, material and spiritual, surrounding his early years: and from these exterior circles, scrutinised with penetrating skill, and exhibited in vivid lines, M. Renan makes what approaches are possible to the irrecoverable life within. The aspect of nature that looked down upon the infant Christ, the simple social life of a Galilean village, the Oriental training, less by book than by oral wisdom and human intercourse, the lessons of the synagogue, of the festivals, of local tradition, of national faith, are all presented to us in a series of pictures as fascinating as they are faithful. The author's familiarity with the whole theatre of the history gives a special value to such a sketch as the following:

"Nazareth was a small town, situated in an elbow of country opening wide to the top of the mountain-group which bounds the plain of Esdraelon on the north. At present its population, which may well have remained without great variation, is from three to four thousand. The cold of its winter is keen, and the climate very healthy. Like all the Jewish villages of that time, the town was an aggregate of cottages without physiognomy, and must have presented the dry and poor aspect belonging to the villages in Semitic countries. The houses, it seems, differed little from those cubes of stone, without pretensions to elegance within or without, which, in our day, cover the richest parts of Lebanon, and which, amid vines and fig-trees, are still very agreeable. The neighbourhood too is delightful, and no spot in the world was ever so made for dreams of absolute good. Even in our days, Nazareth is a delicious retreat,—the only place perhaps in Palestine where one feels a little relief of soul from the oppressive burden of an unparalleled desolation. The people are kindly and cheerful; the gardens are fresh and green. Antoninus Martyr, at the end of the sixth century, draws an enchanting picture of the fertility of the neighbourhood, comparing it to Paradise; and there are valleys on the western side which fully bear out his description. The fountain, which once collected round it the life and brightness of the little town, is destroyed; its cracked channels yield now nothing but turbid water. But the beauty of the women who gather there in the evening,—a beauty noticed as early as the sixth century, and regarded as a gift of the Virgin Mary,—is strikingly preserved; it is the Syrian type, with all its languishing grace. Mary doubtless was there almost every day, and

cases,—and they are only a sample,—either account may be taken, but not both, without outraging probability. In choosing between them, shall we say, then, that the fourth gospel may have been written by the Apostle John, to *correct and complete* the others, and so deserves preference in case of variance? If so, why did he, with whom the mother of Jesus lived, not tell us her real name, instead of merely remarking that it was her sister who was called Mary? and also the real names of her sons, if, as M. Renan supposes, Matthew, confounding them with the cousins, had given them wrong? A gospel which on these points, specially known to the Apostle, creates instead of clearing confusion, can never have come from his correcting hand.

took her place, pitcher on shoulder, in the line with her forgotten companions. Antoninus Martyr observes, that the Jewish women, elsewhere disdainful to Christians, are here full of graciousness. And, to the present day, religious animosities have less life at Nazareth than elsewhere.

Contracted as the horizon of the town itself is, a short climb brings you to a plateau swept by a perpetual breeze, and looking down on the highest of the houses; and thence the perspective is splendid. On the west the fine lines of Carmel open out, abruptly terminating with a point that seems to plunge into the sea. Next appear the double summit above Mageddo; the mountains of the Sichem region, with their holy places of the patriarchal age, the Gilboa hills, the picturesque little group associated with the sweet or awful memories of Shunem and of Endor; Tabor, with its fair form swelling like a bosom, as the ancients said. A depression between the Shunem hill and Tabor opens a glimpse of the Jordan valley and the high plains of Peræa, which form a continuous line on the East. On the North, the Safed hills, trending to the sea, intercept the view of Acre, but leave to the eye the outline of the bay of Khaïfa. Such was the horizon that lay around Jesus,—the enchanted circle, cradle of the kingdom of God, that for some years stood to him for the world. Nor did his life ever take him far from the bounds familiar to his childhood. For yonder, Northwards, a glimpse is caught, almost on the flank of Hermon, of Cesarea Philippi, his furthest point of advance into the Gentile world; and here, Southwards, the more sombre aspect of these Samaritan hills foreshadows the dreariness of Judæa beyond, parched as by a scorching wind of desolation and death.

Should the world, grown wiser in its reverence for the germs of sacred things, yet Christian still, ever want authentic 'holy places' instead of the mean and apocryphal sanctuaries consecrated by rude ages, it will build its temple on this height of Nazareth. There, on the spot where Christianity arose and in the focus of the Founder's agency, should the great church be raised in which all Christians might pray. There too, on the soil where Joseph the carpenter sleeps and thousands of forgotten Nazarenes who never looked beyond the horizon of their valley, would be a better station than any in the world beside for the philosopher to contemplate the course of human affairs, to find solace for their contingency, to gain assurance of the divine end which the world pursues through countless falterings and in spite of the universal vanity" (pp. 25-29).

On Joseph's death while Jesus was still a youth, Mary removed, our author supposes, from Nazareth to Cana, her original home: and there we are to think of the young prophet as maturing into manly life, as exercising his father's trade, and as making the first tentatives in his religious career. This conjectural history is doubtless suggested, though in no way necessitated, by John's "first miracle" at Cana. Without stopping to criticise it, we advance to the more solid ground of the proper ministry of Jesus. His whole public life is reckoned, according to the Johannine scheme, to extend over three years (p. 270, note), closing with the passover of A.D. 33. But our author seems hardly to have made his measurement very exactly: for he takes Jesus, already surrounded by disciples and in the exercise of his ministry, to the passover at Jerusalem in the year A.D. 29 (p. 206, note): and establishes him yet earlier, apparently by several months, in formal relations with the Baptist on the Jordan (p. 105); to which still a Galilean prelude is prefixed, sufficiently prolonged to form a body of disciples who accompany him to Judæa (pp. 77-90. 104). The chronology is thus extended (without, apparently, the author being aware of it) to between four and five years. This whole period divides itself, in M. Renan's view, into two grand stages, separated rather by a moral than an external division, yet furnishing a distinct pause in the natural development of the drama. The first is the season of growing conceptions and deepening fervour in Jesus, during which not only his piety set into its characteristic forms, but his ideas of his own mission passed out of their indeterminate state and took possession of phrases unalterable and definite. It brings us to the spring of the year A.D. 31. The second, extending thence to the end, adds no new ideal element, but is occupied with the struggle to realise his inner thought in the outer world, and gain for it the victory to which sooner or later it was appointed. During the first stage, John the Baptist exercised a dominant influence, and, if not himself the most conspicuous figure, regulated the movements of his greater successor. In the year A.D. 28 his reputation as a second Elijah, on whose rugged model he formed himself, had spread through Palestine; and stirring the heart of Jesus, who had already become the centre of a school, induced him to change the scene of action, and settle, with his disciples, in the immediate vicinity of the prophet of Judæa. There, accordingly, on the banks of the lower Jordan, the two schools exercised their functions side by side during the first half of the year A.D. 29; except that in the spring we find the Galileans visiting Jerusalem for the Passover.* They returned however, and continued to baptize like John, till, during the absence of Jesus for fast and prayer in the desert, the Baptist was arrested and imprisoned in the mid summer of A.D. 29. Informed of this on issuing from his retreat, Jesus breaks up from Judæa, and, adopting Capernaum as his centre, devotes himself to Galilee for the next twenty months or so; vainly trying to win his native town; preaching in the village synagogues; reporting his progress to the doubting messengers of John; and only retiring for an interval to a desert

* John ii. 13.

place on the news of the Baptist's execution in the year A.D. 30. This again, like the imprisonment before, is the signal for fresh and bolder speech, and upon a more conspicuous theatre. At the passover of the year A.D. 31, he makes his most important visit to Jerusalem; dissipates there all his illusions of reverence for the reputed sanctities of priest and temple; and with a settled antipathy to the whole type of metropolitan religion, closes the first stage of his career, and retreats for relief into his native province. Thus far then his public life includes two periods of action in Galilee, alternating with two in Judæa: the transitions, except the last, having their cause in the history of John the Baptist.

Quitting Jerusalem in the spring of A.D. 31, repelled by its pretentious and hollow life, and not without presentiment of its fatal enmity, he throws himself for eighteen months into a bolder and more excited ministry in Galilee; declaring open war against Pharisaism and the Law; hinting at his own probable death, but also at his speedy and glorious return; not declining the Messianic titles or the repute of miracles increasingly thrust upon him; and organising his chief disciples into a college to multiply the voices of his message and the ramifications of his influence. In the autumn of the year A.D. 32 he leaves his native hills to return to them no more, sending his disciples before him to the Feast of Tabernacles at Jerusalem, and following alone, to evade the snares laid for him by hostile members of his family. Several months were passed in the capital, till after the Feast of Dedication towards the end of December; his usual place of resort being Solomon's Porch, where the incidents of the hour alternately entangled him in controversy and drew forth lessons of divine wisdom. One interval still parted him from the last act, and Jerusalem from its supreme crime. In January A.D. 33, he spent a few weeks in Peræa and near the Jordan, not without a last returning glow of public enthusiasm and personal ascendency. The miracles of Galilee were renewed; and the reception by Zaccheus at Jericho was but an example of the spirit he every where met. In February he is recalled to Bethany by the illness of Lazarus; who, really convalescent before the arrival of Jesus, conspires with his sisters to get up a sham resurrection, and consenting to be shut up in the sepulchral cave, duly acts the part of resuscitated corpse. Jesus, more than half imposed upon, acquiesces in the dangerous repute of the miracle, and becomes at once the object of warring passions from the neighbouring city; revered by the multitude, dreaded by the aristocracy of the Temple. As early as the beginning of March his death was resolved on. A short retirement to Ephraim does but keep the storm suspended, he is aware, over the approaching Passover. On returning by the northern road he announces his near death: the congenial home at Bethany, the devotion of Mary, even the triumphal entry into Jerusalem, cannot deceive him: the sadness never deserts his tone again; though the incidents of those closing days,—the betrayal, the seizure, the trial, the cross,—assail in vain his lofty serenity and trust. His body was hastily interred in a provisional tomb, and left over the Sabbath. Next morning it was found to be absent; and, probably on an impulse given by the excitable and visionary Mary Magdalen, the story obtained currency that he was risen from the dead.

This second stage of the public life thus consists of a final eighteen months in Galilee, followed by a closing half-year in and near Judæa, and chiefly in Jerusalem.

Without exhibiting M. Renan's ground-plan of the great drama, it would be impossible to explain adequately his theory of the character of Jesus. But as it is chiefly in subordination to this ulterior point of higher interest that we have sketched the outline of his narrative, we shall not pause to examine it in detail, but shall venture one or two remarks on the distribution of its larger masses and the handling of its main difficulties.

Preferring as we do the simplicity of the synoptic narrative, we find our author's protracted chronology difficult to fill; we feel ourselves tossed about in an objectless way between two scenes of action, Galilee and Judæa; we miss any progressive sequence in the drama; the development of which, amid the fermentation of Jewish enthusiasm and the heats of oriental passion, was less likely to hang back season after season than to hasten to its end. Matthew's story in two acts, of the provincial prophet winning the villages of his country for the kingdom of heaven, and then perishing at Jerusalem, has a naturalness in it which looks much more like history than the rambling intricacies of our author's scheme. Most of these, but not all, arise from his embarrassing pledge to the fourth gospel. His account of the earliest relations between Jesus and John the Baptist does equal violence to all the records, and substitutes for them a purely imaginary picture. One of the few points on which the Johannine and the synoptical recitals concur is this, that when Jesus was drawn to the scene of baptism on the banks of Jordan, he went alone and undistinguished; that that visit was the means of first indicating him as marked out for a divine function; that the two signs of his selection were the testimony of the Baptist and the descent of the Spirit in visible or audible form; and that not till after this inauguration was any disciple called or any beginning made of his works or words of power. The whole scene stands forward as the appropriate prelude to his public life: and the prophet's instant recognition of him as his superior is given as a supernatural foresight of an unsuspected vocation. Strip the narratives of this idea, and their meaning is entirely lost. But, according to M. Renan, Jesus goes to the Jordan already surrounded by his school; he has for some time been teaching and gathering disciples in Galilee; and the Baptist's "good reception" of him is due to a reputation established and the fellow-feeling of a kindred work. It is a welcome extorted not by the future, but by the past. And then the two "schools,"—both of them constituted at a distance from each other before they meet,—sit down together as neighbours for many months, without apparent distinction of message or usage, and, in spite of some mutual jealousies among the followers, kept in good relations by the deference of Jesus to the superiority of John (p. 107). What now is the inducement thus to turn the history upside down? Simply this. The fourth gospel brings Jesus and the Baptist together *twice;* first (i. 10-34) like the synoptics, prior to earliest rudiments of Christian action; then (iii. 23-30) after the passover of A.D. 29, and shortly before the prophet's imprisonment, when the ministry of Christ was in full operation and his followers around him. By throwing away the first of these, and introducing the Baptist to the Christians with the second (though it refers back to the first and builds entirely upon it), our author obtains the extraordinary results we have described. The passage which he retains is one of the most questionable specialties of the fourth gospel; that which he rejects is not only a modified version of the tradition sustained by the synoptics, but is a minute account of day-by-day transactions, which, if really proceeding from the apostle, cannot be discredited without fatally impairing his historical authority. Had M. Renan, who calls Jesus "the imitator of John" (p. 107), represented him as receiving his first impulse from the rugged energy of the new Elias, and merely placed the greater spirit, in virtue of its ready susceptibility and its unfound depth, at disposal for awhile of the sterner and the less, we could understand the temptation to such inverse construction of the personal relations assumed in the gospels. So far, contact with the Baptist would remain the starting-point. But to interpolate the term of intercourse with him as an episode between two acts of an independent public ministry in Galilee, to make it the means of at once interrupting and deteriorating a sacred career already begun, turns it into an arbitrary arrest of natural development, in defiance of whatever evidence we have. The two missions, it seems to us, must be conceived as having some ground of separate operation. If they were not distinct in their idea, if both of them were alike announcements of an impending Messianic crisis, without indicating the personal agent in it, they must either have been successive in time or separate in place, the one taking up what the other dropped, or else dividing the work in different fields. Their co-existence for many months in the same district, with independent organisations and indistinguishable teaching, would leave the more recent of them without any adequate *raison d'être.*

Another feature of our author's biographical program occasions some natural disappointment. If there are any moments in the experience of the Galilean prophet which, as inevitably critical, we watch with intensest interest, they are those which present him to Jerusalem, and bring around him the representative persons and fermenting ideas of the nation. These times we expect to be fullest in incident, deepest in significance. Nor is there any want of room in them for the play of action and character. Some six months in A.D. 29 were spent, we are told, at a spot on the Jordan whither the city population freely came, and whence the disciples accompanied their master to the first passover of his public life. Two years later, at the same annual festival, occurred his "most important sojourn" at Jerusalem. And the whole of the autumn and part of the winter of A.D. 32 were passed in the city. The last of these visits is partially filled in by transferring to it incidents which the synoptics refer to the crucifixion week. But the other two remain nearly blank; and the only details given, the "cleansing of the Temple" and the interview with Nicodemus, are transposed from the second to the first, where the fourth gospel places them. As these Jerusalem visits appear in that gospel alone, and as M. Renan can receive neither its miracles nor its discourses as historical, there is scarcely any thing left in occupation of them; and precisely the great crises of the drama, passed in very focus of trial, are little else than empty spaces of possibility. Once away in Galilee, we are again surrounded by the stir of life and the fulness of human detail.

In every way it would be far better, we think, to be, on critical grounds, independent of the fourth gospel, than to adopt it as a main-stay, yet cut it down to the slenderest proportions, and even transmute its very substance. Above all do we feel this in our author's treatment of the raising of Lazarus. Rather than refer the recital to the post-apostolic age, he refers it to an apostle who cannot have given it in good faith. Rather than dismiss it as unhistorical, he receives the history and blackens it; turning the pretended house of mourning into a chamber of plotters; the confidants of Jesus into his deceivers; his crowning miracle into a wretched trick, of which, having been at first the victim, he at last accepted the success. If the history cannot stand, let it be taken down, stone by stone; but to build it up again in this style is to substitute for the credulity of piety the credulity of cynicism. That a man, dwelling in the innermost circle of Christ's personal affections, should consent to be buried alive in order to force him into imposture and advance him by its fame; that the sisters who had tended his illness, and to whom his pale features were the memorials of breathless watching and of answered prayers, should contrive this clever mode of turning his sunk cheeks to good account; that the funeral rites, the lying notices to friends, the visits of condolence, and all the shameful mockery of woe, should be got up and got through without a slip in the hypocrisy; that the central figure, so simple and sublime, he who was so impatient of the appetite for miracle and had mercy for every thing but falsehood and pretence, should stoop, when his sorrows had been practised on, to whiten that unclean sepulchre and by connivance decorate the cheat; that when the fraud was plainly preparing the cross for him and threatening it to Lazarus, the secret should still have been kept, and have been finally handed down to history by an apostle nearest to the scene if not behind it;—involves, as it seems to us, a complication of improbabilities rarely united in a single hypothesis. We are far from desiring to test it by compelling the author to put the story unconditionally under one or other of the two categories,—"imposture" or "enthusiasm." We own the truth of those more subtle readings of human nature which modern interpreters apply to religious phenomena, and which allow for many intermediate shades between pure sincerity and calculating artifice. In minds capable of being absorbed at times in divine realities, yet descending again to the inevitable human level, there is a kind of double consciousness which too readily carries with it two ethical weights and measures; and may often blend strange contradictions of faith and doubt, of artlessness and scheming, of self-homage and self-surrender. Still, there are limits to the possible combinations of feeling and motive: there is such a thing, in the creations of the drama and the reproductions of history, as truth of character: and, refine as you will upon the varieties of our nature, laws of harmony remain, by neglecting which you may cover your canvas with a monstrosity. Partly in reaction from the narrow logic of books of "Evidences," partly from a pantheistic tendency weakening the lines of human personality as well as of the Divine, modern critics of historical religion appear to us increasingly liable to lose the tact of psychological probability, and put the elements of humanity together *ad libitum*. The instance which we have just adduced from M. Renan's book is not, we think, its only example of this wildness of fancy.

We have to thank him however for at least a definite conception of the individuality of Jesus; and for the firm and sincere application of it as a key to the evangelical history throughout. The ecclesiastical theory of the person of Christ, making him the unique synthesis of two natures, is fatal to any living apprehension of him as he was: inasmuch as it lifts him out of every analogy, and, in the absence of all measures of verisimilitude, leaves us at the mercy of any impression delivered to us. How should we know what would agree with likelihood in such a being, and what would contradict it? Accordingly, the mixed products of successive and even opposite traditions are poured upon our ear from Scripture, without any consciousness of inconsistency, or any such desire to clear the image as we should feel in an undivine biography. The process of metaphysically glorifying a nature unsettles the outline of its moral type. The Christ of the fourth gospel is already pale and characterless. And three centuries were devoted to wrapping up his real history in fold after fold of dogma, and rendering him invisible except through a refracting atmosphere of ideas: and any one who sincerely tries, by removing these, to reproduce his actual figure, as he lived and thought, as he looked and spake, among the villagers who loved and the city-priests who hated him, brings an incipient health and truth to the sicklied imagination of Christendom. Without being able to accept the portrait on M. Renan's canvas, we own the force and grace with which it is drawn, and the reverential feeling which has seldom failed to guide his hand. Evolving Christianity in its essence from the personality of its Founder, and only in its transitory form from the ideas afloat in the atmosphere of the times, he restores the just balance of causation which Strauss's theory had disturbed, and recalls the religion from the cloud-region of myth, to the homesteads and fields of human history.

Three stages are marked in the development of Jesus' character and views: we may call them,—the Ideal,—the Messianic,—the Passionate and Thaumaturgic. A deep and tender piety, fed by the solemn and winning aspects of nature around him, rendered thoughtful by the rich sentences of Hebrew wisdom, and humane in the school of domestic love, took early possession of him and moulded his whole belief, affections, and will. One simple formula condenses the essence of it all: God was a Father; not distant and hard to find; not even external, coming in vision or by word; but a Father within, communing with the pure in heart, and abiding with living, pitying, loving presence in our humanity. This characteristic faith,—remote alike from the Jewish and Pagan type,—was indigenously his; not learned by tradition, not found by reasoning, but presenting itself as a clear consciousness of God, blending in one the light that shows and the vision that sees. He thus felt himself in direct relations of sonship to the Father, not specially his, but such as all men would find true. From this central faith flowed all his conceptions of the government of the world, the maxims of duty, and the spirit of human life. The universe was no mechanism of relentless Fate, nor even an empire of inscrutable Will, but the theatre of a moral drama, a home of domestic discipline, ruled with impartial love. In the face of this sublime affiliation, common to all, the distinctions of social life disappear, and no ranks have any reality except the gradations of inward similitude to God: the only rich is the poor in spirit: the only great, the servant of all: the supremely wise are the pure in heart: and the sole hierarchy is hierarchy of graces. The same truth is the solvent of enmities, as it is of distinctions: your anger knows not what spirit it is of, and observes not the Eternal Father's ways: does not the sunshine sleep and the rain descend on the offender's fields as well as on your own? Reserve the severities for sins in which you cannot be deceived,—your own; if hand or eye betray you into wrong, be as unsparing as you will. But leave a brother's guilt to Him who seeth in secret: and never shut the fountains of pity and forgiveness. Humility, self-denial, disinterestedness, may well be called the special Christian virtues: for they come spontaneously from the soul that lives filially with God, and are the fruits of faith that were most welcome to the eye of Christ himself. With a spirit thus tempered, he carried his affections behind the showy veil of life, and redressed the strong world's scorn by searching out the little and the weak: he loved the child, the poor that rested in their lot, the fallen that were in tears for their sin. His lessons moreover, even where they seemed to say what the wise and humane had said before, escaped the level of all ethical maxims, and rose into a diviner light and glow. Drawn from the contemplation of Infinite Perfection, they aspired thitherward again: hence their unspeakable poetic depth of tone; from his lips the rule of duty is a breathing of humility, a sigh of eternal hope, a vision of ineffable beauty. To find the Founder of the true kingdom of God, the kingdom of the gentle and lowly, we must go, says M. Renan, to

"the Jesus of these early days,—days chaste and without alloy,—when the voice of his Father resounded in his breast with purer tone. There were then some months, perhaps a year, when God truly had abode upon the earth. The voice of the young carpenter suddenly assumed an extraordinary sweetness. An infinite charm diffused itself from his presence; and those who had previously seen him no longer recognised him. As yet he was without disciples, and the group that pressed around him was neither a sect nor a school; but already there is a common spirit discernible there, something gentle and penetrating. His winning character, with doubtless one of those charming figures at times presented by the Jewish race, threw around him a circle of fascination, which hardly any one, among those kindly and simple people, could escape. Paradise would have been actually brought to earth, only that the ideas of the young Teacher went far beyond that level of moderate goodness above which it has hitherto been impossible to raise mankind" (pp. 79-81).

And here is the nursery and the theatre of this pure life:

"Among the influences that formed this far less austere, less harshly monotheistic spirit, if I may venture to say so, was an aspect of nature truly delightful, which gave an idyllic character and charm to all the Galilean visions. The dreariest country in the world perhaps is the country near Jerusalem. Galilee, on the contrary, was very green, very shady, very bright, the true country of the Song of Songs and the lyrics of the poet 'after God's heart.' During the two months of March and April the ground is a dense mass of flowers, unmatched for freedom of colour. The animals are small, but charming in the extreme. Slender and sprightly turtle-doves, blue blackbirds so light as to perch upon a grass-blade without bending it, crested larks that come and almost put themselves under the traveller's feet, the little river-tortoise with its quick and gentle eye, storks with their grave and modest air,—laying aside all fear, allow the close approach of man, and seem to call him. In no country of the world do the mountain-lines dispose themselves with more harmony and stir the mind to higher thought. Jesus seems to have particularly loved them. On the mountains occurred the most important acts of his divine career: there it is that he was best inspired; there that he had secret converse with ancient prophets, and appeared to his disciples' eyes already transfigured" (pp. 64, 65).

During the time of his fresh enthusiasm, the Messianic visions of the Jewish apocalyptic literature,—the books of Daniel and Enoch especially,—slept in the background of his imagination; or threw forward only their ideal elements, their images of pure worship, of compensated sorrow, of everlasting righteousness. But from the moment of contact with John the Baptist, an unfavourable change began. Into the kingdom announced to be so near it became necessary to look with distincter scrutiny: its blank outline must be filled: its chief figure must be determined. It could not coexist with tetrarchies and hierarchies and procuratorships as they were, and carried with it suggestions of political revolution. The Messianic circle of ideas drew more closely round Jesus: and though insurrectionary force was uncongenial to him,—though the heroism of Judas the Gaulonite came from the thought 'God is *King*,' while now it was the truth of truths that 'God is *Father*,'—yet somehow,—in ways that would declare themselves,—the kingdoms of this world would have to vanish and leave room for the divine age which would wait no more. On returning from the Jordan, this prejudicial influence of the sterner prophet on the gentler became evident. His preaching was more and more definitely about the "kingdom" to come: and its advance in force and decision was at the expense of breadth. He did not refuse the Messianic titles; speaking of himself as the "Son of Man," and suffering others to draw the inference contradicted by his birth and call him "Son of David." With deepening sympathies for the village people among whom he moved, and delight in the simple love they gave him, he met the frowns of the decorous classes with less reserved antipathy: he openly disregarded their outward usages of homage to religion in their daily meals and their periodic fasts: he took pleasure in breaking through their Sabbath rules: he let a strange mixture of people draw around him by the natural ties of inward trust and need, and paid no regard to "respectable" objections. In the body of more intimate disciples, whom he now organised into a fraternity, the majority were quite poor and untaught; and its aristocracy consisted of a customs' officer and a land-steward's wife. The native affinities of good and pious hearts, the immeasurable superiority of Jesus, the resistless charm of his word and look, and his deep insight into character, held them to him as by a divine spell.

"It was in truth," says M. Renan, "childhood in its divine spontaneity, in its brilliant bursts of simple joy, that took possession of the earth. Moment by moment, they all believed that the kingdom so longed for was on the point of dawning. Each saw himself already on a throne beside the Master. They allotted the seats: they reckoned the days. This is what they called the 'Good News' (Gospel): the doctrine had no other name. An old word 'Paradise' which the Hebrew, in common with all the Oriental tongues, had borrowed from Persia, and which originally denoted the royal parks of the Achæmenidæ,—gave the sum of the universal dream:—a delightful garden prolonging for ever the charming life spent here below. How long did this intoxication last? We cannot tell. No one, while this magic vision ran on, measured time any more than we measure a dream. Time was stopped: a week was an age. But whether it filled years or months, so fair was the dream that humanity has lived on it ever since, and still our consolation is to gather its attenuated perfume. Never did so much joy lift the heart of man. Humanity for a moment, in this the most vigorous effort it has made to rise above its planet, forgot the leaden weight that holds it to the earth and the sorrows of life below. Happy he whose eyes were permitted to see this divine blossom open, and to partake, were it only for a day, this unexampled illusion! But happier still, would Jesus say, is he who, free of all illusion, can inwardly reproduce the celestial vision, and, without millennial dream, without imaginary paradise, without signs in the heaven, can, by the rectitude of his will and the poetry of his soul, create anew in his heart the true kingdom of God!" (pp. 192-194.)

Once having committed himself to the realisation of these visions, Jesus could not for ever linger in his beloved Galilee. They pointed to the citadel of the nation's history; and thither he must carry them to win a further way. But Jerusalem, by its very look, stripped them of their joy: the temple-buildings, the priestly pomps, the Pharisaic sanctities, had no charm for him: the keen malicious eye, the quibbling intellect, the professional contempt of the scribe, disturbed him. His disciples, derided for their patois and their rusticity, were uneasy and out of place; and his own spirit, alone lofty and simple amid the odious grimaces of conventional religion, could hardly move with freedom and effect. The chief influence of his visit (A.D. 31) was reflex upon himself: he renounced allegiance to the whole system that had crystallised itself into the Jerusalem he saw: and having vindicated the forgotten *idea* of the temple by whipping out the traffic from its courts, left his protest behind, and resought clearness and composure on the familiar beach and hills. Even they had come to be invested in a light less pure. He had claimed the Messianic character: he had let it mean more than he could always hope; he had broken with the Law, and, beyond the basin of the lake below him, he stood alone. A shadow was on his path. He had a baptism to be baptised with: and how was he straitened till it was accomplished!

The next stage took its commencement in this recoil from Jerusalem. Surrounded once more by those who trusted him, he was unable to retreat, and found courage to advance. What though the proud heirs of the kingdom would not make ready for its approach? It should be taken from them and given to others: for Gentiles and Samaritans too were God's children, and had often a truer heart of faith than Israel. What even though his way should lie through hands of violence and he might have to die? The pious dead too were to live again to share in the kingdom to come: and Messiah beyond the verge of death would be in the right place to lead the way for their return. And so, our author thinks, Jesus advanced to bolder self-assertion, and compensated incipient forebodings of the cross by predictions of return in glory. The higher titles of Messiah sounded with fuller sweetness in his ear: he more freely fell in with the demand for miracles, and bore with the uneasy exigencies and feverish half-faith which they imply; sustained by the belief that through prayer and fasting such works were given to men. In his most exalted moments, however, there is not the slightest approach to those conceptions of Incarnation or equality with his Father in heaven, by which the exaggerations of a later time sought to glorify him: on the contrary, he distinctly repels such idea: he is simply and at the highest "Son of God,"—as all men may become in various degrees.* With the expectation of his own death and return came the assurance, solemnly announced, of the end of the world within that generation: a marvellous belief, the disappointment of which the religion could never have survived, but for the imperishable spiritual elements mingled with its illusions and remaining as its essence. The more definitely Jesus became committed to these views, the more imperative was the necessity of action in advance: he sent out therefore bodies of disciples in all directions, empowered to speak and act in his name; associating them as partners in his miraculous power, he evidenced the sincerity of his own feeling with regard to it: they were to be safe from the scorpion's sting and the poison cup; and to carry healing to the sick as well as hope to the heavy-laden. It is impossible, M. Renan thinks, to relieve Jesus, at the expense of the Evangelists, from the weakness

* The judgment of M. Renan on this point, being that, not of a theologian, but of an impartial scholar, who brings to the Scriptures all the knowledge that can clear and none of the prepossessions that can obscure their doctrinal meaning, is so important, that we quote it *in extenso:* "That Jesus never dreamt of giving himself out as an incarnation of God himself, is beyond all doubt. Such an idea was completely foreign to the Jewish mind: there is not a trace of it in the synoptic gospels: we find no indications of it except in some portions of John's gospel which cannot be regarded as reflecting the ideas of Jesus. At times Jesus even seems to take pains to repel such a doctrine. The imputation of making himself God or the equal of God, is treated, even in John's gospel, as a calumny of the Jews. In this last gospel, he declares himself less than his Father. Besides, he avows that there are things which God has not revealed to him. He deems himself more than ordinary man, but separated by an infinite distance from God. He is Son of God: but so are, or may become, all men in various degrees. All are every day to call God their Father: all, when risen from the dead, will be sons of God. In the Old Testament divine sonship was ascribed to beings whom no one ever affected to put on an equality with God. The word '*son*' in the Semitic languages, and in that of the New Testament, has the widest meanings. Besides, the idea of man which Jesus had is not that low idea which a cold deism has introduced. According to his poetical conception of nature, a single breath pervades the universe: the breath of man is that of God: God dwells in man, lives by man, in the same way that man dwells in God, lives by God. The transcendent idealism of Jesus never allowed him to have a very clear notion of his own personality. He is his Father; his Father is he. He lives in his disciples: he is every where with them: his disciples are one, as he and the Father are one. With him, the spirit is every thing: the body, which makes the distinction of persons, is nothing" (pp. 242-244).

implied in the pretension to miracles; but quite probable that it was the result of a genuine though not unfaltering illusion. Indications are not wanting of a certain uneasy consciousness on this matter, as if the answer of experience was liable to fall short of his full faith. His prayers and inward strife before the act, his frequent wish for privacy during it, his prohibition to report it afterwards, his inability amid the cold unbelief of Nazareth, his sharp rebuke of the desire for signs, are all natural, if the effects which, in his fixed idea, ought to arise were slower or less certain to appear than was good for the faith: while, on the other hand, the real influence, on the nervous disorders brought to him, of his soothing and authoritative presence, his look, his word, his touch, would afford sufficient confirmatory phenomena to sustain his inward persuasion. Still, the thaumaturgic character, like all the more definite Messianic pretensions, had its miseries for him: and the near escape of death looked welcome. He became excited and passionate, provoked by opposition, terrible in invective, advancing from defence into attack that left him no retreat: yet withal, on the first invitation from any thing pure and simple, returning, only with sadder voice, to a tone of singular sweetness and repose. With an infinite delicacy of mind, catching every shade of feeling, and drawing women and children towards him with unspeakable attraction, he united an unsparing harshness towards opponents: and it was inevitable that the irritation of the Pharisaic bourgeoisie, whom he abhorred as the very antithesis to his religion of the silent heart, should at length come to a head, and bring the catastrophe which his last visit to Jerusalem almost courted. For himself it was time to close a career no longer sustainable. Almost without fault of his, his conscience had lost its transparency: he had become committed to impossibilities: but in accepting the relief of martyrdom, he did not despair of his work: love for it and faith in it enabled him to rise above suffering and identify his darkest hour and his sublimest triumph.

It is impossible not to perceive in this sketch a gradual declension of character: the brilliant and dewy morning is overcast with noonday clouds; and the bursts of sunset light shoot through wild winds and threatening storm. The struggle of ideal faith to penetrate and mould the actual world involves, it is said, an inevitable descent: it can wield mankind only on condition of falling in with their illusions: and in deadly contest with them it has no effective force, but by clothing itself with the energy of their passions. Forced from his early dream of undefiled religion into the narrower conditions of the Messianic doctrine, Jesus fell into a false position; and as its necessities closed around him, was urged, by partial loss of inward clearness and simplicity, into a more feverish enthusiasm, solving by self-sacrifice a problem else inextricable. We venture to affirm that this theory has not been drawn from the history, but is a preconceived formula applied to it; and that no semblance of support can be given to it, except by transposing the evangelists' memorials to suit its exigencies, and forcing upon them a grouping which they will not bear. Left to their own natural voice, they attest, we believe, a moral order the very reverse; exhibiting, in the person of Jesus, an ascent from the higher levels of his inherited faith to an ever loftier sense and wider view of the spiritual relation between man and God; and with this, an inward sincerity steadfast against increasing strain, and leading up at length to the last sacrifice.

How does M. Renan know that Jesus had his year of "idealism," and then exchanged it for Messianic visions? John the Baptist, we doubt not, is responsible for this fancy: he is the preacher of the "kingdom:" from him the impulse passes to his successor; and as the contact between them does not stand at the beginning of our author's chronology, there is an antecedent stage to be provided for, which, being itself imaginary, is not unnaturally treated in this poetical way. To find materials in illustration of this earliest teaching, our author resorts to the Sermon on the Mount: he selects from it the Lord's Prayer and some of its purely ethical and spiritual sentences: he leaves behind him the verses which say any thing Messianic of the "kingdom of heaven:" and, possessed of his "ideal" anthology, he carries it backward past the Baptist, and prefixes it to what the gospels tell us of the ministry of Christ. The residuary elements of the Sermon, which have any tincture of the Jewish theocratic idea, he holds in reserve, as examples of the post-Baptist preaching. There is no pretence of any critical ground for this re-distribution of parts: it does not result from any discovery of the incidents to which the words of Christ, collected yet unarranged by Matthew, most naturally belong: and, in the case of the Lord's Prayer, which it transposes to a time prior to the gathering of any regular disciples and to any contact with the Baptist, it doubly contradicts the statement of Luke (xi. 2), that the prayer was given *at the disciples' request*, on the ground that *John also had taught his disciples to pray*. In fact, this ideal period on the threshold of public life is simply an artist's fiction: and, once set up, it draws to it at will whatever is congenial. Historical truth however resists this appropriation, and claims its stolen treasures again for their own place. The very saying which appears as the motto on the brow of this young time, "The kingdom of God is *within* you," belongs to the life's last chapter, not the first. And when, to adorn and consecrate this shrine of his fancy, our author has laid his hands on all that seems available, what he leaves witnesses against him scarcely less than what he takes. The very deepest words of Christ, the lessons and images held in everlasting remembrance, the parables that never tire,—the Good Samaritan, the Returning Prodigal, the Pharisee and Publican,—the incidents of divinest meaning,—the Rich Youth, the passionate Penitent, the blessing on the Child, the Widow's mite,—are scattered over his later ministry, and even grow in number to the close.

As the ideal essence of Christ's life cannot be exhaled and condensed into the first stage, so neither can the passionate elements be thrown preponderantly into the last. M. Renan's evidence of an increasing exaltation, enthusiasm, and harshness towards the end is gained only at the expense of chronology. The passages cited in support of the idea (ch. xix.) are almost all drawn from the address to the Twelve in Matt. x.: they are picked out from the midst of others already adduced in proof of just the opposite mood: and they belong to a time prior to the Baptist's death, and to the day of parables (Matt. xiii.). The demeanour of Jesus in his last days seems to us quite at variance with the phenomena of excitement and eager rush to the release of death. The ensnaring questions brought to him in the temple day by day are met with collected thought and quiet feeling: nor can our author himself, in reciting the answer about the tribute-money, refrain from exclaiming,—"Deep words; decisive of the future of Christianity! Words of marvellous justice and perfected spirituality, which have established the separation of spiritual and temporal, and laid the foundation of true liberality and true civilisation!" (p. 348.) The only apparent exception to the serene temper of that time is the invective against the Pharisees (Matt. xxiii.): which however does not arise as an expression of personal irritation against opposition, but as the recoil of a guileless and tender spirit from the type of character most odious to it and most blighting to the public conscience. The discourse moreover, transferred in great part by Luke (xi. 37) to a much earlier occasion, is of doubtful chronology: and has probably been intensified not a little by the sympathetic anger of the reporters. Of the examples usually cited to support the charge against Jesus of harshness and self-assertion,—the reply to his mother at Cana (John ii. 4),—the repulse of an application from his mother and brethren (Matt. xii. 48),—the cleansing of the temple (Matt. xxi. 12; John ii. 14);*—there is not one that, according to our author

* For this incident however M. Renan chooses an original position. The fourth evangelist places it at the beginning of Christ's ministry (Passover of A.D. 29); the others at the end (the last Passover): our author assigns it to

himself, did not occur in earlier stages of his ministry. Nor is there any thing to justify the statement that he acquiesced more and more in the claims upon him as a thaumaturgist. No part of his ministry is less marked by miracle than the last: no part is more full of it than the first. True, there is in the Johannine gospel a certain progression of supernatural acts, not in their frequency, but in their magnitude: and with our author's view of the raising of Lazarus,—which constitutes their climax,—he may well treat the ingenuous Galilean days as gone. But this artificial construction should itself induce us to rely rather on the synoptical accounts, and to hazard no conclusion to which they refuse support. The difficulty of the miracles, whatever it be, is equally diffused over the whole history: and encounters us in full force at the feast of Cana and the synagogue of Capernaum, no less than at the grave of Lazarus. We wonder that M. Renan has not made more use of his own just remark (p. 294) that, in the early memorials of Christianity, we find the thaumaturgic pretensions grow, as the time-distance increases from the person of Christ. This surely indicates that with him they were at their minimum; and that the responsibility for them rests much more with the reporters of the second age than with the Agent in the first.

The time and sense in which Jesus assumed the Messianic character, and propagated the Messianic ideas, are so difficult to determine that the problem might be deemed hopeless, but for a few streaks of light detected within it by the refined in-

the middle (Passover of A.D. 31). In his account of that second visit to Jerusalem, he omits the only incident,—the Bethesda cure,—by which the evangelist marks it (John v. 2); and supplies its place by transferring from the first passover its two characteristics,—the cleansing of the temple, and the visit of Nicodemus. We readily concede that so high-handed an act of authority as the expulsion of the traders from the temple-court is unsuitable to the opening days of the public life of Jesus; but why the choice given us by the synoptics,—of placing it at the end, when the breach with Jerusalem and the heart-weariness, with its insincerities, were complete,—we cannot understand. Again: in John this incident is immediately followed by the remarkable saying, "Destroy this temple made with hands, and in three days I will raise up another made without hands" (ii. 19: comp. Mark xiv. 58). The synoptics do not append this saying, which comes in only at second-hand, as part of the testimony against Christ at his trial, and is called "*false*" evidence. If the saying was uttered, it self-evidently belongs to the cleansing of the temple, as John has it; it is plainly an expression of sublime impatience with the material sanctuary and all the hollow pretences which it sheltered, and of longing to deal,—apart from such hindrance, —with the naked human heart, which, in almost no time, would at the appeal of Christ become a purer shrine. 'Away with your manufactured symbol, that stands instead of the love of God: and soon enough I could show you a holier place of prayer, emerging from the spirit.' Not perceiving this meaning, which connects the saying with the cleansing of the temple, M. Renan divorces the two, and assigns the words to Christ's last days. The enigmatical expression and the depth of the sentiment caused the fourth evangelist to misunderstand, and the rest to disbelieve, the saying. It affords us a glimpse of the things they could not tell us.

struments of modern criticism. To suppose, with M. Renan, that his mind was first turned in this direction by John the Baptist, and reduced from a lofty spirituality into the narrow channels of theocratic zeal, seems to us quite arbitrary. That the burden of their preaching was the same,—"the kingdom of God is at hand,"—indicates, not any imitation of the one by the other, but simply the one great thought of the time, that was in the very air. The phrases flung from the incisive voice of the ascetic on the Jordan were repeated from gentler lips in Galilee, because there was but one message to be delivered: and had there been a thousand prophets in the villages of Israel, they must all have been as a chorus with a common song. The monotheistic faith which had emerged into singular purity from ages of eventful strife, and which had gathered from its heroic traditions and its prophetic guides the sublime assurance of a Providence in history, turned all the religion of that generation into a theocratic vision: the heathen ages approached their term: the world was ripe for judgment; and would soon be cleared for the reign of Everlasting Righteousness. So possessed had the national mind become with this conception, that its images were every where: they peered through words of Scripture that were quite innocent of them: if they were not in the lines of prophets, they were found *between* them: they had created a literature for themselves,—sheltered by the names of Daniel, Enoch, Esra: they had coined a language for themselves, and given it universal currency,—"waiting for redemption," "looking for the consolation of Israel,"—"the kingdom of God,"—"the son of Man,"—"the son of David," "the last days," "the end of the ages," "the day of wrath," "the days of refreshing," "the regeneration." Into this mould all the piety of the place and time inevitably flowed: it gave a channel now to the molten fire of some scorching fanaticism, and now to the sweet waters of a fertilising inspiration. That Judas the Gaulonite, that John the Baptist, that Jesus of Nazareth, shared this common element, however differently they used it, cannot be doubted. If Satan had sent an emissary of temptation, if God had sent a messenger of redemption, without it, both alike would have been without a medium of approach to the souls they would reach, and would have returned to their place frustrated. Jesus then had nothing to learn, still less to unlearn, from the Baptist, on this head: it was because that stern voice echoed his own thought that he went to Jordan: it was because he too would publish the same tidings that he preached in Galilee. The difference alleged between them, viz. that from the first the one disclaimed, while the other claimed, the place of personal Messiah,—is probably the after-creation of disciples interpreting by events. If it was the distinction of Peter to have first breathed the truth of what Jesus was; if this confession was reserved, as the records tell, till the last journey to Jerusalem; if, still, the startling statement was to be held as a secret and "told to no man;" he cannot possibly have appeared all along clothed with Messianic pretensions. Could we indeed remove altogether the retrospective haze of interpretation with which the formed doctrine of the compiling evangelists has enveloped the history, could we see and hear the great realities as they arose, it may be reasonably doubted, whether we should ever find Jesus directly identifying himself with the Messiah whom he preached; and should not rather see that his definite investiture with that character was the later work of disciples to whom he was "declared to be the Son of God by his resurrection from the dead." From the first, he preached the Messianic kingdom as near: to the last it is doubtful whether he gave himself out as Messiah. We can find no date when he began the former topic; nor any when he passed, with intenser self-assertion, into the latter.

Even if we could feel sure of having in the synoptical gospels the unaltered language of Christ, we should still be unable to speak confidently of his state of mind, unless we could determine the precise import of the phrase "Son of Man." It is commonly assumed that, like the other titles, "Son of God" and "Son of David," this term,—occurring some fourscore times and always on the lips of Jesus,—is tantamount to "the Messiah," and uniformly employed with reference to the Book of Daniel and in the sense which interpreters had put upon it there. If so however, the three titles would be interchangeable, and could be resorted to indifferently. Yet "Son of Man" is the only one which Jesus himself uses: "Son of David" is given him only by others, the blind by the wayside, the children that cry 'Hosanna;' it is evidently the *popular* designation: "Son of God" is applied to him by unearthly beings, and seems to be characteristic of *superhuman testimony;* being used (1) by the Spirit at his baptism, (2) by the Devil in the Temptation (Matt. iv. 3), (3) by the evil spirits in the demoniacs, who "knew him" (Matt. viii. 29), (4) by Peter in his "confession" (Matt. xvi. 16), who is expressly said to have been led to it by revelation. This rule indeed is not absolute; for the phrase bursts from the disciples after the walking on the sea (Matt. xiv. 33): but on the whole it is evident (1) from Peter's confession that this term alone is the full equivalent for "the Christ," (2) from the other instances, that to discern Jesus in this character was a matter of superhuman, secret, or exceptional knowledge. The abstinence then of Jesus from the use of this term requires to be explained. It looks very like an *avoidance* of that unhesitating claim of Messiahship which M. Renan attributes to him.

The term "Son of Man" evidently falls short in some way of the Messianic meaning, and has a less limited application. M. Renan (pp. xi. 132) indeed says that we know perfectly from the book of Enoch that it was a mere synonym for the Messiah. But it so happens that the particular section of that work in which alone it occurs (viz. The Similitudes, ch. 37-71) is exposed to reasonable suspicion of being a Christian addition to the original production, as late as the closing decades of the first century:* and by that time the phrase had certainly settled into its purely personal meaning. In the gospels themselves (written after the doctrine had set and possessed itself of the phraseology) the term is often,—in John always,—thus used. But there are instances which clearly escape from this rule, and betray a wider significance in the phrase, rescuing it from its restricted place among the titles of Messiah. When Jesus inquired of his disciples (Matt. xvi. 13), "Who do men say that the Son of Man is? and they said, Some, John the Baptist; some, Elias; and others, Jeremias, or one of the prophets;" and when further he asked, "But whom say ye that I am? and Simon Peter answered, Thou art the Christ, the Son of the living God;" it is evident, as Baur has well pointed out,† that the expression "Son of Man" cannot mean specifically "the Messiah," but is large enough to cover several alternative personalities; and that, in order to pick out from among these possible significates the Messiah in particular, Peter has to employ the phrase "Son of God." His daring to find, under the safe and unpretending designation which Jesus applied to himself, the Messianic character which it did not put forth, constitutes the startling feature of his own confession. The peculiar humanistic sense of the phrase comes out clearly in several deep and pathetic passages, where Jesus at once takes and consecrates the common level of our life, with all its needs and affections: *e.g.* "The foxes have holes, the birds of the air have nests; but the Son of Man hath not where to lay his head"

* The date seems fixed at some point later than A.D. 79, by an allusion (ch. 67) to a volcanic mountain in the West, apparently Vesuvius, and the hot sulphur-springs at Baiæ. Vesuvius, it is well known, was not an active vent till the eruptions which destroyed Herculaneum, A.D. 79. See the whole case ably made out, though not without some overstraining, in Hilgenfeld's *Jüdische Apokalyptik*, 148 seqq. The use, in the same section of the book of Enoch, of the phrase "Son of the *woman*," to denote the Messiah savours strongly of Christian influence.

† See an excellent paper, "Die Bedeutung des Ausdrucks ὁ υἱὸς τοῦ ἀνθρώπου," in Hilgenfeld's *Zeitschrift* for 1860, pp. 274 seqq.; and compare Hilgenfeld's critique in the same *Zeitschrift*, 1863, pp. 327 seqq.

(Matt. viii. 20): "John came neither eating nor drinking, and they say, He hath a devil. The Son of Man came eating and drinking, and they say, Behold a gluttonous man and a winebibber, a friend of publicans and sinners" (Matt. ix. 18). The whole sentiment of such passages would be lost, were we to read "Messiah" for the "Son of Man." On the other hand, where announcement is made of the "coming of the Son of Man on the clouds of heaven," and "sitting on the throne of his glory," we have the expression in the mere Jewish or Messianic sense familiar to the disciples, and not in that which characterised it in the genuine speech of their master. The contrasts presented in this group of phrases were, at a later time, artificially resolved by a dogmatic key. When the contemplation of the risen Christ had produced its counterpart in the idea of his preëxistence, and his life on earth was conceived as a disguise of heavenly glory, the opposite turns of meaning, by which even the same title appears now to claim and now to disclaim, were distributed between his two natures. To import such ideas into the synoptical gospels is to blot out the simple historical Christ, and over that grand figure to paint a stiff ecclesiastic form, with nimbus round the head and clouds beneath the feet, instead of the firm step of nature and the living light of our humanity.

Jesus, we conceive, took the designation "Son of Man" rather in avoidance than in assertion of Messianic claims; because it carried him furthest from the national expectations embodied in the term "Son of God." An indeterminate consciousness of his Divine call drew him with sympathy towards an indeterminate phrase; which echoed the innermost secret of his nature, and said for him how little his eye was drawn to any thing out of the plane of human life; how its tender lights of need and love and sorrow, shed from the smallest and the darkest things, found in him the seats of unspeakable Pity, and made him desire only to be one with all he saw; and which yet, at the same time, by this very intimation of a distinctive humanism, gave him in some sense a representative character, and answered to his feeling that he was not his own, but called to be the organ of a higher will. An ordinary man would have no occasion to designate himself as human. But one who continually referred to supramundane things, who announced an approaching kingdom of heaven, might well wish, in speaking of one world, to keep his place in the other, and to let it be understood that,—whoever he was,—his work was here; and he was one with those whom he was sent to prepare. If he penetrated, through the obstructions of Rabbinical interpretation, to the true meaning of the vision in Daniel most associated with the phrase, he would see that, as its brute forms were but symbols of the great empires of the unregenerate world, so, when "*one like* the Son of Man" was substituted by the Ancient of days, that figure also stood (not for any person, but) for the *realm* of final Righteousness, and signalised its character by making it no longer *brutal*, but *human*. In this view, "the kingdom of God" was the reign of humanity: and he who proclaimed it fell in with its nature, by asking only to be Son of Man. It was the name too by which already the Divine word had addressed the ancient prophet:* and why should not the organ of a living inspiration rest in it as his own?

This name however, though recommended to the feeling of Jesus by such characteristics, has certainly another side. Its vagueness saves it from asserting, but also prevents it from excluding, the Messianic attributes. Whether, under cover of it, these were held in reserve; or whether, without being at all intended at first, they were afterwards developed from it in the mind of Jesus himself, so that he became the Messiah whom he preached, we do not think there are reliable materials for deciding. Even where, according to the evangelists, he says things about "the Son of Man" in the obviously Messianic sense, it is by no means evident that he is speaking of *himself*: the language is usually what it would be if the person were some one else. He does not say, "ye shall see *me* coming on the clouds of heaven;" and the avoidance of the first person in such connexions is the more noticeable because it contrasts him with the disciples, who are described as asking him, "What is the sign of *thy* coming, and of the end of the world?" (Matt. xxiv. 3.) This distinction, we are aware, cannot be absolutely carried through: but that it survives at all, after the large accumulation of free composition round the historical nucleus of the gospels, is highly significant; and justifies the question, whether, after all, the Messiahship may not rather have been put upon Jesus, than claimed by him.

We are not however particularly anxious to relieve his life of this claim. In announcing the kingdom of God, he doubtless shared the Messianic illusions of his native land: and it is only part of the same phenomenon, if his profound personal consciousness of union with God expressed itself in terms of the same theory. Spiritual insight, though carried to the highest limit of inspiration, can only sanctify, not cancel or transform, the scenery of objects, the picture of the world and its history, the images of what has been and what is yet to come, by which the mind is environed. Moral perfection, within the bounds of our nature, has not to wait, till the universe is scientifically

* See Ezekiel ii. 1, 3, 6, 8, and passim.

conceived: the tones of Conscience may be infallibly interpreted without knowing how long the world is to last: the true relation between the human and the Divine may be revealed, though the measures of space and time at the disposal of fancy are ever so inadequate. It is not with the objects thought, but with the ways of thinking, that the truth, the beauty, the goodness of the inner life have to do: and the essence, as of genius, so of religion, come whence it may, lies in subjective harmony and creativeness. The seat of original power is ever in the unconscious background of the soul, in that which thinks and reveres and loves, and not in the elaborated things which, thus moved, we purposely construct: we spend ourselves on what we *do;* God, if any word of his issues from us at all, speaks through what we *are.* And so, while the whole Messianic drama that engaged the early Christianity, and more or less fixed the gaze of Jesus himself, has dispersed as a cloud-picture, a divine light, of which neither he nor others dreamt, has emanated from his person, and has toned anew all the colours and the shadows upon life ever since.

It was inevitable that contradictions should arise between the outer and the inner kingdom of God in Christ; between the exigencies of the Messianic theory and the promptings of a conscience under holiest inspiration. M. Renan thinks that he went with his published doctrine and compromised his private sincerity. Reversing this judgment, we maintain that the theory gave way, and the inward reverence disposed of his life to the last sacrifice. The people around him were for carrying out the doctrine and pushing on to the theocracy: he restrained and corrected them, not by refuting their assumptions, but by the intuitive recoil of higher affections from methods unworthy of him. The multitudes wanted "to make him a king:" and he withdrew to the mountains to pray. His disciples were always taking care of his dignity and his repute: they drove the children away; he took them in his arms and blessed them: they were scandalised at the presence of a woman who was a sinner; he accepted her passionate homage, and put their officiousness to shame. His apostles had the orthodox susceptibilities towards Gentiles and Samaritans, who had nothing to do with "the kingdom:" he loved to draw forth their faith, to commemorate their gratitude, to offer himself to their reception, and rebuked the fiery anger at their refusal. Drawn by the thirst of compassion and the trust in simplicity, he lived among social elements that could do nothing to realise any Messianic dream. The moment he was brought by the theoretic program of "the kingdom" to a point at which popular favour might be turned to account, and the place of leader of the saints of God seemed to invite, an infallible purity of feeling rectified the traditional conception, and made him shrink from any but spiritual methods. The time came,—it is marked by the Transfiguration, —when persistency in this holy abstinence could plainly lead to but one result: the very moment of Peter's exulting confession is the moment of the Master's foreboding of Calvary: and Peter's instant expostulation shows how sharply the two feelings clash. The conflict of that crisis is little penetrable by us: must he deny the part that the apostle gave him?—that might be to betray his appointed part; *who* precisely he was in the Divine reckoning he could not tell; but that he was the organ of his Father, and had a witness to bear, he knew assuredly: out of that inner guidance he must live on: if it disappointed apocalyptic visions, apocalyptic visions must step aside and wait: men should force nothing upon him: and if already in view there was "a decease which he must accomplish at Jerusalem," it would but associate him with Moses and Elias, immortal prophets who also were in reserve for the great day of the Lord. So far therefore as the Messianic idea affected him then, it affected him thus: that rather than aim to realise it unfaithfully, he dismissed it to the other side of death, and would not suffer an imagination of God's outward Providence to disturb the clear tones of his inward Spirit. And so the Messianic theology, without formal cancelling, was from hour to hour neutralised and negatived by the pure ascendency of diviner light. And the *via dolorosa* was all the darker, that it had no ideal light of theory upon it, but was rather a passage right away from theory, into a night that was only not terrible because it was the hiding-place of God. That the great controversy and agony of Christ's spirit was essentially of this nature is suggested even at an earlier period than the transfiguration. Whatever other meaning may be drawn from the remarkable scene called the Temptation, it plainly denotes the dismissal of seducing proposals from the Messianic side,—the rejection of all questionable means,—of ostentation or compromise,—for advancing the kingdom of heaven. That Satan of the wilderness, abashed before the pure eye of the Son of God, departed "for a season." Doubtless there were moments when he returned: he spoke again in Peter's word, "Be it far from thee, Lord: this shall not be unto thee." But the answer is ever the same, "Get thee behind me, Satan: thou savourest not the things that be of God, but those that be of men." And these are words plainly revealing the nature of the conflict in the soul of Jesus. They are not the words of one embracing death because it cut the knot of a hopeless entanglement, and ended the fever of a conscience no longer transparent: but of one to whom the path of sacrifice was the only heavenly road; who must decline deliverance by "self-assertion" not compelled by inward authority. The feeling which they express is not, that he has become committed to pretensions which at all hazards he must press into the advance: but just the opposite resolve, of abstinence, in the face of death, from every claim, even though it might be true, which would turn outside the "kingdom within," and make dependent upon "signs" the divine things he had to signify. It is needless to point out how that resolve was kept. The last period is full of a sad and tender inspiration. The reported miracles visibly abate. He parries questions about his "authority" without a self-assertive word. He speaks the pure truth of heaven, and applies it straight to men and things around, heedless whom it may provoke. He brings his unsullied "idealism" into the very throng of Solomon's porch, and abashes beneath his clear eye the priests' officers, if not the priests:—and falls at last through that sublime saying about the built and unbuilt temples, which expresses the imperishable essence of his religion.

Perhaps, after all, M. Renan's suspicion of a decline in the character of Jesus from its first pure enthusiasm springs less from study of the history, than from a certain melancholy theory of his own, to which more than once he gives pathetic expression. "At bottom," he says, "every ideal is a eutopia." Rather would we say, "At bottom every ideal is an inspiration." He looks with sympathy indeed, but with poetic sadness, on the aspirations of devout and prophetic men after a more satisfying life and a more righteous world than ours; and regards them as unsubstantial fancies of the human mind. We know not why we should part with the natural trust that they are divine glimpses rather than human illusions, escaped rays from the higher light instead of dreams painted on the night; or cease to recognise, in the intuitive visions and untiring prayer of the supreme spirits of our race, the border-land of communion between the immortal thought and the mortal eye that scans it. Here surely, if any where, on the commanding summits and in the unclouded moments of prophetic minds, is the meeting-place of Man and God, where the real meaning of the world is seen, and the stream of tendency may be widely traced. And if it be so, then the so-called "idealist" is, in the end, the truest realist: for the essence of the universe,—the Eternal Will,—is on his side: he speaks to the most enduring affections: he touches the latent powers whose time it is to wake. Nor can we allow that "every ideal must lose something of its purity" in its aim at realisation. On the contrary, we say, it is cleared and ennobled by its perpetual strife with resisting conditions; *suffering*, it may be, under limiting necessities and painful incompleteness, but in proportion as it is faithful, made perfect by suffering; glorifying reality without quenching itself. Did our author mean no more than that in actual execution something must always remain behind the original thought, he would truly enough describe the hindrances of a refractory world. But the application of his maxim gives it a more questionable meaning. It is his general formula for proving that Jesus could not fail, unless he died in his early "idealism," to descend to a lower level of conscience; humouring, for instance, the popular demand for miracles, and otherwise tampering with veracity. He could not otherwise, it is said, have acted on mankind at all; and we have no right to find fault till we have done as much with our scruples as he with his imperfect sincerity. In this sense we must dispute both the fact and its maxim. Jesus, far from condescending to any moral compromise with the Messianic idea, declined its requirements, and became a sacrifice to his refusal; he could not stoop, but he could die. Instead of sinking deeper and deeper into the traditional illusion, he rose higher and higher above it. If, like a mirage inseparable from the atmosphere of his land, it still hovered before his eye, he followed it not, but step by step surrendered himself to the guidance of the Holiest within. As he thus advanced, it receded from him into the distance: it passed beyond the margin of this life; and so, flying before his personal perfection, began that retreat from the earth which left at last the spirituality of the gospel disengaged from the dreams of Judaism. As for his action on the world, he acted on *that* age precisely because he *sincerely* shared some of its transitory ideas; he has acted upon every other, because he was faithful to a divine light, lonely for the moment, but revealed in him for all time. Not humouring and connivance, but truth in every way,—truth with his age, truth with his God, truth with himself,—was the condition of his power, as indeed of all moral power. The managers of the world, hour by hour, must act by adaptation to lower minds; its saviour and inspirer, who lifts it into a new mood for ever, must be the pure organ of a Will higher than his own. He will never reach the seats of any fresh original reverence in others but by artless simplicity of faith and devotion; he is what he is because he just reports eternal things which he did not make and cannot alter: did he even think for a moment of trimming them to his will, he would sink from the prophet to the charlatan. In *administering* an established system, resting on existing pieties, there may be fearful mixtures, as the history of every priesthood shows, of enthusiasm and artifice; but to extend such experience to religious *creation*, to suppose that the purest truth can flow from the courses of a turbid conscience, and the highest worship be raised from the wreck of a ruined "idealism," is to throw all ideas of moral causation into the dreariest confusion. This is to us the most painful feature of M. Renan's book. That he is Platonist in taste does not restrain him from cynicism in morals; his imagination lingers in the upper world of divine ideas, but his belief keeps its footing on the ground, and trusts no power but the mixed motives of an infirm and self-deceiving humanity. We venture to say that his *real* world lies in the wrong place for an historian of religion; the true causes of what he seeks he leaves behind in his dream-realm, and descends for them to a level where they are not to be found. His moral construction is, in consequence, deficient in compactness. He combines incompatible attributes in one person, and then apologises by commonplaces about the contradictions of human nature. At one time he seems to attribute the marvellous success of Christianity to the fortunate errors and fanaticisms, perhaps even unscrupulousness, of its Founder: at another to the sublimity of his character and the imperishable truths at the heart of his religion. That ultimately he will rest, with less wavering, in the higher doctrine of moral dynamics, we cannot but hope when we read such a comment as the following on the words of Jesus to the woman of Samaria, "Woman, believe me, the hour is coming when ye shall neither in this mountain, nor yet at Jerusalem, worship the Father;" "but the true worshippers shall worship the Father in spirit and in truth" (John iv. 21, 23):

> "The day when he pronounced this word he was truly Son of God. He spoke for the first time the sure word on which the edifice of eternal religion shall rest. He founded the pure worship, of no land, of no date, which all lofty souls will practise to the end of time. His religion that day was not only the religion good for humanity, it was Absolute Religion: and if other planets have inhabitants endowed with reason and morality, their religion can be no other than that which Jesus proclaimed at Jacob's well. Man has not been able to abide by it, for the ideal is tenable but for an instant. The word of Jesus has been a gleam in a dark night; it has needed eighteen hundred years for the eyes of mankind (what do I say?—of an infinitely small part of mankind) to accustom themselves to it. But the gleam will become the full day; and, after having run through the whole circle of errors, mankind will return to that word as the imperishable expression of its faith and its hopes" (pp. 234, 235).

CURRENT LITERATURE:—BOOKS OF THE QUARTER SUITABLE FOR READING-SOCIETIES.

1. Fortune's Journey to Yedo and Peking.

2. Eleanor's Victory. By M. E. Braddon.

   [It is difficult to say why people should read Miss Braddon's novels, and easy to show why they should not be read. Yet they are, and will be so.]

3. Alexander's Incidents of the Maori War.

4. Andrew Deverell.

   [An amusing book by an American. Ill-written, but not without interest. He writes to a young lady to ask her to wait and marry him, and she does wait.]

5. Ansted's Great Stone Book of Nature.

6. Shakespeare's Home. By J. C. M. Bellew.

   [A careful book on a subject of which but little can be known.]

7. Browning's Poetical Works.

   [Reviewed in Article VII.]

8. Carey's late War in New Zealand.

9. Border and Bastille. By the Author of "Guy Livingstone."

   [Written with energy, but saying little.]

10. Carey's Four Months in a Dahabeek.

    [A dahabeek is an Egyptian boat, and Mr. Carey amused himself there, and amuses his readers.]

11. The Footsteps of Error. By Dean Close.

    [The author's name suggests the nature of this book.]

12. Davis's Tracks of M'Kinlay across Australia.

    [Interesting, though rather heavily written.]

13. Chesney's View of the Virginian Campaigns.

    [Interesting and valuable.]

14. Davidson on the Old Testament.

    [Reviewed in Article I.]

15. Denise. By the Author of "Mademoiselle Mori."

    [A very interesting novel, written with artistic grace.]

16. The Fairy Book. By Dinah M. Muloch.

    [An excellent set of fairy tales, happily without morals.]

17. Fawcett's Manual of Political Economy.

[A very clear, comprehensive manual, and, what is more, readable and animated.]

18. Captain Gronow's Recollections. Second Series.

[Amusing enough.]

19. A Study of Hamlet. By Dr. Conolly.

[A curious attempt to discuss Hamlet's sanity or insanity, as if it were a reality.]

20. Hind's Introduction to Astronomy. New Edition.

[An established work of high accuracy.]

21. Incidents in my Life. By D. D. Home.

[Curious, at any rate, whether true or untrue.]

22. A Residence in Georgia. By Mrs. F. Kemble.

[A most instructive book on American slavery, written long ago from personal knowledge.]

23. Kingsley's Sermons on the Pentateuch.

[Animated and vigorous, though suggesting many questions which it does not solve.]

24. Essay on Government. By Sir G. C. Lewis.

[Reviewed in Article X.]

25. Lowth's Wanderer in Western France.

[Amusing enough.]

26. Maurice's Claims of the Bible and Science.

[With more of Mr. Maurice's faults and fewer of his merits than most of his writings. He states two opposite opinions, which are intelligible if not satisfactory, and then a third of his own, which may be satisfactory, but is not intelligible.]

27. Mommsen's History of Rome. Vol. III.

[The best part of M. Mommsen's valuable History, now translated for the first time.]

28. Monat's Adventures among the Andamans.

[Interesting, though not without defects of style.]

29. Notes on the Pentateuch. By Andrews Norton; with a Preface by the Rev. J. J. Tayler.

[A most valuable and timely republication.]

30. Phillimore's History of England in the time of George III.

[An animated but otherwise unsatisfactory work.]

31. Remarkable Misers. By Cyrus Redding.

32. Romola. By George Eliot.

[The most powerful of George Eliot's novels since *Adam Bede*, and the best historical novel since the best of Sir Walter Scott's.]

33. Does the Bible countenance American Slavery?

[Written with Mr. Goldwin Smith's usual vigour.]

34. Stephen's Criminal Law of England.

[A very interesting book to all who wish to know *why*, as the author suggests, they may legitimately "kill, torture, and imprison their fellow creatures." It gives a general account of English law, but is not technical. There are some excellent abstracts of French criminal trials.]

35. Christian Names. By Miss Yonge.

36. Life of General Stonewall Jackson. By the Author of "Life in the South."

[The time is hardly come for a Life of General Jackson.]

37. Our Old Home. By Nathaniel Hawthorne.

[An interesting account of England, a little in the style of Washington Irving, but with caustic criticisms of far greater power both on the Americans and the English.]

CPSIA information can be obtained
at www.ICGtesting.com
Printed in the USA
LVHW040402110522
718423LV00001B/146

9 783375 004101